THEY CAME TO SAN FRANCISCO
TO ESCAPE THE PAST . . .

Kendra—nineteen and beautiful, looking for a man to help her forget her years as an unwanted child.

Marny—an audacious redhead, with a talent for cards, declaring her independence by setting up a gambling casino.

Pocket—seeking to dull the ache of a love betrayed.

Ted—strangely silent about his reasons for leaving New York, but ambitious for money and love.

THEN THE CRY ECHOED
FROM THE MOUNTAINS—GOLD!

In just three years, San Francisco would grow from a muddy village to a rich, brawling city. *Calico Palace* is the story of those who found fortunes and failures, violence and love in the wild, breathless fury of the Gold Rush.

Books by Gwen Bristow

Calico Palace
Deep Summer
The Handsome Road
This Side of Glory
Tomorrow Is Forever

Published by POCKET BOOKS

CALICO PALACE

by

Gwen Bristow

PUBLISHED BY POCKET BOOKS NEW YORK

Except for historical personages, all characters in this
story are fictitious.

 POCKET BOOKS, a Simon & Schuster division of
GULF & WESTERN CORPORATION
1230 Avenue of the Americas, New York, N.Y. 10020

Published by arrangement with Thomas Y. Crowell Company, Inc.
Library of Congress Catalog Card Number: 72-106584

ISBN: 0-671-82471-6

First Pocket Books printing June, 1971

17th printing

Trademarks registered in the United States and other countries.

Printed in the U.S.A.

For Louis, Bobby, and the girls

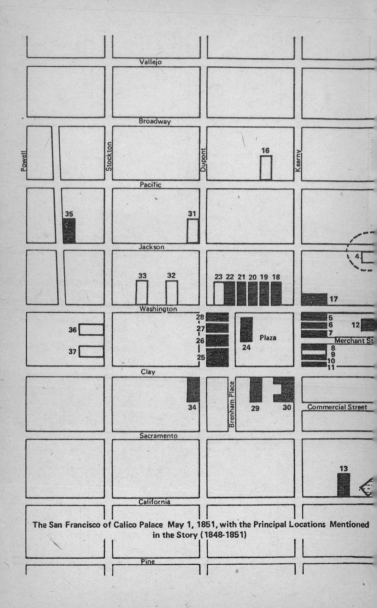

The San Francisco of Calico Palace May 1, 1851, with the Principal Locations Mentioned in the Story (1848-1851)

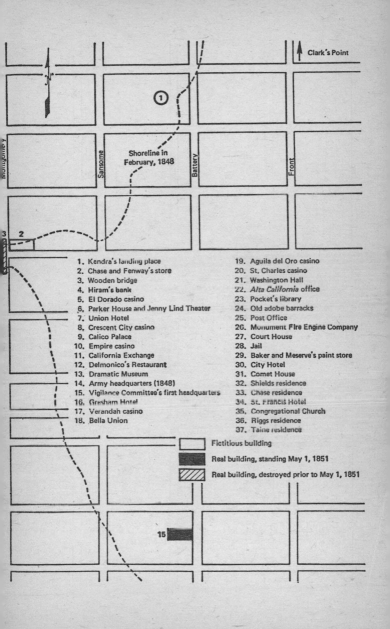

Clark's Point

Shoreline in
February, 1848

Montgomery

Sansome

Battery

Front

1. Kendra's landing place
2. Chase and Fenway's store
3. Wooden bridge
4. Hiram's bank
5. El Dorado casino
6. Parker House and Jenny Lind Theater
7. Union Hotel
8. Crescent City casino
9. Calico Palace
10. Empire casino
11. California Exchange
12. Delmonico's Restaurant
13. Dramatic Museum
14. Army headquarters (1848)
15. Vigilance Committee's first headquarters
16. Gresham Hotel
17. Verandah casino
18. Bella Union

19. Aguila del Oro casino
20. St. Charles casino
21. Washington Hall
22. *Alta California* office
23. Pocket's library
24. Old adobe barracks
25. Post Office
26. Monument Fire Engine Company
27. Court House
28. Jail
29. Baker and Meserve's paint store
30. City Hotel
31. Comet House
32. Shields residence
33. Chase residence
34. St. Francis Hotel
35. Congregational Church
36. Riggs residence
37. Taine residence

☐ Fictitious building

■ Real building, standing May 1, 1851

▨ Real building, destroyed prior to May 1, 1851

CALICO
PALACE

1

The good ship *Cynthia* was on her way to California. The *Cynthia* was a beautiful ship, her sails tall and singing in the wind, her figurehead a white goddess crowned with a crescent moon.

The *Cynthia* had left New York in October, 1847. For two months she had been sailing south, and now she was coming close to Cape Horn at the tip of South America.

On the quarterdeck at the after part of the ship, Kendra Logan stood by the rail watching the gray sea around her. Kendra was nineteen years old. Her figure was slim and firm, and her face, while not beautiful, was a face people looked at twice. She had a straight nose and a stubborn chin and a humorous mouth; her eyes were deep blue with black lashes, and her dark hair grew to a point like an arrow on her forehead. When they got a chance, men liked to drop a kiss on that arrow of hair. A mere peck on the forehead, why that was the way a man would kiss his old teacher, or his aunt. Or so they said.

Kendra's dress and cloak and scarf were all blue like her eyes, and all swirling around her in the wind. As a gust harder than usual struck her she turned from the rail and looked up at the men working among the great sails high against the sky.

These men had never spoken to her and as long as they were on the *Cynthia* they never would. Cabin and quarterdeck were forbidden to sailors, and passengers were not allowed anywhere else. The men worked so hard that they had little energy left for wishful dreams, but as Kendra looked up, drops of sea mist beading her eyelashes like tiny pearls around her blue eyes, a sailor high in the rigging paused to gaze yearningly down upon her. A big fellow with a rust-colored beard, he caught her eye and grinned. He was quite unabashed; his whole attitude said you couldn't blame a guy for looking.

1

Kendra knew she ought not to smile back, but she smiled anyway. As his grin brightened in answer, she dropped her eyes regretfully and turned toward the sea again. During their two months on shipboard her mother had warned her often enough that she must ignore the sailors as if they were not here. Kendra supposed the ban was necessary, but she wished it were not. That man would be fun to know. She wondered how he liked being here on this cold gray sea, sailing toward a dreary country off at the end of the world.

But at least, he had chosen to be here, and she had not. Kendra was going to California because she could not help it. The United States was at war with Mexico, and her stepfather, Colonel Alexander Taine, had been ordered to duty in a town called San Francisco. Alex had sailed on a troop transport that had no place for women, so Kendra and her mother were following him on the *Cynthia,* which though a merchant ship took a few passengers. Kendra's own father had died young and she had grown up in boarding schools. But now her schooldays were over, so for the first time she was going to live with her mother and stepfather at an army post.

She did not like the prospect. In spite of all the pretty pretending that enfolded this journey, Kendra knew they did not want her there. They had lived without her all these years, and they were accepting her now only because she could no longer be tucked away at school, and nobody else wanted her either. Kendra was young and her experience was small, but she was not stupid.

Long ago Kendra had made up her mind that she was not going to feel sorry for herself. But she could not help wishing there was somebody who cared what became of her.

Standing here in the wind that was blowing her to California, Kendra wondered what her life there would be like. She could not make a picture in her thoughts. She had never spent much time with her mother, and she hardly knew Colonel Taine at all. As for California, nobody knew anything about California. Half the gentlemen in Congress had already said the place was not worth having and it was sheer waste of the taxpayers' money to send an army there.

Listening to the crash of water and creak of ropes, Kendra thought of the ship's figurehead, the goddess crowned with the crescent moon. The goddess could not be seen from here, but Kendra suspected that her gleaming whiteness was by now tarnished as gray as the clouds above. Here near Cape

2

Horn the weather was bleak and dark. At night they saw ghostly globes of light hovering about. Loren Shields, the jolly young supercargo of the *Cynthia,* had told Kendra the sailors used to think these were wandering souls. No, Loren didn't know what they were, he didn't think anybody knew, but he was pretty sure they weren't spooks.

A hatch banged shut, and she saw Loren Shields coming out on deck. Bundled up in his thick coat, his cheeks pink and his light hair blowing, Loren waved and came toward her.

Though he was twenty-six years old Loren was the type that Kendra privately classified as "nice boy." He was not an exciting young man, but she liked him. It was almost impossible not to like Loren, simply because he *was* so nice—so courteous, so friendly, so agreeable. He lent her books, and told her the lore of the sea, and was often available for games. Kendra had been surprised that he had time for this, but Loren explained that the word "supercargo" meant what it said: he was supervisor of the cargo. This kept him busy in port, but at sea he often had leisure.

As he reached the rail the ship lurched, and they both got a spatter of sea water. Loren caught the rail with one hand and Kendra's arm with the other, and when she had steadied herself he released her and pointed out to sea. Away out, half obscured by the mist, Kendra saw a great jagged cliff standing high in the water. Bringing his lips close to the blue scarf over her head Loren shouted above the wind, "There's Cape Horn!"

Kendra was not a timid girl, but she shivered. Cape Horn was a rock fourteen hundred feet high, jutting out of the end of South America to divide the Atlantic and Pacific Oceans. Here the winds were violent, and they nearly always blew from the west, hurling the sea against the ships that tried to pass from the Atlantic to the Pacific, as the *Cynthia* would be trying now. But as he saw Kendra's tremor Loren gave her a reassuring smile.

"There's no reason to be scared!" he exclaimed into her muffled ear.

Kendra remembered that Loren had been around the Horn before—*doubled* the Horn, she corrected herself. Seafaring folk said "double" the Horn, not "go around" it. Loren was speaking again.

"It's cold up here. Come below and get warm."

She went with him down the companionway. Once, as the *Cynthia* pitched and Kendra almost stumbled, Loren caught her elbow to steady her, but as he had done on deck, almost instantly he let it go. Loren treated a lady with respect; he had none of the impish daring of that sailor who had grinned at her from the rigging. She still thought the sailor would have been more fun to know.

As they were out of the wind now and could speak easily, Loren paused to encourage her.

"We won't have any trouble, Kendra. There's not a better ship afloat than the *Cynthia,* and Captain Pollock is as fine a navigator as ever lived."

What a nice boy he was, Kendra thought for the hundredth time. Loren added,

"Besides, there's another reason—I mean—oh anyway, we'll be all right."

He was—why, he was *blushing,* thought Kendra, or was that extra pink of his cheeks due to the wind? But whatever he had been about to say, instead of saying it he was hurrying her into the cabin.

Here they found Kendra's mother, Eva Taine, with the other two passengers, Bess and Bunker Anderson. The Andersons were a middle-aged pair who lived in Honolulu, where Bunker managed a branch of a New York trading firm. They had been playing a card game, but the sea had grown so rough that they had given up. Eva was sewing. Catching sight of Kendra, Eva greeted her with a bright smile. She always did. Kendra smiled back. She always did. Kendra and her mother had never felt at ease together, but they pretended.

Eva was thirty-five years old. She did not look like Kendra; Kendra looked like the father she could not remember. Eva was a really beautiful woman, with large dark eyes, brown hair always smooth and shining, and an air of gracious composure. Nobody was ever surprised to hear that she was a colonel's wife. When Loren said Cape Horn was in sight Eva put aside her work, exclaiming that she wanted to see the famous rock. Bess and Bunker Anderson offered to go up with her.

Loren, saying he had to check some records, went to his own quarters. Kendra took off her wraps and waited in the cabin.

The cabin of the *Cynthia* was a handsome place, paneled in hardwood, with a skylight for daytime and whale oil lamps

4

for night. The ship's steward served meals at the table under the skylight, where Captain Enos Pollock sat at the head and the officers and passengers along the sides, in chairs bolted down to hold steady in rough weather. From her reading of sea stories Kendra had thought all you got to eat on a long voyage was salt meat and hardtack, and she had been surprised to find how good their food was. They did have salt meat, but this was varied with fresh, for they had brought along live pigs and poultry, kept in pens on the forward deck. They also had cheese and sausage and smoked fish, potatoes, onions, split pea soup, pickled cabbage, and dried fruit. On special occasions Captain Pollock even brought out a decanter of wine, though he never touched it himself.

Kendra was interested in food. She liked to cook. She liked to try new recipes, and invent others, and make surprises out of leftovers nobody else wanted to bother with. In her grandmother's home, during her vacations from school, when things got dull she always went into the kitchen.

But here on the *Cynthia* she could not cook. And she was *not* going to sew. Kendra hated needlework, and Kendra was a decided young person. She either did something or she did not do it. She never went halfway.

Eva could sew expertly, as well as knit and embroider, and she had accomplished a good deal since they left New York. On the table lay her present piece of work, a handbag of brown linen, embroidered with her initials in a design of autumn leaves. Eva never wasted time. She was always so *right*, Kendra thought rebelliously. In all her life Eva had done only one foolish thing, and this was to marry Kendra's father.

It had happened when she was fifteen years old. Eva lived in Baltimore. The youngest in her family, and the only girl, she was pretty and pampered and used to having her own way. One morning she was out on a horseback ride with a boy named Baird Logan, aged eighteen. Eva and Baird imagined they were in love, and all of a sudden they decided it would be a devilish adventure to run off and get married. They rode to a justice of the peace in a little town near by, added several years to their ages, and the justice, a silly old man with weak eyesight, accepted their fibs and married them. Eva rushed home and packed a few clothes in a bag, scribbled a note, and slipped away without being observed. Off they went for a honeymoon jaunt.

5

In a week, their horrified parents found them and brought them back. Their two fathers summoned a lawyer and told him to have the marriage annulled. Baird and Eva made no objection; they were tired of their escapade and willing to forget it. But before the annulment process could begin, Eva found that she was going to have a baby.

She wept and stormed. The two fathers paced the floor and wondered how they could ever endure the scandal. The two mothers moaned, each to her own offspring, "After all I've done for you, *this* is my reward!"

But the fact was there. Baird and Eva had to stay married. The parents provided a pretty little house for them to live in. Baird's father said Baird could go into the family importing business. But nothing could keep the pretty little house from being a hideous prison.

Eva was barely sixteen when Kendra was born. By this time she and Baird hated each other. They quarreled without end. Baird started drinking, and one night, before Kendra was a year old, he rode horseback home from a party through a winter storm and caught pneumonia. In a few days he was dead.

Baird's mother, a woman of spirit, said it was her duty to take Kendra because Eva was a fool and Eva's mother must be a fool too or she would not have brought up such a fool of a daughter. Eva was glad to get rid of her unwanted baby, but Kendra's grandmother did not want her either. She was merely doing her duty. As soon as Kendra was old enough, her grandmother sent her to a school in New York.

Nobody had ever told Kendra all this. Everybody was kind to her. Her grandparents, her aunts and uncles, the family friends—all the grown people were kind. But grown people *talk*. They drop remarks while you're sitting on the floor with your doll. They look at each other across you, and sadly shake their heads. You're just a child, they think you don't understand. But you do understand. Ever since she could remember, Kendra had known she was a child nobody wanted.

When Kendra was four years old, Eva married Alex Taine and they went to a post west of the Mississippi River, where the army kept the frontier safe from Indians. No place for a little girl, said Eva. Alex agreed. He had no interest in Kendra. He had never seen her, and he expected to have children of his own. In this he was not disappointed, for he and Eva

6

became the parents of two handsome sons. They had left the boys at school in New York this year, because Alex wanted Eva with him and there were no schools in California.

Kendra had seen Alex only three or four times in her life, when he and Eva visited their friends in the East. Kendra had discerned, however, that he was not at all like Baird Logan. Alex was a graduate of West Point. He was not reckless or impulsive; he planned his time and paid his bills and did what was expected of him. So did Eva, now. Eva had learned; never again was she going to make a fool of herself. She and Alex had lived at various frontier posts. She liked this. It was adventure, but a safe sort of adventure; at a frontier post, she had the whole United States Army on her side.

All these years, Kendra had stayed at school. When Eva came to New York for a visit she and Kendra would take a drive, and stop for ices and macaroons. They never knew what to say to each other and they were both relieved when it was over. On vacations Kendra would stay with her grandmother.

And then, last summer, Kendra finished school. She came back to her grandmother in Baltimore, and about this time Alex was ordered to San Francisco. He sailed on the troopship, and Eva engaged a stateroom on the *Cynthia*. But while Eva was in New York waiting for the ship to sail, Kendra's grandmother had a stroke and died.

This was why Kendra was now on her way to San Francisco. Her other grandparents—Eva's parents—had died some years before, and there was nobody Eva could leave her with. Kendra's aunts and uncles were as sweet as ever. They said, if this bereavement had to take place what a mercy that it happened while Kendra's mother was here to take care of the dear girl. What they meant was, they were not going to be bothered with Eva's ill-gotten brat.

Eva came to Baltimore, gracious and well dressed as always. She said she would write Alex at once and send the letter by one of the couriers who carried army dispatches. She would be delighted, said Eva, to have her charming daughter with her.

Like the aunts and uncles, she did not mean what she said. Eva did not find her daughter charming. Other people might admire Kendra's blue eyes and the dark hair growing to an arrow on her forehead. But Eva did not. Kendra looked like

7

Baird Logan, and every glance at Kendra reminded Eva of the trouble she had made for herself when she ran off with him.

As Kendra sat here in the cabin of the *Cynthia*, she remembered how Eva had suggested, in her own tactful way, that Kendra drop the surname Logan and let herself be called Kendra Taine. "As long as you lived with a grandmother named Mrs. Logan," said Eva, "calling yourself Logan was a matter of course. But I am Mrs. Taine. Your being named Logan will be—well, puzzling. You understand, don't you?"

Kendra understood. She knew her mother regarded that first marriage as a bit of childish folly and wanted to be reminded of it as little as possible. Kendra resented this. And Kendra was no more like her mother in nature than in looks. Eva had tact and grace; Kendra was forthright as a storm. The only way she knew to answer was to say what she meant. She said,

"I won't tell people my name is Taine. Maybe you're ashamed of Baird Logan but I'm not. He was my father and my name is Logan and it's going to stay Logan till I get married."

Eva knew when she had lost. Smiling pleasantly she replied, "Very well, Kendra."

They had not referred to the matter again. Those pleasant, tactful smiles of Eva's were part of the endless pretending that made it possible for them to live together. Kendra hated pretending.

"Now why," said Loren's voice beside her, "should you be so gloomy?"

Kendra started. Loren stood by the chair next to hers, smiling down at her. He looked so amiable, so brotherly, that he made her feel like talking. But she was not going to tell him what she had been thinking about. She detested people who whined, and anyway, Loren would not have understood if she had told him. Loren had grown up in a small New England town. His home had been the easy-going sort, with wide fireplaces and comfortable old furniture and a lot of children and parents who loved them all. He simply would not have been able to comprehend the sort of lonesomeness Kendra had felt all her life.

He stood looking down at her, his eyes bright in his happy face. Loren's eyes were a clear light brown, like cider. Kendra said,

8

"Loren, I was just thinking—how far is it from New York to San Francisco?"

This was something Loren did know about. He answered promptly, "By way of Cape Horn, seventeen thousand miles."

Kendra gave her head a shake. "It's a long way. It's such a long way it scares me. It makes me feel like a nobody. So—unimportant."

"But you *are* important!" he exclaimed impulsively. "Here on the *Cynthia*, you're more important than you know." He caught his words. "Well, it's getting late. I'd better see if the captain has any orders."

He went out. Kendra looked after him with a puzzled frown. This was the second time he had started to say something and had broken off.

Now what, she wondered, could he have been talking about when he said that on the *Cynthia* she was more important than she knew?

2

Now began the battle of the Horn. Day after day the *Cynthia* creaked and tumbled as she fought to get from the Atlantic Ocean into the Pacific, while the wind raged against her.

The sailors dragged at the great ropes, and the sea flung icy waves across the decks, blinding and choking the men and leaving salt in the cuts on their hands. In the cabin the four passengers sat gripping their chairs, lest they be pitched out to go rolling around like marbles. They had no heat, and at night they had no light, for the oil lamps were too dangerous to be lit on so frantic a sea. Through the days they sat in the gray glow under the skylight, at night the darkness was so thick that Kendra felt as if she could almost gather it in her hands. They went to their berths as usual, but they could not sleep much, for the waves kept shaking them awake.

Now they did have meals of hardtack, and cold, very cold, salt beef. Nothing else, for it was nearly impossible for the cook to keep a pot steady on the fire. Once in a while he did manage to make coffee, but by Captain Pollock's orders this went to the struggling men on deck.

By morning of the fourth day Kendra's nerves were wearing thin. The night had been so rough that she felt bruised all over, and both she and Eva were glad when the time came to get up and go into the cabin. The steward brought them another meal of salt beef and seabiscuit, and water that tasted rusty from having been stored so long in the tank. The mate came in, ate his breakfast hurriedly, and went out. Captain Pollock was still on deck.

Her hands clenched on her chair, Kendra thought how alone they were in this terrible passage at the bottom of the world, how many vessels had split where the *Cynthia* was fighting now, how lost were even the names of the people whose bones had broken on the rock of Cape Horn. Across the table sat Eva, with Bess and Bunker Anderson, grimly enduring the ups and downs. Loren came in and sat by Kendra.

"The men on deck aren't scared," he told her. "Half of them have sailed with Captain Pollock before. Coming back to the same captain is the highest tribute they can pay."

Kendra smiled. He did make her feel better. Loren, who had also sailed with Captain Pollock before, went on.

"He's a strict master, but I was glad he wanted me again. A young fellow can learn a lot working with a man like him."

Captain Pollock came into the cabin and asked Loren to have the steward bring him some breakfast. Except for a nod he paid no attention to the passengers. The steward brought him beef and biscuit, and Pollock ate in silence, eating because he had to eat, all his thoughts outside with his ship.

Captain Pollock was thirty-six years old, a man of stalwart build, with a sailor's ruddy weatherbeaten cheeks and a sailor's farsighted blue eyes. His hair and beard were chestnut brown, his hands large and strong, his shoulders broad; in his own rugged way he was a handsome man. He wore nautical blue with brass buttons, and excellent shirts and boots, all kept in order by the steward, part of whose duty it was to act as the captain's personal attendant.

Just now his clothes were soaking, his hair and beard and eyebrows frosted with salt. He had no leisure for words or rest. As soon as he had finished his bread and beef he strode across the cabin and mounted to the deck again.

But though abstracted, he did not seem worried. He simply looked like a man who had a job to do. Kendra thought the very sight of him was enough to make anybody feel more confident. She said so to Loren, who had returned to the chair beside her.

Loren agreed. He told her Pollock had been at sea since he was sixteen years old, and had been captain of his own vessel since he was twenty-five. He had been around the world four times, and not once had the underwriters been called on to pay a dollar's insurance for a vessel or cargo under his command. At last the magnificent *Cynthia* had been built, especially for him. This was her maiden voyage.

"And how he does love this ship!" Loren exclaimed.

As he spoke, Loren glanced across the table, where Bunker Anderson was telling Bess and Eva an anecdote of his trading days in China. Lowering his voice Loren added, "Kendra, the other day I almost told you something and then thought I shouldn't. But now I think I should. It will make you less concerned." She listened with interest, and Loren said, "Captain Pollock is glad to have you on the *Cynthia*."

Kendra puckered her forehead. "You mean he's glad to have me, more than the others?"

Loren nodded. With another glance across the table to make sure the others were not listening, he said, "You bring good luck."

Kendra's eyes widened in astonishment. "Me? Why?"

He answered simply, "Because you're a pure young maiden."

Kendra burst out laughing. She was a pure young maiden —in her sheltered life she had never had much chance to be anything else—but she had a practical mind. For the captain to think this would bring good fortune to the *Cynthia* simply struck her as absurd.

"Oh Loren," she exclaimed, "you don't believe any such thing, do you?"

Loren answered soberly. "Kendra, I'm talking about what *Captain Pollock* believes. I've known him to turn down a passenger and sail with an empty stateroom, because he didn't think the passenger was the sort his *ship* would approve of. And now that he's got the *Cynthia* he's stricter than ever."

As she was still perplexed, Loren tried to explain.

To Pollock, he said, a vessel was a living creation. Of course, like people, vessels differed in their worth. Many a

11

dirty old whaler deserved nothing better than grease-buckets and sailors from the waterfront dives. But if a captain should treat a proud ship like some wastrel of the seas, this would be like forcing a fine woman into—into shame, Loren said modestly. She would never forgive you.

Pollock gave his ships the respect they deserved and they rewarded him. This was what he believed and he made no secret of it. If other seamen laughed at him he pointed to his record.

"And the odd part of it is," said Loren, "he's not a bit like that ashore. In port he likes to take a few drinks, drop a few dollars at a gambling spot, meet girls, have a good time. There's a gambling parlor in Honolulu where he goes often. Folks say he admires the hostess."

Kendra felt a twinge of amused astonishment. On shipboard Captain Pollock was so lordly and austere; she wished she could see how he acted around that girl in the gambling parlor. Loren was saying,

"But he wouldn't have her on the *Cynthia*. He believes a girl like that would offend the ship, and the ship would punish him."

Loren thought a moment and went on.

Though fond of women's company ashore, Pollock was not married nor had he ever been known to have a serious love affair. "All his life," said Loren, "he's loved nothing but ships. All his life he's been dreaming of the perfect ship. And now, I guess he's got her."

Kendra nodded gravely. But with a wise crinkle in his pink cheeks, Loren said,

"You still want to laugh, don't you? Well, maybe you're right. But I told you because I don't want you to be scared about doubling the Horn. Captain Pollock knows he can do it, but having you on board makes him extra sure. That's a real help, Kendra."

Kendra looked at him straight. She said, "I'm not scared any more, Loren."

This was true. Whether because of Loren's talk or the captain's assurance, she was no longer scared. Through the rest of the day she listened to the screech of ropes and crackle of sails and the men shouting above the wind. It all reminded her that these men were strong and skillful, and Captain Pollock, though he might have a few strange ideas, was a master

12

who knew his business. For this, and not because he had a virgin on board, the *Cynthia* would reward him.

And she did. That evening, not long before midnight, Kendra heard a bang as of a hatch closing hard. Captain Pollock came into the cabin, bringing a gust of air and the smell of the sea. The captain's nose was red as a strawberry, his coat dripped and his boots squashed as he walked. But his blue eyes were joyful and there was a warmth like a glow around him. He paused, giving himself a shake like a wet dog. Bunker Anderson called to him above the resounding sea.

"Well, captain, so we're in the Pacific now?"

Pollock nodded. Half buried in his salt-crusted beard was a smile of triumph. He had done this before and his smile said he had no doubt he would do it again, but every time the battle was hard and the victory good. Without speaking, he glanced around at them all as if assuring them he was glad to have them on board. As his eyes came to Kendra they paused. The pause was a mere point of time, but it was a piercing point. She felt it all over.

Then Pollock turned and went to his own stateroom. The job was done. The captain could rest.

—It *is* true, Kendra thought. He does believe my being here was a help. Because I'm pure like the *Cynthia*.

She remembered the ship's figurehead, the goddess crowned with the crescent moon. For the first time she realized that the ship's name, Cynthia, was an old Grek name for the moon goddess, ever young, ever virgin.

—Absurd, thought Kendra.

But somehow, it all made her feel uneasy.

The ship sailed up the west coast of South America. Every day the sun grew warmer as she drew nearer the port of Valparaiso, where she would stop for food and water. Two weeks above the Horn she came into harbor.

When you approached Valparaiso by sea the first thing you saw was a hill, so steep that the street was cut like a letter Z across the front of it. There on the Z you saw two houses, one on the lower arm of the zigzag and one on the upper. White houses with red tile roofs, they caught the sun and shone like two lights from the cliffside.

But they were houses where girls received sailors on shore leave, and no nice woman had ever noticed them. Bess Anderson had warned Eva; and Eva, tactful as ever, had warned Kendra. Kendra dutifully said, "Yes, mother." She felt like saying "Rats!" In talkfests at school she had heard of such places but she had never thought she would see any. But since the two houses were right there in front of her, why pretend she did not see them? She felt like a fool.

The waterfront was crowded with the native population, gay in their bright clothes and bangles. Also waiting on the wharf was a group of Yankee traders and their wives, many of them friends of Bess and Bunker Anderson. These traders lived here all the year round, and rushed to meet any vessel flying their flag. One couple asked the Andersons to be their guests, while another, Mr. and Mrs. Carlow, invited Eva and Kendra. With her usual grace Eva accepted.

It was a pleasant visit. They picked peaches and grapes in the courtyard, took carriage drives through the foreign streets, and met other Americans in town. And not once did anybody mention the two white houses on the hill.

They were in port four days. As the ship sailed out of the harbor Kendra stood by the rail and looked again at the two white houses. She wondered what sort of girls lived in those houses. Girls taught by mothers who were themselves in the trade? Or had they—any of them—been properly brought up?

Nice girls did get into trouble sometimes. More than once Kendra's schoolmates had brought back scandalous stories from their vacations. ". . . and she belongs to a *good* family, my dear!"

Kendra had read novels about such "unfortunates." In a book the girl would die—usually she pined away, though sometimes she jumped off a bridge. Kendra did not believe that in life they got out of the way so conveniently.

She wondered what became of them.

From here they sailed directly for San Francisco. Because of the way the winds blew, ships bound for San Francisco often went first to Honolulu, but the *Cynthia* would not, as she was bringing supplies for the California troops. She would go to Honolulu later, then on to trade in the ports of China.

New Year's day, 1848, was fair. Before long they were in the tropics, and now they sailed under a sun so fierce that the boards of the deck were sometimes too hot to be touched. Early in February Loren told Kendra they were coming close to San Francisco Bay.

14

He said frankly that the settlement on the bay was nothing but a scraggly village. The native Californios had named the spot Yerba Buena—good herb—for a plant that grew there, from which they brewed a medicine. But most of the people in town were Yankees and they found this hard to pronounce, so generally they called the town by the same name as the bay, San Francisco.

Loren and Kendra were sitting at the table in the cabin. He went on,

"The town's not much, but the bay is splendid. Look."

He had laid his hands flat on the table, his fingers overlapping, his thumbs pointing at each other.

"Suppose my hands were the California coast," he said. "My thumbs would be two peninsulas. The little space between the tips of my thumbs is the entrance to the bay. And on the inside of my right thumb, looking east across the bay to the mainland, there is San Francisco."

Kendra was surprised to learn that San Francisco faced east. A Pacific port, she thought it ought to face the Pacific Ocean. Loren laughed and said this was what most folks thought, but it didn't.

Two weeks later the *Cynthia* sailed into the bay and dropped anchor. Her voyage from New York had taken a hundred and thirty-two days.

This was remarkably fast. The average time for such a voyage was a hundred and sixty days. But no ship of Captain Pollock's had ever been average, and his beautiful *Cynthia* had outdone all the rest. Kendra wondered if he really thought this was because the *Cynthia* had carried a pure young maiden.

Anyway, the voyage was done. On a murky day in February, 1848, Kendra had her first look at San Francisco.

15

3

Loren had said the bay was splendid, she did not know why. All she could see was a lot of restless gray water, and streaks of fog like an army of ghosts marching past.

It was about ten o'clock in the morning. Kendra was on deck waiting to go ashore—a long way, for the water in front of San Francisco was so shallow that no seagoing vessel could come within a mile of town. The air was damp, the wind blowing hard.

She was alone. Alex had come out earlier, in a boat bringing the army quartermaster to confer with Captain Pollock about the stores the ship had brought. On deck Alex had shaken hands with Kendra, and greeted Eva with an affectionate kiss as if she had been away for the weekend. He genuinely loved her, but he would have died before showing it in front of other people. Alex was forty-five years old, handsome in a dark romantic way, the sort of man who looks well in a uniform. Kendra took about ten minutes to classify him as a high-minded bore.

As soon as the tide turned, Alex and Eva went ashore in the army boat, leaving Kendra to come in on the ship's boat with Bunker and Bess. Loren had gone below with Captain Pollock, but he had left his field-glass with Kendra so she could look around.

Kendra put the glass to her eyes. She saw two other seagoing vessels, a brig called the *Eagle,* which Loren had said came from China, and a smaller brig called the *Euphemia,* which she learned later was just in from Monterey. Close to shore were several little launches, which he had told her plied between the town and the ranch country. The fog was clearing, and a watery sun was pushing through, so she raised the glass to look at the land.

This was the strip that Loren had represented by his right thumb as his hands lay before him on the table. The whole strip looked like a jumble of hills, splotched with clumps of

16

weed and a few trees bent and twisted by the merciless wind. On the shoreline she saw a spot where the water had scooped out a cove shaped like a half moon. Around this half moon stood three hills, enclosing it like the side of a broken cup, and across these three hills sprawled San Francisco.

Kendra thought she had never seen a town so *steep*. The houses were scattered from the waterfront to the top of the highest ridge. The largest buildings—warehouses and trading posts—were on the waterfront. She could see about a dozen big warehouses, for the main business of San Francisco was that of selling supplies to vessels in the Pacific trade. Also near the beach she counted six hovels with the word "Saloon" painted across the front. Men were going in and out, while other men loafed on barrels and boxes by the doors.

Farther up she saw a long squat building of brown bricks, on the roof of which a board said "City Hotel." Near by were two false-fronted white frame buildings—not very white —with signs saying "Beds." (From the look of them, all Kendra could think of was bedbugs.) A few men on horse-back were jogging about.

She saw a few little wooden dwellings that looked solid enough to keep out rain. But except for these, the rest of the "buildings" were shacks and sheds, made of rough boards, flattened tin cans, sides of packing boxes, and anything else that men could nail together. Around them blew shreds of fog, like wet rags in the air.

With Bunker and Bess Anderson, Kendra went ashore in the ship's boat. The sailors rowed them to the north side of the moon-shaped cove, where a man who owned a warehouse had laid stones in the water to make a landing. Here as in Valparaiso, Bunker and Bess were met by friendly traders, and Bunker introduced the two nearest, Mr. Chase and Mr. Fenway. Kendra said, "How do you do." While the Andersons chatted with their friends she looked around, trying not to show her sick dismay.

In front of the stores and warehouses she saw a muddy strip where hoofprints and horse-droppings suggested a street. The "street" was littered with trash—cans and rags, papers trodden into the mud, a broken piece of harness, an old shoe somebody had thrown away. Kendra could hear flies buzzing over piles of empty bottles around the saloons. Her nose wrinkled at the stinks of privies, and dead fish rotting on the beach.

17

And here were the loafers she had seen, unwashed and uncombed and smelling of liquor. Leaving the barrels and boxes they had been sitting on, they came as close to her as they dared, and stood staring at her with greedy eyes.

Kendra felt a touch on her elbow. She started, but relaxed as she recognized a trader, the one Bunker had introduced as Mr. Chase. He was a short, thick man with a kindly smile.

Mr. Chase drew her aside. "I know how you feel, miss," he said with sympathy. "My wife, now, she was mighty upset when we came here from Valparaiso. But it's not as bad as you think." With an embarrassed glance at the staring men, he cleared his throat and went on. "Now those fellows— let me explain."

He told her a recent census had shown that about nine hundred people lived in San Francisco, and among them men outnumbered women three to one. And the census takers had counted only the men who *lived* here—not the soldiers of the garrison, nor the ranchers who came to town for business, nor sailors ashore.

So she could understand, couldn't she?—men here were mighty lonesome.

Here a proud smile broke the gravity of Mr. Chase as he caught sight of something over her shoulder. Kendra turned, and saw coming toward her two lieutenants of the United States Army. They were young, they were good-looking, they were scrubbed and barbered and as correct as if they had come only yesterday out of West Point .As they halted before her and bowed, they looked so much alike that for the moment she distinguished them by noting that one had brown eyes and the other blue.

The brown-eyed one spoke first. "Miss Logan? Lieutenant Morse, at your service."

The blue-eyed one said, "Lieutenant Vernon. The colonel has given us the honor of seeing you home, Miss Logan."

Kendra began to understand what Mr. Chase had told her. Morse and Vernon were so excited at being her escorts that they could hardly keep their dignity as officers and gentlemen. Gallantly they led her to a hitching post where their horses waited, and gallantly helped her into a saddle.

They rode along the soggy waterfront street, Morse and Vernon talking with all their might. This beach road, they said, was called Montgomery Street in honor of the naval hero who had first raised the American flag in San Francisco.

18

They pointed out a rickety building grandly called the New York Store, and another store named the Bee Hive, and Buckelew's watch repair shop near the landing point, and the tailor shop of Lazarus Everhard. Farther on they showed her the store owned by the two traders she had met at the point, Chase and Fenway.

"Everybody is so glad to see you!" Morse exclaimed.

"Now," Vernon said joyfully, "we can have the dance!"

"We've been planning the dance a long time," said Morse, "but we wanted to wait for you."

"We're going to have it," said Vernon, "in the parlor of a new boarding place, the Comet House—" He broke off. "This is the corner of Clay Street. We turn here."

Clay Street was a streak of mud leading straight up a hill. Kendra flinched. "Good heavens! It's like riding up the side of a steeple!"

But she could not help herself, so she started up. Like the beach road, this "street" was a mere track with no distinction of road and sidewalk. As they came to the City Hotel, Morse told her this was the general meeting place of the town. "We drop in there," he said, "to hear what's happening. If anything," he added with an angry little laugh.

"Nothing ever happens in San Francisco," Vernon agreed vehemently.

Across from the City Hotel was the town square. The men said that in Mexican days this had been called the plaza, and most people still called it that. The plaza was an open space slanting down the side of the hill. In the plaza was an old adobe building, which they told her had once been a Mexican customhouse and now served as an army barracks.

They rode past shanties with crudely painted signs of carpenters, cobblers, blacksmiths. Kendra saw a few men in flannel shirts and muddy black trousers, plodding up the hill, and two or three women in sunbonnets and gingham aprons. San Francisco did look like a place where nothing ever happened. In her mind she said—I'll *make* something happen. I'll do *something*.

But in a town like this, what?

"Tell me about the people who live here," she said hopefully.

"Well, the traders," said Morse, "and a few settlers who came out in covered wagons, and quite a colony of Mormons. They came by ship from New York."

"And drifters," said Vernon, "and runaway sailors."

"And crackbrains," said Morse. "The kind who invent perpetual motion machines, or think up schemes for getting gold out of sea water."

"One of those," Vernon remarked, "is roaming around right now. Only it's fresh water this time. A creek somewhere near Sutter's Fort—that's across the bay. This fellow has a tin box with gravel in it. He says the gravel is gold."

Kendra felt a spark of interest. "Gold? Where did he get it?"

Laughing, Vernon explained. "He says the creek bed is made of gold instead of sand. He wants somebody to lend him money to buy provisions, so he can go back and scoop up a million dollars."

"Does anybody believe him?" she asked.

"Oh no. We're always getting that sort. We let 'em talk. Breaks the monotony."

They were nearing the top of the hill. Beyond it Kendra could see more hills, reaching in long dim waves toward the sea. A muddy track ran across the face of the slope, parallel to Montgomery Street at the bottom. Along this track stood a row of dwellings, square like boxes and painted a glaring white. Morse and Vernon told her this was Stockton Street, the neighborhood of the Mormons. An enterprising Mormon carpenter named Riggs, after building a house for his own family, had built another next door for rent, and Colonel Taine had taken the second house. They rode along till they came to it.

This house was square and white like the others. The ground around it consisted of soft black mud, in which Mr. Riggs had laid a line of stepping stones.

Eva came across the porch, brisk, cheerful, as much at home as if she had lived in San Francisco a year. She greeted them cordially.

"Come in, there's a fire burning and I've made coffee." As they went into the hall she gestured toward a door at one side. "Kendra, this is our room, and yours is the one behind it." She opened a door at the other side of the hall. "Now this," she said merrily, "is our dining room, living room, library, drawing room—we're going to be very grand and call it the parlor." Laughing, she exclaimed, "Isn't it all *dreadful?*"

Kendra thought it certainly was.

Barely finished, the house smelled of raw lumber and fresh paint. The hall ran through from the front door to the back. On each side were two rooms—the bedrooms at one side, on the other the general room that Eva was blithely calling the "parlor," and behind it the kitchen. This was all.

Kendra went to look at her bedroom. She found it a small room with two small windows. Light came in dimly, and she could hear the panes rattling in the wind.

There was a narrow bedstead, so clumsy that she felt sure it had been made in one of the workshops she had passed on her way up the hill. To serve for a chair there was a wooden box, and for a dressing table another box on which stood a pitcher and washbowl.

Kendra thought of her grandmother's home in Baltimore, red brick with white woodwork and marble steps, and in front a lawn and flower beds. She thought of her own room there, the dainty furniture, the ruffly curtains, the soft deep rug by her bed.

—And my mother, she thought, *likes* living in such places as this.

From across the hall came the sound of voices and the aroma of coffee. Leaving her gloves and bonnet on the bed Kendra went into the parlor. The furniture here consisted of a rough table, and more boxes for chairs. Eva and Alex, with the two lieutenants, were drinking coffee from tin cups, while a plump rosy woman about thirty years old bustled around with the pot. Eva introduced her as Mrs. Riggs, wife of the carpenter, and said she had agreed to come in every day and help with the housekeeping.

"We're going to be quite comfortable," said Eva. "Mrs. Riggs says the New York Store has chairs, brought around the Horn. I can get calico from Chase and Fenway, to make curtains and bedspreads. And I'll stuff cushions for the chairs, and braid rugs for these bare floors."

Alex smiled proudly at the two younger men, and Vernon said, "The colonel told us, Mrs. Taine, 'Wherever she goes, she brings civilization in her hands.'"

Kendra had never stuffed a cushion, she had no idea how one went about braiding a rug and she did not think she could ever learn. But she was finding out why her mother liked the frontier. It was not merely the adventure. Like an artist who enjoys his power to take a hunk of clay and turn

21

it into something beautiful, Eva enjoyed her talent for turning a shack into a calico palace.

After a while the lieutenants said goodby. Eva said she had put a meal on the stove and Mrs. Riggs had been watching it for her. She went into the kitchen to say they would have lunch now. Mrs. Riggs brought in the dishes, while Kendra waited expectantly. For one thing, the time was well past noon and she was hungry; for another, after being limited so long to shipboard fare she was eager for something new. She had been wondering what people ate in San Francisco.

She came to table, and her hope fell flat. They sat on boxes and ate off tin plates borrowed from the army stores, but this she would not have minded if the food had not been utterly dull: boiled beef, boiled cabbage, boiled potatoes. Kendra ate because anything was better than nothing; but Alex must have noticed her disappointment, for he remarked that food in California was generally dull. People lived on beef from the ranches, beef and more beef till they were tired of it. They had little else. The errand boy from Chase and Fenway was going to bring a box of groceries later today, but Alex could not say what these would be.

When they had finished, Alex went to the army headquarters on the beach. A soldier had ridden up the hill, leading a horse for him and bringing Eva the two weekly papers, the *Californian* and the *Star*. Eva was not, however, interested in the local news. As Alex rode away she told Kendra she wanted to step next door with Mrs. Riggs.

"Mrs. Riggs is going to show me her household arrangements," said Eva. "If that errand boy brings the groceries, tell him to leave them in the kitchen."

She went out. The newspapers lay on the table. Kendra picked up the *Star*.

She read that two men had been arrested for robbing a bowling alley. Another man, presumably more honest, had opened a workshop for making chairs and tables.

She saw advertisements for most of the stores she had passed this morning. Chase and Fenway offered brooms, buckets, nails, axes, paint, brandy, gin, combs, tobacco, pans, soap, wine, and matches. The tailor, Lazarus Everhard, announced that he would make army uniforms. The New York Store urged everybody to buy Vegetable Pills, a remarkable remedy guaranteed to cure smallpox, gout, consumption, and female troubles. The Bee Hive had corkscrews, garden seeds, gunpowder, men's hats, and women's shawls.

Just here Kendra looked up.

And there he stood.

She did not know—as long as she lived she did not know—if she had just happened to look up then or if she had felt his eyes upon her, telling her to do so. But look she did, and across the page of the *Star* she saw him.

He stood in the doorway, a strange man, the most beguiling stranger she had ever seen, watching her with a frank audacious pleasure. As their eyes met, he smiled.

He was about thirty years old, tall, lean, healthy. Standing there with one hand on the door and the other at his side, he had a simple loose-jointed grace. His clothes were practical —leather jacket, plaid wool shirt, trousers of brown twilled worsted tucked into stout boots that came nearly up to his knees. He wore no hat, and his brown hair was tumbled by the wind, one wavy lock falling over his forehead to touch his eyebrow. His gaze at her was steady, his smile wise and experienced, and Kendra felt instantly that he knew more about women than she knew about men. She felt, in fact, that he knew more about everything than she did, which made it an even greater tribute that he should be regarding her now with such admiration plain and undisguised.

He looked straight at her and she looked straight at him. For a moment their eyes held, while he did not speak and she could not. It was only a moment, but it was a moment longer than necessary before he said,

"How do you do. I'm the errand boy from Chase and Fenway."

Kendra started. He did not look like any errand boy she had ever seen. As she dropped the paper on the table he continued,

"I hope I'm not intruding. But the doors were open, so I came in."

He had such an easy way of speaking that he made it easy for her to answer. "It's quite all right," she said. "We were expecting you, Mr.—?"

"My name is Ted Parks," he answered, his smile returning as he went on, "and you're Kendra Logan?"

"Why yes. Who told you?"

"Mr. Chase. He has a good power of description, but he

23

didn't quite prepare me. I hardly expected to find anyone so —vivid."

Ted Parks let his gaze sweep over her. Again, it lasted only a moment, but it was a moment that made her aware of her graceful figure and her dark blue eyes and the arrow of hair on her forehead; it made her feel *discovered,* as if nobody had ever really looked at her before. Then Ted leaned over and lifted a box from the floor beside him. Hoisting the box to his shoulder he asked, "Now where do I put this?"

Kendra opened the door to the kitchen. She was still far from tranquil. The adoration of the lieutenants had not stirred her, not after what Mr. Chase had said about the shortage of girls. But Ted Parks had a splendid impudence, as if he was used to having plenty of girls to choose from, all eager to be chosen. As he followed her into the kitchen Kendra asked,

"How long have you been in San Francisco?"

"Nearly a year," said Ted. With a merry twinkle he added, "But don't think I'm interested in you because girls are scarce. I'm interested because you're you."

He had read her thoughts so clearly that Kendra could not answer, but Ted saved her the need of it. As he set the box on the kitchen table he said,

"I came over from Honolulu."

"Why did you come over?" asked Kendra. She was alert with curiosity.

Ted shrugged. "No reason. I kept hearing about California, thought I'd take a look."

Scatterbrained, she thought. Doesn't plan his life. Alex would never approve of him.

Ted was gesturing toward the box. "Don't you want to see what I've brought? Or maybe you're one of those people who never know what they're eating?"

"I certainly am not!" she retorted. "I like food and I like to cook. Show me."

"I'm so glad you like to cook!" Ted exclaimed. "It's no fun choosing food for people who don't care."

"I'm going to cook our dinners," said Kendra.

In that moment she had made up her mind. She could not make a palace out of a shack but she could make a luscious meal out of any food not absolutely poisonous, and she was

24

going to do it here. She was not going to eat the tasteless kind of stuff her mother had served today. Ted was saying,

"As I suppose you've been told, food in California is mostly beef. So here's the beef, but I found bacon too, and I think later we'll have ham. And here are some relishes and seasonings." He took out curry powder and ginger, mustard and cloves and nutmegs, olives and raisins and dried apples. "It's early for most vegetables, but I did find onions and turnips."

"I'll make a beef stew with onions," said Kendra. "The next day we'll have a curry."

"I'm glad you like curry. This came from China on the *Eagle*."

"And I'm glad to have these dried apples," she said. "I'll make a pie."

"May I give you a hint?" asked Ted. He took up the box of raisins. "Soak a few raisins overnight in wine and add them to the pie filling."

"What a good idea! Who told you that?"

"Oh, a woman I used to know," Ted answered, and quickly changed the subject. "Did the army boys tell you about the dance they're planning?"

Kendra nodded, wondering about that woman he used to know. But he seemed already to have put her out of his mind. Standing with the table behind him, his hands resting on the edge, he asked,

"Dance with me?"

Kendra promised, hoping she did not sound too eager. Ted said,

"I'm invited because I was recommended by Mr. Chase, who's a leading citizen." His forehead wrinkled humorously as he spoke. On impulse Kendra began,

"Tell me—" She stopped, and he prompted her,
"Yes?"

"Why are you an errand boy?"

A grin creased his lean cheeks. "Because," he answered, "I'm too bone-lazy to be anything better."

As he said it, this seemed the most logical and amusing reason in the world. They both laughed, and Ted said,

"I like your name—Kendra. Where did you get it?"

"My father gave it to me. He liked unusual names. They say 'Kendra' is based on an old word that means 'knowledge.'"

"Of course!" he exclaimed. "I know the word—*ken*." He

25

nodded reflectively. "And exactly right, too. That's how it was when I saw you."

Puzzled, she repeated, "When you saw me?"

Again, as when he had stood in the doorway, Ted's eyes swept over her. Again, it was a moment that made her feel as if she had just been discovered. He quoted,

" 'Then felt I like some watcher of the skies,
When a new planet swims into his ken . . .' "

Her breath caught in her throat. Again, she did not know how to answer, and again he saved her the trouble. He said,

"What an expressive face you have."

Kendra put up her hand and felt it. "Do you really like my face?"

"Oh very much. Those black-lashed blue eyes, the way your hair grows, everything. Do you look like your mother?"

"No, like my father. They say I'm like him in many ways. I don't remember him."

"I think you missed a great deal," Ted said gravely. At her questioning look, he added, "Because you are an unusual and winsome person. If you are like him, he must have been an unusual and winsome person."

Kendra felt a start of pleasure. Back home, the Logans thought of her father as the family disgrace. Before she could answer they heard footsteps in the hall and Eva's voice exclaiming,

"For pity's sake, Mrs. Riggs, who do you suppose tracked in all this mud?"

"That's my mother," Kendra said under her breath.

Ted gave a long slow shrug. Hands in the pockets of his leather jacket, he sauntered into the hall. Kendra was observing that he did nothing in a hurry. She heard him say,

"I'm afraid I'm the culprit, Mrs. Taine."

With respectful courtesy he told her who he was, apologized for his carelessness, and bowed himself out. Later that day Eva remarked that Ted Parks seemed surprisingly well bred for a man in his position.

4

That evening, when Kendra said she wanted to cook, Eva heard her with glad surprise. Eva regarded cooking as a disagreeable duty. That anybody should *want* to cook astonished her. She was also astonished that Kendra had a talent for it. Kendra's utter lack of skill at handicrafts, which Eva did so well, had led her to fear that Kendra had no talents at all.

"Why Kendra," she exclaimed, "can you cook a whole meal? All by yourself?"

Kendra said she could, all by herself. "When you go to buy calico," she continued, "let me go with you, for groceries."

"My dear," Eva said fervently, "I shall be delighted."

Overhearing them, Alex smiled with more warmth than Kendra knew he possessed. "You are a thoughtful young woman, Kendra," he said. Kendra guessed that with all Eva's other gifts for bringing civilization to the wilds, that dreadful meal of boiled beef and cabbage was typical of what she put on table.

The next day was foggy and cold. But Eva wanted to start her shopping, so Alex sent up the horses, and two army officers as escorts. The four of them rode down to Montgomery Street and went into the trading post of Chase and Fenway.

Both partners came forward in welcome. They made an odd contrast: Mr. Chase brisk and stocky and good-natured, Mr. Fenway tall and thin and languid, with a mournful look as if he were always hearing sad music. Eva was so charming that Mr. Chase blushed with pleasure and even Mr. Fenway's dismal face relaxed in a smile. Opening a side door Mr. Chase called, "Parks! Come take care of these ladies!" Ted came out and said he would be happy to do so.

Kendra went with him into the storeroom and he showed her around. She did not buy much, for she had the foodstuffs Ted had brought her the day before, but now she knew what she could count on. She went home and prepared the dinner

27

she had planned yesterday: a beef stew with onions, and for dessert a dried apple pie, made as Ted had suggested, with raisins soaked in wine and added to the pie filling.

Alex ate dinner with astonished relish. Afterward he said, almost respectfully, that he would like to bring some of his army friends to dinner now and then. Kendra said of course, and Eva said they would be welcome. After this, he invited his friends often, and as they discovered Kendra's menus and Eva's charm they told him he was the luckiest man in town.

The mornings were foggy, the afternoons windy and sharp. With army escorts Kendra and Eva rode down to Montgomery Street nearly every day. They did much of their shopping at Chase and Fenway's. Eva liked the store, because Ted was so obliging, and because Mr. Fenway saw to it that the place was swept and dusted and the hinges did not squeak.

The building had two main rooms, the front room for trade and the back for storage, and a smaller room used as an office. Across the front room was the counter, and at one side a stove around which men with time on their hands smoked and yarned.

In the storeroom the walls were lined with over-full shelves, and the floor crowded with crates and barrels not yet unpacked. Kendra liked to take her basket and browse in here. It was not a simple task, for as the boys unpacked they piled goods wherever they found space on the shelves, so that prunes and sardines stood among hatchets and shoes and candles; but she enjoyed it, especially when Ted had time to come in and help her.

While Kendra chose the foodstuffs, Eva would often go shopping elsewhere. (It was not wise, she said, to give too much business to one firm.) Leaving Kendra in care of Mr. Chase, Eva would take both the army escorts with her. She did not want to be seen riding with only one man (she said this was all right for a young girl but not for a married woman; it might cause talk). On days when she did not leave the store Eva waited for Kendra in the front room. Seated on a box, with traders and officers around her, she laughed and chatted with them, her manner exquisitely balanced between an artless warmth and the reserve becoming a colonel's wife.

The door to the storeroom was always open, and Messrs. Chase and Fenway and the packing boys came in and out, but Ted and Kendra had many chances to talk. Ted was interesting, and he never spoke again of any "woman he used to know." When the *Cynthia* sailed for Honolulu, Kendra did not miss her shipboard friends at all.

The *Cynthia* left sooner than Captain Pollock had intended. Part of the ship's cargo consisted of goods ordered by Honolulu merchants, but he had planned a longer delay in San Francisco, to give himself and his crew a rest. However, he was leaving now because the garrison at Monterey had sent up a plea for help.

Captain Pollock told Kendra and Eva about this when he called to say goodby. He was in high spirits, laughing as he described his mission, for on shore Pollock was not as formal as he was at sea. He was being sent to Honolulu, he said, to get salt meat and dried split peas for the sailors on the battleships at Monterey.

"The naval supply is running low," he explained, "and the boys are grumbling. They hate all this fresh food from the ranches."

Kendra and Eva were surprised, but Pollock was not. Knowing seamen, he knew they liked the food they were used to at sea.

He said he had been told to come back as soon as possible. An average voyage to Honolulu was three weeks each way, but the *Cynthia* would probably do better than this. As he talked, Kendra mischievously wondered if his good humor at leaving for Honolulu might not be due to the prospect of seeing that gambling hostess Loren had told her about. But the lieutenants were waiting to escort herself and Eva to the store, and Ted was there, and she hardly thought of Captain Pollock again.

She was liking Ted more and more. At home, Kendra had met young men who flirted and told her she was pretty. But she was not used to having anybody, man or woman, take a genuine interest in her as a person who stood out from all the other people in the world. This was what Ted did. She found herself talking to him with more enjoyment than she had ever felt with anybody else.

He was more interested in talking about her than about himself, but when she asked him he said he came from New York, where he had worked for a legal firm. Everybody had told him he had a fine chance to rise in the world. All he needed was diligence, promptness, perseverance, and various

29

other virtues he did not possess. He had been utterly, unbearably bored.

"So one day," he said, "I took a ship for Honolulu."

They were in the storeroom. Kendra held her basket, while Ted was carrying a bag of new potatoes from Sutter's Fort. Sutter's launch had come down a few days before, and Ted had put aside these potatoes for her as soon as they were brought in. As he spoke, Ted shrugged.

"There you have me, Kendra. Hasty, impetuous, reckless, no ambition to be President, just living life as it comes along."

They both laughed. Ted reminded her that tomorrow night was the time set for the dance.

"I have some packing to do tomorrow," he went on. "Sutter's agent brought an order for tools, to be sent up by the launch. I should be finished before dark, but if I'm not I'll quit anyway."

There was a pause. Kendra asked suddenly, "Ted, if you could do anything you pleased, what would you do?"

"Go places," said Ted. "Not the regular spots but—oh, the inside of China, the lonesome islands, the dim far countries." He gave her his happy smile. "And I'd take you with me."

At this moment Mr. Chase came blundering in to ask Ted if he had shown the young lady that cheese from the Columbia River country.

They went back into the front room. Here Eva was holding court. Her clear, friendly voice drifted across to them.

"I tell you, boys, it's sheer nonsense. My husband told me a man came to the quartermaster's office the other day, bringing some of those shiny flakes. He wanted to know if they were gold. The quartermaster looked at them carefully, and said they were nothing but yellow mica."

Standing by the counter with pencil and notebook, Ted was totaling the cost of Kendra's purchases. He glanced at her sideways. "I'd rather have a dance with you than a bag of gold," he said softly. "There'll be two men there tomorrow night for every woman. But you're going to dance with me twice. I said twice."

The next evening was cold, with a hard wind blowing the clouds across the moon. Kendra brushed her hair till it glistened, and put on a dress of white silk printed with little blue flowers the color of her eyes. With Alex and Eva she

30

rode horseback to the scene of the ball, the Comet House on Dupont Street. When they had given their wraps to a soldier on duty they went into the parlor, a room with garish flowered wallpaper and pink-shaded whale oil lamps.

Kendra had never been to a dance like this one. The men present were army officers and their friends: traders, ranchers, officers of the vessels in port, sixty men in all. The women were all the wives and daughters that could be scraped up. There were two army wives besides Eva, all who had made the long journey to San Francisco. Mr. Chase brought his wife, a lady stout and good-natured like himself, but he had brought no daughter because his three children were all sons. (Mr. Fenway, who had neither wife nor child, was absent.) Also there were women of the Mormon families, and several native Californians of Mexican descent, wives of British and Yankee traders.

Altogether, to dance with the sixty men there were twenty-seven women. Only three of these, Kendra and two Mormon girls, were not married. While they danced, the extra men stood along the walls and gazed—no, thought Kendra, they *gawked*. They were not so bad as the loafers on the waterfront, but they did make her think of some farmers she had seen once, yearning over the prize pigs at a fair.

Kendra had so many pleas for dances that she could say yes to only a few of them. But somehow, without any appearance of pushing, Ted found her and claimed her, and got her.

Ted was good-looking in his black suit and white shirt and his well cut shoes. The music was provided by the army band, and they played well. Just now they were playing a frivolous little tune and singing the words that went with it.

"Love is like a dragonfly,
Here today, tomorrow gone,
Love's a teasing passerby,
Blows a kiss and hurries on . . ."

Ted and Kendra danced. Never had Kendra been so aware of a man's arm around her, or of how the two of them almost melted together as they followed the music. Ted looked down at her, his gaze lingering on her dark blue eyes and the arrow of hair. Bending his head closer he whispered, "You're beautiful."

31

Kendra laughed happily. "I'm not really beautiful," she said. She said it because she wanted to hear him say again that she was.

But Ted had a way of saying what she did not expect. His arm tightening around her, his eyes on her with that same intentness of their first meeting, he answered softly, "My dear, every woman is as beautiful as some man thinks she is."

And then before she could even catch her breath, the music ended and Lieutenant Vernon came to tell her she had promised him the next dance.

Vernon, like Loren Shields, was a nice boy, such a nice boy that Kendra felt guilty because she was begrudging every minute she had to give him. She liked Vernon, and it was not his fault that she was falling in love with somebody else.

Her own thought startled her. Was she falling in love?

She danced with Lieutenant Morse, and with several other men whose names she forgot as soon as she heard them, but at last Ted managed to claim her again. By this time the room was hot and the lamps were smoking. Several of the merrymakers had been helping themselves at the table of wines and brandies in a corner, and were dancing with more enthusiasm than grace. Kendra did not care. Ted had asked the musicians to repeat the dragonfly tune, and Kendra thought any time she heard it again she would remember how Ted looked this minute, and the feel of his arms, and the skill with which he guided her among the crowded couples around them.

It was now long past midnight, and when this dance ended Alex said it was time to go home. They rode through the wild night wind, half a dozen officers riding with them. Along Dupont and Pacific Streets the groggeries were lit up, and above the wind came sounds of drunken hilarity. Kendra thought,—I'm glad I don't have to go to all that trouble to be happy.

She was happy, happier than she had ever been. As she lay in bed that night she thought how glorious it was to be *wanted*. Ted did not know how she had yearned to be loved. She had not known it herself until now, when she found out what she had been missing. As she fell asleep she was thinking maybe she was fortunate not to have had any love before, because if she had, she would never have known this joy of discovery.

5

The next day was dark and cloudy. They had slept so late that Eva said they would not go shopping, but would dine on whatever they had at home. Eva had finished her parlor curtains, and she and Mrs. Riggs began hanging them at the windows.

In the mud and fog of San Francisco, Eva was turning their bare little house into an oasis of comfort. The bedrooms now had curtains and matching bedspreads; here in the parlor there were chairs at the table and rocking chairs by the hearth, each with its cushion stuffed with Hawaiian moss. Eva made everything in bright colors. They needed color, she said, in such a gray town as this.

Kendra sat by the fire, a copy of the *Star* in her hand. She was pretending to study the grocery advertisements, but actually she was dreaming in the firelight, remembering last night. "You're beautiful . . . . Every woman is as beautiful as some man thinks she is."

She heard a sound of horse's hoofs. A moment later a visitor ran up the steps and pounded on the front door. Mrs. Riggs went to open it, and in came Ted, hatless and wind-blown, grinning proudly as he paused in the parlor doorway and held out a loosely wrapped package.

"How do you do, everybody!" he greeted them. "Mrs. Taine, I've brought your dinner."

Eva stepped down from the stool she had been standing on. "Why, how kind of you, Mr. Parks!"

"I brought it now," said Ted, "because it won't keep. Shall I put it in the kitchen?"

Kendra had sprung to her feet. "I'll come with you."

They went into the kitchen and Ted laid his package on the table. With a flourish he opened the wrapping and showed her a cut from a fresh-caught salmon.

Beef was so abundant in California that few people bothered to go after anything else. Kendra exclaimed with plea-

33

sure. Coming to the door, Eva added, "This will be a real treat, Mr. Parks."

"Glad you like it," said Ted. He gestured toward the basin on a stand in a corner of the kitchen. "May I wash my hands?"

"Certainly," said Eva, and Kendra asked,

"How did you get this?"

"Luck. Some fellows took out a boat, came back this morning with more salmon than they could eat. Brought the surplus to the store. I'd have been here earlier but I had to finish packing those tools Mr. Sutter ordered. The captain of the launch wants to start back at daybreak tomorrow."

Eva glanced toward the window. "He's a brave man. Aren't we about to have a storm?"

"You never can tell," said Ted, scrubbing his hands. "Sometimes the clouds hang like this for days with never a drop of rain." He grinned over his shoulder. "I like San Francisco, Mrs. Taine, but you're not going to catch me defending the climate."

Eva laughed, thanked him again for the salmon, and returned to the front room to go on hanging the curtains. Replacing the towel on its rack Ted said to Kendra,

"Shall we step outside and take a look at the weather?"

She agreed, and Ted opened the door to the hall. He smiled at her, Ted's sweet, beguiling smile, which always gave her such a happy glow when she saw it. As she started to go past him into the hall her arm brushed his.

Without quite meaning to, Kendra paused beside him. Ted looked down at her, his eyes tender and soft as they had been last night at the dance. Again he smiled, slowly, with a look of wonder, as if he had not seen her for a long time and had forgotten she was so enchanting to look at. Kendra did not move. She could not. It was as if she had been caught in a shining web. Slowly, Ted put out his hand and touched her hair. In a low voice he said, "How lovely you are."

For an exquisite moment they stood still, looking at each other. Then it happened. Ted's hard bony hands gripped her shoulders and brought her to him. Kendra felt herself go limp with delight. Her eyelashes brushed his cheek, their lips touched, then with a violent movement Ted sprang back from her, and words came out of his throat like gasps of pain.

34

"Good God, what am I doing?"

He threw her away from him so roughly that she slipped and had to catch the table to keep from falling. Already Ted was rushing away. She heard the clack of his boots in the hall and across the porch and down the steps.

Dizzy with hurt bewilderment, hardly aware that she was moving, Kendra followed him into the hall. In his haste to get away Ted had left the front door open, and she saw him leap on his horse and go dashing down the hill. He did not look back. She could hear the whirring sound of the wind, and through the doorway she saw the fog, blowing past in waves like water.

In a vacant lot near by several small boys were yelling joyously as they built a fort of sticks and clods. A Mexican woodcutter came up the hill, leading a burro loaded with firewood for sale. A wagon creaked into sight, bringing barrels of drinking water from the spring at Sausalito. In another minute the driver would stop here to make his regular delivery, and Eva or Mrs. Riggs would come out to let him in.

While she was not thinking clearly some instinct told Kendra she did not want them to see her now. Unsteadily she crossed the hall and went into her bedroom. As she closed the door she remembered the words of the song the band had played last night.

> Love is like a dragonfly,
>   Here today, tomorrow gone,
> Love's a teasing passerby,
>   Blows a kiss and hurries on . . .

—Oh Ted, Ted, she cried silently, is that what it means to you?

Though the clouds continued thick all day it did not rain. Kendra cooked the salmon, but she could eat very little of it. When Eva remarked on her lack of appetite Kendra said she thought she was still tired from being up so late at the dance. Speaking of the dance nearly choked her.

All night she was miserably restless, tossing from side to side, waking and dozing and waking again, thinking of Ted.

Did he want her or didn't he? She had felt so sure! Kendra knew there were men who thought it amusing to win a girl's

35

love and then throw her away. But Ted's smile and the warm light in his eyes, the caress in his voice, the eagerness of his simplest greeting—if all these had not been real, never had a girl been so deceived. And that almost-kiss, the shocked dismay of him as he pushed her back—what *did* he mean?

Here as elsewhere, Kendra could not go halfway. When she wanted something she wanted it. And she wanted Ted. If she could not have him she meant to know why. She meant to ask him plainly—Do you love me or don't you?

Any answer would be better than not knowing.

In the morning, thank heaven, there was still no rain. Kendra washed her face over and over with cold water to clear her eyes, for if she did not look well Eva might not let her go out. At breakfast she said the weather was so threatening, she thought they ought to shop early. Eva agreed, and as soon as Alex reached headquarters he sent Morse and Vernon to escort them.

Ted was not in the front room of the store. Mr. Fenway, who had been standing by the stove with several other men, ambled over, saying, "Good morning, ladies, good morning, gentlemen." He spoke like an undertaker greeting the mourners at a funeral.

Strolling to the office door, Mr. Fenway put in his head and solemnly announced that Mrs. Taine and her daughter were here. Out came Mr. Chase, loudly bidding them welcome. He came out alone.

So Ted was avoiding her. Kendra felt a surge of anger. But maybe he was not in the office. She could hear voices from the storeroom, and men rolling barrels in by the back door.—Of course, she thought, he's in there with the packing boys.

Mr. Chase walked briskly over to where she and Eva and the lieutenants stood with the men by the stove. His chunky face was alight as he asked, "You folks want to see some gold?"

There was a rustle in the group. Mr. Chase was holding out his pudgy hand, on the palm of which was a rag creased as if it had been tied in a knot. The men gathered to peer at it, all but one of them, a lanky fellow standing with one foot on a box and his elbow on his knee. The stranger wore a blue flannel shirt and mud-spattered black trousers. Every pocket of his clothes was bulging—notebooks, money, keys, knife, comb, pencil, red bandana, blue bandana, shoehorn,

36

riding gloves, and a thousand other things. He had a week's beard sticking out of his lean jaws like pine needles, but his eyes were quick and likable, a warm hazel, and as he watched the other men crowding around the gold he had a friendly smile.

"Now wait a minute, fellows," Mr. Chase was urging them. "Let the ladies have a look, and the soldier boys. Here you are, folks. This gentleman here, name of Pocket, brought this stuff to town. Took it to Buckelew's watch shop down by the point, and Buckelew now, he knows gold and he's got jeweler's scales to weigh it." Mr. Chase nodded firmly. "It's gold."

Oh, why didn't he stop gabbling, Kendra thought, and call Ted? The rag was a fragment torn from an old shirt. In it lay about a teaspoonful of dirty yellowish grains. Morse and Vernon murmured doubtfully—after all, the quartermaster had said this so-called gold was mica—and Eva touched the grains with a gloved finger, asking,

"Where did you get this, Mr.—I'm sorry, I didn't catch your name."

With a little start, the lanky stranger took his foot from the box and stood up straight, like a man unexpectedly called upon to make a speech.

"My name is Sylvester Brent, ma'am," he answered politely, "but everybody calls me Pocket."

"And no wonder," mumbled Mr. Fenway, with a disapproving look at his visitor's overstuffed apparel. Pocket, his eyes on Eva, smiled bashfully and stroked his bristly jaw.

"If I'd known I was to meet fine ladies, ma'am, I'd have gotten a shave. Excuse me please. But you asked about the gold. I'm a clerk for Mr. Smith, at his store up at Sutter's Fort. Men have been bringing in stuff like this. They want to use it for money."

"Where do they get it?" she asked with interest.

Pocket shifted his weight from one foot to the other. "They say they pick it up around the sawmill, ma'am."

"Sawmill?" Eva repeated.

With shy courtesy Pocket explained. "Well ma'am, settlers are coming in, and they want lumber for their houses, so Mr. Sutter sent some men up to the hills to build a sawmill on the American River. They found bits like this in the river and in the cracks of the rocks, and they say it's gold."

"It's gold," Mr. Chase insisted.

37

Restlessly Kendra tapped her foot. *Where was Ted?*

"It don't mean a thing," remarked Mr. Fenway. His voice was like the drone of a bee.

"What's that?" demanded Mr. Chase. "I tell you, this is gold."

Mr. Fenway looked around like a man about to say a thing or two. "How much gold is up there, Pocket?" he asked.

"I don't know, sir," Pocket answered in his polite innocent way. "I don't reckon anybody knows."

"Well, don't get excited," cautioned Mr. Fenway. "This is not the first time it's happened around here."

Mr. Fenway spoke with gloomy importance. His slow sandy voice went on.

"Five or six years ago it was, that was before Chase got here, he wouldn't know. Down near Los Angeles. A ranch hand pulled up some wild onions and saw grains like these on the roots. Word got around. Men quit work and went out to look for gold. Well, the grains on the onion roots were gold, but—" Mr. Fenway wagged his hand at them in warning—"*but* there wasn't enough to matter. Hunting from dawn to dark, a man couldn't find enough to pay for a bowl of beans." Mr. Fenway nodded with satisfaction. "Well, Pocket, I guess you never heard of that."

Pocket smiled modestly. "No sir, I never did. I wasn't here then. I came out with a wagon train last summer."

Kendra could bear their chatter no longer. She touched Eva's arm.

"Excuse me, mother, but don't you think I'd better get the groceries?"

"Oh yes, of course," said Eva. Kendra began, "Mr. Chase, will you call—" but Mr. Fenway was already drawling,

"I'll take care of you, miss."

He moved languidly over to the counter, took her basket from the shelf, and waited by the door to the storeroom. As she followed him Kendra saw the big back door standing open, and a delivery wagon driving away. The boys who unpacked the goods were busy in there, and no doubt Ted was with them. Promising herself to get rid of the others somehow, she went in with Mr. Fenway.

The boys were three young fellows known as Bert, Al, and Foxy. As she came into the storeroom they looked around, grinned at the pleasing sight of her, and said, "Howdy, miss." Ted was not there.

The storeroom was dim and cold. The room reminded her of a vault and Mr. Fenway reminded her of a ghost. Kendra took a dozen steps, Mr. Fenway accompanying her in sepulchral silence. She could curb her eagerness no longer. In a carefully level voice she asked, "Where is Ted Parks this morning, Mr. Fenway?"

With a sad shake of his head Mr. Fenway answered, "Ted Parks is gone."

Kendra thought she was going to fall. She steadied herself against a barrel. "Gone?" she repeated faintly. "Gone where?"

"Say, Foxy!" called Bert's voice behind her. "Don't put those candles so near the edge of the shelf. They'll roll off. Push 'em back."

Mr. Fenway had turned toward another shelf close at hand and was reaching for a box. Over his shoulder he answered Kendra's question.

"Gone to Sutter's Fort. On that launch." With a sigh he droned on. "Don't know what's come over young men these days. In my time we didn't walk off a job without notice. Parks had easy hours, good pay, room over the store to live in. No gratitude. He comes in here yesterday, says he's leaving. Packs his duds and walks out. Times have changed. Now miss, we've got these nice dried pears from Oregon—"

6

Life went on, but life without Ted was dull and cold. One day was like another. Nothing happened.

Kendra continued to prepare the meals because it was something to do, and the army men continued to tell Alex he was the luckiest man in town. Kendra received several proposals of marriage from lonely young officers, most of whom she hardly knew. She declined as gently as she could. They were fine young men. But no matter how hard she tried she could not think of herself getting into bed with any

39

of these fine young men. With Ted she could think of it; she had thought of it often, without trying.

Now and then she heard people talking about the gold from Sutter's sawmill, but usually they agreed with Mr. Fenway that it would not amount to much. A few waterfront loafers, always looking for an easy way to get rich, roamed off to the hills. But sensible folk, warned by the fiasco down south, were not excited.

There was no news of Ted. To take his place Chase and Fenway hired a young man named Hodge, from Missouri. Hodge did his duty, but he had not Ted's winning manners nor his schooling. Ted could write well phrased business letters and read the Latin terms in contracts, both feats beyond the power of Hodge. They missed Ted.

Kendra wished she had a friend to talk to. But she had not. Certainly not her mother. They did not know each other well enough.

But with April the weather brightened, and the *Cynthia* came in from Honolulu. Kendra felt a lift of her spirits. It would be good to see Captain Pollock and Loren again.

The morning after the *Cynthia* arrived, Captain Pollock came to call. Kendra was on the porch when she heard the sound of hoofs and saw him riding up the hill.

He rode up Clay Street, and at the corner of Stockton he turned his horse. As he rode he looked awkward, and Kendra was surprised, for she had never seen Captain Pollock look awkward at anything. But of course, she rebuked herself, seamen were nearly always poor riders because they had so little riding to do. You could not expect a sea captain to ride like an army man who spent half his life in a saddle.

A short way past the corner a dwarf oak grew by the side of the road. Here Captain Pollock dismounted, tethered his horse to the tree, and started walking. Before he had taken six steps Kendra knew something had gone wrong.

She watched him with puzzled wonder. Now she could tell that his way of riding had not been merely a seaman's clumsiness. And the way he walked was not merely the uncertain land-walk of a man just off a ship. He was *different*.

Whether on sea or land, usually Captain Pollock strode over the world with masterful sureness. But not today. Today his head was bent, his shoulders slumped. He was carrying two packages wrapped in red and gold paper, no doubt gifts he had brought from some palmy shore, and his footsteps

40

crunched on the ground as if these two small packages made a burden almost too heavy to be borne. His whole attitude was so despondent that when he came near the steps and looked up at her, and she saw the lines of strain above his ruddy beard, and his usually steel-bright eyes cloudy like the eyes of a man who had spent a sleepless night, this only confirmed what she had guessed already. Something had gone wrong.

Captain Pollock was trying to act as if nothing was the matter. As he reached the steps he took off his blue cap, and bowed, saying gallantly, "What a pleasure to see you again, Miss Logan!"

With a smile that she hoped was hiding her concern, Kendra showed him into the parlor and went to call her mother. Eva came in and gave him a cordial welcome.

Pollock responded with stiff courtesy. Trying though he was to seem normal, he was finding it hard to do. He handed Eva and Kendra the gifts he had brought. These proved to be lacquered boxes, which later would serve to hold gloves or handkerchiefs, but which were now filled, one with Chinese tea and the other with slices of sugared ginger. They thanked him, and Eva added, "I hope we'll see you often while you're in port, Captain Pollock."

"Won't you come to dinner," asked Kendra, "one evening soon?"

Captain Pollock shook his head. "You are very kind, but I must say no. I'll be in port only a short time, and I have much to do."

He spoke so crisply that Kendra felt uncomfortable. It seemed clear that he had made this call solely for the sake of good manners and would be glad when he could get it over with. Eva was saying pleasantly,

"But you'll come back to San Francisco, I hope, before you leave the Pacific entirely?"

Captain Pollock said yes. His plan was to go on to Canton and several other Oriental ports, and call at San Francisco again next spring, before returning to New York.

Eva said she would be glad to see him then. There was some conversation about what ports he expected to visit, but he was so ill at ease that even she could not help feeling chilled. There was an awkward pause. To fill it in Kendra asked,

"Captain Pollock, how is Loren Shields?"

41

As she spoke Loren's name the captain gave a start. His answer was almost gruff.

"Mr. Shields," he said, "is no longer with us."

Kendra caught her breath in astonishment. Loren was a man who did his work well. Light-hearted he was, but not light-minded. He would never have broken his contract. Nor could he have been dismissed except for some outrageous breach of duty, and she could not believe him guilty of any such thing. Something had certainly gone wrong.

Eva too was startled. She asked if Loren had stayed in Honolulu.

Captain Pollock said no. Loren had returned to San Francisco on the *Cynthia,* but upon arrival their contract had been dissolved by mutual consent.

His answer was brief to the point of terseness. Observing that he did not care to discuss the matter, Eva tactfully changed the subject by asking if he would not take a cup of tea, with some cinnamon wafers Kendra had baked yesterday.

Captain Pollock declined. He said he must leave them now. As master of a ship newly arrived he had many imperative duties.

When he had gone Eva spoke to Kendra, mystified. "What *is* the matter with him?"

Kendra said she too had been wondering, but she had no idea.

When Alex came in that evening he said the *Cynthia*'s return voyage from Honolulu had been unfortunate. Her journey out had been quick—only seventeen days—and the voyage back had begun well. But on the way she had met a storm, which had blown her off course and lengthened the voyage to twenty-three days.

Eva said this must have been the reason for Captain Pollock's dejection, but Kendra did not think so. She could understand that Pollock would be disappointed, but she could not believe the storm alone would have made him so depressed. Pollock had been twenty years at sea. He knew the noblest ship ever made could not defy the wind. Besides, this did not explain his break with Loren. Certainly Loren had not blown up the storm.

The next morning brought that rare delight, a day of unclouded sun. The wind had cleared the sky; the bay was a

42

great wide glitter of water, and the dingy little town of San Francisco looked like a smudge on a golden world. Kendra and Eva rode down the hill escorted by Morse and Vernon.

Both men were talking eagerly. They were planning another dance, and Eva had promised to help with the decorations. Vernon told her the New York Store had Chinese lanterns and other Oriental ornaments, brought over on the *Eagle*. Wouldn't she like to see these?

Indeed she would, Eva exclaimed. "Shall we go to the New York Store?" she asked Kendra.

"Why don't you go there," Kendra suggested, "and leave me at Chase and Fenway's? They have a much better selection of groceries, and Mr. Hodge is so helpful."

She said it with a bright smile, to hide the fact that this was not her real reason. Her real reason was that at Chase and Fenway's she had her best chance to hear of Ted. Mr. Fenway had said Ted had "packed his duds" and left, but this was not strictly true. In his hurry Ted had not packed all his duds. Hodge, who now occupied Ted's former room over the store, had mentioned that Parks had left various objects behind him: shirts and shoes, a razor, and even Hodge said respectfully—some books. An honest fellow, Hodge had stored all these in a box and put the box under the bed, in case Parks should come back. Kendra kept hoping he would.

Not knowing any of this, Eva agreed to Kendra's suggestion. They all four went into Chase and Fenway's, for Eva would never have let Kendra go in alone. She wanted it seen that her daughter was always well protected.

Mr. Fenway was roaming about with an oil can, anointing the locks and hinges. At the counter Mr. Chase was bargaining with a rancher who had brought produce to town. The packing boys were lugging boxes from the storeroom, and the fellow called Pocket sat by the stove, reading the *Star*. Pocket had already sent a boatload of goods up to his employer, Mr. Smith, but Smith's partner, the Mormon leader Sam Brannan, had gone to Sutter's Fort and had told Pocket he could stay a while in town. Pocket was more neat these days than when he first came in with his rag of gold. He now got regular shaves and kept his trousers brushed, and today he wore a new plaid shirt, though all his pockets bulged as before.

Kendra had seen so few sunny days in San Francisco that she was astonished at the difference the sun made in the

43

store. The bare boards of the walls seemed almost to glisten. From a side window a brilliant shaft of light slanted across the front door, brightening the entrance and deepening the shadows at the side. As Kendra and the others came in, the door swung silently shut behind them, but the men in the store heard the sound of military boots, and turned.

Seeing Kendra and Eva in the beam of sun, Pocket laid down his newspaper and politely stood up. Pocket liked women, and Kendra had several times heard the packing boys say how much women liked Pocket. Mr. Fenway sauntered forward, and Eva told him she was going to leave Kendra in his care while she went with Morse and Vernon to see the Chinese decorations at the New York Store. She laughed tactfully. "You'll forgive me for taking business to your competitor, Mr. Fenway?"

"They need some business at that store," Mr. Fenway said with mournful satisfaction. "I hear they're having a hard time getting rid of all that Chinese stuff." This thought cheered him so much that he continued to look pleased for two or three seconds before returning to his usual gloom.

When Eva had gone, Hodge gave Kendra her basket and she went into the storeroom. The boys had brought out several boxes holding tobacco, matches, playing cards, and other small items for which they had constant demand, and were now arranging these on the shelves behind the counter. They grinned admiringly as she passed, and Pocket looked up to give her a shy smile.

The storeroom was dim and cheerless, for it had only two small windows and these were on the side away from the sun. Kendra chose what she wanted, but it was dull work without Ted and in a few minutes she was done. She went back to the door leading into the front room.

After the gloom of the storeroom the sun across the main entrance was almost dazzling. Kendra paused in the doorway to let her eyes get used to the light.

Mr. Chase had gone out with the rancher. At the shelves behind the counter the boys were working little and talking much, while Hodge and Mr. Fenway conferred with another customer, a dusty character addressed as Mr. Ingram. In spite of his earthy appearance Mr. Ingram seemed to be a valuable patron, for in one gnarled hand he held a paper on which was written a long list of items he wanted to buy. Pocket, back at his newspaper, was rubbing one hand over

44

his newly shaved face as if he could not get used to the smooth feel of it. Pocket had a clean-cut jaw and strong features, and since she had been seeing him whiskerless Kendra had observed that he was quite a handsome man.

All of a sudden, as if he had heard his name, Pocket turned toward the front door. Kendra could see his face in profile. His lips parted with a quick intake of breath, and he smiled, like a man who opens a smudgy window and sees a rainbow.

There had been no sound of the door's opening—there never was—but now it did seem to Kendra that she too had heard something, a faint rustle maybe, but it had been so faint that she had hardly noticed it. Now she turned her head and saw what Pocket was looking at.

Full in the flood of sunshine stood a girl.

Any girl was an event in San Francisco, but this girl, anywhere, would have taken a man's thoughts away from what he should have been doing. She had red hair and green eyes and a sumptuous figure, and she wore a green silk dress that matched her eyes, and a fashionable straw bonnet with green ribbons. Her face was not perfect, but the look of it was warmer and more tempting than orthodox beauty. It was an unexpected face—full lips, short impudent nose, and freckles. She had so many freckles that she looked as if somebody had sprayed her with powdered gold.

Her eyes were green as clover, and from under the brim of her bonnet the wind had blown wavy locks of hair, copperred, the shade and shine of a new penny. As she stood there in the sunbeam, slowly and with an air of merry mischief she untied the green ribbons and took off her bonnet. Her red hair caught the sun like a torch, her freckles almost twinkled in the light. She was not beautiful, but she was spectacular, and Kendra wondered what such a woman was doing out here at the end of the world.

Pocket had not paused to wonder. Dropping his newspaper, he had sprung to his feet and was going with long strides to meet her. He reached her with hardly a sound—surprising, what quiet habits he had—and with a shy and likable smile, he spoke, "May I take your bonnet, ma'am?"

The stranger's clover-green eyes sparkled upon him. No doubt she was used to making conquests, but she was not tired of it. "Thank you," she said, and handed him her bonnet with winning grace. As Pocket took the bonnet she added,

45

"I'm looking for—" but she had no chance to finish, for by this time the other men had seen her too, and now the whole room was astir.

The three packing boys were staring, Foxy murmuring, "Lord, look athere!"—and the others making comments of their own. Hodge seemed to have forgotten his dusty customer, but it did not matter because the customer was staring too, forgetting the list in his hand. Even Mr. Fenway had started forward, and was now pushing aside a barrel that stood in his way. They had all taken a step toward her, but Mr. Fenway looked around with an air of stern rebuke, reminding them that he was boss here and *he* would greet his visitor. He reached her and his long figure crumpled in a bow.

"Good morning, ma'am," he droned. "My name is Fenway. Can I be of service?"

Hodge and the customer, Foxy and Bert and Al and Pocket gazed in rapture. The freckled charmer managed to include them all in the smile with which she answered,

"Why Mr. Fenway, you're the very man I'm looking for. You and Mr. Chase. Is it convenient for you to talk to me?"

Mr. Fenway solemnly assured her that it was most convenient.

Kendra, in the doorway of the storeroom, made up her mind to stay there and keep still. Something—she did not quite know what—told her that this buoyant redhead had made Mr. Fenway forget that she herself was anywhere around. If he should be reminded of her presence this scene would fade off, and she wanted it to continue.

The redhead was saying to Mr. Fenway,

"You are very kind to a stranger, sir. My name is Marny—oh, just call me Marny, everybody does. I feel as if I know you already, Mr. Fenway, because I've met so many of your friends—I've been with a gambling parlor in Honolulu. I came in two days ago, on the *Cynthia*."

"Ah," said Mr. Fenway, "the *Cynthia*." He nodded, enjoying this reminder of misfortune. "You had a bad voyage, I'm told."

Marny smiled and shrugged. "Why yes, but we got here, and that's what matters."

Kendra did not hear what Mr. Fenway said next. She was thinking—*a gambling parlor in Honolulu.*

She was remembering what Loren had told her at Cape

46

Horn. She could almost see and hear it all again—the wind and the roaring water, the gray glow from the skylight, and Loren telling her Pollock was happy to have her on the *Cynthia* because she was a pure young maiden. And then—

"There's a gambling parlor in Honolulu where he goes often. Folks say he admires the hostess. . . . But he wouldn't have her on the *Cynthia*. He believes a girl like that would offend the ship."

Kendra had never been inside a gambling parlor and nobody had ever told her what sort of person a gambling hostess was supposed to be. But Loren had certainly implied that this hostess would not be welcome on the *Cynthia* because she was not a pure young maiden.

Kendra remembered the ship's figurehead, the goddess crowned with the crescent moon. Cynthia the moon goddess, ever young, ever virgin. She remembered how she herself had laughed at Pollock's fancy.

And yet, on the long hard voyage from New York, with herself on board, the *Cynthia* had met with no mishaps and had made notable time. But on the short easy voyage from Honolulu, with Marny there, the *Cynthia* had been stormed off her course.

—And so, thought Kendra, Captain Pollock believes the ship was insulted by having Marny on board. And now he's frightened. Maybe his fine record is over.

—Oh, what nonsense! But he believes it.

—And there *was* a storm.

But how, she wondered, had Marny ever been allowed to board the *Cynthia?* Was this what had caused the captain's break with Loren? Loren would take the applications for passage, but he knew how Pollock felt. And even if he had not known, in this as in everything else the captain had the final word.

Every answer seemed to be the start of a new question. Kendra felt more baffled than before.

7

In the front room of the store, Marny was making a debut. The beam of light had moved, and still shone upon her as if it had been put there to follow her about. Against her freckled cheeks the light caught her hair in penny-red sparkles. Foxy had brought a pack of cards from the shelf and was holding it out to her. Smiling her mischievous smile, Marny was taking off her gloves and handing them to Pocket to be cared for along with her bonnet. Mr. Fenway was inviting her to come in closer to the stove and get warm.

"You are so thoughtful, Mr. Fenway," said Marny. She had a beautiful speaking voice. She added, "We'll both come in." As she spoke, to Kendra's surprise and apparently to the surprise of everybody else, she turned toward the dark corner beyond the beam of sun, and said gently, "Delbert?"

Now they observed that she had not come in alone. A man was standing in the shadow on the far side of the sun-beam.

The gleam on Marny had been so bright, and she herself was such a striking figure, that the man might have stood there a long time before anybody noticed him. As she spoke he took a step out of the shadow, calmly, as though it had been her business and not his to take the light.

He looked as if he had always been calm and always would be, because the world did not contain anything important enough to get him excited. Calmly he took off his hat, calmly he gave a nod to the other men. He had glossy dark hair, chin-whiskers neatly trimmed, a calm narrow mouth and a nose like a parrot's beak. He wore a black suit and white shirt, and shoes spotless except for the street dust. Hat in hand, he seemed to be waiting for whatever was going to happen next—not that he cared, but one must get through the day somehow. His boredom was so different from the radiant aliveness of Marny that Kendra wondered how she could put up with him.

48

But put up with him she did, for she was saying with perfect grace, "Mr. Fenway, may I present my friend Delbert?" With an air of elegant weariness Delbert bowed, and Marny suggested, "Why don't you sit there by the stove, Delbert?"

Moving with courtly indifference Delbert went toward the stove, and taking up the newspaper Pocket had left, he sat down on a box and began to read. Marny appeared to forget about him. Followed by her courtiers, she moved into the warm atmosphere between the stove and counter, and held out her hand to Foxy. "Now," she said, "the cards."

The men gathered around her, all business suspended, watching. With his blue bandana Pocket dusted a space on the counter and reverently laid Marny's bonnet and gloves upon it. Her eyes dancing around at her adorers, Marny began opening the case that held the cards. Her hands looked strong and firm, the skin very white and as freckled as her face. The fingers moved with expert speed. She took out the cards. Delbert continued to read the paper.

Taking a step to the counter Marny cut the deck, holding the two halves on end, her thumbs almost touching between them. There was a zip and a zip, and the pack was shuffled. For a moment she held up the cards and looked at them, with a smile. It was a smile of affection. These cards were friends of hers; her fingers went through them, touching them gently, softly, as if each card had a personality of its own and she loved them every one.

Holding the pack in one hand, she flexed the fingers of the other hand above them, then brought the upper hand down in a light firm grasp. With a quick movement she dropped the lower hand and lifted the other. For an instant the pack stood up in a column as though the cards had come alive to do her bidding. She brought her hands together and did it again, only this time she moved her hands horizontally apart and the pack opened out like an accordion. While the men watched in delight, she did it over and over, up, sideways, and in columns slanting to the right and left.

She took the pack in one hand and raised the hand to the level of her shoulder, holding up the cards. After a moment of stillness she gave a twitch of her wrist and the cards fanned out. Anybody can fan a deck, but in Marny's hand the cards were spread so perfectly that the edge of every card was exposed as much as its neighbor and no more, and the fan was firm between her thumb and her finely disciplined fingers. With another twitch she brought the deck together again.

The men sighed with admiration. Pocket grinned proudly, as if he had discovered her all by himself. Even Mr. Fenway murmured approval. Delbert smothered a yawn.

But they were not looking at Delbert, they were looking at her. "You sure can handle 'em, miss," Hodge exclaimed.

Foxy's eyes were bulging. Foxy was a lean, gangling youth, loosely put together, with big hands and feet and a good-humored ugly face. Almost breathlessly he asked, "Will you deal us a game?"

With a glance at Mr. Fenway, Marny smiled and shook her head. "Not now. Not here. Later."

"What games do you deal, miss?" Foxy asked eagerly.

Marny's green eyes flashed around the group. "You name it, boys, I'll deal it."

Pocket took a step closer. "Are you going to stay in town, Miss Marny?"

"I'm thinking of it. I might take one of those tables at the City Hotel. If I do," she invited, "will you drop by?"

Pocket said gently, "I don't gamble, Miss Marny."

Her eyes widened in amused surprise. Before she could answer Foxy exclaimed, "Well, everybody else does. You'd better stay, miss."

Marny nodded thoughtfully. "They tell me," she said with a question in her voice, "that in San Francisco, you haven't got any pious folk who think it's wicked to play cards."

"Wicked?" the men repeated together, and Foxy added, "If there's any such folks around here nobody told me anything about 'em."

"In Honolulu, we've got some really stiff-necked people," said Marny. In a wondering voice she went on, "And boys, when the whaling ships get to port after six months in the Arctic, and the sailors come ashore, you know what those prigs want them to do?"

The men shook their heads.

Marny said, "They want them to meet at a church sociable and have cookies and tea."

The men hooted. Mr. Fenway mumbled that the prigs didn't know much about sailors. The dusty customer, Mr. Ingram, who had not opened his mouth since Marny came in, did not open it now, but his lips moved in derision. Mr. Ingram stood with his thumbs in his pockets, his battered hat on the back of his head, silently enjoying things. Delbert folded back a page of the paper and continued to read.

"Well now," said Marny, "nobody believes the sailors are going to spend their shore leave sipping tea. They want some lights and music, and some excitement. And besides the sailors, there are the men who live in Honolulu all the year round. They want a place where they can have some fun after business. And everybody knows they're going to get it."

The men noisily agreed, and Marny laughed. The locks of red hair danced, and her freckled face had a glow of intimacy, as if she were confiding in her best friends.

"But you know, boys, there's always somebody around to take advantage of a situation like that. In Honolulu it's the police. They made us pay to be let alone."

"Ah," said Mr. Fenway. He sighed with doleful wisdom, as if he had known it all the time.

"And the squeeze," said Marny, "pinched. We got tired of it. Men from San Francisco told us this was a grand new town just starting to roar."

Her hearers nodded vigorously.

"So we thought we'd look it over. They told us the best place to get the facts was an important store called Chase and Fenway's—"

"Well, well," said a hearty voice at the door, and Mr. Chase came thumping in. "My name's Chase—somebody asking for me?"

They all started at once to make the introductions. Kendra, at the storeroom door, wished she dared go out and join them. It seemed to her that Marny was doing no harm. She was merely enjoying life in her own way; and Kendra, who had not been enjoying life in any way at all since Ted left, burned with envy.

Marny laid the cards on the counter. With a bewitching smile she put her hand into the big rough hand of Mr. Chase.

Mr. Chase blinked as though dazzled. He bowed over her hand, so low that for a moment Kendra thought he was going to kiss it. "A pleasure, ma'am," he rumbled. "A pleasure."

"Thank you sir," said Marny. Turning her head toward the stove she said in a voice like silver, "Delbert?"

Delbert put down the paper and stood up. For an instant Kendra wondered if Marny had hired him to follow her around, for it really would not have been safe for her to go about the streets alone. But no, Marny was presenting him to Mr. Chase as her associate in the gambling business.

Basking in her charm, Mr. Chase said he and his partner Fenway were honored to be of service. If the lady and gentleman would step into the office—

They all four went in, Mr. Chase holding Marny's right elbow and Mr. Fenway her left, while Delbert walked behind. As the office door closed, Hodge told the packing boys to get about their work. Hodge himself returned to his conference with the weather-beaten Mr. Ingram. Pocket sat by the stove and picked up the paper, but he did not read; he sat dreamily gazing in front of him as though he could still see Marny's freckled face.

But Marny was gone, the streak of sun no longer shone through the window, and without those two bright presences the place was dingy again. The boys began lazily to take more goods out of the boxes they had set in front of the shelves. Another stroller wandered in from the street, bought a box of matches, and sat down by the stove for a smoke. Kendra began to roam about the storeroom, looking for anything else she might use. On a shelf near the back door, so high that she could barely reach it by standing on tiptoe, she saw a bottle of lemon extract, which gave her an idea of making lemon-iced cupcakes.

The back door was shut and bolted, and near it stood several barrels not yet opened. Kendra set her basket on one of these and reached for the bottle of lemon extract. How quiet it was in here, and how noisy everywhere else. From the front room she heard the boys jabbering. From outside she heard the thud of horses' hoofs, and the bang of hammers and clatter of planks as a new saloon went up. As she put the bottle into her basket she heard another sound from beyond the back door.

She started, and listened. Her heart began to thud like the hoofs on the road outside. What she was hearing was a whistled tune.

She caught the tune only in fragments, for the wind was blowing the notes around, but it was a tune she would have recognized anywhere in the world. The whistler was coming nearer. He was whistling "Love is like a dragonfly."

The dance and the gaudy lights and the crowded floor, Ted's arm around her and his caressing eyes looking down into hers as the band played the dragonfly tune and he whispered, "You're beautiful. . . . Every woman is as beautiful as some man thinks she is."

—Don't be a fool, Kendra told herself. Anybody can whistle that tune. Anybody, anybody—

At the same time her hands were pushing at the bolt. The door swung open. And there was Ted, just reaching the foot of the steps as he walked along. At this moment, as if her eyes had called him, he looked up and saw her.

Here at the back was a flight of broad shallow steps up which barrels could be rolled to the door. Kendra stood at the top of the steps. As Ted saw her he stopped.

Ted's face was brown, as if he had been living in a place where there was more sun than often shone in San Francisco. His whole appearance was different. Usually so neat, today he looked unkempt, his clothes frayed and his boots cracking. But as he stood there his eyes went over her with yearning, he gave her the smile she knew and loved so well, and to Kendra it was as if he had not changed at all. For a moment he stayed where he was; he turned his head aside, as though trying to pull himself away from her; he looked at her again, and slowly, almost unwillingly, he began to climb the steps. It was as though he was being drawn by a force he could not withstand, like a man honest but hungry, walking toward a purse he knew he was going to steal.

Kendra quivered with happiness. Ted was here again, and this time she was not going to let him go. Not without her.

As he reached the top step Ted almost pushed her into the room, and shut the door. He did not say anything and neither did she. They swept into each other's arms. This was the kiss Ted had run away from, the kiss they should have had, that cloudy day hardly a month ago though to Kendra it seemed a hundred years. For a moment she felt a radiant joy. But again, her moment did not last. Again, Ted thrust her away from him, demanding,

"Why the hell can't you get out of my life?"

"Because I love you," she said.

The words did not surprise her at all. It was as though she had been planning to say them, just like that.

Ted clenched his fists against the door behind him.

"I love you too," he said. "I didn't mean to. I never dreamed—" He broke off, and burst out defensively, "And I didn't intend to see you this morning."

"Then what are you doing here?" she exclaimed.

53

"I came to pick up my things."

"Why were you whistling the dragonfly tune?"

"Was I? I didn't know it."

"You were thinking about me," Kendra said.

"I've thought of nothing else since—" Ted stopped, listening to the voices in the front room. "We can't talk here."

Kendra spoke quickly. "We can talk tomorrow afternoon. There's going to be another dance at the Comet House. My mother intends to go over there with Mrs. Chase to see about the decorations. You can come to see me while she's out."

"Kendra, this is all wrong," said Ted.

"You'll come to see me tomorrow?"

"All right!" said Ted. "I'll be there."

Then he pushed the door open and rushed down the steps and away.

Kendra waited where she was. She felt tremors of joy. Ted was with her again and this time he was not going to leave her.

Her thoughts were clear and straight. She wanted Ted. She had not known how much she wanted him until she saw him walking toward the back steps.

She began to laugh. This was the year 1848, a leap year, and she had remembered the old saying—A lady may propose marriage in a leap year, and if her lover refuses he must give her a silk dress. Kendra did not want a silk dress. She already had several. But she wanted Ted and she meant to have him.

8

"Tell me!" Kendra persisted. "Why did you go?"

"You know why. To get away from you."

"But why did you want to get away from me?"

"Because I'm no good, Kendra! No good for you, no good for anybody. How often do I have to say it?"

"Do you love me?"

"Would I have run like that if I didn't?"

"If you love me, then why did you go?"

54

"Oh Lord," said Ted, "now we're starting over."

They stood facing each other in the parlor. The room had a happy look with Eva's bright rugs and curtains, and a bowl of wild yellow poppies on the table. Eva and Mrs. Chase, with several army officers, had ridden over to the Comet House. In the back yard Mrs. Riggs was hanging out laundry.

Ted strode over to the front window, stared out a moment, turned around and came back.

"Kendra, I didn't mean to start anything but a mild flirtation that day when I brought the groceries. But I came to the door of this room, and there you were, and we saw each other. It was like a lightning flash. You remember."

"Yes," said Kendra. "I remember."

"I should have left then," said Ted. "I should have gone to Los Angeles, gone back to Honolulu—anywhere away from here."

"Then," she asked clearly, "why didn't you?"

"How did I know what was going to happen?" he demanded. "I thought I knew all about men and women. I used to laugh when I heard of men so in love they were helpless. I didn't know it happened like this."

"I didn't know it either," said Kendra. "But it does happen, it *has* happened, to you and me both. Oh Ted, where have you been?"

He answered shortly, "To the gold country."

"The gold—" Kendra caught her breath. "Why didn't you tell me you were going there?"

"I didn't know I was going there. All I wanted was to get out before I made any more trouble. I would have taken any boat going anywhere. The only one sailing that day was Sutter's launch. I took the launch to the fort—saw the men bringing in gold from the sawmill—"

"Then it's true, Ted? There really is a golden river?"

Ted nodded. A light broke over his face. When he spoke his voice was awestruck. "Kendra, it's true. Not just one river," he went on eagerly, "but miles and miles of rivers. Nobody knows how many. The sands are speckled with gold, the cracks in the rocks are lined with gold. Look."

Ted was wearing his leather jacket, worn and bedraggled now. From a pocket he took a small buckskin bag that had once held tobacco. Loosening the drawstring he poured on the table a pile of yellow grains. "Gold dust," he said.

Kendra moved the grains with her finger. She picked up

55

a pinch and rubbed it between her thumb and fingertip. When Pocket had brought that rag of gold to the store she had not been excited. But now something curious began to happen inside her—a flutter, a sort of pain, and yet a sort of pleasure too. It ran down from her chest through her middle and made her legs feel quivery; it ran up to her head and gave her a tingle at the back of her neck. Her voice like his was awestruck as she asked,

"And there's really so much gold? You *know?*"

With a slow smile at her, Ted nodded. Kendra felt the same intimacy of their first meeting, the sense that their thoughts had met and joined. In a low voice, like a conspirator sharing a secret, Ted answered her question. "Kendra, at a ravine called Shiny Gulch, I've already picked up three hundred ounces of gold. I've put most of it on deposit with Mr. Chase. Part will pay for my outfit, and he'll keep the rest for me. And there's more of it, and more and more. I've seen it."

Kendra picked up another pinch of gold. She put it into the palm of her hand and looked down at its glowing promise. She thought—I'm tired of being nobody's child. Now I can show them. Alex, my mother, all those aunts and uncles who think my father was the family disgrace. They'll be proud to know me when I come back. I'll have a carriage with matched black horses, I'll have a fur cloak and a muff pinned with a spray of opals. I'll have Ted—he's clever, he's handsome, he's sophisticated and charming. I'll have everything.

She looked up. With barely breath enough to speak, she asked,

"Who else is up there at that place called Shiny Gulch?"

"Workmen from Sutter's Fort, a few ranchers, some of the local savages. The word will get around, of course, but it's not around yet. I'm going back. I had to come to town to buy supplies. I've made friends with a fellow named Ning, at least that's what they call him, his right name is Ingram—"

"Ingram?" she repeated, "He was in the store yesterday, buying a lot of things."

"We need a lot of things," said Ted. He was talking fast, with boyish eagerness. "Boots and blankets, shovels and pans, food—it's a wild country, we'll have to carry everything we intend to use."

Ted explained that Ning knew a lot about gold mining.

56

Ning had grown up in Lumpkin County, in the mountains of north Georgia, where gold had been discovered years ago.

"He knows what we need," Ted hurried on. "We'll go back as soon as we get our outfit, and then—Kendra, before the end of summer I'll be rich. The gold is there. I can do anything I please, buy anything, go anywhere. Remember once I told you what I'd do if I could?—sail to the lonesome islands, the dim far countries—"

She remembered. He had told her this, and he had added, "I'd take you with me." Ted was still talking, telling her about this marvel of the hills. Gold in the waters and under the rocks, gold in flakes and specks and even in lumps among the pebbles of the earth. Gold, waiting for somebody to come and pick it up.

And Ted loved her. He had said so. He was saying it now.

"Oh Kendra, it's such fun to tell you all this! You understand it, you understand how I feel, you always did. I've missed you so!"

"I've missed you too," she told him joyfully. "But now you're here, and when you go back—"

"Yes!" he cut in, almost angrily. "I'm going back. And this time I'm leaving for good."

"No!" she cried in sudden fright.

"Yes!" he repeated vehemently. "I'm getting out of here. You're the first girl I ever loved and I hope to God you're the last. I'm not going through this another time."

He took a long step toward the door. But Kendra had never had a subtle thought in her head nor a subtle speech in her mouth. She rushed to him and locked her hands around his wrist.

"Ted, you love me! You said you did!"

"That's why I want to leave you. If I didn't care what became of you—but I do care." He broke off and looked longingly down at her. "Why do you have to be so lovely now when we're saying goodby?"

"We're not saying goodby, Ted."

"Kendra," he urged, "I'm lazy, I'm useless, I'm unreliable, I'll never amount to anything—"

"I don't care. We'll have all that gold from the rivers."

"Oh Kendra, the trouble is not money! The trouble is me. I'm not good enough for you. And you're a nice girl. You'll want to be married."

"Of course. We can be married here, now. The head

57

magistrate—what do they call them in California?—the alcalde. He can marry us."

"Then you'll be stuck with me the rest of your life."

"That's what I want."

"Oh my dear," said Ted, "don't be in such a hurry to make a fool of yourself."

Again, hands thrust into his jacket pockets, he walked to the front window and back to her. Kendra looked up at his tumbled hair and the lock that kept falling over his forehead; his roguish face, now drawn into lines as if he were fighting her and himself and everybody else in the world. There on the table lay the buckskin bag and the beckoning pile of gold dust. Ted was gazing at her with a look that was wistful and tender and yet strangely frightened, as if he wanted to escape and could not. Suddenly Kendra asked,

"Ted, why did you come back to San Francisco?"

"I told you," he answered—"to get supplies."

"You could have bought those at Sutter's Fort. Why come all the way down here?"

"The prices are better here," said Ted. "At the fort, everything has been brought up the Sacramento River, or by land around the bay. That makes things expensive."

"Everything you buy here, you'll have to take back the same way. So why come to San Francisco?"

"Another reason," said Ted, "was that I wanted to leave my gold in a safe place. Mr. Chase will keep it locked up for me."

"Wouldn't Mr. Sutter have kept it for you? He must have a safe or some sort of strongbox."

She took a step closer to him. Standing very near him she looked up directly into his eyes.

"Ted, why did you come to San Francisco?"

Ted looked down at her a moment without answering. As on the first time he had ever looked at her, he made her aware of her every feature—her dark blue eyes, the arrow of hair on her forehead, her slim strong body, eager and demanding before him. All of a sudden Ted turned on his heel and struck the table such a blow that everything in the room seemed to tremble.

"All right," he blurted. "I came here because of you. I tried to get away from you. God knows I tried. I went up to Sutter's Fort and that wasn't far enough. I went beyond the fort, up to the sawmill in the mountains. That wasn't far

58

enough. I went beyond the sawmill to Shiny Gulch. I panned gold from dawn to dark, trying to get so tired I'd fall down and go to sleep instead of thinking about you. It didn't work. I wanted you too much. But I did try, Kendra!"

She was laughing now. "Oh Ted, what makes you so serious? I love you and you love me and I'm not concerned with anything else. Why should you be?"

Ted did not turn around. Slowly he pulled the petals from a yellow poppy on the table. "Kendra, I know the kind of fellow I am. I'll wreck your life."

She said stubbornly, "It's my life."

He began to argue, with himself as well as with her. "Kendra, you don't want to go to Shiny Gulch! It's wilderness. Men are sleeping outdoors on the ground. They fry bacon over campfires—"

"I'd like to try that."

"But the discomforts!" said Ted. "Ants and grasshoppers, washing clothes in the river—"

"I want to go with you," said Kendra.

She said it forcefully because she meant it. Every word he spoke made her more eager. Her eagerness was in her words and her voice and in the urgent atmosphere around her. Ted could not doubt it nor withstand it. Abruptly he turned around, and his hands gripped her shoulders so fiercely that he hurt her.

"Is it my fault I can't go back without you?" he exclaimed. As he drew her to him she heard him say again, "God knows I tried."

And so, on a bright April afternoon, the American alcalde of San Francisco read the wedding ceremony. He read it in the parlor of the little house on Stockton Street, in the presence of Alex and Eva, several army officers, and other friends they had made in town. Mr. and Mrs. Chase were there, also Mr. Fenway, sitting with a dour look as if he did not approve of people's getting married. Afterward there was an hour of wine and wafers and good wishes, then Alex and Eva went to spend a few days with Mr. and Mrs. Chase. Ted and Kendra were left alone.

For Eva had said firmly, "You are going to do this right. No slipping off to the alcalde's office."

In this Alex had concurred. Alex would have felt disgraced if a marriage in his household had not been rightly performed. A good Episcopalian, he would have preferred a clergyman; but there were none available in San Francisco except the Mormon elders, and no military chaplain nearer than Monterey. Alex agreed that the alcalde would have to do.

As for the marriage itself, Alex and Eva would have chosen one of the young army men, but if Kendra wanted to marry Ted Parks, why shouldn't she? Ted was a man of education and good behavior. He did not get drunk; he did not spend his evenings loafing around the gambling tables at the City Hotel. And Shiny Gulch, wherever that was, could not be much more primitive than some of the frontier posts where Alex and Eva themselves had lived. When Ted and Kendra got tired of roughing it they could always quit. Before the *Cynthia* left New York, Congress had authorized a contract for regular steamboat lines on both the Atlantic and Pacific coasts, to be connected by a railroad across the Isthmus of Panama. Soon, coming home would be easy.

The fact was (and Alex and Eva both knew it) they could not have prevented the marriage if they had wanted to. American women were so scarce in California that they could do about as they pleased. When a wagon train came near Sutter's Fort, if word got out that there was a girl in the party, or a woman whose husband had been killed by Indians on the way, men rushed out to meet the wagons and propose marriage before she had had time to take off her sunbonnet. Married women too had their own way. Nearly every week the papers carried notice from some angry husband saying his wife had left his bed and board. In the older communities of the States, such an announcement would have made a woman an outcast. Here it merely meant that she set up housekeeping with a man she liked better, and life went on.

If Ted and Kendra wanted to get married, all they had to do was walk into the alcalde's office and say so. Alex and Eva admitted this to each other. What they did not admit quite so frankly was that they both felt a certain relief. Eva was not by nature maternal. When Alex had wanted her to leave their two sons in New York so she could follow him to California, it had required no great wrench for her to do so. She was fond of the boys, but she was in love with Alex. As for Kendra, all Eva had ever felt about Kendra was a guilty embarrassment, and this was all she felt now. Both she and Alex were glad to have Kendra married to a suitable young man.

So Eva said, "All right, Kendra." After giving Kendra some good advice about what a bride ought to know (Kendra thought—She sounds like a teacher explaining French verbs), Eva added, "You'll be married here at home, and you and Ted can have the house to yourselves until you leave town."

Kendra would have been willing to spend her wedding night in the covered wagon Ted had bought for the journey to Shiny Gulch, but she was glad to have it this way instead. The house did look like a honeymoon cottage, with its pretty rugs and curtains and the cushioned chairs by the fireplace. She would start her marriage like a bride in New York or Baltimore.

And then such an adventure as no bride in New York or Baltimore had ever looked forward to. Then—up to the land of the golden rivers!

9

It was a happy time they had in the little house on Stockton Street. They were in love, and now Ted spoke no more of doubts. He was a joyous and adoring lover, and Kendra had never been so glad she was alive. Now at last, at last, she was imporant to somebody.

Ted and his partner Ning wanted to leave soon, while there were still only a few men scattered in the fields of gold. Kendra bought sunbonnets, and sturdy shoes for climbing over the rocks; and horn spoons, which Ning said were best for outdoor eating. These were made of cattle horns cut spoon-shaped at the big end while the pointed end was left for a handle. Ning told her a horn spoon was useful all day long. A man could use it for scraping up flakes of gold, then at mealtime the pointed end would spear his bacon and the spoon end mix his pancakes.

Mr. Chase sold her all these with indulgent smiles, convinced that she and Ted would soon tire of this foolishness and come back to town. Mr. Fenway warned her that the savages back there in the woods were a miserable lot, full of sin and vermin. But Mr. Chase said, "Now now, don't get her scared. All youngsters ought to have a little fling before they settle down."

Kendra laughed at them both. Ted loved her and wanted her, and more, he needed her. He told her there were men in the gold fields so impatient to get rich that they would not take time to prepare decent meals. They tried to live on bacon with dough fried in the bacon grease, and then groaned with bellyaches.

"But I needn't worry," said Ted. "I've got the best cook in California."

Ning came to dinner, and he too said Kendra was going to be mighty handy. Ning ate with his knife and poured his coffee into the saucer to cool, but Kendra liked him. In her present glitter of mind she was in a mood to like everybody, but even in her soberest moment she would have recognized that Ning was no fool. With him as a guide they need not fear.

He went with her into the yard and taught her to build a cookfire outdoors. Kendra knelt beside him and watched as he laid two green sticks in a V, placed two smaller sticks across them and piled twigs on the cross-sticks.

"Keep in mind, have the open end of the V toward the wind," said Ning. "Now you squat by this open end, like so. Before you strike your match, make your hands like a cup upside down—no ma'am, don't do it till I've showed you, this is tricky—and light the little twigs from below. Wait till it's burning good before you put on any sticks of real firewood. Now ma'am, you can try."

Kendra tried, scorched her fingers and got her nose full of smoke, coughed and laughed at herself and tried again, and at last she did manage to make her fire burn. It was fun.

Ning had made up a party to go to Shiny Gulch. This was safer, as the journey would take them through a lonesome country. He had carefully interviewed their traveling companions. Ning had himself made the long journey across the plains to California, and he knew some people were good travelers and some were bad. The bad travelers would not do their share of the work, they would not obey the leader, they were always complaining, always having a fuss with somebody. The good travelers—well, Ning said Kendra would be a good traveler. He also said if he had not thought so he would have gone back to Shiny Gulch alone and let Ted shuffle for himself.

Ted told Kendra that besides themselves and Ning, there would be eight persons in the party. One of these would be Pocket, who was tired of waiting to hear from his employers, Smith and Brannan of the store at Sutter's Fort. Pocket wanted to go to the fort himself and find out what was happening there, and maybe move on to the hills and pick up a little gold.

"I'm glad he's going with us," said Kendra. "I like him. Who else besides Pocket?"

They were sitting at table after dinner. Ted was in a happy mood. Kendra had served him a meat pie, and now they were sipping coffee while the fire crackled and the wind outside was like music.

Ted continued. Another of their traveling companions would be a sailor—not a deserter, but a hardy honest fellow who had worked his way out from New York. "On the *Cynthia*," Ted added with a chuckle, "and he told me to ask if you remembered him. Said you flirted with him one day at Cape Horn."

Kendra began to laugh as she thought of the big sailor with the rust-colored beard who had grinned at her from the rigging. "Of course I remember. What's his name?"

"Hiram Boyd. He's from the country somewhere near New York. Wanted to come to California, had no money to pay his way, signed up as a seaman on the *Cynthia*."

Ted said Hiram and Pocket would be in charge of the packhorses and spares. They both understood horses, and Pocket especially was a crack shot. Pocket had grown up in the Kentucky hills, where a boy learned to shoot as soon as he was big enough to tote a gun. He would be mighty useful if they met horse thieves or other troublemakers on the way.

"Pocket and Hiram," said Kendra. "That's two. You said eight. What about the others?"

"The others—" Ted began to refill his coffee cup, giving her a teasing look across the pot as he asked, "Kendra, how straitlaced are you?"

"I don't think I'm straitlaced at all," Kendra said with some surprise. "What do you mean?"

"Remember that girl from Honolulu?" asked Ted. "You saw her at the store."

Kendra set her cup in the saucer with an eager rattle. "Why Ted! Is Marny going with us?"

"Yes, Marny and her partners." Ted was laughing. "I see you don't mind."

"Mind? I think it's wonderful. I've never known any people like that. Why are they going to Shiny Gulch?"

"To set up a gambling tent. Delbert spoke to Ning—"

"Don't tell me," said Kendra, "Delbert can open his mouth and talk."

"Yes he can, and quite sensibly too. He said that since they were strangers here they needed guides to the gold country. He offered to pay a good price if Ning and I would guide them."

Ted spoke practically, but Kendra felt a thrill. Ted was saying,

"When I lived in Honolulu I used to drop into Marny's place once in a while to play cards. Marny's good-tempered and she minds her own business. She and her friends won't give us any trouble. So—" Ted shrugged.

As she cleared the table Kendra wondered how a girl ever happened to choose the career of dealer in a gambling house. She wondered where Marny came from and how she had learned all she knew. This was going to be a real adventure. Strange to remember that she had not wanted to come to California.

The next day Loren called to see them. As Captain Pollock had said, Loren had come to San Francisco when the *Cynthia* returned from Honolulu, but he had left the ship when she reached port. Loren congratulated Ted, whom he had not met before, and gave Kendra a basket of wild strawberries. These grew in the open lands above town, and were brought in by Mexican boys.

Today Loren wore a business suit that made him look quite unlike the blue-clad seafarer who had shown her Cape Horn, but he had the same pink cheeks and the same genial candor. He said he had been down to Monterey to consult a friend, who had recommended him to a San Francisco trading firm. He was planning to work there a while, and make up his mind whether to stay in San Francisco or seek another position on a vessel going back to the States. No adventurer, Loren was not interested in looking for any hills of gold.

As Ted knew Kendra was eager to hear what Loren could tell her about Marny, he went indoors to check a supply list, and left them together on the porch. The wind was blowing and the air was clear, so they could look down and see the *Cynthia* at anchor in the bay. Kendra asked how Marny had boarded the ship.

Leaning back comfortably in one of Eva's rocking chairs, Loren gave her a good-natured smile as he asnwered, "She came aboard like anybody else."

Kendra frowned. "Then she didn't—sort of—*slip* out of Honolulu?"

Laughing, Loren shook his head. He was such a cheerful fellow, thought Kendra, so easy to be with. "Nobody can 'slip' out of Honolulu," said Loren.

He explained. Honolulu, halfway between Asia and North America, was the central Pacific trading point. People were always coming and going. But this made it an inviting spot for drifters who wandered in and then wandered out, leaving debts and other obligations piled up behind them.

To stop this, the Hawaiian government had decreed that when a person wished to leave the country, he must get an exit permit. Any sea captain who took a passenger without this would find himself in rich trouble if he ever came to Honolulu again. When you applied for a permit, notice was published in the Honolulu papers. Thus, if you were running away from anything, your creditors could notify the passport office, and your permit would be refused until your affairs were settled.

Shortly before the *Cynthia* reached Honolulu, Marny's partners had left for California to look over the territory, leaving her to close the gambling rooms and follow them. Marny had applied for and received an exit permit, to be ready for the first California-bound vessel that had good accommodations. When she read in the papers that the *Cynthia* was in port and would take passengers on her return voyage to San Francisco, Marny asked for passage.

She did not do so in person. A man named Galloway, a merchant who had been doing business in Honolulu for years, was planning a business trip to San Francisco with his wife. As Marny had a lot to do before the ship sailed, she asked him to buy her ticket when he bought his. Mr. Galloway had reason to be grateful to Marny. Once when he had been playing vingt-et-un at her place she had observed the dealer using a daubed card. The players had not seen it and might have gone on losing money, but Marny had promptly stopped the game and returned all they had lost that evening, while the dealer was thrown out by two burly employees known as the Blackbeards. Remembering this, Mr. Galloway was glad to do her a favor now. His wife was too young and pretty to be jealous, and he did not know Captain Pollock well enough to be aware of his scruples.

All this Loren had learned after the ship sailed. In Honolulu, Mr. Galloway came into his office and said he would like to take one of the *Cynthia*'s staterooms for his wife and himself, and the other for a friend. He presented the exit permits, all in order. But Marny's permit had been issued in her full legal name: "Miss Marcia Roxana Randolph, native of Philadelphia, U. S. A." It did not occur to Loren that this meant the red-headed enchantress of the gambling parlor.

It did not occur to Captain Pollock either. Loren submitted the names of Mr. and Mrs. Galloway and their friend Miss Randolph, and received the captain's approval. Pollock knew Mr. Galloway was a respectable man of business. He did not know Miss Randoph, but he assumed that the three of them were traveling as a party, since it was hardly proper for an unmarried woman to take a journey unchaperoned.

Here Kendra interrupted the story. "If Captain Pollock meant to be so proper himself, he shouldn't have 'assumed' anything."

"Maybe I shouldn't have either," Loren said, laughing a little, "but I was working so hard with the cargo I didn't have much time for the passengers. When Marny came on board I checked her ticket, showed her the stateroom, and didn't think of her again."

"You didn't recognize her?" asked Kendra.

"How could I? I'd never seen her before."

"You had never been to her gambling place?"

"Never. I don't mean I'm righteous, I just don't like to waste money that way. But when Captain Pollock saw her, he simply would not believe I hadn't known who she was when I let her board the ship."

"When did he see her?" Kendra asked.

Loren said not until the next day, for Marny had not come to table that evening. This surprised nobody; passengers often had no appetite for the first meal or two on shipboard. When Pollock did catch sight of her, strolling in the sunshine of the quarterdeck, the ship was well out to sea. Pollock had stormed into his own quarters and sent for Loren.

"He was in a rage," said Loren. "I couldn't persuade him that I was as surprised as he was." Loren turned his chair so as to face Kendra, speaking with puzzled thoughtfulness. "And do you know, there *was* something surprising about her. I had been told Marny was a siren who sent men out of their heads. But the Miss Randolph who came on board that day looked like a perfect lady and talked like one. She wouldn't have attracted any attention at a church tea party."

Remembering Marny's opinion of church tea parties, Kendra was astonished. This did not sound like the girl she had seen in that gush of sunshine.

Loren said Captain Pollock had summoned Marny and asked what she meant by daring to board his ship.

"What did she say?"

"She talked back to him," said Loren, "like a soldier. And not," Loren added humorously, "like a perfect lady. Marny has—I guess you'd call it a double personality. I never knew anybody like that before."

"What did Captain Pollock expect to do?" Kendra asked wonderingly. "He couldn't throw her overboard like Jonah and hope a whale would come along."

"No," said Loren, "but he did threaten to turn the ship back to Honolulu and put her off. She told him if he did she'd take him to court and he wouldn't get his precious *Cynthia* out of the harbor for six months. When he accepted her money for a ticket he had made a contract to take her to San Francisco. And of course, she was right."

"Then what happened?" Kendra asked.

"Then," said Loren, "for ten days we had smooth sailing. The weather was perfect. Marny spent most of her time on the quarterdeck. At meals she was pleasant and quiet. And yet—" Loren frowned and bit his lip—"everything was going well, and yet there was a kind of tenseness on the ship. You might almost say Captain Pollock *knew* something was going to happen. And when the captain is uneasy everybody else is."

Kendra nodded. She remembered how, at Cape Horn, the captain's confidence had given confidence to her. Certainly it would work the other way.

"And then, eleven days out of Honolulu," said Loren, "the storm broke. That storm was really a shocker. We came through it, but by the time the wind calmed down and we got back on course—Kendra, Captain Pollock was like a man with a demon. The storm was her fault, and my fault for letting her come on board, and Mr. Galloway's fault for buying her a ticket."

"How did Mr. Galloway like that?"

"He was amazed. He had seen Captain Pollock in Marny's gambling place, he couldn't understand that this was any different from having her on the ship. But the person Captain Pollock was really angry with was Marny herself."

"How did she take all this?"

"She laughed at him."

"To his face?"

Loren nodded. "She told him he was the biggest fool she had ever seen."

Kendra reflected a moment. She thought making fun of the captain directly was not wise. "Did you laugh at him when he blamed you?" she asked Loren.

"No, I couldn't," he replied soberly. "I know him better than she does. I understand how seriously he takes this. But I can tell you, the rest of the voyage wasn't comfortable. By the time we got to San Francisco I knew he and I couldn't work together any longer. So I told him I was willing to tear up our contract."

Loren left soon after this, and Kendra went indoors to make a shortcake with his gift of strawberries.

While they were at dinner that evening she repeated Loren's story to Ted. As she finished she noticed that Ted's lips were quivering with amusement. "What are you laughing at?" she asked.

Ted said, "Loren is too nice to tell you all that went on aboard that ship. Or possibly he's too nice even to realize it. But I'm not."

"What went on?" Kendra echoed. She gave him a puzzled look across the shortcake.

"Simple," said Ted. "Between Honolulu and the storm, Pollock and Marny spent a night together."

"Oh—I see!" Kendra nodded. Now that Ted had said this, it seemed so plain that she wondered why she had not thought of it herself.

Ted smiled, that cool little flicker of a smile that amused her so much. "Didn't Loren tell you Pollock liked to go to Marny's place in Honolulu because he liked Marny?"

"Why yes. He said that on shore Captain Pollock was different about everything."

"I believe it," said Ted. "Agreeable sin—on shore yes, on shipboard no. But in Honolulu, Marny was surrounded by men. Probably at least one of them had a prior claim and was ready to defend it with a gun."

Kendra listened. Ted went on.

"But on the ship she had her own stateroom and Pollock had no rivals. The minute he saw her he knew fate had caught up with him."

"But how could he know Marny would be willing?"

"Darling," said Ted, "Marny doesn't think of these things the way you do. To her, I'm sure, it was a trivial incident. On shore it might have been the same to Pollock. But not on the ship. When the storm came he knew it was because his virgin *Cynthia* had been insulted."

"So then," Kendra exclaimed indignantly, "he said the storm was Marny's fault, not his."

Ted shrugged. "Plain old human nature, Kendra. When we do what we shouldn't we always try to blame somebody else. Started with Adam. Don't you remember, when the Lord asked him about eating the forbidden fruit, he said, 'That woman Eve, she gave it to me, it's her fault.' So with Pollock. My dear, would you think I was a pig if I asked for another slice of strawberry shortcake?"

Kendra laughed happily. "You'd better eat cake while you can," she warned him. "Cooking outdoors, I won't have much chance for baking."

"Make it a *thick* slice," said Ted.

Two days after this, on the twenty-fifth of April, 1848, Ted and Kendra set out for the land of gold. They had been married nine days.

10

There were several ways to go from San Francisco to the golden hills. On Ning's advice his party planned to go by land, riding down to the southern tip of the bay and then north and northeast by way of Sutter's Fort. This would take longer than sailing a launch up the Sacramento River, but Ning reminded them that none of them knew how to sail a launch, except maybe that sailor from the *Cynthia*, and he couldn't do it by himself.

They loaded wagons with their food supplies, their clothes and bedrolls, guns and tools; and a lot of beads and face-paints for trading with the savages. Most people called these savages Digger Indians, but Ning would not. Ning knew the stalwart red folk of the prairies. He said calling these creatures Indians was an insult to his friends. As he was firm about it, Ted suggested that they call this variety the Aborigines. Ning had never heard this word before and found it hard to say, so he shortened it to Ab. From there on, to Ning himself and the rest of his group, a California wild man was an Ab.

The party met early in the morning at a level spot below town. There were three covered wagons, twenty horses, and eleven travelers. The travelers were Ning, Ted, and Kendra; Pocket, and the sailor from the *Cynthia*, Hiram Boyd; Marny and Delbert, with two men and two women who worked for them. These assistants were the two burly fellows called the Blackbeards, who had thrown out the cheating dealer from the gambling room in Honolulu, and a pair of pretty Hawaiian girls who were probably not their wives.

One of the wagons belonged to Ning and Ted, the other two carried the goods and gambling equipment of Marny and her friends. Pocket and Hiram, who had less to carry, had loaded their supplies on packhorses. Ted told Kendra she would ride horseback while he and Ning took turns driving their wagon. Riding a horse was the easiest way to get anywhere in California, for there were no roads and a wagon bumped unmercifully over the ground.

At night Ning would take his bedroll and sleep outdoors, as he was used to doing, while Ted and Kendra would drop curtains at the front and back of the wagon cover and have it to themselves. These curtains were made of Chinese grasscloth, brought from Canton on the *Eagle*. They were strong, and artfully woven to let in air but keep mosquitoes out.

Marny and Delbert were on horseback too, while the Blackbeards drove their wagons. This was the first time Kendra had seen Marny and Delbert since that day in the store, and their helpers she had not seen at all. The Blackbeards looked so exactly alike that at first sight of them Kendra decided they must be twins (she found later that she was right). They were a fierce-looking pair, with black hair and thick black eyebrows, and beards like black cabbages on their chins.

The Blackbeards looked like sons of a pirate, but Ted said their father had been a New England storekeeper. He had bequeathed them the plain surname Thompson, but their romantic mother had given them the first names Marmaduke and Murgatroyd. Marny, who by long study had learned to tell them apart, called them Duke and Troy.

Apparently Duke and Troy had inherited their father's head for business and also their mother's streak of romance. Before they were out of their teens they had gone off to look for adventures in the Pacific, and now they were as canny a pair of card players as you were likely to meet.

Each Blackbeard had his Hawaiian girl on the wagon seat beside him. The girls were a striking pair, with bright jetty eyes and golden skin. Marny called them Lulu and Lolo. Duke was the protector of Lulu, Troy of Lolo.

All the men wore heavy cotton shirts and corduroy riding breeches, and carried guns in holsters at their belts. Kendra and Marny wore riding dresses of sturdy dark cloth, with leather gloves, and straw bonnets made deep-brimmed to shade their eyes. The Hawaiian girls were dressed in flowered chintz, with ribbons binding their hair.

As the party gathered, Ning rode up and down astride a fine roan gelding, inspecting the wagons, making sure all packs were securely strapped, every horse in good condition.

"Quiet, folks!" he ordered.

71

Pointing his riding crop at each in turn he repeated their names, beginning, "Ted Parks, Mrs. Parks." Ted waved from the wagon, Kendra from her horse. Kendra loved hearing herself called Mrs. Parks. It made her feel welcome. In this group she had a place. She had never before had any feeling of belonging to a group, or belonging anywhere.

Ning went on, presenting the company and assigning their places in line. As Marny's name was spoken she flashed her merry smile and called, "Howdydo, everybody!" Delbert, on a steed so black it looked like a mount for the Prince of Darkness, bowed with a bored formality. The Blackbeards nodded, the Hawaiian girls raised their hands in greeting.

Ning introduced Pocket and Hiram Boyd. Pocket gave them a bashful smile, as if not used to being noticed in public. Hiram pulled off his hat and waved it above his head like the leader of a cheering squad. Hiram was not handsome but he was attractive in a rough-hewn way—strong broad shoulders, enormous hands puckered by wind and sun. He had left his rust-colored beard at a barber shop in San Francisco —though on this journey Kendra had no doubt that he would soon grow it again—and now she could see that he had a rugged face with a strong nose and jutting chin, what some people would call a fighting chin. His hair, like his beard, was a rusty brown, thick and untidy. He sat his horse well, and he had brought the spare horses into line with easy skill. Kendra remembered what Ning had said about good travelers. Certainly Hiram would be one.

Ning shouted, "Catch up!"

This was the signal on the Western trails. It meant they were starting to move. Ning rode ahead to lead the line, and the others fell into place: first Ted's wagon, then the two wagons driven by the Blackbeards, one behind the other. After the wagons came the packhorses and the spares, linked by long braids of leather and guarded by Pocket and Hiram. Kendra, Marny, and Delbert had been told to ride alongside the train in any order they pleased.

Kendra looked around. Delbert was riding near the first wagon. He rode calmly, saying nothing, lost in his thoughts— if he had any, which she was beginning to doubt. Marny, near the line of horses, was watching with interest the way Pocket and Hiram were managing them. Kendra wondered if she would get to know Marny on this journey. She hoped so, though she could not think how to open a conversation. She could not go up to Marny and say, "I've never met anybody like you and I'm dying of curiosity."

Well, there must be a way. Ning had said they would be about two weeks on the road. Anything might happen.

The ride was pleasant that morning. Once past the fog-ridden hills of San Francisco they came into a land of sun and grass and April flowers, and trees lively with birds. To her left Kendra could see the bay streaked pink and silver by the sun, to her right the hills that divided the bay from the sea. On the hills she saw herds of grazing cattle, and little houses of plank or adobe where the ranchers lived. Sometimes she saw a man on horseback, or a woman carrying water, or a child who waved as they rode by.

Once she caught sight of a dozen Abs, staring from beyond a line of bushes. They were ugly creatures, a dark grayish brown, their hair sticking out in all directions from their heads, their little beetle eyes batting greedily as they looked at the horses, which they would have liked to eat. They wore tatters of cloth and strings of beads, but not much of either, and they were so dirty that Kendra could smell them as she rode by. Ted had told her that except for stealing anything they could carry, the Abs were harmless unless some fool let them have liquor, but she was glad when the train had left them behind.

These first days were going to be easy. Ning had said they would rest early and often, to keep the horses fresh for the hard pulls ahead. The army couriers made forty miles a day, but those men rode horseback with no burdens but a few clothes in their saddlebags. With wagons, said Ning, twenty miles was enough. And Kendra's meals would be no problem, for she had brought baked ham and beef and other foods ready to eat, enough to let her ease gently into the ways of cooking outdoors.

There was only one detail that worried her, but worry her it did. She liked roughing it this way. But she *was* a civilized person, and there were certain private necessities that ought to be *private*. On a journey such as this, what did you do? Just slip behind a bush and hope nobody would pass?

Well, she would soon find out. Ning kept his word about an early rest, for it was still long before noon when they came to a stream lined with willows and he called that they would stop here. He had divided the party into two messes. Kendra would prepare the meals for Ning and Ted, Pocket

73

and Hiram, while Marny's group would be responsible for their own. Kendra dismounted, Hiram took charge of her mare, and she went to the wagon for the coffee pot. Ted, unhitching the team, called to say he would gather wood for the fire. When he had put the horses in Hiram's care he started off to look for sticks.

Kendra climbed into the wagon, took the coffee pot from the corner where she had carefully put it this morning, and came to the front to climb out. To her surprise she saw Marny, standing by a front wheel as if waiting for her. Marny had taken off her bonnet, and in the sun her hair was like a crown and the freckles almost danced on her nose.

"Won't you share my bathroom?" asked Marny.

11

Marny's voice was demure, but about her lips and her green eyes there were mischievous flickers that added plainly, "We're in this together, let's manage together."

A hundred thoughts rushed into Kendra's head. She had never spoken to—or been addressed by—a woman of easy morals. The nearest she had ever come to it was that day in the store, when she had watched Marny manipulating her cards, and she did not know if Marny had noticed her then or not. She did know that if Eva had been in her place now Eva would have given Marny a cold gaze, replying, "No, thank you," and would have gone back into the wagon and stayed there until Marny had taken her impudent presence somewhere else.

But as she thought of this, Kendra wanted to laugh. For of course, Eva would not have been here at all. Eva would not have consented to be part of a group that included such people as Marny and her friends.

—And I, thought Kendra, am not Eva. I'm me.

She said, "Thank you, I'd like very much to share it. But what do you mean by a bathroom?"

Marny pointed with her crop. Looking around, Kendra saw a clump of bushes around which the Blackbeards were draping a piece of cloth like a long sheet. On the sheet was painted in big black letters, "Ladies Only."

"I have all the needed utensils," said Marny, "including a wash-basin. Just bring your own towel."

As fast as she could, Kendra took a towel from the wagon pack and scrambled down. "What a good idea!" she exclaimed. "Who thought of it?"

"Me," said Marny. She said it with a little smile of amusement, as if to add,—Who do you think has the ideas around here?

As they started toward the clump of bushes, behind them they heard the men laughing. Marny said calmly, "They'll get used to it."

When they reached the bushes Kendra saw that the two ends of the sheet had been sewn around two stakes, and now these were stuck into the ground behind the clump, providing an entrance to the "bathroom" and privacy on all sides. Marny gestured with a slim freckled hand.

"You go in first. You're my guest."

This was a strange way to have an introduction, but an introduction it was. Kendra went into the bathroom, and when she came out she said, "I do thank you!" Marny smiled and answered, "You're welcome, see you later," and they were friends.

Kendra spread out her towel to dry. She started the fire, brought water from the creek, and tied the coffee beans in a cloth so she could grind them between two stones as Ning had taught her. While the coffee was brewing she took out the "eating pans," stout pans with wooden handles, easily held by men sitting on the ground. When she had filled the pans with beef and ship's bread and olives and dried figs, she called that dinner was ready.

While she was working she had noticed that Delbert was not as useless as she had thought. He and Pocket were guarding the camp. On opposite sides, they walked up and down, speaking to nobody, holding their guns ready. When Ning had finished his dinner he took Pocket's place, and one of the Blackbeards relieved Delbert. Ning told the others to stretch out and rest.

An hour later they began the afternoon ride. When they stopped for the night, again the Blackbeards put up the sign around more bushes, again Kendra and Marny shared the bathroom. Lulu and Lolo went in after them. As the girls passed they both politely said, "How do you do," and Lolo added to Marny, "We've started the fire."

"They speak good English," Kendra said to Marny.

"Oh yes," said Marny. "They went to a mission school. Not that it did them much good, I'm glad to say."

Kendra saw Ning bringing an armful of sticks. "I'd better go now," she said, "and get my own fire started."

"You're better than I am," Marny said with a smile. "I'm tired and I'm going to rest. But you're going to cook."

Kendra said she did not mind, though in fact she was tired too. Her riding masters had made her a good horsewoman and the hills of San Francisco had made her a better one, but she was not used to riding all day long. She could not help feeling envious as she scorched her face over the frying pan and saw Marny sitting under a tree with Delbert, sipping wine and playing a card game while Lulu and Lolo cooked supper for them.

But just then Ted, on guard duty, walked past her fire and took the chance to say softly, "Sweetheart, you're great." A moment later the other men of their mess came hungrily to the fire. Kendra filled their eating pans with ham and applesauce and hot fried potatoes. Hiram grinned and said, "This is better food than I'm used to," and Pocket said, "It sure is good, ma'am," and Ning said, "I told you she was gonta be handy," and Kendra thought she would not have changed places with anybody else on earth.

That night, on her bedroll in the wagon, she slept as if a black curtain had fallen over her. In the morning she was awakened by Ted's putting a kiss on the tip of her ear, and she said to herself, "Oh, I'm happy, happy, happy! I'm married to the most delightful man in the world and I'm on my way to a mountain full of gold."

When they mounted their horses, she and Marny rode side by side. Marny was easy to talk to. "Did you see me in the store," Kendra asked, "when you came in that first day?"

"Oh yes. I liked having you there. You looked so fascinated."

"I *was* fascinated. I'd never seen anybody handle cards like that."

"I like cards," Marny said simply.

"I don't know much about them," Kendra said, a little

shyly. "Oh, I know games like whist—parlor games—but not—" She hesitated.

Marny smiled. "But not games like faro and twenty-one? You can watch us at Shiny Gulch when we set up our tent."

"What sort of tent are you bringing?"

"Just a shelter, but I want it bright. I'm bringing some red calico to drape around, and lots of candles. And I'll have a sign. But first I must think of a name. Golden Bar—we'll have a bar, naturally—only that isn't quite right."

A tent in the wilderness, Kendra thought, a tent with many lights and bright calico hangings—men would have fun there, whether they played cards or not. Marny would see to this. Marny had a talent like Eva's for taking a shack and some calico—Kendra said, "Calico Palace."

Marny burst into laughter like a happy child. "Calico Palace! That's it! Thank you! I'll tell Delbert."

Kendra glanced at Delbert, serene in his solitude. "Why does Delbert keep to himself?" she asked.

Marny answered with a merry green sparkle. "Delbert doesn't like the human race."

"Not anybody? Why not?"

Marny laughed. She had a soft, silken laugh. "Darling, he decided long ago that people were pests."

"But he likes you," said Kendra.

"He doesn't really like me," Marny returned good-humoredly. "He just thinks I'm less objectionable than most."

Kendra wanted to ask, "Why do you like him?"—but she did not feel she knew Marny well enough. Instead she inquired, "Is Delbert his first name or his last? I mean, like John Delbert or Delbert Smith?"

"Just Delbert. He writes 'John Delbert' when he's required to give a full name, like on the Hawaiian passport, but otherwise he's just Delbert. I don't know why—I suppose he thought it was an elegant way to name himself."

"Name himself? But what's his right name?"

"Oh dear, I don't know. Wouldn't surprise me if he'd forgotten it himself by now."

Kendra was so startled that she could not think of anything to say. Marny and Delbert had shared a wagon last night, and yet she did not even know his right name. Kendra wondered how it felt to be so frivolous. She wondered if Marny really thought, as Ted had suggested, that the affair of the *Cynthia* had been a trivial incident. Kendra could not imagine

77

how anybody could think going to bed with a man was trivial, but Ted usually knew what he was talking about.

But however Marny regarded it, to Captain Pollock the incident had not been trivial. Pollock thought Marny had insulted his ship.

—Oh, moonshine, thought Kendra. Still, he's in love with that ship. In love, the way any other man would be in love with a woman. But what can he do to Marny? Nothing. All the same—maybe I'm as silly as he is but all the same—I'll feel better when he's on his way back to New York.

That evening they made camp at the southern tip of the bay. In the morning, their third day out, they turned north. The country was wild and green and nearly empty. Here and there an Ab peered from behind a tree, or a group of Mexican horsemen went by on some errand of their own. Nobody else. They saw cattle grazing, and in the distance deer and elk, running away as the wagons rumbled by. Ning warned Kendra and Marny to ride close to the train, and be careful. Here east of the bay they might meet wandering no-goods— runaway sailors, deserters from the army, all sorts of men who found it advisable to keep away from the law.

Kendra was realizing, better than ever, how wisely Ning had chosen his company. Hiram and Pocket did their work well, Delbert continued an excellent guard by day or night. Delbert might not think highly of his fellowmen but he did value the coins he and Marny had packed as capital for their gambling venture, and he had no intention of letting any outlaws get near. While they were washing in the bathroom at noon Marny told Kendra that Delbert used to play cards on the Mississippi River boats. "In that trade," said Marny, "a man has to be quick on the draw if he wants to survive."

"Was he playing on the river boats when you met him?" Kendra asked.

"No, I met him on the way to Honolulu. He boarded the ship at Valparaiso. Delbert likes to roam."

Marny buckled the belt of her riding dress. Kendra observed that Marny carried a little firearm of her own, in a pocket on this belt. "May I look at that?" asked Kendra, who had never handled a gun in her life.

Marny held out the gun and explained how it worked. It was a tiny Colt revolving pistol, a .28 caliber six-shooter, with

78

a barrel only two and a half inches long. "Isn't it a dear?" said Marny.

"Is it loaded?" Kendra asked with awe.

"Of course. What would it be good for if it wasn't?"

As Kendra gave back the gun, rather fearfully, Marny fondled it, smiling.

"This was a present," she said, "from the man who ran the best gambling parlor in New York. A Frenchman from New Orleans, named Norman Lamont. I used to be one of his dealers. When I decided to move to Honolulu I wanted him to come too, but he wouldn't. He wanted to go back home. He said New Orleans was the best gambling town in the country."

"But you didn't think so?" Kendra asked. She wanted to hear more. All this was a matter she knew nothing about.

"I don't know—I've never been there," said Marny. "But I do wish Norman had come to Honolulu. He could have been with us now, going up to the gold fields. Smartest gambler I ever saw."

Marny paused, thinking back.

"There never was anything between Norman and me," she added thoughtfully. "He always had a girl of his own. But I admired him. He had real talent."

"More than Delbert?" Kendra asked.

"Yes," Marny answered with amusement, "but don't say I said so. Life is dangerous enough as it is."

Kendra laughed and promised. She added admiringly, "And you can really shoot?"

"Certainly." Marny gave her a knowing smile. "You've never had to take care of yourself, my dear, but that's what I do all the time."

That afternoon as they rode, Kendra wondered how it would feel to be in need of a gun. She had never taken care of herself. As a child, while she had not been loved, she had been well cared for. The journey to California was a long one but she had made it on one of the finest ships in the world; San Francisco was a rude town but she had not once been in the street unguarded. And now she was on her way to a wilderness but she was going there with Ted.

She and Marny were riding together, with Hiram on the other side of Marny. Marny was saying, "If there isn't such a lot of gold, we'll come back and set up shop in San Francisco."

"There's plenty of gold," Kendra exclaimed. "Ted saw it."

Hiram chuckled dryly. "I believe him. If I didn't I shouldn't be here." His big hand gestured toward his own two packhorses. "Everything I own is on those."

"You're a brave man," said Kendra, "to risk everything."

Hiram shrugged. His russet beard had begun to grow and the prickles glistened in the sun. "I came to California," he answered genially, "to seek my fortune. I'm a minister's son. As you may have heard, ministers send their children to school but they don't make 'em rich."

How strong and self-reliant he looked. He was now telling them he had packed some Chinese firecrackers, to scare any Abs who might come prowling around his belongings. Marny, as usual, was laughing.

Kendra envied them both. Hiram and Marny sounded like such independent people. People who did not need anybody, who were complete in themselves.

—And I, thought Kendra, am not complete. I need other people. I want to be loved. I *need* to be loved.

Ning was driving the wagon today and Ted was on horseback leading the train. Kendra hurried her mount and caught up with him. She felt a sudden fright at the thought of how much she did need Ted. Without him she would be lonesome again, as lonesome as she had been all her life. But as he saw her riding into place beside him Ted puckered his lips to blow her a kiss, and Kendra thought,—I am not alone any more. I need him, yes, but I've got him.

12

The next day they ran into a shower, which slowed the wagon teams and swelled the creeks they had to cross, so they did not go far. But the morning after this was clear. Ning had them up at daybreak, and by eight o'clock they came to the strip of water called Carquinez Strait. This strait, about eight miles long and two miles wide, linked two inland bays, all part of the eastern branch of the great bay, reaching in to meet the Sacramento River. Here an enterprising giant named Semple, straight from Kentucky and seven feet tall, ran a ferry to the settlement of Benicia on the other side.

Semple lived across the strait at Benicia, but he kept a boat on this side, and a supply of barley and corn for horses, guarded by several youths who were the only visible inhabitants. These guards would take a man across to Benicia, but if a party was waiting, Semple himself came over on the return trip and took charge. His ferryboat was a broad flat-bottomed affair, big enough to carry a dozen horses. For each horse he charged a dollar, for each person fifty cents, and six dollars for a wagon.

Along the waterside the country was bright with flowers and lacy with willow trees. The men stopped the wagons near a creek that ran down into the strait about half a mile from the ferry landing. The Blackbeards enclosed a group of willows with the "Ladies Only" sign, and Ning went ahead to arrange for the crossing.

This was their fifth day out. They were now twenty-three miles from San Francisco. Twenty-three miles as the crow flies, but they had traveled nearly ninety miles to get here, because, not being crows, they could not fly across the bay.

Ning told Marny and Kendra that getting the horses and wagons over would mean four trips. Kendra suggested that she go over on the first trip, to start dinner and have it ready by the time the crossing was done.

"No ma'am," Ning replied firmly. "You ain't gonta let loose no smell of cooking till you've got men to guard the pot. Otherwise you'd have every do-nothing in the neighborhood coming up to sponge a meal."

Ning made sense, as usual, so Kendra sat with Marny on the grass and looked on. The ferry guards took the first horses over, with Hiram to watch them on the other side. On the next two trips the boat carried the Blackbeards with Lulu and Lolo, Delbert and the two wagons loaded with everything he and Marny had brought (including the "Ladies Only" sign, now rolled up and stowed away), and Ning to supervise the camp. Still waiting to cross were Marny and Kendra, Ted with his own wagon, and Pocket, who had stayed to help him guard the team.

By now it was past noon and the sun was hot. Ted and Pocket, tired from the work of getting horses and wagons on the ferry, were enjoying the luxury of having to watch only a single team and wagon. Pocket had tethered the horses to a tree by the creek, and rested near by while they cropped the grass. Twenty yards away Ted lay stretched in the shade of the wagon, his gun at his side. Between them Marny and Kendra sat under a tree, their big riding skirts spread around them, watching the ferry as it made its way over the water toward the fifteen or twenty shacks that composed the town of Benicia.

The birds chirped and pecked at the grass, and a thousand bees were buzzing among the flowers. "I have only one complaint," said Marny. "I'm hungry."

Kendra was hungry too. She remembered the dried fruit in her wagon. "I'll get some figs," she said, and began to stand up. "Oh—*rats!*"

"If you mean damn," said Marny, "why don't you say so?"

"Damn!" said Kendra.

"What happened?" Marny asked laughing.

Crossly, Kendra showed her. As she stood up she had stepped on the hem of her riding skirt, and ripped several riches of the seam where the skirt was gathered to the belt.

"No tragedy," said Marny. "Easy to mend. Haven't you got a sewing kit?"

"Yes, my mother made me bring one, but I can't sew."

Marny smiled understandingly. "I'll mend it. Bring me a needle and thread."

Kendra brought the sewing kit from the wagon, and went with Marny into the cluster of willows that had served as their bathroom. Here she took off the skirt, and watched as Marny competently stitched up the tear. "I wish I could do that!" she exclaimed.

"You can't have all the talents, darling, it wouldn't be fair. You should see me trying to cook. My best coffee tastes like mud." Marny snipped the thread. "There, that's as good as new. Put on your skirt and you can go out in public again. Oh my Lord," she broke off—"see what we've got now!"

On the last line her voice had dropped to a frightened whisper. Closing one hand around Kendra's wrist, with the other she pointed to the grassland beyond the willows.

Out there in the sunshine Kendra saw two men, tattered and shaggy-haired, who had rambled down from the wooded hills. Their clothes were dirty and their shoes broken; one man was bare-headed and the other wore an old hat on the side of his head. They were still a good way off but they were coming nearer.

Kendra smothered a gasp of dismay. Still whispering, Marny added,

"Sailors. I know by the way they walk, I've seen hundreds in Honolulu. Some of those deserters Ning warned us about. Kendra—our men don't know they're here."

Through the willows Kendra saw Pocket, his back to them, retying a loose tether. In the other direction Ted lay on the grass by the wagon, but the sailors were approaching from the opposite side and he had not seen them. Apparently they had not seen him either, and they had not noticed herself and Marny behind the willows. But they had seen the wagon and they were heading for it. A covered wagon meant travelers, and travelers carried stuff worth stealing. Maybe they thought this wagon, waiting its turn for the ferry, had been left unguarded—foolish, but some people were fools. The sailors' pockets sagged as if they held guns. Knife-handles stuck up from their belts.

"They want the wagon," Kendra whispered. Her lips were dry with fear.

"Wagon your grandmother," Marny retorted. "They want us."

Kendra started with terror. "They haven't seen us!"

"They will," Marny said wisely. "And when they do, they'll forget about the wagon."

Kendra thought of the little gun in the pocket of Marny's belt. "I don't want you to hurt anybody—but couldn't you shoot so as not to hit them? Ted and Pocket would hear the shot."

"I could fire, of course," Marny said doubtfully, "but those men would know the shot came from this direction and they'd shoot back. And they wouldn't be squeamish about not hitting anybody. I'd feel safer with some helpers. If Ted and Pocket would only look around!"

Ted and Pocket, however, had noticed nothing amiss. For though the wagon seemed untended, the sailors were taking no chances. They were walking carefully. On the thick grass their footsteps made no sound. The birds chirped, and in the clover the bees made a song of their own. Kendra shivered. Those birds and bees had seen the sailors—if only their songs were words, calling Pocket and Ted! Words—the wish gave her an idea.

With one hand she reached for the skirt she had taken off to be mended, while her other hand closed on Marny's elbow.

"We can step outside," she whispered. "Then we can pretend we don't speak English and don't know what they're saying. That will give us time, and the men will hear us talking."

Marny's face brightened. Dangerous or not, Marny enjoyed adventure. "I get it. No spik Inglis. But let's not go out together. I'll hold them—you put on your skirt and run to call Ted in case he doesn't hear."

Kendra nodded agreement. Marny stood up and pushed aside a willow branch. She stepped out into the sunshine, took a few idle steps, and paused before a cluster of blue lupin. Bending over, she reached as if to pick the flowers, and the sailors caught sight of her.

As she had foretold, they forgot there was a wagon in the world. They rushed toward her, and in front of the willow group they met her. They could have seen Kendra too if they had looked through the willows, but they did not look; they saw nothing but Marny with her green eyes and her freckles and her lissom figure and her blaze of hair.

Quivering all over, Kendra drew on her skirt.

The bareheaded man loudly kissed both his hands at Marny, the one with the hat pulled it off with what he thought was a gallant bow. The first said, "Howdy, beautiful!" The other, "Say, ain't you a sight to behold!"

Marny looked at them blankly. In a toneless voice she said, "No spik Inglis."

They were not listening. They were gazing, and making plans to make love. They both began to talk at once. "I'm named Joe," said the man who had kissed his hands. "He's Bill. What's your name?"

"Where'd you come from?" demanded Bill. "Where you going? Where'd you get that red hair?"

"Where'd you get all them freckles?" asked Joe.

Marny answered, "No spik Inglis."

"We been everywhere all over the world," said Joe, "but we ain't seen nothing like you."

Marny said impassively, "No spik Inglis."

Bill and Joe were not very bright, but they did begin to hear what she said. "She don't speak the language," Bill said to Joe. "Foreign lady."

Joe nodded. With a broad smile that showed several broken teeth, he inquired, "Mamzell, parlez-vous français?"

His accent was dreadful, but Kendra had learned enough at school to recognize that he was trying to speak French. Whether or not Marny knew this, she remained blank.

"She don't speak French neither," said Bill. "Lemme try." With another low bow he asked, "¿Habla español, señorita?"

Marny gave him no answer.

"Hell," Joe reproved him, "she ain't no Mex. There ain't no red-headed Mexes."

"Well, she's something, ain't she?" Bell exclaimed. "Look, lady, we been all over. Sprechen Sie deutsch?"

Marny continued to look blank.

But Bill and Joe had sailed the seven seas, they had made love to girls in a hundred ports. They spoke no language well, but in their travels they had picked up a smattering of tongues in half the countries of the world. Bill demanded, "Parlate l'italiano?"

"I told you," said Joe, "she ain't no Mex, I bet she ain't no Dago either. And she sure ain't a Chink." He pointed his grimy finger at Marny. "Look here, lady. You can talk something. Snakker De norsk? Spreekt U Nederlandsch? Come on now, wake up and *talk!*" As he spoke he clapped his dirty hand on her shoulder and gave her a shake.

Angrily Marny wrenched herself free and swallowed the plain English words she felt like saying to him. Behind the willows Kendra was trembling so hard that her fingers were having trouble pushing the buttons through the buttonholes. She did not know what languages those men were speaking but she did know Marny could not hold them at bay much longer. In another moment Marny would have to start talking, and how was she going to do it? She could not gabble "Fe fi fo fum"—they would know she had been making fools of them, they might really start shooting. Joe was now demanding,

"Er De dansk? Oh, come on now, lady!"

With a grin of inspiration Bill twirled his hat and suggested, "Maybe—Roosky?"

Kendra gathered up her unwieldy skirt. —Run, she commanded her legs. Run and don't fall down.

"Talk!" Joe was yelling at Marny. "I said, talk!" He grabbed her again.

Again Marny jerked herself out of his grasp. She did not

like to be rudely handled. Now she was no longer amused, she was mad. Being mad, she had an inspiration of her own.

She began to talk.

"Amo, amas, amat!" she retorted angrily. "Amamus, amatis, amant!"

"Huh?" said Joe.

13

Joe and Bill stared at each other.

Marny stamped her foot. "Gallia est omnis," she flung at them, "divisa in partes tres."

"Hey, what's that?" asked Bill.

Though Kendra had barely heard what Marny was saying, she did realize thankfully that Marny had hit upon a language the men had not heard before. Through the willows she saw Ted. The voices had roused his attention and he had moved to a spot where he could see the sailors, but though he held his gun he was not firing. For heaven's sake, wondered Kendra, why not? He might not want to kill anybody but he could at least have fired into the air so those men would know Marny was not alone. Marny was vigorously talking back to them.

"Quo usque tandem abutere, Catilina, patentia nostra?"

The sailors stood with their mouths open, but saying nothing because they could not think of anything to say. Marny rattled on.

"O tempora! O mores! Senatus haec intellegit, consul videt, hic tamen vivit!"

On and on she went, to the greater and greater bewilderment of her hearers. Without listening any longer Kendra ran to Ted. As she reached him she stopped short, seeing with amazement why he had not fired.

He could not. He was choking with laughter. His gun shook so that he dared not pull the trigger.

"Ted!" she exclaimed. "What on earth—aren't you going to help her?"

For a moment Ted's laughter smothered his words. When he could speak he said, "That girl doesn't need any help."

Marny's voice came to them. "Arma virumque cano, Trojae qui primus ab oris—"

Ted turned to Kendra. "Do you know what she's saying?"

Kendra shook her head.

"She is speaking," said Ted, "Latin."

"Latin!" Kendra echoed. "But where did she learn—"

"How would I know?" he retorted, with wonder equal to hers. "A stray flossy who deals cards in gambling houses out at the end of the world—"

"Italiam fugo profugus," continued Marny, "Lavinaque venit—"

Ted went on, "The most beautiful classical Latin I ever heard. She has quoted Caesar and Cicero, and right now she's giving them the opening lines of Virgil's *Aeneid*. Kendra, where do you suppose she—"

A shot cracked from the creekside. Bill's hat fell out of his hand and Bill himself flung up his hand with a yell. But there was no mark on his hand. The bullet had hit nothing but the hat. It was a splendid piece of marksmanship, and now Pocket was following the bullet from the bank of the creek.

Joe grabbed at his knife, but it was too late, for now at last Ted fired too, aiming high, for while he was a fair marksman he had not Pocket's consummate skill. As he fired he sprang to his feet and went toward the sailors from one side as Pocket approached from the other. Bill and Joe were cornered, and even more so when Marny produced her own little gun, and Pocket, now at her side, ordered, "You fellows get away from here. Get a long way from here."

The sailors blinked. "We didn't mean any harm!" said Joe.

"You didn't do any harm, either," said Ted, "and you're not going to. Back!"

They backed, Ted and Pocket prodding them with the guns. Leaving the shelter of the wagon Kendra went over to Marny, who was now sitting on the grass, mirthfully watching the sailors' retreat. "Marny," Kendra said with awe, "you're marvelous!"

Marny looked around and gave her a broad wink. Together they watched till the sailors had run out of sight among the trees. Ted and Pocket came back.

"Thanks, boys," said Marny.

"Don't thank us," said Ted, "you did the job."

Marny picked up Bill's hat from the grass beside her, and ran her finger along the tear the bullet had made in the brim. "Pocket," she said with admiration, "you do know how to use that cannon." She threw the hat away and held out her hand. "Help me up."

He took her hand in his. "Say, Miss Marny," he exclaimed as she stood up, "Ted told me—you're educated, aren't you?"

Marny pushed back a lock of shining red hair. "Right now, I'm kind of limp. I'd like some refreshment. Among all those pockets of yours, Pocket, have you got a flask?"

He smiled regretfully. "Sorry, Miss Marny, I don't drink."

She gave him the same look of tolerant amusement she had given him in the store when he told her he did not gamble. "Do you smoke, Pocket?" she asked.

"No ma'am," he said gently.

"What do you do for fun?"

He gave her a smile of disarming candor. "Well ma'am, I sure do like women."

Marny burst out laughing. "And I like men," she said. "You're all right, Pocket."

Ted was laughing too. Like the other men of their group, Ted had not shaved since they left San Francisco and now his face looked like a good-humored cockleburr. "I have a flask in the wagon, Marny," he said. "Come along. And where did you learn Latin?"

Marny gave them all a merry green glance. "Darlings, anybody who's been thrown out of as many schools as I have, couldn't help learning a little something on the way." She put a freckled hand on Ted's arm. "Now where's that flask? Bis dat qui cito dat—that means if you hurry up, one drink will seem like two."

She and Ted walked toward the wagon. Ted climbed in, and a moment later reappeared with the "flask," a canteen bought from the army stores, as no glass container was likely to withstand the bumps of the journey. Pocket returned to the horses. But Kendra stood where she was. All of a sudden she had had an idea about Marny.

Loren had told her, "The Miss Randolph who came on board that day looked like a perfect lady and talked like one." She herself, before those two white houses on the cliff, had reflected that nice girls did get into trouble sometimes and she did not believe they all pined away like the girls in story books. She remembered the drawings that illustrated those stories—a girl slinking off as a grim-faced father pointed the way into a snowy night. In those illustrations, it was always snowing.

But absurd though they were, the stories and drawings must have been built around a core of truth. Otherwise there would not be so many of them.

And now here was Marny. Had somebody—an implacable father, a whole self-righteous family—turned her out of doors like that?

Marny and Ted were walking back toward her, both of them sipping drinks Ted had poured into their tin cups. Pocket came back too, pausing a moment to scan the horizon and make sure the sailors were staying out of sight. Reaching Kendra, Marny gave her a quizzical smile. "You're mighty quiet," she observed.

Kendra started. "Oh—I was just thinking how beautiful these wild flowers are. I wish I knew some beautiful words to say it."

Smiling, Marny suggested,

"When daisies pied and violets blue,
    And lady-smocks all silver white,
And cuckoo-buds of yellow hue
    Do paint the meadows with delight . . ."

"Say," Pocket exclaimed as she paused, "that's *pretty!*"

Marny laughed softly. "Do you like poetry, Pocket?"

"I guess I do, ma'am. Only I don't know much. Who made up that one?"

"Shakespeare."

"I've heard of him," Pocket said gravely.

Marny sat on the grass again, while Pocket watched her with interest. "Miss Marny," he asked, "where did you come from?"

"Philadelphia."

"Why'd you leave?" asked Pocket.

Kendra, standing to one side, inwardly winced. He should not be asking! Couldn't he realize that a girl like Marny might not want to discuss her past? Kendra glanced at Ted, but he too was waiting for what Marny would say. Marny herself merely gave Pocket a roguish look as she asked,

"Pocket, were you ever in Philadelphia on Sunday?"

Ted began to laugh.

But Pocket soberly shook his head. "No ma'am. What happens in Philadelphia on Sunday?"

"Nothing," said Marny. "I mean *nothing*. People stay home and read good books."

Ted sat down on the grass beside her. "Is that how you learned so much?" he asked.

"Why don't you let her alone?" demanded Kendra.

The two men turned to her in astonishment. Kendra hurried on.

"Can't you understand?—it's none of our business! Maybe Marny doesn't want to tell you about herself. Marny—Marny was well brought up!"

She stopped abruptly. Ted and Pocket had heard her with faces suddenly grave, even a little guilty, as if agreeing that maybe they did have too much curiosity about Marny's affairs. But Marny herself had begun to laugh, with a silvery merriment that made the brandy tremble in her cup. Reaching out her free hand she took Kendra's hand and squeezed it.

"Kendra, you are a darling, you are adorable, and you are as artless as the flowers. Sit down." She drew Kendra to the grass beside her, and Pocket sat down too. Marny went on,

"Kendra, back in Baltimore, you must have known people to shake their heads regretfully and say, 'There's one in every family.' "

Kendra frowned. "One—?"

"The one who's never mentioned."

Kendra did remember that she had heard this phrase, or others like it, spoken in hushed voices that she was not supposed to hear. ("And the younger brother, what is he doing now?"—"Sh! Don't ask about him. Around the family, he's never mentioned.") So Kendra nodded, and Marny looked humorously from her to the men.

"Dear people," said Marny, "around my family, the one who's never mentioned by tactful visitors is me."

They were all listening. A mischievous glint in her green eyes, Marny asked,

"Shall I tell you the story of my misspent life?"

"Yes ma'am!" Pocket exclaimed. "Please do, Miss Marny."

Marny laughed gently. She said,

"Darlings, on the outskirts of Philadelphia is an institution called Landreth University. A noble place. Towers of ivied gray stone, fine old trees, walks winding among lawns and

90

shrubbery. My father was Dr. Virgil Randolph, professor of Latin and Greek at Landreth. My mother was the daughter of another man of learning who had also studied in those hallowed halls. Their marriage pleased everybody. Their home was a brick house on a tree-shaded street. They had aunts and uncles and cousins and ancestors and they were all fine people. Every one of them.

"In fifteen years Dr. and Mrs. Randolph had three sons and two daughters. The children were bright and handsome and well behaved, and their parents and all the relatives were proud of them. There was not a family in Philadelphia more respected than the Randolphs. They were a credit to the community and a credit to the human race. And believe me, they knew it.

"Everything was going well with the Randolphs. And then, when her youngest child was ten years old, Mrs. Randolph was dismayed to find herself again having delicate symptoms."

Marny paused. Kendra and Ted and Pocket began to laugh. Pocket said,

"That was you?"

"That was me, Pocket," said Marny. "I started making trouble before anybody even saw me."

Taking a sip of her brandy, Marny continued,

"My mother was deep in her forties. She was not only dismayed, she was embarrassed. So was the family. No nice woman should be having a baby at that age. But I was born, and they tried to make the best of it. But then, before I was very old, they found that I was like a bee buzzing around in their well-ordered life."

Marny gave a sigh.

"I wasn't sickly, I wasn't stupid, I wasn't bad-tempered. But I was *different*.

"It wasn't merely that nobody else in the family had red hair and green eyes. Whether or not they liked the way I looked, they could understand that I was made that way. But nobody in the family was bubble-headed and gigglesome and frivolous like me. This they could *not* understand. Shall I go on?"

"I'm fascinated," said Ted.

Kendra and Pocket were fascinated too. Marny laughed as she remembered. What beautiful laughter she had, Kendra thought. You could see a flower and smell it; if you could also *hear* a flower, it would sound the way Marny laughed.

"One day when I was a tiny child," said Marny, "I ran in with muddy hands and smeared a book of etiquette lying on the table. It was a book that belonged to my grown-up sister Claudia, who was going to be married and wanted her wedding to be just right. I didn't know what a book of etiquette was, but they said I had an instinct for attacking such things. It was as if I'd been possessed by a naughty little demon.

"Another day I found a tray of glasses filled with red wine, ready to be passed to guests. The wine looked lovely and it smelled delicious and I tasted it and I liked it. I thought it was much nicer than jam. I still think so. When my grown-up brother Ovid came in to get the tray he found half the glasses empty and he found me dancing around and trying to sing, gloriously fizzled at the age of four. I thought it was great fun but he didn't."

Marny sighed.

"Not long after this I came across a pack of cards somebody had left lying on a table. The cards enchanted me. I loved to lay them out in patterns, long before I knew what they were for. But after a while I made friends with a boy whose father was a janitor at the university. He taught me some card games. My sister Doris found us gambling for pennies on the back steps. The family decided I needed a governess to keep me in order.

"I had several governesses, one after another. The poor dear things wouldn't stay. They tried to change me but I couldn't be changed. The family sent me away to a boarding school. I did well in my lessons. I'm quite bright and I like to study, I really do, but one night I was discovered on a back balcony being kissed by the gardener's boy. They sent me home.

"More schools, more disgraces. I couldn't stay away from cards and handsome men. My parents were killed in a boating accident, but my brothers and sisters and aunts and uncles and cousins all kept trying to uplift me. It was no use. I didn't want to be uplifted.

"Still, I didn't want to bring any more trouble on them. I had a little legacy from my father and I took it and got out of Philadelphia."

"To Honolulu?" asked Ted.

"Not at first. I went to New York. I didn't have any trouble finding work, I have a talent for cards. I was a dealer at Norman Lamont's card parlor—I've told Kendra about him. But New York was too close to Philadelphia. Men who knew the family would drop into Norman's to play, and they recognized me, and they talked, and the family was embarrassed as much as ever. I decided I'd better go a long way off. Norman wanted me to move to New Orleans when he did, but I thought I should go even farther. I really didn't dislike my family. I was sorry for them, keeping their heads in mothballs. I thought the greatest kindness I could do them would be to get out of the country and out of their lives. So, here I am."

Marny looked around.

"My friends, I'm light-minded and trifling, and my character is not worth a damn, but I like what I'm doing and I like all of you. I like you much better than I liked the people I used to know in the halls of learning. And I hope you like me. Do you?"

"Yes ma'am," Pocket said firmly. "I like you."

"I like you too," said Ted.

For a moment Kendra said nothing, then she spoke thoughtfully.

"Marny, I like you better than if you were the kind of mistreated girl I thought you were. You knew what you wanted to do and you did it, all the way. I don't like halfway people. I like people who have courage."

"Thank you, dear," said Marny. "If you mean guts, why don't you say so?"

"Guts," said Kendra.

14

This was the twenty-ninth of April. On the second of May, a week out of San Francisco, they saw the Sacramento River twinkling behind the tangle of trees and vines along its bank. Through the tangle they caught distant glimpses of the high white walls of Sutter's Fort. But between themselves and the fort lay the river, and clouds of mosquitoes swarming upon them so fiercely that they wished they had never heard of gold. This was another reason why Ning had told them not to travel by water. He knew that in spring the mosquitoes on the Sacramento were a greater plague than all the Abs and runaway sailors in California.

Here on the river bank Ning received his first surprise of the journey. Mr. Sutter had a dugout canoe to bring visitors across, but Ning had warned the men that they would have to cut logs and make a raft to carry the wagons. But hardly had they begun to unpack their tools when they heard shouts from the water, and saw coming to meet them a raft moved by poles and a cable stretched from the opposite bank. On the raft were two sturdy bearded fellows, pointing upstream. Following their direction Ning found the place where they had tied the cable on this side.

The men sprang ashore. Between slaps at mosquitoes they said their names were Bates and Cunningham. They were Mormons from New York, and had come out on the same vessel that had brought the rest of the Mormon colony to San Francisco. Bates and Cunningham wanted to go gold hunting, but lacked money to buy supplies, so had chosen to earn it by ferrying other gold hunters across the river.

"Fine idea," said Ning. "I guess we'll have to unload the wagons?"

"Right," Bates agreed. "They'll be too heavy to take over unless they're empty."

"Well, let's get busy, boys," said Ning. "Bates, you can help with our wagon, and you, Cunningham, give a hand to Delbert there."

The men set to work, and Ning spoke to Kendra. "I'm gonta send you and Marny over on the first crossing," he told her, "with Pocket and one of the Blackbeards to stand guard. You can start dinner. But look out for the dinner hunters. Don't give away a bean."

"I understand, Ning. I won't give away a bean."

He nodded approvingly. "You know how to take orders. You're a good traveler, Miss Kendra."

Oh, she liked being here, liked hearing herself called a good traveler. And as if she had needed anything more to make her happy, all of a sudden a sharp wind came out of the north and blew the mosquitoes downstream.

Carefully holding her skirt with one hand and Cunningham's elbow with the other, Kendra stepped from the river bank to the raft. After her came Marny, with Pocket and

Blackbeard. The crossing, though teetery, was short and safe. As she stepped ashore Kendra felt her heart bump with excitement. About three miles away, she could see the most famous structure in California, Sutter's Fort. And coming to greet them was a group of horsemen led by the great Johann Augustus Sutter himself, the most magnificent humbug who ever crossed the western mountains.

Sutter was forty-five years old, a man of blustering charm. He had a fine curling beard, and thick dark hair balding back from his forehead. His clothes were impressive: black suit and white linen shirt, wide blue silk cravat tied with a flourish, boots gleaming, heavy gold watch chain looped across his middle. A forceful man, hearty with other men, courtly with women, Sutter usually smelled of brandy and he loved to talk.

Pocket had told Kendra and Marny a good deal about him. Sutter came from Switzerland, and had reached California nine years ago. His pockets were empty but visions of grandeur filled his head. The Mexican government gave him a grant of wilderness (some people said ten thousand acres, some said fifty thousand). Here he built his fort, the start of a kingdom where he meant to be king.

Beyond this, nobody knew much about him, for though he spoke four languages and talked about himself in all of them, he was seldom entirely sober and his yarns had a bubbly sound. He came, he said, of a noble Swiss family, but had had to flee his native land because of his liberal ideas. (This puzzled those of his hearers who were familiar with Switzerland. They said they had never heard of any man's being expelled from that free country merely for speaking his mind.)

After countless adventures and hairbreadth escapes (which he loved to describe) Sutter said he had joined the guard of King Charles of France. In defense of his new country he had fought many battles and received many wounds (he would gladly show the scars). But misfortune still pursued him. A revolution dethroned King Charles, and again, said Sutter, he had had to seek a new homeland. After more heroic exploits he had at last reached California. And now he was happy to see his friends coming into the country around the fort. If they wanted to look for gold in the mountains he was glad to have them do so.

This last, Pocket had said, was flubdub. The fact was that

95

when the sawmill workers found something they thought was gold, Sutter had sent one of his clerks to Colonel Mason, military governor of California, trying to claim the find for himself. As the gold had been found on public land, Colonel Mason said he had no authority to give it to Sutter nor anybody else. The clerk then came to San Francisco and showed the gold around, until he finally found a man who believed him and they went back to the hills to dig for themselves. (The clerk's name was Bennett, and Kendra learned later that he was the "crackbrain" Morse and Vernon had told her about the day she arrived.)

Never mind Sutter, said Pocket, let him talk. He enjoyed it and you couldn't stop him anyway. If he liked to imagine the gold seekers were there by his permission, what harm was it? He stood to make a lot of money as they came by the fort and spent gold dust there.

Riding with two of his henchmen on either side of him, before he was near enough to start talking Sutter pulled off his hat and waved. As he recognized Pocket, he loudly welcomed him back. He was noisily glad to meet Blackbeard, and to Marny and Kendra he bowed low, exclaiming that it was a joy to greet such lovely ladies. Hiram swam their horses over the river, and he and the Mormons went back on the raft, while Sutter, talking with all his might, led the girls and their escorts into the primitive splendor of his domain.

They had seen already that the Sacramento River flowed south. Now they saw that another river, called the American, came down from the hills and flowed into the Sacramento almost at a right angle. In the corner where the two rivers met stood Sutter's Fort, placed far enough from the banks to be safe in times of flood.

Sutter had marked off a rectangle five hundred feet long and a hundred and fifty feet wide, and around it he had set up a high whitewashed brick wall three feet thick. Inside this wall he had built a second. The space between the walls was roofed, and divided into rooms used as living quarters for the guardsmen and shops for the workers.

The main entrance was wide enough to admit a covered wagon. However, it was not easy to get inside if Sutter did not want you there. Along the outer wall cannon pointed in all directions, and the entrance gates were so vast that it took several men to move them. At two corners were watchtowers, from which the guardsmen could see anybody who came by land or water. Pocket whispered to the girls that underneath one of these towers was a dungeon where Sutter locked up any man who misbehaved. The dungeon was dark and damp, but its real horror was several million fleas. After a few hours among the fleas the toughest wrongdoer was yelling that if they would let him out he would be good as long as he lived.

Inside the walls was a well, and storehouses stocked with food and guns. Here also was a tall two-story house, headquarters of Sutter himself, where he received his guests and issued his orders.

Outside the walls they could see Sutter's spreading empire. The air smelled of animals and liquor and people, and rang with noise—shouts of men and lowing of cattle, bang of hammers and creak of wheels, and now and then a shot as some fellow tried his gun. Here they saw the beginnings of a town: trading posts and scattered dwellings, where children scampered and women in sunbonnets hung out clothes or cooked over outdoor fires. Farther out, stretching into shadowy distance toward the mountains, they saw Sutter's wheatfields. Tending the fields were Abs, bossed by a mounted troop of their own tribal chiefs. These chiefs had brought in the fieldhands and now kept them from running away. They were rewarded by being dressed in many-colored "uniforms," called by the title of "capitano," and given food and squaws in abundance. Sutter, said Pocket, got more work out of the Abs than any other landowner in California.

After making terms with Sutter, Pocket led them to a camping place near the American River. While Kendra made her cook-fire Pocket brought water, and went to Sutter's storehouses to buy grain for the horses and vegetables for Kendra's beef stew. Having thus spent enough money to make them really welcome, Pocket left Blackbeard to guard the horses and the simmering kettle, while Pocket himself stuffed another bandana or two into his pockets and took the girls to see Smith and Brannan's store, where he used to work.

The store was a good-sized structure with a trading room and a storeroom. Pocket introduced the clerk in charge, a friend of his named Gene Spencer, one of the Mormons who had come out from New York. Leaving Gene to tell Pocket what had been going on in his absence, Marny and Kendra walked around.

The front room was like that of Chase and Fenway's, except that it displayed far more goods. The shelves behind the counter were crammed almost to the cracking point, and the space in front was so full of barrels and boxes that there was hardly room to move. Holding their skirts close around them to avoid snags, Kendra and Marny made their way to the storeroom. Here they stopped and stared.

The front room had been crowded, but this room was almost literally *stuffed*. Merchandise was hung from the ceiling, piled on the shelves, stacked in every foot of space on the floor. They saw hams and beef and tobacco, flour and whiskey and salt fish and pickles, coffee and cornmeal and bacon and beans; pots and pans and wooden bowls, picks and shovels and crowbars, knives, matches, horn spoons, men's boots and shirts and breeches, saddles and blankets and guns and bullet molds. As they turned from the storeroom door Gene Spencer broke off his chat with Pocket and gave them a teasing grin, as if he already knew what they were going to say. They said it.

"This place," said Marny, "reminds me of Pocket's pockets."

"Who on earth," exclaimed Kendra, "is going to *buy* all this?"

Gene chuckled. He was an agreeable young man, with a more sophisticated air than most of the others around Sutter's Fort. "The men from San Francisco, Mrs. Parks," he told her, "on their way to look for gold."

"Do you really think there'll be so many?" she demurred. "We've just come from San Francisco. They talk about gold there, but—Pocket will tell you—hardly anybody thinks it's important."

Gene smiled sagely. "They will."

"I think maybe he's right, ma'am," Pocket said in his slow gentle way. "Gene, tell the ladies what you were telling me."

Gene explained. They knew that Smith's partner, the Mormon leader Sam Brannan, had left San Francisco some weeks ago. He had said he was coming up to Sutter's Fort on business. His business was, that he had heard those rumors of gold and wanted to find out if they were true. They were.

So Mr. Brannan had rushed about the country, buying everything he could find that would be useful to men in the mountains. When the store was so full that it would hardly hold another bag of beans, he had started back to San Francisco. He was on his way now. When he got there he was going to announce the news of gold. He would announce it so loudly and so vigorously that every living soul in town would hear and be impressed, and men would start for the hills.

And here at the entrance to the gold fields they would find his trading post, ready to sell them what they needed to buy. Sam Brannan knew there were other ways to get gold besides scraping the earth for it.

They listened with mingled amusement and admiration. Marny asked Pocket what he was going to do now. "Will you get your old job back," she said, "or go on with us?"

"I'll go on with you, Miss Marny," he answered. "We were lucky to get started when we did."

Kendra spoke to Gene Spencer. "Aren't you coming up to the hills at all, Mr. Spencer?"

"Oh yes, Mrs. Parks, later, when Mr. Brannan gets back. For the present—" he laughed candidly—"I'm pretty well paid to stay where I am. Already, business is good." Glancing from her to Marny and then to Pocket, he asked, "Shall I show them, Pocket?"

Pocket wrinkled his forehead, pinched his chin, considered, and finally said, "Well, it's not modest, but they're right strong-minded ladies."

Gene got down on his knees and unlocked a safe that stood behind the counter. Reaching into the safe he took out an earthenware chamber-pot.

It was a fancy pot with a lid, painted with bright red roses. Holding the pot with both hands Gene lifted it to the counter and took off the lid. The pot was half full of gold.

"We haven't got anything else to hold it," he apologized softly.

But Kendra and Marny were gasping, not at the pot, but the gold. In a voice of awe Marny asked, "Mr. Spencer—all that gold—may we touch it?"

"Why sure, ma'am," said Gene with a chuckle.

They gathered up the gold in their hands. The gold was in grains and flakes and little pear-shaped nuggets and oblong bits like melon seeds. It was cold and heavy, it tinkled against the sides of the pot, it ran glittering between their fingers.

Kendra felt the same tingles she had felt when Ted showed her the bag of gold in San Francisco. She could almost see her fur cloak, her muff with the spray of opals, the new

99

respect of the aunts and uncles who thought her father was
the family disgrace. She and Marny looked at each other
across the chamber-pot. They both smiled slowly. Kendra
wondered if Marny too was thinking about the day when she
would go home, carrying bags of gold.

15

Bringing the wagons and supplies over the river was a long
hard job, and by the time they had finished, the men ached
with weariness. They jumped into the river to wash off the
sweat of the day, gobbled the beef stew Kendra had cooked
for them, and by dark they were sound asleep, all but Pocket,
who went off to see a girl he remembered from his days at
Smith's store.

Ning roused them early. "Gotta make Mormon Island
today," he said. "So get going."

They grumbled, but being good travelers they obeyed.
Before they had gone far they knew why Ning had made
them get an early start, for the riding was a rough stony
climb that grew harder every hour.

At sunset they came to a place where the American River
turned and bent back around a big piece of land shaped like
a tennis racket. This was Mormon Island. It was not really
an island, but at times of high water it looked like one
because then the river overflowed the handle of the racket.
Two Mormons had found gold here, and now they and their
friends were scratching in the gravel and getting rich.

The two leaders of the camp came along the handle to
meet the new party and make sure they meant no harm. As
Ning had been here before, the Mormons recognized him,
and helped stake the horses among the wild oats by the river.
Sure, they said, there was plenty of gold. They were taking
five to ten ounces a day each, and one of them showed
Kendra a bottle that had once held pickled onions and was
now full of gold dust. That night Kendra dreamed about
golden flakes dancing in the air like fireflies, and in the

morning as she was waking up she heard Ted exclaim, "What are you laughing at, when you've hardly opened your eyes?" She did not know she had been laughing, but as she looked up at his quizzical whiskered face she laughed again.

Today the riding was even harder than yesterday. Ahead of them the ground rippled upward—a hill, a valley, another hill, and so on and on, each hill higher than the last. The sun was hot, the horses sweated and strained as they dragged the wagons. Sometimes the train had to stop for repairs. "When we get that gold," said Hiram, as he and Pocket tightened a shaky metal tire, "we sure will have earned it. Pocket, what are you going to do with all your money?"

"I'm going to spend it," said Pocket, "on a whole lot of beautiful women."

"I bet you'll do exactly that," said Hiram. "And it's not," he added, "a bad idea."

He and Pocket sent yearning glances toward the girls. Kendra was brewing coffee to cheer the men while they worked; Lulu and Lolo were mending clothes for the Blackbeards; Marny was practicing with a deck of cards. She practiced at every stop.

Now they were close to the mighty mountains. The earth had turned from brown to red. They made their way around bushes and pine trees, and vast outcroppings of rock. At last, shortly before noon on Saturday, the sixth of May, their twelfth day out of San Francisco, they came to a rock standing like a castle on top of a hill. Past that castle, said Ning, they would go down into Shiny Gulch.

Kendra thrilled all over with impatience, but Ning was not going to hurry. First, he said, they must have their midday meal, and let the horses rest. Kendra managed to keep calm enough to cook, and as they ate she realized how wise Ning had been, for they had been riding since dawn and they were all famished. When they were done Ted brought water from the rivulet trickling down the slope, and she began to scrub the pans.

She felt strong and happy. Everything was going well. The weather was clear, nobody had quarreled, the horses were all healthy. She was not going to have a baby—not yet, anyway—so she did not have that to worry about. She saw Marny coming toward her, red hair glimmering and skirts awhirl in the wind. Marny was humming a tune, blithely but not well. Music was not one of her talents.

She paused by Kendra. "Excited?" she asked.

"Aren't we all?" asked Kendra.

Marny agreed. "Even Delbert," she said, "is showing a flicker of interest. Come on, I'll help you pack those things, then we can get going. Pocket is saddling our horses now."

Kendra doused her fire, carefully as Ning had taught her, and gathered up her utensils. She and Marny carried them to the wagon, where Ted was hitching the team and whistling "Love is like a dragonfly." They mounted their horses, and a moment later they heard Ning call "Catch up!" The train started around the rock castle and down the other side of the hill.

Kendra and Marny rode side by side. The mountain air was clear as glass, the trees were scattered, and they had a good view down into the gulch.

They were looking north. On both sides of them long mountain ranges shot up toward the sky. Below, between the ranges, they saw an open strip two or three miles long and about a thousand feet wide, sloping upward to a point where the two ranges came together. At one side of the strip, along the foot of the range to their left, the earth had cracked open, making a deep ravine about a hundred feet from rim to rim. This was Shiny Gulch.

And shiny it was, the sun glowing on the red earth and sparkling on the stream that bubbled among the rocks at the bottom. Along the sides of the gulch they saw fallen logs, and tangles of brushwood, and great rocks jutting out of the earth. In the strip between the edge of the gulch and the mountain range they saw more rocks, and trees that had fought the rocks as they grew, till the rocks were split and the trees twisted into crazy shapes. But rough as it was, this strip was the only place in sight that had any claim at all to being level, so it was here that the gold hunters had made their camp.

Kendra and Marny could see two covered wagons and three tents, and here and there a lean-to made by tilting logs against a flat-sided rock. Among these various shelters they saw the smoke of campfires, and doll-sized figures moving about. They counted twenty-seven men, three women, and six children. Most of the men were down in the gulch, gathering gold. Kendra could not see just how they were doing it, but she felt the tingles down her back, and she and Marny gave each other the same awestruck glances they had exchanged across the chamber-pot at Sutter's Fort.

In the camp on the rim the women were washing clothes and tending fires, and even the children seemed busy too. Gazing as far as she could, Kendra did not see a single soul who looked idle.

And why, she asked herself, should they want to be idle? Their life was rough but it had the shine of romance. They had been drawn here by a dream. And unlike most dreams, this one was coming true.

As she and Marny looked down, close to them the wagon wheels bumped over the ground. Sticks and stones, loosened by their passage, rattled down the slopes. All around them was the pungent fragrance of pines in the sun. But they were hardly aware of anything but the camp below.

Then suddenly Hiram was riding beside them. As they looked around he gave them a joyful grin. His beard had little golden flashes, and around his eyes were lines of delight.

"Isn't it grand," he exclaimed, "to see all this?"

Kendra nodded vigorously, and Marny said, "I love it!" Hiram went on,

"Nobody ever saw anything like it before. I feel like—oh, what do I feel like?"

"Like Columbus!" Kendra exclaimed. "Discovering."

"Yes!" agreed Hiram. "We—and those people down there —we're discoverers. And it's our secret—have you thought about that? Back in the States, nobody knows anything about our gold."

Kendra gave a start. She had not thought of this.

Marny had not thought of it either. They talked it over.

East of the Rocky Mountains, nobody knew there was gold in California. People back home could not possibly know, for months to come.

Because, how could anybody tell them?

There was no regular communication between California and anywhere else in the world. Kendra knew this, but in the excitement of the past few weeks she had forgotten it. Now she remembered. Telegraph lines reached from the Atlantic Coast to New Orleans and St. Louis, but no farther west. The westernmost post office on the continent was in the town of Independence, Missouri.

Between Independence and San Francisco lay two thousand miles of country, unmapped and almost unknown. To cross that country with a wagon train, as Pocket had done, took four or five months; to come from an eastern port by sea, as Kendra had done, took as long. And it would take as long to go back, no matter how splendid the news you brought. At intervals the army garrisons sent couriers with military dispatches, but even the best equipped army men took months to go from California to the States.

Of course, the people back home would hear about California gold some day. But it would take a long, long time.

She wondered how long.

16

Ted, driving the wagon, leaned out to call to them. "Say, girls! What's the matter? Catch up!"

With a start of guilty laughter, they saw Ning turning the train to go around a barrier of rocks. In a moment the curve of the hill shut off the view.

The riding grew more and more rough. They went around rocks and trees, and bumped over ledges jutting like steps along the hillsides. Several times they had to stop while the men took axes and hacked a way through tangles of brush. When they finally rode into the camp it was late afternoon. The horses were panting, the men's faces dripped with sweat. Kendra felt her underclothes so soaked that they clung to her skin like the peel of an orange, and Marny sighed, "I feel like I've been beaten up by experts."

In the camp it was time for supper. The gold diggers were gathering around their fires, and the air was rich with smells of woodsmoke and bacon. But at sight of the new party, men and women alike dropped their frying pans and flocked around. Of the diggers at Shiny Gulch, only two or three had come from San Francisco. The rest had been workmen at Sutter's Fort or settlers in the country close by, and had seen the sawmill men offering gold dust to pay for drinks and guns. Several of them recognized Ning, and they nearly all knew Pocket.

Turning his horse toward Kendra, Pocket introduced two men named Will Gibson and Nathan Larch. He said they had come out last summer in the same wagon train as himself. They were married men, and had brought their wives and children. And here were the ladies, Sue Gibson and Hester Larch. Mighty fine folks.

Will and Nathan wore overalls spattered with mud from the gulch, Sue and Hester were hard-muscled women in sun-bonnets and shapeless dresses. They all four had skin like leather and they looked tough as mules, but they had a big noisy vitality that reached out like warm hands in the wilderness. "Glad to see you," Nathan Larch shouted to Kendra, and Will Gibson boomed, "Howdy, ma'am, make yourself at home." Several tousle-headed children jumped around, yelling for supper. Hester and Sue told them to mind their manners, and said to Kendra, "Now anything we can do, Mrs. Parks, just let us know."

They were, as Pocket had said, fine folks. Kendra smiled back at them and thanked them for their welcome. But she was so tired that smiling was an effort, and she could not help feeling relieved when Hester and Sue called their families to supper at the campfires.

Ning had told the others to wait while he and Hiram rode off to find a good site for their own camp. Kendra thought now she would have a few minutes of restful silence, but she had forgotten that when she and Marny looked down from the hilltop they had counted three women at Shiny Gulch. Hester and Sue were two of them. Now the third woman had planted herself beside Kendra's horse and was examining Kendra with critical eyes. This woman did not look like the other two. She was a small plump creature about thirty years old, shaped like a sausage roll. She wore a blue gingham apron, and she had yellow curls drawn up high and pinned in a bunch, so that she looked as if she were wearing a lot of wilted daffodils on her head.

"My name," she announced sternly, "is Edith Posey." She added with emphasis, "*Mrs.* Edith Posey."

"How do you do," said Kendra.

"You're not going to like it here," snapped Mrs. Edith Posey.

"Why not?" Kendra asked.

"Up here," said Mrs. Posey, "we *work*."

Kendra brushed away a gnat that had lit on her nose. "I'm used to work," she returned.

Mrs. Posey shook her head so hard that the yellow curls bobbled. "You don't look it. You look like a New York society girl. Where'd you come from?"

Kendra almost told Mrs. Posey to mind her own business, but desisted because she was so tired and it took less energy to give a plain answer. "I was born in Baltimore," she said. "I went to school in New York."

"I told you so," said Mrs. Posey. She nodded sharply and the curls nodded with her. "Society girl. You won't like it."

At this moment Mrs. Posey's ears caught a ripple of laughter. She turned her head, and her round little mouth tightened as she got a good look at Marny.

Like Kendra, Marny had stopped her horse and was waiting for Ning. While she waited, a cluster of men had gathered around her. Marny had pushed back her bonnet, and the sun glinted on her hair. She was laughing with her admirers. Tired though she was, Marny was never too tired to enjoy such a welcome.

Mrs. Posey viewed her with alarm. After a moment she turned back to Kendra. "And who's *that?*"

This time Kendra smiled without trying. "Her name is Marny."

Mrs. Posey gave her head a toss that sent a shiver through the curls. "And what," demanded Mrs. Posey, "is *she* doing here?"

Kendra said, "She's going to set up a gambling tent."

Mrs. Posey gave a righteous start. "Gambling tent! We'll see about that."

Losing interest in Kendra, she turned, and as fast as her short little legs would carry her she hurried over to the group around Marny's horse. The men parted to let her through, reluctantly but with resignation, as if they knew it was no use to object. Mrs. Posey slapped her plump little hand on the arm of one of them. "Orville Posey," she exclaimed, "supper's on."

The men chuckled, and Marny joined them with a soft little laugh that did not amuse Mrs. Posey. She led her husband off by his elbow, though it gave the effect of her leading him by the nose.

A few minutes later they heard a big jovial voice shouting "Ready!" Hiram came riding back, waving his hat above his head and as usual giving the impression that he filled up even more space than he did. "Ning has picked our campsite," he called. "Catch up!"

Marny kissed her hand to her new friends as the train fell into line. Hiram led them to the far upper end of the open strip, close to the point where the mountain ranges came together. Here the ground was steep, but Ning explained that this was a good safe place to keep the horses. Down at the lower end of the gulch, beyond the turn where the stream went around a hill, a village of Abs had gathered to pick up the offal of the camp, and there was nothing an Ab liked so much as a roasted horse. Better keep the whole camp between them.

And here, right at the edge of the gulch, was a clear level spot that would do for Kendra's cook-fire tonight. Tomorrow they would fix her a permanent cooking place.

At the work cook-fire Kendra felt another tremor of weariness. She had to cook supper, this was her job, but she was so tired that she dreaded it. Ted was anchoring their wagon with logs under the wheels. Hiram walked over and helped her dismount.

"I came to tell you," said Hiram, "give us a cold supper tonight."

She started. "What do you mean?"

"I spoke to Ning," said Hiram, "and he agreed. Salt beef and hardtack and some dried fruit—we're so hungry, those will taste like a feast. Don't do any cooking except to make coffee."

Kendra gave a grateful sigh. "Oh, thank you, Hiram! I'll give you a big breakfast in the morning, to make up."

Marny came over to say she had found a place for their bathroom. Kendra felt better when she had washed off the dust, or at least part of it. Back at her level space on the edge of the gulch, she gathered sticks while Ted brought a pail of water. "Now I've got to help Hiram and Pocket with the horses," he said. "Shout when you're ready."

He left her, and Kendra knelt to set the sticks and light the fire. When she had put on the coffee pot, she stood up to stretch her cramped legs and look down into the gulch. The gold hunters had quit work for the day. The gulch was empty, and quiet but for the rush of water at the bottom. Farther downstream she could see paths the men had cleared so they could make their way down to the stream with its

107

golden sands, but up at this end the sides were rough, broken only by rocks and bushes sticking crookedly out of the bumpy earth.

Raising her eyes Kendra looked around her. Their campsite was about a quarter of a mile from any other, for few people cared to make the hard climb to this high end of the strip. Down where most of them were camped, she could see tired men already going to sleep, their hats over their faces to shut out the last rays of the sun.

On the other side of her, near the spot where the mountains closed in, Ted and Hiram and Pocket were tethering the horses. Lulu and Lolo were busy at their own cook-fire. The Blackbeards were anchoring their wagons as Ted had anchored his, and near one wagon Marny and Delbert stood looking over the territory, no doubt choosing a place to set up their gambling tent.

Already, standing at the edge of the gulch and looking around, Kendra felt almost rested. "I like it here," she said to herself. "I have friends. I belong." She added with decision, "And no matter what happens, I'm never going to let myself get lonesome again."

She stamped her foot on the ground.

"I'm never going to be lonesome again," she repeated. "I'll be hot and dusty and tired, but I *won't* be lonesome. I'm just beginning to live and I'm going to *live*. I'm going to live every minute."

She stamped her foot again. This time she stamped so hard that the rim of the gulch gave way and she felt herself falling.

From somewhere above her she heard Marny give a cry, but she hardly noticed it. Her fall was too fast and too terrifying. The earth, soaked by the melting of the mountain snows, was still soft; as Kendra slipped downward the stones and young growth came out easily, and fell with her instead of holding her back. She felt herself thumping and heard her clothes tearing, and the rocks and clods clattering down beside her. Her knees and elbows were scraping raw, dirt was filling her eyes and mouth and nostrils. A bush caught in the neck of her dress, giving her a hard scratch and drawing the dress so tight around her throat that it nearly choked her.

But this gave her an instant's delay. The skin was torn

108

off the sides of her hands, and the grains of dirt in her eyes were making her shed tears so that she could hardly see, but she caught blindly at the bush and clutched the stems. By good fortune this bush was an old one, well rooted, and she had grasped it near the ground. The roots held, and the pause gave her a chance to breathe.

Above her she heard voices. Though she was too confused to catch the words, the sounds gave her comfort. Her friends would get to her somehow, if she could hold on to the bush. But, she wondered in fright, could she hold on?— hanging here by her bleeding hands? The collar of her dress chafed painfully into the place where the bush had cut her neck, but she managed to look down. Below her, not far from her dangling feet, a ledge broke the side of the gulch. It was a shelf of stones and earth about three feet wide, and it looked solid.

Kendra heard her breath coming in choking gasps. She heard another sound too, close to her ears—the roots of the bush were firm in the ground, but the stems she held were cracking under her weight. Catching her lower lip between her teeth she loosened her hands from the stems and let go, and slid down upon the ledge and fell there in a heap, sore and bruised and ragged, but on steady ground again.

For a moment she could not do anything. Stones and dust and lumps of earth tumbled after her, and fell upon her and all around her, but she hardly noticed. She felt as if every organ in her body had been shaken out of place and was hurting from the shock. Her hands were stinging, and she saw bloodstains on her skirt.

With an effort she lifted her hands to her neck and unfastened the top button of her dress so she could breathe more easily. This was a help. She moved her shoulders. The shoulders hurt, and her hips hurt, and her knees felt bruised, and her upper arms were stinging as if they too had been scraped raw. She felt so many hurts that only now did she realize that Ted was calling her name, over and over above her head.

Vaguely she looked up. Ted was there on the edge of the gulch, close to the spot where she had slipped. He had thrown himself on the ground as if to get nearer her, and he was shouting,

"Kendra! Can't you hear me?"

Kendra managed to nod. With another effort she called back, "Yes, I can hear."

"Hiram has gone to get a rope," called Ted. "Understand?"

Kendra's head was beginning to clear. She nodded again.

"He'll make a noose," Ted went on, "with a good strong sailor's knot. You'll put the noose around you, and we'll bring you up."

Kendra called back that she understood. As she looked up she saw with surprise that Ted was not very far above her. Her fall had seemed so long that she felt as if she should be nearly down to the bottom of the gulch. But now, though she was still too confused to judge the distance, she could see that it was not as great as she had thought. It would not be very difficult for the men to bring her up.

Too bruised to feel like moving, she sat as she was. More pebbles, loosened as she scraped down the slope, fell around her.

Worse than feeling shaken and sore, she felt ashamed of herself. Through the whole journey, twelve days from San Francisco, she had been a good traveler. And now, just as they reached Shiny Gulch, she had gone and done a stupid thing like this, and discommoded the whole company. Her hands would have to be bandaged and maybe it would be days before she could make a fire or lift a kettle again. Bruised as she was, maybe she could not even walk.

Her dress was torn in a dozen places and so dirty that an hour's scrubbing would hardly get it clean. In her lap, as well as all around her, were rocks and sticks and leaves and lumps of red clay. Near her right knee she saw a lump not as red as the others. The lump was about the size of an egg, but unlike an egg it was rough and uneven. It did not look like a clod, it was more like a rock with scraps of red earth clinging to it. A shiny sort of rock—in a spot where there was no dirt on it, the side caught the sunset with a little soft glow. Kendra picked it up.

Her breath caught in her chest with a gasp so hard that it hurt. This was not a rock. No rock this size would be so heavy. Her hands still oozing blood, she took a corner of her skirt and rubbed the dirt off the lump. The gasps of her breath came harder and faster. The pain in her chest swelled till she felt as if she were going to explode. The hand that held the lump began to tremble.

110

Above her, Marny was calling some words of encouragement. Ted shouted that Hiram was right now making the noose in the rope. Kendra hardly heard them.

They had been little more than an hour at Shiny Gulch. And she had made the first find. Her torn, tingling hand was holding a really magnificent nugget of gold.

17

The next day was Sunday. Ning had said the fellows generally didn't go after gold on Sundays, but got rested up like the Good Book said they should. Today they came to see Kendra.

She had spent a restless night, for it seemed that every time she moved, something hurt. When the light of the morning finally woke her for good, she found herself alone, for Ted had gone out to start the fire and make coffee in her place. She felt bruised and sore all over. But when he brought her a cup of coffee, and a piece of hardtack with bacon fried for her by Ning, she began to feel better. And now that she was fairly holding court she felt almost well.

Her wounds bandaged by Ted, her hair combed by Marny, Kendra lay on her bedroll in the wagon with a blanket over her knees, and under her head another blanket folded and covered with the blue scarf she had worn over her hair at Cape Horn. Ted had rolled up the wagon cover so she could look out—or rather, so everybody else could look in.

They all wanted to look in, for nuggets like hers were rare. Most gold came in bits like those she and Marny had seen at Sutter's Fort. Though envying such good fortune, the gold hunters were glad of it too, like men at a gambling table who see another player win a big stake from the house. Every man in the camp came up to touch her for luck.

They were frontiersmen, with horny hands and workaday heads, but they knew finding gold was a matter of chance. A man could work all day and find an ounce, or work an hour and find a pound. And sometimes, as had happened to

111

Kendra, gold would fall upon him without his having worked at all. Gold meant luck. And the way it looked to them, Kendra had come to camp in a rosy cloud of luck.

They said this. They kept on saying it until by afternoon Mrs. Posey thought it necessary to come up and tell her it wasn't so. Mrs. Posey made her plump little legs carry her all the way to this high end of the strip, and poking her head into the wagon she gazed at the nugget in Kendra's bandaged hand. After a moment she shook her scrambled curls in warning. "Well, don't get the idea it's going to happen like this every day. You're no better than the rest of us."

As she spoke Mrs. Posey looked past Kendra, between the curved wooden slats that held up the wagon cover. Now that the cover was rolled up, she could look through the wagon and see what lay on the other side.

"Now what," Mrs. Posey demanded, "is That Woman up to?"

Kendra turned her head—a painful movement, as the cut on her neck was raw and sore—but in spite of the discomfort she began to laugh. Already, before they had been twenty-four hours at Shiny Gulch, Marny was in business. The tent for the Calico Palace could not be pitched until a space had been cleared of brush. But Marny had set up two barrels, across them she had laid boards knocked out of the side of a packing box, and over the table thus made she had placed a cover of green baize. Here she had set stacks of gold and silver coins, and a pair of scales to weigh the gold dust that was already gathering in little piles before her.

To the delight of about a dozen men, Marny was dealing cards. Beside the barrel at one end stood Delbert, army canteen in hand, doing double duty as bartender and guard.

Kendra answered Mrs. Posey. "I don't know much about gambling games. But I think she must be dealing vingt-et-un —twenty-one—because she told me it was a game that didn't need any special equipment."

"Gambling!" said Mrs. Posey. "And on Sunday too! Shameless creature. If my Orville—"

Her little blue eyes scanned the group. But her Orville was not there, possibly because he knew he'd better not be. After a moment's watching, Mrs. Posey trotted off. Reaching the sinners, she halted to scold. Kendra could not hear much of what she said, but she could see that Mrs. Posey's words were not recalling the men to virtue. Several of them smiled tolerantly, others shrugged with annoyance, the rest paid no attention. The game went on.

The table was on lower ground than the wagon, and Kendra could look down and watch Marny's hands. She thought she had never seen such beautiful hands at work. They were quick, rhythmic, sure. The fingers all moved in harmony. Marny's hands dealing cards were like music made visible.

She saw Hiram placing a bet. Ted was there too, but after a while he came up to the wagon to ask how she felt. "Ning and Pocket are cooking supper," he told her. "They say the food won't be as good as yours, but it'll be eatable."

"Tell them I sent my thanks," said Kendra, "and I'm sorry to make trouble."

"No trouble," said Ted. "They're glad to help out." He pinched her ear. "The coffee should be ready by now. I'll bring you some—where's your cup?"

Kendra looked after him fondly as he went off. She wondered why Ted had been so reluctant—almost frightened—about getting married. Well, it didn't matter now. He seemed to have forgotten his qualms, and she was not going to remind him. They had been married twenty-one days. It had been the happiest time of her life.

Kendra's fall had given her a hard shaking, but it had done her no real damage, so in a few days she was up and ready to work. She had plenty of work to do, but here in the fresh mountain air she had almost endless energy, and her meals were easier than they had been on the journey. The men made her a permanent cooking place: a trench, over which they set up a frame made of two forked logs with a crossbar held in the forks. From the crossbar they hung a branch with a deep notch cut in the lower end, strong enough to hold her kettle. She kept a fire going in the trench, and when she made a stew the kettle hung over the fire; when she fried bacon her pan stood on two green sticks laid crosswise. To take care of the foodstuffs the men set up two other frames, higher and stronger than this one. Here they hung their cases of meat and dried beans, out of reach of prowling animals.

More men came into camp, alone or in groups, but there was plenty of room and plenty of gold. Some men worked as partners, helping each other and sharing their findings; others were loners, who stayed by themselves and spoke to nobody if they could help it.

A loner used a pan. He scooped up the sand and water and swirled the pan with sharp regular motions of his wrist, until the lightweight sand splashed out and the heavy grains of gold were left at the bottom of the pan. Or he searched the rocks by the waterside till he found a crack where he could split the rock with a pickax. In the crack he nearly always found gold. Sometimes the gold was like a silken lining, and he scraped it off the rock with his knife. Or sometimes he found a little pile of golden flakes, which he would rake out with his horn spoon and store in the bag or bottle that held his treasure.

Ning and Ted, Pocket and Hiram, had agreed to work as a team. Under Ning's direction they built a contrivance he remembered from his mining days in Georgia: a log hollowed and open at one end, with wooden bars tacked at intervals across the bottom. When they had finished, Ning made them mount the thing on rockers. It looked like a cradle, built for a baby nine feet long.

Ning said some fellows did call it a cradle. But mostly it was called a rocker because it really did rock the gold right out of the earth. He explained how the four of them would manage it. Two men would bring loads of dirt, and dump the dirt into the rocker. A third man would bring water and pour it over the dirt, while the fourth man would gently, carefully, rock the cradle and let the mud flow through. The principle, said Ning, was like that of the pan—the gold was heavy, and would sink, and catch on those bars they had nailed to the bottom. The dirt, being lighter, would flow with the water out of the open end.

There was only one drawback, Ning warned them the day they finished. This was that a rocker required them to work together, day after day. Sometimes men couldn't stay at it because they quarreled. If they could keep the peace, four partners with a rocker could take out a sight more gold than four loners with picks and pans. But they had to get along.

They were waiting for supper. Kendra was stirring a kettle of beans and salt pork. Ted had gone to bring drinking water, while Ning and Pocket and Hiram, weary but proud, sat contemplating their new machine. As Ning spoke, Hiram laughed good-naturedly and Pocket said, "I think we'll get along, boss."

114

"I think we will," Ning said gravely, "because I picked you out myself and I generally pick 'em pretty good." He took off his hat, scratched his head, and put the hat back on.

"We've done fine so far," Hiram remarked.

"Yes, we have," said Ning. "You've behaved mighty well, boys." As he spoke he gave a quick, meaningful glance toward Kendra.

Kendra felt her cheeks burning. Ning did not realize that she had heard what he said, or that out of the corner of her eye she had seen the look he gave her. She kept her head bent over the kettle, so they would think her color had been caused by the fire.

She heard Pocket say, "Well, boss, I've been called a skirt-ruffler and I guess I am. But I know when I'm not wanted."

Hiram did not think it necessary to say anything. Kendra felt relieved to see Ted coming up with the pail of water. He set it down so the men could dip in their cups, and she called that supper was ready.

She ladled out the pork and beans, and while the men talked about the rocker she looked down at the space that had been cleared for the Calico Palace. Delbert and Marny had thought the job of clearing would take only a day or two. But the work was harder than they had expected, and the Blackbeards had insisted on using part of every day to pan gold, so though they had been here nine days they were only now ready to set up the tent. Marny, however, had wasted no time. Every afternoon she stood at her table, to be ready when the first gold diggers quit work. Kendra could see her now, her hair shining and her hands flirting among the cards.

They finished supper. Pocket said he would help Kendra wash up, while the others used the last daylight to drag their rocker up to the place where Ning had decided they would start work in the morning. Pocket was on his knees scrubbing the eating pans with grass, and Kendra stood pouring a last rinsing water into the kettle, when they heard short little footsteps padding close. They looked up to see Mrs. Posey, carrying a basket of chips she had gathered to start her fire tomorrow. Mrs. Posey stopped with a glare in her little blue eyes.

Pocket stood up courteously, but she paid him no attention. To Kendra she snapped, "Here comes That Woman."

Kendra was tired. She felt short-tempered. Never very

115

tactful, she said what she thought. "Marny's not hurting you. Why don't you mind your own business?"

"It *is* my business!" Mrs. Posey retorted. "She's an insult to every respectable woman here."

"Well, I don't feel insulted," Kendra said shortly, "and I think I'm respectable."

Pocket's mild voice added, "Marny's a real sweet girl, Mrs. Posey. She's not making any trouble."

Apparently feeling that it was no use to talk to a man where Marny was concerned, Mrs. Posey continued to ignore him. She blazed at Kendra.

"She's a disgrace to this camp. You ought to be ashamed, taking her part."

"Howdy, everybody!" said a voice near by. Pausing beside them, Marny smiled amiably. "Good evening, Mrs. Posey."

"Don't you speak to me. Brazen baggage."

Marny looked thoughtful. She said clearly, "Mrs. Posey, you're pinguescent."

Mrs. Posey started. "I'm nothing of the sort. Stop using such words and insulting a decent woman."

Her eyes blinked in baffled rage. Kendra had no more idea than Mrs. Posey what Marny was talking about, but she thought Mrs. Posey's anger was funny and she could not help showing what she thought. Mrs. Posey glared.

"And it wouldn't surprise me a bit," she sputtered, "to find that you're no better than *she* is."

She spoke the last words over her shoulder as she hurried away, full of wrath and righteousness. Kendra plucked at Marny's sleeve.

"Marny, what did you say to her?"

"I said she was pinguescent," Marny returned. "She is. 'Pinguescent' means 'getting fat.' "

Kendra burst out laughing, but Pocket spoke in a voice of gentle rebuke.

"Miss Marny, you've got no more manners than a jaybird." He shook his head. "And a jaybird," Pocket continued gravely, "has got no manners at all."

Marny's reply was serene. "Pocket, I respect your judgment. But Mrs. Posey is a public nuisance."

"Oh, she's just stupid, Miss Marny."

"She's wicked," Marny said with conviction. "And you, Pocket, are too innocent for your own good."

Pocket did not bother to contradict her. He poured the

116

rinsing water from the kettle and they all three started walking up the strip. The light had faded, and fireflies danced in the gloaming. Ted came down the strip to meet Kendra. They said good night, and Kendra walked with him toward their wagon.

As they walked, Kendra wondered about Mrs. Posey. She was so unlike Pocket's two friends of the wagon train, Sue Gibson and Hester Larch. Mrs. Posey and Orville had come out from New York on the Mormon ship, though they were not Mormons. Orville had been a neighborhood storekeeper in New York, but he had not done very well. When Mrs. Posey learned that the Mormons were selling the extra space in their ship she had persuaded him to borrow money from his brother to take passage, hoping he woud do better in a new land. She intended to see to it that he did. Cards were not part of her plan.

Sue and Hester were different. They often passed Marny's table and paused to watch the play. Both their husbands took a hand sometimes, and Sue and Hester seemed not to mind. But Sue and Hester were frontier women who had fought their way across the plains. They had driven ox-teams and fired on marauding Indians; they did not need to be always bossing somebody because they did not need to prove how good they were. Kendra shrugged as she walked along.

18

During the next two days Kendra watched eagerly as Marny and her friends set up the Calico Palace. In their clearing they had left two young pine trees that stood about thirty feet apart. The Blackbeards had nipped the branches off the trees and cut the tops, leaving the two trunks standing for tent poles. Across these, for the ridge pole, they laid a wooden bar they had brought with them in sections, and over the the frame thus made they draped the tent. Waving from another tree-trunk close by was a strip of cloth on which Marny had printed in big black letters, "Calico Palace."

Marny would have preferred red paint, but she had no paint red or otherwise. She had done the lettering with charcoal, and she would have to renew it often. But as she said, giving the place a name gave it a personality.

The tent was ugly and drafty, and the walls sagged. But it was there. It dominated the camp of Shiny Gulch. It was the first thing a newcomer saw as he approached, and it was the most imposing structure this side of Sutter's Fort.

The tent had no floor. The earth inside was lumpy and soft, but Marny said the men would soon trample it hard. She and Delbert set up tables made of packing boxes, and for seats they used wooden tubs that had once been packed with salt pork for sailors. At the end away from the door they placed the "bar," which was merely Marny's board-and-barrel table set up again. Behind the bar stood the casks holding their liquor, served by being drawn out through a bung-hole and poured into a tin cup which the drinker was supposed to bring for himself.

They announced ahead of time that their supply of liquor was small. They had only what they had brought with them, and a little more they had been able to buy from peddlers who sometimes drove wagonloads of goods to the mining camps. For this reason, they said, drinks would be limited to three per man.

Marny privately told Kendra they had set the limit to keep order.

"During these first few weeks," she said, "I want us to get a lily-white reputation. No drunks, no brawls, just good clean fun. Later, when they can't do without us, we can send down to the fort for all the liquor we need. That store of Smith and Brannan's has it by the barrel. I saw it."

On Wednesday, the seventeenth of May, their eleventh day at Shiny Gulch, Marny and Delbert opened the Calico Palace. Pocket and Ning and Hiram went there, and Pocket came back to report to Ted and Kendra. He said there was no reason why Kendra should not go there too if she wanted to see it. Everything was as orderly as Marny had promised. Sociable fellows were at her table playing twenty-one; loners sat in silence at another table where Delbert was dealing faro, with one Blackbeard as case keeper while the other acted as general guard of the establishment. There were also several other tables, rented by the hour to men who wanted to play their own games, betting against each other instead of the house. Lulu and Lolo were tending bar. Now and then some man made a hopeful remark to one of them, but a glare from Blackbeard usually persuaded him that this was not wise. If he was not so persuaded, Blackbeard escorted him out and told him to sit under a tree and think it over.

Ted and Pocket went with Kendra to the Calico Palace. She sat near the bar on a pork-tub turned upside down, while Ted bought a drink and Pocket discovered that Lulu and Lolo also sold, of all things, tea. For a drink they charged a dollar. For a cup of hot water—not too hot—with a few tea leaves in it, they charged fifty cents, but a man had to pay for two cups whether or not he drank them both, for a dollar was the smallest sum accepted at the bar. If he paid with gold dust instead of coin they sold him the drink or the tea for enough dust to balance a little weight they placed on the scale. If he had forgotten to bring his own cup, and had to use one supplied by the bar, he paid an extra charge.

Nearly every man in camp dropped in that evening, though not Orville Posey. Nathan Larch and Will Gibson came in, but Hester and Sue, not as bold as Kendra, paused at the entrance and stood looking. The Blackbeard guard reported their presence, and took Delbert's place at the faro table while Delbert went to the door and asked the ladies to come in and have a cup of sherry as his guests. They did come in, giggling like young girls and enjoying it. At the same time Ted brought Kendra a cup of sherry, served by order of Delbert. The three sipped sherry beside the bar, and thus, despite Mrs. Posey, the stamp of respectability was put upon the Calico Palace.

Hester and Sue left after a few minutes, saying they had to get back to their children. Pocket asked Kendra if she wanted to walk around. Leaving Ted explaining to Will Gibson how they had made their rocker, Pocket and Kendra roamed about the tent.

Drab though it was on the outside, Marny had done a good deal to make the inside bright. On the bar and card tables she had set abundant candles, around the door she had hung loops of red calico, and on the canvas wall at each side of the bar she had pasted pictures from fashion magazines. The fashions were long out of date, for she had cut them from old magazines that packers in the States had stuffed into crates to fill up odd spaces. But they were pictures of pretty women, and Marny's customers were men.

119

The tent was full of men. Tobacco smoke drifted about in curly blue patterns, and everybody seemed in good humor. They smiled broadly as they stepped out of Kendra's way, bowing and saying "Howdy, ma'am."

When she had seen the Calico Palace itself, Kendra guided Pocket's willing elbow toward Marny's table. This stood near the entrance, so every man who passed would see Marny and be tempted to come in. Kendra and Pocket stopped at one side. Marny did not glance around. When she dealt cards she did it as if there was nothing else in the world.

Standing there in the smoky light Marny had a look of tantalizing elegance. Her dress was a plain dark cotton, the sort that could be scrubbed again and again in a creek, but its very plainness set off her figure and her sparkling hair, her white skin and her freckles. As her eyes flicked from the cards to the players and back again, they were like the eyes of a prankish cat. It occurred to Kendra that Marny was rather like a cat. She had the calm self-reliance of a cat; like a cat she was fond of luxury but could manage very well without it; she moved with the silken silence of a cat; and like a cat, she loved herself best.

Several more men came up to the table, and Kendra whispered to Pocket that she thought they ought to make room. They walked back to the wooden pork-tub beside the bar. Ted stood a little way off with Will Gibson, still discussing the rocker. They waved at Kendra as she sat down, and Pocket said to her,

"Well ma'am, the bar owes me another cup of tea. Do you want it?"

Laughing, Kendra shook her head. "Thanks, Pocket, but I thought you said the tea was too weak to be worth drinking."

Pocket, however, set a high value upon money. He answered, "It's not worth drinking, ma'am, but I've paid for it. So excuse me please, while I get it."

Pocket went to the bar for his tea. Half a dozen men stood there, among them Delbert, relaxing while the Blackbeard guard relieved him at the faro table. But Delbert, though his hand rested on the holster at his belt, was not watching the scene in general. His attention was fixed on one man at the bar, who was talking with all his might.

The speaker was a man named Ellet, who had recently come to Shiny Gulch from another camp farther up the river. Ellet was a big hairy fellow with sharp small eyes and enormous dirty hands. His hair grew down to his shoulders, his vast shaggy beard covered his chest and reached nearly down to his waist. He wore buckskin breeches, red flannel shirt, and a short sleeveless leather jacket, and he talked in a booming voice, emphasizing his important words by clapping his right fist on the palm of his left hand.

All the men at the bar were listening. Even Pocket paused to hear what was being said. Kendra eased the pork-tub nearer.

Ellet was talking about the Big Lump.

"Here's how it is, boys. We find the gold in the rivers, or in the rocks and dirt close to the banks. We know the gold was brought down by the water. But—" he paused impressively—"brought down from *where?*"

There was a murmur in the group. Ellet went on.

"Boys, there's some place it came from. Now don't that make sense?"

The men looked at one another and back at him. Yes, that made sense.

"Now look," said Ellet. "We know the little rocks and pebbles in the water, they've been broke off from the big rocks farther up. In flood times the rivers bring them down, in quiet times they sink to the river beds. Now don't it seem reasonable that these here little pieces of gold in the water were broke off the same way, from a big gold lump in the mountains?"

Somebody gave a whistle.

"I tell you, boys," said Ellet, "most of them mountains is still the way God made them. They ain't never been walked on by human feet. But one of these days, somebody'll go up there and explore. Somebody's gonta find it. The Big Lump."

Four or five men began to talk all at once. Delbert said nothing. The other men were so busy giving their own opinions that none of them seemed to notice him. But Kendra was not talking, and she noticed.

Over Delbert's face had come a look like the look of a hungry animal. He wet his lips. His eyes grew narrow. He listened. It was the first time Kendra had ever seen him shaken out of his massive calm. The change did not make him pleasant. It made him frightening .The other men went on talking.

They asked, Was it possible? Was it really there, the be-

121

ginning and the parent of all this glory, the Big Lump? Some said it wasn't so, couldn't be so. Others said it could be so, and probably was.

After a while, Pocket had something to say. Pocket had one of those quiet well-pitched voices that can penetrate a hubbub.

"Suppose it's there," said Pocket, "and somebody finds it. It won't be worth anything."

"Huh?" said the men.

They said it all together. They were shocked. Pocket sipped his tea. He continued,

"The only reason gold and diamonds and suchlike are valuable is that they're scarce. If some man finds that Big Lump, and starts bringing down gold by the ton, pretty soon a gold bar won't be worth any more than a copper cent."

Here there was more talk. Again they all had something to say, and said it in many words. All but Delbert. For a time he continued to listen. After a while he did speak, but he spoke slowly, in a low voice, as if talking to himself.

"But suppose a man found it," said Delbert, "and did not tell?"

The other men, all gabbling, seemed not to hear him. But Kendra heard, and his words gave her a shiver. She thought—a man who found a golden mountain and kept it to himself, a man who could chip off gold whenever he wanted, as much as he wanted, and was the only man on earth who knew where it was—

Delbert said nothing more. He stood where he was, thinking. But Kendra said to herself the words she was sure were in his mind.

"The man who had the Big Lump—he could be king of the world."

19

Ted had not heard the talk about the Big Lump. "Absurd," he said when Kendra told him. "Anyway, aren't we doing well enough where we are?"

Kendra thought they certainly were. Their rocker had begun by washing out thirty-three ounces of gold the first day. The next day they took forty ounces, the third day nearly fifty. By the first of June the four partners had gathered five hundred ounces, and the whole summer lay ahead.

"We can go to those strange far places," Ted exclaimed to Kendra, "and soon! Kendra, would you like to see China? Or maybe a real South Sea island, where the girls wear grass skirts and dance on the beach?"

Kendra thought of her carriage with the matched black horses, her fur cloak, her muff with the spray of opals. "We can go back to the States," she said. "To Baltimore—New York."

"Oh Lord no," he protested. "I hate New York."

"Why Ted! Don't you want ever to go there again?"

Ted laughed a little as if in apology. "But darling, we've been there! Wouldn't you rather see something new?"

Kendra laughed too. It was like the dreaming glory of fairy tales. Shiny Gulch was what they called a placer. The Spanish word "placer" meant pleasure, delight, and now men were using it to mean any spot where they found gold scattered around them, waiting for them to pick it up. Kendra felt as if she were living on a magic island, cut off from past and future, without need to think of either one.

They were glad they had reached Shiny Gulch when they did, for they had made their start before the real rush began. Throughout the month of May men had been coming into camp, some to stay, others to wander on looking for placers yet unfound; but these had come in groups of two or three, mostly from the fort or the ranch country near by. Then all of a sudden the little camp almost exploded. Parties from

123

San Francisco began pouring in, twenty or thirty men at a time, lusty and noisy and eager for gold.

It began in June. Kendra was resting on the grass near her cook-fire, reflecting that somebody had better go down to the fort and bring back some food, or pretty soon she would have nothing left to cook. The hard outdoor work gave the men vast appetites, and they were eating their supplies twice as fast as they had expected. She decided to make a salad of dandelion greens to go with supper this evening. The dandelions at Shiny Gulch were like no others she had ever seen: the flowers were great fluffy wheels the size of a silver dollar, and the little young leaves were delicious. Kendra had made up her mind that she and her friends were not going to get scurvy from lack of plant food. She had never seen a case of scurvy, but she had been told it was a dreadful illness.

She was about to get up and gather the salad leaves when she heard a voice shouting, "Miss Logan!—I mean, Mrs. Parks!" Running toward her she saw Foxy, the packing boy from Chase and Fenway. Kendra was almost surprised that he recognized her, for living outdoors had browned her face, and instead of the city clothes she used to wear she had on a dress of heavy dun-colored cotton with a checked gingham sunbonnet pushed back and hanging by its strings around her neck. But Foxy knew her and was glad to see her. With a grin that stretched all the way across his long buck-toothed face, he grabbed her hand and shook it hard, and began to talk, as volubly as he used to talk all day at the store.

He said he had reached Shiny Gulch several hours ago, with a party from town. While they were looking for a place to make camp somebody had told him that she and Ted were here. "And that red-headed lady with the freckles, is that her tent yonder?"

Kendra told him the Calico Palace was not open for business so early. However, she added, Marny was probably there, arranging the tables and the bar.

Foxy said he had brought a little present. He gave her a can of coffee, to Kendra's delight as her own supply was running low. Then Foxy candidly let her know that his gift was not entirely disinterested. She had a fire already made—maybe if he brought Marny, Mrs. Parks would brew a pot of coffee for all three of them? He sure would enjoy having a nice cup of coffee with his lady friends.

Kendra consented, and Foxy set off to find Marny. When he came back with her, Kendra filled their three cups and they sat under a tree. Kendra inquired about her mother and Alex.

Foxy told her Colonel and Mrs. Taine were fine. They had come into the store together one day a little while back; Foxy could not remember just when, because so much was happening, it was enough to mix up a fellow's head.

He said Hodge had left town with him, and so had the other two packing boys, Bert and Al. The boys were down yonder making camp with the rest of their party. Hodge had gone up to the sawmill, to see the place where the first gold had been found. "Myself," said Foxy, "I think he's plumb crazy to go up there. That place is old now. I'd rather find a spot not so worked over. Maybe a new placer, a *new* one."

"With all this digging for new placers," Kendra said, "you men are going to turn the country inside out before summer's over."

Foxy paused a moment to look around and listen to the clang of picks and pans. "Well, I'll stop a while anyway, till I learn how things are. Looks like they're pretty busy around here."

Kendra said yes, everybody was busy around here. Marny asked about Messrs. Chase and Fenway.

Doing fine, said Foxy. All the traders were doing fine, selling supplies to men leaving for the placers. Did Mrs. Parks remember that sailor boy, Loren Shields? He was working for Chase and Fenway now. They paid him good, but Foxy thought it was pretty silly of him to stay in town.

Loren had already told Kendra he preferred a steady life to a venturesome hunt for gold. She asked, "Why is it silly if that's what he wants to do?"

"Why Mrs. Parks," said Foxy, "the town's dead. Men like Mr. Chase and Mr. Fenway, at their age, they must be mighty near forty, it's all right for them, but why should a young fellow like Loren stay there? Ted was smart to leave when he did. I wish I'd gotten out early, like him. When was it he first came up here—March?"

Kendra nodded. With a shrug, Foxy continued,

"Well, I'm not the only one who wasn't smart. Back then, hardly anybody believed it. Folks didn't really start believing it till around the first of May, and most folks not even then. First week or two in May, men were creeping out of

125

town, I mean really creeping like they were ashamed of themselves, making up reasons why they had business across the bay so people wouldn't laugh at them if the whole thing turned out to be a flop. Some soldiers and sailors deserted, not many, but a few."

Foxy scratched his head and tried to justify himself for having hesitated like the rest.

"Nobody had any reason to leave, really. Town was booming. Must have been fifty buildings going up—stores, warehouses, houses for people to live in. And a fine new hotel, the Parker House on Kearny Street facing the plaza. The editor of the *Star* went up to the sawmill, came back and wrote a piece for his paper. Said there wasn't enough gold to make any difference, like that time around Los Angeles. Said if men had any sense they'd stay on their jobs.

"And then—do you remember Mr. Brannan, that rich Mormon who lives in the big house on Washington Street corner Stockton? Well, he went up to see about his store at Sutter's Fort. Came back to town after you'd left."

Kendra and Marny exchanged glances. They were remembering the store at Sutter's Fort, and Gene Spencer's telling them how Brannan had stuffed it for men on their way to the mines. Brannan knew men would soon crowd up to the mines; he was going to see to it that they did. Foxy went on.

"Well, one day me and Bert and Al, we were working in the storeroom at Chase and Fenway's, and we heard a commotion outside. We thought it was just somebody drunk and hollering, but the noise came nearer and the commotion got bigger and we went out and looked. And who did we see running down the street but this here Mr. Brannan, and he looked like he was drunk and crazy both. He had a quinine bottle full of gold dust and as he came running he was waving this bottle over his head and yelling 'Gold! Gold! Gold from the American River!'"

"Bright young man," murmured Marny.

Foxy spoke in a voice of awe.

"Ladies, you never saw anything like it. He was yelling so loud you could hear him half a mile, and men were running out of their stores and workshops all along the street to see what the fuss was about. But he didn't stop, he kept right on running and hollering and waving that bottle over his head. So the men started running after him to find out if it was really gold.

126

"I tell you, by this time his face was so red it was shining, and with him running and all those other men tailing after him, it was like a comet going down the street."

At the memory, Foxy mopped his forehead with his sleeve.

"Well naturally, he couldn't keep going forever. By the time he got to the waterfront he had such a crowd after him he had to stop. Me and the other boys, we went out too, and we all huddled up around him wanting to see that bottle of gold. Soon as he got his breath he showed the bottle around and told us we could pick up that much in practically no time.

"So, me and the other boys, we decided we'd go up there and get some gold. But everybody else decided the same thing."

Foxy spoke impressively.

"Ladies, as the word went around that day, it looked like every man in town quit what he was doing. The carpenters working on the Parker House, they threw down their hammers right where they stood, left their saws in the boards they were sawing. Didn't even wait for the wages due them. Just walked off. And the same with all those other buildings half built.

"It was like that all over. The shoemakers and clerks and stable boys and the gamblers in the City Hotel and the cooks and bakers and the teacher at the school and the doctor who ran the drug store—they left. It was like somebody had said *Boo* and the whole town had gone off in a puff of smoke. At the market on Kearny Street, the market man put up a sign that said 'Help yourself,' and he went off, leaving his meat and produce right there. And he wasn't the only one.

"But Mr. Chase and Mr. Fenway said they were going to stay in town and sell their goods. Mr. Chase told us boys if we'd wait two or three days and help him, he would give us our whole outfit, boots and shirts and picks and shovels and jerky and salt pork, all free for nothing. So we stayed on. Men were buying food and clothes, and picks and pans and knives and shovels and horn spoons. They bought anything that would hold gold dust—bottles and cooky jars and jam pots and snuffboxes and tea canisters, anything. Mr. Chase kept putting up the prices but they didn't care.

"We ran out of everything they could possibly use at the mines. But they kept coming in, begging us to sell them things we didn't have any more. A man came in with a bag of money and said he'd pay fifty dollars for a shovel. Just a plain shovel he could have bought for a dollar before the rush began. But we didn't have any. I had the shovel Mr. Chase had given me for staying on, but I hid that in a box of cabbages."

Marny and Kendra laughed appreciatively as they listened. Kendra filled the coffee cups again.

"And, folks," said Foxy, "you should have seen the trouble they were having, getting out of town. Any man who had any kind of boat could make money taking people to Sutter's Fort. All along the beach they sat, with their bundles of food and clothes and their picks and pans, hoping for boats. Not just men, but whole families, even ladyfolks with babies that couldn't walk yet, sitting on boxes, waiting.

"So me and the other boys, we decided to go by land, around the bay like you did. There was a lot of people going that way, with horses and mules or covered wagons, or even walking and carrying their outfits on their backs. We got around the bay all right, but when we had to cross Carquinez Strait—you must know, you crossed there, didn't you?"

"Why yes," said Marny. "By Semple's ferry."

"Did you have any trouble getting over? I mean, was anybody there ahead of you?"

She shook her head.

"When was that?"

"About the end of April," said Kendra. .

"I guess it was about three weeks after that when we got there," said Foxy. "And do you know what? There was two hundred and forty-three wagons—I counted 'em, didn't have anything else to do while I waited my turn to go over. All those wagons were waiting to cross, besides the horses and mules and the men who rode them and the other men who had walked all the way. I didn't count the people, couldn't, they kept moving around, but I guess there must have been five or six hundred, men and women and children and babies, waiting for the ferry."

The girls marveled, thinking of the strait as they had seen it, the wide green landscape with the willows and wild flowers, and the ferryboat splashing on the quiet water.

Foxy sighed. "And nobody to run that ferryboat," he said, "but Semple."

"What about those young men," Kendra asked, "who worked for him?"

"He didn't have any young men when I was there," Foxy returned. "I guess they were off to the diggings. He was working day and night, still is, I reckon. I don't know what he does for sleep, but if he lives through this he sure will be rich because he puts his prices higher every day and still the people pile in. Us boys were lucky because we didn't have a wagon to take over. The boat carried two wagons at a time, and on each trip Semple would tuck in a few extra men like us. So we didn't have to wait but three days to cross."

Foxy sighed.

"Then," he said, "we came to Sutter's Fort."

"Are Bates and Cunningham still running their raft?" Marny asked.

"No, I heard tell of them but they're gone now, gone prospecting. Mr. Sutter has a rowboat, with a crew of them so-called Indians—"

"We call them Abs," said Kendra.

"Abs? Well, the Abs take this rowboat back and forth across the river, and it's all right if you can stand the lice. But you have to stand 'em because that's the only way to get over, and when you do get over you find the river around the fort is full of men who came over before you, washing off the lice, so that's the first thing you do yourself."

Foxy chuckled ruefully in remembrance.

"The fort," he said, "was full-to-busting of people on their way to the mines. And that store of Smith and Brannan's, you should have seen the business."

Kendra and Marny nodded in amused understanding. "Was Gene Spencer still there?" Marny asked.

"Yes ma'am, he was there, but he said he was coming up to Shiny Gulch pretty soon. That store sure is raking in money. And gold dust, pounds of gold dust. And you know where they keep that dust—oh gee, excuse me, ladies—"

Kendra and Marny began to laugh. "That's all right," said Kendra. "We saw it."

"Saw *it?*" repeated Foxy. He began to laugh too. "There's a whole row of 'em now."

"Marvelous," said Marny. "Go on."

"Well, we rode to Mormon Island. There's forty or fifty men there, rocking cradle things like the one your menfolks are rocking up yonder. They told us every man of 'em was taking at least half a pound of gold a day. So now we want to get to work too. Mrs. Parks, do you think Ted would explain to us about that cradle?"

Kendra said he would be glad to do so.

Foxy looked along the strip, a slow grin spreading over his bony face. "It sure is wonderful," he said. "Half a pound a day. But there's some," he added eagerly, "who say there could be even more. Ladies—have you heard anybody talk about a Big Lump?"

"Why yes," said Marny. "They talk about it at my place. Every day or two I hear of somebody who's gone to look for it."

Foxy sighed. "Gosh! I say, Marny, do you believe that?"

"No," said Marny, "I don't believe it." She gave a shrug. "They used to shout with joy at a hundred dollars a day, now they complain because they aren't picking up a million dollars a month. So they go looking for the Big Lump. Some people," said Marny, "are just plain greedy, and they're going to be sorry for it."

20

In the next few days Kendra heard more talk about the Big Lump, but not from Delbert. What he talked about—when he talked at all—was his need for more liquor to sell at the bar. A man known as Stub Crawford, a weasely character with a dirty face and a voice like a cat's meow, came up to Shiny Gulch with a load of liquor, expecting Delbert and Marny to buy it at a fancy price. Delbert bought one drink, tasted it, and threw the rest on the ground. "That stuff," he said, "would pulverize tin."

To the rage of Stub Crawford he refused to buy so much as a pint. Delbert had no scruples about selling rotgut, but he agreed with Marny that the Calico Palace ought to keep its good reputation. Now and then a peddler came up with a keg of drinkable gin or brandy, enough to keep the bar in business. Marny told Kendra the Calico Palace was doing better than they had dared to expect. More men were coming in every day to hunt gold, and they found it. They found it in such abundance that many of them forgot it had any value, and spent it or gambled it away as fast as they gathered it up.

Even Ellet of the great beard, who had started the talk of the Big Lump, seemed to have forgotten it, for Ellet too was getting rich where he was. He had brought two wagonloads of goods from the fort, and opened a trading post.

He set up his business at the lower end of the strip, about three miles below the high end where Ning's party had made their camp. Ellet placed the post here because the Ab village stood close by, around the turn of the stream. The men at Shiny Gulch—and even more the women—did not want the Abs roaming through the camp, scattering stinks and vermin, and carrying off anything that caught their fancy. Everybody, however, was willing to trade with them because the Abs came to the trading post with their hands full of gold.

Through their uncounted centuries in California, the Abs had not paid much attention to the bright sand they saw in the creeks. But now these strange new people wanted it. In return the strangers offered all sorts of delights: raisins and tobacco and face paints, colored glass beads the size of walnuts; dried beans, which the Abs pounded into a delicious paste with fresh grasshoppers; silver coins, which they loved to pierce and hang around their necks.

For a handful of beans or raisins, Ellet charged them as much gold dust as he could pick up between his thumb and his two first fingers. As Ellet had big hands, this was a good deal of gold. For coins the Abs would give even more. The bigger the coin the more they wanted it. Ted had a silver dollar he had been carrying as a luck piece, but now he took the dollar down to the trading post, where an Ab joyfully bought it for its weight in gold. Ellet kept ten per cent of the gold as his commission, and all three were happy.

Kendra wondered about the rightness of these transactions. She did not ask anybody, for she liked to answer her own questions. When she had made up her mind she told Marny what she thought.

"It's as fair as any other trade," she said. "It's as right for Ted to take gold for that dollar as for a jeweler to take gold for that spray of opals I'm going to buy. It's as right for Mr. Ellet to take gold for beans as for a man in New York to take it for caviar. What's anything worth except what somebody is willing to pay for it?"

131

They were sitting on the grass, waiting while Ted saddled a pair of horses so he and Kendra could ride down to the trading post. Their food supplies had to be replenished, but the men dreaded going all the way to the fort to buy more and leaving the rocker while other men gathered gold. Kendra had suggested that if they would spare Ted for an hour or two this afternoon she would see what Ellet had for sale.

Ted brought the horses, and he and Kendra rode down the strip. About two hundred men were here now, working with picks and pans in the water or with rockers and shovels on the hills. By this time there were also about thirty women in camp. Most of these were sturdy sunbonnet pioneers like Hester and Sue. But several, Ted had told her, were the sort you might expect in a place where there was such a surplus of men. As they rode they saw Mrs. Posey washing clothes, and Kendra asked what she was doing about those women.

With a chuckle Ted said he didn't think she was doing anything. "My dear," he added, "it's not Marny's morals that Mrs. Posey objects to, it's Marny's sizzling self. Haven't you noticed, she objects to you as much as she does to Marny."

Mrs. Posey did not look up to greet them. They rode on.

The trading post was a rawhide shed. Close to the mountainside Ellet had set up poles with the bark still on, laid crosspieces over them, and made a roof of rawhides thatched with leaves. The mountain made the back wall of the shed, and more hides hung at the south side, for shade. The other two sides were open. In the shed, a wagon stripped of wheels had been turned upside down for a counter. On this Ellet had placed a tin cup to serve drinks to men who did not bring cups of their own, and a pair of scales for weighing gold.

Near the shed Stub Crawford sat on a rock, smoking. Kendra had not been close to him before, and now she thought whoever had called him Stub had named him aptly, for he did look like a useless leftover. Stub was a smallish fellow with a sour little face, dandruffy hair and black fingernails, and clothes that looked as if he had been wearing them for weeks. As she dismounted, his nasty little eyes crept over her as if he could see through her dress.

Ted and Kendra went into the shed, and Ellet came around the wagon-counter to welcome them. "Howdy, folks! Come right in. Make yourselves at home."

Though not much cleaner than Stub, Ellet had a big hearty

132

friendliness that made him far more agreeable. With a backward glance at Stub, Ted asked, "What's he doing here?"

Ellet shrugged his big shoulders. "Oh, the damn fool. Keeps begging me to buy his liquor. I don't want it, got my own. Told him to set up a saloon for hisself, but he won't take the trouble. Too lazy to work, too lazy to pan gold, grumps all day long because the Lord ain't running the world to suit him."

To give Kendra time to look around, Ted said he wanted some kerchiefs to keep the sun off his neck. Ellet had a variety of goods—salt pork and jerked beef, salt cod and herring, coffee, seabiscuits, liquor, flour, dried peas and beans, besides mining tools and trinkets for the Abs. But the minute she had set foot in the shed Kendra had known she was not going to eat anything that came out of it. Ellet was affable enough, but she had never smelled a stench like that of his trading post and she had never seen so many crawling things in one place. Already she felt as if they were crawling on herself. Maybe they were.

The shed was fiercely hot, and the smell was making her sick—stale food, stale sweat, hides reeking because they were only half cured. She heard a greedy buzzing of flies, and saw black beetles creeping in and out of the cracks in the barrels.

A man came in carrying a pail, saying he wanted flour. Genially booming, "Sure, right here," Ellet reached into a barrel—it had no top—and brought up flour in a tin scoop. Kendra saw a cockroach wiggling in the flour as Ellet dumped the scoop into the pail. The customer paid with gold dust. Kendra looked after him as he walked off, wondering if he had seen what she had. Maybe he had not, maybe he did not care. Well, she cared. Outdoor living had made her less squeamish than she used to be, but she was not going to eat cockroaches. She thought of the store at Sutter's Fort, where she and Marny had talked with Gene Spencer. It had not been elegant but it had been reasonably clean. At least it had not smelled like this.

She said, "I'll wait for you outside, Ted."

She went out and mounted her horse, and when he had paid for his kerchiefs Ted followed her. He was laughing. "I don't blame you a bit," he said as they rode away. "Ellet is not a bad fellow, but we'll get our food supplies from the fort."

Ted went back to work at the rocker. When Kendra had

133

scrubbed off the memory of the trading post, she built up her fire and put on a kettle of beans and jerked beef, seasoned with the sage that grew in thick purple beds on the hills. While the stew was simmering she filled a pot with leaves of the wild mustard plant and set it on the fire with a scrap of her shrinking store of bacon.

The shadows were lengthening, but the sun had not yet gone behind the hills. As she looked down the strip Kendra could see other women stirring their kettles, and children bringing sticks for firewood, and men gathering in groups with their pots and pans. Other men were going into the Calico Palace, to buy a drink or to risk their day's takings with Marny. The air was full of coffee and bacon, and whiffs of salt fish bought at Ellet's trading post. Ted and his friends were dragging their rocker up to the spot where they would let it stand for the night. They all four waved to her, and went on to a pool behind a jutting wall of rock, where they liked to take a plunge after their hot day's work.

Kendra put on the coffee pot and set the eating-pans by the fire to be ready when the men appeared. The odors of sage and bacon and wild mustard were making her hungry.

She heard a sound of hoofs, and looked around. Riding up the strip on an ugly sort of nag she saw Stub Crawford. He had a saddlebag, from which he was trying to sell liquor to the men around the campfires. But not many of them were buying it; evidently they had heard of the dreadful quality of his liquor and those who wanted a drink could get a good one at the Calico Palace, for no more than Stub wanted them to pay. As he drew near Kendra, Stub dismounted and ambled toward her, carrying a tin canteen that smelled of booze.

"Howdy," he greeted her in his fretful voice.

Kendra, bending over her kettle, glanced up at him with distaste. "Good evening," she said. She said it with a snap, and returned to her task of stirring the beans, to let him know he was not welcome.

But Stub was not one to take a hint. "Where's your men-folks?" he drawled.

"They're taking a bath," Kendra answered shortly, wishing Stub would take one too.

Stub wiggled his nose. "Mmm-mhmmm!" he murmured. "What's that you're cooking?"

"Beans," said Kendra.

"And meat too, ain't it? Sure smells good," said Stub. He

134

sniffed hungrily. "And coffee. And—what's that?" He pointed his dirty finger.

"Wild mustard," she said tersely, wishing her friends would hurry.

"And bacon. I smell bacon. Aw!" Stub whimpered. "Help out a pore man, can't you? Just a little somp'n?"

"No," said Kendra.

Stub stuck the canteen into his pocket. He drew nearer. "Oh now, you could spare a *little* somp'n."

"*No!*" said Kendra. "Go away."

Stub was pleading. "How can you be so mean? A pore man that ain't got nothing to eat and nobody to care about him. What makes you so stingy?"

Kendra turned to face him, the ladle from the bean kettle in her hand. "Go *away!*" she ordered him. "Let me alone. I'm not going to give you anything."

She spoke clearly, in a voice that meant what it said. A drop of gravy fell from the ladle and splashed on the ground.

"Let me alone!" she repeated through her teeth.

But Stub bent and picked up one of the pans that stood waiting. "Aw, you'll never miss it," he whined like a spoilt child. "Just a little bit." He reached for the ladle she was holding.

"*No!*" retorted Kendra, and gripped the ladle with all her might. But Stub wanted supper and saw no reason why he should not have it. With a cackling laugh he wrenched the ladle out of her hand and gave her shoulder a push. Kendra fell backward on the ground.

No man had ever touched her roughly before. Blazing with fury, a gasping noise of rage in her throat, she sat up. Pan in one hand and ladle in the other, Stub was about to help himself to beans.

But he never did. Kendra heard the crack of a gun. Stub let out a howl, the ladle dropped, the pan tumbled on the ground and went clattering away toward the gulch.

Several men, their attention roused by the shot, were running toward Kendra to offer help. But she did not need it. From the direction of the pool Pocket was walking toward her, pistol in hand. Pocket was smiling sweetly. Finishing his bath before the others, he had come around the rock that hid the pool, in time to see what Stub was trying to do and prevent his doing it. With the same exquisite marksmanship he had shown when the sailors had approached Marny at Carquinez Strait, he had shot the pan out of Stub's hand without hurting the hand itself, as he had shot the hat out of the hand of the sailor.

Yelling with terror, Stub was running toward the spot where he had left his horse. The canteen fell out of his pocket and the booze trickled out onto the ground. The other men burst out laughing. Kendra laughed too, in admiration and relief.

"Pocket, you're a wonder," she exclaimed as he reached her.

Pocket put the gun into his holster. "Glad to be of service, ma'am."

"Weren't you afraid," she asked in some disquiet, "you might kill him?"

Pocket answered with innocent surprise. "Why no ma'am," he said. "I never kill anybody," he explained, "unless I mean to."

Before Kendra had time to ask him if he had ever killed anybody, Ted and Ning and Hiram came running from the pool, pulling on their clothes as they ran and calling out to ask what the shooting was about. Kendra explained, Pocket borrowed an eating-pan from somebody, and she served the supper.

When they had finished and the men lay on the grass talking, they agreed that Pocket and Hiram would ride down to Sutter's Fort with packhorses and bring back food supplies. While they were gone Ning and Ted would work the rocker, and the gold they took would be shared with Pocket and Hiram when they came back.

Ning said this would be better all round, for Pocket and Hiram would take the gold they had already gathered, and leave it at the store for safekeeping. Here at Shiny Gulch, so far there had been no thievery. Men left gold at their camping places, in bottles and cans and anything else that would hold it. But with no-goods like Stub Crawford moving in, they'd better be on guard.

The long June day was still glimmering. As she looked at the glow on the peaks Kendra thought how well she felt. She was tired, they were all tired, but there was nothing wrong with being tired at the end of the day. All it meant was that they would sleep soundly and be ready for tomorrow.

Tomorrow they would have to eat beans and jerky again, but she would flavor the stew with wild dill instead of sage.

136

And she would fill a pan with an herb Ning had shown her. This was a charming little plant three or four inches high, with a stem that went up straight through a round flat leaf, and then, half an inch or so above the leaf, produced a little pink flower. Ning said the plant had no name he had ever heard of. But the leaf made a good salad, so they called it "miners' lettuce."

Hiram, who had been lying flat, lazily watching the clouds, raised himself on his elbow. "Hey, what's that?"

The others looked around, all now hearing a clatter of hoofs. Foxy was riding up the strip as fast as his horse could carry him, shouting as he rode. Evidently he was giving an alarm, for men were dropping their pans, and women grabbing their children.

Hiram was already running to find out what the trouble was. As they scrambled to their feet Ted's arm went around Kendra's shoulders. Farther down the strip she saw Marny and Lolo come to the entrance of the tent, Delbert just behind them. Hiram met Foxy, heard his news, and came dashing back, his big feet pounding on the earth as he ran.

"That damned Stub Crawford," he panted, "has trundled his rotgut down around the turn and is trading it to the Abs."

His hearers gasped with anger. A drink that would merely give a white man a glow would turn an Ab into a dangerous beast, and every man in camp knew it. Hiram continued,

"Ellet tried to stop him but Stub was on a whining jag— nobody would help a poor fellow make a living, and when he was hungry and begged for food some ruffian tried to kill him—"

"Bastard," said Pocket. "Excuse me, ma'am."

"If Pocket had *tried* to kill him," Kendra said indignantly, "he'd have done it."

"The Abs are going wild," said Hiram. "If we don't go down and hold them where they are they'll be all over camp."

Along the strip groups of armed men were already gathering. Above their voices Kendra was almost sure she could hear the howling of the drunken savages down below. Her mind told her she could not, they were three miles away, but her ears thought she could all the same.

Ning had been conferring with Delbert and the Blackbeards. He told Kendra that she and Marny and the Hawaiian girls would spend the night in the tent, with Delbert on guard outside. Ning and the Blackbeards would also stay behind as camp guards, while Ted and Pocket and Hiram would join the posse.

Ted walked with Kendra down to the tent and kissed her goodbye. Inside, she saw that the gold had vanished from the tables and the liquor from the bar. On the bar burned a single candle, and at either end of the tent Marny had laid a bedroll, one for Lulu and Lolo, the other for Kendra and herself.

Kneeling by the first bedroll, she told the girls to go to sleep. A moon was rising, she said, and the men outside could see any approaching danger. Her manner was so calm, her voice so warm and soothing, that before long she had quieted their fears and they lay down.

Kendra sat on the other bedroll. This one was near the bar, and the candle flickered above it. She looked up as Marny came to join her.

"How level-headed you are, Marny!" she exclaimed.

"Thanks," said Marny, and sat down on the bedroll too, her arms around her knees. "But really, I don't think we have anything to be scared of. The Abs are a long way off. Ning's guarding your gold, and ours is out of sight. As soon as we opened the Calico Palace I fixed up a hiding place, in case we should ever need one."

There was a pause. Lulu and Lolo, reassured by Marny, were falling asleep. The sounds of the voices outside were dwindling, as the men who were to guard the Abs went down to the village and those who were to guard the camp paced in silence. Kendra was glad Marny had a safe hiding place for her treasure. It was like Marny to be prepared.

She spoke thoughtfully. "Marny, you never leave anything to chance, do you? You always think ahead."

In the half-dark she saw Marny pull reflectively at a lock of her red hair. "Well, I'd not say always—nobody can foresee everything—but I do try to arrange things the way I want them. Now what, pray, are you laughing at?"

For Kendra had begun to laugh, trying to smother her laughter but not succeeding. "I just this minute had an idea," she returned. "It came to me as I was saying you don't leave anything to chance."

Marny was laughing too. "What is it, Kendra?"

"You planned to get aboard the *Cynthia* without Captain Pollock's knowing it until the ship was out to sea. You arranged for everything to happen just the way it happened. Didn't you?"

Marny answered in a voice quivery with mirth. "Of course I did. I knew he wouldn't want me aboard because he's a prig and I'm a bad girl. But the only other vessel due to leave for San Francisco was a dirty old tub full of rats, and I wasn't going to sail on that."

"So you told your friend Mr. Galloway you were too busy to buy your own ticket, and wouldn't he please buy it when he bought his—"

"Right, dear."

"—in the name of Miss Marcia Roxana Randolph."

"That *is* my name," said Marny.

"But Loren didn't know it nor Captain Pollock either and you knew they didn't. And you knew Loren had never been to your gambling place and was almost certain not to recognize you, but to be doubly sure you dressed and talked like a lady on her way to a church tea party—"

Marny said demurely, "I was well brought up. I'm not a lady but I know how to act like one."

"But Captain Pollock would have recognized you, so you didn't go to table that evening nor the next morning. You weren't seasick, were you?"

"No, I felt fine. I just wanted to keep out of sight. I'd brought some fruit with me, I ate that."

"So by the time he saw you, it was too late." Kendra sighed with admiration. "You planned every single detail."

Marny shook her head. "No I didn't, Kendra," she said soberly. "Up to here, you're right. But I didn't plan anything else. If you've guessed so much you've probably guessed the rest of the story, and that just happened."

Kendra had not meant to speak of this. She was too modest to bring up a subject that belonged to Marny's private life. But since Marny had brought it up herself, she answered,

"I didn't guess that. Ted did."

"Well, Delbert didn't, and if you told him he wouldn't believe it, he thinks he's too captivating."

There was another pause. They could hear the sigh of the wind, an occasional call of a bird or the rustle of a night-prowling animal, and now and then a voice outside saying things were all right. Evidently the men who had gone down to the Ab village were holding the Abs there. Marny spoke softly as she went on.

"Kendra, I knew Pollock had given me yearning glances, but then so had most of the other men who came into our place in Honolulu. I didn't know he was so excited about me. Maybe I should have thought of that, but I didn't. All I thought about was getting to San Francisco. But a voyage, day after day and night after night, you know how dull it can get."

Kendra remembered her own dreary weeks at sea. She remembered how careful Loren had been not to touch even her elbow unless it was needful. She understood this better now than she had then. "Yes," she said, "I know."

"And at night," said Marny, "the stateroom was dark and stuffy and I was restless. When I couldn't sleep, I would put on a wrapper and go sit in the cabin under the skylight. There was more air in the cabin, and I could watch the stars and the clouds, and hear the men on deck, and see the moon come up. The moon was beautiful, getting bigger every night. After a while I would get sleepy and go back to bed. I never bothered anybody."

There in the dim flicker of the candle, Marny sounded so innocent.

"Then one night, Captain Pollock came into the cabin. He didn't expect to find me there. He stopped, he stood looking at me, and I looked at him. We could see each other perfectly well. He was dressed, but he wasn't wearing his coat, and his shirt was open at the throat and it made him look so different—you know how formal he is all day. As for me, I was right under the skylight, and the moonshine was pouring through. And my hair was down and I had on nothing but a nightgown and a silk wrapper over it—"

Marny paused a moment. Kendra could almost see her there, in her light silk robe, her hair shimmering and her green eyes shining under the moon. Marny said,

"So, things started to happen. After a while I said—oh, whatever one says on these occasions, you never remember afterward."

Marny turned, and through the flickers she looked at Kendra squarely.

"Kendra, I didn't plan that when I took the *Cynthia*."

"Of course you didn't," said Kendra. "Are people supposed to plan things like that?"

With a whisper of laughter, Marny shook her head. She continued, "Well, the next morning I was waked up by the wind screaming in the sails. The ship was tossing like a handkerchief. The storm had started."

140

Marny shrugged and shivered.

"I really did get seasick after that, and I was scared half to death. And then that crazy fool said I caused the storm! Does he think I'm a witch?"

Kendra felt the same uneasiness she always felt before this aspect of Captain Pollock, but she did not want to admit it. She said, "Let's hope he makes a million dollars trading in China and goes back to New York and stays there."

"Right," said Marny, and yawned. "Meantime, let's go to sleep."

They had not undressed, but now, as everything was quiet, they decided it would be safe to do so and sleep in their chemises. They carefully placed their clothes on the bar so they could get dressed on a moment's notice if they had to, and lay down on the bedroll under a blanket Marny had provided. From outside they could hear Delbert's steady footsteps as he walked up and down, guarding the tent.

"Delbert is a good watchman," Kendra remarked.

"Delbert loves money," said Marny.

Kendra spoke abruptly. "Marny, are you in love with Delbert?"

Marny began to laugh. "Good heavens no. I'm not that big a fool."

"Then—why do you like him?"

In the darkness Marny's laughter was soft and candid. "Well, I like money too." After a moment she added, "And Delbert doesn't *talk*. Kendra, my whole family was full of words. They talked all the time. They talked in languages old and new. They quoted everything from the ancient Greeks to the morning paper. They talked *to* me, *at* me, *about* me. Why can't you be like the rest of us? What's going to become of you? Oh dear, what are we going to *do* with that girl? It's refreshing to live with somebody who doesn't give a damn what becomes of me and keeps his mouth shut."

After a moment Marny added,

"Besides, dear, you know the facts of life. He's rather good there too. Now go to sleep."

141

21

Not all the Abs had had a chance to try Stub's liquor, and before morning a drunken stupor had overtaken most of those who had. However, to be sure, the guards kept watch till sunrise. They came back red-eyed and weary and sputtering with rage. After being up all night they would now have to sleep, and this meant the waste of a day. Not a Sunday either, but a workday that should have been full of gold. If Stub ever showed his rat-face around here again—

Some of the men had wanted to shoot him last night. But Pocket had insisted that it was enough to march him a mile down the river with a warning that they would shoot him if he ever came back. Pocket said he did not like to kill people unless it was really necessary.

They had to rest that day, but the next morning Pocket and Hiram, with Delbert and one of the Blackbeards, took the packhorses and set out for Sutter's Fort. They were strongly armed, for the horses were carrying three thousand ounces of gold. When she had told them goodby Kendra went to look for mustard leaves. The sun was hot, and gathering the wild plants was hard work. But they stretched her food supply, now so scant that if Pocket and Hiram didn't come back soon she feared she would have to buy from Ellet, cockroaches and all.

The very next day, however, Foxy approached her to ask if she would buy some provisions he and his friends had brought with them. The boys had decided to move on and look for richer diggings. Who could tell, maybe they would find the Big Lump. The farther upstream they went the steeper the way would be, and the mules had to carry their picks and pans. No use piling on bulky foodstuffs. They were taking only jerky and hardtack. Foxy wanted to sell Kendra a bag of potatoes and another bag of dried peas.

Kendra knew she ought to tell him that if he tried to live on jerky and hardtack, with no vegetable food at all, he would

142

get scurvy. But she knew that Ning and other frontiersmen had said this till the townsmen were tired of hearing it. She also knew she ought to say that if he would stay in one place and work he would be more likely to get rich than if he kept looking for some marvelous spot where he could pick up a hundred ounces a day. But like the warnings about scurvy this had already been said, and still many men spent more time looking for new placers than they spent gathering gold after they had found one. And nobody wanted free advice anyway, and she did want the peas and potatoes, and Foxy wanted to sell them, and if she didn't buy them somebody else would.

So she bought them. She paid with gold dust, ten times what she would have paid for peas and potatoes last spring in San Francisco, and she and Foxy were both happy with their bargain.

Several days later Marny also had a happy surprise. A peddler came up to Shiny Gulch driving a wagon holding a little salt pork and a lot of good wine and brandy. The peddler told them their friends had reached the fort before he left. All fine, he reported.

Marny bought his liquor, and lifted the limit on drinks at the Calico Palace. The peddler then divided the pork among several purchasers, and turned back toward the fort rejoicing.

Marny rejoiced too. But Kendra, standing with Marny in front of the tent, looked sadly at the small piece of pork in her basket. "Why on earth," she exclaimed, "didn't he bring more meat?"

"There wasn't room in the wagon," Marny returned with some surprise.

"But he should have brought more meat and less liquor."

"Why?" asked Marny.

"Because people *need* food. They don't *need* liquor."

"Kendra dear," said Marny, "he's not in business to do good deeds. He's in business to make money. And people will pay better prices for things they don't need than for things they do."

"That doesn't make sense."

"I didn't say it made sense," Marny replied serenely. "I said that's the way people are. I get two ounces a quart for liquor—who'd pay two ounces of gold for a quart of milk?"

Of course, Kendra thought with a start, she was right. Kendra asked, "Why are people that way?"

"I don't know," said Marny. "All I know is, that's the way they are. It's time to set up my bar."

With a wave of goodby, she turned and entered the tent. Kendra went back to her own campsite, where Ted was resting on the grass after his afternoon plunge in the pool. She sat down by him to tell him he must get a haircut and a shave. The men in camp cut each other's hair now and then when it grew long enough to be a bother, but these were clumsy jobs at best, and Ted had not used a razor since they left San Francisco two months ago. His beard was an inch long and it stuck out in all directions. Now, however, a barber had come to Shiny Gulch. He had brought shears and razors, and had spread the news that while he expected to pan gold on weekdays he was going to add to his income by barbering on Sundays.

Ted demurred. Why should he get a shave? The man would charge an outrageous price and his beard would only grow back.

Kendra insisted. "If you had a nice neat beard like Delbert's—"

"My darling," Ted answered with a lazy stretch, "that's as much trouble as keeping clean-shaved."

"Your head," said Kendra, "looks like a bunch of straw with eyes in it. And when you kiss me your whiskers scratch."

"But sweetheart, it's natural for a man to be whiskery."

"If you'll go to the barber Sunday morning," said Kendra, "and get a shave and haircut, I'll have a clean gingham shirt all ready for you."

"I'd rather you gave me a new pair of boots," said Ted, looking sadly at those he was wearing. Bruised by rocks and water, boots and shoes wore out faster than anything else in the gold fields.

"They'll bring those from the fort," said Kendra. "Go to the barber Sunday morning and at noon I'll have a regal dinner. Peas cooked with chunks of pork, and fried potatoes —or would you rather have them boiled?"

After a few more protests Ted yielded. Kendra was learning that if she really made up her mind to something Ted would yield, as he had when she wanted to get married and he did not. They seldom disagreed, but when they did, she liked knowing she could get her own way.

Sunday morning the barber set up shop under a tree. His chair was a fallen log, his razor strop hung on the tree trunk, and leaning against the tree was a piece of cracked mirror in which he showed his customers the change in their faces. Many of the men scoffed at the idea of getting dandified in the wilderness, but others liked it, and most of the married men, such as Ted, went to the barber whether they liked it or not. Shaved and shorn, wearing his clean gingham shirt, Ted did look well as he came back toward the cook-fire, where Kendra was preparing the dinner she had promised.

Ning stroked his grizzled chin and said it was all kind of interesting and he might drop around to the barber one of these days himself. Regarding Ted, Kendra spoke her admiration. "You look the way you did the first day I saw you," she said.

He smiled at her happy face. "And you," he answered, "are the prettiest woman here."

"I am not pretty. Nutshell brown, wearing a sunbonnet and a faded dress and these clumpy shoes—"

"Against that tan," said Ted, "your eyes are a real sapphire blue, and as you bend over that kettle you're as graceful as a flower." He sniffed at the rising steam. "And you can cook too!"

They had a luscious meal. When they had finished, Ning and Ted stretched out on the grass, their hats over their eyes. Kendra sat under a tree, and through the waves of the afternoon heat she watched the camp keeping Sunday. Some men were dozing, some washing their clothes, others going in and out of the Calico Palace. A loner was playing solitaire on a flat rock. Another man sat on a log reading his Bible. Most of the women had gathered in groups to chat, and brag about how much gold their husbands had taken during the past week. Two little girls were cradling dolls they had made of sticks. A short way down the strip, between Kendra and the Calico Palace, Orville Posey sat under a tree, watching a group of small boys playing leapfrog.

Orville seemed to be enjoying their game. Kendra, watching, began to enjoy it too. But then she caught sight of Mrs. Posey.

Mrs. Posey had been washing her cooking pots at one of the high pools, where the water fell over the rocks with such force that it did half the work. Now, carrying the pots, she was on her way down to join Orville. As she came near Kendra she paused to look with disapproval at the noisy children. Mrs. Posey, who had none of her own, disapproved of children in general. She spoke sharply to Kendra.

"Shameful, isn't it?"

"What?" Kendra asked in surprise.

Mrs. Posey tightened her lips and tensed her plump little person. Her yellow curls trembled on her head. "Playing games on Sunday!"

Kendra shrugged. "What do you want them to do?"

"They ought to be quiet," said Mrs. Posey. "Here comes Nathan Larch. Somebody ought to speak to him. Letting his own son break the Sabbath."

Kendra drew a sharp breath. Mrs. Posey always brought out her temper at its worst. "Why don't you let other people alone?" she snapped.

"Why don't you mind your manners?" Mrs. Posey snapped back. With another shake of the curls she toddled on over to where her husband sat passing Sunday in proper idleness.

Nathan Larch, riding up the strip, called to Kendra. When she went to meet him he told her the men were back from the fort. Nathan had just been down to the trading post and had seen them coming around the turn with several new gold seekers. Nathan was now on his way to the Calico Palace to play cards, and seeing her he thought she'd like to know.

Kendra thanked him and went to tell Ning and Ted. Before long she too saw the party, ten or a dozen men and a string of packhorses, making their way up the strip among the trees and tents and wagons. Pocket and Hiram caught sight of her and waved.

The newcomers scattered; Delbert and Blackbeard rode toward the Calico Palace. Pocket and Hiram came on up to their own campsite. With the help of Ning and Ted they set about unloading their horses.

Yes, they said, they had had a good journey except that the sun had nearly roasted them. Yes, the gold was all safely on deposit with Smith and Brannan. The day they left Sutter's Fort the temperature there had been a hundred and six. Yes, they had brought plenty of beans and salt meat and coffee, and new boots for them all—and such prices as things cost these days! You wouldn't know the fort, full of men coming and going, and oh Lord was it hot.

To unload the horses and picket them in reach of grass and water took more than an hour. Worn out with heat and hard work, the four men flopped beside Kendra in the shade of a tree. Hiram gave her a weary grin.

"Kendra, I'm ashamed to be around you, dirty and sweaty as I am. Forgive me. I'm just too tired to wash."

Sitting on the grass by him, Kendra smiled. "It's all right, Hiram."

"She's a nice lady," said Pocket.

Reaching into some stuffed corner of his raiment, Pocket took out a tin box holding dried apricots, a gift he had brought her from Sutter's Fort. Kendra exclaimed, for it had been weeks since she had had such a luxury as dried fruit. How at ease she felt with these friends of hers. Strange to remember she had been married less than three months. Everything that had happened in that small time seemed more real than all that had happened before. And she felt so well—not a mere absence of sickness, but an extra awareness of being alive. She still was not going to have a baby and she was glad of this. Getting pregnant now would change things, and she did not want any change before the end of this golden summer.

"Shall I make coffee?" she asked.

"Coffee, hell," Ted said with a chuckle. "They need a drink. I'll take my canteen down to Marny's and get it filled."

"What a brilliant idea," murmured Hiram. He lay on the grass, his big hands clasped under his head, his jutting chin pointed skyward. Ted went off toward his wagon to get the canteen.

"Ted looks so gentlemanly," Pocket said to Kendra, "with his beard gone."

As Kendra told him about the barber Pocket stroked his own hairy chin. "Maybe I'll get him to shave me next Sunday," he remarked. "Why, here comes Miss Marny!" Tired as he was, he sprang up.

Marny was coming toward them with Gene Spencer, the clerk they had seen at Smith and Brannan's store. While Pocket went to meet them Hiram explained that Gene had come up to Shiny Gulch with their party, to try his luck at gold digging. Mrs. Posey gave a frosty stare as Marny walked past her, while Orville dutifully gazed over to the other side of the gulch. Pocket introduced Gene to Ning, who had not been to the store when they came by the fort, and Marny said,

147

"It's hot and I'm tired of dealing. When Gene came in I decided to rest and hear the news."

"Did you meet Ted?" asked Kendra. "He went to buy drinks."

"No," said Marny, "we were peeking into our wagon, where Delbert is now sleeping like a baby. But Ted didn't need to buy liquor, I've brought some." She showed them a coffee pot, which she had filled from one of the casks at the bar. "Hold your cups, boys."

Hiram sat up. "Between the two of you, we'll be nicely boozed up before dark."

"After that ride to the fort and back," said Marny, "you deserve it. Hold your cup, Gene."

He grinned. "Well ma'am, a *good* Mormon would say no, but I guess I'm not a very good Mormon."

"But you're good company," said Marny, pouring his drink. "Kendra?—oh come on, you can thin it with water, a teaspoonful won't hurt you. Ning?"

Ning held out his cup and she gave him considerably more than a teaspoonful. Pocket gently declined. Marny poured a drink for herself.

"Cheers!" she said as she raised her cup. "Kendra, isn't it good to have the fellows back safe!"

Kendra said it certainly was. Gene spoke to her, a little shyly.

"You're all such old friends—I hope I'm not in the way, Mrs. Parks."

"Of course not!" she exclaimed. "I'm glad to see you again, and I want you to meet Ted."

"On the way up," said Gene, "I heard a lot about Ted. And about Ning too."

Ning sipped his drink, and his leathery face brightened with enjoyment. "I hear you're getting crowded at the fort," he remarked.

"Well, no matter where they're headed," said Gene, "it seems they all come by the fort. Looks like the whole country is on the way to the hills. As soon as the gold news hits a town, they leave. Monterey is empty, and San José too. I don't know if the news has gone all the way to Los Angeles yet."

"Have they heard it in Honolulu?" asked Marny.

"They're getting it about now," said Gene. "Two schooners

left San Francisco for Honolulu the last week in May. They'll spread the word."

"The schooners almost didn't leave," said Hiram. "The captains had to give big pay raises to keep the seamen. All the vessels are having crew trouble. The men go ashore in San Francisco, they hear about gold, and they run."

"They're even deserting the army and navy," said Pocket. "Tell them about Colonel Mason, Gene."

Gene said Colonel Mason, military governor of California, was making a tour of the gold country. There were rumors that the fighting had ceased in Mexico, and officers with Colonel Mason had told Gene they were dreading the day when they would get word of a treaty of peace.

"But why?" Kendra asked in surprise. "Don't they want the war to be over?"

"No, Mrs. Parks, they don't," Gene answered seriously. "I mean, they don't want to get any official bulletin *saying* it's over. Because then all the volunteers will have to be mustered out, and there aren't enough men of the regular army to keep order, the way things are going. The thievery is awful."

"That's odd," said Marny. "Nobody steals gold up here."

"Not gold," said Gene. "They expect to find plenty of that. But they steal horses and mules, to get here. Same for launches and rowboats, or anything that will take them across the bay. Same for cattle—they raid the ranches for meat. And when they start for the mines they're in such a hurry they gallop right across fields and ruin the crops. And all over California, married men have walked out and left their families. They expect to come back with bags of gold and maybe they will, but in the meantime the kids haven't got anything to eat."

Gene sighed. Marny started pouring another round of drinks.

"And everybody," said Gene, "wants Colonel Mason to do something. The ranchers want guards. The traders want their boats. The shipmasters want their sailors. The women want their husbands back."

Ning twisted his lips to one side in a half humorous, half sympathetic smile. "What's he gonta do?"

"Lord knows. He's sending a report to Washington, but it'll take months for the courier to get there and more months to bring back instructions. And in the meantime, if he loses half his men—" Gene shrugged.

"He's doing his best," said Hiram. "But I don't believe there's a man on earth who would know what's best to do."

Gene chuckled suddenly. "You know who's one of the officers touring the mines with Colonel Mason? That quartermaster, Captain Folsom—the one who looked at gold in the early days and said it was yellow mica."

They all laughed. "Have a drink, Gene?" asked Marny.

"Not yet, thanks, I haven't finished this one. Well—Lord bless my soul! Here comes a man I used to know way back in New York." Gene began scrambling to his feet. "Timothy Bradshaw, as I live and breathe! When did you get to California?"

Gene was taking a stride forward, his hand out. The others turned to look, for they had met nobody in camp named Timothy Bradshaw. But they saw only Ted, in his battered boots and trousers and the clean gingham shirt Kendra had washed as his reward for getting his whiskers off. He was carrying the canteen he had had filled at the Calico Palace bar.

Ted had stopped short. He looked like a man who had been kicked in the stomach. It seemed to Kendra that his face had turned a strange color. Certainly it had a strange look, hostile, nothing like the look of careless good humor she was used to. Ted began to say,

"I'm sorry, I believe you have made a—"

At the same moment, as though to stop their speaking any more, Hiram had sprung to his feet and was saying, "Gene, let me introduce—"

But neither Gene nor Ted was hearing him. A broad grin on his face, Gene had clapped his hand on Ted's shoulder. "This is a real surprise! Is Della with you?"

"I told you—" said Ted, but his lips were so stiff that he could hardly make plain words, and Gene had already turned his head to speak to the others.

"Hiram, Pocket—why didn't you tell me Tim was at Shiny Gulch? I used to work right in the same office with this fellow!"

By this time Ted's shock had eased enough to let him speak clearly. He said,

"I don't know what you're talking about."

His voice was as harsh as the scrape of a horn spoon on a rock. His face was lined, as if he had suddenly grown

150

older. His hand holding the canteen looked tense enough to crush it.

By this time they were all standing, Ning and Hiram and Pocket and Marny, and Kendra too. Kendra did not remember getting to her feet. It seemed to her that she did not remember anything about this whole day except Gene's springing up to greet an old friend. "Timothy Bradshaw, as I live and breathe! . . . Is Della with you?"

Her throat was dry and her mouth had a bitter taste. She was conscious of the rub of her clothes on her skin. She felt hot all over, and then in spite of the warmth of the day she felt cold. She did not know what Gene's words meant. She did not know who Della was. But she did know her magic island was breaking to pieces under her feet.

As Ted spoke, Gene's grin had faded. He took his hand off Ted's shoulder, and his sunburned face showed a blush of embarrassment as he stammered, "Gee—what—what's wrong, Tim?"

Quietly, Pocket said, "Maybe *you're* wrong, Gene."

Gene shook his head, plainly mystified. "But gosh—I never —what's the matter, Tim? Are you sick or something?"

In that same strange voice Ted said, "I don't know you."

Gene passed a hand over his forehead. "Well, say, I never was so surprised in my life. I could have sworn—if you're not a ditto for Tim Bradshaw—"

Through her daze Kendra heard a rustle of skirts. Marny came a step closer and took Kendra's hand in hers. Kendra felt it but did not turn. She was staring at Ted as if under a spell.

Gene was talking, floundering around among his own words. "Tim Bradshaw was a fellow—I mean this was back in New York before I took the Mormon ship—I knew him well—went to dinner at his house—his wife was named Della and she was a good cook, had an idea about apple pie—she would soak raisins in wine and put them in—"

That first day in San Francisco, when the errand boy had brought the box of groceries. "May I give you a hint? Soak a few raisins overnight in wine and add them to the pie filling."—"What a good idea! Who told you that?"—"Oh, a woman I used to know."

Gene stood looking helplessly at the ring of faces around him.

Hiram spoke firmly. "You heard what Ted said, Gene."

151

Gene scratched the back of his neck. "Ted?" he repeated.

"This man's name," said Hiram, "is Ted Parks. You made a mistake."

Gene gave a bewildered look at Kendra. She had told him she wanted him to meet "Ted."

Kendra heard herself speaking. Her voice sounded rough in her own ears.

"He did not make a mistake, Hiram."

She felt Marny's hand tighten on hers. At the other side, she felt Ning take her free hand in his. She noticed how different their hands were. Marny's was smooth as silk; Ning's hand felt like the bark of a tree.

There had been an instant of silence after she spoke. But only an instant. Now Gene was exclaiming,

"Gosh, I'm sorry!"

"Damn your soul," said Ted. He turned around and strode off, toward the highest end of the strip where the river flowed down around the higher mountains. He did not look back. He simply walked on and on till he was out of sight among the trees.

For the first time since Gene had sprung up to greet Ted, Ning spoke. He said,

"Well, boys, it looks like I don't pick 'em as good as I thought."

Kendra felt as confused as dust in the wind. Her only clear thought was that she had to run away and hide somewhere alone, and get used to knowing that she was alone again, and would be alone as long as she lived. Jerking her hands from Marny and Ning, she turned to go, but before she could do so she felt herself held again. This time it was the big powerful hand of Hiram, and he had grasped her shoulder with a grip she could not break.

"You're not leaving yet," said Hiram. He spoke in a voice of command.

"Yes, I am!" she cried. "Let me go!"

"No," said Hiram. "Not until I've said something. Wait, Gene. You hear this too."

With his free hand he beckoned Pocket and Ning and Marny. They all came close. Holding Kendra where she was, Hiram spoke.

"Kendra, we are your friends."

The others nodded. Hiram went on.

"I want to make this clear. Gene, since we've been at

Shiny Gulch Kendra has worked as hard as any of us, maybe harder. She has cooked three meals a day. She has walked all over these hills looking for sage and dill to flavor our tasteless dried meat, and wild salads to keep us well. There's been a lot of scurvy in the gold camps but we haven't had any. Kendra has been as hot and tired as we have, maybe hotter and tireder, but she's never said so. Not once has she opened her mouth to complain. She's what Ning calls a good traveler."

Nobody said anything. They were all listening. Kendra saw Ning's lips move in that odd little smile of his, which told that he agreed without his having to say it.

Hiram looked at Kendra.

"Now, Kendra, I'm going to say something to you. We like you and we respect you. Whatever is behind this, it's a matter for you and Ted. Whatever you do, it's all right with us. And this I promise."

He looked at the others, one by one, and back at her.

"Kendra, we are the only persons who heard what Gene said, and nobody else is going to hear it. We'll keep our mouths shut. Promise, Gene?"

"Sure," said Gene. He spoke sincerely. "You can count on me not to make any trouble, ma'am."

Hiram said, "Ning?"

Ning spoke out of the side of his mouth. "I never was one to blab, Hiram."

"Pocket?"

Pocket said, "Right."

Hiram glanced at Marny. With a slow smile Marny spoke, not to him but to Kendra.

"Kendra, the other evening I told you, I'm not a lady but I know how to act like one. Well dear, I'm not a gentleman either but I know how to act like one. That's all."

Kendra wondered why she was not crying. It would be such a relief to feel tears in her eyes, to feel anything besides this whirling confusion in her head.

Hiram smiled down at her, and behind the stubble of his beard and the sweat streaks down his forehead, his rugged face looked almost sweet.

He took his hand off her shoulder. "Now you can go," he said.

"Thank you, all of you," said Kendra. "Thank you."

She was surprised to hear herself speaking so steadily. She added,

"Please, don't anybody come with me. Let me manage this by myself."

"Of course," said Hiram.

She turned and went away, in the direction Ted had gone, up toward the highest end of the strip where the river came down around the higher mountains.

In the group she had left there was a hard silence. Then Ning asked,

"Any liquor left in that coffee pot of yours, Marny?"

"Plenty," she said, and held it out. "You're welcome to the liquor, boys, but bring me the pot when you've finished. Now I'd better get back to work."

She turned, about to walk toward the Calico Palace. As she did so she stopped, and the men heard her swear, softly, angrily, obscenely. They were astonished. Marny had heard most of the ugly words in the language but this was the first time they had heard her use them.

They looked where she was looking. During the past few minutes they had been so intent on their own subject that they had taken no notice of the rest of the camp. But as they saw what Marny was seeing, their lips too moved in words like hers. Close to their circle, within easy earshot, stood the round little pinguescent figure of Mrs. Posey, with her curls like a lot of wilted daffodils on her head.

Mrs. Posey saw them looking at her. For a moment she looked back at them. Then, with a smirk of delight, she turned and trotted off down the strip.

Pocket shook his head. "That woman," he murmured, "is a public nuisance."

"Q.E.D.," said Marny. "That, my friend, is short for Quod Erat Demonstrandum, and *that's* Latin for 'I told you so.'"

22

When she opened her eyes in the light of daytime and found herself alone on her bedroll in the covered wagon, for an instant Kendra had a feeling of surprise. It was like the morning after her fall down the gulch, when she had wakened alone because Ted had slipped out early to start the fire and make coffee in her place. She remembered how bruised and stiff she had felt that morning.

Today again she ached all over. Her head beat with a dull rhythm as if somebody were pounding the wagon with a stick. But as memory pushed its way into her mind she knew that this time she was not suffering from any damage to her body. This time the wounds went deeper than that.

Memory pushed in, hard and cruel. The moment when Gene Spencer had recognized Ted. The hours afterward, when she had been alone with Ted, finding out that through these golden weeks she had been living with a dream lover in a dream world. The pain growing worse and worse until she had cried out, "Leave me alone! Stop explaining. Stop talking. Just leave me alone!"

Then the night, when every hour seemed twice as long as the one before. And at last the glimmer of dawn as she had dropped to sleep from sheer exhaustion.

Kendra wondered how long ago that had been. The day was bright now. The sun was shining on the curtains of Chinese grasscloth, so artfully woven to let in the air but keep mosquitoes out. She felt uncomfortably hot. This meant the morning was well advanced, for here at Shiny Gulch, no matter how hot the sun, the nights and early mornings were cool. As she sat up and caught her throbbing head between her hands she could hear the sounds of the camp—horses stamping, men shouting, the rush of water and the clank of pickaxes on the rocks. They were the sounds she had been hearing every day, only now they were different. Everything

155

was different because she was different herself, and she would never be the same again.

Maybe if she had a good wash in cold water her head would stop thumping and she could think. As she was used to doing every morning, she slipped her bare feet into her shoes, threw a blanket around her, gathered up her clothes, and ran to the bushes where she and Marny had set up their bathroom. On her way, through the undergrowth she caught glimpses of men at work down the strip. She wondered where Ted was.

—I don't care, she told herself.

But even as she said it she knew she did care, or she would not be wondering.

Their green bathroom was shady and cool. Here stood their bathtub, the lower half of a brandy keg sawed in two by the Blackbeards. Beside it were two pails of water the Hawaiian girls had brought in.

The cold bath did make her feel better. She rinsed the tub, refilled the pails at the little waterfall near by, and left the bathroom in order for the next user. The familiar work loosened her muscles and cleared her mind, and made it easier for her to think. She had to think. She could not talk to anybody yet.

She found a place to sit, under a tree, out of sight of the camp. The wind blew pleasantly on her face. Around her were the odors of greenery and wild herbs and fresh-turned earth. She heard the drone of bees and chirps of birds, and squirrels rustling about as they looked for acorns. She ran her fingers along the earth beside her. Faintly damp, it felt soft and gritty at the same time. Her hand loosened a pebble, and sent it rattling along the ground. A mosquito lit on her wrist and she gave it a slap.

The sting of her own slap on her skin roused her as though from a doze. As if all the hours since yesterday had been crowded into an instant, they came back.

She was not married to Ted and she could not be and now in black disillusion she did not want to be. Ted had a wife in New York and her name was Della and he had left her because she bored him. No, there was hardly a chance of Della's having died. She was one of those violently healthy people who would live almost forever. And no, he could not possibly have divorced her. Not unless he had caught her taking a lover, and there was no hope of Della's ever doing

156

that. Not after she had roped a husband and could sit on her bottom and get fat while he paid the bills. Once a woman like Della got hold of a man he was caught for life, bound to put up with her and her two wet-nosed brats.

Who was taking care of them now? Ted didn't know and didn't give a damn. The brats were whiny and spoilt and messy like Della herself and the thought of all three of them made him sick.

"Ted, why did you marry her?"

"I've nearly cracked my head trying to think of an answer to that one."

As he had told her, Ted had worked in a law office in New York. Gene Spencer had been a clerk in the same office. Ted had liked Gene, had invited him to dinner, and one thing Della could be counted on to do was put a good meal on table when there was a handsome young man around to enjoy it. Quite different from the warmed-over slops she served when only her husband was there. No wonder Gene had remembered the pie.

Gene had gone to another job in Brooklyn and Ted had not seen him since. Ted knew Gene was a Mormon, but he had not known Gene had taken the Mormon ship to California. He had not thought about it at all.

No, Ted could *not* go back to New York. Not ever. Because if he did he would be locked up for embezzlement.

He was not in the habit of stealing. But he had been so sick of Della. For months, all he had thought about was that he had to get free of her. But how?—if he left her she could drag him into court, and she would, no doubt about Della. The only way would be to go off to some place so far away that she could not find him. And this cost money. A lot of money.

Then one evening he was in the office catching up on some work. He often stayed late and had dinner at a restaurant because it was no fun to go home. Another man was working late too, a cashier. This fellow went out to mail some letters. Ted was alone. The fool had left the safe open. Ted caught sight of a pile of cash.

Here was his chance. Never again would he have one like it. That damned idiot of a cashier, he should have known better. The temptation was too great. Ted gathered up the money and walked out.

Leaving everything behind him, he went directly to the

157

waterfront and asked what boats were leaving tonight. He took one for Boston. He had no idea where he would go from there, anywhere would do so long as it was far away. In Boston harbor was a ship about to sail for Honolulu. Ted paid his fare and went aboard.

Kendra did not remember how long it had taken him to tell her all this, nor how many questions she had asked. She did remember that they had been here in the grove, out of sight of the camp and of their own wagon. Ted had walked up and down, now and then pausing to stand in front of her as if to make a speech in his own defense. She had seen the sunset red beyond the trees. She remembered saying,

"And your name is not Ted Parks."

"My name is Timothy Parker Bradshaw. I thought if I changed it, there was less chance of her finding me."

Here Kendra recalled her own shock at learning that Marny did not know Delbert's real name. How foolish, how *young* she had been then! Marny did not know Delbert's name, but Marny knew she did not know. She had not been a child bedazzled by a handsome stranger.

—How stupid I am, Kendra thought.

She asked, "When you went to the fort last spring—when you ran away and left me in San Francisco—was Gene Spencer at the fort then?"

"I don't know. I was there only a day or two before I came up here to look for gold. I didn't know Gene was in California till today."

"You've met nobody else who knew you?"

"Nobody. And Gene wouldn't have known me if you hadn't pestered me to get a shave. If I had kept my beard I would have recognized him first. Then I could have gone somewhere else."

"And did you plan to spend your life like that?" she demanded. "Always running away?"

What a useless question, she thought as soon as she had asked it. Of course he had not planned it that way. By this time she was realizing that Ted never planned anything. He acted and then thought about it.

And now she was having to face all this, and most especially to face the fact that she had made a fool of herself. She asked desperately,

"Ted, *why* did you go through that marriage ceremony with me when you knew all the time—"

158

"Good Lord," he burst out, "you all but got into bed with me. I'm not made of marble."

This she knew very well now. He was not made of marble and neither was she. But she felt a surge of anger. She was realizing something else.

His self-pity, so easy, and to her amazement, so sincere. Everything was somebody else's fault and he was the victim.

Della had been a fat lazy bore. It had not occurred to him that he might not have been a perfect husband. The cashier had been a fool to leave the safe open. He had snatched at his only chance to get away—it had not entered his head that he might have worked his passage on a ship, like Hiram. She had made him get his beard off just as Gene Spencer reached camp. She had trapped him into this marriage that was no marriage at all. None of it had been his own doing. Not once had he blamed himself.

Nor did he now. Her anger must have blazed in her face, for he spoke again, this time not defiant but pleading.

"Kendra, I tried to put some sense into your head! I told you I was no good. I tried, Kendra! God knows I tried."

Kendra spoke slowly. She quoted what Ted himself had said to her, on a happy firelit day that now seemed so long ago. "Started with Adam. That woman Eve, it's her fault—"

"Oh, stop!" he exclaimed.

"I won't stop," said Kendra. She felt a cold hard rage such as she had never felt before.

"I told you," he cried, "it would be the mistake of your life. I gave you every argument—"

"Every one," she cut in, "except the one that might have worked. The truth."

"I did love you, Kendra!"

"Not enough to be honest with me. Not enough to tell me the facts, then say, 'Now do you want me?' You could have done that."

Again Ted stopped pacing, and stood in front of her. "If I had done that," he asked, "would you have said yes?"

"Wait a minute," Kendra answered. "Let me think."

It seemed to her that she had to look at herself more closely than she had ever done, be more honest with herself than she had ever been. If Ted had told her the facts, would she have gone through that ceremony, and come with him to the hills of gold? Would she have done this, knowing that he had deserted not only a wife but two children, knowing that

159

her marriage was almost certainly not lawful, that any day somebody from New York might recognize Ted—would she?

After a long pause she said slowly, clearly, "Yes, I believe I would."

Ted gave a start of puzzled astonishment. "Then," he exclaimed, "why are you so blistery mad with me now?"

"Because you didn't give me a chance to choose," she returned. "You didn't tell me the truth. You haven't any—" She remembered the word Marny had teasingly told her to use, and she said, "You haven't any guts."

Still puzzled, Ted shook his head. Kendra went on.

"If you had told me the truth—I was so in love with you, I wanted you so much, I think I would have said, 'Yes, I'll do it. It's nobody's business but my own. It's wrong and maybe I'm wrecking my life but this is what I want to do.'"

She drew a short hard breath.

"But you didn't tell me. You wanted me as much as I wanted you, but you didn't love me enough to let me make up my own mind. Do you understand?"

To the end of her life Kendra never knew whether Ted understood this or not. He could not answer. As she talked, her anger had risen. Now she spoke sharply, full of scorn.

"You're a halfway person. That's what I can't stand. A coat with one sleeve, a house without a roof, a bridge that stops in the middle of a river—who wants those? Things are no good unless they're *done*."

"What makes you so merciless?" he begged. "Kendra, I was in love with you! I tried to tell you—"

"You did not try. And whatever you call trying, now you can stop it. I'm not married to you and I'm through with you. If you think I'm going to sleep with you tonight in the wagon or anywhere else you're wrong. I don't have to and I won't."

"You don't have to," he said with a tired sigh. "What do you want me to do?"

"Leave me alone!" she cried. "Stop explaining. Stop talking. Just leave me alone!"

"All right," said Ted.

He turned and walked into the shadows among the trees. She heard his footsteps crunching on the ground.

That had been last night.

Now she had to face today. Now she sat here under the

tree, hearing the birds and squirrels, feeling the heat even here in the shade, wondering what she was going to do next.

It seemed to her that there was only one thing she could possibly do. Go back to San Francisco. Tell Alex and Eva what a blunder she had made and ask them to take her in again.

—Oh God, she thought, how I dread that! But where else can I go?

—Face one problem at a time, she told herself. The first problem was how to get to San Francisco. She would have to endure one more talk with Ted, to arrange this. One more talk, then they would say goodby.

"Oh, Ted!" she said, and her voice broke with a little sob. It was the first time today she had spoken aloud. As she heard her own words, it seemed to her that she had two separate hurts. One was what she had learned about Ted, the other was memory of the joy she had had with him. One emotion was as real as the other, and they were there side by side, doing battle within her. She hated Ted for what he had done to her, but she had loved him, and she was finding out that love did not go when it ought to go.

Suddenly she realized that the air was pungent with the odors of coffee and bacon and roasting beef. The day had reached noon, and men in camp were cooking their midday meal. With a twinge of surprise Kendra recalled that she had eaten nothing since that Sunday dinner of dried peas and pork and potatoes—had that been only yesterday?

Last night she had not wanted food, but now she was hungry. She stood up and walked out of the grove, down the open strip. In the gulch a few men were still working, but most of the miners were gathered around fires with their pots and pans. As she came nearer, several lifted their hands in greeting. Kendra waved back. It was cheering to know she had friends, no matter how casual they were.

At their own cook-fire Hiram was doing the work. He had strung chunks of beef on a long peeled stick, and set this over the fire, the ends resting on stones at either side of the trench. Now and then he turned the stick so the meat would be broiled on all sides. On the crisscrossed sticks, the coffee pot was steaming.

Catching sight of her, Hiram ran forward. "Howdy!" he said heartily as he reached her. "Had anything to eat yet?"

161

—Oh thank God, she thought, he's not starting right off to talk about Ted. She answered, "Not yet, and I'm starved."

"Beef isn't ready," said Hiram, "but the coffee is. Come on and have a cup."

They went to the fire. Kendra sat on the ground and he poured coffee into her tin cup. Her spirits rose as she sipped it. What a joy, the day's first cup of coffee. When he had given the beef a turn Hiram sat by her, linking his big hands around his knees. How vital he was, with his muscles and his thick waves of hair and that rusty-gold beard looking as if it had exploded from his chin. It occurred to her that she had never seen Hiram indoors. He did not seem to belong indoors. With his size and energy, he would make any room seem to shrink when he came into it.

Near the edge of the gulch she saw Ning beside the rocker, while Pocket lugged up water to wash the dirt. They were having a hard time working the rocker with only two men. Hiram turned and shouted to them to make this the last washing, as the beef was nearly done. Kendra wondered where Ted was. She had to know; she might as well ask now.

As she set down her empty cup she drew a deep breath and began,

"Hiram, I've got to get this over somehow. I want to ask about Ted."

He smiled through his shining beard. "Sure. Go on."

"I've got to talk to him one more time," she said. "Where is he, Hiram?"

Hiram turned and looked at her hard. His whole face changed with astonishment as he answered, "Why Kendra, Ted is gone."

"Gone?" Kendra repeated.

She had not thought he would go like that, leaving her alone without making any provision for her safety in this camp of strange men. She stared at Hiram. His thick eyebrows drew together in surprise.

"By—the—great—horn—spoon," he said slowly. After a moment he asked incredulously, "Kendra—do you mean you didn't know that?"

"I didn't know it," said Kendra.

"We were surprised, Ning and Pocket and I," said Hiram. "We wondered what plans you two had made, but he didn't want to talk so we didn't insist."

"When did he go?" she asked.

162

"Early this morning. He said he was setting out for another camp, didn't say which one. He took a saddle horse and two packhorses with supplies. Lucky there was plenty of everything from the fort. He left you a poke of gold, gave it to Ning to keep for you." Hiram spoke as though appalled. "Kendra, we couldn't believe you didn't know."

Kendra said again, "I didn't know."

Her voice was hard and toneless. She felt her lips moving in a tight little smile. Without seeing herself, she could feel that it was an ugly smile.

"You had made no plans?" Hiram asked, still almost unbelieving.

Kendra shook her head. As if in need of something to do, Hiram stood up and turned the meat.

Why on earth, she wondered, had she been surprised, even for a minute? They had made no plans. But now, again, she was reminded that Ted never planned anything. He had not considered what Della was going to do when he left her, now he had not considered what she herself was going to do. How she was to live in a mining camp with no protector, how she would get from Shiny Gulch to Sutter's Fort, from Sutter's Fort to San Francisco—he had not thought of that.

Ted had not changed a bit. He had run away again.

23

It was afternoon when Kendra learned that her personal life was not private. After sharing the men's dinner she had felt more cheerful, and told them she would wash up. She had finished this, and was resting in the shade when she saw Lolo, her black hair bound with a ribbon and her flowered dress still bright in spite of sun and wear.

Lolo came up to her. "Please, Mrs. Parks, Marny says will you come and talk for a few minutes?"

Kendra thought,—I wish she wouldn't call me Mrs. Parks. I am not Mrs. Parks. I'll tell her so. Oh, why? She's not doing any harm.

163

Aloud she answered, "Why yes, Lolo. Where is Marny?"

Lolo said Marny was down near the tent, by the tree where she had set up her first gambling table. Kendra went to find her.

Under the tree, Marny stood before an up-ended box. She was practicing a game called monte, played with a special Mexican deck. Several cards were laid out on the box, and Marny held the rest of the deck in her hand, but her practice had been interrupted. Mrs. Posey had dropped by for a chat.

Kendra paused. They had not seen her. Mrs. Posey was looking at Marny, Marny was pointedly looking down at the cards. The sun falling through the tree made bright coppery flickers in her hair. Kendra heard Mrs. Posey say,

". . . and what's his real name? I didn't catch it exactly— Bradford, Bradley, Brandon?"

"He told me," Marny replied without looking up, "his name was Ted Parks."

Mrs. Posey giggled. "Oh now, you know better than that! You were right *there*. You *heard* what that man Gene Spencer called him."

"I wasn't listening."

"But you heard, I just know you did! And this girl Kendra—" Mrs. Posey bent forward with intimate glee— "are they really married?"

Marny took a card from the deck in her hand and held it poised over the cards on the box, as if deciding where to place it. "I didn't witness the ceremony," she returned. "I didn't witness yours either. Are you really married?"

"Oh dear, what a question!" tittered Mrs. Posey. "Everybody knows I'm a married woman. But do come on! Tell me! Are they married?"

Carefully placing the card, Marny said, "If you're so much interested, why don't you ask Kendra?"

Mrs. Posey's plump little hands began to flutter. The yellow curls bounced on her head. With another self-conscious giggle she began, "Well now really—"

Kendra had been getting madder with every line she heard. Now she stepped forward, deliberately breaking a twig with her foot so they would know she was there. For the first time Marny raised her eyes, sparkly green in the light. Mrs. Posey turned around with a start. For once in her life she did not know what to say.

But Kendra did. Kendra was so angry that her words came out with no effort at all.

"If you can't mind your own business, Mrs. Posey, can't you at least keep out of my way?"

"That," said Marny, "is a good idea. Keep out of my way too." She fanned the cards in her freckled hand and snapped the deck together again. "I've got work to do."

Mrs. Posey drew herself up to her full height, which was not very high. With all her dignity she replied, "So have I. Honest work. Decent work. I'm not cheating men out of their money—"

"I don't cheat," Marny said tersely.

"—and dragging them down to the gutter," fumed Mrs. Posey. "And as for *you*," she continued, turning upon Kendra, "I always knew you were a sham. I knew your fine society airs were a lot of false jewelry. You pretending to be better than other people! I've told you before and I tell you again, it wouldn't surprise me to find out you're no better than *she* is! Well," she announced to the air, "I'm no fine lady but at least I know my husband's *name!*"

Marny sighed and spoke. "Verba, verba, ad infinitum ad nauseam."

"What?" Mrs. Posey demanded.

"That means," said Marny, "if you don't stop talking I'll throw up."

Mrs. Posey's little blue eyes flicked in contempt from Marny to Kendra and back again. "If you want to be so snotty it's all right with me. Goodby, both of you."

Marny shrugged. Kendra said, "Goodby, Mrs. Nosey."

Without waiting for any more words Kendra turned and ran over the rough ground to the tent, pushed aside the flap in front and went in. The tent was empty and dim. She ran to the back, where the boards across the barrels formed the bar. She put her elbows on the bar and put her face into her hands and burst into tears.

She felt torn and helpless and sick at heart. Ted had made her so happy and now he had crumpled up before her and was gone. And already she was wondering where he was and if he had taken enough food with him and who was going to cook it. She tried not to care. But she cared.

It would have been so much easier if only she had been left a shred of pride. She could have made up a story to explain why Ted had left Shiny Gulch—he had gone to hunt

165

venison, to check a report of rich diggings on Weber Creek, or to see a new type of rocker they were using at Horseshoe Flat. For reasons such as these the population of every mining camp was constantly shifting. Nobody would have doubted what she said; nobody would have cared anyway.

But now—Kendra sobbed in despair. Somehow Mrs. Posey had gained a smattering of the facts, and now she would talk to everybody who had ears, and what she did not know she would make up. Oh, to get out of here! To double Cape Horn again, to leave California forever! Kendra fumbled for her handkerchief. The handkerchief was a big blue bandana like those Pocket carried, because in a mining camp a kerchief was more often needed to mop a sweaty forehead than to dry weeping eyes.

"Kendra," said Marny's voice.

Kendra gave a start. Marny had walked around to the back of the bar.

"Here," she said, pushing a tin cup across. "It's a good white wine, light and dry. Calms the nerves."

Kendra took a sip. The wine was delicious. She murmured, "Thank you. I'm sorry—but that woman—"

In the half light of the tent she heard Marny laugh gently. "Darling, if Mrs. Nosey—oh, what a beautiful name for her —if Mrs. Nosey had your figure she wouldn't dislike you so much. Now don't you want to know why I asked you to come and talk to me?"

"Oh yes. I'd forgotten that."

Still standing at the bar, Marny spoke practically. "Kendra, I know you want to go home to your mother—"

"I don't!" Kendra burst out. "I've got to go back to her, but I don't want to."

She blurted out some facts about her loveless childhood and her dread of returning to a mother who had never wanted her. Marny responded with real fellow-feeling.

"I didn't know that, but I do know what you mean. I certainly wouldn't want to see my family again unless I came back in a blaze of glory."

She paused a moment and went on.

"Well, you'll have time to get used to the idea, because here's what I wanted to tell you. You can't ride to San Francisco alone. You can go when we go, but we're not leaving yet. Business is too good. In the meantime, you can't sleep alone up there in the grove. It's not safe. 'Beauty provoketh

166

thieves sooner than gold,' said Shakespeare, and he was right as usual. Let's have the Blackbeards move your wagon down here, close to mine."

"How thoughtful you are," said Kendra. "I'll pay them for their work," she added hastily. "I'm not asking any favors."

Marny began to laugh. "Don't be so quick on the draw, Kendra! I'm not offering you a favor. I was about to ask for one."

"I'm sorry, Marny." Kendra tried to steady herself. "What did you want?"

Marny rested an elbow on the bar. "Well dear, I have some problems. Lolo is pregnant. Poor kid, I've told her everything I know but maybe she didn't listen and anyway nothing works all the time. Her Blackbeard—Troy—is quite fond of her, says he's going to marry her. But cooking in this weather is hard work and I'd like to make things easier for her. I wondered if you'd let me share your meals."

"Why yes!" Kendra exclaimed gladly. "I haven't had time to think about meals."

"Well, I have," said Marny. "I spoke to Ning about it this morning. We made a plan and we hope you'll approve. You're to cook for Ning and Pocket and Hiram as before, and now for me too. That's four. We'll pay you a salary."

"A salary? From my best friends?"

"You don't owe us anything. We're making it a straight business proposition. Two ounces of gold a week from each of us, that's eight ounces together. Agreed?"

Again Kendra felt tears spring into her eyes. Eight ounces of gold a week was a better salary than most men earned in New York or Baltimore, but this was not the reason for her tears. In a low voice she said, "That will be wonderful. I'll be independent—no burden on anybody."

"You'll never be a burden on anybody, Kendra," Marny said quietly. "Well, that's settled. Lulu and Lolo will have only the Blackbeards to cook for."

Kendra had a sudden thought. "But what about Delbert?"

Marny moved away from the bar. She sat on one of the upside down pork tubs that served for chairs at the Calico Palace.

"Kendra, you are not the only one who has had—shall we say—a change of fortune."

"What are you talking about?"

167

"I'm saying, dear, I too am about to be deserted. Left high and dry on the beach. Thrown away like an old shoe."

Kendra made a gasping sound of comprehension.

The night she had come here with Pocket, had sat on a bottom-up pork tub, had heard Ellet talking at the bar. The look of Delbert as he listened—ugly, sensual, like the look of those men who had stared at her that first day on the beach in San Francisco.

She said, "The Big Lump?"

"Right," said Marny.

"When did he tell you this?"

"Last night."

Kendra was amazed at Marny's composure. She seemed to be accepting this as she would have accepted a change in the weather. "Is he going alone?" Kendra asked.

"Oh no. It seems he has been dreaming of the Big Lump ever since he heard of it, but he wasn't convinced it was real. Then at Sutter's Fort he met three men buying an outfit for an exploring trip. Smart fellows, he says. They're sure it's there, somebody is going to find it, why not themselves? Delbert was well supplied with dust, could pay his share and more, so they were glad to have him join the party."

"Did those men ride in with the others yesterday?"

"Yes. And now they're ready to set out."

"But what are you going to do about—" Kendra swept her arm up and around—"all this?"

"We'll split what we've made already, and I'll carry on here."

"Do the Blackbeards want to go with him?"

"No, thank heaven. They're a pair of canny Yankees, they don't believe in any Big Lump."

Kendra struck the bar with an angry fist. "How can you be so calm? After all the time you and Delbert have been together—don't you *care?*"

"Of course I care, Kendra. We worked together in Honolulu, we came together to California. We've been partners. I've never cheated him out of a penny. Now he's leaving me in this wild country with this enterprise on my hands, and no warning. I think he's an absolute rotter."

"Wouldn't you like to break his neck?"

"Why yes, but why worry about it?" Still sitting on the pork tub, Marny rested her elbows on her knees and cupped

168

her chin in her slim strong hands. "I suppose he can't help being the way he is."

In a wondering voice Kendra asked, "Marny, have you ever been in love?"

"Oh yes, often," Marny said. "But never really."

Kendra did not answer. She had nothing to say to this.

Delbert and his new partners rode on to look for the Big Lump. Kendra cooked as before, with Marny sharing the meals. Mrs. Posey talked.

Ted had been gone a week when Hester Larch and Sue Gibson came up to Kendra as she was putting jerked beef into water to soak before being cooked. Hester and Sue had been washing, and carried baskets of damp clothes ready to be hung out to dry. As Kendra looked up Hester spoke.

"We just wanted you to know," she said, "how sorry we are."

"Edith Posey told us," said Sue. "Now dearie, if we can help at all, you say so."

Kendra tried to speak evenly. "Thank you. But I—I'd rather not talk about it."

"Naturally," said Hester. She smiled, pushing some stray locks of hair under her sunbonnet. "And don't you pay any attention to what anybody says," she added kindly. "We know you didn't do anything wrong."

They meant well. But as she watched them hang their clothes Kendra shivered with rage at Mrs. Posey.

The following Sunday, while Hiram and Pocket were scrubbing their own clothes in the pool and Kendra sat in the shade watching the camp, a young man paused before her to give her a bashful bow and say, "Good morning, ma'am."

He had a brand new shave and haircut, and his red neck showed a white streak where the hair had been. His shirt was clean and his water-cracked shoes had been brushed, and he stood holding his hat with both hands. Kendra vaguely remembered having seen him around, and as he looked harmless she answered, "Good morning."

Turning his hat between his hands the stranger began, "Well ma'am, I heard about your—husband, only it seems he wasn't really your husband, and I thought—my name is Frank Turner and I thought—"

"You thought what?" Kendra almost gasped.

"I thought maybe you and me—don't get me wrong, ma'am, I mean everything to be all honest and legal—there's an alcalde down at Sutter's Fort, he could hitch us up—"

Kendra's mouth fell open and stayed open. To receive a proposal of marriage from a man she had never spoken to was so astounding that for a moment she thought Frank Turner must have come straight from Marny's bar. But as she stared up at him he took her silence for leave to go on talking, and he was not drunk. He was merely lonesome, and she was that rarest of treasures in California, an American woman not attached to a man. He said again, he wanted to marry her, all legal and right. Kendra began to shake her head.

"Please ma'am," Frank Turner begged as she did so, "I'm no loafer nor convict nor anything bad. I worked my way to California on the brig *Rainbow* out of Salem, two years ago. I've been living in Monterey, always had an honest job, ask anybody—"

Kendra managed to speak. "No, no—I don't want to get married!"

"—and I've been right lucky at the diggings, ma'am, nearly four hundred ounces already—"

Kendra was standing now. It was all a shock, and yet she felt an almost overwhelming impulse to laugh. If that hat in his hands had been a bouquet he would have looked like a stage yokel calling on his lady-love. She tried to be considerate. "You are very kind, sir—it's an honor, I'm sure—but I don't even know you."

"We could get acquainted easy, ma'am."

"Thank you, no," said Kendra.

She had to say it several times before he would accept it. At last she got rid of him, but as he went shambling in disappointment down the strip she looked after him with apprehension. It was not hard to foresee that this was only the first of many such offers she was bound to receive as her story went around. Mrs. Posey, she thought. Damn Mrs. Posey.

24

Marny was receiving offers too, from men eager to take Delbert's place in the wagon if not at the faro table, but she too was declining. The Calico Palace was doing well, and for the present Marny was content to sleep alone.

Meanwhile, Kendra found that she was not the only person at Shiny Gulch who had reason to dislike Mrs. Posey. Because of her, Gene Spencer was suffering vast annoyance.

Innocent though he was, Gene's conscience gnawed at him for the trouble he had caused. And now Mrs. Posey was making it worse. As Marny had refused to discuss Kendra's affairs, Mrs. Posey was pestering Gene. Mopping the back of his neck, Gene said, "I've already talked too much," and would say no more. But while this disappointed Mrs. Posey it did not quiet her tongue. Up and down the camp she told all she knew and a great deal that she did not know. Now men were applying to Gene for details.

Like Frank Turner, these men had long been distressed by the scarcity of American women. Like Frank, several of them came right over to Kendra and proposed marriage. But unlike Frank, others among them did not want to marry her. What they wanted to know from Gene was, would she be available without marriage? What had really happened between her and that so-called husband?

Before long Gene packed his outfit and rode out of Shiny Gulch. Not to another gold camp; Gene had found that gold camps were not to his liking. He rode back to Sutter's Fort and his old job at Smith and Brannan's. Loudly and sincerely he said he wished he had never left it.

Kendra was not sorry to see him go. She liked Gene, but his presence was embarrassing.

As those hot dry weeks went by, Kendra was in no wise happy. But she did have compensations. Her friends liked her, and she was taking care of herself. She got another poke, a buckskin bag Hiram bought for her at the trading post, and every week as it grew heavier she felt a joy at being beholden to nobody. Right now it was a bleak sort of joy, but nonetheless a prideful sort.

Still, nothing eased the way she felt about Ted.

Day after day she tried to think why the remembrance of Ted should bring her such longing for him. She had told him she was through with him and she had meant it, but she kept remembering how delightful it had been to be with him. She despised him for his cowardice but she kept thinking— Oh dear heaven, how I miss him! She resented his having let her live in that dream world, but she could not forget how happy she had been while she lived in it.

She remembered the first time she had seen Ted, the splendid impudence of his gaze, the sense of intimacy that had come to them before they had known each other ten minutes. Was this love at first sight? It must have been.

She told herself— Love at first sight ought to go as fast as it came. Then why doesn't it? Why is the going so slow? Why so hard? Why does love hurt this way? Why doesn't it *go?*

Day after day she repeated to herself—I hate the thought of him.

But instantly the opposite would come—I'd give all the gold in California to have him back. No, I don't want him back. But I do.

This conflict Marny could not understand. Marny was friendly with all the warmth of her generous heart. But like other people who have never been in love, Marny had no knowledge of that ecstatic and unreasonable pain. She could not see why Kendra felt as if she were being torn in two.

As they sat together in the scorching afternoon, Marny tried to put some sense into Kendra's head.

"Kendra, you're sure you're not pregnant?"

"I'm sure I'm not."

"Then," said Marny, "you've got nothing to worry about."

"It's not worry," said Kendra. "It's—a battle."

"Kendra," Marny said with patient affection, "the world is the same as it was before you met Ted. Nothing is different except that you're wiser than you used to be."

Kendra looked out over the gulch. The time now was August. The weather had grown so hot, and the work so hard as the streams narrowed through the rainless summer, that Ning had ordered the men to take a rest every afternoon. Ning and Hiram lay asleep under a tree, and in another shady

172

spot Pocket was sleeping too. Kendra looked back at Marny, and Marny continued,

"When you leave Shiny Gulch you'll go right back to where you were. The alcalde in San Francisco will annul the marriage. When Alex is transferred back to the States you'll go along. Nobody there will know. You won't tell. From the way you've described Alex and Eva, I'm sure *they* won't tell. You'll meet other men, you'll marry one of them."

Kendra shook her head. "I'll never have the courage to try again."

Marny smiled. "Kendra, do you know why gambling is such fascinating fun? It's because, sometimes you lose. If you won every time, gambling would be no more of a thrill than washing your hands. Darling, make another play. This time you might win."

Kendra pushed her hand up through her hair. Marny sounded so reasonable. —But just now, thought Kendra, I don't *feel* reasonable.

Marny went to the tent to put the tables in order for the evening. Kendra stayed where she was.

The once green country around Shiny Gulch had turned brown. The grass was brittle, the flowers had dried up, the wild plants that used to vary her dinners were nearly all gone, and the few she could find were so tough and harsh-flavored as to be almost unfit to eat. As Kendra looked around, she saw Pocket beginning to wake up. He yawned, stretched, got to his feet, and began to stroll around as if to limber his muscles before the other two woke and were ready to work again. Pausing to take a drink from the water pail beside the rocker, he caught sight of Kendra. He came over, asking,

"Mind if I sit down, ma'am?"

Pocket had not been to the barber lately, but though his face was nearly hidden behind a wilderness of whiskers this could not hide his likable smile. Kendra smiled back. "I'm glad to have you," she said.

Pocket sat down beside her. He rummaged in his pockets for a knife, picked up a stick, and began whittling. Around them sounded the usual bangs and clanks. From down in the gulch came a shout as some man made a lucky find. Ning and Hiram slept on. After a while Pocket spoke.

"Miss Kendra, if you don't want to talk about your trouble it's all right with me. But if you feel like talking, that's all right too."

She turned herself halfway around toward him. It had been a month now since Ted left her, and in that month not once had Pocket or Hiram or Ning asked her to talk about him. She had welcomed their restraint. But now, somehow, Pocket had sensed that she needed a confidant. Pocket had such a kind and simple heart—sometimes people like him understood life better than more sophisticated people like Marny. Without any prelude Kendra asked,

"Pocket, is it possible to love a person and not love him at the same time?"

Pocket said, "Why of course it is, Miss Kendra."

He spoke as simply as if a child had asked him if it was possible for rain to fall in one place while the sun shone in another. Kendra felt a vast relief. He had seen at once what Marny had not seen, in spite of all her own attempts to make it clear. Kendra put her hand on Pocket's wrist. The sleeve of his shirt was torn, and grimy from the morning's work; the wrist under the sleeve was hairy and strong. "How do you know, Pocket?" she asked.

"Because," he answered, "I felt like that once, myself."

Looking across to the mountains on the other side of the gulch, Pocket put away his knife and linked his hands between his knees. When he spoke again his voice was like that of a father speaking softly by the cradle of his sleeping child.

"I figured this might be your trouble, Miss Kendra. That's why I thought I might help. The others—well, Hiram, he's a fine fellow, I never met a finer, but he's never been really hit by love. Ning, I guess he never will be. Marny—not yet anyway. But you have, and I have."

He paused, still looking at the mountains.

"Where was this, Pocket?" she asked. "At Sutter's Fort?"

"No ma'am, it was back in Kentucky. That's why I joined that wagon train coming West. I had to get away from it."

He picked up a twig and began breaking it into little pieces.

"I sure never thought," said Pocket, "I'd want to leave home and not go back. I was doing fine. My father and mother had died but I lived on my grandpa's farm. It was a real handsome farm, big white house, lots of horses, and it was all coming to me. Then I met this girl."

He threw away the remnant of the twig. With one hand he pulled up a long dry weed.

"I'd been liking girls since I was half grown, I still do, but I never thought one of them would knock me over like that.

174

But she did. I was really in love. I don't reckon I'll ever feel that way again. Then I found out. I was luckier than you. I found out before I married her."

Pocket crushed the weed in his fist.

"Miss Kendra, I haven't talked about this since I got to California. There was another man. She didn't want me, never had. She wanted the farm. The big house, all those horses, that good fat land. A fellow told me, my good friend. He thought I ought to know. I was furious, called him a liar. But then I thought, I'd better make sure. I made sure. I found her where he said I would. I found her and that other man together, making love."

Pocket stopped. Both his hands were fists now, striking each other softly between his knees. His forehead was tight, his eyes were strange. Kendra had never dreamed that the gentle Pocket could look like this. Listening, she almost held her breath.

Pocket said, "I shot that man, right there."

He stopped again. His blazing eyes still looked across to the mountains. In a low voice Kendra asked, "What about the girl, Pocket?"

"I wanted to shoot her too," said Pocket. "But I couldn't. I loved her too much." He turned and looked at Kendra straight. "That's why I know how you feel. I hated her, but I loved her. And this is what I want to tell you now." He spoke earnestly. "It hurts. It hurts something terrible. But it doesn't last forever. It doesn't, Miss Kendra."

She asked tensely, "Pocket, why do we feel so?"

Pocket smiled a little. As if it had been a release to talk about his own experience, he was again his quiet gentle self. "I spent a lot of time," he said, "trying to understand that. Coming over the plains, you get time to think. I hated that woman like I never hated anybody. But I loved her too. There was a real smart man with us, a preacher coming out to a mission church in Oregon. He was older than I was, had been to college. I talked to him. He told me what I'm going to tell you now."

She waited.

"Look down there," said Pocket. He indicated a loner swirling sand and water in a pan, looking for pay dirt. "Do you love that man, Miss Kendra? Or hate him?"

"Why no," she returned. "I don't even know him. I don't care about him one way or the other."

175

"That's it," said Pocket.

She frowned, not comprehending. Pocket held out his hard dirty hand. He explained.

"Love and hate, Miss Kendra, are not two opposite things. That's what the preacher told me. They're like the front of your hand and the back of it, two sides of the same thing. They both mean, this person *matters* to me."

A light began to dawn upon her. "You mean—that loner—" She stopped to think.

"You don't love him," Pocket said as she paused. "You don't hate him either. You don't care anything about him. That's the opposite of love, and the opposite of hate too. Not caring."

"And you mean—some day I won't care?"

"That's right, Miss Kendra. Some day you won't love Ted or hate him either. You just won't give a damn."

"It's hard to believe, Pocket! If I saw Ted this minute—"

"You're not seeing him this minute," Pocket interrupted her forcefully. "Maybe you'll never see him again. But if you do—I mean this, Miss Kendra—if you do see him again, whether you still care or not, *pretend* you don't."

"I'm not good at pretending," she said.

"In this," Pocket said sternly, "you've got to be. Any time you think about Ted, tell yourself, it's over."

"And some day—it will be over?"

"Yes ma'am," said Pocket.

She wondered if he was right. Just now, this was not easy to believe. But right or wrong, Pocket had let her know she was not alone.

"Pocket," she said after a moment.

"Yes ma'am?"

"Pocket, you like women, don't you?"

He smiled a little. "Why yes ma'am, I like women."

"Some men wouldn't, after what happened to you."

He shook his head. "Country stuff. I'm not that big a yokel."

"What do you mean, country stuff?"

"Oh Miss Kendra, I've seen them. One crop fails and they say nothing will grow around here. Some Frenchman comes along selling tools, then he rides off with the money and the tools fall apart and folks say, 'See now, this proves all Frenchmen are a bunch of swindlers.' " Pocket spoke contemptuously. "They see one and they think they've seen all. Country

176

stuff." He looked at her directly, across his whiskers. "Don't you be like that, Miss Kendra."

"I'll try, Pocket," she promised. "I mean it."

For several minutes they were silent. Then through the dry sunny air they heard Hiram calling.

"Hey, Pocket! We're getting back to the rocker."

"Be right there," Pocket called back.

He stood up, held out his hand, and drew Kendra up too. "Thank you, Pocket," she said in a low voice. "You've done a lot for me."

"Glad if I could help, ma'am."

"Marny has tried," said Kendra. "She's been a dear. But Marny didn't know what I was talking about."

Behind the wilderness of whiskers Pocket chuckled softly. "Miss Marny has a lot of education, I mean Latin and Shakespeare and things like that. But she's still got a lot to learn."

25

But the hurt did not go away. It stayed, and stayed, and stayed.

Still, Pocket had promised that in time the wound would heal. And unlike many well-meaning talkers, Pocket knew what he was talking about.

Time, thought Kendra. Time. She put her fingers on her wrist, where her pulse was ticking away the time. Enough ticks—how many thousands more?—and she would not care any longer about Ted.

Fortunately, she did not have much leisure to think. Her task of preparing the meals was growing constantly more difficult. The jerky from the fort was so hard that unless she pounded it to pieces between two stones it would not absorb water no matter how long she boiled it. Once in shreds, and cooked with dried beans, the jerky made an edible if not a savory dish. Sometimes she could add vegetables from a peddler's wagon—a pinch of gold dust for six carrots or two red onions, usually dry and wrinkled with age. When she could not get even these, Ning told her to scatter clover leaves on each serving of stew.

"You folks never had scurvy," Ning warned them, "and as long as I'm running this outfit you ain't gonta have it. Eat that clover."

They said "Yes, boss," and obeyed.

But now after four months without rain, clover was hard to find. Over the beans and jerky, Ning said it was time to leave.

At first, Pocket and Hiram shook their heads. The land was rich with treasure. Some men were putting up cabins so they could stay all winter in the hills and be on the spot, ready to start work again, as soon as the snow was gone.

Marny too was reluctant. She spoke to Kendra. "I'm raking in dust by the bagful. Do you think we ought to go so soon?"

"Yes," said Kendra. She spoke with determination, to convince herself as much as Marny. She dreaded facing Alex and Eva, but she could not postpone it forever. "I don't want to get scurvy," she added. "What good is a bag of gold if you're too weak to carry it?"

At last, when Kendra served them jerky and beans with not one clover leaf because the clover had all dried up, Hiram spoke thoughtfully.

"I've been told," he said, "that a man who has had scurvy once would eat grass like an ox to keep from having it again."

"In a few more weeks," said Ning, "there won't be no grass."

Hiram sighed.

"And in case you ain't noticed," Ning continued, "our horses are already lean from lack of it. If we want them to carry us out of here we'd better start."

Marny looked down at the shriveled old beans in her pan. "Well boys, a smart gambler knows when to quit. Let's go."

Ning nodded approval. "It don't pay to be greedy. Count what you've got."

Later that day, they counted. Hiram told Kendra they had done well. With the gold they had left on deposit at Sutter's Fort, and what they had gathered since then, the men would have about a thousand ounces each. They could not say what this would be worth in San Francisco, for men lately arrived at the mines had told them the price was going up and down

178

every week. But at any rate, said Hiram, a thousand ounces was good profit for a summer's work. As for Marny, when she had collected her share of what Delbert had put on deposit at the fort, and added it to what she had made at the Calico Palace since then, Hiram had an idea that her gold would total even more than this.

Kendra had less than the others. Ted had left her a poke, but the poke held only about thirty ounces because nearly all his dust had already been sent for safekeeping to the fort. Her friends had been paying her a salary for eight weeks, so she had earned sixty-four ounces, and she still had the nugget she had found the day she fell into the gulch. This was enough. All she wanted now was to get away from everything that reminded her of Ted, to go back to the States and hurry time away, so her hurt would heal.

They made ready for the journey, not a simple matter any more. In the early days thievery of gold had been almost unknown, but now there were tales of bandits on the trails, watching for miners going home. Ning told them to look as grumpy as they could, as if they had had no luck. And at the same time, said he, contrive unexpected ways of carrying their gold. "And just so there won't be no disputing," he said firmly, "we'll each carry our own. Put it in your saddlebag or anywhere you please, but fix it so it don't look like gold."

Gold did not take up much room—he told them a ton of it could be put into a bushel basket—but gold was heavy. Anything small and heavy would call attention to itself. Kendra and Marny conferred and for the first time since Gene Spencer recognized Ted, Kendra found herself having fun again.

Marny showed her where she had hidden the gold dust not needed on the gambling tables. She had put it into flat little cloth bags, and tacked these inside the pork tubs that served for chairs. "At first," she said, "I thought of dropping the bags into the brandy kegs. Then I thought, somebody might steal the brandy. But who'd steal a greasy old pork tub?"

Now, however, they had to hide gold in something smaller than pork tubs. Kendra sent Hiram down to Ellet's trading post for flour. "I don't care how dirty it is," she said, "we're not going to eat it." She heated stones in her fire-trench to make an oven, and baked bread of flour and water and saleratus. Making a cut in the first loaf she tucked in her nugget, and the soft bread closed around it.

179

Hiram also bought slabs of Ellet's fly-specked salt meat, and Kendra slashed the meat and put gold inside. It was Pocket's idea to carry gold in a coffee pot under a layer of stale grounds. Nobody would be surprised by stale coffee grounds in a pot. Many men at the camps made coffee by putting fresh grounds on top of the old and pouring in water, until they had filled the pot with grounds and the water tasted like coffee no longer.

While Kendra baked bread Marny cut up old clothes and stitched more little bags to hold gold dust. Several of these they put into Kendra's loaves, others into sacks of flour, which they would carry as if to make pancakes on the trail. Marny made other bags the size of her little finger, so she and Kendra could roll them up in their hair and hold them in place with hairpins.

"You girls are right bright," Ning said with a grin. "Got any ideas about the dust we're gonta pick up at the fort?"

"Simple," said Marny. "We'll get pregnant."

"Ma'am?" said Ning.

"I mean, if we can't hide it any other way, we'll each wear an apron with a bag of dust underneath."

Ning burst out laughing. "I declare, Marny, you'll get along."

"I always have," she said.

At Ning's instruction each of them put a few ounces into a little buckskin tobacco bag. These bags were to be hung around their necks and tucked under their clothes. "When you gotta pay for something," said Ning, "pull out your poke and do it slow and stingy, like this is all you've got. Take out the dust a pinch at a time, and squint at every grain on the scale. Talk poor-mouth. Look shabby."

They promised to talk poor-mouth. Looking shabby was no problem; they could not possibly have looked anything else. Most of their clothes were too tattered to be worth loading on the pack-horses. Kendra and Marny each chose one dress, the least dilapidated they had; Kendra washed and Marny mended them, and they stowed the dresses in one of the packs so as to be at least fairly neat when they rode into town. Kendra in particular did not want to look like a ragamuffin when she had to face Alex and Eva and tell them they must take her in again.

As they had so little to carry they sold their wagons. After standing all summer the wagons were not as stout as they had been, but they would do as sleeping shelters for men who planned to stay here all winter. Marny sold her surplus liquor to Ellet. Now they were ready to go.

Early one morning in the third week of September they rode out of Shiny Gulch. In the party were nine persons: Ning and Pocket and Hiram, Marny and Kendra, and the two Blackbeards with Lulu and Lolo. The men had let their hair and beards grow wild. They wore their ragged shirts and trousers and their broken shoes; the girls their tired old dresses, and sunbonnets from which all color had long since faded out. Ning said they could expect a short ride and an easy one. Their journey from San Francisco to Shiny Gulch, with loaded wagons, on a route that led steadily uphill, had taken twelve days. The journey down, with horses lightly packed, should take only six or seven.

They rode down the strip, past men calling that they'd better change their minds and stay, and other men kissing their hands to the girls and lamenting the end of the Calico Palace. They passed Mrs. Posey, scrubbing the pan in which she had fried bacon and pancakes for breakfast. As Mrs. Posey glanced up, Kendra looked the other way. Marny, calmly and deliberately like a bad child, poked out her tongue.

Kendra thought of the day she had come to Shiny Gulch, in the green of May. How different it was now—brown, teeming with people, the hills torn and scarred by men digging for gold. But she had a feeling of homesickness. A chapter in her life had ended. What lay next she did not know, but she did know that when the time came for her to go eastward around Cape Horn she would not be the same girl who had doubled the Horn going west. She would be older, in more than time. And wiser? She hoped so.

Marny cast a wistful look at her old Calico Palace, torn and dirty now, and flapping in the wind. Already men were pulling the tent apart so they could use the canvas to make shelters against the winter storms. "I had a good time there," said Marny. "But never mind. When I get to San Francisco I'm going to open a real palace."

They went past Ellet's trading post, and past a group of Abs dressed up in gaudy junk they had bought for its weight in gold. And on past the turn of the stream, where two loners were silently twirling their pans. Then on, through the blowing dust, out of sight of Shiny Gulch.

Marny glanced around to make sure nobody was near

enough to hear what she was about to say. Moving her horse close to Kendra's, she spoke in a low voice.

"Kendra, on this ride, do something for me."

"Of course," said Kendra. "What do you want?"

Marny spoke with grim humor. "I want a chaperone."

"What on earth—"

"Kendra, don't pretend you're as innocent as an unborn calf. I'm still mad with Delbert and I'm not in the mood for a man. Pocket and Hiram are grand fellows, but they're men. So is Ning. When we put out our bedrolls, stay by me. Stay by me day and night all the way. I don't want any trouble."

Kendra glanced at Pocket and Hiram, busy with the pack-horses. The dry weeds crackled under the horses' hoofs. "Do you really think they'll bother us?"

"Not you, dear. They wouldn't offer you anything but marriage and I don't believe any of them is in a marrying frame of mind. But I'm a doxy."

"You're not!" Kendra exclaimed. "You're a fine person— why call yourself by such an ugly word?"

Marny gave her a stare of mock seriousness. "Dear me, lady, I thought *that* word was real cultured."

Laughing in spite of herself, Kendra promised that they would stay together. After supper that night she laid her bedroll close to Marny's. The men had to take turns keeping awake for guard duty, and as each man was relieved he tumbled down and fell asleep in dusty weariness. This, Marny remarked as Kendra made coffee in the morning, might have been one reason why their own sleep had been untroubled.

That afternoon they reached Mormon Island, now a bustling camp of about two hundred men and a few women. The next day they rode to Sutter's Fort.

The fort had changed. Long before they got there they saw the dust before them hiding the walls like a curtain. From beyond the curtain they could hear yells and shouts and firing of guns and lowing of animals, and when at last they rode into the dust cloud, they found a howling confusion of men and women and mules and cattle and swarms of flies. Most of the men and a good many of the women were drunk. Or at least, from the way they were singing and staggering and quarreling they seemed to be. Kendra saw Marny's hand go to her gun, and wished she had a gun of her own.

Ning said they would not go inside the walls of the fort itself, but would go directly to Smith and Brannan's store, to buy food for themselves and their horses. With him as leader, they made their way through the pandemonium. The Blackbeards fiercely sheltered the Hawaiian girls, while Pocket and Hiram, holding their guns in sight, moved to ride close to Marny and Kendra. Marny murmured, "Thanks for the fireworks, boys." Hiram grinned, and Pocket said softly, "Glad to use 'em any time they're needed, ma'am."

They passed many so-called trading posts—crude shacks or tents or sometimes merely counters set up outdoors. Most of the traders seemed mainly concerned with selling liquor. Piles of bottles lay around, flies buzzed over them and bugs crawled among them, and men in various stages of drunkenness sat or sprawled or lay in sodden heaps on the ground. They called out as the girls rode by. Some of them said "Hi, you beauties!" Others used phrases Kendra had never heard before and hoped she would never hear again.

But when at last they reached Smith and Brannan's, the store looked like an oasis of calm. The building had always been strong, but now the windows had stout wooden bars, and shutters that could be closed and padlocked. At the entrance stood a guard with his gun ready. The men going in and out looked respectable. A few of them were even escorting women, hardy sunbonneted women carrying market baskets.

Ning gave instructions. Hiram and the Blackbeards, with Lulu and Lolo, would stay outside to guard the horses and packs. "Me and Pocket will go in with the other two ladies," Ning went on, "and see about fodder for the horses and somp'n good for Miss Kendra to cook." He smiled at Kendra, such a friendly smile on his whiskery earth-brown face that though she was tired and sweaty and crusted with dust, she smiled back. "And then," said Ning, "we'll stand guard while you folks go in and pick up whatever little things you might need."

They agreed, understanding that the "little things" would be their own deposits of gold dust.

The door guard told the men to put their guns into the holsters before going in. They obeyed, and he let them enter.

The front room was crowded with people and merchandise. Behind the counter stood six clerks, all well armed. One of the clerks was Gene Spencer.

Gene hurried over to serve them. While Ning loudly complained about the prices, Gene drew a box from under the

183

counter and put in beef and bacon, along with squash, potatoes, onions, cans of coffee, and a bag of corn for the horses.

"All right, folks!" he called when the box was full. "Now we'll go into the office and settle up. Come along."

Another clerk stepped out from behind the counter and picked up the box, and they all followed Gene. The office was a small room furnished with a table, a bench, and a strongbox in one corner. On the floor was a stack of ledgers, and on the table were a pen and ink, a candle, and scales for weighing gold. The room was dim and stuffy, for it had only one window, and though the shutters were open, wooden bars were nailed across the window close together, leaving only slits to let in light and air.

The clerk carrying the box set it on the floor. Gene closed the door and locked it. In a low voice he said, "I guess you've come to get your dust."

"Right," said Ning.

"Fine," said Gene. "This is my friend Curtis. We call him Curt."

Curt was a big muscular fellow, and while he did not look surly he did look stern, like a man with an important job to do. Moving to stand near another door, this one evidently leading to a back room, Curt took a pistol from the holster at his belt. He said nothing. He simply stood there.

Gene said to the others, "Take off your guns."

Ning and Pocket and Marny obeyed. Gene raised the lid of the strongbox.

"Put 'em in here."

They obeyed again. Gene spoke to Kendra.

"What about you, Mrs.—er—"

"Call me Kendra," she said, smiling as brightly as she could.

"Well, Kendra," said Gene, using her name quickly as if glad to know what name to use, "haven't you got a gun?"

"No," she answered, "I haven't."

"Better get one, ma'am," said Gene. "It's dangerous country."

Locking the strongbox, he looked around at them all.

"And by the way," he said tersely, "keep your hands in sight. Curt knows all the tricks. If you need something out of your pocket, let me know and I'll take it out for you. Get the point?"

They got the point. While they stood with their hands in

184

front of them, Gene searched among the ledgers until he found the right one. Turning the pages till he came to their names, he sat down on the bench and began to calculate the deposit charges. After a few minutes he stood up.

"Ready, Curt," he said.

Holding his gun in one hand, with the other hand Curt unlocked the door to the back room. Even smaller than the office, this room was airless and midnight dark, for it had no windows at all. Gene lit the candle, and carrying it, he took a step toward the door. "You stay here," he ordered, "with Curt." They stayed, but he had to leave the door open so he could breathe, and by the candlelight they could see what he was doing.

In the back room were three large heavy safes. Setting the candle on the floor, Gene knelt and opened one of these. Inside was a jumble of containers—bags, bottles, tin cans, glass jars, chamber-pots—anything that would hold gold dust. Gene took out a chamber-pot, closed the safe, and got to his feet. Holding the pot in both hands he came into the office, and Curt locked the door behind him.

Gene grinned around at them all. "Ladies first?" he asked.

"Sure," said Ning.

"Start with Kendra?" Gene suggested.

"I haven't anything on deposit here," she said.

Still holding the pot, Gene gave her an astonished look across it. "Why yes you have!" he exclaimed, then as she caught her breath in surprise he said, "You didn't know?"

Kendra shook her head. She looked from Gene to Ning and Pocket and Marny, but they knew no more about it than she did. Pocket spoke to Gene.

"When we brought in the dust, we left Ted's whole share on deposit in his name. Has he been here since then?"

"Why sure," Gene answered. "I thought he'd told you." The pot was heavy, and he set it on the table. Awkwardly patting Kendra's shoulder, he went on, "Tim Bradshaw—I mean Ted—he's not a bad fellow, ma'am. He came to the store one day not long after I got back from Shiny Gulch. Said he'd come to get the dust Pocket and Hiram had put on deposit for him. But he said he wanted only half of it, we were to keep the other half for you."

Kendra felt a choke in her throat. Gene went on.

"When the charge is paid you'll have about two hundred ounces. That's not bad, ma'am—"

185

He said no more because Kendra had crumpled up on the bench and was crying helplessly into her grubby red bandana kerchief. Ted was not a bad fellow. Then what was he? She did not know; her heart was asking more questions than her mind would ever answer.

Ted had run away because he could not face her. But he had left her half his gold. After this, how could she ever reach the tranquility Pocket had promised her, when Ted would hurt her no more because she no longer cared? Oh, life would be so much simpler if people were only good or bad, instead of such a mixture of both.

She heard Ning saying, "Gene, you can put Kendra's dust into one of those coffee cans."

Kendra jerked up her head. "No!" she cried.

Gene was already reaching into the box for one of the cans he had put there to disguise the fact that they would be carrying gold out of the office. "What's wrong?" he asked.

"I don't want it!" she blurted.

Pocket put a gentle hand on her shoulder. "Miss Kendra, you did earn it."

Kendra looked up at him, shaking her head. A tear rolled down and dropped off her chin. "I don't want it," she repeated.

As she spoke she heard Marny say to Pocket, "Let me tell her something. And you—all of you—get back. This is private."

The men drew away. Marny sat on the bench by Kendra and spoke into her ear.

"Kendra, listen to me. Are you listening?"

Her voice was low but forceful. It reminded Kendra that Marny was her friend. "Yes," she said, "I'm listening."

"My dear," said Marny, "this dust, added to what you have already, will give you about three hundred ounces. That's a neat little fortune. Maybe you don't want it, but there's something else you do want."

Kendra looked up. She had begun to be interested. "Yes? What?"

Marny smiled, and her green eyes were wise and cool. "You haven't told the boys," she said, "what you told me about Colonel Taine and your mother. How you've dreaded going back to them because you feel you won't be welcome." Marny spoke impressively. "Kendra, if you come back with three hundred ounces of gold—you'll be welcome."

Kendra gave a start.

Marny said, "Even if the price of gold is down a little, three hundred ounces still means thousands of dollars. More than an army colonel is paid in a year."

Kendra felt a tingle all over. It was exhilarating, like a rubdown after a cold bath. She turned to speak to the others.

"I'll take it," she said. "I'm sorry I made a scene."

"She was a little shocked, that's all," said Marny. "Gene, you can measure the dust."

Gene poured a handful of gold on the scale, added a little, pinched out a little, added a little more, and kept on till he had the right amount. He spread a sheet of newspaper on the table, and from the box of groceries he took a can holding coffee beans. Prying off the lid, he emptied the coffee beans on the newspaper and poured Kendra's gold into the can. This done, he filled the can with coffee, replaced the lid, and brought the can to Kendra.

"Careful," he warned as she held out her hands. "It's heavy."

Kendra took the can, and to her own surprise she began to laugh. How strange, and how laughable, to hold a coffee can that weighed nearly thirteen pounds. She would have to think of more ways of hiding gold. She could put some into her canteen—that was a good idea, gold under the drinking water.

"Will you sign the receipt, please?" asked Gene.

Kendra took up the pen. This was the first time she had been asked to sign her name since she had found that she was not Mrs. Ted Parks. Setting her lips tight, she wrote, "Kendra Logan."

Involuntarily Gene frowned. He had never heard her called Kendra Logan. "Is that your name, ma'am?"

"It is now," said Kendra. She felt suddenly proud of herself, as if she had seized her courage and walked over a shaky bridge.

She moved aside so Marny could take her place by the table. Gene turned a page of the ledger.

"Your friend Delbert brought in the dust, Marny. I guess you know—" he paused questioningly.

"Oh yes, I know," she returned with a smile as she sat down by him. "He brought in eleven hundred and thirty-eight ounces. It was half his and half mine. That means, today I have on deposit here, five hundred and sixty-nine ounces, less the charge."

Gene turned red. Then he turned white. Then his face grew splotchy as if somebody had been pinching it. His hands fidgeted with the pen. He bumbled,

"Gosh, Marny—I don't know what to say—"

Pocket put his hands on the table and leaned forward. With an authority in odd contrast to his usual mildness he ordered,

"Say it, Gene."

Wetting his lips and mopping his forehead, Gene demanded of the air, "What's the matter with me? Why do I always have to bring the bad news?"

Waiting for no more, Pocket turned the ledger around. He looked down at the page and then up at Marny. She met his gaze directly. Pocket said,

"Marny, Delbert left you twenty ounces."

Kendra gasped. Ning let out an ugly word. Gene sighed miserably. Curt, standing by the door to the safe-room, said nothing. His job was to stand guard, not to talk.

Marny's eyes had narrowed to slits. Kendra remembered an angry cat she had seen once, crouching in a corner. The cat's eyes were narrowed like that, with the same baleful green gleam. After a moment of furious silence Marny spoke.

"That means, Delbert stole from me, five hundred and forty-nine ounces." '

Pocket said, "That's what it means, Marny."

Gene mopped his forehead again. "Gee, Marny, how could I know he was stealing it? I thought—he told me—" Poor Gene floundered wretchedly.

"Just what did Delbert tell you, Gene?" she asked in a cold level voice.

"Well—" Gene began, and lost his words again.

"Go on, Gene," ordered Pocket.

Gene doubled his hands into fists as if to give him strength. "Well—the day he got here he brought in his dust and I weighed it and put it in the safe. But the day before we all started up to Shiny Gulch together, Delbert came in again. He told me he'd changed his mind about leaving so much dust. He said he'd been foolish to bring it here, because gambling was a chancy business and the house might have a run of bad luck when it would need plenty of reserves on hand. He said he was going to take back most of what he had put in the safe."

She nodded slowly. "I understand. That was when he had decided to leave me for good and go Lump-hunting."

"He took out all but this twenty ounces," said Gene. "He said this was to take care of you in case the Calico Palace went broke."

Marny's lips moved silently. Kendra suspected that at least part of what Marny was saying about Delbert consisted of words she herself did not know.

"I thought it was—considerate of him to leave you anything," Gene lamented. "Damn, I seem to have bungled things all round. I guess I'm stupid."

Marny laid her hand on his unhappy fist. When she spoke her voice was smooth. "You're no stupider than I was, Gene, when I trusted him in the first place. Now measure what he left me and I won't bother you any more."

Gene spoke from under a burden of guilt. "No, no, I really was a galoot." Suddenly he glowed with righteousness. "I tell you, Marny—to make up, I'll pay the deposit charge on that twenty ounces myself."

"Oh, don't be silly," she retorted. "You did what a bank is supposed to do, you returned a deposit on demand. I'm not destitute. Figure the charge."

Gene glowed even more brightly. This time he had the brightness of one who has earned a reward in heaven without putting himself to any inconvenience on earth. "You're a grand girl, Marny. Next time I come to San Francisco I sure will drop by your place. You'll be having a card parlor there, I suppose?"

"Oh yes. Glad to see you any time." Marny too glowed brightly. Hers was the brightness of one who has gained a friend and a customer. She knew Gene was likely to spend far more in her card parlor than the small deposit charge on twenty ounces.

Gene poured her gold into the weighing pan on the scale. While he concentrated on his task, Pocket gave Marny an admiring smile.

"You're taking it mighty well," said Pocket.

She smiled back at him. "Don't worry," she said. "Somewhere in the world there's some chump of a man who's going to pay me for this. Trust me, Pocket. I'll find him."

189

26

Ning stayed at Sutter's Fort. If they hadn't learned to manage without him by now, he said, they deserved to get hurt. The others went on.

The rest of their journey was hot and tiresome, but not difficult. As they rode down, they met new gold seekers on the way up: men from far places such as the islands beyond Honolulu, and young fellows just mustered out of the volunteer troops. Here and there they saw other men skulking apart, trying to keep trees and bushes between themselves and the beaten track. The volunteers said these were deserters. Some of them were sailors who had run away at their first glimpse of gold dust, leaving their vessels stranded. Others were men who had deserted the army or navy, hoping to pick up fortunes and get out of California before they could be caught.

Because of these and others like them the way back was dangerous, but the men never all slept at once. Marny also took her turn at guard duty. At mealtimes, while Kendra cooked, Marny kept watch so the men could rest. She carried her little gun. "This," she said to them tersely, "may look like a toy. But I assure you, gentlemen, it's not."

Pocket gave her a respectful grin. "I shouldn't like to have you mad with me, Marny," he said.

"I'm not mad with anybody right now," said Marny. "Except Delbert, of course."

But she accepted even Delbert with grim humor. She made up a song, and warbled in her blithe tuneless voice as they rode along.

> "Thought he was wonderful,
> But I was blunderful,
> Now I feel thunderful—
> *Damn!*"

190

"Miss Marny," Pocket said to her, "not only have you got manners like a jaybird, but when you sing, you *sound* like a jaybird."

"What delicate ears you have, Pocket," said Marny. "All right, I'll stop singing. I'll just be glad he's out of my way."

As they made camp the evening before they were to ride into San Francisco, Kendra felt tremulous. Tomorrow she would have to go to Alex and Eva. She broiled the beef, and cooked potatoes and carrots they had brought from the fort, but she had not much appetite.

The next morning she and Marny put on the dresses they had washed and mended at Shiny Gulch and saved for this day. They braided their hair closely, so the wind would not blow it to pieces, and tied on their best sunbonnets. In front of her cracked piece of mirror Kendra decided that she looked well. Her face was darkly tanned, but this only accented her blue eyes, and after these months of rough outdoor living she was as firm and flexible as a young tree. And she had three hundred ounces of gold.

As they left the camping place, Hiram rode beside her. She looked him over—reddish brown hair and beard, hands crusty from work, torn shirt and shabby breeches and broken boots —he was not at all like the spruce young officers who used to ride with her. But she liked him better. Hiram was a person in his own right. One glance at him and you saw his ruggedness, you felt his abounding vitality. Hiram did not try to be impressive. He did not need to.

After a while he spoke to her.

"Kendra."

"Yes?"

"This may be my last chance," said Hiram, "to tell you how great you've been this summer. Kendra, you've got guts."

His words made her throat hurt and her eyes sting. "Thank you, Hiram," she said in a low voice. "You've been a mighty good friend to me."

"I like you," said Hiram. "And I wish you well."

"And I wish you well!" she exclaimed. "Hiram, what are you going to do now?"

"Pocket and Ning and I are planning a business, at the settlement growing up around Sutter's Fort. While Pocket and I are buying tools and equipment in town, Ning will set up the workshop."

"Making what?" she asked.

191

Hiram grinned proudly, like a man with a good idea. "Rockers," he said.

He went on to explain. As she knew, the military leaders had smiled when they first heard the talk of gold. But when they realized that the talk was true, they had written letters to be sent home.

President Polk and Congress were in Washington, and neither Commodore Jones of the navy nor Colonel Mason of the army had authority to send a battleship around Cape Horn merely to carry a letter. But they did the best they could. For couriers, they chose two resourceful young men, Midshipman Beale and Lieutenant Loeser. Beale and Loeser were now on their way. They were traveling separately, but their orders were the same: Go by any route you can, no matter how often you have to turn on your tracks. Take any means of travel you can find, no matter what you have to pay for it. Only get there. Get there and tell them the news.

"And when the news gets around," said Hiram, "can't you imagine what it's going to be like? Men will start coming here from the States the way they're coming now from the islands. So we're taking a hint from Sam Brannan. Right in front of the placers we'll have a shopful of rockers, ready made."

Hiram's strong confident smile shone at her through his rusty beard.

"I told you," he said, "I came to California to seek my fortune. I meant it. I still mean it."

"You have a thousand ounces of gold!" she exclaimed.

"I want more than a thousand ounces," he returned quietly. "I want ten thousand. I want to be *rich*, Kendra."

She looked him up and down, thoughtfully. "You will be, Hiram. You're the kind of man that gets what he wants."

He flashed her another smile. "I hope you're right."

Pocket and Marny came riding up, to discuss the problem of where they would all sleep tonight. Men they had met on the way had said San Francisco was crowded to the bursting point. Pocket suggested that they rent space in a vacant lot, and set up a tent if they could buy one. If they could not get a tent they would simply have to spread their bedrolls in the open.

While they talked, Kendra was making up her mind that Marny was not going to sleep on the ground again. Marny could share her room in the house on Stockton Street. Alex and Eva would know nothing about her except that she was a friend from Shiny Gulch, and by the time they learned more Marny would have had a chance to find a place of her own.

The track made a turn, toward the yellow-brown hills half swathed in mist. Now they could see San Francisco, growing like a toadstool and just as ugly. As they came nearer they could see it more plainly, the gaunt slopes, the shacks and shanties and tents stuck over them like bugs on a pile of potatoes. Then as they climbed a hill they saw the deserted vessels swinging at anchor in the bay.

Because of the fog and the curving shoreline they could not be sure how many there were, but Kendra thought there must be thirty or forty of them. The crews had run off to the gold fields, and here stood their argosies, helpless and forlorn. She looked at Hiram, and they both shook their heads.

The track led across the sandbanks at the southern end of town and brought them into Kearny Street. The street was crowded with men who all seemed to be going somewhere in a hurry. Most of them wore red shirts and dark corduroy breeches, and carried picks and shovels over their shoulders. Among them were a few frontiersmen in buckskins, and traders in business suits, and miners in scraps and tatters, just back from the hills, and in this last rag-tag group were undoubtedly some of the richest men in town.

Wagons and handcarts and wheelbarrows creaked by, horses and mules thudded over the choppy ground; in empty lots men stood on barrels, surrounded by bales of goods which they were offering for sale in thunderous voices; and the men in the street all seemed to be talking, shouting to be heard above the din. Kendra thought of her first ride through these streets, in the days when nothing ever happened in San Francisco.

They saw the unfinished buildings Foxy had told them about. Saws were still in the boards, hammers lay unclaimed, nails were rusting on the half-made floors. A few men were working on a few buildings, but only a few. Along the street, signs offered jobs to cooks, waiters, bartenders, men to cut wood or take care of horses. But remembering how she had felt when she found her nugget, Kendra understood why few men wanted regular jobs. When a man worked for wages he knew what to expect. At the placers, any day something wonderful might happen.

They stopped in a lot next to an unfinished building. Hiram and Pocket said they would go on to Chase and Fenway's

193

and put their dust on deposit. When they came back they would guard the packhorses while the Blackbeards went to deposit their own dust. As soon as the Blackbeards returned, Hiram added, he would ride with Kendra up the hill and see her safely to the home of Colonel and Mrs. Taine.

Meanwhile, Hiram continued, didn't Kendra and Marny want their dust put on deposit too?

"I'll go with you," said Marny.

"Don't you trust us?" asked Pocket.

Smiling sweetly, Marny shook her head.

"Do you trust us, Kendra?" Hiram asked.

"Yes," she answered. "But—" She put her hand on his arm. "Deposit it in the name of Kendra Logan. Explain why I want it that way. And tell them I don't want to talk about it."

"Right," said Hiram.

Kendra gave him the saddlebag where she had carried her gold, and watched the three of them ride away. Lulu and Lolo and the Blackbeards had dismounted, and were making a lunch of beef and hardtack from their supply bag. Lolo's Blackbeard—Troy—came over and asked Kendra to join them, but she declined. She had something else to do.

She was going to ride up the hill now, without waiting for Hiram. She did not want anybody with her when she had to face Alex and Eva and tell them about the wreck of her marriage.

She turned her horse. Troy urged her to wait, but Kendra shook her head. She was a determined person when her mind was made up, and it was made up now. She rode out of the lot and along Kearny Street to the corner of Clay, and here she started up the hill. She remembered that she had once said it was like riding up the side of a steeple.

Along Clay Street she saw new signs, new shacks and sheds, and new groups of men talking about gold. The men looked at her with curiosity but they did not stop talking.

The porch of the City Hotel was full of men. In front a sign announced that a South American brig, now in the bay, would be sold at auction this afternoon. "Just right," a man was shouting, "for taking supplies to the camps!"

In the plaza she could see more signs, offering more deserted vessels and their cargoes "for cash or gold dust." Around the army barracks in the plaza she saw no soldiers, and she recalled what she had been told about desertions.

194

She came to Stockton Street. Here, high above the water-front, the air smelled damp and clean as she remembered it. She had an odd, surprising sense of coming home.

She rode past the dwarf oak where Captain Pollock had left his horse when he came to call, the day after he arrived from Honolulu. As she looked toward their little square white house she felt a flutter, wondering if Alex or Eva would be on the porch. But as she looked, she started and caught her breath.

The porch was full of men. Most of them had on red shirts and corduroy breeches.

In front of the house several horses were waiting at the hitching post. As she drew near, a big bearded fellow came down the steps and was about to mount one of the horses when he caught sight of her. Astonished, he pulled off his hat and bowed, exclaiming, "Howdy, ma'am!" As she stopped her horse he inquired with rough politeness, "Looking for somebody, ma'am?"

"Yes—thank you," said Kendra, wondering if she was showing how bewildered she felt. "I'm looking for Colonel Taine."

"Colonel?" the man repeated with a frown.

"Colonel Alexander Taine. Doesn't he live here?"

Slowly, the stranger shook his head. "Not that I know of, ma'am. Still, I've just come down on a boat from Oregon, I wouldn't be sure." Turning, he called to the others, several of whom had now come down the steps. "Any of you folks know of a colonel living around here?"

He received nothing but head-shakings. Another man suggested,

"Might ask Mrs. Beecham." He said to Kendra, "They come and go, ma'am. You know how it is in a boarding house."

Kendra started with dismay. "Is this a boarding house?"

"Yes ma'am," said still another fellow in a red shirt. "Run by Mr. and Mrs. Beecham. But there's no army officers living here."

They all seemed eager to help, or at least to take part in the puzzle. Somebody had gone indoors to bring Mrs. Beecham, and now she came across the porch, a strong lean woman in a gingham apron.

Mrs. Beecham was brusque, but not unkind. She had never heard of Colonel Taine. She and her husband had come down

195

from Oregon in a wagon. Hadn't known about gold before they left home, but when they got here they figured there was need of a good eating place so they bought this house from Mr. Riggs—

"Mr. Riggs!" Kendra exclaimed. "I know him. I'll ride to his house and ask."

Mrs. Beecham shook her head. "It's not his house any more, lady. It's another boarding house, run by Mrs. Fairfax. The Riggses sold these houses because they were joining a train of Mormons leaving for the Salt Lake. That was quite a spell back—I guess you've been away?"

Kendra had heard the saying "her heart sank." She had never known what it meant. But now she felt as if there were a lump in her chest, heavy, sinking.

"Yes," she said, "I've been away."

She looked up at Eva's little calico palace. All at once she felt homesick for Eva's bright curtains and bedspreads, the rugs she had braided for the floor, the gay flowered cushions she had stuffed for the chairs. —Oh why, thought Kendra, why don't we appreciate things while we have them?

At this moment a gentleman came to the steps. As Kendra saw him, the word in her mind was *gentleman*.

He looked like a man who would be at home in the best hotels, a man who liked money and horses and beautiful women and was an expert on all three. Among these backwoodsmen and red-shirted miners he was like a fine sword among a lot of hunting knives. Though not conspicuously tall he was strongly built; he wore a suit of good cloth and cut; his age was probably somewhere near forty. About the last it was hard to be sure, because while his face was still youthful his hair was almost perfectly white. It was thick wavy hair, not yet receding from his forehead, and its whiteness was made more striking by his dark eyebrows and dark eyes, and a deep outdoor tan suggesting that he had not been long in San Francisco.

But he had not come down from the mines; those well-kept hands of his had never wielded a pick and shovel. As he drew near Kendra, his eyes gave her that flash of appreciation which is in no way rude but is merely a man's instinctive tribute to a comely woman. He spoke to her gravely.

"Good morning, madam. My name is Warren Archwood. Perhaps I can be of assistance."

His calm courtesy was reassuring. "Thank you!" she exclaimed, and added by way of explanation, "Mrs. Taine is my mother."

"I was about to suggest," said Mr. Archwood, "that you inquire at the army headquarters. The whereabouts of a colonel must certainly be known there."

"The army headquarters—of course!" said Kendra. "Is it still where it used to be?"

The wind blew a lock of Mr. Archwood's white hair across his brown forehead. As he pushed back the lock he said with a smile,

"I don't know where it used to be, but I doubt that it's still in the same place. Everything in San Francisco is moving and changing. However, I know where it is now, in a cottage on Montgomery Street." He drew his riding gloves from his pocket. "I'll ride down there with you."

"You don't have to do that!" Kendra protested. "I can find it."

"You are too young," said Mr. Archwood, "and—pardon me—too pleasing, to go about alone. My horse is here, still saddled. I'll go with you."

Without more conversation he mounted one of the horses at the hitching post. They started riding. To keep the conversation away from herself Kendra said,

"You seem to know your way about, Mr. Archwood."

"I'm forced to be idle," he explained genially, "so I've been exploring the town." He told her he had come from New York on the ship *Huntress*, which she could see in the bay. He had brought a shipment of goods, part consigned to Chase and Fenway, the rest to a firm in Honolulu. But the *Huntress* could not go on to Honolulu because her crew had run away.

"We left New York last April," said Mr. Archwood. "How could we have known what to expect?"

—Last April, thought Kendra. That's when I was getting married to Ted. How could I have known what to expect?

Thinking of that happy time, she remembered Eva's telling her that when she and Ted got tired of California they could come home on one of the government-sponsored steamboats. Aloud she said to Mr. Archwood,

"Maybe you can go home on one of the passenger steamers. Congress authorized those last year, to run up and down both coasts."

"Yes, I know," he returned. "They were laying the keels for those steamers when I left New York. The first one should

197

get here before long. But—" he smiled quizzically, looking at the deserted vessels in the bay—"will she get out?"

Kendra returned his smile. He was so friendly and so courteous, he was making her feel more cheerful every minute. "With all you have on your mind," she said, "it's good of you to help me find my family."

As she spoke she realized that this was the first time she had ever called Alex and Eva her "family." Mr. Archwood, with casual good humor, was saying,

"My plight is not as sorry as you think. I really came to the Pacific for the adventure of it. The business could easily have been handled by somebody else."

He told her his wife had died several years ago, leaving no children. In New York he had not been exactly lonely, for he had many friends, but he had grown tired of the same restaurants, the same theaters, the same hotels. He liked travel, but he had already visited most of the interesting places on both sides of the Atlantic. So he had decided that this time he would travel the other way.

"I wanted something surprising," he said. "True, what I found is more surprising than I could have imagined, but I'm enjoying it."

On Montgomery Street he guided her to the cottage he had spoken of. An army private stood on the porch, leaning against the wall by the door. He did not look like the smart young soldiers Kendra had seen last spring; he needed a shave and haircut, and his uniform had a bedraggled air. Mr. Archwood went with her up the steps. The private came to meet them.

"This lady," said Mr. Archwood, "is looking for Colonel Taine."

"Colonel Taine?" the soldier repeated doubtfully. But as he spoke his face brightened. "Oh, are you Mrs. Parks?"

Kendra winced at the name. "I am Mrs. Taine's daughter."

"Oh yes ma'am, we've been expecting you. If you'll wait here, I'll speak to Lieutenant Vernon."

In all this strangeness, it was good to hear a name she knew. She thanked the soldier with a smile as he turned to go indoors.

When Vernon came out she saw that he too was different. He was not unkempt, but his boots were worn and his uniform frayed, and his face had lines of weariness. He addressed her and Archwood politely, but without the eagerness of those

198

days when nothing ever happened in San Francisco. Today he was simply too tired.

"I hope you and Ted had a good summer at the mines," he said.

"Well enough," she answered, and changed the subject. "Can you tell me where to find my mother?"

"Ah—then you didn't get her letter?"

Kendra felt a sudden alarm. "Letter? What letter?"

"She gave it to a man setting out for the placers," said Vernon. "He said he might go to Shiny Gulch, but evidently he didn't. But don't worry," he went on. "The letter isn't lost. Mrs. Taine thought he might not find you, so she left a copy here."

Kendra was feeling a chill all over. "But where is she?"

"Colonel Taine was transferred," said Vernon, "to Fort Monroe." At her look of bafflement he explained, "Hampton Roads, Virginia."

Kendra heard herself echoing, as though from the bottom of a well, "Hampton Roads, Virginia."

He might as well have said "Zanzibar."

27

She thought of the runaway crews. "How did they get out of San Francisco?"

"The order came before the place was quite as crazy as it is now," said Vernon. "Colonel and Mrs. Taine took a schooner to Monterey, and sailed from there. I'll bring you the letter."

He went indoors again. Mr. Archwood began to chat with the private, giving Kendra a chance to adjust to what he recognized as a stunning blow.

Kendra turned away from them, and stood twisting her hands together. She had an eerie sense of having been here before. It was that old feeling of being in the way, unloved, the child nobody wanted.

Vernon brought her Eva's letter. The letter was addressed

199

to "Mrs. Ted Parks." When they took ship for the other side of the continent, it had not occurred to Alex and Eva that she might want to go with them. They had thought she was securely married.

Vernon still thought so. Right now he was saying he wished he could stay with her and hear about the adventures she and Ted had been having at Shiny Gulch. But he could not take the time. The ranks were so depleted by desertions that the loyal men had more duties than they could possibly take care of. He smiled wearily. "Remember how we used to complain of nothing to do?"

Kendra tried to smile back.

Vernon went in. She stood where she was, feeling like one of those deserted ships in the bay.

But something inside her head began to demand of her,

—What's so awful about it? You never did like living with Alex and your mother anyway. You have three hundred ounces of gold. You can go to Chase and Fenway's and ask them where to rent a room, then you can think about what to do next.

She told Mr. Archwood she would like to go to Chase and Fenway's. Again he said he would go with her. Again, though she protested, she was glad to have him.

As they rode, she looked up at his bright dark eyes, his tanned face under the white hair. He was not asking her any questions and she was grateful, but she said,

"Mr. Archwood, you are so kind—I should give you an explanation."

He answered quietly, "You don't need to. I think I know what the trouble is."

"But how can you?" she exclaimed.

"I heard the soldier call you Mrs. Parks," he said, "and I saw the name on your mother's letter. A man who had dinner at Mrs. Beecham's table a few days ago, told me about you. He had been at Shiny Gulch, heard the story from a friend of yours—"

"A *friend?*"

"Why yes—a Mrs. Cosey, Mosey, Posey—"

"I call her Mrs. Nosey and I hope she falls down the gulch and breaks her fat neck!" Trembling with anger, Kendra told him about Mrs. Posey's eavesdropping. "My name is Kendra Logan. And it's terrible to have everybody in town concerned with my private life!"

To her amazement, Archwood began to laugh.

"Now what is it?" she demanded.

"Dear lady, I'm laughing at your fears. Nobody is concerned with your private life. They're concerned with gold, and how to get their cargoes unloaded, and gold, and how to man their vessels, and gold, and gold, and gold. I heard what that man said, but I wouldn't have thought of it again if I hadn't met you. He was a harmless lout—I believe his name was Turner."

Kendra remembered the fellow named Frank Turner at Shiny Gulch, who had asked her to marry him. She wondered how much her story had been garbled by the time he told it.

They reached Chase and Fenway's. In the store a dozen men were buying supplies for the mines. Mr. Chase and Mr. Fenway were both there, and a clerk she had not seen before. As she and Archwood came in, Mr. Chase called a greeting. A few minutes later he and Mr. Fenway came to meet them.

Mr. Chase said Hiram Boyd had been in, and had told him about—well, Hiram had said she didn't want to discuss it but he sure was sorry things hadn't worked out. Mr. Fenway shook his head and sighed, as if he had expected no better.

And now, Mr. Chase inquired, what could they do for her?

"I'd like some advice," said Kendra. "Or are you too busy?"

"Not a bit of it," exclaimed Mr. Chase. "Watson!" he bawled to the clerk. "Take care of things."

They all four went into the office, and Mr. Chase gave them chairs by the desk. As he sat down he pulled out a bandana and mopped his forehead. It was a pleasure to rest a minute, he said. A man had to do his own work these days. You couldn't get help, or when you could, you had to pay them outrageous wages to keep them down from the gold fields. That clerk Ralph Watson, good fellow but—oh well, no use complaining. "Now what is it you want to know, Miss Kendra?"

Kendra asked where she could rent a room.

Mr. Chase, Mr. Fenway, and Mr. Archwood looked at each other. Mr. Chase shuffled his feet uncomfortably. Then, as if with an inspiration, he said,

"Archwood, didn't you buy some property?"

Regretfully, Archwood explained his situation. Like Hiram,

201

he foresaw a rush to California as the gold news spread around, and like Hiram he meant to take advantage of it. He had bought two lots, to hold for rising prices. But one of these, on Kearny Street facing the plaza, was vacant. The other, around the corner on Washington Street, had a small wooden dwelling, but before he bought it this house had been rented to four miners who had come down to rest and get cured of scurvy before going back to dig more gold. The men were still living there. They had paid the rent in advance and they refused to get out.

For the present, at Mrs. Beecham's boarding house, Archwood said he was sleeping on a cot in a room he shared with three other men. Mrs. Beecham had crowded cots into every room of the house, and served meals on a table set up on the back porch. Mr. and Mrs. Beecham slept in what used to be the kitchen, and she cooked outdoors.

Mr. Chase said he and Mrs. Chase would have been glad to have Kendra stay with them, but their house was full. They had three bedrooms. One of these was occupied by Mrs. Chase and himself, another by their three sons. The third—the room where Alex and Eva had stayed last spring so Kendra and Ted could have the house on Stockton Street —was now sheltering two unfortunate friends of Mr. Chase. They were traders who had brought some goods up from Valparaiso and could not go back because their vessel was stranded in the bay. Also living in the house was a young woman from Oregon. Her husband had left her to go gold hunting, and she had pled to be allowed to do housework in return for a place to live. They had put a mattress for her on the floor of a clothes closet.

"And by the way," said Mr. Chase, "you've got some clothes in that closet, Miss Kendra. A trunk your mother asked us to keep for you, things that were too nice for you to take to Shiny Gulch."

He spoke hopefully, and she guessed that in the crowded state of his home, the sooner she removed her trunk the happier he would be. She managed to say, "Thank you, I'll take the clothes as soon as I have a place to put them."

Mr. Chase mopped his forehead again. Mr. Fenway gloomily said nothing.

Mr. Chase explained that Mr. Fenway had long boarded with a married couple named Brunswick. He still had his room, but he was now paying them ten times what he had

202

paid last spring, to keep Mrs. Brunswick from crowding a lot of other men into the room with him.

Of course, continued Mr. Chase, he was not going to let Miss Kendra sleep in the street. If she couldn't find any other place, his wife would put up some sort of couch somewhere—

Mr. Chase paused helplessly. He wanted to be kind, but it was plain he thought his burdens were too great for his strength.

Kendra was tired. She was sick with discouragement. She wanted to break down and cry.

"Well now, well, well," said the doleful voice of Mr. Fenway.

Mr. Fenway's long spidery body was sprawled over his chair. His face would have befitted a man viewing a shipwreck.

"Miss Kendra," droned Mr. Fenway, "can stay right here."

His hearers all brightened with surprise. "Where, Fenway?" demanded Mr. Chase.

"In Loren's room," Mr. Fenway said solemnly. "Loren works for us," he said to Kendra. "Maybe you didn't know. He lives upstairs. Right now he's in Honolulu, buying goods for us. You can have his room till he comes back."

Kendra gasped her thanks. Mr. Chase rubbed his hands delightedly. Fine idea, he exclaimed. And quite respectable. There was another room upstairs, occupied by the clerk Watson, and Watson was a married man and his wife was with him. "Now is there anything else, Miss Kendra?"

The promise of a bed to sleep in tonight was so cheering that Kendra felt strong again. "I'd like to have my friend Marny stay with me," she said.

Mr. Chase frowned. "Marny?"

"She's been here before," said Kendra. "In fact she came in a little while ago, with Pocket and Hiram Boyd."

Mr. Chase's round jovial face had gone dark with shock. "Oh now, Miss Kendra! What my wife would say!"

"Who is Marny?" Mr. Archwood asked with interest.

Kendra did not answer him. She was answering Mr. Chase.

"I've been in trouble, Mr. Chase," she said, "and Marny has been my friend. If I have a place to stay I'm not going to let her sleep on the ground."

"Miss Kendra, honestly—if my wife thought I was letting in a woman like that—" He stopped, his pudgy hands fluttering.

There was a moment of silence. It was broken by the languid voice of Mr. Fenway.

"Marny can stay here," he said.

"Now, Fenway—"

"Marny seems to me like a pleasant sort of girl," droned Mr. Fenway. "And if Miss Kendra wants to help her out, I think it's a right neighborly thing to do."

Kendra heard him with new respect. She had thought he was the backward member of the partnership. But it was Mr. Fenway who had offered her Loren's room, and Mr. Fenway who was now telling Mr. Chase to stop worrying about his wife. Kendra gave him a grateful smile. Mr. Fenway did not smile back; that would have been too much trouble. In his mournful manner he said, "Well, I guess that's settled."

Mr. Chase sighed and yielded. "If my wife ever finds out—"

"Maybe," Mr. Fenway suggested gloomily, "you'll find she's got more sense than you think." Slowly, as if it were a great effort, he began to stand up. "Well, I guess we'd better get back to work. Archwood, if you'll come with us you can bring Miss Kendra her key."

They went out, and in a few minutes Mr. Archwood came back with the key. "Mr. Fenway says you are to use the staircase leading up from the storeroom. At the top you'll see two doors. The door on the left leads to the room of Mr. and Mrs. Watson, the one on the right is yours." As he handed her the key he added smiling, "I admired the way you stood up for your friend."

"I thought it was good of Mr. Fenway to say she could stay here," Kendra answered. "I was surprised, though, that Mr. Chase gave in so fast."

Archwood gave her a glance of wise amusement. "Mr. Fenway," he said, "owns the ground this building stands on. Mr. Chase doesn't."

Kendra began to laugh, and Archwood laughed too.

"May I come back tomorrow," he asked, "and see how you are?"

She told him he certainly could. Mr. Archwood walked with her through the main store and the storeroom to the stairs at the back. As he left her, Kendra felt another wrench of homesickness. She remembered what fun she and Ted used to have as they chose groceries here in the storeroom, how they used to talk and talk—

—Stop it, she ordered herself, stop it!

She hurried up the stairs, and at the top she unlocked the door to Loren's room. As she went in, she realized that she and Marny were fortunate indeed.

The room was probably as comfortable a place as she could have found in San Francisco. In front of her was a real bed with mattress and pillows; at one side a washstand, and tilted against the wall, a metal bathtub. She also saw a wardrobe and chest of drawers, a table with a chair beside it, and a bookcase full of books. And with delight she observed, pushed into a corner, a charcoal brazier, small but adequate if she wanted to heat water, brew coffee, or fry bacon.

Oh, Mr. Fenway was kind to let her and Marny stay here. She hoped Loren would not mind their using his room.

Then suddenly she remembered that this had not always been Loren's room. Before Loren, this had been Ted's room. Ted had slept in that bed, had sat in that chair. She felt tears burning her eyes.

—Oh Ted, Ted, she thought desperately, won't I ever get away from you? Why does it hurt so much? Why does love cling like this? Why won't it *go?*

28

With a great effort she pushed Ted out of her thoughts. —Get busy, she told herself.

She found bedclothes in the chest of drawers, made the bed, and started out to bring water from the well behind the store. Halfway down the stairs she heard a commotion in the front room and an angry voice shouting her name. When she went to see what was going on she found Hiram storming around, demanding to be told if anybody knew where she was. At sight of her he grabbed her shoulder, exclaiming that he had been looking for her all over town and what did she mean by going off without him? Kendra told him how Mr. Archwood had helped her. Hiram made it plain that he thought she had been a blundering fool to need, or take, any help but his own.

He did, however, have the grace to say he was glad she and Marny would have sleeping quarters, because nothing was so hard to find in this demented town as a tent fit for human occupation. He said he would bring Marny to the store.

In a little while he was back, with Marny and the makings of a dinner. In a better humor now, he built a fire outdoors near the well and did the cooking himself. Kendra had observed already that most people in San Francisco now did their cooking outdoors. Sleeping space was too precious to be wasted on kitchens as long as the rains held back.

After dinner Hiram went off, taking their horses to a livery stable for safekeeping, while the girls carried water up to their room and washed off the dust of the day. Then at last, wearing the battered remains of what had once been nightgowns, they had a chance to talk. Lying on the bed with the pillows at her back, Kendra described her search and her meeting with Mr. Archwood.

Marny sat by the table, idly shuffling a deck of cards. As the story ended she stood up. Going to a window she raised the shade and stood looking down at San Francisco—lights fluttering from tents and shanties, dust blowing in the wind, men sleeping in the dust because they had nowhere else to sleep. "Kendra," Marny said after a moment, "are you interested in Mr. Archwood?"

"Interested?" repeated Kendra. "What do you mean?"

"You know what I mean. The way a woman gets interested in a man."

Kendra started. "Of course not!"

"Well," said Marny, "I am."

Kendra gave a little gasp of surprise. "But—you've never even seen him!"

"This time last year," said Marny, "I'd never seen a gold strike. But when I heard of one, I was interested."

Kendra sat up. "I thought you weren't in the mood for a man."

"I wasn't. I am now. For Mr. Archwood, that is. But you saw him first. Do you want him?"

"For heaven's sake," exclaimed Kendra, "no!"

"You made a good impression on him," Marny reminded
206

her. "If you should give him any encouragement he might want to get married."

"Oh, stop!" Kendra said shortly.

"Wait a minute, Kendra. This town is delirious and it's going to get worse. And it may be months before any of these vessels get out of the bay. You can't go back to the States now. A man is a mighty good thing to have around."

"I don't want a man."

"Kendra, *think*. I'm giving you first chance. Do you want Mr. Archwood?"

"No."

"Sure?"

"Yes."

"Well then," said Marny, "I do."

She gathered up the cards from the table, played with them a moment, laid them down, and turned from the window. Almost as if to herself she murmured,

" 'An army have I mustered in my thoughts
Wherewith already France is overrun . . .' "

"What's that?" asked Kendra. "More Shakespeare?"

"Yes."

"Marny, what are you up to now?"

Marny answered slowly, as if thinking while she talked.

"Well, dear, at present I'm—what might be called—an unemployed adventuress."

She picked up the cards again and looked down at them as she went on.

"Delbert really gave me a jolt when he went off with that dust of mine. It takes capital to start a new Calico Palace and I'm not sure I have enough. Mr. Archwood sounds like just what I need."

Thoughtfully, she began to review his charms.

"Money to invest. Manners of a gentleman. No wife to clutter things up. Owns a vacant lot. And the lot faces the plaza—ideal place for a gambling parlor. He has to wait here until some of those runaway sailors come back, so he might as well use the time. And he came to California looking for experiences."

Kendra thought again that Marny was really like a cat. A charming and lovable cat, to be sure; but even the most lovable cat had a genius for finding the warmest spot in the room, and taking it. After a moment of silence Marny fanned the cards in her beautifully expert fashion and snapped them together again.

"Kendra," she said, "I think your friend Mr. Archwood is about to fall in love."

The next morning they woke to find the sun already sending darts through the mist. It was going to be a cheerful day. While coffee steamed on the brazier Marny made a proposal.

On a day like this, she said, dining outdoors would be a frolic instead of merely something they had to do. Hadn't Archwood told Kendra he would come by to see how she was? When he arrived, would Kendra invite him to dinner? "I'll provide the food and drinks," said Marny, "and help in every way I can."

Kendra had never been asked to help a doxy get a man. She was fascinated, and at the same time uncertain how to play her part. "But at dinner," she said—"will you want me there?"

"Oh yes," said Marny. "Let's invite Hiram and Pocket, and make it a party. We'll carry the brazier outside, and have charcoal broiled steaks—right? And do you need any clothes? When I went to Shiny Gulch I left a trunk in a warehouse belonging to the New York Store."

Kendra told her about the trunk Eva had put in care of Mrs. Chase. Marny said she would hire a cart and bring this at the same time as her own.

She brought the trunks; she also brought steaks, potatoes, and yellow squash; bread and butter, and some really excellent French wine she had procured by telling Mr. Fenway she wanted the best no matter what it cost. She said Hiram and Pocket would be here. In fact, they were already here. She had not told them that the purpose of the dinner was to enchant Mr. Archwood, but she had told them they were to dine on charcoal broiled steaks. They had come over with some tall sticks and several bolts of mosquito netting. Now they were making a pavilion, in which dinner could be cooked and served without bother from flies.

Kendra went down with Marny to look. "It's luxury!" she exclaimed, while Marny said, "I love you all," and meant it.

The men finished the pavilion and went off to buy new shirts for the party. Kendra was unpacking her trunk when Serena Watson, wife of the clerk, came up to tell her Mr. Archwood was in the store.

Kendra went down. Marny had told her what to do.

She led Mr. Archwood into the storeroom, where there was less bustle than in front. They sat on goods-boxes, while Kendra thanked him again for his help yesterday and said she and Marny were quite comfortable in the room over the store. After a few minutes' talk she asked him if he would not come to an early dinner this afternoon and meet the friends who had been with her at Shiny Gulch. Mr. Archwood accepted gladly, saying the meals at Mrs. Beecham's were pretty dull.

"We'll have dinner behind the store, by the well," said Kendra. "This way, I'll show you."

They went out by the back door. And there, on a bench by the well, demurely hemming a handkerchief, was Marny.

Marny wore a dress of plain gray muslin. She knew the value of simplicity, and besides, she wanted Archwood to notice herself and not her clothes. The sunlight made flashes in her hair, and as she stitched, her deft freckled hands were all grace. Kendra introduced Mr. Archwood. Marny greeted him like a perfect lady. While she went on sewing, they chatted about the welcome bright weather, and she said she was glad he was coming to dinner.

In a few minutes Mr. Archwood was aglow with happy surprise. From the arguments between Messrs. Chase and Fenway yesterday, he had learned enough about Marny to be interested. But Chase and Fenway had not spoken of her exciting figure, her green eyes and red hair and freckles. And they had not said—they did not know—that when she felt like it Marny could blend her tempting looks with the manner of a young lady from a finishing school. Mr. Archwood wanted to know her better.

They had dinner at five o'clock. Kendra and Marny had set up the brazier in the pavilion, and built a campfire to cook the vegetables. For seating they had spread their old bedrolls on the ground; for napkins they had bought some unbleached muslin and cut it into squares. Their plates were miners' eating-pans; their forks and spoons were cut from cattle horns; their knives were the sort miners were demanding these days, small and sharp, equally useful for slicing steak, scraping gold out of a crack in the rocks, or slitting a man's throat.

Kendra thought the whole scene had a wild splendor—the great sunset over the hills, the smoke wandering up through the mosquito net, Archwood with his urbane elegance and the other men in their red shirts and corduroy pants; the firelight flickering on Marny's hair and on her hands as she poured the wine. Kendra herself had put on one of the frilly aprons she used to wear when she served the officers Alex brought home to dinner. Here by the campfire it gave her a piquant charm.

Archwood sat on a bedroll eating steak from a pan, sipping burgundy from a tin cup, and for the first time really sharing the excitement of California gold. He had never seen a placer. He had no idea how a man twirled a pan to part the sand from the gold flakes. He did not know what a rocker was. He asked a hundred questions and the others liked answering. Hiram and Pocket told him about their scheme to set up shop at Sutter's Fort.

When they talked about Sutter, Archwood's eyes widened with surprise. Now, instead of being merely a listener, he had some news of his own. As he heard of Sutter's grandiose tales he began to laugh.

Expelled from Switzerland for his free opinions? A soldier in the guard of the king of France?

He told them a fellow passenger of his on the ship *Huntress* had been Sutter's son Johann, and young Johann had never heard any of this. Johann said his father had run away from home because he was about to be jailed for debt. He had left a wife and four children behind him. For fourteen years they had not heard from him, not until last year when he had sent them a letter saying he was now lord of a great property in California. Young Johann had set out for the new country, to see what his father was really doing here.

Archwood's hearers, who had suspected something of the sort, laughed merrily.

Neither of the girls talked much, but they were both enjoying the party. Kendra was happy because again, as at Shiny Gulch, she was needed. Without her there would have been no party. Marny too was happy. While the men talked she listened with a warm amusing friendliness, the way of a woman used to liking people and having them like her back. She did not need words. She was there, and every man of them knew it.

When the main meal was over Kendra rinsed the tin cups and poured coffee. Marny produced more tin cups and poured brandy. Archwood and Hiram accepted, Pocket as usual shook his head. The brandy was of equal quality with the burgundy she had served earlier.

For a while they lingered around the fire, talking with lazy after-dinner enjoyment. When the sunset was fading into the dark, Archwood said it was time to go. Outside the pavilion he drew Kendra aside. After thanking her for the best meal he had had since he left New York, he again offered his services in any way he might be of use in the days ahead. He spoke sincerely. She had no doubt that he liked her. But she noticed with amusement that it was Marny he was speaking to when he asked if he might call again.

When he had gone out of sight Marny said to Kendra, "You did the cooking, so now it's our turn. Go on upstairs. The boys and I will clear up."

Pocket was already drawing water from the well, Hiram building up the fire to heat it. Kendra gratefully left them to their task. They cleared up, and Marny and Hiram finished the brandy.

29

Archwood did call again, the next day. This time he and Marny sat together on the bench by the well and she told him about her plan to open a gambling parlor.

For several days, in long conversations on the bench, they talked it over. Marny made him a clear business proposition. While she let him know that the proposition included her own dramatic self, primarily she offered him a chance to make money. Archwood liked to make money, but hitherto his interests had lain in the fields of commerce. He had been into gambling parlors only as a player. Until now he had never thought of himself as concerned with one.

But Marny's offer promised the adventure he had been looking for. And Marny herself would have been an adventure even without the gambling parlor. However, Archwood was in no hurry.

"Answer me this," he said. "And speak the truth. I can usually tell when people are lying. Do you run a straight table?"

Marny's eyes looked squarely into his. "Yes," she said.

Archwood looked back at her with an unswerving gaze. "Always?"

"Yes," said Marny.

"Why?"

"Several reasons. For one thing, I don't want to get shot. For another, when you cheat there's no fun in the game. But mainly I don't cheat because I don't need to."

Archwood was smiling shrewdly. "Go on. You were about to say something else. Why don't you 'need to'?"

"Because I can win by my wits," said Marny. "I have card sense. That's a talent. Either you have it or you haven't. And I can remember which cards have turned up. In plain words, I'm good."

He was laughing, with admiration. "I like that. I mean, I like you for saying it. I've no use for people who belittle themselves."

"And I have the surest hands in the business," said Marny. "Look."

Holding out one hand, she showed him. In the curve between her thumb and forefinger, where most people have only a bit of cushiony flesh, years of practice had given Marny a muscle like a steel spring.

"You *are* good," he said.

"Yes," said Marny. "Some things I can't do. I can't cook, I can't play a piano or sing a tune. But when I deal cards, I never make a mistake."

Archwood was convinced. Within two weeks after he and Marny had met each other, workmen were leveling a spot at one side of Archwood's empty lot on Kearny Street. Marny told Kendra they planned to set up a small tent in this corner. Thus she could go into business promptly, and continue while they were putting up larger quarters. This should not take long, she said, for workers were getting easier to find. At the upper placers the rains had begun. More men were coming to town, and not all of them brought pokes full of gold. Even in this first rich season some men had been unlucky; others had blithely drunk and gambled away all the gold they found. Now they had to take jobs before they could buy supplies to go back and look for more.

212

Meanwhile, the Blackbeards with Lulu and Lolo were living at the back of Archwood's lot, in a shelter they had made of canvas and packing boxes. Hiram and Pocket slept on their bedrolls outdoors. Marny and Kendra, in their room over the store, were faring about as well as anybody could fare in the dusty disorder of San Francisco.

Chase and Fenway had so much business to attend to that for days at a time they seemed to forget the girls were there at all. When they did meet, Mr. Chase was affable. (Apparently Mrs. Chase had raised no objection to Marny, or possibly she did not even know Marny was living in the store.) Mr. Fenway looked as sad as usual, but when he passed he did manage to say a dismal "Good morning." The clerk Ralph Watson and his wife Serena were proving a likable pair.

The Watsons had come out during the summer with a wagon train from Missouri. Upon hearing of gold, Ralph's first thought had been to set out for the hills. He had desisted partly because of the high pay offered him by Chase and Fenway, but mostly because of the urging of his wife. Serena was a sturdy young woman but she was a heartbroken one. She had borne a baby in a covered wagon, and the baby had not been strong enough to live through the rigors of the desert. Serena wanted no more adventures. To the joy of Marny and Kendra, she was an energetic young woman, glad to earn gold dust by doing laundry and sewing for her new neighbors.

Archwood found a tent, small but strong, for the Calico Palace. He also managed to buy enough lumber to put a floor under it, and to order a bar and card tables made in a furniture shop. Before long he and Marny would be ready for business.

But they were not as happy as they might have been. To the exasperation of them both, the miners who had rented Archwood's house on Washington Street still refused his offer to refund the rent and would not budge. Archwood had to continue living at Mrs. Beecham's in a room with three other men, while Marny stayed with Kendra in the room over the store. Nobody could suggest a place for them to live because there wasn't any. Every shack and shanty in town was full. The City Hotel, built to accommodate forty persons, was now housing a hundred and sixty. They slept in two shifts, half of them at night and half in the daytime. They never had time to air the beds, and the bugs were swarming.

213

As Loren was expected back from Hoolulu before long, Marny said that when the miners did get out of the house, Kendra could live there with herself and Archwood. Kendra exclaimed gratefully, "Thank you! And I'll cook dinner every day."

"Wonderful exchange," said Marny.

While she was glad to cook dinner in return for a place to live, Kendra wanted to be altogether independent. She had come to San Francisco with three hundred ounces of gold, but prices were soaring. She told Marny she would like to make cupcakes and cheese rolls, to be sold at a coffee table in the Calico Palace.

Marny was doubtful. To her, the words "cakes and coffee" sounded like a church social. But Kendra reminded her that men had to eat. They could not eat gold. They could, however, exchange gold for food, and they would if the food was good. Hers would be good. Archwood's two lots, on Kearny Street and Washington, touched at the back in the middle of the block. This meant that she could bring in her cakes and rolls several times a day, hot from the oven. "They'll be sold," she insisted, "before they're cool."

Marny began to be interested. Though Lolo was going to have a baby, Lulu was not, so Lulu could sell the cakes. Marny said she could put the table just inside the entrance of the tent, where the odors would tempt men to come in from the street. A noble fellow who thought he did not gamble would step in for a snack. Once the noble fellow got inside, he would ramble over to watch the play—no harm in that. Then he would lay a bet, a little bet, only a dollar or two, just for fun—

"It's an idea," said Marny. Her eyes had a soft glow like the eyes of a purring cat.

At last the miners moved out of Archwood's house and took a launch back to the gold country. Marny had bought some usable if not stately furniture, and she and Archwood and Kendra moved in.

Archwood ate Kendra's dinners with relish, but otherwise he did not notice her much. He had a great deal to do, all new and interesting; and he had Marny, also new and interesting. He was charmed by her linking of bedroom art with drawing room grace, and equally charmed by her talent for making money.

Marny opened her gambling parlor on an evening in November, 1848. It was a neat little tent fifteen by twenty-five feet, with a floor of redwood planks and the words "Calico Palace" in bright red paint on the outside. Facing the entrance, so every man who walked past on Kearny Street could see her, Marny dealt her card game. In front of her was a pile of treasure—lumps of gold, Yankee dollars, British sovereigns, gold and silver coins from Mexico and China and Peru. As coins had to be brought in by the ships, there were not nearly enough of them in town. People were used to taking any sort they could get.

Also near the entrance Lulu sat by a table spread with Kendra's cupcakes and cheese rolls. Coffee pot and teakettle steamed on a brazier beside her. At a spot farther back the Blackbeards took turns, one dealing while the other kept guard. There were two tables for rent, and at the back was the bar. The bartender, known as Chad, was a stoutish man with a thick neck, curly black hair, and a pink jovial face. Chad had been lured from the bar at the City Hotel by the promise that he could sleep in the tent, on a bug-free cot with clean blankets.

Two Mexican youths strolled about, strumming guitars. Archwood had found them and he told Marny they played well. She said, "I'll take your word for it." As far as Marny was concerned music was merely another kind of noise. Not that she minded it, so long as it brought in the gamblers.

Everybody who worked in the tent wore a gun. The men had big murderous-looking pistols at their belts, Marny wore the pretty little Colt given her by the gambler from New Orleans, Norman Lamont. But they rarely had any disorder. The Blackbeards were competent guards, and Chad was glad to help when needed because he liked a quiet life. Archwood came in often to look things over, but he seldom stayed long. Gambling was not his talent. His kingdom lay in the account books, and he had no complaints. Every launch that came down the river brought more men from the mines. Here in town they were squandering gold in a crazy carnival.

A week after the gambling tent opened, Hiram and Pocket said goodby. Drinking coffee in Kendra's kitchen, they told her and Marny they planned to leave tomorrow to start their workshop at the fort. They were going to cut down trees, make rockers, and get rich.

215

Marny wished them good luck, gave them each a kiss to remember her by, and went back to her card table. Leaving Lolo to watch the fire, Kendra walked with them to the hitching post in front of the house.

His hand on his horse's bridle, Hiram scowled down at her. "You're all right here, Kendra?" he asked.

"Yes," she assured him, and as he still looked doubtful she added, "Really I am, Hiram."

"You have a gun?"

"Yes."

"Where?"

"Under my apron."

"Let me see it."

She took the gun out of its holster and gave it to him. This was a gun Archwood had bought from a man who had run short of coins to gamble with, a little Colt with a barrel four inches long and a revolving cylinder with five chambers. Hiram examined it, nodded with approval, and gave it back.

"Stout little weapon. Do you know how to use it?"

"I'm learning," said Kendra. "It still scares me, but I'll keep trying."

"Keep trying till you know how," Hiram ordered her sternly. He shook his big shaggy head. "I don't like all this," he said. "Your living next to a gambling spot that's half saloon. But——" He shrugged. She had nowhere else to go and he knew it. He added, "As I've remarked before, Kendra, you have guts."

Standing by his own horse, Pocket spoke in his wise quiet way. "Folks need guts around here," he said.

The men mounted their horses. Pocket smiled at her gently. But Hiram was still scowling. His big hand on her shoulder, he said,

"You're sure you don't mind being here, Kendra?"

She smiled up at him. "I'm sure, Hiram. I'm quite safe. They never leave me alone in the house. I'm busy, I'm independent, I'm happy here."

At last Hiram smiled at her too. He squeezed her shoulder. With Pocket, he rode away toward Kearny Street. At the corner they waved goodby, and Kendra waved back.

As she watched them go, she felt shivers. She had said she was all right, she was happy here.

It was the biggest lie she had ever told.

216

30

She was not all right. She was scared and lonely and half sick with wondering what was going to become of her. Hiram had said she had guts. She felt about as gutsy as a bowl of jam. The best she could do was pretend it wasn't so. She pretended to herself as well as to other people.

Kendra was not good at pretending, and she could do it now only because her days were so full that sometimes she herself was hardly aware of her own thoughts. She cooked the meals, and between meals she made her cakes. At best this would have left her scant leisure; but as it was, she not only had to cook, she had to search for something to be cooked.

Flour and sugar and meat she could buy, but fresh foods were rare and sometimes she could not get any at all. The boats that used to bring produce from the ranches now stood idle for days or weeks at a time, waiting for men to sail them. While some miners had run short of gold and so had to take jobs, most men still carried heavy pokes and wanted to celebrate instead of work. When she looked out of a window and saw a launch approaching, Kendra ran to call one of the Blackbeards. If he found any milk on board, or eggs, he was to buy them at any price. Sometimes he found them, sometimes not.

However, she did her best with what she could get, and in spite of Marny's fantastic prices men bought her cakes as fast as she could bring them in. Kendra worked nearly every minute of every day, but this was the way she wanted it. Work kept her from thinking. It was like a drug.

But like any other drug, hers could not always hide the truth. She knew her work kept her from thinking and she knew what it kept her from thinking about. About how lonesome she was, and how scared.

This fear was not what she had felt at Cape Horn. That fear had been real, certainly, until Loren with his cheerful confidence had eased it, but that had been the simple bodily fright that any animal in danger might feel. This fear was more complex, more shattering. She felt like a lost child, among strange people, strange sights and noises in meaningless confusion.

Never had she felt so alone. Kendra was used to being lonely, but at Shiny Gulch, while she had still believed in Ted, she had found out what it meant not to be lonely, and this made loneliness harder than ever to bear. It was not Marny's fault. Marny was as friendly as ever, but Marny had the exhilaration of her cards. She also had Archwood's backing. "He won't last," Marny whispered to Kendra, "but as the smart old Roman said, *Carpe diem*. Which means, Make hay while the sun shines."

Marny's spirit had never been deeply stirred. She would not have understood Kendra's yearning terror now, any more than she had understood, last summer, Kendra's pain at the loss of Ted.

"I believe Pocket would understand how I feel," Kendra said to herself. "Hiram? I don't know."

But Pocket and Hiram had gone to the fort. She had nobody to talk to.

Archwood was making plans to go to Honolulu. This was no longer an impossible dream. Men who had come from the islands last summer were now willing to sail the vessels that would take them home. Also there were deserters, who had gathered their pokes of gold and wanted to get away before they could be caught. The captains were so eager to move their ships that they would take almost any man they could get, asking no questions. Archwood took passage on the ship *Rhone,* which now had enough crewmen to promise a sailing before the end of the year.

His purpose in sailing was twofold. The Calico Palace was not the only gambling tent on the plaza, but Marny had made it the most enticing one, and it was over-full every evening. Archwood was eager to put up a building large enough to take care of all these men who wanted to risk their gold. But his problem was how to get something to build with. There was a sawmill in Bodega, north of the bay, and the sawmill had lumber in plenty, but there was no plenty of sailors to bring it down. However, men newly arrived from the islands had told him Honolulu was not yet swamped with gold. There he would find an abundance of brick and lumber. Also, while in San Francisco the price of gold was bobbing up and down every day, in Honolulu gold was still worth its normal value in coin. Archwood had therefore determined to leave for Honolulu as soon as he could, taking his gold dust with him. He would buy what he needed and bring back the change in real money.

He offered to take the girls' dust too, and change it for coins. Kendra consented gladly, and Marny gave him her share of the dust they had earned in the Calico Palace, keeping back only coins to gamble with. Kendra was surprised that Marny had become so trustful. She said so, over a pot of chocolate while Marny was taking a rest from her card table.

The weather had turned cold and damp and they sat in the kitchen. This was the only warm room in the house, for firewood was as hard to get as every other article requiring men's labor.

At Kendra's remark Marny gave her a wise look across the cups. "Darling, he'll come back. He hasn't sold his lots yet because prices are going up. He won't sell the lots until he's ready to go back to New York, and he won't go back till he's bored, and right now he's not bored. Look."

She set her cup on the kitchen table. Reaching inside her dress she drew out a little bundle wrapped in a handkerchief, and put it into Kendra's hand.

The little bundle had the weight of gold. While Marny watched her, Kendra unwrapped the handkerchief and took out a gold chain, of a length to fit around a woman's throat. Attached to the chain, under little caps like acorns, were five fat lumps of gold, so pure and soft that Kendra felt as if she could almost have dented them with her fingernail.

"The newest thing," said Marny. "A nugget necklace. He had it made for me at Buckelew's watch shop."

"It's lovely!" said Kendra. "Not lovely like anything I've ever seen before. But like—like California."

"Exactly," said Marny. "I'm proud of it."

She took the necklace and stood up.

"You know, Kendra," she said thoughtfully, "I used to think I'd never want to go back to Philadelphia. But some day, I might. To—show my trophies." She touched the nuggets with affection. "I'm beginning," she said, "to understand the Indian braves, going home with scalps on their belts."

Kendra remembered that once she had felt like this. She had wanted to go back to her aunts and uncles, with a fur

219

cloak and a muff pinned with a spray of opals. And Ted. Now she did not care if she ever went back or not.

She thought—I wish I could be like Marny. But I can't. I don't want a nugget necklace. I want somebody to love me.

To hide her face she stood up and put a stick of wood into the stove. Marny said,

"Those cupcakes smell so good! I wish they were ready. I'd like one."

"They'll be done in about twenty minutes," said Kendra. "I'll bring them over."

Marny put on her shawl and left for the tent. A few minutes later Lolo came in to watch the fire. Leaving her at work on a garment she was making for her expected baby, Kendra went into a front room and looked out toward the bay.

Dark against the sky she could see the tall masts of the deserted vessels. She wondered how many of them would ever go to sea again.

Still, more kept coming in. Some came from ports where people had not yet heard of California's gold; others were brought by captains thinking, "It can't happen to me." Out there in the bay Kendra could see a schooner called the *Hope*, which had arrived yesterday from Honolulu, full of gold-hunting passengers. The passengers had come ashore, and no doubt the crewmen had already started to slip away.

The cakes were done now, so she went back to the kitchen. Arranging the cakes on a big tray, she covered them with a cloth and started toward the tent.

The ground was rough and she had to take care about every step. Ahead of her the tent was full of light, a bright island in the gloom of the day. She could hear the guitars. Those Mexican boys did play well, whether Marny knew it or not.

The back entrance of the tent was a flap behind the bar. As she came near she heard a thud, somebody kicking a rock out of the way. Kendra glanced around. Ambling toward her, shoulders hunched and hands in the pockets of his dirty coat, was the sponger from Shiny Gulch, Stub Crawford.

With a start, Kendra made for the flap. But Stub was already in front of her.

"Howdy," he drawled in his peevish voice.

"Let me pass!" said Kendra. She spoke sharply, holding her tray like a shield before her.

Stub sniffed at the hidden tidbits. "Seems like you've all the time got somp'n good," he whimpered. "How's about giving me some?"

"No!" retorted Kendra.

She was trembling. She had her little Colt with her, but now she was realizing with terror that she did not have it at hand. She had never really expected to shoot anybody; she carried the gun only because her friends had said she should. The Colt was hidden under her apron. To use it she would have had to throw down her tray, fumble with the holster— before she could have drawn the gun Stub would have knocked her down as he had done before. Clutching the tray, she demanded,

"Let me pass!"

She took a step to one side. Stub took one too, keeping himself between her and the tent. He was grinning. His mouth had a greedy look of wetness.

Kendra cried out, "Chad! Chad!" But the tent was full of noise and Chad did not hear.

"What you got under that cloth?" Stub asked hungrily.

Her nose caught liquor on his breath, and the stinks of his sweat-ridden clothes and his skin long unwashed. But Stub's nose caught only the fragrance of the cupcakes.

"Sure smells good," he said, "and you're gonta give it to me. You're gonta give it all to me."

He reached both his dirty hands across the tray and clamped them on her arms, holding her where she was.

"You ain't been nice to me, you ain't," he whined at her. "Last time I saw you, you set all them bullies on me. Now that wasn't nice of you, not nice at all. I was a poro hungry man and you sent them rowdies after me with their guns. This time—"

Kendra had been gathering her strength. Now with all the force at her command she gave herself a wrench and pulled her arms out of his grip. The tray went down on the ground and rolled over, scattering the cakes among the rough weedy clods. But instantly Stub grabbed her again.

"Now you quit that," he ordered. "Throwing away good food right in front of a pore hungry man. I'm gonta get it yet. And that ain't all I'm gonta get. I'm gonta get me a sweet little kiss—"

Kendra looked frantically around her. On the street she saw a group of men going toward the tent, but they were not looking her way. Struggling to free herself from Stub, she tried to scream. Her voice came out in a gurgle. Not hearing her above the street noises, the men went in. Stub held her, enjoying his triumph, prolonging it by repeating, "A sweet little kiss, maybe more than one sweet little kiss—"

Across his shoulder Kendra saw another man walking along Kearny Street toward the Calico Palace. He walked briskly, head up and shoulders erect, a man who had nothing to hide. As he came into the glow from the tent she saw his bright cider-brown eyes and pink cheeks, and a mighty wave of thankfulness rolled over her as she recognized Loren Shields.

Again she cried out, and this time gladness made her voice strong.

"Loren!" she called. "Loren! Make him let me alone!"

The next thing she heard was a yell. Stub Crawford tumbled down on the ground, and Loren, fists clenched and face distorted with rage, was exclaiming,

"Kendra, my dear girl, what—"

She did not hear the rest of his words. She found herself leaning against him, weak with fear and relief and joy, and she sobbed on his shoulder as he held her up with his arms around her. On the ground, Stub was holding his near-broken head and bawling that somebody was always being mean to him.

At that moment the flap of the tent was pushed back. Chad's curly black head came through, and she heard his voice demanding,

"What the hell is going on out here?"

Kendra raised her head. She did not answer. She could not. But in a few blunt words Loren explained. Hands on hips, Chad profanely told Stub what he thought of him.

"And all these fine cakes," barked Chad, "and the fellows clamoring for them—"

Chad was down on his knees now, picking up the cakes from the ground, dusting them with his bartender's apron, and setting them one by one on the tray. They could be sold as usual—what was so awful about a little dirt? Watching him, Kendra began to laugh. It was slightly hysterical laughter but it soothed her nerves. Chad, solemnly in earnest, got up from his knees and carried the rescued cakes into the tent.

"Show me where you live," Loren said to Kendra, "and I'll see you home."

They started walking across the lot, toward the door to the kitchen. Loren's arm was still around her shoulders.

His presence gave her a sense of safety such as she had not felt since the day she lost Ted. She asked,

"Loren—how did you happen to be here just when I needed you?"

"I came in from Honolulu yesterday," he said, "on the *Hope*. I didn't know what had happened to you until this afternoon, when Mr. Chase told me. As soon as I heard, I started right over to see you. Thank God I got here when I did."

Behind them, they heard Stub grunting and groaning as he stumbled to his feet. They stopped and looked around, and saw him running away, across Kearny Street and across the plaza and out of sight. Loren turned back to Kendra.

"And now," he said, "I'm going to take you out of this mess."

He smiled down at her, tenderly.

"Maybe you don't know it," he went on, "but I've been in love with you ever since we were both on the *Cynthia*. Only I was too big a fool to say it, so I lost you. I'm not going to lose you again."

31

Two weeks later Kendra married Loren Shields. With this, her world changed.

Loren gave her the love and security she had yearned for. He gave her a gracious life almost unmatched in the crudeness of San Francisco. She married Loren in December, 1848, and before New Year's Day she knew she had made the second big mistake of her life.

Over and over she asked herself why. Sometimes she thought she understood. She had been so alone and so frightened, and Loren had come to her like a rescuing hero. But every time she remembered this she asked again, despairingly, "Why, oh why was I such a fool? Why didn't I know better?"

For if she had needed anything to make her sure of it, marriage to Loren showed her all over again that the only man she wanted was Ted.

Loren loved her. As he had told her that evening while they crossed the lot behind the gambling tent, he had loved her since they had been together on the *Cynthia*. He had not said so because he knew the risks of shipboard romances.

When you first go to sea, Loren told Kendra, the older men all warn you about these. They say: By the time you've spent six or eight weeks in the masculine monotony of a trading vessel any woman looks good, and a really desirable girl looks like Helen of Troy. No matter how much in love you think you are, never get involved with a girl on a voyage. Wait and see if it's the real thing. It usually isn't.

Loren himself had found that the old seamen were right. More than once he'd been attracted by a pretty passenger, only to find when he reached port that it was nothing but her uniqueness. He would forget her in a week.

So he left Kendra in San Francisco, and went with Captain Pollock on that errand for the military. Thought he'd wait, come back to San Francisco, and see if she still seemed as charming as before. But in the meantime there was that trouble about Marny and he gave up his berth on the *Cynthia*. He had to start a new career. He went down to Monterey to consult a trader there, and while he was gone Kendra married Ted Parks.

"So of course," Loren continued, "I put you out of my mind in that sense. But I tell you, Kendra, I was a mighty disappointed man."

He smiled at her fondly.

"But now, if your marriage wasn't real, here I am."

Everything was done smoothly. Loren went to the alcalde and got a legal annulment of Kendra's first marriage. Mr. Chase was pleased about it all, so pleased that he offered to have the wedding in his own home. Mrs. Chase served wine and wafers, and Mr. Fenway looked on as dolefully as before, as if he wished people would stop doing this sort of thing.

Several days beforehand Marny gave Kendra a present of an embroidered silk shawl from China.

"I won't be there for the ceremony," she said. "If Mr. Chase didn't want me in his store he'd want me even less in his parlor. But I'll be thinking about you, and wishing you all sorts of happiness."

She spoke sincerely, though as Kendra found out later, Marny was doubtful about the wisdom of this marriage. Marny did not understand why Kendra should still love Ted, but Kendra did love him and Marny knew she did. However, her opinion had not been asked and she did not give it.

The fact was that Marny did not believe her opinion would be worth anything. Marny was not one of those people who think themselves competent to offer other people advice on every subject under heaven. If she had seen Kendra playing a poor game of cards she would have said so. Cards Marny knew about. But she did not know about marriage, she was wise enough to know she did not know, and she kept her mouth shut.

After the wedding Kendra and Loren went to their own home, a luxury Loren had secured by a union of good luck and good sense. A trader who owned a house on Washington Street, near Stockton, wanted to move to Canton. For three months he had been waiting for a vessel to take him there. At last the captain of the ship *Rhone,* about to sail for Honolulu, announced that he had enough seamen to go on to Canton. The trader engaged passage and sold his house to a land speculator. The new owner had put the house into the care of an agent, to be rented while he waited for the price to rise.

The house was a story-and-a-half cottage, plain but solidly built. The rent would have paid for a mansion in the States. But Loren earned a good income, and in Honolulu he had changed his gold dust for coin, the article more wanted than anything else in San Francisco. Loren went to see the house agent, a gentleman named—or at least called—Mr. Reginald Norrington.

Mr. Norrington was a short squat fat man who did business in a smoky little office on Clay Street. He had black hair around a bald spot, a greasy moonlike face, plump fluttery hands, and few charms except a gift for making the best possible terms for his clients. In spite of the high rent he wanted for the cottage, decent dwellings were so scarce that several persons had already asked him for this one. However, they had offered him gold dust. He was hesitating. Then Loren, several days before his marriage, walked into Mr. Norrington's office and showed him enough gold coins to pay the rent for six months ahead. Smiling all the way across his moony face, Mr. Norrington said his client would be proud to have a tenant of such fine repute as Mr. Shields.

Loren had planned everything for Kendra's convenience. He told her he had to make frequent buying trips and it would not be safe to leave her alone. He had asked Chase and Fenway's clerk, Ralph Watson, with his wife Serena, to live in two rooms on the first floor. They were delighted, for they were sadly cramped in their little room over the store. Serena would do housework. Thus Kendra would be relieved of drudgery, and when he was away she would have a man in the house.

Kendra was not unhappy. Loren was so kind, so cheerful, so considerate, that he was easy to live with. And he loved her. But though she tried to love him back she could not. She knew now that love was not made by trying. If it did not go when it ought to go, neither was it there when it ought to be there.

Several days before Christmas Loren told her there was to be a ball Christmas evening at the Comet House. Wouldn't she like to attend?

When she heard his words Kendra felt a shock that went through her like a knife. To dance again in the parlor where she had fallen in love with Ted—she could not, she simply could not. Exclaiming that she smelled something burning, she ran out to the kitchen and waited till she could control her voice. When she came back she said to Loren,

"Instead of going out let's do something unexpected. Let's have a good old-fashioned Christmas dinner and invite some friends. Wouldn't you like that?"

Loren brightened at the idea. "I'd like it very much. But wouldn't it mean a lot of work for you?"

"Oh, Loren, don't be so careful of me! You know I never mind cooking, and Serena can help."

He laughed in anticipation. "I don't think there's a turkey in town, but we can get a ham—"

"Fine," said Kendra.

Dinner was a great success. The guests were Mr. and Mrs. Chase, and Mr. Fenway, and Lieutenants Morse and Vernon. The lieutenants apologized for eating so much, but said it was the first good meal they had had in months. Mr. and Mrs. Chase agreed that Kendra was a rare cook. Even Mr. Fenway

226

uttered praise. Loren, presiding over his first dinner party in his own home, beamed with pleasure.

New Year's Day was cold and cloudy with flurries of rain. But again Loren and Kendra were host and hostess, for more than ever San Francisco was a town of lonely men. Business firms in other Pacific ports were sending agents to open branches in the land of gold. A few of these newcomers had wives, most had not; all were homesick, all hated the mud and rawness around them and longed for the ways of civilized men. On the first day of 1849, groups of lonely young fellows set out to bring one of these pleasant ways to San Francisco. They dressed up in formal suits and kid gloves and polished boots, and went slopping through the rain to make New Year's calls on the ladies.

Kendra had been warned by Loren to expect them, so she was ready, sitting by the fire with cake and wine on a table at her side. The young men brought her gifts of books and candy, walnuts and dried fruit. They paid her flowery compliments, wished her a happy New Year, bowed and went on, leaving tracks of mud all over the carpet.

Kendra did not mind the tracks. Like her work for the Calico Palace, all this kept her from thinking too much.

A week after New Year's, Loren went to Oregon on another buying trip for Chase and Fenway. Mrs. Chase promised him she would see to it that Kendra was not lonely while he was away. She began by inviting Kendra, with Ralph and Serena, to a musical party.

Mrs. Chase was a jovial, friendly soul. She was not highly educated, but she liked to read a good story, she was clever at party games, she enjoyed music and she had an inborn good taste about it. Among the newly arrived businessmen were some good amateur performers, and Mrs. Chase told Kendra they would provide the entertainment.

The evening appointed was mild and clear. Mr. and Mrs. Chase lived near Kendra, only a few steps farther up the hill. As Kendra set out with Ralph and Serena they saw the sunset afterglow, and Ralph said there would be a moon to light their way home. The walk was easy, and the parlor was bright with candles and firelight. Mr. Chase came hurrying to take their wraps, inviting them to warm up with cups of chocolate or glasses of wine.

Mr. Fenway was there, and half a dozen of the new traders. Two of these gentlemen were married and had brought their wives. Also present was that precious rarity, an unmarried girl about eighteen years old, daughter of one of the married couples. Her name was Ada Lansing. Ada was escorted by one of the bachelor traders, who was glowing with pride at this mark of favor.

As Kendra was the only other woman without a husband at her side, the other bachelors flocked around her. One of them set a chair for her in a warm spot near the fire, another brought a footstool, still another a cushion for her chair. It was all quite agreeable.

Mrs. Chase had not been able to get her heart's desire, a piano, but they did very well without it. The four bachelors played guitars and sang as a quartet. They had joined for their own entertainment, but they were genuinely musical and worth listening to. After several songs, they rested while one of the married men, Mr. Dean, played his violin. It might have been better if he had had a piano accompaniment, but he was good and deserved the applause they gave him. Then the young lady, Miss Ada Lansing, favored them with a solo while her escort played the guitar.

Ada Lansing could not sing, and her song, which concerned shrill references to moonlight and dew, was not worth singing anyway. But she was young and pretty, and the gentlemen listened with their souls in their eyes. All but Mr. Fenway. Kendra, sitting next to Mr. Fenway, noticed him squirming. A moment later, as Ada sang blissfully on, Mr. Fenway growled out of the corner of his mouth,

"That's the third time she's flatted and she's not *that* pretty."

Kendra bit on her handkerchief to keep from giggling. Fortunately, in another moment the song came to an end. Applauding dutifully, she avoided the eyes of Mr. Fenway.

After another interval of guitars, Mr. Chase announced that they would now have a song by Mrs. Dean, wife of the man who had played the violin. Kendra shivered at the prospect of what they might hear now and what Mr. Fenway might say about it. But while Mrs. Dean had not Ada's pretty face, she had a good voice and knew how to use it. She gave them a pleasant ballad, and this time the applause was real and they begged for more. Mrs. Dean sang again, simply and well.

The room was getting stuffy, and Mr. Chase opened a

228

window. The guitar players performed again. This time they sang a mischievous song beginning,

"If there's one thing really nifty it's a gentleman of fifty
When a thoughtful girl is contemplating love,
For *if* a man of fifty had been reasonably thrifty,
He's got just what thoughtful girls are thinking of . . ."

The audience laughed, all but Ada Lansing. Ada had expected to be asked for another song. Since coming to San Francisco she had received so much adulation that she now took it for granted that she would be the center of any gathering she favored with her presence. She forgot that this group had come to hear music, which she could not provide. All she understood was that Mrs. Dean had been encored while she herself had not. Ada rustled her skirts petulantly.

The quartet went into a mirthful chorus.

"For love without cash means a diet of hash,
Then love gets thrown out with the rest of the trash . . ."

When the chorus ended they decided they had been cynical long enough. Changing to a happier mood they began a song about spring and flowers.

Kendra was listening with pleasure. She was no singer herself (and unlike Ada Lansing, she knew it), but she liked music. Mr. Chase had told her pianos would be coming in soon. Kendra hoped she could get one. She and Loren would both enjoy it. He liked music too. She was finding that they had many tastes in common. Oh, she was a fortunate woman, she ought to be thanking heaven for Loren's warm affection instead of dreaming about spangles of fool's gold—

The guitar players began another tune. Kendra felt herself going tense. A tremor ran over her skin. Her hands felt damp. Her lips tightened. The men were playing the gay, lilting melody of "Love is like a dragonfly."

That dance at the Comet House. The smoky lamps, the garish wallpaper, music by the army band. Ted's arm around her, his whisper in her ear. "You're beautiful. . . . Every woman is as beautiful as some man thinks she is."

—Oh God, make them stop! Make them play something else. Why does love hurt like this? Why doesn't it *go?*

The men were blithely singing.

"Love is like a dragonfly,
     Here today, tomorrow gone,
Love's a teasing passerby,
     Blows a kiss and hurries on . . ."

Kendra's hands clenched each other in her lap. She felt
rigid as a rock. Thank heaven nobody was looking at her.
They were watching the singers, tapping their feet to the
happy music, enjoying the song.

At last—it seemed like a thousand years—the singers
changed to another tune. Kendra did not know what tune
they played and she did not hear the words they sang. She
sat there, trying to draw deep breaths and make her heart
stop pounding, trying to unclench her hands, relax her taut
knees, loosen her stiff lips, silently pleading—Make them
keep on singing! Give me time!

They did keep on singing; she did not know how long, but
she wished it had been longer. She heard the applause, she
joined it. She heard the others thanking the singers and she
realized that this was the end of the program. She heard
Mr. Chase saying to her, "And now, ma'am, a glass of sherry?
Real Spanish sherry this is, came a long way."

Kendra took the wine. To her own surprise she found
herself saying, "Thank you," and a moment later, "It's delicious, Mr. Chase."

Mrs. Chase was passing toasted crackers with cheese, dishes
of olives and nuts, and pretty little cakes. Kendra managed
a few nibbles. She kept thinking,

—Nothing lasts forever. Before long I can get out of here.
I can be alone. Oh thank God I'll be *alone*. Please don't let
Loren ever guess this. Please, please let me get over it, some
day, somehow.

At last it was time to go. They began thanking Mr. and
Mrs. Chase for a pleasant evening. Kendra said the proper
phrases, and found herself on her way home with Ralph and
Serena. It seemed a long way, but they got there and said
good night.

Kendra went upstairs to her room. She saw a faint glow
in the grate. They had plenty of fuel now, for a ship had
come in with a cargo of coal and Loren had bought enough
to last the winter. Kendra built up the fire and watched the
little flames run among the coals. She heard Ralph try the

230

front door to make sure it was locked, and his footsteps as he went to his and Serena's bedroom downstairs.

She took off her clothes, but she was not sleepy. She had never felt more wide awake. Lighting a candle, she put on a dressing-gown and sat in front of the fire. The flames crackled cheerfully. Outside, the wind was rising. Kendra put her head into her hands and forgot about the fire and the wind and all the other sounds in the house and out of it; she forgot everything but Ted and how happy he had made her for a little while.

—Why can't I cry? she wondered.

It would be such a relief to cry. To do anything. Anything but sit here and remember, sit here with her hands holding her throbbing temples, her heart thumping in her chest, her spirit torn into little pieces of pain because she missed Ted as she had never missed anybody else, she wanted him as she had never wanted anything else in her life.

There was a knock on the door. Kendra started. The knock came again and she heard Serena's voice.

"Mrs. Shields?"

—What on earth, Kendra thought. Why does she have to bother me *now?*

With an effort she went to open the door. "Yes, Serena?"

Serena was holding a woolen wrapper around her. There was a smile of apology on her rosy innocent face.

"I'm sorry to trouble you, Mrs. Shields, but I thought this might be important. It's a letter for you."

Kendra heard her with a puzzled frown. "A letter?"

Serena held out a folded paper sealed with wax. "A strange man knocked at the front door," she explained, "and Ralph answered. The man gave him this and asked him to take it to you."

A hundred cudgels began to beat on Kendra's head. She took the letter, and managed to say "Thank you." Serena went downstairs. Closing the door, Kendra went back to her chair by the fireplace.

She broke the seal and unfolded the paper. As she saw the writing her hands began to shake so that the paper rattled between them. Her eyes clouded; it was several seconds before she could steady them enough to read.

Kendra my dear,
   Tonight I heard that song again. Love is like a

231

dragonfly. If you don't know what it did to me—but of course you know.

I came down from Sacramento yesterday on the schooner. My plan was to take the first boat for Honolulu. I had no plan to see you. I had asked about you, was told you had married Loren Shields. A good chap, I suppose; I saw him only once, but at any rate I understood that you were done with me.

So I thought I would go on to Honolulu and let you alone.

But this evening I walked over to see Mr. Chase. You may remember, before we went to Shiny Gulch last year I put my first gold dust on deposit with him. This evening I went to ask him what time he would be in the store tomorrow so I could get it. But I found his house all lit up and saw horses tethered outside. He was giving a party. I could not see indoors because of the curtains, but I could hear music. Somebody had opened a window. The music was good. I didn't want to interrupt, but there was no harm in stopping a few minutes to listen.

Then I heard it. They were playing guitars. They began to sing that song.

And I was back with you at that ball in the Comet House, dancing to that tune and falling in love.

I thought if I didn't see you again I would go mad. I walked to the nearest bar, told them I wanted to see Loren Shields on business, asked where he lived. They told me, and they told me I could not see him now because he was out of town.

Kendra, a few lines back I said when I heard you had married Loren I understood that you were done with me.

But are you, Kendra?

After all there has been between you and me, can you throw it away?

I am waiting in front. Come down and open the door. Come down, Kendra.

Ted

32

Kendra stood up. She walked to the end of the room and back again, holding the letter with both hands. Her hands came together and clasped each other, crushing the letter between them. She looked at the curtain covering the front window. If she should blow out the candle this room would be almost dark, no light but the glow from the fire. Not nearly as bright as the moonlight in the street. She could push the curtain aside and see Ted waiting there. Waiting for her.

It would be so easy. All she had to do was slip downstairs and open the door. If she went softly, Ralph and Serena would hear nothing, suspect nothing. Her bedroom was at the front of the house, theirs at the back, and the rising wind would blur all other sounds. Nobody would ever know.

—Nobody, thought Kendra, but me.

She looked at the bed with its smooth white counterpane. The whole room was like that. Smooth, seemly, well ordered. Like Loren and Loren's gentle embraces. Nothing about this room reminded her of that rude bumpy covered wagon she had shared with Ted.

—Nobody would ever know, Kendra thought again. Nobody but me.

—But I would know.

She twisted her hands together, hearing Ted's letter scrunch between them. She seemed to hear her own voice, an angry scornful voice speaking angry scornful words under the trees at Shiny Gulch.

—You're a halfway person. That's what I can't stand. A coat with one sleeve, a house without a roof, a bridge that stops in the middle of a river—who wants those? Things are no good unless they're *done*.

The crumpled paper dropped out of her hands and fell on the floor. She struck her fist on the mantelpiece. The candle shivered, her shadow shook on the wall. She wondered,

Was I talking to Ted that day? Or to myself?

She began walking again, making a path up and down the room. Again her thoughts took words.

—Kendra, you are not a halfway person. What you do, you *do*. You've always been that way. Always, except for Ted. You love Ted and you hate him too. And Loren? You don't love Loren and you don't hate him either. But you do respect him.

She remembered what Loren had told her just before they were married. He had been in love with her, but while he was in Monterey she had married Ted. "So of course," said Loren, "I put you out of my mind in that sense."

She remembered. He had made a courteous call, to congratulate Ted and bring her a basket of wild strawberries. Then he had gone away, and he had not tried to see her again until Mr. Chase told him about the breakup of her marriage to Ted. Loren was not a halfway person.

—And you, Kendra, she told herself, you are not going to be one either.

She picked up the wadded letter from the floor. She was not going to read it again. If she read it again she might lose all her courage. She tore the paper into shreds and threw them into the fire. Taking her candle she went out and made her way down the stairs.

The house was dark and ghostly. Outside, the wind blew hard. In spite of her woolen dressing-gown Kendra shivered as she went along the hall to Ralph and Serena's room at the back. Thank heaven they had not yet gone to bed. She could see a line of light under the door, and she heard them moving around.

She knocked. After a moment the door cracked open and she saw Serena's startled face.

"Why, Mrs. Shields! Is something wrong?"

"Nothing's wrong, but I'm afraid I'll have to trouble Ralph to go to the door again. The messenger who brought this letter is waiting for an answer, but it concerns a matter of business that will have to wait till my husband comes home. I don't know anything about it."

From inside the room she heard Ralph's voice. "Something you want me to do, Mrs. Shields?"

He sounded both dutiful and irritated. Ralph was no doubt almost or quite ready for bed.

"Yes, please," said Kendra. "I hate to ask you, Ralph, but

234

it's getting very cold and if the poor fellow waits much longer he'll catch pneumonia. Tell him I said there is no reply."

"All right, Mrs. Shields, I'll tell him. Soon as I can put on my shoes and find my overcoat."

"Thank you so much," said Kendra.

She turned and ran up the staircase and into her own room. The candle blew out as she hurried; she did not care. Her eyes were burning and her throat felt sore. She wanted to scream. She almost did scream. Throwing the candle on the hearth, she clenched her teeth on her sleeve to keep quiet.

Downstairs, Ralph was not trying to keep quiet. She heard him tramping along the hall and opening the front door. She waited tensely until she heard him come back. Glad his chilly chore was over, Ralph shut the door with a bang. She heard him push the bolt and tramp back down the hall.

Kendra had wondered why she could not cry. She did not know; she knew only that now she could. She was crying already. Now that Ted had heard her answer she broke down utterly, and fell across the bed while great wrenching sobs tore through her with a force like pain.

She was crying as she had never cried before and she could not stop. She cried until the sobs wore themselves out and she lay limp on the bed, exhausted, her cheek on the wet pillowcase.

After a while she realized that she was cold. The fire had died down, and there was nothing left in the grate but a few embers glowing among the ashes. Kendra turned down the coverlet and got into bed. The sheets were like slices of frost. From outside she heard the wind, that wild San Francisco wind, wailing and groaning around the hills.

Her body ached all over. She remembered Marny's remark as they rode into Shiny Gulch that first afternoon. "I feel like I've been beaten up by experts."

She had felt that way too, that day. But she had not minded because she had been so happy. She tried to remember what it was like, that expectant sense of adventure. She could not remember.

How dark it was. The moonlight was gone. The wind must have blown in more clouds from the sea, for now she heard the rattle of rain.

The rain had a sort of rhythm, a soothing sound. The sheets

were getting warm. Kendra's taut muscles began to loosen. After a long time she fell asleep.

When she woke, the rain was still coming down. Through the windows came a gray light that reminded her of the *Cynthia*'s cabin at Cape Horn. She could not tell what time it was. A clock stood on the bureau, but she had not thought to wind it last night and the clock had stopped at a quarter past three.

Kendra stretched and turned over. The air on her face was cold, but the bed was warm and comfortable. She had not slept enough and her eyes ached from last night's tears, but she felt better than she had felt last night. She turned back the covers, shivering as the cold air struck her, and put her feet into her slippers. They were soft fleece-lined slippers made in Scotland, a gift from Loren when Chase and Fenway had bought some goods from a British brig.

How cold it was! Maybe Serena had coffee on the stove. Serena would no doubt have been up long ago to give Ralph his breakfast before he went to the store. —At least, thought Kendra, I'm glad I don't have to go out in this rain.

Hugging her dressing-gown around her, she opened the door. Up the stairs drifted the odors of coffee and bacon, and the sound of footsteps. Kendra went to the head of the stairs and called, "Serena!"

Serena ran out of the kitchen and came to the bottom step. "Oh Mrs. Shields, you're up at last! I was getting worried about you. Are you all right?"

"Oh yes," Kendra assured her. "The rain kept me awake last night, that's all. What time is it?"

"Why, it's after ten," said Serena. She added, "I hope Ralph got to work all right. He said if the mud should be too bad this evening he'd sleep in the store."

"Good idea," said Kendra. "Is there any coffee left, Serena? Will you bring me a cup?"

Serena nodded, and a minute later she brought the coffee. Not the most polished of attendants, as she came upstairs she had spilt some coffee into the saucer, but frontier living had made Kendra less fastidious than she used to be.

But though not urbane, Serena was a kindly soul. "Don't you want to come down and let me fix you some breakfast?" she was asking. "You can get warm in the kitchen."

Much as she would have liked to get warm in the kitchen, Kendra did not quite yet feel able to bear Serena's cheerful chatter. She said she would like to wash before breakfast, and asked Serena to heat a pot of water. Serena went down, and Kendra began to sip her coffee.

She looked at the ashes in the grate. Somewhere among them was Ted's letter. Setting down the cup she went to the front window, drew back the curtain, and stood looking out at the rain and the mud. Out there, Ted had been waiting for her last night.

—Now he's gone, she thought. I sent him away. I suppose I'll never see him again.

All of a sudden she found that she did not care.

It had happened. What had happened to Pocket, what he had promised would happen to her, had happened at last. She did not love Ted any more. Nor did she hate him any more. She simply did not care.

Amazed at her own self, Kendra let the curtain drop. She went to the washstand and bathed her burning eyes with the icy water in the pitcher. What, what had become of the yearning she used to feel?

She could not answer. She did not know. But whatever the reason, that old ache was gone. She thought of Ted. She remembered how he looked, the tone of his voice. She remembered how he had disillusioned her, and the self-pity of him as he tried to say it was everybody's fault but his own. She remembered how she had fallen in love with him and how she had stayed in love with him. Why had that love taken so long to go? Again, she could not answer. All she knew was that she was not in love with Ted any more.

But neither did she bear him any ill-will. Ted had ceased to matter. She was free.

Kendra sat down on the foot of the bed, not thinking, but merely being aware of things around her—the fragrance of coffee, her warm dressing-gown, her soft fleecy slippers, and in this town of shacks and tents, her own house firm against the rain. And Loren.

She asked herself, now did she love Loren?

No, she did not. But she respected him and she trusted him.

—I am not in love, she thought. I suppose I'll never be in love again.

She missed being in love. Something was gone out of her, something vast and important. But in its place had come a curious kind of peace.

33

Now that her thoughts were no longer full of Ted, Kendra was surprised to notice how much was going on around her. In these first weeks of 1849, every man, woman, and child in San Francisco was tingling with expectancy.

She could sense it everywhere. At home, on the street, in the trading posts, people were talking about one subject and only one. The steamer from New York. They were talking about the steamer and wondering who would be on board. "Wouldn't it be fun," exclaimed Marny, "if the steamer should bring somebody we know!"

For at last, at last, the gold fever had reached their countrymen on the Atlantic side. At last, real Yankee Americans were on their way from the States to look for gold in California.

True, during the past year hundreds of newcomers had poured in. Among them had been many Yankees. But these Yankees had not come directly from their own country. They had come from Hawaii, Oregon, Mexico. True again, some men had come here from the States since the gold fever began. But these were men who, like Warren Archwood, had not heard of gold before they left home. They had come out for other reasons, and heard about gold after they got here. A workman named Jim Marshall had found gold at Sutter's sawmill in January, 1848; now it was January, 1849, and so far not one single person had come from the United States to look for gold.

But now they were on their way. They had learned about gold from the two military couriers who had been sent to tell them.

As Hiram had said to Kendra when they rode in from Shiny Gulch, these two men had set out last summer with reports for the national government in Washington. Commodore Jones of the navy had sent Midshipman Beale,

Colonel Mason of the army had sent Lieutenant Loeser. Both men carried official letters. They also carried samples of gold.

Beale got there first.

He made a toilsome journey down to Mexico, across to the eastern side of Mexico, and up to Washington. He reached Washington in September. Here he gave his letters to the authorities, and showed them the sample he had brought with him. They said the stuff looked like fish-scales, but they sent it to the Mint. The Mint reported that the fish-scales were twenty-two carat gold.

Rumors of gold had already seeped into the States. Seamen who had left the west coast last spring before the storm really broke had told the yarns they had heard on the waterfront. Landsmen had shrugged and said, "Oh, you know how sailors talk." Men in the army and navy, sending letters home by the ship captains, had mentioned that some fellow had found gold in the hills. Several such letters had been printed in the home town papers. The homefolks had remarked, "California sure does sound like a fine place." Nobody had been excited.

Even after Beale got there, the homefolks did not get really excited. Not right away.

His news was announced by a Washington paper, the *Union.* A few days later it was repeated by the Baltimore *Sun.* Somebody brought a copy of the *Sun* across Mexico, and a week after Mrs. Chase's party a vessel came from a Mexican port to San Francisco with this copy on board. The new weekly paper, the *Alta California,* quoted what the *Sun* had to say.

(Kendra thought the new paper was aptly named. *Alta* meant Upper. The Mexicans had long used the word to distinguish this region from their own province of Baja, or Lower California.)

The *Alta California* was published every Thursday in an office on Washington Street, a short way down the hill from Kendra's home. On the third Thursday of January, 1849, Kendra read what the Baltimore *Sun* had said about Mr. Beale and his report of gold.

The *Sun's* article was deceptively calm. The man who wrote it was either dazed or doubtful. Without exactly saying so, he seemed to be warning his readers—Now let's not lose our heads over this.

Kendra was not surprised. She thought of Morse and

239

Vernon telling her about the crackbrain who had come to town with his box of gravel. She thought of the quartermaster, saying this so-called gold was yellow mica. And Mr. Fenway, looking at Pocket's rag of gold dust and saying it didn't mean a thing.

But that man in Baltimore had been writing last September. Now it was January. Another vessel had brought news that the army courier, Lieutenant Loeser, had reached the port of Callao in Peru. From there he had gone on to Washington, carrying a box of gold and letters in which Colonel Mason described his own visit to the mines. Kendra said to Marny, "That column in the *Sun* must have been like a puff before an explosion."

And any day now they would be hearing about the explosion.

They had long known about the steamboats that were going to connect the east and west coasts. On the fourth Thursday in January the *Alta* announced that the first of these steamers had left New York last October. The steamer had sailed three weeks after Beale had reached the States with his news. In San Francisco, everybody began exclaiming to everybody else, "There will surely be some gold-hunters on board!"

Through the wind and the rain they waited for the steamer. They climbed the hills and strained for sounds over the foggy water, hoping to hear the steamer chugging toward the bay. The rain kept on pouring. One day they even had a flurry of snow. January sloshed into February, and still the steamer had not come.

They passed the time somehow. Every night the saloons and gambling tents were full. Marny said men were gambling even more recklessly than they had gambled at Shiny Gulch. Warren Archwood came back from Honolulu with his cargo of brick and lumber. He brought enough to put up a building several stories high, with living quarters on an upper floor, but this was not possible as long as the ground was a sea of mud. For the present he built what people in San Francisco were beginning to call a "cloth house"—a frame of wooden beams with heavy canvas nailed over it. The "house" had a board floor, and several extra rooms divided by "walls" of canvas, which men could rent for private games.

Archwood also built a smaller cloth house for Lolo and her Blackbeard, Troy, and their baby son, born the first week in February. A few days before his birth a schooner had

240

brought news from the States that General Zachary Taylor had been elected President, so they named the baby Zachary in the President's honor and called him Zack for short.

Marny was happy about the way things were going. Her cloth house was larger than the tent and more festive. She hung whale oil lamps from the beams overhead and hid the ugly canvas walls with curtains of bright red calico. At each end of the bar she set a model of the picturesque Chinese sailboat called a junk, and in the junk she put smoking sticks of punk for lighting cigars. "Try the punk from the junk," Chad would say to the customers.

They liked it, as another of Marny's amusing ideas. Marny, however, told Kendra that the real idea was to keep them from dropping lighted matches on the floor. In this gimcrack town fire was a constant danger. Marny was taking no risks if she could help it.

"So far, we're doing fine," she said to Kendra. "And look what Warren brought me from Honolulu."

She showed Kendra a gold pin made like a woven basket, with jewels of many colors above the edge like flowers.

"A nice new scalp," said Marny, "if I should ever go back to Philadelphia."

Several days after this, Loren came home from Oregon. Kendra put her arms around him and shed tears on his shoulder. Loren was touched by her tears. But since he was a happy-minded man who had never thought to look deeply below the surface of things, he was also astonished.

"My darling girl," he exclaimed, "you weren't worried about me! I had a perfectly safe journey. The *Malek* is one of the stoutest brigs in the coast trade—didn't you know?"

Yes, she knew. It had not been fear for Loren's safety that had kept her sobbing through that dreadful night. But she could not tell him this. Nor that her tears now were tears of thankfulness for the simple strong goodness of him, which she could be glad of even if she could not fall in love with it.

In the second half of February the rain stopped. The sun appeared and the mud began to dry. With Serena, Kendra made frequent trips down the hill to lay in supplies in case she had to stand another deluge.

Mr. Fenway told her sad stories about the launches coming down from the gold country, bringing men half dead from scurvy and fevers. Barefooted, frostbitten, sick, with blood-

241

shot eyes and trembling hands, the poor fellows lay on deck begging stronger men to help them carry their loads.

"Loads of what?" Kendra asked.

"Gold," said Mr. Fenway. "They can't eat it, can't wear it, can't use it to keep off the snow. Now they're so sick they can't even carry it."

Kendra thanked heaven that she and her friends had taken Ning's advice and left the hills in time. Mr. Fenway, never loth to find some comfort in other people's troubles, was telling her that all this had made his own life easier.

"Here's all they need," said Mr. Fenway, his big bony hand holding out a bottle of lime juice. "We're getting this stuff in casks now from these British vessels. We pour it into empty gin bottles and keep it for sale. It's bringing us quite a lot of business."

He spoke with gloomy satisfaction. By this time Kendra had learned that Mr. Fenway—like herself and no doubt like a lot of other people—had worked out his own way of finding content.

34

The next morning there were clouds on the hills, but by the time Kendra and Loren had finished breakfast the day was bright. Ralph and Loren set out for the store. While Serena cleared up the kitchen Kendra went upstairs to attend to the bedroom.

As she was slipping a pillow into a fresh case she heard quick footsteps on the stairs. Almost before she could turn around Loren burst into the room.

Loren's light hair was all a-tumble, his cheeks looked even pinker and healthier than they usually did. He was almost breathless with his news.

"Kendra! The steamer!"

Kendra dropped the pillow. "In the bay?"

"Not yet. But she's been sighted. Come on, we'll have a look—bring the spyglass."

Ralph had brought Kendra's horse around to the front of the house. Already the streets were full of people, on horseback and on foot. They were all shouting, laughing, hurrying in whatever direction they thought would give them the best chance to see the steamer as she puffed through the narrow gate between the two peninsulas that enclosed San Francisco Bay.

Over the racket Loren called,

"Let's ride up the hill to get a look. We'll have time to come down to the waterfront before she drops anchor."

It was not easy to ride up or down or crosswise, for everybody was getting in the way of everybody else. But Loren and Kendra struggled through, with Ralph and Serena close behind them. They rode up and up, beyond the last scattered tents and houses, and climbed a ridge from which they could see out to the strait between San Francisco and the upper peninsula. As they paused, Kendra was surprised to see how many other people had thought to come the same way. On all sides of her, riders were straining their eyes toward the strait, while behind them still others were plodding up the hill. Spyglass at his eyes, Loren had begun to search the distance.

The wind was sweeping the hilltop with nothing to break its force. But this same wind had cleared the air, so that Kendra could see down to the water and across to the slopes on the other side. Also she could see that Loren was trying to tell her something. But every soul around them seemed to be talking at once. Between the noise and the wind, Loren had to repeat his words several times before she understood that he had sighted the steamer and was offering her the glass so she could see it too.

Eagerly Kendra put the glass to her eyes. At first she could see only the faroff hills and the whitecaps tossing on the water. Then, as she turned this way and that, she found the steamer, and as she found it she felt a shock.

Before she left home Kendra had seen many steamboats on the rivers. But these had been smart little craft with paint always new and brasswork polished every morning. This steamer in front of her was the ugliest thing she had ever seen on water.

She saw it all at once—a squat ungainly vessel with a big paddlewheel and a smokestack belching out clouds of smoke. Along with the smokestack she saw three masts sticking up like giant black toothpicks; she supposed they were there to carry sails if the engines gave out. And the steamer was not only ugly. She was also a mess. She was scratched, battered, stained with salt and blistered with sun.

—She looks, thought Kendra, as if she hasn't been scrubbed or painted since she left New York. And that was last October. Twenty-one weeks ago.

But then Kendra guiltily reminded herself that this was the first steamboat ever to make her way from the Atlantic Coast of the United States all around to the Pacific side. No wonder the crewmen had had no time to keep her looking pretty. They had been too busy just getting here.

But the steamer was here. And she had brought an astounding lot of people. Watching, Kendra saw men and women packed on deck, more of them than she thought could possibly have been crowded into the berths inside. Loren knew more about vessels than she did, so giving him the glass she cupped her hands and shouted to him through the wind.

"How many passengers was she built to carry?"

After a study of the steamer he shouted back, "About a hundred."

"There must be," she exclaimed, "at least three hundred of them on deck!"

"Three hundred?" Loren repeated. "I'd say nearer five."

"Where," Kendra demanded, "did they all sleep?"

As he knew no more about this than she did, Loren could not answer. Kendra wondered if they had used the berths in shifts, as men were using the beds in the City Hotel. She saw an astonishing number of women, and shivered as she thought of what those women must have had to put up with in a ship so crowded that they could hardly have had any privacy at all.

The people on deck were milling about, as eager to see San Francisco as the people on shore had been to see the steamer. Beckoning Ralph and Serena, Loren proposed that now they ride down toward the waterfront and watch the boat come in. They made their way down and stopped their horses at a spot from which they could look over the point where Kendra had landed from the *Cynthia*'s rowboat last year.

At the reminder Kendra felt a start. The *Cynthia* had brought her to San Francisco in February, 1848. Now it was February, 1849. In that year how much had happened! A year ago she had never heard of Ted, nor of Marny. She had not dreamed that the creeks of California were flowing over golden sands. She had not dreamed that one day she would be married to Loren Shields.

A year ago this had been a village of nine hundred people. Today—she did not know how many were here now, nobody had time to count them, but there were thousands. A year ago mighty few people in the whole world had heard of a town called San Francisco. Today mighty few people in the whole world had not heard of it.

She caught sight of Marny and Archwood, on horseback, a little way farther down the slope toward the waterfront. Marny had already seen her and was waving. Kendra and Loren waved back. After some trouble they maneuvered their horses so that they were all together, watching the show.

Marny wore a new spring bonnet and a riding dress with a big rippling skirt. Pinned to the bosom of her dress was the jeweled brooch Archwood had given her, but in this crowd she was taking no chances; she also wore the belt that carried her little Colt pistol. Marny's red hair was blowing rakishly around the brim of her bonnet, and her green eyes were big and bright and vivid. She was nearly breathless with excitement.

Archwood was interested but not excited. With his usual air of urban elegance, he was smiling faintly as he watched. Archwood kept himself a bit aloof from San Francisco. He was enjoying his adventure here, but his home was still New York.

Marny, who had brought a field glass of her own, looked at the steamer and whistled softly.

"So many people!" she exclaimed. The wind here was not as strong as on the hilltop and she could talk without effort. "Loren, Kendra," she went on, "don't you think there *must* be somebody we know?"

Archwood gave her a glance of amused indulgence. "Marny can't get that out of her head," he said to them. "I've told her there are several million people who might have boarded that steamer, and the chance of our knowing any who did—" He shrugged.

"I don't care," said Marny, "we might know some of them!"

Archwood smiled. He liked all this. Archwood might laugh at Marny, but one reason why she delighted him was her talent for enjoying whatever went on around her.

Kendra was glad the steamer was arriving on a sunny day.

245

The water of the bay was so bright that it dazzled her eyes. She thought even the deserted vessels did not seem as forlorn as when she had looked at them through the rain. And the ships of war, about to give the Commodore's official greeting to his countrymen, were magnificent.

In the bay were five ships of war besides the Commodore's flagship. From the moment he had received the report that the steamer was in sight he had been preparing his welcome.

Some men of the navy had deserted but many more of them had not. Now these stood proudly at their posts. They had emblazoned their vessels with every flag and pennant they could find, and they had manned every gun. The ships had bee stationed in two lines, the smallest of them nearest the Gate, the next larger opposite and farther in, and so on until the largest, the flagship itself, would be the last that the steamer would pass. The men at the guns stood ready to fire salvos.

The steamer came in between the two rugged strips of land that enclosed the bay. The watchers began to cheer. On the hills and rooftops, leaning out of windows and shoving on the waterfront, they yelled their welcome, they waved flags and scarfs and pages of newspaper. The steamer came on. Spewing smoke, she whiffed and belched and at last she drew into line with the first of the waiting warships. The sailors shouted, the guns gave a broadside salute. The steamer growled and went on, passing one ship on her left and another on her right. The guns thundered, the smoke rolled up in great black clouds, the wind blew the clouds to shore. Loren choked, Archwood began to cough. Kendra felt her eyes pricking with tears. As she dried them she heard Marny say, "The damn thing is throwing soot all over my bonnet!"

But it was quite wonderful. They all agreed to this. They coughed and wiped their eyes and laughed and said hoarsely that it was a great day and they wouldn't have missed it for a fistful of gold.

The first Forty-niners were here.

35

When the smoke cleared, they saw the steamer anchored near the Commodore's flagship. She had brought several army officers and their wives, and already boats from the flagship were receiving them. The rest of the passengers waited, clutching such baggage as they had managed to cram on the steamer along with themselves. If they waited long enough the crew would row them ashore. But already men with boats of their own were rowing out, to bring in those willing to pay for the ride.

It was now almost noon. The watchers on shore were crowding as close as they could to the waterfront. Marny was not the only one saying, "Maybe the steamer has brought somebody I know."

Ralph and Serena moved a little way off to join some friends of their own. Kendra and Loren, Marny and Archwood, stayed where they were, in sight of the point. Several peddlers were walking around, selling dried fruit, walnuts, and jars holding pickles or candy drops. Others offered wine and gin, each of them carrying a tin cup which he passed from buyer to buyer with the utmost democracy.

Kendra and her companions would have liked some refreshment, but they did not feel tempted by what was being hawked around them. Kendra proposed that Marny and Archwood come home with Loren and herself. "I have cold meat," she said, "and cheese, so there'll be no trouble putting a lunch on table."

But neither she nor the others wanted to leave yet. The first boats were coming in, the first passengers were stepping ashore. At sight of them the waiting onlookers began to murmur with shock and sympathy.

Kendra thought she had never seen people who looked tireder, dingier, more bewildered, or more miserable. Men and women, they looked as if they had been starved of sleep and food. Men and women, they looked as if they had been wearing the same clothes for weeks. Whatever had been their circumstances at home, today they were unwashed, uncombed, exhausted, and in wretched disarray.

Loren spoke to Kendra. "They must have had a mighty hard time getting here."

Looking at their haggard faces, Archwood said, "I don't understand why the captain took so many passengers aboard."

Loren could not reply to this. He did not understand it either.

Marny was exclaiming in amazement. "They keep on coming! Boat after boat—where did they *put* so many? And aren't they the worst looking—" Her voice broke into a squeal. "Look! Oh look! Norman!"

She began to call out, in a tone of delight.

"Norman! Norman Lamont!"

In the general hubbub, nobody six feet away could have heard her, and none of the steamer's passengers had yet come so close. Marny caught Archwood's hand with such force that she nearly threw him off his horse.

"Warren Archwood, I told you so! Don't ever laugh at me again. I told you so, I told you so—"

"What are you—" Archwood was demanding, but if she heard him she gave no sign of it. She had thrust her horse's bridle into his hand and was scrambling to the ground.

"Wait for me, all of you," she ordered. "Here, Warren, take the glass—I was never so happy in my life—I told you so!" Her voice rose again. "Norman!"

If she said any more they could not hear it, for by this time Marny was too far away. Holding up her skirt, she was running downhill toward the point. The road was full of people,—but Marny was making her way among them with such delighted energy that she was speedily getting where she wanted to go. She had thought to pull off her bonnet, so the sun on her red hair would flash like a beacon. Waving the bonnet over her head, she was trying to catch the eye of somebody below.

Through her own glass Kendra had a clear view of what was happening.

As Marny waved the bonnet above her torchlike hair, a man laboring upward from the landing place caught sight of her. He stopped as if in shock. His chin dropped, his eyes widened. For a moment he stared in disbelief. Then a sudden

248

smile lit up his face. As Marny pushed nearer, he began to laugh in joyful amazement.

The stranger was a lean dark fellow with black eyes, sharp nose, and black hair going gray. He had a black moustache and a small pointed beard, both sadly untended now. He wore no hat, and his suit was rumpled as if he had slept in it. With one hand he lugged a heavy-looking carpetbag, with the other he had been helping a girl who was climbing the road beside him, carrying a bag of her own. But at sight of Marny he had let go of the other girl, and now was waving eagerly, as glad to see Marny as she was to see him.

The girl beside him was young and slender, but like the other women from the steamer she was so bedraggled that it was hard to tell if she was pretty or not. The man said something to her, apparently a few words of explanation. The girl gave a weary nod, and again they both began to climb. While they pushed upward Marny elbowed her way down toward them, and when at last they met, Marny and the man caught each other in a joyous hug.

Kendra lowered her glass and turned to Archwood. Holding his own glass to his eyes, he was watching in surprise and displeasure. Archwood was not a man who would make a scene in public, but his face had darkened angrily. Whoever that stranger might be, Archwood was not happy at the way Marny was greeting him.

Kendra put her hand on his sleeve. "Mr. Archwood," she said, and again, "Mr. Archwood! May I tell you something?"

A memory had popped into her mind. A few minutes ago she had noticed the belt in which Marny wore her little gun. The first time Marny had shown her that gun they had been in their leafy "bathroom" on the way to Shiny Gulch. Marny had said,

"This was a present from the man who ran the best gambling parlor in New York. A Frenchman from New Orleans, named Norman Lamont. I used to be one of his dealers."

Marny said Norman had gone back to New Orleans because he thought it was the best gambling town in the country. She had added,

"There never was anything between Norman and me. He always had a girl of his own. But I admired him. He had real talent."

Now as both Loren and Archwood turned to her with puzzled faces, Kendra said,

"I think I know who Marny's friend is. A famous gambler —Marny told me about him."

She explained that Marny had been one of Norman's dealers in New York.

"I don't know the girl with him," Kendra added. "Maybe she's his wife."

"Possibly," said Archwood. Kendra was glad to observe that he spoke with a flicker of amusement.

Putting his glass to his eyes again, Archwood turned back to look for Marny. With Norman and his girl friend, Marny was making her way back up the hill. Marny had taken the bag from the girl and was now carrying it for her. She raised her free hand in a gesture to Kendra and Loren and Archwood. Kendra and Loren waved back. Archwood waited, to hear what Marny herself was going to say.

He did not have to wait long. Marny came hurrying up, half out of breath. Dropping the bag, she grabbed Archwood's hand.

"Warren, our fortune is made! This is Norman Lamont, the smartest sporting man that ever turned a card!"

She spoke with such innocent exuberance that it was plain even to Archwood that in Norman he himself had no rival. Archwood held out his hand.

"How do you do. My name is Warren Archwood."

Norman smiled. As she watched him, the word that came to Kendra's mind was *sharp*. Norman's look at this new acquaintance—and probably at every new acquaintance—was a look of appraisal. He seemed to be asking—What use can you be to me? But his smile was quick, and there were crinkles of humor around his eyes.

—Sharp, thought Kendra, maybe too sharp, but I can see why Marny likes him. I like him myself.

Norman was saying to Archwood, "Marny has been telling me about the gambling tent. Sounds interesting."

His accent had a trace of French. It was not the accent of a man who had recently learned English; Kendra judged that he had grown up speaking both languages, so that his French was likely to be slightly American, as his English was slightly French.

Marny had turned to the girl. She told them this was Norman's friend Rosabel (she said nothing about her being

250

his wife, and they had not expected her to). She said Rosabel could play the piano. Marny had not met Rosabel before, and this was all she had had time to learn as they came up the hill.

Rosabel was a brunette with a well-shaped nose and chin, and eyebrows so thick and silky that they were like strips of black velvet above her eyes. Her face was dirty and so was her dress and so was the tattered scarf she had tied over her head. But Kendra could see now that she was a handsome wench and also she had the look of a clever one.

—Of course she's clever, thought Kendra. If she were stupid Norman would never have brought her here.

Rosabel smiled up at them, saying, "Pleased to meet you, I'm sure."

Her speech had no trace of French, nor was it typical of anything else. It was merely rather common. Her manner was friendly, with a saucy self-confidence. No doubt Rosabel's schooling had been scant. But she had her own sort of education and she knew how to make the most of it.

While Norman and Rosabel were getting better acquainted with Archwood, Loren spoke to Kendra in an undertone. She had invited Marny and Archwood to lunch—was there enough to take care of these other two as well? "They can tell us," said Loren, "about the voyage of the steamer, and what's been going on in the States."

As Kendra was as eager as Loren to hear what they had to tell, she said she could manage, and gave the invitation. They accepted with enthusiasm. Marny said this was one day the Blackbeards could open the Calico Palace without her, and they would all four come to lunch as soon as Norman and Rosabel had had time to go home with her and get washed.

With Serena's help Kendra set out a meal. It had to be hastily prepared, but if the food on the steamer had been as meager as she suspected, she thought it would make little difference what she served as long as there was plenty of it.

When her guests arrived Norman and Rosabel wore borrowed clothes because, as they said, their own were not fit to be seen. Archwood's coat was too wide for Norman, Marny's skirt was too long for Rosabel, but they did not care. They were happy because they had reached San Francisco alive, which many times during the journey had seemed

251

doubtful. They were happy at sitting down before a table with knives and forks and napkins. And as Kendra had foreseen, they were ecstatic at having all they wanted to eat.

Loren told them not to try to talk until they had finished their lunch—a needless remark, for they had not thought of trying. But at last they had had enough. Loren brought out brandy, Kendra poured coffee and told Serena to leave the dishes. They all went into the parlor. Rosabel saw the sofa and with a sigh of joy flung herself upon it. Norman sat on the floor, his back against the wall. As there were only four chairs besides the sofa, Loren and Ralph sat on the floor too. Kendra and Serena and Marny took three of the chairs, and Archwood—who was not fond of floor-sitting—gratefully took the one left over.

Sipping coffee and brandy, they listened. Norman and Rosabel, with sighs and shudders and—now that it was over—with laughter, told them how the first Forty-niners had come to California.

36

"Well, it was this way," said Norman. "Those men who had organized the steamboat line, they were a smart bunch. Their *plan* was good."

Norman lounged on the floor, his shoulders against the wall, his hands with the brandy glass dangling between his knees. As he paused, Rosabel nestled deeper among the sofa cushions, luxuriating in the first comfort she had known in months. Norman went on, his French accent giving a piquant turn to his words.

"The plan was like this. Now that California was American, they figured that a lot of Americans would want to come here—to live, or just to look it over. And these people would like a quicker way to get here than taking wagons across the plains, or ships around Cape Horn. The quicker way would be to go across the Isthmus of Panama."

His listeners nodded. Norman said,

"So in New York these men organized the steamboat line. They planned to send steamers from New York to Chagres."

"Chagres!" Rosabel echoed in a voice of horror.

"Chagres?" Marny repeated. "Where's that?"

"I never heard of it," said Archwood, "but probably Loren knows. He's a seaman."

Loren nodded, but made a gesture toward Norman, who explained.

"I hadn't heard of it either, but"—he said with a shiver—"I sure do know about it now. Chagres is a port on the Atlantic side of the Isthmus. The plan was that a steamer would set out from New York, stop at New Orleans to take on anybody who wanted to start from there, and go on to Chagres. The passengers would get off and the steamer would go back to New York."

"Then what?" asked Loren.

"Well, at the same time," said Norman, "the steamboat men were building some other steamers to operate on the west coast. These would go from New York around South America to San Francisco. Once they got here, they would stay on the Pacific side, running up and down between San Francisco and Panama City." He glanced at Loren. "I guess you know—I didn't—Panama City is on the Pacific side of the Isthmus."

Again Loren nodded. Norman took a sip of brandy and continued,

"The people on their way to California would cross the Isthmus from Chagres to Panama City. At Panama City they would get aboard one of the steamers that ran between there and San Francisco."

"How were these people," asked Marny, "going to get across the Isthmus?"

From the sofa Rosabel gave a shuddering sigh. Norman began to chuckle, but at the same time he shuddered too.

"The plan was to build a railroad across," he said. "But until they could do this, a traveler would have to make his own way from one side to the other. But they said the Isthmus was only about fifty miles wide, so this wouldn't be too much trouble." He gave an expressive Latin shrug. "The fact is, I saw all this in the papers but I didn't pay much attention. I wasn't thinking about California. I had a nice business in New Orleans—card parlor, good dealers, music by Rosabel—"

Marny glanced at Rosabel, evidently calculating how her talents could best be used at the Calico Palace. Norman went on with his story.

He said the first Pacific steamer, the one they had seen this morning, fittingly named the *California*, had left New York last fall, bound for San Francisco. Midshipman Beale had brought his news of gold, but he had not stirred much excitement. The *California* had berths for a hundred people. If anybody in New York had wanted to buy a ticket to the land of gold, he could have done so. But nobody did.

However, the captain of the steamer, Mr. Forbes, had been told that on his way up the Pacific Coast he was to stop at Panama City. Here he would meet a group of Americans on their way to San Francisco. These people were not looking for gold. They were army officers with their wives, men sent to fill government posts, directors of the steamboat line who wanted to look over their new territory, and four clergymen going out to set up churches. There were also two or three young men of business, who intended to join the growing Pacific trade. One of these had his wife with him, and he had chosen to go this way because of the agreeable companions she would have on the journey. Not wanting to make the long voyage around South America, these twenty-odd persons had planned to sail to Chagres on the first steamer of the Atlantic line, and cross the Isthmus to Panama City.

Captain Forbes set out on his journey. He did not expect it to be easy. No vessel had ever steamed its way around South America. Captain Forbes knew this voyage would test his worth as a seaman and as a commander. But he expected the test to concern wind and waves and unruly sailors. The poor man had no idea what lay ahead of him.

He sailed from New York on the sixth of October, 1848, bound for Panama City and San Francisco. Eight weeks later, on the first of December, the steamer *Falcon* left New York, bound for New Orleans and Chagres. On board the *Falcon* were the ladies and gentlemen who expected to cross the Isthmus and meet Captain Forbes on the other side.

They had a pleasant journey to New Orleans. The *Falcon* was a brand-new vessel equipped with every luxury of travel, and they were looking forward to their days in port. General Persifer Smith, who was on his way to take command of the army in California, had spent several years of duty at a post near New Orleans and while there he had married a local girl. General and Mrs. Smith had promised to guide their fellow travelers on sightseeing tours of the town.

As Norman got this far, his lips began to twitch. "But in the meantime—" he said, and glanced at Rosabel.

"Things were happening in New Orleans," said Rosabel.

Lying on the sofa, she raised herself on her elbow. She and Norman looked at each other. They both began to laugh. Norman said,

"I suppose you folks know about that army courier, Lieutenant Loeser. The fellow who went to Washington with letters from Colonel Mason and a box of gold."

They said yes. Kendra added that the last time she had heard of Loeser had been when she read the *Alta's* report that he had gone as far as Callao in Peru. Norman said Loeser came from Callao to New Orleans, where a newspaper editor sent a reporter to ask him the latest news from California.

Loeser showed the reporter the box he was carrying to President Polk. A little box that had once held tea, now it held two hundred and twenty-eight ounces of gold.

"Look at it," Loeser said to the newspaper man. "Handle it. And you can print in the paper—men are coming in every day from the placers, bringing so much gold that they can hardly carry it. I've seen them."

The newspaper printed the interview.

New Orleans caught fire. All of a sudden, in the streets, the taverns, the banks, the gambling rooms, everywhere you went, people were talking of nothing but California gold. Everybody in town wanted to go to the placers

Loeser took a coastwise boat for Washington, but behind him the fire continued to blaze. A few days after he left, the New Orleans *Picayune* published an article headed "Ho for California!" This article gave more details about the steamers that were to sail from New York to Chagres, every one of them stopping at New Orleans on the way.

"By this time," said Norman, "the town was wild."

"In the shops," said Rosabel, "the salesmen were so excited that their hands trembled when they tried to measure a yard of ribbon. When you went to a show, so many people were whispering about gold that you could hardly hear the actors. One man even told me girls in California were wearing nugget necklaces—"

"They are," Marny said smiling.

Archwood asked, why had New Orleans exploded in front of Loeser, when Washington and Baltimore had shown only mild interest in Beale?

Norman could only guess. Maybe it was because Beale had been needed to prepare people's minds. Maybe it was because Loeser's report, based on Colonel Mason's own tour of the placers, carried move vivid details. Or maybe it was a difference in the two men themselves. Norman could not say. All he could say was, New Orleans was the first town in the United States to get the gold fever, and New Orleans really got it.

And the way to New Orleans was the *Falcon*, with half her berths still empty. The steamboat line had an office in New Orleans, and when people inquired there they got a clear answer. If you wanted to go to the gold fields you could buy a ticket. This ticket would entitle you to passage on the *Falcon* from New Orleans to Chagres, and then passage on the west coast steamer from Panama City to San Francisco. (Crossing the Isthmus, said the clerks, was up to you.)

The questioners hardly heard this last remark. What they did hear was, if you bought a ticket on the *Falcon* you could go to San Francisco.

But the *Falcon* was almost here.

The passengers already on the *Falcon* had had months in which to put their affairs in order and prepare for their voyage. But if you were going to board when the *Falcon* stopped at New Orleans, you had only a few days to make ready.

Only a few days—and this was no short and easy journey. From New Orleans to the Isthmus was about two thousand miles; from the Isthmus to San Francisco was nearly four thousand miles farther. And those miles meant dollars. That ticket cost money. A lot of money.

Norman had said everybody in town wanted to go to California. But in New Orleans or anywhere else, it would be a rare man who could drop his whole present life so suddenly. Men of property could not wind up their business in a week or two. Men of no property could not pay their way. Dutiful fathers were not going to abandon their families and run off to the end of the world. Fathers with no sense of duty were not often the sort to have saved up so much cash.

And if there were few men ready for such a jaunt, there were even fewer women. A woman was less likely than a man to have a purse full of money; she was more likely to want security instead of wild chances; and she was even more likely to be serious about such obligations as children and aged parents.

The only people who could scramble aboard the *Falcon* would be those who had no ties and no cares. Or at least, none that they bothered about. They would be people who could throw away the past and laugh at the future. But they had to be people with ready money.

Were there any such people? Yes, of course. The professional gamblers, and the most reckless of their lady friends. People like Norman and Rosabel.

37

The *Falcon* steamed placidly into port at New Orleans. And here, bags packed and tickets in their hands, she found a hundred and sixty persons ready to start for the land of gold.

They were a varied company. Among them were troublesome rich boys whose families had bought their passage to get them out of the way; men of the hopeful sort who are always chasing rainbows and who always seem able to borrow money for it; even a few responsible citizens who wanted adventure and had nothing to keep them at home. But by far the greatest number—about two-thirds of them all—were gamblers from New Orleans and the Mississippi River boats, and the girls who worked with them. And of course, said Norman, women—

Here Norman cleared his throat and glanced at Kendra, as if just remembering her presence. "Excuse me, Mrs. Shields," he said.

Kendra gave him a smile. "Go ahead, Norman. It's all right."

"It *is* all right," Marny assured him. "Kendra has lived at a gold camp, which is more than you have. You can talk."

Loren laughed and agreed. Thus encouraged, Norman laughed too and talked frankly. While in New Orleans, he said, Lieutenant Loeser had spoken of California's excess of men. So, naturally, among those who had bought tickets on the *Falcon* were several of the town's most enterprising madames of parlor houses. As the trip was so costly, most of them planned to look for girls after they reached San Francisco, but not all were willing to leave so important a matter to chance. In particular, one keen-witted madame known as Blossom had thoughtfully chosen the four most engaging girls in her establishment and was taking them with her. They were all named for flowers—Lilac, Iris, Clover, and Daffodil.

"And they *were* pretty," said Norman. "And not stupid. Hardly as smart as Blossom, but they knew their way around."

All these people had tickets entitling them to passage from New Orleans to Chagres, and then to San Francisco, on the steamboat line. They were all determined to go there.

The captain of the *Falcon* warned them that his vessel, only half as large as the *California,* had berths for only fifty passengers. Half of these berths were already taken. Such a crowd as themselves would be most uncomfortable. Did they mind?

They did not.

Very well, said the captain. A berth meant for one could always hold two, and if they were willing to sleep in hammocks, on bare planks—?

They were.

Well then, let them do it. The voyage to the Isthmus would take nine or ten days. He would get them there.

And so the little steamer *Falcon,* jammed with nearly two hundred people, left New Orleans.

Marny got up from her chair, took the seat cushion and plopped it on the floor and sat upon it.

"I am breathless," she said. "Four clergymen, a general, all those fine ladies—do go on."

Norman and Rosabel spoke together.

"It was dreadful," said Norman.

258

"It was funny," said Rosabel.

Norman continued,

"The captain couldn't force the old passangers out of their berths, so he had to pack us into what was left. This meant they were more cozy than we were, but they were mighty unhappy all the same. The food was awful—salt meat and hardtack, there was no room to carry luxuries—and the ship was so crowded we could hardly move, but this wasn't the real trouble. The trouble was, they were the steady sort, and we—" He shrugged again, and looked at Rosabel as if asking for words.

Rosabel lifted her black velvet eyebrows and spread out her hands. "My dears, the general had brought three men-servants to shave him and shine his boots and wait on him. And the general's wife had brought a maid of her own, a real elegant lady's maid like in a show. Those army ladies were used to being treated with *respect*. On military posts I guess everybody steps aside to let them pass. They sure didn't like us. They sat in a huddle with their embroidery and pretended they didn't see us—"

Kendra choked into her handkerchief. She was remembering how she had been ordered not to see those two white houses on the cliff at Valparaiso. She thought of Eva on the *Cynthia*, with her pretty sewing; Eva in San Francisco, the colonel's wife. She pictured Eva among those motley travelers. Yes, Eva would have gone on with her pretty sewing. She simply would not have seen them.

"And those ministers!" said Rosabel. "They were young men and they weren't bad-looking, but they sure were pious. One Baptist, two Presbyterians, and the other—what was he, Norman? Doesn't matter. Anyway, they set out to reform us. They couldn't understand that we were doing all right the way we were. We sat on the floor and played cards—for money, of course, what's the fun of it otherwise? —and they thought this was wicked. And we played on Sunday and they didn't like that either. I had brought my banjo, and we sang songs, and they didn't like our sort of songs. They didn't like anything we did."

Kendra caught Marny's eye. They both bit their lips to keep from giggling. They both suspected that Rosabel, out of respect for the company, was omitting to say that the real basis for the consternation of the clergy was neither songs nor gambling, but the fact that Blossom and her flower

259

garden had gone right into business as soon as they came aboard.

Rosabel said, "We were crowded and cross and the weather was as hot as the inside of a cow. But then we got to Chagres." She gave a long deep sigh. "And after that, everything that had happened on the *Falcon* seemed like bliss."

The *Falcon* dumped her passengers at Chagres. The captain, having done all he had promised to do, turned his vessel around and left them there.

Seven degrees above the equator, Chagres was a swampy village on a river bank. In Chagres it was always hot and nearly always raining. The few hundred people who lived here were the mixed-up descendants of Indians, Negroes, Spaniards, and sailors of many races whose vessels had touched here in years past. Their homes were huts made of canes, often raised on stilts because of the swampy ground. The *Falcon* reached Chagres in the last week of December, but now as usual the weather was so hot that the people wore hardly any clothes, and some of them no clothes at all.

"The army ladies," said Norman, "were horrified."

"I was horrified myself," said Rosabel. "I never saw such ugly people."

She made a face and continued,

"The town is filthy. It swarms with every kind of vermin you ever heard of or saw in a nightmare. Every afternoon it rains, then the sun comes out and everybody starts to steam. I never smelled anything like it. There was no place for us to stay, nothing to do about our baggage except sit on it with a gun so nobody could steal it. They have a few little trading booths that sell things from the ships, and we bought umbrellas, but there weren't nearly enough. We were all so miserable together it actually made us kind of friendly."

"What did you eat?" asked Kendra.

"Stuff we bought at the trading booths. Mostly hardtack and jerked beef. Dreadful."

Kendra smiled in sympathy, remembering all the jerky she had eaten at Shiny Gulch. Norman took up the tale.

"We couldn't find anybody who spoke English, but some of us from New Orleans could get around in Spanish and we asked how to cross the Isthmus. They said we should take boats up the Chagres River as far as it went, and get mules to carry us the rest of the way. The only kind of boat they have is a thing called a bongo."

He explained.

"They take a big log—I mean *big,* the trees down there grow ten or fifteen feet across the trunks. They hollow out this log till they have nothing left but a slab of wood at each end, then they put up a sort of awning made of palm leaves, because the sun would kill even the natives if they didn't have some kind of shade on their heads."

He paused, and Rosabel said,

"You pile into the bongo, ten or a dozen people and your bags. We threw away a lot of stuff, not room to take it along. There aren't any seats in a bongo so you sit on the bags. And each bongo is poled up the river by three or four boatmen. And those men, my dears—"

She drew a long breath like a groan.

"They are big, they are mean, they are always yelling and quarreling and fighting, and they are stark naked. On that trip up the Chagres River they did not wear one single thing."

"They wore hats," said Norman.

"Excuse me, gentlemen," said Rosabel.

She cuddled into the sofa cushions as if her memories had made her tired. Norman said,

"Well, here we went, a string of bongos poled by those naked savages. They poked along at about one mile an hour. Every time we came to a patch of shade they stopped to rest. Nothing could make them work harder. We offered double wages, extra food—they would *not* hurry."

Norman gave a sigh of his own.

"The trees hung over the water and dangled great big vines, sometimes such a tangle of vines that we couldn't get through, and the men had to hack a way. They had brought big long knives for this."

"We were scared half to death," said Rosabel. "Those creatures with those knives, yelling and howling all day long. They couldn't keep steady. One bongo would hit another and that one would hit the next one, and so on down the line. They would all hit and scrape and bounce, and we had to hold tight to keep from being thrown into the water, and those men would stop poling and we had to sit there while they yelled and waved those knives. Every one of them was shouting that somebody had hit his bongo on purpose and they were all threatening to kill each other."

"We wouldn't have cared," said Norman, "if they had only killed each other, but we were scared they were going to kill *us*. We had money and food, and anyway they looked like the sort who might have killed somebody for the fun of it. We never all slept at once."

"Where did you sleep?" asked Kendra.

"Huddled up in the bongos, or on the ground by the fire. We couldn't cook much because the rain kept everything so damp. Mostly we nibbled on hardtack and jerky. But we tried to keep a fire going at night, because of the mosquitoes, and to scare away animals. Sometimes we couldn't even keep that much fire going."

"One night," said Rosabel, "those savages had a monkey roast. Made me sick. It looked like they were tearing babies apart. But then it rained, and put out their fire too."

"How did you get out of the rain?" asked Kendra.

"We didn't," said Rosabel. "We bunched together under our umbrellas, or under the bushes, and then steamed. It was like being boiled alive."

"We were on that river," said Norman, "three days and three nights, every minute of it plain horror. That's the time it took us to go thirty miles. When we'd gone that far we came to a village called Cruces. This is the end of the river."

"Cruces was worse than Chagres," said Rosabel.

"Right," said Norman. "Hotter, wetter, dirtier. And nobody in Cruces knew *anything*. Chagres is a port, the people have to do a little something. In Cruces they don't even move. They just sit and sweat. They are there because they were born there and it's too much trouble to get out."

He gave a long low whistle.

"This," he said, "is where we were supposed to get mules to take us to Panama City. Hell, damn, by—oh, excuse me, Mrs. Shields. Here we were, nearly two hundred of us, and there weren't that many mules around. Or donkeys or horses or anything else that could carry us. And some people who had animals wouldn't sell them. Not for any money—and no wonder, what could they buy in a place like that?

"But we had to get out, and fast. The place is a pest-hole— malaria, yellow fever, smallpox, everything. Two or three of us were already sick.

"The boatmen were going to take the bongos back to

Chagres—that's easy, the current carries them down—and some of our crowd said they were going right back to Chagres and back home. Said they wouldn't move another yard through this hell if they never saw a speck of gold."

Kendra smiled as she listened. She knew nothing about Norman's talent as a gambler, but she was recognizing the trait that made Marny admire him. He had it, and so had Rosabel. They were not halfway people. It had not occurred to either of them to turn around at Cruces. They had set out for California and they meant to get there. Norman was saying,

"Those fellows had their minds made up to go home. They wanted to sell us their tickets on the Pacific steamer, Panama to San Francisco. Most of our party wouldn't buy them. Said we had our own tickets, who'd want any extra? But—"

Pausing, Norman sent a flash of his black eyes toward Rosabel. She laughed under her breath, and added,

"But Norman said there might be somebody at Panama City who would want to go to San Francisco, and would be glad to buy a ticket on the steamer. So we bought the tickets from men who were going back. Of course it was a gamble—"

"Norman Lamont," said Marny, "is the smartest gambler I ever knew. I've been saying so for a long time."

Norman accepted her praise with a comradely smile. Evidently he had a similar opinion of her.

"We spent a day in Cruces," he said, "buying all the mules and donkeys we could. We didn't dare stay longer because we knew we'd catch our death if we did. We had left a lot of our baggage in Chagres, now we had to throw away more because we couldn't carry it. Rosabel and I got a mule and a donkey, and they had to carry us and our stuff too. And we were lucky. Some men paired up and bought one donkey for both, and took turns riding it. Some of them walked the whole way with their bags on their backs.

"We had to spend a night there, lying on the wet ground and slapping mosquitoes. Some of the ladies cried all night, and some of the men never stopped swearing. Blossom gathered her girls together and put her arms around them and they sat there in a bundle of misery. Next morning we started out."

With a desperate look, Norman poured brandy into his glass.

"Cruces to Panama City," he said, "is only twenty miles, but it's twenty miles of mountains, rocks, bugs, heat, rain, torment. Away back, three hundred years ago when the Spaniards used to carry treasure across the Isthmus so their ships could take it to Spain, they made a sort of trail. But now the trail is overgrown, and piled with rocks that have rolled down the slopes. And steep——!" He whistled again.

"We climbed over mountains made of solid rock," said Rosabel. "They were so steep that they went almost straight up in the air. In the steepest places those old Spaniards had cut notches, like steps, so the mules could climb without sliding backwards. These mule staircases were so narrow that only one mule could go up at a time. Sometimes a pack would drop off a mule and people's clothes would fall out and their money too, gold and silver coins clattering down the mountain and rolling into the cracks between the rocks.

"Then when we got to the top of the mountain we had to go down the other side the same way. It was so steep, some folks fell over the heads of the mules and got hurt. We had to tear up clothes to make slings and bandages for them. Blossom knew how to do this. She showed me how and made the other girls help. One man fell so hard he broke his bones all to pieces. He screamed and screamed and at last he shot himself.

"After that," Rosabel continued grimly, "I walked. I let the mule carry my bags but I *walked*."

She laughed suddenly.

"My dears, I wish you could have listened to those men! I've heard a lot of blue words but I never heard so many at one time. Army and non-army. Blossom and the girls too. The ladies wept and sobbed and prayed and begged the ministers to pray for them. The ministers did pray. They prayed for us all, even those who played cards on Sunday.

"Those fifty miles across the Isthmus," she said clearly, "took us a week. Seven days. And there's a lot of minutes in seven days and every minute I thought I was going to die and I thought, What good will it do me to have a solid gold tombstone? But at last we got to Panama City."

"When you got there," said Marny, "were your troubles over?"

Norman and Rosabel broke into sardonic laughter. Like Norman before her, Rosabel reached for the bottle.

38

"Panama City," said Rosabel, "is a town of two thousand people and forty million bugs. It is hot and wet and sticky and when we got there they were having an epidemic of cholera."

"Have you ever seen anybody die of cholera?" Norman exclaimed. "Well, I hope I never have to again."

He continued. He said the people of Panama City were more civilized than those of Chagres, and in general they were a good-natured lot. But like most people who live in the smothering heat of the tropics, they spent most of their time drowsing in the shade, and moving as the shade moved. They had no idea what to do when a mob of Yankees exploded into town like a bunch of firecrackers.

The *Falcon*'s passengers burst into Panama City one day early in January, 1849. They demanded food and shelter and a steamboat to take them on their way .

Food? Well, the town had a market. Shelter? There wasn't any. Panama City had no hotel. As for the steamer, nobody knew anything about it.

Most of the Americans had to sleep outdoors, on the ground. Only a few of the most persistent, like Norman and Rosabel, managed to get lodgings.

"We went around and around," said Rosabel, "until we found a woman who would rent us a room. The room had fleas in it, and cockroaches and spiders, but at least it kept off the rain. And the house had a well, so we could wash. We kept as clean as we could because our people were getting sick."

"The whole Isthmus is a plague-spot," Norman said shortly. "Some of our friends died right there on the ground. The natives dragged their bodies off and threw them into the sea.

"All we could talk about or think about was getting away. There were no boats in the harbor except rowboats and fishing smacks, nothing fit to put to sea. We simply had to wait for that Pacific steamer and hope we'd live till it came in. The town has an old wall, about twenty feet high and I guess pretty near twenty feet thick, left by the Spaniards. Part of it has broken down but part is still there. On the ocean side of the wall they left some big guns, real cannon, two or three tons apiece. Every day all day you could see men straddling those cannon, watching for the steamer."

Norman gave his neck a stretch as if to cast off a burden.

"But those first days were simple," he said. "Pretty soon it got worse."

"What now?" Marny exclaimed.

Norman answered, "More people."

"They started coming in before we'd been there a week," said Rosabel. "A new crowd came in nearly every day."

"They told us," said Norman, "the whole United States had gone wild about gold. The President had shown Loeser's gold to Congress, and papers all over the country had printed Colonel Mason's report. Everybody wanted to go to California.

"But this was midwinter and they couldn't drive wagons across the prairies till the snow was gone. If they wanted to go to California right now, they had to take a boat. When the second steamer of the Atlantic line left New York she was packed with people like the *Falcon* at New Orleans.

"Of course they didn't know what they were getting into, any more than we had. That steamer got to Chagres a few days after we had left to go up the river. She dumped them all, like the *Falcon,* and went back for more. And those poor fools started across the Isthmus, like us.

"And in the meantime, other ships loaded with gold hunters had set out from Boston and Norfolk and Charleston and New Orleans and the Lord knows where else. They brought more people to Chagres. And all those people started across the Isthmus.

"Like in our group, some of them gave up at Cruces and went back home, some of them died on the way, but a lot of them got to Panama City somehow. By the time we'd been there two weeks, there were more Americans in town than natives. The family we were living with doubled and redoubled our rent because the people coming in were offering to pay practically any price to get under a roof.

"And we were all waiting for that one Pacific steamer, the *California.*"

Norman ran his hand over his black hair. He had a bewildered look, as if he could hardly believe what he himself had seen. He said,

"And in the meantime again, that steamer—Rosabel, pass me the brandy."

Laughing a little, she obeyed. Norman offered the bottle to Marny, but she shook her head.

"No thanks, I've got to deal this evening. Go on, Norman. What was the steamer doing?"

Norman told them the steamer had been having a good voyage. About the time that Norman and Rosabel were getting out of Chagres in a bongo, the steamer *California* had reached the port of Callao in Peru.

Captain Forbes stopped here to take on fresh food and water. To his astonishment, fifty Peruvian men came to him, saying they wanted passage to San Francisco.

The captain did not understand it. One or two passengers would not have surprised him, but fifty was an astounding number. Why on earth, he asked, did all these men want to go to that little village up the coast?

The Peruvians were surprised at his ignorance. They asked, Didn't he know? Hadn't he heard that in California people were running about, picking up lumps of gold like children gathering seashells on the beach?

No, Captain Forbes knew nothing about it.

As Kendra had read in the *Alta*, Loeser had stopped in Callao on his way to Washington. He had told his news of gold, and people in Callao had been talking about it ever since. But when Captain Forbes had left New York, Loeser had not yet reached the United States. The gold talk there had been no more than a gentle buzz. Captain Forbes had hardly heard it. Now he and his crewmen listened in wonder.

The steamboat line had been licensed by the government to carry Yankee mail and Yankee passengers. There was no rule forbidding Captain Forbes to take foreigners if he had room for them, but the understanding was that he would always give precedence to United States citizens.

However, every passenger berth on the *California* was empty. Captain Forbes had reserved space for the twenty-odd persons he expected to meet at Panama City, but his vessel was built to carry a hundred. When the steamer left Callao fifty of her berths were occupied by these men of Peru.

On the eighteenth of January, Norman and Rosabel and

their weary friends heard a shout from the men straddling the cannon on the wall. The steamer! Oh, that splendid steamer, with her red paddlewheel and her American flag! The steamer anchored in the deep water and lowered a boat to take the captain ashore.

Now Captain Forbes received what was probably his greatest shock since he first went to sea. Instead of a dozing village he found a place of horror. Instead of twenty ladies and gentlemen and a few elegant maids and valets he met thousands of frantic people, pleading for passage to San Francisco. When he stepped off the boat, Captain Forbes was nearly crushed by the mob that rushed upon him.

He saw men and women lying in helpless groups on the ground, dying of dirt and bad food and tropical diseases. Nobody could tell him how many had died and how many more were sick. Some of the Americans had left, to re-make the dreadful Isthmus crossing and go home. Others, afraid to try the crossing again, said they would take any vessel going anywhere if only they could get off the Isthmus.

"The poor man," said Rosabel, "didn't know what to do. I bet he wished he'd stayed home."

The others agreed with her. "But what *did* he do?" asked Kendra.

They said the captain had handled the problem about as well as anybody could have. After a day or two of utter bewilderment—for which nobody could blame him—he announced his decision. The officials of the steamboat line approved, and General Smith promised the authority of the army to help him enforce it.

The captain said that in common humanity he had to rescue as many of these people as his vessel could carry. She could not carry them all. He said he would take them in the order in which they had the right to come aboard. Those who had first right to take the steamer were those who held through tickets to San Francisco on the steamboat line, tickets they had bought at an office of the line in the United States.

The men from Peru would have to get off. They objected so violently that the sailors had to pick them up and carry them to the boats that would take them ashore. Once the steamer was empty, the captain said the passengers would come aboard in order of their precedence. First he would take the military personnel, the officers of the steamboat line, and the men who had been sent out to fill government posts.

268

Next, the men and women who held the through tickets. They could come aboard in the order in which their tickets were dated, until there was not room on the steamer for one passenger more.

This meant that after the officials, the first to board would be the four clergymen and the businessmen who had bought their tickets in New York. Next would be the merry throng who had boarded the *Falcon* at New Orleans.

Now went up cries of pious fury.

Among the people who had reached the Isthmus by steamers later than the *Falcon,* or by vessels not belonging to the steamboat line at all, there were some worthless fellows and more than one adventuress. But there were also men of good connections and even two or three respectable married couples. That they should be left behind while the captain stuffed his boat with gamblers and barmaids, with Blossom and her flower garden—they said it was unthinkable. It was wicked. It was an affront to the morals of men and the virtue of women. It was a threat to the American home. And if they ever got back to their own country they were going to take the whole thing to court.

Captain Forbes shut his mouth tight and shook his head. The officers of the steamboat line stood firmly behind him. They were responsible for people who held tickets on boats of the line. They were not responsible for people who had flocked to the Isthmus by other means, hoping the Lord would open a way for them to go farther.

"Ah!" said Marny. "I'm beginning—to understand." She spoke slowly, awesomely. "I see—why Norman was so smart."

She looked at Norman with eyes aglow. He smiled back at her. Well pleased with himself, he accepted her admiration as no more than his due.

"Right," Rosabel said laughing. "Because now, the most precious object on the Isthmus was not a diamond necklace nor even a bag of money. It was a ticket to San Francisco. They were willing to pay anything. I mean *anything.* And Norman had been buying tickets. From people who quit at Cruces, from other people who gave up and started back from Panama City."

"Weren't you afraid," asked Archwood, "that somebody would kill you to get a ticket?"

"Of course," said Norman. "But everybody who had a

ticket, or a bunch of tickets, was afraid of the same thing, so we stuck together."

He explained that several other gamblers had followed his example and bought tickets from people who wanted to turn back. Norman and some of his old friends from New Orleans formed a club. For safety, four of them came to sleep in the room Norman occupied with Rosabel; others established themselves in the courtyard of the house. They were all armed, and two of them were always awake and on guard. The family who lived in the house could do nothing about them. By this time the natives were so bewildered that they were almost stupefied. They had never known the world contained such people as were now pouring into Panama, people who were so active or who made so much noise or were so determined to get their own way. The Panamanians longed for the good old days, and sighed when the Yankees told them the good old days were gone forever.

The gambling club began doing a brilliant business. The men pooled their funds and bought every ticket they could get, stateroom or steerage, often at two or three times the original cost. Some of the tickets they raffled, others they sold outright at fantastic prices. People bought the tickets with their last gold and silver coins, agreeing to take any sort of accommodation as long as they could get aboard the steamer. Several men paid twice the normal cost of a first-class stateroom to be allowed to sleep on a coil of rope on the deck of the *California.*

At last, on the first day of February, 1849, the *California* steamed away from Panama. She was so stuffed with human beings that she had little more than standing room aboard, but she left behind six thousand more people who wanted to go to San Francisco.

Her voyage took four weeks. It was about as dreadful a voyage as any vessel ever made. Food was scant, water was rationed by the cupful. The passengers were crowded like beans in a basket. They were so wretched that everybody hated everybody else. They snarled and quarreled all day long.

"We couldn't move," said Rosabel, "without bumping into each other. And when we tried to sleep other people kept stumbling over us. I thought, if only I could get *out,* and walk around a little—"

270

"Couldn't you get off at all?" asked Marny. "Didn't the boat stop anywhere for water?"

"Why yes," said Rosabel, "at a place called Mazatlan, and again at Monterey. The army people got off, but most of us were scared to. We had to take our tickets with us, because we couldn't come back on board without showing them, and by this time the gold news had spread around and everybody in the world wanted to go to San Francisco. We were afraid somebody would knock us down in the street and take our tickets. So we stayed on board and suffered."

"But now you're here," said Marny, "and you can come right over to the Calico Palace."

Norman's shrewd black eyes met the eager green eyes of Marny and he began to laugh. Looking around at the others he said,

"She hasn't changed a bit. When she wants to do something she wants to do it right *now*. What was it you used to say, Marny? Vivimus—"

Marny laughed too, but she stood up and began to put on her bonnet, which she had hung on the back of a chair. "Dum vivimus vivamus," she returned. "Which means in plain United States English, we won't live forever so let's get busy."

39

Norman got busy. He was an enterprising man, and anyway, there was nothing else he could do.

When he first looked around him Norman said frankly that he did not like this town and did not think much of Marny's Calico Palace. Norman had spent his life in civilized cities. He was used to card parlors with mirrors and carpets and crystal chandeliers and paintings of beautiful women. While he had known that San Francisco was a frontier village, he had not imagined such a flapping hodgepodge of tents and shanties and cloth houses, set on such bleak windswept hills. Like other men who came to San Francisco in 1849, when he actually saw the fabled city of gold Norman had a shock of dismay.

But he was here, and Norman was not a man who gave up easily. Unlike Archwood, Norman was not looking for adventure. He was looking for gold, and there was more gold in this rag city than in any other city in the world. He told Marny he would join her in the Calico Palace.

"I came here planning to stay at least a year," said Norman, "and I'm not going back without giving the place a try."

Marny flicked him a glance from her leaf-green eyes. "Norman dear," she said, "it may be a long time before you *can* go back, even if you want to."

She led him to a window and pointed to the empty vessels swinging in the bay.

"Do you think," she asked, "that the crew of the *California* is any more noble than those other crews?" The steamer had been in port only two or three days, but she spoke with confidence. "I'm a cool gambler, Norman, but it doesn't take any courage for me to bet you a hundred dollars that there is not one man aboard the *California* now."

Marny lost her bet. There was one man aboard the *California*. Exactly one. He was an engineer, who had been persuaded by Captain Forbes to stay aboard at exorbitant pay and take care of the engines. As for the rest of that sturdy crew who had brought the steamer through the Straits of Magellan and up the west coast of the two Americas, every man of them had deserted to the gold fields.

Norman accepted Marny's hundred dollars. Also, with shrewd good humor, he accepted the Calico Palace with its canvas walls and red cloth hangings, and said he would do his best. And Norman's best, like Marny's, was very good indeed.

Before long, Norman and Rosabel were as well known in the Calico Palace as Marny herself. Norman dealt cards and Rosabel provided music. She played first on a guitar, but when a British vessel came in with pianos, the Calico Palace bought one of the first for Rosabel. She played with skill. Rosabel might be a waif, but she was a clever waif and she had a genuine talent for music.

Loren bought another of these first pianos for Kendra. She was glad to have it, and she accepted it without the vague sense of guilt she had so often felt before Loren's eager generosity. For now she had something to promise him in return. She was going to have a baby.

When she told him, Loren heard her with such delight as she had seldom seen before. Loren had grown up in a happy family and he missed it. San Francisco, with all its crowds, was a lonesome place. What a joy, he exclaimed, to have a family of his own!—and was Kendra all right? There was a good doctor in town, a man who had come here after years of practice among the Yankees in Valparaiso. Kendra assured Loren that she felt well, but he said it wouldn't hurt to have Dr. Rollins make a call.

Dr. Rollins proved to be a man in his forties, agreeable and competent. He said Kendra was perfectly well. She was glad of this, not only for herself but because she did not want to be a burden during the months ahead; she wanted no flaw to mar Loren's joy in the coming baby.

The baby made her feel more adequate than she had felt since she married Loren. Her yearning for Ted had gone, but it had left an empty space behind it. What she felt for Loren —admiration, affection, respect—did not fill that emptiness. These were not love. She knew the difference.

The doctor told her to keep lime juice on hand and drink a cupful every day when she could not get fresh vegetables. Tucked into some corner of the *California* had been packets of garden seeds, and these were now advertised for sale. Kendra inquired about them at Chase and Fenway's. Mr. Fenway gloomily advised her that with vegetables bringing such prices as they were, a garden here in the middle of town would be stripped as soon as the green shoots came up. Very well, said Kendra, she would grow radishes and carrots in window boxes. Upstairs windows.

"Real good idea," said Mr. Fenway. "Plant a flower or two at the front of the box. They'll think it's just some silly woman trying to make things pretty around here."

He gave her a surprisingly humorous glance.

A day or two later Loren came in with a husky strong-faced man he introduced as Dwight Carson, a building contractor from Honolulu. Dwight Carson was now constructing a wharf. He had promised to put up several business buildings as soon as he could find enough men to do the work, but Loren had secured him to look at the upstairs windows and provide a carpenter to make the boxes. Kendra knew the price was outrageous, though Loren would not tell her what it was. When she asked, he only smiled and said, "Don't worry. I can take care of my family."

Dwight Carson proved to be a friendly fellow. He had practical sense and he knew his business, and he provided well-built window boxes, more spacious than Kendra had thought possible. And if his price was high, she could not blame him for getting rich while he could.

Dwight told her one of the buildings he had contracted for was a new Calico Palace. He said he could have started it tomorrow, but he could not get carpenters. Even when he could find men willing to take steady jobs, and when he was paying them all they asked for, some fellow would come to town with an extra big nugget and they would throw down their tools and go off to look for one like it.

Kendra sympathized. She did hope he could build the Calico Palace soon. She knew how much Marny wanted it.

On the first of April the second steamer of the line, the *Oregon*, came in from the Isthmus. By strict and clever management, she got out of the bay twelve days later.

The captain of the *Oregon*, Mr. Pearson, had been warned of what had happened to the *California* and he had vowed that it was not going to happen to him. He dropped anchor under the guns of the battleship *Ohio* and put his most unruly sailors in irons. Thus they stayed, until they and all the other men had agreed to take the steamer back to the Isthmus, at wages ten times what they had signed up for.

In spite of their promises, Captain Pearson kept his steamboat under the guns until he was ready to leave. Then the *Oregon* steamed away, carrying ten thousand ounces of gold and nineteen passengers bound for home.

The departure of the *Oregon* gave Kendra a chance to send a letter to her mother. She wrote that her marriage to Ted had proved a disappointment and had been annulled, and said she was now married to Loren Shields. She gave no details and she did not tell Eva about the baby. She would save that for her next letter. One shock at a time, she thought. She was not sure how Eva was going to like being told that she was to become a grandmother at the age of thirty-seven.

Spring was here and the weather was clearing. As she planted her window boxes Kendra could look down the hill and see the deserted hulks rocking on the water. Nearly every day she saw more vessels come in, and at last, on the first of May, she saw the *California* get out. After two heartbreaking

274

months, Captain Forbes was taking his steamer back to the Isthmus. Like the captain of the *Oregon* he was paying his men extravagant wages, but his vessel was moving.

The *California* carried nineteen thousand ounces of gold, to be sent across the Isthmus and taken to the Mint. She also carried several homebound passengers. Most of these were army officers, including Lieutenants Morse and Vernon, both of whom had been assigned to posts in the United States. The lieutenants had called to say goodby to Kendra. They said they were sorry to part with her, but they could not conceal their delight at getting away from the weary drudgery that had been all they had known in San Francisco. Also aboard the *California* was the wife of General Persifer Smith. Mrs. Smith's elegant maid had run off to the gold fields with a man she had married on two days' acquaintance, and Mrs. Smith herself wanted no more trials.

While the steamers left a host of empty vessels behind them, by this time not all of these were still on the water. Men like Dwight Carson were buying the best, and turning them into the structures that everybody needed but nobody could build. With a few workmen the builders could get, they dragged the vessels to the beach. Here, after a little carpentry, the vessels became rooming houses, warehouses, restaurants, saloons, and every other sort of "building" needed by the people crowding into town. And men like Dwight Carson were getting rich.

The carpenters who rebuilt the ships got their pay every evening in gold dust. Whether or not they came back to work in the morning usually depended on how lucky they were at the gambling spots. As the night came down, the streets around the plaza blazed with light and shook with noise. The light poured through the cloth walls of Marny's Calico Palace and other calico palaces like it, so much light that it looked as if the whole street were on fire. Nearly every one of these places had a band, and the musicians played whatever tune they chose and played it as loud as they could, so that a dozen different tunes were always blaring over the plaza together. The men must have liked it, for every night they clustered around the card tables with pokes of gold in their hands.

Rosabel, trying to play real music on her piano, said the discord was driving her mad. Marny, dealing her cards, was not troubled at all. Marny could not tell good music from bad; besides, her power of concentration was such that she

275

hardly heard it. She stood by her table, her eyes and her mind and her beautiful hands concerned only with her cards. Men tried to talk to her. This disturbed the players, but if Marny heard the talk she rarely noticed it. If a man became obnoxious she gave a signal to whichever Blackbeard was on guard near her table, and he hustled the sinner outside. The Calico Palace was the most orderly gambling spot on Kearny Street, and Marny and her friends intended to keep it so.

Once in a while she said something, but her words were few and terse. When a croaker stood at her elbow, complaining about the country, the climate, and his own general discontent, Marny went on shuffling and dealing without giving him a glance. She had heard croakers before. They were men who had come to California expecting to see lumps of gold lying about on the ground, to be gathered with no more trouble than picking flowers. When they found that gold digging meant work they decided they had been lured here and cheated, and they loudly said so.

The bettors told the croaker to move on. He did not move, but went on croaking. San Francisco was a big sham. Dirty and cold and full of fleas. He was here and all the ships were stuck in the bay and he couldn't get out and he wished he was dead. "Hear what I say?" he demanded. "This place is a big cheat. You're all a lot of big cheats. Liars and robbers and no-goods—"

Marny lifted her hand in the signal to Blackbeard. As he reached her she indicated the croaker, still grumbling at her side.

"This guest," she said clearly, "is not welcome." She turned her eyes back to the gamblers. "Place your bets, gentlemen."

They laughed approvingly. A moment later the croaker found himself in the street.

It was not always so easy. One fellow planted himself by Marny's table and began making obscene remarks which he thought were clever. The other men told him to shut up, but he was too fond of his own wit to do so. For several minutes Marny paid him no attention. At length, tired of being ignored, the man gave her a pinch. The card in her hand, which should have been dealt face down, fell on the table face up and spoiled the deal. Marny got mad.

Whatever could be done with a pack of cards, Marny could do. The gamblers had never seen her use a card as a weapon, but they saw it now. Her green eyes snapped up toward the

276

man's face. With a lightning-quick movement she tossed a card, so sharply that the corner of it struck him like a knife, and blood began to trickle from a cut just below his eyebrow.

With a yell, the man clapped his hand over his stinging eye. The gamblers laughed with joy and Marny gave the signal. As Blackbeard took out the offender one of the players picked up the card, dirtied now with a heel mark, and handed it to her. With a smile of thanks Marny swept up the rest of the cards and handed them to the other Blackbeard. He gave her a new deck, she shuffled and dealt again. "Sorry for the ruckus," she said evenly. "Place your bets, gentlemen."

Kendra heard about these episodes, from the talk at Chase and Fenway's or from Marny herself. Now and then she met Marny in the store; oftener, Marny walked up the hill and told her about the doings in town.

As she listened, Kendra felt twinges of envy. Her own life was so protected. This was how it should have been, she knew; a woman who was going to have a baby had no business taking part in the lusty rowdiness of the plaza. Loren was giving her exactly what he thought she wanted, which was exactly what she should have wanted—safety, ease, sheltering. Loren liked Marny, but he felt no interest in the razzle-dazzle of Kearny Street and it never crossed his mind that Kendra might feel any.

Still, Kendra was happier than she had been since last summer at Shiny Gulch, and she was glad about the baby. She told Marny,

"I never dreamed I would love a baby so much before I even saw it."

Marny looked around Kendra's parlor. The ships had brought furniture and curtains, rugs and silver and glass, and Kendra had them all. "Your baby will start life in luxury," said Marny. "I don't believe there's another woman in San Francisco who lives as well as you do. I know I don't. If we ever get our new building—" She shrugged.

"Is there any chance of starting it soon?" Kendra asked.

"I doubt it. Dwight Carson is doing the best he can, but—" She shrugged again.

They heard laughter from the kitchen, where Serena was entertaining Marny's escorts, Troy Blackbeard and Lolo and baby Zack. The Blackbeards liked to escort Marny on these visits because Kendra always had something good to eat on hand and they got a treat at the kitchen table. As Troy and

277

Lolo had been married by one of the ministers who arrived on the *California,* they were now a respectable pair and Serena enjoyed their company.

Marny said it was time for her to go down the hill and get ready for her evening at the card table. When she had left, Kendra went into the kitchen to prepare a dessert for dinner, dried apricots stewed with citron and raisins.

While they sat at table that evening, Loren told her a launch from the placer country had brought Chase and Fenway's packing boys, Bert, Al, and Foxy. The boys were in the same state as so many others coming back from the hills, rich with gold and sick with scurvy. Foxy had staggered into the store this morning, begging for lime juice at any price. He said the other two were even sicker than he was. Loren and Ralph Watson, carrying bottles of lime juice, had gone with him to the lodging where the boys were paying high prices to lie in dirt and misery.

Loren said the place was a bug-ridden flophouse. Not even a house, he corrected himself; it was merely a canvas roof supported by four walls so badly put together that light came in between the planks. Along the walls were shelves, each shelf about three feet above the one below it, and each man had a space of about six feet on a shelf.

He said half the men lying on the shelves were drunk, the rest were groaning with scurvy and other illnesses they had brought back from the hills of gold.

Kendra shivered. "What did you do?"

"We gave them the lime juice," said Loren, "and we brought the boys' gold back to the store and put it in the safe. They'll be all right after a few days of wholesome food."

"Are they finished with the mines?"

"They certainly are," Loren answered. "The three of them say with one voice they never want to see a placer again. They want to come back to work in the store. And they can, we need them."

"Where will they live? You can't let them stay in a place like that."

"Of course not. We'll set up three army cots in one of the rooms over the store. Not luxurious, but better than what the boys have now."

Kendra felt a nip of guilt. She told Loren about the time she had bought potatoes and dried peas from Foxy because he wanted to go farther up in the hills with no provisions but jerky and hardtack. "I should have warned him about scurvy," she said.

But in Loren's eyes Kendra never did wrong. "My dear girl," he urged, "you know perfectly well he had heard that before. If you hadn't bought his vegetables he'd have sold them to somebody else."

"All the same," said Kendra, "I'm going to help those boys get well. Dr. Rollins says dried fruit helps scurvy, and we have plenty of that. I'll make some pies and send them down by Ralph."

"Do you feel strong enough for the extra work?" he asked anxiously.

"Oh yes, I feel fine. And the doctor says the best thing I can do for myself is keep active."

"Then make the pies." He smiled fondly at her across the table. "You are a most thoughtful person."

He began to praise her concoction of apricots stewed with citron and raisins. For the thousandth time Kendra asked herself—Why can't I fall in love with him? He's the finest man I've ever known and he loves me more than anybody else ever loved me. Yet I like him but I don't love him. I can't and I don't.

Loren was right about the packing boys; they were young and hardy, and after a few days of good food they were up and ready to work. Kendra saw Foxy in the store one morning when she had walked down with Loren to choose foodstuffs. Loren had gone into the office with Mr. Chase, and Kendra sat by the counter waiting till he was free to escort her home. Mr. Fenway was selling a pick and shovel to a would-be miner, and around the stove a group of croakers sat smoking and voicing the usual complaints.

Foxy came out of the storeroom, bringing packages to be stacked on the shelves behind the counter. Seeing Kendra, he leaned over the counter to speak to her.

"Say, Mrs. Par—Mrs. Shields," said Foxy, "it sure was nice of you to send us boys all that good eating. I guess we never had thought about how important it was, good eating."

"Are you well now?" she asked. "All three of you?"

"Oh yes ma'am, we're fine. But I tell you, nobody'll catch me going up to those mines again. Hardest work I ever did, all that digging, and in the winter was it cold! Snowed so hard

279

that the passes were blocked and we couldn't get down to Sacramento, and we had nothing to sleep in but a lean-to, and nothing fit to eat—no ma'am, I've had my lesson. And scurvy! When you get scurvy your joints swell up and hurt, and your mouth gets all raw inside—I tell you, it's not worth the gold. We lived through it, but not everybody did. Quite a lot of men died up there last winter. Oh, and that reminds me—you remember that fellow Delbert? The one that used to go around with Marny?"

Kendra gave a start. It had been a long time since she had heard Marny mention Delbert's name. She wondered how Marny felt about him now.

It was not likely that Foxy knew anything about Delbert's theft of Marny's gold. All he knew was that Delbert and some others had gone looking for the Big Lump. Kendra asked, "What about him, Foxy?"

Foxy rested his elbows on the counter. His ugly buck-toothed face was sober, but at the same time eager with the eagerness of one who has news to tell. "Delbert's dead, Mrs. Shields. I guess I ought to tell Marny. I'll go over to the Calico Palace one evening soon, and tell her."

Kendra felt no grief for Delbert. She wondered if Marny would feel any. "What happened to him?" she asked.

Foxy spoke importantly. "Well ma'am, it was kind of funny. I don't mean funny to be laughed at," he apologized quickly, "I mean *strange*—sort of—" Foxy fumbled through his limited stock of words. "What I mean is, you know Delbert and some other fellows went looking for the Big Lump—"

Kendra felt a sudden tenseness. She heard Mr. Fenway giving directions to a pair of new arrivals who had come in to ask where they could board a launch for Sacramento. "Go on, Foxy," she said.

"It happened not far from where we were," said Foxy, "so we heard all about it. Delbert and his partners had a big quarrel. I don't know what about, but they all got mad. They were standing close to a creek and one of the other men gave Delbert a punch and Delbert fell into the water. It wasn't a big creek, not over his head, but he couldn't seem to get up and make his way out. Couple of the men jumped in to help him—nobody had meant to kill him, I guess—but Delbert was down in the water and by the time they dragged him out it was too late. And then they found out why he couldn't get

280

up when he fell. They found he was wearing a sort of shirt under his clothes, a leather shirt with strap-down pockets—and Mrs. Shields, those pockets were *stuffed* with gold. You never saw so much. Hundreds of ounces. And the gold weighed him down. Once he fell into the water he couldn't push himself up—do you see?"

"Yes," Kendra said in a low voice, "I see." She tried to recall how much gold Delbert had stolen from Marny. She could not remember the exact amount, but it was enough. Enough to kill him. She asked, "What did the other men do with the gold, Foxy?"

"Why, they divided it up," said Foxy. "They said this was nearly as good as finding the Big Lump. I'll have to tell Marny. I hope she won't be too upset."

"I don't think she'll be too upset," Kendra said. She felt herself smiling, and wondered if Foxy thought she was a cold-hearted woman, smiling as she heard of a man's death. She wondered again how Marny would take the news.

Two days later she found out. Loren had heard about it at the store, and he told her.

Foxy went to the Calico Palace, eager to tell Marny about Delbert before she could hear the story from somebody else. Elbowing his way to her table, he stood with several other men watching the game. Foxy was not aware of Marny's talent for fixing her mind on her cards so that she was almost unconscious of everything else. After a moment's watching he exclaimed, "Evening, Marny!"

She did not look up. One of the other watchers warned him, "Don't bother her while she's dealing."

Foxy was restless. He tapped his foot on the floor. He had brought big news, and he wanted to be noticed. Marny did not notice him.

Foxy said eagerly, "Marny, I've got something to tell you."

Marny did not turn. She said, "Place your bets, gentlemen."

The coins clinked down. The eyes of the other onlookers bulged at the array of gold and silver. But Foxy persisted, "Marny, this is *important*."

Troy Blackbeard came over to him. "Let her alone," he ordered. "Don't interrupt."

"But I've got something to tell her!" Foxy argued. "Marny!" he exclaimed. "Marny, that friend of yours, Delbert —remember?"

Marny did not lift her eyes. She went on with the deal.

"Let her alone," Blackbeard said again.

"Marny!" Foxy insisted. "Marny, Delbert is dead."

Marny asked, "Cards, gentlemen?"

"Marny," urged Foxy, "don't you hear me? Delbert is dead."

One of the gamblers spoke with annoyance. "Oh, be quiet, fellow. Save it for later."

Marny turned up her own cards. She paid the winners, gathered up the coins of the losers, and dealt again. Foxy demanded,

"Marny, aren't you even *interested?* I tell you, Delbert is *dead.*"

Marny's eyes did not flicker from the cards. But now at last she answered. She said, "May he rest in peace, that son of a bitch. Place your bets, gentlemen."

Foxy felt Blackbeard's hand closing on his shoulder. In another minute he was outside, blinking at the glare of Kearny Street.

40

On the fourth of June the third steamer of the line, the *Panama,* came into the bay. She brought Yankee newspapers that had been carried on muleback across the Isthmus, and Yankee dollars of gold and silver—nobody in California trusted paper money. She also brought three hundred gold seekers. They were squeezed into space meant for eighty, and they reported that thousands more were waiting on the Isthmus.

The next day, Marny came up the hill with Duke Blackbeard and Lulu. Unlike his brother Troy, Duke had not married his Hawaiian charmer. But Serena thought he had, and she cordially led them into the kitchen for cake and coffee. Kendra and Marny went into the parlor. Here, after a few minutes of chat, Marny announced,

"Kendra, I'm having a little problem with my gentleman friend."

Kendra started. "You mean Norman Lamont?"

"No, dear, I mean Warren Archwood." Smiling regretfully, Marny explained, "Warren is getting homesick."

"Don't tell me he's tired of you!"

"Not of me, but of everything else. He's had the adventure he came for, so now he's noticing that this town is a dirty stinky place. He's lonesome for New York."

Marny stood up and walked over to a long mirror that hung on the wall opposite a window, reflecting the roofs that went like steps downhill toward the bay. Looking not at the roofs but at herself, she remarked,

"After a winter in this rainy town my freckles are fading. Kendra, Warren wants me to go back with him."

Kendra hated to think of doing without Marny. But it was no business of hers to protest, so she asked, "Does he want to marry you?"

Marny began to laugh. "Of course not. He wants to take me as a trophy. A scalp at his belt: He wants me to deal in one of the fancy gambling parlors in New York, so other men will see what a treasure he brought back from California. —Look at her! Any of you would be glad to have her, but I've *got* her."

Kendra laughed too. She liked Marny for being so clear-headed about herself. "Will you go with him?" Kendra asked.

"No," said Marny. She adjusted a lock of red hair before the mirror, came back to her chair and sat down.

Kendra said how glad she was. "I'd have missed you," she added.

Marny said, "He keeps asking—Don't you miss New York? The restaurants, hotels, theaters, fine stores? Don't you miss living in luxury, driving down Broadway in a carriage?"

"Don't you?" Kendra asked keenly.

"Of course I do. Don't *you* miss living in a clean well-mannered town? Don't you miss having all the fresh food you want, instead of raising radishes in a window box?"

"Yes," said Kendra, "but I don't miss any*body* in the States. And there's nobody in the States who wants me back."

"Right," said Marny. "That's how I feel. My brothers and sisters and aunts and uncles and cousins are a bunch of self-righteous moth-eaten relics and they can stay on their side of the Rocky Mountains and I'll stay on mine."

Kendra thought of the property Archwood had bought in

283

San Francisco, expecting the price to rise. Well, the price had certainly risen. He could sell his lots now for two or three times what he had paid for them last fall. She asked Marny if this was what he intended to do.

"Oh yes, he'll sell them," Marny said. "Norrington, that moon-faced little real estate agent, is taking care of it. I wish Norman and I could buy the ground under the Calico Palace, but we need our cash to bank the games. We'll have to pay rent to somebody. Still, we shouldn't complain. We're doing fine."

There was a pause. Marny walked back to the glass. Looking at herself again, she said thoughtfully,

"I'll miss Warren when he leaves. However"—she touched the jeweled pin on her dress—"I'll have a lot of pretty things to remember him by."

As she looked into the mirror, behind her own reflection she could see the roofs, and beyond them the tops of the masts on the vessels in the bay.

"The fog has blown off," she said, "and the sky is all clear. Kendra, I believe if we went upstairs we could see all the way across the bay to the other side."

"Let's go up and look," said Kendra. "We can use Loren's glass."

They went upstairs to the bedroom. Kendra opened the window on the side looking toward the bay. From here they had an unbroken view down to the water, and as Marny had said, to the hills on the other side.

Kendra brought the glass, gave it first to Marny and then had a look herself. The water of the bay was dancing in the sun. In front of the town the deserted vessels swayed with the tide. In spite of the number that had been beached and put to use, the water here was still so crowded that in high winds the vessels sometimes struck one another, and it required expert seamanship for a captain entering the bay to move his own vessel safely among them. Looking down at the hulks, Kendra asked,

"How does Warren Archwood expect to get out of here?"

Marny reminded her that the *Oregon* had gone, and so had the *California*. "With the wages the line is offering now," Marny continued, "Warren is sure that before long the steamers will be making regular runs between here and the Isthmus. As long as a man knows he's coming back every few weeks he can sign up for one round trip at a time, and whenever he wants to quit and go to the gold fields, he can do it. It's not like taking a ship all the way back to the States."

Kendra still held the glass to her eyes. The vessels out there had such a sadness about them, standing gaunt and empty against the sky. She asked,

"He doesn't mind crossing the Isthmus?"

"Oh, it won't be agreeable, but he says it isn't as bad as it was at first. Now that mail is being sent across, and gold, the parties crossing are protected by army guards."

"Marny!" Kendra exclaimed.

Marny gave a start of astonishment. "Yes? What?"

Kendra was still looking out toward the bay. With her free hand she caught Marny's wrist.

"Wait," she said—"I'll give you the glass in a minute, but first let me be sure—"

Nearly breathless, she stared out toward the water.

A ship was coming into the bay. She was a tall proud ship, her sails billowing in the wind, her figurehead a white goddess crowned with a crescent moon.

Kendra handed the glass to Marny.

Marny looked, and caught her breath. "Why Kendra! Is that the *Cynthia?*"

"Yes, it is. Back from China."

They watched as the *Cynthia* threaded her way among the lost ships. She moved with stately confidence, guided by a master.

"So," murmured Marny, "our friend Pollock is with us again." She laughed shortly. "What do you suppose he wants this time?"

"Water and supplies," said Kendra, "and maybe he's brought goods for trade. He said he was coming back."

She told Marny about the day Pollock had brought gifts from Honolulu to Eva and herself. Eva had asked him if he expected to visit San Francisco again before returning to New York, and Pollock had said yes. His plan had been to spend a year or so trading at Canton and other Oriental ports, and call at San Francisco on his way home.

Now he was on his way home. But Kendra exclaimed,

"I don't understand him! By this time he must have heard of what happens to ships that call at San Francisco! Why do you suppose he came here?"

"Because he's got rocks in his head," Marny answered with

285

curt amusement. "He wanted to come to San Francisco, so he came to San Francisco. Things happen to other men's ships but not to his."

Kendra did not answer. If Marny laughed at Pollock's fancies, maybe Marny was right. Maybe Pollock would get his ship out and back to New York. Maybe, after a year in the Orient, he had let Marny slip out of his mind.

Still, Kendra could not help feeling her old sense of foreboding.

But the *Cynthia* had rare good fortune.

Three men of her crew ran away as fast as they could. But only three. Two of these were Yankees who had been engaged in Canton. They were members of a growing group, men who boasted as soon as they came ashore that they had signed as seamen only to get a free trip to San Francisco, planning to desert as soon as they got there. The third deserter was one of the regular crew who had signed articles in New York, contracting to stay with the ship until she came to New York again; but the rest, though they were paid and given shore leave, came back to the ship.

Captain Pollock had a ready explanation for their loyalty. The *Cynthia* was a vessel far superior to most of those in San Francisco Bay, or for that matter, anywhere on the seas. Even before he was captain of the *Cynthia,* Pollock had been well known for giving his men better food and quarters than most captains. He had larger crews than average, so that the men were not overtaxed. As a result he had his choice of many applicants, and his crews were the ablest men on the waterfronts. If they chose to stay with him now, Pollock was not surprised.

Loren told Kendra this. He told her too that Pollock seemed to have forgiven Loren himself for letting Marny board the *Cynthia* at Honolulu. A day or two after reaching port Pollock had come into Chase and Fenway's. When he caught sight of Loren, Pollock had greeted him cordially. At dinner that evening Loren described their meeting.

"No sign of resentment," Loren said. "Since he left San Francisco he's had a good year. With all going well, I suppose he figures the *Cynthia* has forgotten that episode with Marny, and he might as well forget it too."

Kendra hoped this was right. She asked, "Did you tell him you and I were married?"

"Oh yes," said Loren. "He said he was glad to hear it. Altogether, he seemed happy and full of energy."

"What was he doing at Chase and Fenway's?" Kendra asked.

Loren reminded her that Pollock was not only a fine seaman but an astute man of business. He had come to Chase and Fenway's to discuss his cargo. Most of his cargo was intended for delivery in New York. But before he left Canton, Pollock had heard of San Francisco's housing need. As he was planning to stop there for water and supplies, he had quickly moved to take advantage of this need. He had brought some thousands of Chinese bricks. He had also brought several readymade wooden houses, walls packed flat, doors and windows ready to be put in their places, the whole needing only a few hours' work to be assembled and set up. And perhaps most important of all, he had brought as passengers five expert Chinese carpenters.

"Carpenters!" Kendra exclaimed. "We must tell Dwight Carson. Right now, so he can hire them before somebody else does, and start the Calico Palace."

Loren smiled at her across the table. "I've already told him. I went by his office before I came home."

"Oh Loren, you dear! Marny wants it so."

"I know," said Loren.

Kendra thought of the flophouses such as the one where Foxy and his friends had stayed. "Maybe," she said, "you should have told Dwight Carson to use those carpenters for a decent lodging house, instead of the Calico Palace. But I'm glad you didn't. Marny was my friend when I needed one and I'll never forget it."

"I'll never forget it either, my dear," Loren said gently. "That's why I made Carson promise to start the Calico Palace instead of anything else."

Kendra reflected that even if Loren had urged Dwight Carson to build a lodging house instead of the Calico Palace, Dwight would not have done so. Nobody would pay him as much for that as Marny and Norman would pay him. Gambling and a well stocked bar brought in more profit than a lodging house. As Marny had reminded her last summer, people will pay better prices for things they don't need than for things they do.

She herself met Captain Pollock at the store the next day. Catching sight of her at the counter, he came over at once.

287

He said nothing worthy of note, but his manner was easy, with none of the constraint he had shown the last time she saw him. She agreed with Loren that his year of prosperous voyaging had soothed his spirit.

As Warren Archwood had foreseen, the steamer *Panama* had no crew trouble. After two weeks in port she left for the Isthmus, carrying thirty thousand ounces of gold and a group of passengers bound for home. One of the passengers was Archwood. He was sorry Marny would not go with him, but not sorry enough to stay any longer in the ugly golden mishmash of San Francisco.

Archwood and Marny parted friends, but without heartbreak. He said he would write to her, but Marny told Kendra she did not expect him to do so. He had had his California adventure, and this chapter in his life was closed.

Marny had thought she would miss him, but she was too busy. Dwight Carson had started the new Calico Palace, and Marny and Norman were searching every warehouse in town for fittings that would make it as splendid as the gambling parlors they remembered from New Orleans and New York. Marny said she was just as well pleased that Archwood was no longer around. Men were for amusement. When she had so much to fill her days, she was content to spend her nights alone. Kendra wondered how long her fit of celibacy would last, but for the present at least Marny did seem happy.

Not long after Archwood sailed, Loren left on another buying trip up the coast. He told Kendra that Ralph and Serena would take care of her, and she was *not* to go on the street alone. Such characters as were coming in now!— beachcombers from the islands, criminals from the convict colonies of Australia, all sorts of fellows who had never done any honest work and did not mean to start now.

Kendra promised. The weather was dusty and disagreeable, and for several days she did not go out, alone or attended. She heard nothing of Captain Pollock. Ralph went to the store every day, but Ralph had no special interest in Pollock or the *Cynthia* and did not know Kendra had any. So it happened that Loren had been gone a week before Kendra learned that now the *Cynthia* too had been deserted.

Marny told her. Escorted by Duke Blackbeard, Marny came up the hill for a chat, but at first she did not think to mention the *Cynthia*. Marny thought Pollock was a blockhead and this was the end of her interest in him and his ship; she was interested in the Calico Palace.

"Kendra darling," said Marny, "I'll never finish being thankful to Loren for sending us those Chinese carpenters. Dwight says they're steady and sensible and they really know their trade. Of course the language is a problem, but they're learning."

Kendra had brought in a coffee pot. While she poured, Marny watched her, smiling.

"Motherhood is becoming to you," said Marny. "You look positively blooming."

She went on to tell Kendra about a man from Sydney who had come to the bar last night wanting a particular sort of mixed drink. He tried to tell Chad, but Chad came from Boston, and he and the Australian simply could not understand each other's way of speaking. At length an Englishman, who had lived in both Australia and the United States before coming to California, offered to act as interpreter. Understanding at last, Chad mixed the drink. The man from Sydney gave him a good tip and gratefully bought a drink for the Englishman, and all three were happy.

"It's not true what people are saying, that all the men from Sydney are jailbirds," said Marny. "I've met several who are quite nice. But I must say, until I got mixed up in this gold rush I never dreamed there were so many different ways of speaking English. Some of these sailors—oh, speaking of sailors, I have some news."

"Tell me. Since Loren left, I don't know anything except what's printed in the *Alta*."

"The *Alta* doesn't print this sort. Too commonplace. Just one more ship stranded in the bay."

"Not the *Cynthia!*" Kendra exclaimed.

"Yes, the *Cynthia*. She's empty."

"But what happened?" Kendra asked. "I thought—we all thought—"

As she paused, Marny nodded. "Yes, I heard it over and over. Pollock's men were different. They were staying with their ship. It couldn't happen to the *Cynthia*."

"But it did!" said Kendra.

"Yes, it did."

"Tell me about it."

"Well, dear," said Marny, "the way they're telling it along Kearny Street, Pollock did have the smartest sailors on the sea. Too smart to do what so many others have done, steal the ship's boats and slip off in the middle of the night without waiting for their pay."

"But Pollock's men were paid," Kendra protested. "They came ashore."

"But when they got on shore," said Marny, "they inquired around. They were smart enough to want the facts about gold hunting. They found out that men going to the placers needed boots and clothes and tools and bacon and cornmeal and all that other stuff we saw at Smith and Brannan's store. Also they found out about California prices. The men talked it over, and decided a bigger grubstake was worth a few days' wait." Marny smiled. "You see, Pollock had heard how hard it was to get laborers, so he had promised them extra pay for unloading his bricks and readymade houses. The men agreed. When they got that extra pay they went ashore again. And puff!—they vanished."

"And what," Kendra exclaimed, "is Pollock doing about it?"

Marny shrugged. "What can he do?"

"You haven't seen him?"

Marny shook her head. "No. In Honolulu he used to drop in often to see me, but he hasn't been near me since he came to San Francisco. That's all right. I hope he keeps out of my way."

Kendra stood up restlessly. She went to the window and looked out. From here on the first floor she could not see the bay; above the roofs she could see only the tops of the masts, and she wondered which of these were the masts of the *Cynthia*. She wondered what Captain Pollock was going to do now.

41

It was a week before Kendra saw Marny again. They met by
chance at Chase and Fenway's. The store had received a
shipment of vegetables from Honolulu, and as Loren was still
in Oregon, when Ralph went to work the next morning
Kendra walked with him down the hill.

It was not yet nine o'clock, but the streets around the plaza
were agog. Wagons creaked through the dust, every driver
shouting to the rest of them, "Why don't you look where
you're going?" Auctioneers bellowed; other men hurried
about their business. At sight of Kendra they bowed, made
room for her to pass, and hurried on, kicking rubbish out of
the way. She heard the buzz of flies loud around the garbage,
and though she held her handkerchief to her nose this did
not do much to block the smells.

Kearny Street was closely lined with tents, cloth houses,
even a few genuine buildings. The most imposing of these
was the new hotel called the Parker House, finished at last
after a year of standing half built for lack of workmen. The
Parker House had two stories and an attic, painted white,
with gingerbread trimming. A number of gamblers had
rented space for card tables there, Norman among them. The
Chinese carpenters had torn down the old Calico Palace to
make room for the new one, and Norman did not want to
be idle.

Near the Parker House, Kendra saw the carpenters building the Calico Palace. Quaint figures in blue cotton, with
straw hats shaped like umbrellas, and pigtails dangling halfway to their knees, they were working with the assurance of
men who knew their trade. She saw Dwight Carson supervis-
ing them, but he did not see her; he was too busy to look
around. It was important to make the most of every workman
while you had him. You never could tell when any men, even
these sensible Chinese, might catch the gold fever.

Out in the bay Kendra could see the poor deserted ships. Among them, her masts tall and gaunt and empty, was the *Cynthia*. How forsaken she looked, how desolate.

Kendra felt a rush of sympathy for Captain Pollock. No doubt he had been foolish, coming to San Francisco in the serene belief that what had befallen other captains could not befall him. But who on earth, she asked herself, had not sometimes been a fool? And the *Cynthia* need not be a total loss. So fine a ship could readily be sold for a hotel or warehouse. Pollock could get a good price and then go home by way of the Isthmus, knowing he had done the best any man could do.

At the store, Mr. Chase was selling boots and clothes to two miners who had come to town with full pokes in their hands but only rags and tatters on their backs. By the stove sat two croakers, exchanging complaints. Mr. Fenway was making entries in an account book, scowling as if he were going bankrupt instead of getting rich. As he saw Kendra he closed his book and dawdled over.

Ralph went to his own work in the storeroom, saying he would come back later to see her up the hill. When Kendra had bought what she needed, Mr. Fenway dragged over a chair and gave her a copy of the New York *Tribune*, seven weeks old, brought by the *Panama*. Kendra caught sight of herself in a mirror that hung on the wall behind the counter, a price tag on the frame. Marny had been right—she was flowering in her prospect of motherhood. Her skin glowed, her blue eyes were bright and clear. With a smile at her reflection she opened the newspaper.

Mr. Chase, having sold the miners their new clothes, went to the storeroom door and called Foxy.

"I've got to go out," he said. "You show these gentlemen where to change."

Ambling out, Foxy gave Kendra a grin of welcome. "Morning, Mrs. Shields," he said, and opened a door leading to a hastily built little room at the back. The two miners, their arms piled with apparel, followed where he led. As was now usual with men returning from the mines, they were going to put on their new clothes right here, and throw out the old ones to add to the litter in the street.

As the miners went out Kendra heard the front door open, and saw Pocket and Hiram, down from the settlement at Sutter's Fort, now grown to a busy town called Sacramento.

She sprang up, and as they caught sight of her they exclaimed and hurried toward her.

Pocket and Hiram were lean and brown and hard-muscled. They had brand new shaves and haircuts, and like the miners they had bought new clothes in honor of this visit to town. They looked tough and handsome, but they did not look citified. It was not possible for Hiram's thick rust-colored hair to stay tidy for long, nor for Pocket to wear any garment without stuffing it out of shape.

In high spirits, both men began to talk. They told her she looked beautiful, said Loren was a lucky man, and wished her happiness in her marriage. They said they had come to town on business. Their venture of making rockers was paying them well, and they wanted to put their surplus gold dust on the next steamer to be taken to the Mint in Philadelphia.

By this time gold was as cheap in Honolulu as it was in San Francisco, so a man could no longer send his dust there and change it for its value in coins. He had to send it to the Mint. This was a long and expensive business, but worth doing because real money was so much wanted in San Francisco that a man who had any could loan it at interest of ten per cent a month.

"We got to town yesterday," said Hiram, "and left our gold dust here in the safe while we went looking for a place to sleep."

"Where did you sleep?" asked Kendra.

"Parker House," said Hiram. He growled and added, "If you'd call it sleeping."

Pocket gave a sad sort of laugh. Hiram put both his big hands on the counter and heaved himself up to sit there. Pocket pulled over a box and sat down too, still laughing under his breath. Hiram vehemently continued,

"Has anybody told you about that place, Kendra? A 'bedroom' is a cubbyhole four feet by seven——"

"Hiram could hardly get in," murmured Pocket.

Hiram was still venting his wrath. "——and that cubbyhole has two bunks. Yes, two, one above the other. And the walls between the rooms are nothing but sheets of cloth. If you light a candle your shadow on the cloth shows the neighbors what you are doing. If you speak to your roommate and don't want them to hear, you have to whisper——"

"Hiram can't whisper," said Pocket.

"Most men can't whisper," Kendra said laughing.

Hiram certainly could not, nor did he try. He was roaring,

"The gamblers have taken nearly the whole second floor, and the games go on all night, and the racket—if I ever catch one of those gamblers—"

Kendra felt a flash of mischief. "Here comes one now," she said. The front door was opening, and she had caught sight of Marny, with Norman and Rosabel behind her.

The men saw Marny too. Hiram leaped down from the counter and Pocket sprang up from the box. Rushing to them, Marny joyously embraced them both at once. She called Norman and Rosabel, introduced everybody all round, and explained how Norman happened to be at present one of the Parker House dealers. She was sorry Hiram and Pocket had been kept awake by the gamblers, but she declared that Norman had not been one of them. Not last night. Norman had left his table early because of important errands this morning.

Norman heard her with a faint smile. Norman's business was gambling. If he had left his table early last night, it had been for his errands this morning, not for the sake of anybody else's comfort. Much as he admired Marny's talents he thought her exuberant concern for other people a waste of energy.

The croakers by the stove had quit croaking to look and listen. The two miners came out of the changing room resplendent in red shirts and corduroy breeches and bright new boots, and they too paused. As Mr. Chase was still out and Foxy had been sent back to the storeroom, Mr. Fenway lounged over to offer Norman his services.

Norman explained that he and Marny wanted to be the first to see some furnishings advertised by Chase and Fenway in the latest *Alta*. He supposed these could be seen at their warehouse?

Right, said Mr. Fenway. He would go with Norman and Marny and open the warehouse. However, they would have to wait till Mr. Chase came back; he had gone to look at some goods just unloaded from the *Cynthia*, and both partners could not be away from the store at once.

Very good, said Norman. He had another errand to attend to, so he would do this now. Marny and Rosabel could wait here till Mr. Chase returned, and he would meet them at the warehouse.

Mr. Fenway glanced at Rosabel. "And while she's waiting,"

he said solemnly, "maybe Miss Rosabel would like to see a fine new guitar that just came in."

Rosabel said she would *love* to. Norman went out, and Mr. Fenway went to the storeroom to get the guitar. While he and Rosabel examined it, Marny and Kendra, Pocket and Hiram, sat down to talk. The miners joined the croakers by the stove.

Marny said Norman had gone to look at a roulette wheel advertised in the *Alta* by another firm. If it was any good he would snap it up before anybody else had a chance.

Pocket and Hiram told the girls about Sacramento. A town of tents, they said. Population always changing, men going to the mines or coming back. All of them half wild with excitement, whether of hope or success or despair. Riches thundering out of the hills, yet every day you met men begging the price of a meal.

They said everything at the mining camps was different now. Last year the miners had been men who lived in California and knew each other, in general a pretty decent lot. This year they were men who had poured in from everywhere, some of them good fellows, others trash from the back alleys of the world. It would be a brave man who would bring his wife to a mining camp this year. Last summer, you panned anywhere you pleased; now you had to stake a claim and be ready to defend it.

"And do you remember," said Hiram, "how we used to leave our dust while we worked, and nobody bothered it? No more."

He paused as he heard a tinkle of music. Rosabel sat on the counter, blissfully thrumming her new guitar. The miners and the croakers had turned their chairs eagerly. Rosabel began a song.

"I knew she'd buy that thing," said Marny. "Well, that's what we're here for, to spend money."

Her words about spending money caught the ear of Mr. Fenway. Leaving Rosabel to play her guitar, he came strolling over to say he had a mighty fine painting in the storeroom and maybe Marny would like to have a look.

Marny consented, and he called Bert and Foxy to bring the painting. Rosabel ended her song, the men by the stove gave her rapturous applause, and she began another. At Mr. Fenway's direction Bert and Foxy set the painting against the wall.

About six feet by eight, the picture showed the sawmill in the mountains where the workman named Jim Marshall had first found gold in the water. Marny looked at it thoughtfully, walked a little way off and turned to study it again.

Mr. Fenway told them the artist was a man named Bruno Gregg. He had come around the Horn from New York, bringing oils and canvas with him. His picture was good, wasn't it?

Marny said yes, the picture was good. But she would have liked it better if instead of scenery Mr. Bruno Gregg had chosen to paint a pretty woman with not too many clothes on.

Mr. Fenway sighed. Kendra spoke.

"I think men will be interested in this," said Kendra. "The place where the first gold was found—why, that's a historic spot."

Marny thought a moment, and said Kendra might have an idea there. What did Pocket and Hiram think?

They agreed with Kendra. Hiram added that Bruno Gregg might also be good at painting women. While they talked Pocket spoke to Kendra in an undertone.

"I'd like to say something to you, please ma'am."

She went with him back to the chair she had occupied before. Pocket stood by her, his elbow on the counter. At the other end of the counter Rosabel continued to play and sing for her delighted hearers. Pocket spoke in a low voice.

"I wanted to tell you, Kendra, how glad I am you're married to a fine man now, and happy."

How likable he was, thought Kendra. "Thank you, Pocket," she said.

Pocket went on, "And—excuse me for getting personal, but—about Ted, did it happen the way I said it would?"

"Yes, Pocket," she answered. "Just as you said it would. That's over. I don't care any more."

Pocket smiled, his gentle endearing smile. "That makes me mighty happy, Kendra. I'm glad you're in love again."

Kendra did not tell him she was not in love again. She might have reminded him—he had gone past that episode with that other girl, but he had not been in love again. Maybe he never would be. Maybe all he would ever reach with a girl would be the sort of pleasant affection she had reached with Loren. Well, no doubt this was better than what either of them had had before.

For several minutes they listened while Rosabel went on

singing to the music of her new guitar. She looked pretty as she sat there on the counter, her black curls dancing and her fingers skipping over the strings. Rosabel liked to play and sing and she liked to entertain admiring men.

The admiring men sat facing her, their backs to the stove. There were six of them: Bert and Foxy, the two miners in their bright new clothes, and the two croakers, looking happy now instead of sad. By the side wall Marny and Hiram and Mr. Fenway were discussing pictures for the Calico Palace.

The front door opened, and Kendra saw Mr. Chase. He was holding the door for some important personage to come in. Pocket spoke with regret.

"There's Mr. Chase. Now Mr. Fenway will take Marny and Rosabel to the warehouse."

Kendra looked up at Pocket. "Why don't you and Hiram go along?"

"You don't think they'll mind?" he asked.

"Why no," she said. "I think Marny will like your opinions."

As she spoke, Kendra became aware that something was taking place. Rosabel's music had stopped on a discord. Voices and other sounds were ceasing. One by one the men facing Rosabel were turning away from her. By the wall, Marny and Hiram and Mr. Fenway were turning too. Kendra looked where they were looking, toward the front door. She saw Captain Pollock, the important personage who had come in with Mr. Chase.

But Captain Pollock did not see her. He saw nothing in the room but Marny

He stood looking at her. He stood motionless, a figure of fury and rage and breathless hate.

On Marny's face was a look of shock. In spite of Kendra's warnings, Marny had never until now realized the scope of Pollock's wrath. For a moment the two of them stood without moving, silently challenging each other.

It was only a moment, only a flick of time. But like the time when Pollock's eyes had thanked Kendra for her virgin presence as he doubled the Horn, this was a moment that struck and pierced. Now that Mr. Chase and Pollock had come in, there were fourteen persons in the room. For this instant, not one of them moved or spoke.

Later, all that most of them could say about it was, "Gosh,

297

that man was mad, mad with her—I tell you, it was gruesome."

Most of them knew Marny had come to San Francisco on the *Cynthia,* but they did not know about her adventure with Pollock, nor that he bore her any ill-will. But Kendra knew, and as she saw Pollock now she shivered before him as if before a cloud of evil.

The first of them to move was Hiram. He took a step toward Marny, not a heavy step, but the sound of it was as startling as a crash. Almost at the same time the rest of them unfroze. Mr. Chase demanded, "Say, captain, what's the matter?" Pocket exclaimed, "Who is this man, Kendra? Why is he mad with Marny?"

Foxy and Bert and the strangers all began to ask what was wrong. Rosabel, sitting on the counter, hugged her new guitar as if afraid somebody was going to attack it.

Pollock took a stride toward Marny. He blurted, "Shameless creature!"

With a quick movement Marny had whipped out her little gun. "Keep your hands off me," she ordered.

But neither her gun nor her speech was necessary. Hiram's big powerful hands had already caught Pollock and halted him. Pollock was no weakling, but Hiram had spent the past year doing the hardest kind of physical work, and he stood like an oak tree. Pollock exclaimed,

"Do you know this woman?"

Hiram, still with no idea of why Pollock should dislike Marny, answered simply, "Yes, I know her. Let her alone."

Mr. Chase, looking around at Marny with her gun, at Rosabel with her guitar, at Rosabel's audience blinking in wonder, was asking at the same time, "What are we having here anyway, Fenway? A variety show?"

Now, all of a sudden, they noticed Mr. Fenway.

He was walking across the floor toward Pollock, slowly, dragging his feet, but steadily, like the approach of fate. In his hand he held a big astonishing revolver. Without looking around he answered calmly,

"One thing we're *not* having here, and that's trouble."

Hiram, seeing that Mr. Fenway's gun made his own grip on Pollock needless, let him go. Mr. Fenway took another step toward Pollock, serene with menace.

"Look, you," he droned, "maybe you'd better get out of here."

Wheeling toward him, Pollock demanded, "You're ordering me out?"

"Yes I am," drawled Mr. Fenway, "unless you behave yourself. I know you're an important man. But there's no man important enough to start disorder in my place of business."

"And do *you* know this woman?"

"Sure, I know her. She wasn't raising any dust before you came in."

Pollock shouted, "She is killing my ship."

Standing like an embodiment of vengeance, he looked around to be sure they were all listening for what he was about to say. They were. Pollock pointed to Marny.

"Look, all of you!" he thundered. "Do you see this woman? She has brought evil to my ship. Evil and death. Out there in the bay my beautiful *Cynthia* is dying. Dying, because of this woman. My fair, unspotted *Cynthia*—"

He slumped into a chair, and dropped his head upon his hands. Disconsolate, despairing, he sat there.

As she saw him now, Kendra thought she understood him better than she ever had before. He was a man condemned to watch the slow disintegration of the being he loved. Kendra had never in her life seen anything so pitiful. With an impulsive movement she went to him and put her hand on his shoulder.

"Captain Pollock," she said, "may I speak to you?"

He did not lift his head. He muttered, "What do you want?"

"I want to tell you," she said gently, "the *Cynthia* isn't lost. She's a fine ship. She can still be put to service."

Hiram gave her a nod of approval. But Pollock, still staring down between his knees at the floor, shook his head.

Hiram came to stand by Kendra. Hiram had come around the Horn with Pollock's crew, and they had told him how the captain loved his ship. With a quiet sincerity, he continued the counsel Kendra had begun.

"Captain Pollock, we know it's hard for you to see your ship deserted. But this has happened to other ships, and their captains have turned it to account. You can do the same."

Shaking his head again, Pollock looked up. He gave no sign of recognizing Hiram. Probably, thought Kendra, he did not. Hiram had been only a common sailor, and it was a long

299

time since their voyage. Nor, in his grief, did Pollock seem to recognize Kendra herself. He said,

"Thank you, sir, and you, madam, for your sympathy. I know you mean to be kind. But if you think I am going to force my ship to become a saloon, a brothel, a gambling den—" With a shudder of loathing he exclaimed, "No!"

Like a man without hope, he looked up.

"No!" he repeated.

Now for the first time he noticed Kendra, and she saw a start of recognition on his face.

"As for you," he said to her sadly, "of course you must side against me. You married Loren Shields. Has he told you he was the man who let that woman board the *Cynthia?* That he was the man who insulted my ship and broke her heart?"

Facing his disaster, Pollock could not be comforted. Kendra's eyes met Hiram's. Neither of them knew how to say anything more.

Pollock started to get to his feet, stumblingly, like an old man. Hiram gave him a hand. As he stood up, Pollock said,

"Mr. Chase, Mr. Fenway, forgive me. I am sorry to have made a disturbance. I shall not do so again."

"Come into the office," said Mr. Chase, eager to end this whole puzzling scene. "We have a lot of business to—"

"Later," said Captain Pollock. "I can come back *later.*"

He spoke the last word with a glance at Marny, as if to say he did not care to stay under the same roof with her. Putting away her gun, Marny answered in a level voice.

"It's all right, Captain Pollock. I'm about to go out with Mr. Fenway."

"Come into the office, captain," Mr. Chase urged him again.

This time Pollock yielded. As the office door closed, Foxy edged toward Marny.

"Say," he demanded, "what's that man got against you?"

"He doesn't like red-haired women," Marny retorted. "Says they bring bad luck."

"You get on about your work, Foxy," Mr. Fenway ordered him.

The other men began to scatter. Pocket gave his hand to Rosabel and she wiggled down from the counter. Saying, "I'm ready whenever you are, Mr. Fenway," Marny went to look across the counter into the mirror, and began to adjust her bonnet ribbons. Kendra followed and stood beside her.

"Now what do you think?" Kendra asked.

"You're right," Marny returned. "He does think that ship is alive. And he's in love with her."

"I was hoping," said Kendra, "when we reminded him about the shored-up vessels—but that was no use."

Marny answered tersely. "He's as crazy as a fifty-card deck." She tied the ribbons. "But you're right again, Kendra. He's dangerous."

42

That day in the store Kendra had felt sorry for Captain Pollock. But as the summer went on, her sympathy turned to exasperation.

Kendra believed the *Cynthia*'s crew had deserted because the men wanted to look for gold, not because of any mystical heartbreak of the ship. But this was not the basic reason for her change of attitude. She simply had no patience with people who went off and sulked when they could not get their own way. She could understand Pollock's distress when he found that the *Cynthia* could not finish her voyage—though she thought if he had had any sense he would have stayed away from San Francisco in the first place—but since the ship could not go on, Kendra could not condone his refusal to let her do anything else.

He had many chances. With so much riffraff pouring through the Golden Gate, crimes of all sorts were increasing. Honest folk wanted an adequate prison. The only one they had was a small building left over from the quiet days, so ramshackle that bad men had little trouble breaking out. Several leading citizens had advised that the town buy one of the deserted vessels, anchor it a safe distance from shore, and let convicts serve their sentences there. Mr. Chase asked Captain Pollock if he would sell the *Cynthia* for this.

Turn the *Cynthia* into a jail? Pollock was so outraged that Mr. Chase reported, "For a minute I thought he was going to knock me down."

Dwight Carson offered to buy the *Cynthia* for a business building. Again, Pollock refused.

Mr. Fenway had another idea. The coastwise vessels did a thriving business bringing in food and lumber and firewood. It was not too hard to find sailors for these short voyages, if only because men wanted to earn a grubstake for the mines. Mr. Fenway said Pollock might go into the coastwise trade.

Pollock would not. He would take his ship home, or nowhere.

When Loren came back from Oregon he told Kendra he believed Pollock could at least make a start on his homeward voyage if he really wanted to. A few of the most determined captains were doing it. Nearly every week the *Alta* reported the sailing of some vessel bound for Mazatlan or Callao or some other port down the Pacific Coast. True, they were sailing with scanty crews, often including such men as the captains would never have accepted anywhere else. Loren did not suggest that Pollock try to double the Horn with a makeshift crew. But he did say that if Pollock would take what he could get, and put to sea, with any luck at all he could reach a port where he could find competent seamen.

At the advice that he insult the *Cynthia* with what he called "the sweepings of the waterfront," Pollock was angrier than before.

Pollock would not, in fact, listen to anything Loren had to say. While he had been friendly toward Loren and Kendra during his first days in port, now that his sailors had left him he was friendly no longer. Loren was the enemy who had let Marny board the *Cynthia*. As for Kendra, it was bad enough that she should have married Loren; but when he learned of her friendship with Marny, it seemed to Pollock that she had betrayed his trust.

The *Cynthia* stayed where she was, among the lost ships. Day after day Pollock paced up and down the waterfront, watching her slowly rot on the water.

It was deliberate self-torture, and also it was a kind of triumph. If life would not give him what he wanted, life would get nothing from him. He, Captain Enos Pollock, would make no compromise. He was a man of iron will. He would do what he set out to do, or nothing.

To Kendra, it simply did not make sense. It made no sense to Marny, nor to Hiram and Pocket. During the summer

Hiram and Pocket came to San Francisco several times. Each time they looked to see if the *Cynthia* was still there. She was.

"Pollock's a fool," Hiram said bluntly, as he and Pocket and Kendra talked it over in Kendra's parlor. He ran his hand over his turbulent hair. "You know," he went on, "a lot of this stuff called 'strength of character' is nothing but plain muleheadedness."

Kendra agreed.

"And what's he got against Marny?" asked Hiram.

Kendra made little pleats in the handkerchief lying on her knee. "On the way from Honolulu," she said, "Marny and Captain Pollock had a quarrel. I know what they quarreled about because she told me. Maybe some day she'll tell you."

"And until then," Pocket said, "I suppose it's none of our business."

"I suppose so," said Kendra.

The men yielded good-naturedly. Kendra suspected that they would guess the truth, if they had not already done so. After a moment Pocket remarked,

"Poor captain. I'm sorry for him."

"I was," said Kendra. "I'm not any more. Hiram's right. He's a fool."

"He is," Pocket agreed gently. "That's why I'm sorry for him."

Other people wondered in vain why Pollock blamed Marny for his ship's disaster. Pollock's outburst in the store had been described with gusto by the men who had been there, but they could not explain it. Messrs. Chase and Fenway wondered too. When they—or anyone else—asked Pollock, he would answer only, "That woman is evil. She brought evil aboard my ship. And now my ship is dying."

Messrs. Chase and Fenway, both practical men, did not know what he was talking about.

When men asked Marny why Pollock did not like her, she gave them the same answer she had given Foxy. "He thinks red-haired women bring bad luck."

Some of them believed her. This answer was as sensible as any other.

However, both Kendra and Marny had much to think of besides Captain Pollock and the *Cynthia*.

Kendra was concerned with her coming baby. She felt well, and Loren's loving delight was like a cloak around her. She bought a crib, and cloth for little sheets and blankets, which she hemmed with slow awkward stitches while Serena made baby clothes with quick deft hands that Kendra envied. While Kendra envied Serena for her skill, Serena envied Kendra for her baby. Serena wanted another baby to replace the one who had died on the plains. Kendra promised, "When my baby outgrows these clothes I'll give them to you." But Serena protested, "Oh no! You'll want to save these for the next one."

Marny was concerned with the Calico Palace. Besides the furniture, she and Norman were choosing dealers, croupiers, musicians, bartenders. The artist Bruno Gregg was proving himself adept at painting women in all sorts of tempting attitudes. The building was nearly done, and Marny was aglow with joyful impatience. Several of her friends asked if she was going to change the name, now that the walls were brick instead of calico. Marny shook her head. Like most gamblers, Marny had a streak of superstition. She had been lucky in the Calico Palace and she was not going to tempt fate.

But though happily occupied, Kendra and Marny agreed vehemently that the city of gold was no easy place to live in.

Every day San Francisco was growing richer, dirtier, more stinky, and more packed with people. Except for a few who had made their way by land from Oregon or Mexico, so far all the Forty-niners had come by sea. But now the wagons that had left the States last spring were beginning to arrive. Some of the newcomers went directly to the mines, but not all of them had brought enough money to pay California prices for their picks and shovels and salt pork. They came to town to earn their grubstakes, and they could find no place to live. Angrily they wrote home that they had to sleep on the ground, stifling in the dust.

This was true, though seldom did people put up shelters with such speed as the people of San Francisco were doing it now. The hills were a wilderness of tents—big tents, little tents, sturdy tents, and tents quickly torn to pieces by the wind. Captain Pollock had brought a few readymade houses; now other captains were bringing them by scores. With half a dozen workmen, Dwight Carson could set up such a house in a day, and the residents—usually six or seven to a room— could move in the day after. They would not be comfortable, but at least they would have some protection from the dust.

Now in the summer of 1849 the people of San Francisco were nearly smothering in the dust.

As long as they had had an occasional shower, the dust had been merely a nuisance. But since June they had had no more showers. They had only the dust.

The dust was dark and ugly. It was so deep that when you went outdoors you felt as if you were walking through a pile of feathers. Kendra reached down one day and stroked her hand through the dust. Against her fingers it had a velvety feeling, like fine flour.

Sometimes Kendra thought wistfully of the country back home, where they had rain all the year round. But it was no use to wish for rain. Here in the California summer they might get a spatter—though this was rare enough—but as for real rain, Mr. Fenway warned her sadly that they were not going to see any before November, maybe not before December, so she might as well stop wishing.

Every day was like the day before.

In the night the fog crept in from the sea. When she woke in the morning the fog lay on the town in a clammy wad. Sometimes it was so thick that she could not see the houses across the street; sometimes she could find the sun, a cold ball of light behind the fog. If Kendra had to go out she went now, before noon, and when she came in she and Serena closed the doors and windows and shut every drawer. Serena even wanted to cover the keyholes.

Early in the afternoon the wind began. The wind blew away the fog; and mercifully, said Serena, it blew away the smells. But the wind raised the dust in clouds higher than the chimneys. Every morning Kendra and Serena rubbed the furniture till it shone; by dark they could draw pictures on every chair and table in the house.

Last year during the rainless months the town had been dusty, but last year there had been less traffic and fewer people to stir the dust. And this year the people themselves were making it even worse than it had to be.

These men of San Francisco were the most impatient men on earth. They had come here to get rich and they were wasting no time about it. They said San Francisco had too many hills and too little flat ground. They said the water close to shore was too shallow. So, cut off the hilltops and throw them into the bay. Do it now. They would raise a few more tons of dust, but who cared?

305

They set big mule-drawn scoops to cut down the hills. Every day the scoops tore deeper into the hillsides, and every afternoon as the wind came sweeping around these hills, the dust rose. If you went outdoors the dust blew into your eyes and nose and throat, it choked you and sent tears streaming down your cheeks. It got into your hair like cobwebs. It got inside your clothes and crawled on your skin.

But already the men who cut down the hills had filled in the lagoon where an arm of the bay used to cut across Montgomery Street. Now they were filling the cove in front of town, pushing the waterfront out toward the deep water and making town lots where no lots existed before. Dwight Carson had bought several of these "water lots," as they were called, and Marny said to Kendra, "He's going to be *really* rich before long. Some smart girl is going to marry him and do nothing but spend money the rest of her life."

In the white mornings, before the dust rose, Marny still found leisure to climb the hill and keep Kendra informed of doings around the plaza. All along Kearny Street and the cross-streets on both sides of the plaza, buildings were going up with breathtaking speed. Marny said they would be restaurants, hotels, gambling houses "—and," said Marny, *"houses."*

She told Kendra one of these new buildings, on Washington Street overlooking the plaza, was occupied by Norman and Rosabel's friend Blossom.

"Blossom has several more flowers in her garden now," said Marny. "Mostly from New Orleans. I'm told her business is fantastic."

Kendra was not surprised. The harbormaster kept a careful count of the passengers who disembarked at San Francisco. His figures were published once a month in the *Alta,* and the ratio averaged one woman to thirty-seven men.

Marny liked to come up the hill. This was not only because she enjoyed Kendra's friendship, but because—as she herself said frankly—it was a pleasure to spend an hour or two in such comfort. Kendra had everything gold dust would buy.

While firewood was scarce, charcoal from China was abundant, so Loren put braziers in all the rooms, to protect her from the chill of the fogs. He brought her books and sheet music from the bookshop recently opened in the City Hotel, and the newspapers brought by the steamers. Then in late summer Loren joined the other residents of Washington Street in providing the two greatest luxuries of the year. First, they hired workmen to lay a plank sidewalk that led up from Kearny Street to the top of the hill. Second, they bought a sprinkler wagon that watered the street every morning before the wind raised the dust.

Marny told Kendra that Blossom had made a liberal contribution toward both these civic improvements. "They go past her place," said Marny. "Good for business. Expensive, but worth it."

Kendra knew they had been expensive, though Loren would not tell her how much he had paid as his share. "Don't worry," he said. "I'm not spending anything I haven't got. I don't believe in debt." He smiled down at her, adding fondly, "I can take care of my family."

As always, he spoke the last word with pride. His hand on her shoulder, he bent and kissed the arrow of hair on her forehead.

All of a sudden, Kendra had a feeling of being *caught*. That kiss of Loren's was saying, "You are my dearest treasure." That hand on her shoulder said, "I will never let you go."

When Loren had left her, for a long time she walked up and down the room, asking herself—Why do I feel like this? Haven't I got everything I want? Everything I ought to want?

Yes, she thought, she had everything she *ought* to want. She had robust health. The doctor said he had never seen a woman have an easier pregnancy. Her child would be fine and strong, and she would have the joy of giving it the love nobody had given her when she was a child herself and had wanted it so much.

She had a home admired by every woman who came into it, and every man too. She had genuine friends. She had a husband who adored her, and who was one of the most highly respected men in town. So what else did she want?

—I ought to be ashamed of myself, Kendra thought sternly. I *am* ashamed of myself. Half the women in the world would envy me right now. And the other half? Oh, *stop* this! Mrs. Chase says every woman expecting a baby gets odd fancies now and then. The best way to manage them is to get busy and do something. There's the wind. I'll make sure Serena has closed all the windows.

Even with the plank sidewalk and the sprinkler wagon, they still shut up the house every afternoon because dust blew in from other streets not so well cared for. Serena had closed

the windows, but one window in the parlor was slightly stiff
and she had not quite brought the sash all the way down to
the sill. Kendra could see light through the slit at the bottom.
As she started to draw the sash down the rest of the way, a
little tremor ran over her nerves. Why did that slit make her
think of light seen through the bars of a cage?

43

The new Calico Palace opened on the evening of Saturday,
September first, 1849. The opening was grand and noisy and
destructive. Hundreds of men charged through, in joyous but
not gentle mood. They cracked the mirrors, they whittled on
the card tables, they broke half the glassware at the bar, and
they left behind them a trail of gold dust so thick that Marny
likened it to that other dust outdoors.

In the morning, looking over the wreckage, Marny and
Norman were not dismayed. Most of the havoc had taken
place in the big public room on the ground floor. They had
equipped this room with furnishings they expected to be
destroyed, and had kept better in reserve. By evening they
had hung new mirrors, replaced the nicked tables, put more
cups and tumblers at the bar, and doubled the price of drinks.

Nobody minded. The men thronged in and brought their
gold dust with them. Where would they find a better place to
spend it? The Calico Palace was the most sumptuous building
in San Francisco. It was not well built, for Dwight Carson
had not had enough workmen nor enough time, but it was
bright and warm and gaudy, and this was what they wanted.

The Calico Palace was three stories high, with gambling
rooms on the two lower floors and living quarters on the third.
Here lived Marny, Norman, Rosabel, Duke Blackbeard and
Lulu, Troy Blackbeard and Lolo and their baby, Zack. None
of them had much space or much comfort, but they were
better off than most people and glad of it.

The public room, opening on the street, had tables for

monte, faro, twenty-one; a roulette wheel, and a game of chuck-a-luck. At one side was a platform, on which an orchestra blared forth what passed for music on the plaza. Across the back was the bar, where Chad presided, assisted by several other barmen. Ten chandeliers hung from the ceiling beams, and on the walls mirrors threw the light back and forth in an endless glitter. Between the mirrors hung paintings of pretty women in various stages of revealment. None of them was wholly undressed. Marny and Norman had agreed that a little drapery was more interesting to the customers; as Marny said, it gave them something to look forward to.

There were also two pictures of scenery, both by Bruno Gregg. One was his picture of the sawmill; the other showed men panning gold among the rocks in a river. As Kendra had foretold, the men did like these pictures. Those who had not yet been up to the gold country were curious about it, while men who had already been there were glad to show their superior knowledge by explaining details. The men who most enjoyed this were the "old miners"—those who had been here before '49. Norman said grumpily that the Forty-eighters and the Forty-niners were like the Bourbons and the Bonapartes.

Any man could come into the public room and stay as long as he did not make a nuisance of himself. He could bet any sum he pleased, small or large, buy drinks and cigars at the bar or not buy them. This room was a bright and tempting place, a refuge from the fogs and sea winds, and from the tents and flophouses where most men had to live. They crowded it every evening.

This was as much of the Calico Palace as most of them ever saw. To take part in the upstairs revelry a man had to have abundant gold and he had to be willing to part with it. Marny called the upper rooms the sky parlors, and explained, "We get only the most aristocratic sinners there."

The main parlor was a room about half the size of the public room. The rest of the second floor was divided into small rooms that men could rent for private games. Like the public room, the main parlor had a bar, and mirrors, and game tables, and pictures of women. But here the bar was less dusty, the barmen more mannerly, and the drinks more expensive. Here the play was quieter and the stakes in general higher. And here a man could be sure of seeing at least one live woman—Marny at her card table, Rosabel playing the

309

piano, Lulu and Lolo helping tend the bar. They never all took a rest at the same time.

The girls did not appear in the public room. They were too precious to be wasted there. The *Alta* had said that during the month of August, the Forty-niners entering by the Golden Gate had shown an imbalance of the sexes even higher than usual—eighty-seven women and nearly four thousand men. Clearly, said Norman, men who wanted to look at women— especially pretty women—ought to pay for it.

They paid, willingly. "Some of them," Marny told Kendra, "just stand at the bar and buy drinks and *look* at us. They don't gamble, they don't talk. They just look, until they've bought so many drinks they're seeing us double and I suppose they figure they're getting twice their money's worth."

"Don't they ever try to handle you?" Kendra asked.

"Oh yes, but we always have guards on duty and pretty soon they learn it's not allowed." Marny added that a guard stood at the door, and a man who had once made trouble in the parlor had a hard time getting in again. "But usually," she went on, "it's remarkable how respectful they are. Most of them ask us to marry them. Some men propose marriage every time they come in. Poor fellows, they're so lonesome for women. I feel sorry for them. But not sorry enough to marry them. We're doing fine. And my dear," Marny continued happily, "we're getting the *best* people. Dwight Carson comes up often, and all the rich traders. Even Mr. Chase has been in once or twice. And you may be surprised, but we also have Mr. Fenway."

Kendra was surprised, and said so.

"Mr. Fenway likes music," said Marny. "When Rosabel plays he brings a chair near the piano, and he does enjoy it. When he's listening to the piano he looks more cheerful than I've ever seen him anywhere else."

"Doesn't he ever gamble?"

"Yes, sometimes he plays roulette. He doesn't drink much. Several of our best patrons don't drink much. I wish we had your cakes and cheese rolls again."

She said they liked to have such a solid citizen as Mr. Fenway. He gave tone to the parlor. Because of this, one evening when Mr. Fenway did go to the bar for a drink Norman told the bartender to serve it without charge, but Mr. Fenway declined the favor. He was a self-respecting man, he said sternly, and preferred to pay his way. The bartender

310

poured the drink, and Mr. Fenway handed him the price, solemnly saying, "Thank you, steward."

In San Francisco, bartenders and waiters and doormen were always addressed as "Steward." They preferred this term, and when you were lucky enough to have a man serve you in any way, you treated him with respect. Besides, back home he might have been a lawyer or a teacher or an architect. San Francisco had a vast over-supply of educated men. California was a long way from every other town in the civilized world. By land or sea this long journey was expensive. A banker was more likely to have the price than a ditch digger. Also, once they got here, men used to hard labor usually went to the mines and stayed there. Men of learning, while they often went to dig gold, were likely to come back soon, full of aches and blisters, to look for a less painful way of getting rich. They learned to drive mules or mix drinks, and made more money than they had ever made at their desks back home. Bookshops flourished, and half the men employed in the Calico Palace were college graduates.

Among her applicants for work Marny had met two or three gentlemen from Philadelphia, who recognized her as the professor's wayward daughter. Kendra said to her, "They are probably going to spread word of where you came from. Do you mind?"

With a smile, Marny looked at her squarely. "Do you think I should?"

"No," said Kendra. "I think you have as much right to live your way as other people have to live theirs."

"Thanks," said Marny. "I thought you'd say that." She shrugged. "I don't think anybody will care anyway."

Loren confirmed this. He said men who heard of Marny's background were interested for ten minutes, but few of them for longer than this. Marny was a skillful, straight-playing, and amusing redhead who dealt cards. This was what they cared about.

But while Marny was content, Rosabel was less so. Marny told Kendra that Rosabel was in love with Norman and wanted to marry him; while Norman, fond as he was of Rosabel, did not intend to tie himself down to her or anybody else. "I've told her and told her," said Marny. "Still she keeps hoping."

Marny herself continued to receive proposals of marriage

and continued to shrug them off. Never had Kendra heard her express any interest in getting married.

Marny's interests centered around the plaza. The plaza was dirty and rowdy and full of smells, but it was one of the most exciting spots in the world and Marny was glad she was here.

The best of the resorts around the plaza were those on the Kearny Street side. Here you would see the Calico Palace and another casino called Denison's Exchange. Here was the Parker House, which in spite of its cloth walls and all-night racket brought in a monthly rent of a thousand ounces of gold; and the El Dorado, flashy and noisy but kept in order most of the time. On Kearny Street you could dine in the most excellent restaurants in town. In New York you might not have called them excellent. The plates were thick and heavy and usually chipped; instead of damask the tables were covered with oilcloth, which could be wiped off instead of laundered; for a napkin a man used his handkerchief (if he had one) or his shirt-tail.

But the food was good. The stewards offered you beef and ham and venison, veal cutlets, mutton chops, fish from the rivers and birds from the woods across the bay; potatoes and squash from Honolulu, and now in the fall, fresh grapes from the vineyards above the Golden Gate. You paid far more than you would have paid in New York, but on Kearny Street you expected this.

Where Kearny Street met Washington, on the corner opposite the El Dorado you would see another gambling house called the Verandah. If you turned here and climbed the plank sidewalk you would soon pass Blossom's flower garden. Then you would come to more gambling houses not so well kept as those on Kearny Street—the Aguila del Oro, the St. Charles, and the Bella Union, rowdiest of them all. If a man wanted a really skittish evening (and did not mind the risk of a shooting spree) he could buy a ticket to a "grand fancy ball" at the Bella Union. At the ball he could sample the fanciest drinks and meet the fanciest of the girls who had come across the Isthmus from New York and New Orleans. Next morning his head would be so fuzzy that he could rarely describe just what had happened, but men who had been there always spoke of the goings-on at the Bella Union as "extraordinary."

But if you walked on, past the Bella Union, before long you would observe that Washington Street was getting quieter, and beginning to behave itself. You might have said the change came at a half-and-half building called Washington Hall. As you would expect, this building had a saloon on the ground floor. But on the second floor was a room that sober citizens rented for sober reasons—to raise funds for sick men, or to discuss the proposed State Constitution, which they hoped would make California a state of the Union.

Above Washington Hall was the office of the *Alta California,* and this building was one of the best structures in town. Beyond this you would pass stores selling clothes and books and musical instruments. Then, as you went on up the hill toward Stockton Street, you would come to the neighborhood of little square white houses. This was where Kendra and Loren lived, and Mr. and Mrs. Chase, and other people who rarely took part in the doings around the plaza.

The plaza itself was a mess. The whole square was cluttered with bricks and lumber, bales of goods, and walls of ready-made houses piled up and waiting for workmen to put them together. In the plaza somebody was always shouting. On weekdays the auctioneers offered their goods, on Sundays a preacher mounted a barrel and loudly warned his hearers about their sins.

Early in October, Loren told Kendra that since Pollock would not sell the *Cynthia,* the town council had bought the brig *Euphemia* to be used as a jail. Kendra remembered this brig. Just in from Monterey, the *Euphemia* had been one of the two seagoing vessels she had seen in the bay the day the *Cynthia* brought her to San Francisco. The other had been the *Eagle* from China. Only two of them, and look at the bay now! Less than two years ago, but it felt like a long, long time. In San Francisco things happened so fast, time did not *seem* like time. No more than gold dust seemed like money.

The *Cynthia* was still anchored in the bay, useless. Pollock still walked up and down the waterfront, watching her. She was dying and he was sick with grief, but he would not save her in the only way she could be saved.

While she had small sympathy for Pollock, Kendra was glad to talk about him and take her mind off herself. For the past few days she had been feeling droopy. At first she had thought it was because the baby was getting heavier, but she noticed that other people complained of feeling droopy too. They blamed it on the weather. They said October weather had never been like this.

313

The afternoon winds had stopped. For days now the fog had lain thick and unrelieved. Even outdoors the air was stuffy like the air in a room long unopened. The morning after Loren brought her the news about the *Euphemia,* the fog was so heavy when they woke up that Kendra exclaimed, "It's like living in a bowl of milk!"

Loren called to Serena to bring a cup of coffee to warm Kendra before she got out of bed, and he told Ralph to light the brazier in the parlor. By the time he and Ralph left for work Kendra was as comfortable as she could possibly be, on the parlor sofa with several new books at her elbow. Serena came in to say she had meant to do some laundry this morning, but she didn't think she should because in this heavy gray weather the clothes would never get dry. As she spoke, they heard a splashy noise. Kendra looked around with a start. "Why Serena, is that *rain?*"

It certainly was rain. No spatter this, but a roaring storm lashing the house in fury. Kendra was astonished. She had never heard of a storm in San Francisco so early in the fall. As she hurried to close the front windows she saw that already the dust was turning to soft thick mud, creeping downhill toward the plaza.

For three hours the rain came down. When Loren and Ralph came home the downpour had stopped, but the clouds were gathering again. Both men wore high rubber boots they had procured from the stock of Chase and Fenway. They said the mud on Montgomery Street was ankle deep, and the plaza was like a lake of black oatmeal.

Loren said tons of merchandise, stacked outdoors because nobody had dreamed of rain so early, had been drenched and ruined. Men of business were not only astonished, they were angry, as if Nature had played a mean trick on them. Rain in the first half of October just wasn't right.

Right or not, the rain began again the next morning, and this time it poured all day. The mud was so thick that except on the rare plank sidewalks every step was an effort, and in some places the mud even buried the sidewalks. Men living in tents were miserable, and many of those living under roofs were not much better off, for the rain seeped in through the cracks.

The rain had blocked Kendra's view of the bay, but when Loren came in he told her the steamer *California* had come in from the Isthmus this morning. She had brought American

314

newspapers, and three hundred and thirty-nine passengers. "And most of them," Loren said laughing, "took one look and wished they had stayed home."

For days, people talked about the unseasonable rain. Mr. and Mrs. Chase, who had lived five years in San Francisco, said they had never seen anything like it. Mr. Fenway, who had lived here eight years and was one of the oldest Yankee inhabitants, said such early rain was unwholesome, and he sadly prophesied colds and consumption this winter. The native Californios said the Yankees had brought their own wretched climate with them.

At every bar around the plaza, men began announcing that they had choked in the dust and bogged in the mud and they were sick of it and they were going home.

The steamboat line was well organized now. A steamer left San Francisco every month, bound for the Isthmus, and when passengers reached the other side another steamer met them and took them to their home ports on the Atlantic Coast.

But up to now, while the steamers had always been packed with people on the voyages to California, they had gone back half empty. Now, however, for the first time, the steamboat office sold so many tickets for the homeward voyage that the crewmen said every berth on the *California* was taken and men would be sleeping on deck.

Then, all of a sudden, the sun began to shine.

The mud dried. The air turned balmy. The wind was merely a pleasant breeze, and because of the lingering dampness there was no more dust. In such delightful weather everybody wanted to go outdoors. Women went shopping, and men lined the streets to watch them pass. Boys roamed about selling walnuts from Chile, and strange delicious candies from Hong Kong, and an exciting new luxury, oranges from Honolulu.

There was another grand fancy ball at the Bella Union. Near the plaza a tent shot up, with a sign saying "Rowe's Olympic Circus." Mr. Rowe presented a circus he had brought from the States, a real circus with clowns and acrobats and trained horses, and even two well-shaped female performers. The ladies disappointed their admirers by being married, the tightrope dancer to her partner and the bareback rider to Mr. Rowe himself, but they were live women, and men crowded the benches to look at them.

All over town, tents and shacks were coming down and

three-story buildings rising to take their places. Chase and Fenway began putting up a new store next door to the old one. Loren said they were going to tear down the old store and replace it with a warehouse.

"I'll miss it," said Kendra, but even as she spoke she laughed at herself. In San Francisco it was absurd to waste your thoughts on anything from last year. It was all you could do to keep up with the here and now. The sun poured out of the blue sky, the whole town clinked with gold, and the men who had bought tickets home began to change their minds.

Sipping chocolate with Kendra, Marny said a few men were still planning to leave, but many more wished they had not been in such a hurry. They wanted to return their tickets to the steamboat line. This could be done, but it was a tedious process, so the hasty buyers were offering their tickets for sale around town.

"Is anybody buying them?" asked Kendra.

"Certainly," said Marny. Her green eyes had a mischievous flash.

Kendra asked, "Who?" She was not surprised when Marny answered,

"Me."

Kendra began to laugh. Marny set her cup on the table beside her and looked out at the sparkling day.

"Kendra," she said, "I'm a gambler. We may not get much rain this winter, but even with a little rain this town can be mighty disagreeable. I'm gambling on the chance that it'll be disagreeable enough to put up the price of steamboat tickets."

Kendra remembered the mud flowing down the hill after a storm of only two days. "You're a smart business-woman," she said.

Marny smiled. "Then you don't think I'm wicked?"

"No," said Kendra.

"Some people would," Marny reminded her.

"I'm not 'some people,'" Kendra retorted. "I'm me. I know what I think, and I think it's no more wrong to buy tickets and hold them for a rise than to buy city lots and hold them."

Marny took up her cup again and sipped the chocolate. "That's what I like about you, Kendra. You do your own thinking and make up your own mind."

"That's what I have a head for," Kendra said laughing.

But even as she laughed, she knew she was not going to tell Loren about Marny's buying up those steamer tickets.

316

Loren would not approve. It was only one more incident to remind her that her own spirit was closer to the Calico Palace than to this demure little cottage where she lived. She had let herself be caught between them. She had let herself turn into a halfway person, and she did not like it, and she did not know how to wrench herself free.

44

At noon on the first of November the steamer *California* puffed her way through the Golden Gate and turned toward the Isthmus. As usual on her southbound voyages half her berths were empty. The day was bright, and sunbeams danced around the vessels in the bay. That afternoon Marny went to Chase and Fenway's and locked up her steamboat tickets in the little safe she kept there to hold her own private hoard of coins. Marny never paid for anything with coins unless it was something so rare and necessary that the seller could demand coins instead of gold dust. She put coins into her safe. You knew what coins were worth. You never could tell about gold dust, not in San Francisco.

She went back to the Calico Palace along the plank sidewalk that the gamblers had built on Kearny Street. She dealt cards until shortly after midnight, then she climbed the stairs to her little room on the third floor and went to bed. Unlike the Bella Union and some other resorts around the plaza, the Calico Palace did not stay open till dawn. Marny and Norman had observed that most of the disorders in these places occurred in the early morning hours, when the serving men were tired and the drinking men drunk. They closed early, and kept the peace.

By this time Marny was used to the plaza noise and slept through it fairly well. But the next morning a different sort of noise woke her up. She raised herself on her elbow, hearing the howl of wind, and vessels creaking as the waves rose and knocked them around. When she looked out she saw that the brightness of the past few weeks had gone. The clouds were thick, and as the day went on they grew thicker, until the Blackbeards had to light the chandeliers in the gambling rooms so the players could see the cards. In the late afternoon the storm broke.

The rain poured all night. It poured all the next day, and the next and the next and the next. It poured every day for two weeks. Once in a while it would pause for an hour or so, long enough for people to look up at the sky and say hopefully, "Don't you think it might clear now?" But they hardly had time to patch a leak before the rain started again.

The mud rolled in torrents down the hills. Behind them the torrents left open gulfs that filled with water. In level places the ground soaked up all the water it could. When it could hold no more, great dark pools lay about, and stayed there. In places men laid planks across the pools to serve as bridges, but their work was wasted. After a few hours the planks went down into the mud, out of sight.

The whole town tottered in a sea of mud. The best of the plank sidewalks had been laid on piles, and these could still be used if you wore thick boots and were very careful. But it was not easy, because the sidewalks were so narrow that when two persons met they could barely pass each other without stepping off into the slush.

Except on these rare sidewalks men waded in mud to their knees, swearing tiredly as they slogged along. Sometimes they stumbled, and nearly choked in the mud before they could get up.

In places the mud was six feet deep. Wagons stuck. The mules kicked and strained, bogging deeper as they fought to get out. Sometimes they went down and smothered to death. Their owners tried to drag the bodies away, but the stenches that rose over the mud suggested that some of the carcasses had gone out of sight and were still there. The wagons went down until the wheels could no longer be seen, and nobody tried to move them.

Chase and Fenway advertised rubber coats and hats and boots, rubber tents for men to live in, rubber sheets to cover the beds they tried to sleep in or to tack on the leaky roofs they had to live under. But much as these were needed, few men could reach the store to buy them. Montgomery Street was a sea of mud, black and deep and dangerous, and cut with runnels of rain that made it deeper every hour.

318

Mr. Fenway had an idea.

"Let's bury some of this trash from New York," he said. "That'll make the street solid enough to walk on."

He and Mr. Chase and their helpers set to work. Before long other businessmen up and down the liquid streets were following their example, dragging out bales and barrels of merchandise and sinking them into the mud so the customers could walk.

They all had plenty of stuff that was good for nothing else. For months past, half the vessels that came into the bay had been bringing cargoes of expensive rubbish. Most shippers in the States knew nothing about San Francisco except that it was a town full of gold, and they had not bothered to find out anything else. They had sent out silver-mounted carriage harness for mules dragging wagons up the hills; ruffled white shirts and kid dancing slippers for men who needed overalls and knee-high boots for gold digging; mahogany beds and marble-topped dressing tables for a town where most men slept on shelves in flophouses, with bugs and rats and twenty or thirty other men all breathing the same air; baby beds and rocking chairs and parlor stoves for a town that had hardly a dozen family homes; and tons of bonnets and ribbons and silken fripperies for women who weren't there. Messrs. Chase and Fenway and their friends, who had been supposed to sell these things on commission, now dragged them out and let them slide into the mud.

Men who did not own stores came in, bought piles of this trumpery at low prices, and used it to fill their own streets. At the corner where Kearny Street met Washington, Norman and his gambling friends sank a double line of stoves. The stoves went down easily and made a firm pathway so men could cross from one plank sidewalk to the other.

Swathed in rubber clothes, carrying lunches in rubber bags, Loren and Ralph and Mr. Chase went down the hill and back every day. Mr. Fenway, who had no family to go home to, slept in the store. Often in the evenings, dripping and determined in his boots and raincoat, he walked up to Kearny Street, crossed on the line of stoves, and made his way to the Calico Palace. Here he warmed himself with a few drinks and heard Rosabel play the piano.

The Calico Palace was still doing a good business. It was a bright and cheerful spot. Many men besides Mr. Fenway

319

preferred to kick their way through the mud than to stay in the wretched lodgings where most of them had to live.

As for Marny, she too was damp and cold. Her bedroom was drafty, her clothes seemed never dry, and her meals—brought in from the restaurant next door—were soggy when they reached her. But she had the inner warmth of the gambler who has guessed right. During her breaks from the card table Marny sat in her dismal little room, sipping warmed over coffee and listening to the rain. Thump, thump, rub-a-dub, pour, rattle, rain, rain, rain. As she listened, she knew that every day of it was making her steamboat tickets worth more than they had been worth the day before.

She did not try to see Kendra while the rain came down. But Kendra thought of her often, and of the steamboat tickets, with amusement and admiration.

Kendra herself was as comfortable as anybody could be in such abusive weather. Her house did not leak, and she had a good supply of firewood. Shortly before the storm Loren had bought the scraps from a building recently finished by Dwight Carson.

During the deluge a steamer came in, bringing mail that had come on muleback across the Isthmus. Loren sent Ralph to the post office, a little wooden building high on the Clay Street hill, and Ralph came back with his rubber bag full of mail. Kendra had a letter from Eva, an answer to the letter Kendra herself had written last spring telling Eva of her second marriage.

Kendra read the letter, lying on the sofa in her parlor while the fire crackled and the rain pelted the roof. Eva had written from Alex's post of duty at Hampton Roads, Virginia. It was the same sort of tactful, dutiful letter she used to write when Kendra was at school. Eva was sorry the marriage to Ted had been a failure—"You gave so few details, I hardly know what to say, but I am sure you acted for the best"—and she hoped Kendra would find more happiness with Loren. "I remember him well from our days on the *Cynthia*. A young man of excellent character and gentlemanly bearing." She added some details about life at Hampton Roads, which she was evidently enjoying.

Kendra lowered the pages to the cushion beside her. She heard the rain. She looked down at Eva's letter. Pleasant, almost impersonal. As if she were writing to a cousin she had

320

not seen for years and did not expect to see for years more, if ever.

—As always, thought Kendra, she's glad to be rid of me. I am suitably disposed of. "And how is your daughter, Mrs. Taine?" —"She's married, living in California. Oh yes, she likes it there."

—I'll write her after the baby is born. That will give me something to write about. I suppose we'll each write about two letters a year, and neither of us will be sorry we're so far apart. We have nothing in common. We never had, and we never will.

Kendra felt her baby move. She looked down at the place where the baby was growing, nearly ready now to be born.

"You are going to be loved," she promised. "You are never going to know how it feels not to be wanted."

After two drowning weeks the rain stopped. The weary people looked around. The hills showed long deep slashes cut by the rain, the lower part of town stood in a lake of mud like black molasses. In the mud they saw rags and shoes, bones and bottles and tin cans, potato peelings and eggshells and cabbage leaves and every sort of offal, all rotting together in the mess.

They had to live in it. Except where they could use the few plank sidewalks, there was nothing to do but wade in the mud. And it stank. Never had they been so glad of the wild winds of San Francisco.

They could only hope there would be no more rain until they had had time to make some sort of order out of the chaos around them. Or, said several hundred disgusted citizens, until they had left this miserable place forever.

The steamer *Panama* was in the bay, making ready to leave. The disgusted citizens rushed to the steamboat office and bought tickets home. The tickets at the office gave out, but word went around—You could get a ticket at the Calico Palace. You asked one of the bartenders. He would consider, and reply, "Why yes, I'll try to get one for you." After a moment's pause he would add, "It *may* be expensive."

Men who wanted to leave paid gladly, saying it was worth the price to get out of this filthy swamp. They crowded aboard the *Panama*. Two days after the rain ceased she left for the Isthmus, packed with passengers, half of whom had bought their tickets from Marny.

But over San Francisco the sky was bright again. The hills across the bay turned green, with great yellow splashes of wild mustard blooms. Again the people began to build. They laid plank sidewalks, they threw footbridges over the gulfs, they put up workshops and shelters of every kind. Chase and Fenway moved into their new building. Dwight Carson tore down their old store and set to work on their new warehouse. Workmen were not so scarce as they had been in the summer, for the mountains were covered with snow and men could no longer dig gold.

Kendra did not go into the mushy streets, but she got exercise by walking up and down her front porch. From here on the hill she could look down at the town and its boisterous energy. She could see men laughing, shouting, arguing, drinking from flasks they carried in their pockets, stumbling on the paths and swearing as they tried to stand up again. She could see the plaza and its peacocky resorts; on side streets she could see Chinese restaurants, where slippered men served good food at surprisingly low prices, and Chinese gambling houses where they played games unknown to Caucasians; and on other streets she could see saloons and cheap brothels and lunch counters where men ate standing up while they brushed away flies.

Swaggering up and down, often passing her own porch, were men just down from the mines. You could always tell a miner: bearded, long-haired, shirt of red or blue or plaid flannel, heavy breeches, gun in holster—maybe two guns in two holsters—boots caked with red mud. They kept the red mud sticking to their boots as long as they could. San Francisco mud was black. Only the mud of the placer country was red. Red mud on their boots proved they had been to the mines.

Nearly all these men from the mines were very young. In this same month of November, when the citizens voted on the State Constitution, hundreds of the swashbuckling heroes of the gold camps could not vote because they were not old enough.

But though they were nearly all young, not all the men from the mines were joyous. As she watched them go by, sometimes Kendra felt sympathy that was almost pain. The death rate among the miners was tragic. They had so much to get used to—the labor, the strange climate, the uncertain rewards of gold digging, the dreadful food and liquor, which

322

was all they could get at many of the camps; the nerve-racking newness of everything. They had come into it suddenly. They lacked the background of slow toughening that Kendra and her friends had had that first year, when a gold camp was a safe and neighborly place.

No wonder so many of them could not stand it. They withered and died, or, in shocking numbers, they gave up and killed themselves. As the miners strutted around, much of their exuberance was real. But much of it was nothing but the bluster of scared kids who wished they had never left home.

And these were the men who had lived to get here. Now that the covered wagons were coming in, horrible stories were coming in with them. Stories of jaunty young fellows who had started out with their wagon covers painted "California or Bust," thinking a lot of guns and bravado was all it took to get here, thinking one Yankee could lick six Indians with his right hand tied behind him, knowing nothing about the deserts and mountains ahead of them and too bumptious to ask. People said you could find your way from Missouri to California now, simply by following the graves.

But thousands of them did get here, and many of these prospered. How San Francisco was growing! From her porch Kendra could see the new buildings mushrooming out of the mud, and the vessels hurrying into the bay. When the *Panama* sailed she had left three hundred and seventeen vessels in the bay behind her. Still they came, they came from all over the world, bringing more people and more goods. Kendra could see the wharfs piled with merchandise, waiting to be drenched in the next rain.

On Thanksgiving Day the town was still wallowing in mud; but the sun shone, there were blooms on the wild bushes, and the people made holiday. Clergymen held services for thankful worshipers; the captain of a bark from Boston gave a dinner on board for a group of leading businessmen; the plaza preacher shouted to his hearers to repent, which apparently they did not, for the Calico Palace and its rivals were thronged all day. When Marny sent a bartender to the restaurant for her dinner he brought her turkey with sage dressing, fresh and hot as a holiday dinner ought to be. The men of the Calico Palace went out for their meals, but Marny did not. The restaurants were full of men, and the sight of her would have caused too much excitement. She carried the trays to her bedroom and ate her meals alone.

When she had finished dinner she piled the dishes on the tray to be sent back at once. She was not going to keep any broken pieces of food around to bring in the creeping things that spawned by millions in the damp.

For a minute or two she stood at a window, looking down. Her bedroom did not face the plaza—she had chosen a back room because here she had some protection from the noise—so she looked over the alley between this building and the restaurant, and the back doors of both. The dusk was closing in, but she could see by the light from the first floor windows. What a *dump,* thought Marny. Piles of boxes, bottles, garbage, and mud, mud, mud. Well, it didn't matter. She was here because she wanted to be here, and she was doing what she wanted to do. And while she certainly did not live in such comfort as Loren provided for Kendra, she took care of herself rather well.

Marny slept on an iron cot. It was not handsome, but keeping clean in San Francisco was an endless and sometimes hopeless battle, and an iron cot was not attractive to bedbugs. Unlike most people, Marny slept between sheets. The sheets were never hemmed and never washed. She bought bolts of white muslin, tore off strips of the right length and put them on the cot. When she needed a change of sheets she rolled up the strips and threw them out of the window, and tore off new ones. Like the miners, she also threw away many of her garments. It was easier than washing them. It was also easier, and less expensive, than finding somebody to wash them for her.

She liked it here. She liked the bright raucous merriment of the Calico Palace, she liked the people she worked with. The Blackbeards and the Hawaiian girls were her friends, so were Chad and the other barmen. She liked Rosabel's good-natured cleverness and the cool competence of Norman. Norman had few orthodox virtues—he was not kind or generous or unselfish—but he was consistent with himself. With Norman you knew exactly where you stood. Marny liked this.

And she liked all those beautiful gold coins she was collecting in her safe at Chase and Fenway's. Marny had a high opinion of money. It gave her freedom to do as she pleased, and the triumph of proving herself. Marny shrugged as she

324

thought of her brothers and sisters and aunts and uncles and cousins. For all their prattle about good repute and good behavior, she knew that if she ever did go back to Philadelphia they would have more respect for a rich sinner than a poor one.

It was time she went back to her card table. As she turned from the window she caught sight of herself in the glass. Taking up the candle, she went nearer. She looked well. Her penny-red hair shone in the candlelight, and her cheeks— still somewhat freckled in spite of the San Francisco clouds —had a healthy glow. She wore a dark green dress, not very low at the neck but low enough to set off her nugget necklace. Men liked that nugget necklace. It was, as Marny herself had said, a trophy that belonged to California. Marny liked it too.

She blew out the candle, picked up her dinner tray, and went down to the second floor. Opening a door behind the bar of her parlor, she beckoned to the bartender who had brought her dinner.

"You can take it now, Wilfred," she said as he came to the door.

"Right," said Wilfred, "and I'll stay for my own dinner. If I don't get there soon all the turkeys will be gone and I'll have to eat beef again."

She gave him a smile of comradeship. "Fine, eat turkey while you can. Mine was good."

Another bartender was approaching, this one from Chad's bar in the public room. As Wilfred took her tray and went off, Marny spoke to the second man.

"Yes, Gordon?"

"Fellow downstairs," said Gordon, "has a ticket on the *Unicorn*. Wants to cash it for gambling money."

Marny puckered her lips, calculating. The steamer *Unicorn* was due to leave December first, day after tomorrow, and except for one or two quick showers, there had been no rain for two weeks. However, the ticket would still be good on the next steamer run. "Take it at twenty per cent discount," she said.

He nodded and went out. Marny walked around to the front of the bar. A dozen drinkers greeted her and she threw them a kiss.

Pausing at the bar, she looked around. Everything was going well. Norman had gone out to dinner, and another Frenchman from New Orleans stood at the roulette table

325

replacing him as croupier. Rosabel was playing the piano. Mr. Fenway, ungracefully straddling a chair, was listening as somberly as if he were hearing a dirge instead of a waltz. Near the piano was the faro table, where the players sat in their own blank-faced silence. Two young Mexicans were dealing Monte, and a Yankee who spoke with a Harvard accent was substituting for Marny herself at twenty-one.

Marny could hear the clink of coins and glasses, and here and there the tinkle of a bell as some player summoned a bartender so he would not have to leave his game. In front of the bar a boy about sixteen years old was busy with a broom and dustpan, sweeping the carpet. The cleaning boys each paid half an ounce a day to be allowed to work here. As they swept up the cigar ash and dried mud and other odds and ends, they emptied the sweepings into bags. After work they sifted the sweepings.

Lucky gamblers, misty eyed drinkers, men who had had a good summer at the mines, were not too careful with their gold dust. When they took out their pokes to pay for drinks they rarely bothered about the grains that fell on the carpet. When a boy sifted the sweepings of an evening's work he nearly always found enough gold to pay back his investment several times over. San Francisco was a dirty town, but never were carpets kept so clean as those of the gambling houses around the plaza.

Marny heard the main door open, and the steward saying "Good evening, sir," to a man coming in. She glanced toward the door and gave a start as she recognized Loren.

The wind had spanked Loren's cheeks bright pink, his cider-brown eyes were aglow, and as he took off his hat he smiled with the happy impulsiveness of a man who smiles without realizing that he is doing so. Loren had never been inside the Calico Palace before. As he came in he looked around him with curiosity, like a city boy on his first visit to a farm.

Marny hurried to meet him and caught his hand in both of hers. "Loren! Come in, I'm glad to see you. And I think," she added in a lower voice as she drew Loren toward the bar, "by the look of you, you've brought good news."

Loren nodded with his own engaging eagerness. His joy was like a light. "It's a boy!" he told her.

"And Kendra?"

"She's all right—would I be so glad if she wasn't? She was sound asleep when I left. Mrs. Chase is with her, and will stay till I get back."

"Oh Loren, I'm so happy for you!" Marny exclaimed. She spoke to the nearest bartender. "Pour Mr. Shields whatever he wants, he's my guest. Shall it be champagne, Loren? Fine, I'll have the same." The bartender grinned and poured the champagne. As they lifted their glasses Marny said,

"And I suppose his name is Loren Shields, Junior?"

Loren chuckled. "I haven't made sure yet, but I hope so."

The other men at the bar were listening with a certain wistfulness. So few men in San Francisco had anything like a family, or if they had, they had left it two or three thousand miles away. They congratulated Loren. Every one of them wanted to buy him a drink. He declined, saying he'd better get home sober. He had just come here to tell the news.

"When can I see Kendra?" Marny asked.

Loren was not sure. It would depend on how she felt, and what the doctor said.

Marny said she understood. Loren went on,

"They say Junior looks like me."

This Marny did not understand. As far as she could tell, babies did not look like anybody. They were just bits of squirming flesh. However, as Loren said the baby looked like him, she was willing to say this too was wonderful.

"And born on Thanksgiving Day!" said Loren.

"Perfectly right," said Marny.

Loren agreed.

Marny would have liked to stay at the bar longer and chat with him. Such happiness as his was catching. But she saw that the Harvard man at the twenty-one table was growing impatient. He did not know what news Loren had brought, but he was sure it was not as important as his own Thanksgiving dinner. The turkeys had been brought over live from Honolulu, not too many of them. Like Wilfred the bartender, the dealer feared that if he did not get to the restaurant soon he would miss his share. Marny said it was time she went to work.

Loren said he had to get back to Kendra and his son. But first, he walked over to the piano and stood waiting till Rosabel finished the piece she was playing, so he could tell the great news to Mr. Fenway.

45

Before she went to see Kendra, Marny took Troy Blackbeard as her escort and walked down to Chase and Fenway's new store to buy a present. The day was clammy and dark, but there was no rain. Holding her cashmere shawl close around her, Marny made her way along the plank sidewalk, with Troy keeping his hand on his gun and glowering at men who would have liked to accost her.

Montgomery Street was a barbaric mixture of dirt and splendor. Rats were feasting in the garbage, and Marny's nose met every nasty smell she had ever heard of. But the stores had glittering windows, where she saw bonnets and laces from New York, silks from China, French wines and perfumes, formal apparel for ladies and gentlemen of fashion.

At Chase and Fenway's they found a little plank bridge leading from the sidewalk to the door, so customers could go in without soiling their shoes in the mud. While Marny stood admiring such luxury Blackbeard opened the door. As they went in she looked around with more surprise. The lumbery old store was really gone. The new store had a carpeted aisle down the middle, and on either side glass-fronted counters, and cabinets flaunting more displays. The salesman who approached was a dapper young man, bowing with practiced ease no doubt learned at some emporium in the States.

"Good morning, sir and madam," he greeted them. "Can I be of assistance?"

Marny was not in a spendthrift mood. The man who had cashed his steamer ticket for gambling money had been lucky, so lucky that he had won enough to buy back his ticket at full price and still walk out with a pokeful of gold. This was the hazard of gambling, of course, and Marny tried to be a good loser, but this loss was hard to bear. Big winners had a way of getting flushed with success, and coming back and playing till they lost again. But this man had boarded the

Unicorn and was now on his way home. What she had lost to him was lost forever.

But Marny was fond of Kendra and she meant to prove it. She chose a robe of quilted satin from China, hyacinth blue with silk embroidery in many colors.

"Warm and useful and a work of art," she said softly, stroking it with pleasure. Marny loved the feel of fine silk under her fingers.

Still guarded by Troy, she walked up the hill. At Kendra's home, Serena opened the door.

Serena told them Mrs. Shields was fine. Dr. Rollins was with her now. Not that she needed a doctor any more, but you know Mr. Shields, he couldn't be content unless Dr. Rollins came over every day to say she was all right. Mrs. Chase was here too. Such a nice lady, so friendly and kind. And there was coffee on the stove, and a cake in the cupboard. Of course, said Serena, her cooking wasn't as good as that of Mrs. Shields, but if Mr. Blackbeard would care to try a piece of cake he'd be mighty welcome.

Troy happily followed her into the kitchen. Marny, carrying the robe, went up the staircase that led to Kendra's room. On the landing outside the door Mrs. Chase was waiting for the doctor.

Mrs. Chase, who was not as stiff-minded as her husband liked to believe, smiled at Marny and said Kendra would be glad to see her. A moment later Dr. Rollins came out. A hearty soul with a genuine liking for the human race, the doctor had visited the Calico Palace several times, and he paused to exclaim, "Well, well, Marny! How are you?"

"Fine," said Marny. "And Kendra—she's really had no trouble?"

"Trouble!" he scoffed genially. "Never saw an easier delivery in my life. Nothing to it. Like shelling peanuts. Well, I guess I'd better get along." He rattled down the stairs toward Serena's cake and coffee, while Mrs. Chase looked after him with half humorous exasperation. Giving Marny's arm a squeeze she exclaimed,

"Don't you *hate* men sometimes?"

The force of her remark was largely wasted on Marny, who had never had a baby, had no intention of having any if she could help it, and did not hate men at all.

Mrs. Chase tapped on the door. She said, "Kendra, Marny's

329

here to see you." She added that she would step downstairs for a cup of coffee before going home.

Kendra lay resting against a pile of pillows, in what was probably the coziest bedroom in San Francisco. Near the bed was the crib, where the baby was asleep under a white cover. In the grate a fire was snapping, while the windowpanes reflected a ruddy light that belied the fog beyond. On the bedside table were copies of the *Alta* and its recent rival, the *Pacific News;* several new books, a brush and comb and hand mirror, and a bell to call Serena if she was needed. Kendra's eyes were alert and her cheeks rosy, and she did look well.

Marny said so, and gave her the quilted satin robe. At sight of it Kendra gasped with such pleasure that it almost, if not quite, consoled Marny for her loss to the man who had redeemed his ticket on the *Unicorn.*

"Look at my baby," Kendra went on. "Isn't he beautiful?"

Marny bent over the crib and obediently said the baby was beautiful, though in fact she thought his little face looked like a piece of used soap. She took up one of his hands from the coverlet.

"Babies are so *little!*" she exclaimed.

Kendra gave her a puckery smile. "He *felt* about the size of a clipper ship," she said, and Marny refrained from telling her the doctor had said the birth was like shelling peanuts. But Kendra was adding, "That doesn't matter now, it's over, and—Marny," she said earnestly, "I'm so happy about him!"

Marny sat down in a chair by the bed. Kendra took her hand and spoke softly.

"I didn't know," she said, "I never dreamed, how much a baby makes up for. I knew I was going to love him, but I didn't know how much. It's all so wonderfully surpri:ing."

Marny told her how glad she was. This time all she said was sincere. It was the closest they had ever come to admitting the fact that Kendra's marriage had its dull side. But Marny knew it did, and she had no doubt that Kendra knew she knew and was grateful to her for not saying so.

A week after her visit to Kendra, as she finished a shift at her card table and stood up, Marny saw Hiram and Pocket waiting for her at the bar. As she had thought they were still in Sacramento, she was surprised. She was even more surprised by the looks of them. Not only did they both have brand new shaves and haircuts, but they were dressed like men of the world, in fine black broadcloth suits, white ruffled shirts, kid gloves, boots meant for city streets. They carried high-crowned beaver hats, and even the handkerchiefs trailing from Pocket's pockets were sheer white linen. As Marny came toward them and they saw her green eyes wide with astonishment, both men began to laugh.

Hiram held up his drink. "Join me?"

Marny said a glass of champagne wouldn't hurt her. Glass in hand, she led them into one of the private game rooms not occupied at the moment.

"Now tell me everything," she ordered as they sat down by the table. "When did you get to town? What are you doing here? Where are you staying? And where," she demanded, sweeping her gaze up and down them, "where did you get all that elegance? And for the love of heaven, *why?*"

Still laughing, they began to answer. They had come down from Sacramento on the steamer *Senator*, which had arrived yesterday. They had come down for several reasons. For one thing, San Francisco mud was bad, but the mud of Sacramento was worse.

"That's not possible," said Marny.

They assured her that it was not only possible, it was true. Hiram added, "You've had plenty of rain here, I know. But we've had more. Don't argue," he challenged her sternly. "I was there."

Pocket said Hiram was right. Not only was the mud frightful in Sacramento, but in the mountain passes it was so deep that a double mule team took twelve or fifteen days to drag a wagonload of provisions from Sacramento to the nearest diggings. There were thousands of men spending the winter at the mines, and Pocket, always concerned about other people, fervently hoped the trading posts had laid in a good stock of food before the storms began.

Pocket and Hiram had taken a room at a new hotel called the St. Francis, at Clay and Dupont streets. Had she seen it?

Not yet, said Marny. The place had been open only a week or so. But she had heard that the owners were going to see to it that the St. Francis was the most aristocratic address in San Francisco. They would rent no space for gambling games, and this would at least make the place quieter than the Parker House. Also it would be more expensive.

Right, said Pocket. The St. Francis was the most expensive

hotel in town. And it was a hotel such as he had never seen before. "Nor anybody else either," Pocket murmured.

They told her what it was like. The men who planned the St. Francis had bought twenty readymade houses and had put them together to make a building four stories high. The rooms were divided, not by cloth, but by wooden partitions. True, these partitions were made of boards split almost paper thin, so Hiram and Pocket did not have much more privacy than they had had at the Parker House, but still they were better off. Their room was eight feet by six, spacious for San Francisco; it had a shelf to hold a washbowl and soap, a hook on which to hang towels, and another hook for a looking glass.

"You bring all those for yourself, of course," said Hiram, "and if you're wise you'll also bring your own blankets. But it's the best lodging place I've seen around here. Remember that, if you ever have to stay in one."

"Heaven forbid," said Marny.

They told her what they had been doing since they reached town yesterday. First, as soon as they got off the boat they had gone to Chase and Fenway's to put away their gold. Muddy and unkempt as they were, they had felt out of place among all those handsome exhibits, but Mr. Chase had welcomed them and Loren had hurried over to tell them about Loren Junior. They had bought new clothes, complete outfits from the skin up, and had asked Loren where they should stay and where they could get washed. He had told them about the St. Francis, and recommended a bath-house on Kearny Street.

By this time it was late and they were tired, so they went to the St. Francis as they were and spent the night. First thing this morning they had gathered up their new outfits and had gone to the bath-house.

"Not a bad place," said Hiram. "Fire going all day, plenty of hot water. We scrubbed off Sacramento, we each got a shampoo and haircut and shave, and then we put on our new clothes and looked like gentlemen."

"And smelled like gentlemen," said Pocket.

"You *are* gentlemen," said Marny, "and I love you both. How long are you going to be in town?"

"We're staying," said Pocket. He chuckled and added, "We're going to do gentlemen's work."

Hiram spoke seriously. "Rockers are getting obsolete,

Marny. Of course men are still making lucky strikes, but there's less and less gold to be taken out with simple machines. Now they're talking about quartz-crushers, and sluices, and wing-dams—"

"What are those?"

"I don't know enough to tell you," Hiram answered frankly. "But the placers are getting scientific. What I mean is, the frolic is over. Or soon will be, and Ning and Pocket and I thought we'd better change with the times."

She nodded her approval. "My congratulations, boys. As I've said before, the smart gambler is the one who knows when to quit. What is Ning doing now?"

They told her Ning had used his gold to buy property in Sacramento. He had put up a big sturdy tent on one of his lots and was living there in what he regarded as luxury. When they quit making rockers Hiram and Pocket had wanted Ning to come to San Francisco with them, but he had declined. He said San Francisco was getting to be too much of a big city. Plank sidewalks, bath-houses, buildings three and four stories high—not for him.

Marny nodded. "He's right to do what he wants to do. And you, boys—what is this gentlemen's work you were talking about?"

Hiram said he had invested in a newly organized banking house. The office, on Montgomery Street, was being built now.

"And you, Pocket?" she asked.

With his charming modest smile, Pocket said he had bought a share in Gilmore's Library on Washington Street. Marny had heard of the library. Recently opened, it was in a building downhill from Loren and Kendra's home, near the office of the *Alta California*. Men joined for a monthly fee. Mr. Gilmore subscribed to the local newspapers, and had a contract with the steamboat line to take copies of every other newspaper and magazine, American or foreign, brought in by the steamers. Besides providing the papers, Mr. Gilmore would receive mail for his patrons; he had desks equipped with pen and ink so they could write letters home; and as few men stayed long in any one place, he had announced that the library would also be a clearing house for messages to and from men whose only address was "somewhere in California." The library was a sort of club, where men could drop in and hear the news and make friends. Both Mr.

Chase and Mr. Fenway were members, and so were Loren and Dwight Carson and most of the other leading men in town.

"I think I'll like working there," said Pocket. "I like being with people."

Marny smiled in agreement. Pocket had a natural inborn sympathy for people. She suspected that before the end of winter Pocket would have heard a thousand tales of why men had come to California—unhappy marriages, domineering fathers, sheriffs' warrants just behind them, heartbreak and disillusion and just plain foolishness. Other men would talk and he would listen, and they would be better for having talked to him.

"I think it's a perfect job for you," she said. After a moment's thought she added, "Welcome to San Francisco, boys. Ning is right. We may not be a big city yet, but we sure are on our way."

46

The men wanted to see Kendra too, and as there was no rain the next morning Marny walked with them up the hill. They passed the library of which Pocket was now part owner, and paused to watch a group of workmen putting a new sign over the door. "Gilmore and Brent, Proprietors."

As she read the second name Marny felt a twinge of strangeness. She knew Pocket was rightly called Sylvester Brent, but she never thought of him by any such name. "'It doesn't sound like you, Pocket," she said.

"It is me, though," he returned. "It's the name of my account at Hiram's bank. Everybody calls me Pocket, but they don't want checks signed that way."

They laughed, and walked on up the hill. Kendra, well now and downstairs, was glad to see them. She was even more glad when Hiram and Pocket told her they were going to stay in town. She invited all three of them to come here for Christmas dinner.

Hiram and Pocket whistled with joy, but to Kendra's surprise, Marny shook her head.

"Why not?" Kendra exclaimed, and both men echoed, "Why not?"

"Darlings," Marney answered, "you should know, the children of delight *work* on the days when other people play. Holidays are our biggest days at the Calico Palace."

"But Marny," Pocket protested, "aren't you going to have any Christmas at all?"

Marny shrugged good-naturedly. "I didn't last year."

Kendra felt a pang of conscience. She recalled the Christmas dinner she had given last year for Mr. and Mrs. Chase and Mr. Fenway and the army lieutenants. She had not thought of Marny. She had suggested the dinner only to avoid going to the Christmas ball at the Comet House where she had once danced with Ted. How much had happened since then! And as she had said to Marny, how much a baby made up for! Aloud she said,

"All right, we don't have to have Christmas dinner on Christmas Day. We'll have it on a day when Marny can be with us. How's that?" she asked Pocket and Hiram.

By all means, they said. Christmas came on a Tuesday this year. They decided to have the dinner on Sunday, the day before Christmas Eve, because the store would be closed that day and Loren would be free. Marny said she would take the whole day off. "And let's hope," she exclaimed, "that it doesn't rain!"

They all joined in her hope. Kendra said she would have dinner at two o'clock, so they could leave before the dark blotted out the town. San Francisco had no street lights. Except in the glare of the plaza, people out after dark had to carry lanterns, and even at that the streets were perilous, from mudholes, rats, and robbers.

They happily waved goodby, promising to see each other again in a day or two. But they did not, for that evening the rain began again.

For eight days the rain came down. The wind tore savagely around the hills, knocking down houses, ripping tents from the ropes that held them, raising great waves in the bay and sending helpless vessels smashing against their neighbors. The mud rolled down the hills in such torrents that Kendra wondered if she could have her Christmas party at all.

But at last, in the week before Christmas, to the joy of everybody in town the rain stopped. The weather was still gray and cold, but at least they did not have to look out at that dreary downpour. A man could put on rubber boots and go outdoors and slog around, and this was better than staying inside the bug-ridden flophouses, listening to the stranded vessels groaning like ghosts in pain.

In spite of the mud and fog and swarming rats there was a happy spirit abroad. The bands around the plaza played what they imagined was Christmas music. Boys tramped up and down the firmer streets selling evergreens cut from trees across the bay. The storekeepers decked their windows with pretty trifles for presents. At one corner of the plaza a literary beggar set up a pole, with a sign on which he had printed his own version of an old holiday rhyme:

Christmas is coming but my poke's not fat,
Please drop a pinch of gold here in my hat,
If you haven't got a pinch, a speck goes far,
If you haven't got a speck, you can sweep up Marny's bar.

On Saturday, the day before he was to come to dinner, Hiram appeared at Kendra's front door with an armful of evergreens and a roll of red ribbon, saying he had come to decorate the house. He and Kendra hung sprigs at the windows and tied one to the baby's crib. Hiram said Pocket had gone to the plaza to watch—and hear—an auction of town lots. Pocket liked auctions.

"Pocket," said Kendra, as she tied a red bow on some fir sprays, to be hung on the front door, "likes everything. I think Pocket is one of the happiest people I ever knew."

"He deserves it," said Hiram. "Pocket doesn't let the world get the better of him. Take that episode with the girl back in Kentucky."

Kendra looked up from the ribbon in her lap. "'I didn't know he had told you about that."

"Yes, he told me. Pocket," Hiram said with emphasis, "has what everybody needs most in this world. Guts. A pretty red bow you've made on that fir cluster. Now give it to me and I'll put it on the door."

As he went outside Kendra looked after him, reflecting that Hiram also had guts. He had come to California with a

336

strong pair of hands and little else. And that was before anybody knew there was gold in the hills. She wished he had told her more about himself. He had said very little, only, "I'm a minister's son. As you may have heard, ministers send their children to school but they don't make 'em rich." But in spite of his reticence, she felt that she knew him well. He had the kind of tough gallantry that she liked.

No more turkeys had come from Honolulu, but the men had said they would rather have steaks anyway. On Sunday morning Loren went to church, but he said Kendra positively must not go out yet. It was not raining, but the day was sharp and blustery, and she was nursing the baby and for her to catch cold would be disastrous. So Kendra stayed at home, with Serena to keep her company. She had the steaks, big thick ones, and the charcoal brazier ready; and she had potatoes and turnips, oranges from Honolulu and a raisin pudding, and the best liquors and brandies in town.

They had a merrier Christmas than any of them had had in years. Pocket and Hiram and Marny came to the front door carrying bundles of firewood tied up with blue ribbon— "A present for Junior," they said, "to keep him warm." Behind them in the street a mule driver stood beside a cart that his team had dragged up the rutted mud of the hill. The cart was piled with more firewood, and assorted packages wrapped in paper.

At sight of so much wood, Kendra nearly shed tears of gratitude. Firewood was not only the most expensive gift they could have brought, but the most welcome, now that she had a baby who must be kept warm at any cost. Loren, as delighted as she was, hurried out with a big drink of whiskey to warm the driver. He and the other men helped unload the wood and stack it in the storeroom next to the kitchen, while Kendra and Marny brought in the packages and piled them in a corner of the parlor, to be opened after dinner. Loren came in with Pocket and Hiram, all flushed from the work of wood-carrying. Loren asked, "Drinks, everybody?"

Hiram said "Sure," Pocket said, "Not for me," and Marny said, "Yes, thank heaven, I can even get a little high today, I'm not dealing."

They had drinks and a royal dinner, and came back into the parlor for coffee and brandy. With joyful extravagance,

Loren piled up the fire with the Christmas gift of wood. Kendra brought in the baby and was sure he smiled at the sight of these friends who had brought him so much comfort. When she had taken him back upstairs, they opened the other Christmas presents—woolen scarfs for Loren and Ralph, gloves and slippers for Kendra and Serena, delicacies from China for them all, and a book of Christmas carols.

"Oh Marny—boys," Kendra exclaimed, "you shouldn't!"

"Yes ma'am we should," Pocket said firmly. "Look at what you're doing for us. Here we are, in this miserable town, all mud and rats and strangers, and you're giving us a Christmas like folks at home. It's been so long since I—since any of us —have been in a *home*."

"Do shut up," said Hiram. "You'll make me get a lump in my throat."

"I've already got one," said Kendra.

"All right," said Marny, "let's be practical. Kendra, I'll help you clear up."

Pocket cut into her words with emphasis. "No ma'am you will not. You work all the time. This is your day off. Loren and Hiram and Ralph and I have got it all settled. We men will clear up."

"Oh—" Kendra caught her breath and laughed. "Wonderful. Go right ahead."

Hiram fortified himself with another drink, and the men went out to the kitchen. Wrapped in warmth and luxury, Kendra leaned back in her chair.

"Oh Marny, isn't this fun?"

"I think it's grand," said Marny.

"All that wood!" Kendra said softly. "Marny, I can't tell you how thankful I am."

Marny poured brandy into her coffee. "Don't be too thankful, dear, it's not necessary. I'm sure Pocket and Hiram can afford their share, and I know I can afford mine." She sent Kendra a bright green twinkle across her cup. "I've done well in the business of buying steamboat tickets. One or two tumbles—nothing pays off every time—but mostly this has paid off. In fact, I've made *lots* of money."

They both laughed, but after a moment Kendra sobered.

"Marny."

"Yes?"

"Don't tell Loren how you paid for the wood. He's so glad
338

to have it, and if you told him, he wouldn't feel quite at ease about using it."

"I understand," Marny said quietly. Without further comment she changed the subject. "Look, Kendra, outside. The sun is shining!"

They went to the window. The wind had scattered the clouds and between them the sky was clear blue.

"Beautiful," murmured Kendra. "It seems a long time since I've seen any sunshine."

"Cold and bright," said Marny, "perfect for Christmas. Oh I do hope this weather lasts a while."

Serena came in, saying the men had chased her out of the kitchen. She and Ralph had been to the circus yesterday, and she told them about it. The clown was so funny, and the acrobats were marvelous, and so were the tightrope dancers, and Mrs. Rowe riding bareback standing up on her toes—oh, it was grand. She was still talking about the circus when the men joined them.

"We've washed up everything," Pocket announced proudly, "without breaking a dish. And now," he went on, taking up the book of carols, "let's sing. Kendra, will you play?"

She went to the piano, and Hiram said,

"I haven't sung a Christmas carol since—I can't remember. Kendra, let's have—" He began to sing.

"As I sat on a sunny bank . . ."

Pocket joined him,

". . . on Christmas Day in the morning . . ."

Kendra played the tune. She played "God rest you merry, gentlemen," and then Hiram wanted an old English wassail song. He could sing it, too. Hiram sang well, in a deep rich baritone, and he did it joyously, waving his glass in time to the music.

"Wassail, wassail, all over the town . . ."

They all sang but Marny. Marny, quite unable to follow the simplest tune, curled up on the sofa and sipped brandy. She was quite happy.

At last, when the sun had gone behind the hill and the town was turning gray, they said they should leave. It had been a beautiful day for them, they told Kendra, and she said it had been equally beautiful for her. Hiram and Pocket and Marny started down the hill together. Kendra and Loren, looking after them from the porch, could hear them—especially Hiram—warbling the old wassail song.

"Love and joy come to you,
And to your wassail too,
And God bless you and send you
A happy New Year."

"I think," Loren said with amusement, "to quote Scripture, Hiram is merry with wine."

"As long as he's merry," said Kendra, "who cares?"

Loren said he certainly did not care. It had been a great Christmas party, he had never known a better, and he was glad everybody had had such a good time.

He went upstairs to make a fire in the bedroom, telling her not to come up until the fire was burning well. When the room was warm she went up too, took the baby from his crib and fed him and put him to sleep again. Loren banked the fire carefully, to keep the room warm, as she would have to get up in the night to nurse the baby again. He said he did not like to think of her getting up on such a cold night, but this was a task he could not do for her.

Kendra reminded him of how comfortable everything was. On the chair beside the bed was the quilted satin robe Marny had given her, and a new pair of fleece-lined slippers, a gift from Loren. "I'm as well cared for as anybody can possibly be," she said.

She went to sleep warm and secure. At about four o'clock in the morning she heard a cry from the baby. Loren did not wake. Kendra slipped out of bed, wrapped herself in her warm silk robe, nursed the baby, and tucked him back into his crib. How quiet everything was. The wind, usually so wild on winter nights, had stilled, and from the window she could see stars in the clear cold sky. As Marny had said, lovely Christmas weather. Such a welcome break in the wettest winter San Francisco had had in memory. She slipped into bed and fell asleep again.

Since the baby's birth Kendra had become acutely sensitive to noises in the night. She was sleeping soundly when she heard something.

She raised herself on an elbow, turning her head to look through the darkness toward the crib. But the baby was quiet. The noise came from outside. Now that her senses were clearing she could hear more plainly—men shouting, bells ringing, cries of fright and dismay. Something was going on, something wrong, something terrifying—and just

340

as she realized this Loren woke too, and sat up. "What's happening?" he demanded.

At almost the same moment they heard sounds from downstairs—loud frightened questions from Ralph, a cry of alarm from Serena. In the crib the baby woke now, and murmured. Loren sprang out of bed.

"Stay where you are, I'll see," he said to her, and ran to the window that looked downhill toward the bay.

Kendra sat up too, hardly aware of the shiver she gave as the cold air struck her shoulders. At the window Loren gave a wordless utterance of horror, then wheeled around and spoke to her. He spoke in a voice more fear-stricken than she had ever heard him use.

"God help us, Kendra, the town is on fire!"

Before he had finished speaking she was out of bed and looking out of the window. Down the hill, toward the bay, she could see flames leaping into the air, streaking the sky with fire and smoke. By the dreadful glow she could see the street, and she felt a twinge of astonishment at how many people were already out there, dressed, or half dressed, or barefooted and shivering in their nightwear. She looked downhill again, across the turmoil, and then she heard herself cry out.

"It's the plaza—it's Kearny Street—it's the Calico Palace!"

Loren had already begun to pull on his clothes. In the crib the baby was crying. Kendra took him up, remembered the cold air blowing in by the window, and snatched up a blanket from his crib, holding him against her own body to warm him. Loren was saying breathlessly,

"It's the Calico Palace and a lot of other buildings too. I can't be sure if the fire has gone as far down as Montgomery Street, to Chase and Fenway's, but it may get there any minute. You stay here, get dressed and keep warm. And wrap up the baby, so if you have to run you'll be ready. I'll go down and see what I can do to help."

Kendra hardly heard him. She was gathering up her robe of quilted satin and drawing it around herself and the baby, doing it without thinking about what she was doing, taking care of him by an instinct deeper than thought. What she was thinking, in her own awareness, was how she and Marny had rejoiced that the clouds had blown away and there was no rain tonight.

341

47

Marny had not gone to bed as early as Kendra that night. She was not used to early hours, and she was looking forward to the luxury of an idle evening.

At a side entrance of the Calico Palace she said goodby to Pocket and Hiram. They walked on, and Marny went into the little dark hall from which the stairs led up to the living quarters on the third floor. As she reached a door leading into the public room, she paused to open it a little way. Standing back in the darkness, she looked in.

The public room was full of men. Their voices were loud against the clang of the band and the clinks of bottles and coins. But the racket was good-humored, and everything seemed to be in order. There had been a murder recently at the Bella Union. Four o'clock in the morning, everybody had been drinking for hours, two men at the bar had had an argument, and one of them had pulled out his knife and stabbed the other. And then an inquest, and a lot of ugly stuff in the papers. Bad for business. This, Marny had said proudly to Norman, was what came of keeping the bar open till four in the morning. They hadn't had any murders at the Calico Palace.

She closed the door silently and went upstairs. From Lolo's room she could hear the baby, Zack, murmuring in baby-sounds that Lolo seemed mysteriously to understand. The noise from below did not bother Zack. Nearly a year old now, he hardly knew what quiet was.

Her own room was cold, but as she lit the candle it looked peaceful, and she did not hear any rats scuttling about. When she had undressed she put on her wrapper, a fluffy woolen robe lined with silk; she slipped her feet into a pair of soft cuddly slippers tied with ribbons, and sat down before the mirror to brush her hair. Marny liked to brush her hair. She liked sweeping the brush in long hard strokes and watching the ruddy lights that followed its path.

After a while she began to yawn. It was still earlier than her usual bedtime, but she remembered that she had been up early this morning to help with the presents; or maybe it was Loren's excellent brandy. Anyway, a long night's sleep never hurt anybody. Making sure her door was bolted, she put her little gun on the table by her iron cot.

Marny always put the gun within reach. Besides the fact that she was a tempting woman, the Calico Palace had to keep a fortune in coins on hand for the gambling tables. The coins were kept on this floor, in two safes. The safes were strong, and Norman and the Blackbeards were first-class guards. But with all precautions the Calico Palace was still a dangerous place to live.

Marny blew out her candle, and stored this and her cake of soap in a tin box with a tight cover. The rats liked to gnaw on soap and candles. Having done all she could to assure herself of a tranquil night, she slipped in between the sheets and drew the blankets up around her. The cot was narrow. Marny reflected that it was just as well she was sleeping alone. Drowsily she wondered if she were in the mood for another gentleman friend. —No, she thought, if I were in the mood I shouldn't be wondering. She went to sleep.

When she heard the noise of the fire her first thought was that the sounds meant trouble downstairs, and in her mind she cried out—Don't tell me we're having a murder here too! But almost instantly she heard the bells, and bangs of the gongs that hung at restaurant doors to announce mealtimes; she smelled smoke and saw the weird swirling light, she heard rushing footsteps outside her door, and from somewhere she heard voices yelling "Fire!"—as if anybody needed to be told.

Marny sprang out of bed. When she thought of it later it seemed that in those first few seconds she had acted without any conscious plan, because she could not remember doing anything. She only knew she had done it, and had done it with the speed of terror. She kicked aside her pretty slippers and without pausing for stockings she pushed her feet into the shoes she had worn to Kendra's dinner party. They were not stout shoes, but she had no time to look for thicker ones. She threw on her fluffy woolen robe, and snatching up her gun she put it into a pocket. What roaring of flames, what shouts and screams! The whole town must be ablaze. Marny jerked a drawer open and swept up her nugget necklace and dropped it into the other pocket of her robe. Most of her ornaments were in her safe at Chase and Fenway's—if only the store were not burning too! Tossing back her hair, she thrust in a pair of combs to hold it out of her eyes. The night was cold. With one hand she snatched her cashmere shawl from the wall hook where she had hung it before she went to bed, and with her other hand she pushed back the bolt of the door.

She was wide awake now and her senses were alert. She had a cabinet full of clothes, but clothes were not important. Not even gold dust was very important. But the coins! Coins, brought all the way from the Mint in Philadelphia. Coins, so valued that they brought interest of ten per cent a month. There in the hall were the two safes, two, because Norman had said, "If anybody gets into one, we'll have lost only half."

Norman, wearing shoes and trousers, was on his knees before one safe. A candle in a candlestick stood on the floor beside him; Rosabel, wrapped in a dressing gown, stood beside the candle. Even at this moment Marny felt a touch of thankful admiration that Rosabel was not screaming. Rosabel's mouth was tight with fear, but her hands were steady as she held them out for the poke of coins that Norman was taking out of the safe. Marny heard a clatter of feet on the stairs, and cries from baby Zack as Lolo rushed down with him, not caring if she saved anything else or not.

Marny noticed that Norman's upper arms were getting soft. In fact, while he was not fat, his whole torso was a bit flabby. He was not like Pocket and Hiram, tough with the toughness of labor. What a foolish detail to notice at a time like this. Yet she was noticing everything else too, as though fright had sharpened all her senses.

Norman thrust a leather bag of coins into her hand. "Can you carry this?"

"Of course," she said, and then thought—How? A leather bag would be snatched in a minute. She wrapped the bag in her shawl and tucked the bundle under her arm. Cries of terror rose from everywhere; she heard Norman say sharply, "Well, get out!"

He was right, there was no use trying to save any more,

they would die trying. Lugging her unwieldy bundle, Marny started to flee.

She ran down the stairs, holding up the long skirt of her robe with her free hand. The wall beside her was hot; the fire was coming close. The staircase had never before seemed long or steep, but it did now. Though she was running as fast as she could her journey down to the first floor seemed to take an hour. At last she reached the hall, she rushed past the door of the public room, and then to the outside door by which she had come in, and then at last she was out in the air. Thinking of it later, she remembered that in her thankfulness the air for a moment had seemed cold and fresh, though in fact it had been hot and threatening and full of smoke.

She saw the glare of shooting fires, and as far as her eyes could reach she saw hordes of people milling around. She heard the roar of flames, and voices shouting, and her own voice crying out, "Oh God, please make it rain!"

A thousand others were sending up the same petition. But it did not rain that night. The rain had poured mercilessly upon them when they did not need it; now when it could have helped them it was not here.

Marny pushed her way through the mob, across the plank sidewalk, past the mud-puddles bright with reflected fires. Beyond the sidewalk the mud clung to her shoes like an enemy trying to hold her back. She fought her way on, through the mud, through the teeming throng in the plaza. She had thought the night was cold; maybe it was cold elsewhere, but here near the fire the heat was terrible, and she felt sweat oozing under her woolen robe. She ran on, panting as she ran, and biting back sobs of rage as she thought of all she was leaving behind.

—Stop it, she told herself, don't think about what you're leaving. Take care of what you're bringing out. This poke of money—

The poke, clumsily wrapped in her shawl, felt immensely heavy, though she was in no frame of mind to estimate how heavy it actually was. —Take care of it, she told herself again. And take care of yourself. Get away from the fire.

Above the thunder of flames she heard the shouts of thousands of men around her, and as the dreadful glares came and went she saw them. Thousands. Where on earth had they all come from so suddenly? They were dressed, or in various stages of undress, all yelling, all rushing about in what looked like meaningless confusion. Marny hugged her bundle and elbowed her way among them, telling herself again and again that the only thing to think of now was how to get as far away from the fire as she could.

A man's voice said, "Howdy, Marny!" A rough hand gave her hair a yank. Marny said, "I've got a gun. Get away from me before I use it." The man slunk aside. Marny pressed on. A minute later another man put a hand on her wrapped-up shawl, snarling, "What you got in that bundle, Marny?" Marny snapped, "Clothes. Let me get by."

She pushed past him too, and he troubled her no more. Around the plaza men had respect for Marny. They knew she was no helpless ninny who would crumple up without somebody to take care of her.

By this time her shoes were so heavy with mud that every step was harder than the one before. Her legs ached. Behind her she heard a crash. A wall falling in, no doubt. She did not pause to look around.

—Get away, her thoughts kept pounding, get away. A sudden glare lit up the sky; a flame must have leaped from the site of the crash. By its light she saw, ahead of her, standing a little higher than the heads of the men scrambling around, an auctioneer's platform stacked with boxes and barrels. She pushed toward it. The glare faded, the platform stood almost in the dark. Another burst of flame lit up another part of the plaza. Marny did not look. She made her way toward the platform. Her strength was giving out. She had to rest somewhere, and catch her breath.

A skeleton staircase, hardly more than a ladder built on a slant, led up to the platform. Marny pulled one foot out of the mud and put it on the step. She took her hand out of the gun pocket to support herself, and pulled up the other foot. Panting, she made her way up the steps. On the platform, there seemed to be no room for her to stand or sit. She might have knocked a barrel over the side, but it would almost certainly have fallen on somebody's head, and the last thing she wanted now was to call attention to herself. With the hand not holding the bundle she managed to move several barrels closer together, leaving a small space among them. Here she dropped the bundle, and sat, almost fell, upon it. For the moment she was out of sight,

346

hidden by the barrels around her, as safe as she could be so near the fire and in the midst of such a frantic rabble.

Her breath was coming in such short pants that the air seemed hardly to go down at all. The struggle to get here had given her a pain in her chest and another pain in her side. For several minutes—she did not know how long—she sat where she was, hardly moving, trying only to breathe easily again and give her thumping heart a chance to quiet down.

After a while she noticed that drops of sweat were running down her face. She had no handkerchief. Lifting her arm, she wiped her forehead with the sleeve of her robe, and as she did so she looked up.

Huddled here among the barrels, she could not see what lay directly in front of her, but farther off she could see flames, and showers of sparks, and clouds of smoke swirling in the air. She could hear roars and crackles of fire, and crashes as timbers fell, and screams and shouts from many throats. The smell of smoke was thick in the air. Marny felt intensely hot, but it did no good to push back her woolen robe. There was no coolness in front of such a roaring fire.

The last phrase caught cruelly at her mind. "A roaring fire"—what a cheerful, comfortable sound those words had always had!

She felt stronger now. Taking a long breath of the smoke-laden air, she pushed herself up and stood looking across the barrels toward Kearny Street.

For a moment the street seemed like a solid wall of fire. Then as her eyes accepted the dazzle, she began to distinguish among the burning buildings. Denison's Exchange, near the middle of the block, was hardly anything now but a lot of seething flame. The front wall was gone—this must have been the crash she had heard as she ran toward the platform—and the fire was fairly eating what was left. Later, Marny learned that the fire had started there, and this was why Denison's had gone first. There were a dozen tales about how it started, but nobody was ever sure.

—If people, thought Marny, would only stop throwing matches around—but they won't.

Denison's was wedged between a restaurant on one side and the Parker House on the other. They had both caught fire. The Parker House, built of wood, was burning like a matchbox. Terrified men and women were rushing out, in

347

nightgowns, in their underwear, or holding blankets around them with apparently nothing underneath. In spite of the hideous confusion Marny felt a tickle of laughter as she thought of the embarrassments that were going to follow some of these disclosures of who had been sleeping with whom.

Beyond the Parker House, at the corner of Kearny Street and Washington, was the El Dorado, now housed in a new building four stories high. The outer walls were brick. But Marny could tell that the inside—wood and cloth like other buildings—was fiercely on fire. Flames darted out of the windows, and smoke rolled after them in long harsh coils. Behind the El Dorado she saw the fire pouring eastward, toward Montgomery Street and the waterfront.

Sparks like great handfuls of stars were blowing across Washington Street toward the Verandah and the Bella Union and Blossom's flower garden and other structures higher up the hill. In spite of the mud, in several spots the plank sidewalk was already burning. Men had formed bucket brigades, to keep the buildings wet. Other men were piling wet blankets on the roofs, or tossing liquid mud up the walls. Some people were throwing their belongings out of windows, others had rushed out with their arms full, and were running away. Farther out, in areas that the fire had not reached, men were breaking the buildings to pieces. They were chopping at the walls with axes, using logs as battering rams, working with frantic force to make open spaces that would stop the spread of the fire.

Marny saw all this without really looking at it. The sight was in front of her and her eyes saw it because it was there. What she saw with her thoughts and her heart and all the rest of her was the Calico Palace.

The Calico Palace stood between a restaurant and another gambling house. They were all in flames. The Calico Palace was turning into a wreck. Its outer walls, like those of the El Dorado, were brick, but she knew—oh, how well she knew!—that here too the inside walls were thin and flimsy, and these could burn, and were burning, with a roar like thunder. Marny stood helplessly, and looked.

She saw the fire, she saw smoke curling out of the windows. But she saw more. As though they too were there in front of her, she saw the paintings, the carpets, the mirrors, the costly chairs and tables, the sparkling chandeliers. She heard

348

the rush of the fire. But with it she heard the clink of coins on the tables, the little bells calling the bartenders. She remembered the polished top of the bar under her fingers, the aroma of fine liquors as the barmen filled the glasses. She remembered all these, and she remembered the long hours and days and months she had spent at her card table to pay for them. Dealing cards was *work*. Marny had chosen her career and she had no wish for any other, but it was work none the less. She had done it well and she had the Calico Palace to show for it. Now it was all going up in smoke.

And it was going for good. There was no such thing as fire insurance in San Francisco. Who would be so foolish as to insure a town made of cloth and tarpaper and splinter-thin boards?

A part of herself was dying. She stood here watching it die. Marny did not intend to crawl off somewhere and wail that life was not worth living. But right now, she understood people who did.

The front wall of the Calico Palace crashed into the street, scattering bricks and sending men fleeing in all directions. Now Marny could see the blazing desolation inside. She could not look. She turned her head away.

48

As she turned, Marny saw that the sparks had caught the Verandah roof again, and the fire-fighters were pouring buckets of mud on the flames. From somewhere toward Montgomery Street she heard an explosion. Bricks and pieces of lumber littered the air as men blew up a building, to break the march of the blaze.

All around her, those thousands of people were still surging about. Some of them were fighting the fire, others were dragging goods out of doors; some were running here and there, spending much energy to accomplish nothing; still others merely stood around, enjoying the show, or watching for a chance to make off with goods other people had rescued. On another platform not far from where she stood among the barrels, Marny saw the plaza preacher. He was addressing the crowd, shouting to them that this disaster had come upon them because of their sins. It was a judgment of the Lord upon this wicked city, this Babylon of the Pacific, and they had better repent. Marny wondered if it had not occurred to him that the sinners would have been more inclined to listen if instead of blaming them for the fire he had gone to work to help them put it out.

Just then, above the din around her, she heard a man calling her name. She could not find him at once, for the mob was seething and the light was not steady—a flash here, a dart of flame yonder, a billow of smoke somewhere else. But after a moment or two, with a start of joy she caught sight of Hiram, pushing his big self through the crowd.

As he reached the platform he leaped up to meet her, taking the steps three at a time.

"Marny!" he shouted again as he reached her.

"Merry Christmas," said Marny.

Hiram threw back his head with a roar of wrath.

"Stop making jokes, you damned halfwit. Come down!"

He grabbed her with both hands.

"Don't you know with that light on your hair you're a target for every scoundrel in town?"

For once, Marny had forgotten her hair. Still gripping her arms, Hiram was demanding,

"Why didn't you crouch behind these barrels? What's wrong with your head?"

Marny pushed her hand across her smoke-stung eyes. "Right now, Hiram, my head isn't working very well."

He glanced toward the tottering remains of the Calico Palace. "You poor girl," he returned, "no wonder."

Marny looked up at him. "Besides, Hiram," she retorted, "if I'd been hiding, nobody would have seen me, not even you. I might have had to stay here till day after tomorrow." She gave him a smile. "I'm not *so* stupid."

He smiled back at her, this time with admiration. "You're taking it mighty well, Marny."

"No I'm not," she said. "We opened it the first of September and now on Christmas Eve it's gone. I feel sick and sore. But I'm glad you found me, Hiram. I've got—" With

350

the toe of her mud-caked shoe she touched the bundle on the floor. "I've got something worth saving. Which means, worth stealing."

"Good," said Hiram. "I'll help you save it. Let's try to get to Chase and Fenway's."

She exclaimed hopefully, "Then the store is still there?"

"I don't know," said Hiram. "That's what we came to find out."

As he spoke, Hiram made a gesture toward the foot of the steps. She saw Pocket, looking up at her with his shy endearing smile, like a boy about to escort a girl to a party and hoping he was going to do everything right. Marny blew him a kiss and he blew one back to her. Hiram gathered up the bundle. Its weight told him what was in it, and he smiled his congratulations.

"You have your gun?" he asked her.

"Yes."

"Keep your hand on it. Let's go."

Marny gave a sigh of relief. She did not know how long ago the fire had waked her, but she did know this had been one of the hardest periods she had ever lived through and she felt drained of strength. She wanted to put her money into a safe place, and she wanted to get out of sight of the wreckage. She went down the steps, and with Hiram and Pocket beside her, their own guns in evidence, she began making her way through the multitude.

She noticed that Hiram and Pocket were fully dressed, even to rubber boots to help them through the mud. Evidently they had not, like herself, rushed out with no minutes to spare. "So the St. Francis Hotel is all right?" she asked.

Yes, the St. Francis was all right, they told her, and so was the rest of Clay Street. There was not much wind tonight, but what wind there was had been coming from the south, blowing the fire away from that side of the plaza. They did not know yet whether or not they had lost anything. Their gold, like her own private fund, had been stored in a safe at Chase and Fenway's, and they had been on their way there when they had caught sight of her on the platform. "So," said Hiram, "we turned aside."

"I love you both," said Marny.

She said nothing else; it was all she could do to struggle ahead. They had each given her an arm, and were half leading, half helping her away from the fire, toward Clay

351

Street. Their progress was slow. She was not, like them, wearing high boots to support her ankles, and the long full skirt of her robe trailed in the mud and held her back. But the crowd on Clay Street was not so thick as that in the plaza. Once there, they would be able to walk more easily, down to Montgomery Street.

"We'll cross here," said Hiram.

Marny gathered up her hampering skirt, and waded through the miry mess of the road. At the corner of Clay and Kearney was a restaurant calling itself by the lordly name of Delmonico's, not on fire but in danger. Men were swarming over it, beating out sparks, throwing mud over the walls, hanging wet blankets on the side toward the flames and changing the blankets as they dried in the heat. While they worked to save the building, other men had pounded the door open and now were running off with armfuls of loot—chairs, lamps, liquor, anything that came to hand.

"What a pleasure it would be," Marny murmured, "to shoot them."

"Yes ma'am, it would be," Pocket agreed gently, "but please don't. There's enough trouble around here already."

Marny wondered bitterly if anybody had had time to steal anything from the Calico Palace before it fell in. As the men dragged her farther from the fire she thought she saw a glimmer of dawn in the sky, though in the confusion of flame and smoke it was hard to be sure. Remembering what a happy time they had had yesterday she wondered how Kendra was, and the baby. She could not tell if the fire had climbed the hill, but if Kendra's house was in danger she would have had plenty of time to get out. Only this would not have been good for the baby, taking him out of a warm bed into the chilly dawn. As she thought of this, above the noise she heard Pocket exclaim. "Well, of all people—Loren!"

By the fitful glares they saw Loren walking uphill from the direction of Montgomery Street. He was carrying a child, a small child crying and struggling in terror. Marny saw Lolo running behind him, sobbing with fright, and as she recognized Lolo she also recognized Lolo's little boy, Zack.

Pocket and Hiram called to Loren. He saw them and came on. As he reached them Lolo caught up with him and tearfully held out her arms, and with a gurgle of joy little Zack held out his.

"He's all right," Loren said encouragingly as he gave her the baby. "Just scared, like the rest of us."

Sobbing her gratitude, Lolo took her squalling child. Loren patted her shoulder.

"You're still too close to the fire," he warned. "Better take him farther away."

But Zack was heavy and Lolo was out of breath. Loren indicated a packing case that somebody had dragged outdoors. "Here, sit down and rest. Look out for that nail—it can give him a nasty scratch."

Glad to be told what to do, Lolo sat down on the packing case, holding Zack away from the nail that stuck out of one corner. Pocket spoke to her. With a comforting smile, he suggested that she take Zack to the porch of the City Hotel. He and Hiram had just passed the City Hotel, he told her, and it was not even scorched, for the wind was blowing the fire away from it. A lot of people, including several women, had taken refuge on the porch.

Lolo nodded, promising that as soon as she felt able to carry the twenty pounds of Zack any farther, she would go to the City Hotel. Now that he was safe in his mother's arms Zack's tears were subsiding, and while Lolo soothed him Loren had a chance to talk.

He said both the Blackbeards were fighting the fire. Troy had told Lolo to wait here at the corner, but as the fire drew nearer she was frightened, and with Zack in her arms she ran down Montgomery Street. That street too was full of men, some of them bent on looting, others defending their property from fires and looters alike. Zack, in Lolo's arms, fought in panic. Struggling to hold him, Lolo ran on, hardly noticing where she was going, knowing only that she had to get him away from the fire. As she neared Chase and Fenway's, she bumped into a looter with his arms full. Lolo and baby, looter and loot, fell down in a heap together.

Loren, helping to guard Chase and Fenway's, heard her scream and ran to give help. The looter was swearing at her in rage. He had no interest in her or the child, he wanted to rescue his plunder, and as she tried to rise he knocked her down again.

Loren cracked the looter on the head with his gun, picked up the baby, and when he could make out Lolo's frantic appeals he carried Zack back to the spot where Troy had told her to wait for him. But Pocket was right, this was dangerously near the fire, and he was glad she had agreed to go to the City Hotel.

"How is Chase and Fenway's?" Hiram asked anxiously.

"Safe," said Loren, and his hearers exclaimed in relief. Loren went on, "The fire hasn't come that far and I don't think it will. The problem in that section is looters. I've got to hurry back, to help guard."

"We'll come with you," said Pocket.

"And meantime," said Marny, "how is Kendr—"

"Look!" burst out Hiram. "The El Dorado—look!"

They looked along the street, past the wreckage of nearly everything that had been here yesterday. Next door to the El Dorado the wooden Parker House had crashed in, but the tall brick El Dorado was still standing. Except for the whirls of smoke their view was unbroken. The walls were there, but columns of smoke and fire were rolling out of every window of the four stories. And they saw what Hiram had seen first—a sheet of fire rising from a building behind the El Dorado. The flame rose higher than the roof and towered above it, curving over the El Dorado like a great grasping hand. For an instant, the whole mob in the plaza seemed transfixed. Hiram and Pocket, Marny and Loren, stood where they were, staring in fascinated horror. The brick walls of the El Dorado would not burn. But inside the walls, the heat had risen to a terrible force. As they looked, the El Dorado exploded.

The four walls broke with a boom. Sparks burst out like a magnificent display of fireworks. Bricks, lumber, flaming scraps of every kind of debris, shot up and out in all directions.

From the crowd came screams and howls as fiery pieces of the El Dorado fell and struck. Instinctively, Marny put her arm over her eyes. At the same instant she heard a wordless sound beside her. She moved her arm and looked, just in time to see Loren falling at her feet, close by the packing case where Lolo was clutching little Zack to her bosom. Marny dropped on her knees, thinking she might grab one of these wet blankets to restore him. But Loren was not unconscious. Already he was passing his hand over his forehead with the bewilderment of shock. She heard Pocket exclaim,

"Don't try to move yet, Loren—how are you?"

"All right—I think," Loren answered with a half stunned

attempt to take it lightly. "Something hit me—a piece of brick, I guess—help me stand up—"

"Not yet," Hiram was saying sternly. "Here, we'll make a cushion."

He was setting Marny's bundle on the ground, raising Loren so that the shawl with the money-bag inside would make a pillow for his head and shoulders. A trickle of blood was oozing out of the wound on Loren's temple. They could see burnt flesh around the cut, for the brick that had struck him had been as hot as a blazing coal.

Pocket had already pulled a bandana out of some pocket or other and was holding it over the cut to check the blood. But just then, Marny saw with alarm that the cut in his head was not Loren's only wound. He had fallen against the packing case where Lolo sat, and as he fell, the nail sticking out of the edge had torn a gash in his side. She saw a blood-stain spreading around the rent in his shirt.

"Hiram, look!" she exclaimed. He gave a start and she hurried on. "This is worse than the other. Can we stop the blood?"

"We can sure try," said Hiram. "Damn you, Loren, lie *still!*" he ordered as Loren tried again to stand up. Hiram was pulling off his own shirt to make a dressing.

"Do you need mine?" Pocket asked. "Here it is."

He took off his shirt and tossed it to Marny, saying, "Tear this up." Loren mumbled some apology for giving them so much trouble, and while she tore one shirt to make bandages Pocket and Hiram used the other to stanch the blood. Watching them shirtless, Marny noticed what splendid muscles they both had. Gold digging and rocker making, while not parlor employments, did build handsome men.

She remembered that neither Pocket nor Hiram had ever made an amorous gesture toward her. The thought brought her a touch of surprise, because there were so few men hereabouts who had not. Much as she liked men, it was refreshing to have a few of them treat her as a human being and not merely as a desirable body. What an absurd time to be thinking about such things, she thought as she held out the strips she had torn from Pocket's shirt so he and Hiram could finish bandaging Loren's wound.

"There," said Hiram, having tended Loren as well as he could. "Now if we can get him back to Chase and Fenway's—"

355

"I can walk," said Loren. He sat up, almost angrily, protesting that he was grateful for their help but his wounds were not serious and he was not a baby. "I can walk," he said again.

Pocket grinned ruefully. "Looks like you'll have to," he said. "I don't think even Hiram could carry a grown man through this mud, and certainly not down that sidewalk."

The sidewalk, like others in town, was narrow and shaky. The planks were uneven, with gaps here and there where boards had come off. Hiram and Pocket helped Loren to his feet. Though he said he did not need any more help they could see that he did, and they took his elbows and walked on either side of him. Lugging her bundle, now muddy and bloodstained, Marny trudged beside them.

With Hiram and Pocket supporting him, Loren did manage to slog through the mud, but his steps were slow and painful. He stumbled, he tried not to groan, he did the best he could, but after a little while Hiram and Pocket were not supporting him so much as they were dragging him. It seemed a long, long way. Marny thought of how often she had walked briskly from the Calico Palace to Chase and Fenway's. How easy the walk had been, how agreeable, with Blackbeard proudly holding her elbow, men stepping aside to make way for her, taking off their hats, exclaiming, "Howdy, Marny!"

How short the walk had been then. Now it seemed as if she would never get there. The mud clutched at her shoes, the heat of the fire scorched her face, the smoke was nearly choking her. Men bumped into her and went on without seeming to notice.

But there could be no pause for rest. They had to get Loren to Chase and Fenway's, they had to, they could not let him fall down here and be trampled on.

By this time daybreak was clear in the sky over the bay. Marny saw the masts of the stranded vessels sharp against the dawn. She wondered what Captain Pollock was doing. It had been a long time since she had thought of Pollock at all. There had been so many pleasanter things to think about. She dragged herself along.

With ironic humor, she recalled that Loren was not the only one of them who had to get to Chase and Fenway's. She had to get there herself. She had to go inside, and whether or not Mr. Chase approved she would have to stay there a while, sheltered until she could get some clothes.

356

How often she had said, "I've nothing to wear." Now this statement was not a girlish lament, it was a fact. Her robe was torn and filthy, and scorched in places where sparks had struck it. Under the robe she had on nothing but a wisp of a nightgown, ragged from being stepped on in her flight. She could feel her thin party shoes, broken to pieces under the mud that covered them. And she had the dirty shawl that held her bag of money. Nothing else. Every other garment she had possessed was gone in the ashes of the Calico Palace. She did not own a dress nor a suit of underwear nor a pair of stockings.

As they turned into Montgomery Street they met more desolation. The fire had swept down the hill, and had been moving toward the waterfront when the fire-fighters had destroyed a row of buildings near the corner of Washington Street and Montgomery, blowing up some and tearing down others, to clear a space too broad for the flames to cross. They had halted the fire before it reached Montgomery Street, but the road was strewn with the wreckage they had made. Along the street men stood with guns in their hands. Other men prowled about, looking for anything that might have been left unguarded, while others, as in the plaza, were running about to no purpose except to get in the way.

Marny heard Hiram say to Pocket, "I don't think Loren can walk any farther. If we could make a basket seat out of our hands—"

"Try it," said Marny. "I'll hold Loren on his feet."

Loren murmured again that he was sorry to be such a bother. He leaned on Marny while Pocket and Hiram, gripping each other's wrists, made a carrying seat between them. With Marny's help, Loren managed to sit there. He put his arms around them to keep himself in place.

"Hold your gun, Marny," Hiram ordered, now that his own hands were occupied. "And use it if we need help."

"I'll use it," she answered. She did not add that she had seen blood spreading again around the tear in Loren's shirt. Hiram and Pocket were doing all they could. No use frightening them any more. Keep going.

They kept going. They clumped through the mud, in constant danger of being knocked over by some man running away with stolen goods. Marny held her bundle under her left arm and her gun in her right hand. The bundle felt as if it weighed half a ton. Her arm ached, her legs felt almost numb. —One step at a time, she told herself as she put each foot into the mud and pulled it out again. The longest journey has an end. One—step—at—a—time.

They plodded through the area piled with the fragments of buildings destroyed. At last, they came to the store of Chase and Fenway, windows lighted, plank walk intact. Marny thought she had never seen anything so welcome. Mr. Chase and Mr. Fenway were both standing guard at the main door, and at an upper window she saw the bucktoothed visage of Foxy, on lookout for would-be thieves.

Messrs. Chase and Fenway came forward, full of concern. Loren was not only their most valued employee but a man they liked for his own sake, and they needed no words to let them know he had been badly hurt. Moving with unaccustomed speed, Mr. Fenway unlocked the door. They helped Loren inside, through the front salesroom and into a stockroom behind, while Mr. Chase bellowed to Ralph Watson, guarding a side door, to fix a mattress or something back here so Loren could lie down.

In the front room, Marny leaned against a counter. She let her bundle slide to the floor. She was so tired that she nearly slid down with it. Ralph was saying they had better send one of the boys to find a doctor, and tell Mrs. Shields what had happened. A pity it was, said Ralph, for Mrs. Shields to have her husband get hurt, and her with a baby hardly a month old.

—Maybe I ought to go and tell her, thought Marny. But I can't. I simply can't fight my way up that hill.

"Well, Marny," said a dolorous voice at her side.

Marny looked up and saw Mr. Fenway. He wore a night-shirt and trousers, the tail of the nightshirt stuffed into the top of the trousers, and he looked as doleful as if he had lost everything instead of nothing.

"This is a grievous occasion," murmured Mr. Fenway. "Grievous."

"Yes," said Marny. —For once, she thought, there's so much trouble around that even old Gloom-face must be satisfied.

"I guess your place is gone," Mr. Fenway said sadly.

"All gone," said Marny. She was so tired that it took an effort for her to say even as much as this.

Mr. Fenway regarded her sorrowfully. "You look tuckered

358

out," he said. He dragged out the words as if they were heavy in his throat.

"I feel tuckered out," she agreed.

Mr. Fenway droned, "I guess you'd better come with me."

"Yes," said Marny. She did not know where he was going to take her and in her present state she did not much care.

As she bent to retrieve her bundle he picked it up for her.

"Heavy," he said. "Gold dust inside?"

"Coins," said Marny.

"Better put 'em in the safe," Mr. Fenway advised in his slow monotone. "You never know what may happen in times like these. People." He spoke the last word with a shrug, as if people were a species he did not admire.

She followed him and waited while he unlocked the door of the room where the private safes were kept. Here she unrolled the shawl, took out the leather poke, and stowed it away. The click of the safe's closing brought her a sense of relief, almost of rest. At least this much was done. She did not have to carry that weight any longer. She picked up the shawl and noticed with surprise how light it felt. Mr. Fenway drearily said again,

"You'd better come with me."

He led her through the stockroom. Loren lay on a mattress. Beside the mattress was a basin of water and a bolt of clean cloth, and Mr. Chase was helping Hiram and Pocket dress Loren's injuries. So Loren would be taken care of, she reflected; they did not need her and she could sit down somewhere and rest. She followed Mr. Fenway.

Marny had never been into this part of the new building, and even in her weariness she observed how much better it was than the old one—larger, with more windows and a wide easy staircase. In somber silence Mr. Fenway led her up the stairs. At the top he paused beside a door. He took out his keys again, took one key off the bunch, unlocked the door, and handed the key to her.

"This is where I stay," he said, "when it's too rainy for me to go home. Bad climate we live in. Not healthy. All this fog and damp. You better stay here a few days. Till you pull yourself together."

Marny felt a glow all over. A place to sleep. A decent place. "Mr. Fenway," she said to him, "this is the second time you've given me shelter when I needed it. After I've

359

had some rest, and untwisted my thoughts, I hope I can tell you how grateful I am."

"Bad times these," said Mr. Fenway. "Bad times. Now down by the foot of the stairs is a back door and just outside is the well. You can draw all the water you want, private-like." He took another key from the bunch. "This unlocks the back door. Be sure to lock it every time you come in, and slip the bolt. Can't trust anybody these days." He heaved a sigh. "Well, I better get back on guard before some of those hellcats from Sydney start busting in."

Marny thanked him again. Mr. Fenway did not trouble to reply. With a woebegone look he turned and dawdled his way down the stairs. Marny went into his room and locked the door behind her.

It was a small bedroom with table and washstand and looking glass, all plain and neat in the light of the grim December morning. Marny went to the window and looked out.

The fire was not raging as it had been an hour ago, but it was still burning. Clouds of smoke hung above Kearny Street, and here and there a glow in the smoke showed her where flames had not yet been put out. One of these smoke clouds was lowering above the spot where, this time yesterday, had stood the Calico Palace.

Marny went and sat on the bed, a narrow bug-proof iron cot like her own. She saw her hands, blackened with soot. In the glass on the wall she saw black streaks on her face, ashes scattered in her hair, and the hair itself wild as a jungle vine on her head. She felt loathsomely dirty, and so tired and so beaten that she had no strength to wash.

She could not keep a brave face any longer. Nobody was noticing her. Nobody cared what she did. Marny dropped across the bed and put her face into Mr. Fenway's blankets and began to whimper like a sick child.

49

Marny cried, and crying loosened the knots inside her. As her sobs wore themselves out and she dried her eyes with the sleeve of her robe, she felt better. Getting up from the bed she walked over to the glass.

"I look *awful*," she said aloud.

So she did. The tears had made splotches on her dirty face. The combs that had held her hair had long since fallen out and been lost; all she could do now was push the tangled red locks back from her forehead, which was no use because they immediately fell down again. With some difficulty she pulled her feet out of her broken mud-caked shoes, and looked at the mess—mud between her toes, mud smeared on her insteps and splashed around her ankles. But now that she had let herself give up and shed tears, she felt more like tackling the monumental job of getting herself clean.

She drew down the window shade, poured water into the basin, took off her robe and her bedraggled nightgown, and tore a piece out of the gown to be used as a washcloth. A towel, somewhat used, hung on a nail by the washstand, and she found soap in a tin box where Mr. Fenway had hidden it from the rats. She began to scrub her face.

But it was hard to take off soot with soap and water. She needed oil. The store had oil for sale, but Marny wondered if she had courage enough to put on that filthy robe again, and with her frowsy hair and dirty bare feet, go down and buy it.

As she tried to tell herself that she had better summon courage to do this because she had to, she heard a knock on the door. She called a query.

"It's Pocket," said his voice outside.

With a cry of joy Marny threw the robe around her and opened the door. There he stood. In one hand he held a tin plate, in the other a tin cup, and under his arm a bottle of red wine. With his lovable little-boy smile he said,

361

"I figured you'd need some refreshments, ma'am."

He made no comment on how she looked. If he guessed that she had been crying he gave no sign of it. Marny realized now that she was hungry. Her dinner at Kendra's, only yesterday, seemed long ago.

"I was never in my life so glad to see anybody," she said, and she meant it. "What have you brought me?"

Pocket set the plate on the little table by the bed, and took a horn spoon from one of his pockets. "Nothing but cold beans, ma'am," he apologized. "It's the best I could find. So many restaurants were burnt up, and there was so much stealing from the others, folks are having a hard time trying to eat." He poured wine into the tin cup and held it out to her. "Here, drink this. It'll make you feel better."

Marny thanked him with all her heart. She felt a mild surprise as she thought how Pocket, who never took drinks himself, was always ready to provide them for other people. "How is Loren?" she asked.

Pocket said Loren was in good hands. He was weak from loss of blood, of course, and the cut did hurt. But Foxy had found Dr. Rollins, and the doctor was here now, putting professional bandages on his wounds. Hiram had gone to look for a cart and horse so they could take Loren home, and the doctor was going to give him a dose of laudanum so he would not feel the pain as the cart bumped up the hill. While Hiram was getting the cart, said Pocket, he himself had some free time to attend to her.

"But your own work?" she asked him. "What about the library?"

"That can wait," returned Pocket. "The building wasn't damaged, and Mr. Gilmore can take care of things there. Now what do you need?"

"Pocket," she said fervently, "I need everything. Shoes. Stockings. Brush and comb. Hairpins. Toothbrush. Something, *anything,* to wear. Soap. Towels. Olive oil—"

"Yes ma'am," said Pocket. "All the necessities of life."

"Right," said Marny. "Buy them downstairs and put them on my account. And oh yes—pen and ink and paper. I'd like to write a note to Kendra."

Pocket went down to shop. Marny ate the beans, scooping them up with the horn spoon, and felt stronger with every bean. Before long Pocket came back with his purchases.

He said the store had lots of gloves and bonnets and other

expensive doodads for ladies, but no dresses already made. But he brought her a new robe, thick and warm and a sensible dark blue in color; two regrettable pairs of heavy black cotton stockings, and half a dozen pairs of shoes so she could try them on and find a pair that would fit. He would go down again now, he said, to see if Hiram had brought the cart, and would come back to get her letter so he could give it to Kendra when they took Loren home.

Gratefully, Marny pinned back her tangled hair. She wondered where Norman was, and Rosabel, and how much money they had rescued. A new Calico Palace, they would get it built somehow, and paid for somehow. The very thought was refreshing.

She wrote to Kendra, and told her Loren had been hurt while saving a child. If he had not cared what happened to little Zack he would not have come up to Kearny Street at all, and so would not have been near enough to be struck when the El Dorado exploded. When she had given the letter to Pocket she set about washing herself.

After a while she had another visitor, Ralph Watson. He brought an answering letter from Kendra, and a bundle of clothes. The clothes had been wisely chosen, simple dark dresses and plain underwear.

—Bless you, Kendra, Marny thought as she sat down to read the letter.

Dear Marny,

Loren is still asleep from the laudanum the doctor gave him, so I have a chance to write. Thanks for your letter. I am glad—and not at all surprised—that Loren took care of little Zack. It is what anybody would expect him to do.

We have done all we could to see to it that Loren will be comfortable while he is getting well. Hiram and Pocket carried him upstairs and put him to bed. We moved the baby's crib down to the dining room, because that is close to Ralph and Serena's bedroom and she can pile Junior's belongings on the table and take care of him while I am upstairs waiting on Loren. Dr. Rollins says Loren will have to stay in bed for several days, until he makes up for his loss of blood, but with rest and care he'll be all right. He's as healthy as a colt.

I know you are heartbroken about the Calico Palace,

and to tell the truth so am I. I did want to go there. Now that Junior is born and I am well again I was planning to go in one day and see the mirrors and chandeliers and pictures and all the rest of it. Never mind. I'm sure you and Norman will rebuild, and when the new Calico Palace is open I shall come to see it right away. Mrs. Chase will disapprove and Mr. Chase will be shocked, but I don't think Loren will care. He doesn't try to boss me around.

Serena says Loren is waking up. In a hurry—
Kendra

Marny thought—Kendra, Pocket, Mr. Fenway. How good people are. How willing to help in a time of trouble. Well, not everybody. Not those men I saw last night, running off with everything they could lay hands on. But a lot of people are good.

She spent the rest of the day making herself fit to be seen. Wearing her new dressing gown, she went up and down the stairs, drawing water, heating it on the stove in the stockroom, carrying the pails upstairs, bringing down the pails of soiled water and emptying them into the mud behind the store. Messrs. Chase and Fenway came in and out of the stockroom but they seemed hardly to notice her. They were too busy making money.

Every unburnt store in town was doing a roaring business today. Hundreds of people, like Marny, had nothing to wear. Now, dressed in borrowed makeshifts, they were crowding in to buy clothes. Owners of lodging houses, from the respectable St. Francis to the dirtiest flopperies, came in begging for cots, mattresses, blankets, to take care of people who had been burnt out and now were offering any price to sleep somewhere out of the mud. The restaurants wanted food for clamoring hungry men, and plates and knives and spoons so the hungry men could eat it. All day the clerks hurried about, from the salesroom to the various stockrooms upstairs and down. In the afternoon Marny told one of the boys to bring her a tin box of crackers and another of sardines, and on these she made her second meal of the day.

But busy as they were, the clerks were all eager to talk. Bit by bit she heard the news. A lot of men had been hurt last night, by falls, burns, blows from the axes used to tear up buildings, or like Loren, by the explosions. She heard more

364

reports of looting, and sorry tales of men who had stood by, refusing to give aid—whether to fight the fire, save property, or even help an injured man who could not help himself— unless they were paid for it in advance.

The last burning building fell down about noon. By mid-afternoon the fire was mostly out, though there were still many little flames flickering among the ashes. Men who had owned the fallen buildings were going about with pails of water, sprinkling these little lingering fires, the sooner to set about the work of rebuilding. Foxy, sent on an errand, had caught sight of Norman watering the ruins of the Calico Palace. Foxy had stopped a minute to speak to him. Norman had said he and Rosabel and the Blackbeards and the Hawaiian girls and the baby were jammed into two rooms at the St. Francis, the men in one and the girls in the other, and the St. Francis had taken advantage of the fire to double its prices but what could you do? Learning Marny's where-abouts, Norman had said he would come to see her tomorrow and discuss a new Calico Palace. Marny said she would like to look over the site of the Calico Palace herself.

Foxy exclaimed in dismay. No indeed. She had no idea of the crazy mob she would run into around the plaza. Every looter from last night was there, looking for something else to steal. And half of them were drunk. A lady amid all that riffraff? No. She must positively not show herself on the street unless she had a strong man to take care of her.

In the morning Marny saw the wisdom of Foxy's advice. She had decided that since she had to stay here she would use the time to make some of those clothes she needed. This was Christmas Day, but with so much money to be made in the business of rebuilding, few men had closed their shops or offices, and Chase and Fenway's was open as usual. Wearing one of Kendra's dresses, Marny went into the front salesroom to buy cloth and sewing needs.

Instantly, she found herself in the middle of a mob. These men were not riffraff. They were customers here to do busi-ness; many of them she recognized as well-behaved patrons of her parlor. They were good-natured and they meant no harm. But they were men and she was a woman and they wanted her back among them. They grabbed her, they tried to embrace her, they pulled her hair. One cavalier produced a pair of scissors and snipped off a lock and held it up,

365

announcing that he was going to put it into a gold case and wear it next to his heart. They babbled a thousand questions. When would the Calico Palace be up again? While it was under way was she going to deal cards anywhere else? Maybe she could deal a game right here, right now. They would set up a table, or an up-ended box would do. Would she?

It lasted only a minute or two; if it had lasted longer they would have torn Kendra's dress to pieces. As it was, both sleeves ripped at the shoulders and a button popped off. But before they could do more, Mr. Chase thrust his strong stocky person among them and loudly ordered them to move on. No disorder wanted here. He was holding a gun.

As they fell back, Marny put her hands up to her disordered hair, and managed to smile at them all.

"Let me go now, boys. There's going to be a new Calico Palace. I promise."

She saw Mr. Fenway. He too was holding a gun. With his free hand he took her elbow.

"Shame on you all," said Mr. Fenway. "Pushing and shoving a helpless female. Now Marny, you come along."

The men were protesting that they hadn't hurt her, they had barely touched her. Just wanted to ask a few questions—

Mr. Fenway led Marny back into the stockroom. As they turned to go, she saw Mr. Chase giving her a baleful glance across his gun. She guessed what he was thinking: that she made trouble wherever she went. As she was here by Mr. Fenway's invitation he could not throw her into the street, but the sooner she cleared out the happier Mr. Chase would be. Well, she had nowhere to go, and Mr. Chase would simply have to put up with her. She would keep quiet and out of his way and not enter the front room again. This was the best she could do.

Mr. Fenway asked what she had wanted to buy, and sent Foxy to take her order. When she had told Foxy she wanted cloth and scissors and needles and thread and a tape measure, Marny asked him where he took his meals. Foxy said usually at a restaurant down the street, near the rooming house where he and the other packing boys now lived. She asked if he would bring back meals for her while she was living in the store. He could use a tin plate, and buy a knife and fork for her to keep on hand, so there would not be much for him to carry. Foxy said he sure would, glad to. He figured what she owed the store, and Marny told him to add an extra pinch for himself.

"I'm giving you a lot of trouble," she explained.

Foxy demurred. Ah, he didn't want any pay, he said, he was glad to oblige, but she told him again to take it and he did. Marny's opinion was that no matter how obliging people were, they were even more so when they were paid for their favors.

While Foxy was bringing her supplies from the salesroom Marny pushed several empty boxes together to make a sewing table near a stockroom window. She had begun to work when Norman came in. Norman was carrying something tied up in a rag. Taking off the rag he showed her a shapeless twist of gold, weighing ninety or a hundred ounces.

"This," he said angrily, "is what became of those coins we didn't have time to take out. Melted. Gold coins from the Mint, *melted*." Norman let out his rage in a growl.

He had picked it up yesterday, he said, in the ruins of the Calico Palace. He and the Blackbeards had guarded the site all day, sprinkling the rubble until it was cool enough for them to poke around. Norman was sure this was not the only piece of melted gold that had been found there. He was sure because they had left behind far more coins than could be accounted for by this one lump. But looters were swarming over the wreckage and he couldn't keep his eyes on them all.

As she took the twist in her hands Marny felt a bitter sense of loss. This was gold, it could be exchanged for merchandise, but what they needed for their gambling tables was real money, brought from the Mint. She said she would put the twist into her safe here in the store, and to keep from thinking any more about it she changed the subject.

"How is Rosabel?" she asked.

"Cross as a wet cat," Norman said laughing. "She lost her clothes, and to tide her over she bought a few dresses from the girls at Blossom's love store. And the price they made her pay!" His eyebrows knotted seriously. "Marny, everybody who wasn't burnt out is getting rich from the fire. We've got to start again, soon. *Soon*, Marny."

"You might set up a table somewhere," she said. "But I hear they don't allow gambling at the St. Francis."

Norman growled again. No, they would not let him set up a table there. The St. Francis was *respectable*, Norman said with wrathful disdain. He could set up a table at that new

367

hotel on Pacific Street, the Gresham, but he thought he'd better use all his energy getting a new Calico Palace under way. He had some coins in his private safe here, as she had in hers, and this would start them. Norman had already gone to Reginald Norrington and told him they were solvent, and he would get the rent for the lot the day it fell due. Now for the new building.

Norman was speaking in a rush. He told her, now that the plaza had lost the big gambling houses—the El Dorado, the Parker House, Denison's, the Calico Palace—the lesser spots were booming. The Verandah roof had caught fire five times, but the fires had been put out. Today it was open for business. Same for the Bella Union and the Aguila del Oro and the rest of them. "They're getting our trade," said Norman. "We've got to start building right now."

Norman wanted Dwight Carson, because Dwight was the best builder in town. But the trouble was, everybody else wanted him too. Norman had called at Dwight's office on Montgomery Street, and had found a dozen other men there, all on the same errand as his own. Dwight was considering the offers, taking his time about it like a girl choosing among a throng of suitors for her hand. "Where's that poke you carried out, Marny?" Norman asked.

"Here, in my safe," she answered. Marny knew as well as Norman that neither dust nor the twist of melted gold would be much inducement to Dwight. A man so much wanted would insist on coins.

"At least we have cash on hand," said Norman. "No borrowing if we can help it."

Marny heartily concurred. "Ten per cent a month!" she exclaimed.

"Ten?" Norman laughed aloud. "Since the fire the bankers are getting twelve and a half. That friend of yours, Hiram Boyd, and his partner, name of Eustis, they've got a building on Montgomery Street hardly half finished. But they're doing business today in one room of it, and I'm told men are begging for loans. I don't know why they're lending at twelve and a half a month. I'd charge fifteen. Now tell me, have you been buying any more steamer tickets lately?"

"Why yes. I have them here, in my safe."

Norman looked up at the ceiling and gave thanks. He had been afraid she might not have bought any, or if she had, they had been kept in the Calico Palace and now were lost with everything else. "Oh Marny," he exclaimed, "you do use your head for thinking! Most people don't use their heads for anything but to grow hair."

With a humorous shrug, Marny asked, "What do you want with the tickets?"

"The steamer *Oregon*," he retorted, "is due to sail for Panama the first of January. Men are storming the steamer office. They're sick of the rain, the mud, the rats, and now the fire. They want to ride a mule across the Isthmus and go home. But the steamer line has sold out of tickets. We can sell yours for three, four times what you paid for them. Maybe," Norman added brightly, "maybe we *can* get Dwight Carson before anybody else. If you should see him, don't tell him how much we need him."

Marny answered with a canny smile. "Dwight uses his head for a lot more than to grow hair, my friend. He knows how much we need him."

Norman brought Mr. Fenway to open the room where the private safes were kept. Sitting on the floor, he counted his own coins and Marny's, added the probable value of the steamboat tickets, and locked them all into the safes again. "We're in good condition," he said to Marny as they went back into the stockroom. "I do believe we can outbid the rest of them."

Whistling as he went, he hurried off to report their financial state to Dwight Carson.

As she returned to her sewing, Marny laughed under her breath. She would have been willing to lay a bet that Norman, like herself, had shed tears yesterday. But he would not own up to it today, any more than she would. Today they did not feel like crying. They felt like fighting. So did those others who were hastening to rebuild. There *was* something about this fogbound ratty bug-ridden town. She liked being part of it.

The day after Christmas was raw and murky, but the stockroom was warm and the store was clackety with business. The boys rushed about, lamenting that Loren had to be at home just when they needed him more than ever. Ralph said Loren was doing well and would be back soon, but this didn't help them do the work today. Marny sat by the window, sewing and waiting for news.

369

Right now, Norman was no doubt talking to Dwight Carson.

—That Norman, thought Marny, he's really a cannonball. No more principles than a tomcat, but *smart*. I wonder why Rosabel wants to marry him. Love is strange and wonderful. At least it's strange.

In the midst of her reverie Norman burst noisily into the stockroom. Brushing past the clerks and packing boys, he hurried over to where she sat. Usually so dapper, Norman had been too busy since the fire to care how he looked. His shirt was rumpled, his cravat askew, his pointed beard untended, but his face was full of joy and he was so breathless he could hardly talk.

"Marny!" he blurted as he reached her. "I can't stay but a minute—just wanted to tell you—we've got him!"

"Oh glory!" she cried, and dropped her sewing. "How did you manage it?"

For once in his life, Norman's face went blank. "I don't know," he answered. "'I went by his office again yesterday after I talked to you—"

"When is he going to start?"

"That's what I'm trying to tell you!" Norman retorted. "I went by his office and he'd already started."

Marny gasped. Norman caught his breath and hurried on.

"He had hired a wagon to carry off the ashes, and he was working on a floor plan. And what's more"—Norman spoke with wide-eyed wonder—"he wasn't concerned about price. Said we'd discuss money later."

Marny gave a happy sigh. Norman was still talking.

"He's on the lot now, getting the rubble cleared. He asked where you were staying, and said he'd be over to see you soon as he got things organized. Now I'll get hold of Bruno Gregg and send him here so you can talk to him about pictures. Oh yes, here's today's *Alta*. Now I've got to go."

Norman exploded out of the room, bumping into two of the boys in his hurry. Marny smiled as she looked out at the fog and gloom. She did not know why Dwight had been so amenable, and at the moment she did not care. It was enough to be told the new Calico Palace was on its way.

She began to read the *Alta*. Storekeepers advertised auctions of goods they had carried to safety before their buildings fell in. Others begged for the return of papers locked up in stolen safes, promising to pay rewards and ask no questions.

Several honest men announced that they had picked up property belonging to other people, and said it would be returned if the owners would come and claim it. After the disgraceful scenes she had witnessed that night, Marny liked finding this evidence that there really were some upright folks around.

Her meditations were broken by the entrance of Bruno Gregg. Sketching pad in hand, Bruno opened the door that led from the salesroom, and stood on the threshold looking doubtfully around him, as though not sure he ought to interrupt all this important bustle. Calling, "Here I am, Bruno," Marny went to meet him and brought him to sit beside her at the window. Here in her private nook, ignoring the racket, she began the joyous task of planning the new Calico Palace.

For the rest of that day and most of the next, Marny and Bruno talked about pictures. Besides those that she would hang on the walls Marny wanted him to do some of the new type called transparencies. A transparency was a painting on cloth, hung in a window with a light behind it, to give men in the street a foreglimpse of the delights within. A transparency might show a table with stack of coins, and Marny dealing cards to a throng of happy players, all winning. Or it might show a bar, with men celebrating their good luck while Lulu or Lolo poured drinks. Or Rosabel at her piano, making music while other happy men looked and listened.

Bruno understood. While they talked he made sketches. The next afternoon he came back with completed designs for transparencies to deck all the front windows. He brought her a pack of cards, and when she had posed for several sketches of herself—to the great interest of the packing boys—Bruno said he would start the paintings first thing tomorrow morning. And he would finish them on time, she need not fear.

The next day Marny had a call from Dwight Carson.

Dwight did not burst in, like Norman, nor give a questioning look around, like Bruno. He was too important a personage for either. Dwight was escorted into the stockroom by Mr. Chase, who presented him to Marny with a bow that really gave her a shock, and the formal speech, "Mr. Carson to see you, ma'am."

Marny politely shook hands, saying, "How do you do, Mr. Carson." Dwight, taking the hint, replied, "It's a pleasure." He did not call her by name. The occasion was too stately for him to call her Marny, and neither he nor Mr. Chase had ever thought to inquire what her surname was. But as Mr. Chase withdrew, Marny grabbed Dwight Carson's hands in hers, exclaiming, "Oh, I'm so glad to see you! Thank you, thank you—Norman says you're starting a new Calico Palace for us."

His hands in hers, Dwight Carson smiled down at her, looking directly into her eager green eyes. "For *you*," he said clearly.

50

Marny's eyes widened slightly. She was thinking—Of course, how stupid of me not to have realized this before.

Dwight drew up a chair, and sat facing the window, his back to the room. He spoke in a low voice but his every word was plain.

"What's Norman Lamont to me? He's no better than any other gambler on the plaza."

Marny could have told him that Norman *was* better than any other gambler on the plaza, except herself, and this was why she was partner to Norman instead of somebody else. But Dwight was evidently making a speech he had planned, maybe one he had been planning for a long time. Besides, she was interested in what he had to say. She let him talk on.

"But you—" he continued. "I mean it, Marny. It's not often a man sees such a fine girl as you. A girl who keeps steady and plays straight and stays in good humor through everything. And now to see this happen—makes a man's heart ache for you."

Marny knew how to answer this sort of talk. She spoke softly, gently. "Oh Dwight, you're so understanding!"

"I think a lot of you, Marny," Dwight assured her earnestly. "I've been admiring you for a long time. Not many people are like you. And now—why, any other woman on the plaza would be having hysterics if she'd put as much as you've put into that place and then watched it go up in smoke.

But not you. I want to help you. You don't know how well I think of you, Marny."

Marny thought—I didn't, but I'm a girl who learns fast.

Dwight went on talking. His sympathy was sincere and so was his regard. He was so earnest that Marny had a moment's fear that he was going to ask her to marry him. She did not want to marry Dwight or anybody else; marriage had such a frightening permanence about it. But as he talked on, she felt assured that he was not interested in marriage any more than she was. But he was deeply interested in herself.

Though Marny and Dwight had both lived in Honolulu, they had not known each other there. Dwight had formerly lived in New York. By the time he reached Honolulu, Marny had already left, and he had lived there for several months before the gold rush brought him to San Francisco. He had been into the Calico Palace often, but this was the first time he and Marny had had a real conversation. As he talked, she listened with growing attention.

—He does like me, she was thinking.

Most men who made proposals to her had a wearying sameness. They wanted a woman, and they wanted her in particular because Marny of the Calico Palace would have been a trophy at any man's belt. But Dwight did not want her merely because she was a goodlooking woman who had prestige value.

—He likes *me*, she reflected. I know the difference.

As he talked, and she encouraged him with a few words here and there, she thoughtfully appraised him. Dwight was a rugged fellow, not handsome, but he had a look of humor and his expression showed the quick changes of an alert and attentive mind. He had straight light brown hair, and steely blue-gray eyes that moved eagerly, noting all that went on around him. He looked healthy—good teeth, ruddy skin with an outdoor tinge in spite of the fogs. He wore heavy practical boots and heavy practical clothes, and a gun in a holster at his belt. Nothing parlor-style about him, but he kept himself neat and in order.

Agreeable disposition, she told herself, and good sense. He won't be dull. He cares about me, and right now I need somebody to care about me. Before the fire I wasn't in the mood for a gentleman friend. But now I believe I am. It's been a hard knock. I need a little cuddling.

373

Dwight was saying, "Marny, I guess I think more of you than I've ever thought of any other girl."

She was thinking—I need a little cuddling and I need a new Calico Palace. If I say yes I can be sure of getting the Calico Palace *now*. He has begun the work, but that's only a gesture to prove he means what he's saying. Everybody else on the plaze wants him. He could start six other buildings and have them all going up at once and meet "unavoidable delays" with ours. But if I say yes he'll finish the Calico Palace before he lays a brick for anybody else. He'd better.

She realized that Dwight had paused expectantly.

She said, "Dwight, you're so kind, so gallant! Coming here to see me when you must be the busiest man in town!"

Dwight smiled his appreciation. Marny had no notion of yielding at once; first she wanted to be sure he deserved her. She went on,

"I know how much you have to do, but I wonder if you could spare time to go out with me?"

His face brightened. "Why Marny, I'd do anything for you!" He took her hand in both of his. "Where do you want to go?"

"I'd like to have a look at the plaza. But I'm told there's so much confusion in that neighborhood, I wouldn't be safe going there alone."

Dwight vehemently agreed with this. Of course she must not go there alone. Most positively not. He would go with her, and protect her.

—And show the town what a conquest he's making, Marny thought with amusement. A man who wins a trophy is entitled to some renown.

She said, "Thank you so much, Dwight. It's good of you. I'll run up and put on my bonnet and shawl."

He solicitously asked if she had mud-boots. Marny said yes, she had bought them here in the store because the boys had warned her that the plank sidewalks had burnt or broken in many places and the mud was deep. She promised Dwight she would wear them.

Standing before the glass in Mr. Fenway's room, she decided that she looked well, considering what she had been through. She had bought the bonnet and shawl in the store. They were a pleasant shade of gray that set off her red hair; the bonnet had a green plume that matched her eyes, and she had bought gray kid gloves with pearl buttons. The rubber

374

boots were not pretty but her skirt would hide them except when she had to lift it to cross a miry spot. As she put on her gloves she smiled at her reflection, and went downstairs.

With a proud smile Dwight took her arm and escorted her through the main salesroom, bowing to acquaintances as he went. The men did not surround her now; with Dwight at her side they knew better. Dwight led her through the front doorway, into a day raw and cold and feathery with fog. They walked along Montgomery Street to the corner of Washington, and started up the hill toward Kearny Street and the plaza.

As they walked, Marny looked around her with amazement. She had known the men of the burnt area were rebuilding, but she had not dreamed how fast they were doing it. Kendra and Loren had given their Christmas party last Sunday; the fire had broken out before dawn Monday morning; today was Friday, and this was the first time since the fire that Marny had been in the street. Remembering the devastation she had seen as she sloshed through the mud in that bitter daybreak, she was almost awestruck.

The litter, the ashes, the pieces of buildings torn up to stop the fire, nearly all had been cleared away and wagons were busy hauling off the rest. Marny saw the frames of six or seven ready-made houses already standing on the sites of others lost in the holocaust. Workmen were fitting the doors and windows. The better buildings were being put up with less impatience, but several of these were under way. The air clanged with the noise of tools and the shouts of men wielding them. In lots still vacant, other men walked about, measuring, calculating, drawing plans.

As they reached the corner of Kearny Street she saw the Verandah, scorched but not hurt; and on the opposite corner she saw the beginning of a new El Dorado. Next door, men were unloading a wagon full of bricks on the site of the Parker House. Built of frame, the Parker House had burnt like brushwood; evidently they were going to make it stronger this time. On the site of Denison's Exchange a two-story structure was already half done.

"How in the world," she marveled, "can they do it so fast?"

With a smile of disdain Dwight answered, "Tarpaper and toothpicks."

He told her the owners of Denison's Exchange had made an arrangement with a contractor, signed before the ashes

375

were cold. The contractor had promised to have a new building ready in sixteen days. If he met his contract they were to pay him two thousand ounces of gold; for every day over sixteen he was to forfeit part of his pay. "But the way it's going," said Dwight, "I shouldn't be surprised if he gets it done in ten days instead of sixteen, and they'll be in business. If," he added with a shrug, "*if* a good wind doesn't blow it down."

—Or, thought Marny, if a dropped cigar doesn't set it on fire again.

But though all this was dramatic, she had not come out to look at Denison's or the Parker House or the El Dorado. She wanted to see what was being done about the Calico Palace, and as she tried to look farther along Kearny Street her view was hindered by these other structures and blurred by the fog. She told Dwight she would like to go nearer.

The Calico Palace was what Dwight wanted to show her. He warned her, however, that the plank sidewalk on Kearny Street had sizzled away in the fire, and while there had been no actual rain since then, in these fog-drenched days the mud simply could not get dry. They stood at Washington Street and Kearny, at the corner where the gamblers had sunk a line of stoves to make the crossing possible. Dwight asked her to wait here while he tested the footing.

Marny stayed where she was, standing on a hastily repaired piece of sidewalk in front of the Verandah. She watched Dwight as he made his way along. Dwight's rubber boots came up to his knees, but he moved with care. Some of these puddles covered slush where a man could go down to his waist.

"Well, Miss Randolph!" said a man's voice at her side.

Marny gave a puzzled start. Hardly anybody ever called her "Miss Randolph."

Beside her stood Captain Pollock. He had his usual air of sturdy health, and he was well dressed, still in his dark blue seaman's garb, crisply neat except for the mud on his boots. He had not taken off his cap. This surprised her a little. Most men in San Francisco uncovered their heads and bowed at the sight of any woman at all. Pollock gazed at her, not so much with anger as with angry triumph.

"So," he said, "it has happened to you too."

Marny gave a sigh of annoyance. She would have liked to step off the sidewalk and go after Dwight, but she decided

376

quickly that a minute with Pollock was better than the risk of stepping into a mudhole three feet deep. "Oh, let me alone," she said to him. She added, "You silly fool."

"I shall not detain you," said Captain Pollock. "I was merely about to suggest that now you have some inkling of how I feel, when I look at the wreck of the *Cynthia*."

"At least," Marny returned, "I'm fighting. I'm building again. You won't fight. You may as well go back to New York." She had a sudden mischievous idea. "'If you want to go back," she said sweetly, "the *Oregon* leaves next week and I can sell you a ticket."

Pollock regarded her with hatred. He gave her a slow, contemptuous smile. "As always," he said, "queen of the mantraps."

"Well, yes," answered Marny. "And a pretty good one, if I do say so myself."

At that moment she found Dwight Carson beside her again. Dwight had glanced around to see if she was being bothered, and at sight of Pollock he had hurried back. He took Marny's arm. To Pollock he said,

"Careful, captain. You're jumping a claim."

Marny felt a little jolt in her mind. Dwight was mighty sure of himself, calling her a "claim" before she had even seen the new Calico Palace. She had not made him any promises and she was not going to make any right away. She thought he deserved her, but again, let him prove it.

Pollock was giving Dwight a coldly courteous bow. "I beg your pardon, sir." He strode off, down the hill toward the waterfront.

"I shouldn't have left you," Dwight said to Marny, his voice full of regret. "Did that man say anything rude to you?"

"Oh no," said Marny. "He just has a crack in his head. Scared to open an umbrella in the house, all that sort of thing. Hadn't you heard?—he thinks I brought bad luck to his ship."

"Oh yes, I've heard that. He's scared of red hair." Dwight looked fondly at the coppery tendrils blowing around the brim of her bonnet. "Think of that. Just think of it."

He glanced toward the bay, and the masts of the empty vessels barely visible through the fog.

"I doubt he could move that ship now," Dwight remarked, "even with a first-class crew. Not without a lot of work, anyway. Stuck here since last spring, nobody taking care of her—by now I bet she's splitting at the seams. But he shouldn't worry, he's making a living."

"Doing what?" she asked with curiosity.

"He's opened a brickyard, and bought part of a lumber company. Maybe not doing as well as if he still had his ship, but not suffering." Dwight lost interest in Pollock.

Observing this, Marny said, "Oh, let's forget him, Dwight. Show me what you're doing about the Calico Palace."

While Dwight held her arm protectively, and Marny with her free hand lifted her skirts above the mud, they crossed the road on the path of stoves and then made their way along the squashy roughness of Kearny Street. The street was full of men, hurrying, talking, arguing, panting as they pushed laden wheelbarrows through the muck. It was not an easy walk, but Marny enjoyed it. For now she saw what she had been looking for: Dwight's carpenters rebuilding the Calico Palace. As she saw them she gasped with delight. The foundation was laid, a sturdy foundation of bricks and mortar, and the walls were on the way up.

"Oh, Dwight!" she cried happily.

He smiled down at her. "Like it?"

"Like it!" Marny repeated. She sighed with rapture. "So much done already. And that's not tarpaper and toothpicks."

"You're mighty right it's not," he assured her. "This new building is going to be better than the old one. Thicker walls. Two staircases."

Marny walked nearer, along a pathway of boards that the workmen had laid in the mud. She told him about the transparencies she had ordered from Bruno Gregg, and he told her about the iron shutters he was going to put at the doors and windows to keep the building safe from burglars after closing time. They stood talking until the twilight crept around them, and men began to carry lanterns in the street. As they walked back to Montgomery Street she asked,

"Where do you live, Dwight? You were not burnt out, were you?"

"No, I had good luck, didn't lose anything. I used to live in a room over my office, but lately I've moved into that new hotel on Pacific Street, the Gresham."

"Do you like it there?"

"Oh yes. I've got two rooms all to myself, one of them on a corner."

"*Two* rooms!" she echoed in amazement. Most men in

378

San Francisco, no matter how prosperous, had to share bedrooms with two or three others, as Norman was doing now at the St. Francis. Few were even so lucky as Hiram and Pocket, with one room occupied by only the pair of them.

Dwight nodded proudly. "And good solid walls," he said. "Space. Privacy."

Space and privacy were both so rare that Marny's voice was almost reverent as she exclaimed, "How on earth did you manage to get two rooms of your own?"

"I built the hotel," Dwight returned laughing, "with rooms for myself at one corner. That was part of the contract."

Marny thought of Hiram and Pocket's description of their room at the St. Francis—two bunks in a space eight feet by six, with paper-thin walls on both sides. She thought of her own drafty cubbyhole above the old Calico Palace, and herself now, unwanted, in Mr. Fenway's room over the store. "It sounds delightful," she said truthfully.

"The Gresham is better than the St. Francis," Dwight continued. "Not so many highflown airs about it. And they've got a good restaurant."

Marny said again that it sounded delightful.

But she made him say goodby at the door of the stockroom. She was thinking—Tomorrow, maybe. Tomorrow, probably. She liked Dwight. She liked him very much. She promised to take another walk with him tomorrow, to see the progress of the Calico Palace. But this was the only promise she made. She was not going to do this all of a sudden.

She lit a candle, took off her muddy boots, went upstairs to leave these and her bonnet and shawl, and came down again to the stockroom. A few minutes later Foxy brought her a tin plate of beef and potatoes.

The food did not look appetizing. It was cold, of course, it always was, and somebody had let fall a brush of cigar ash on the beef. Marny was used to eating food that not long ago she would have thought uneatable, but she wistfully remembered the luscious meals Kendra used to serve when they lived in the cottage with Archwood. As these were no longer available, she recalled hopefully that Dwight had said the Gresham Hotel had a good restaurant. She set the plate on her improvised sewing table, and took out her knife and her tin fork and the horn spoon Pocket had left with her. Foxy stood beside her, a grin across his long bucktoothed face.

"Us boys," he announced, "are going to see the Olympic Circus tonight."

"Fine," said Marny. She glanced down at her plate, still untouched. "Do you have to leave right now?"

"No ma'am, Al's going to call me when it's time to go. Why?"

"Because," said Marny, "I believe it would be easier to get this beef down if I had a nip of sherry first. You have some good Spanish sherry on the shelf, haven't you?"

Foxy said yes, he sure had. He brought her a bottle and drew the cork, and she told him to hold out his tin cup, it was no fun drinking alone. Foxy gladly complied, and while they sipped sherry he straddled a goods-box and told her the news. Foxy loved to tell news, any news at all.

The steamer *California* had arrived today, he said, from the Isthmus. Packed with passengers. Nearly three hundred men, Foxy added sadly, and only eight women.

Several of the passengers had come into the store. They had reported that a great throng of people was crowded into Panama City, waiting to come to San Francisco. There were so many of them and so few vessels to carry them that they had settled down for a long wait. Some had gone into business, opening stores, restaurants, rooming houses. A group of literary fellows had even started a newspaper to record the doings of the colony.

Al put in his head and called that it was time to get going if they wanted to see the circus. Foxy went off.

Marny finished her sherry and began her dinner. The food tasted better than it looked, but not much better. However, she felt in good spirits. The Calico Palace was on the way up. Dwight Carson was an agreeable fellow. She was going to move out of here tomorrow, she was almost sure of it now, and move into the Gresham Hotel. When she had finished the beef and potatoes, and washed the plate so it would have no attraction for rats, she took out the pack of cards Bruno had brought her yesterday and laid them out on her sewing table to tell her fortune. The cards promised a rosy future concerning a large building and a man with light hair.

She slept well and woke in a cheerful mood. The morning was white with fog, and the water in her pitcher was so cold that she wished she had never formed the habit of washing. Fortunately she could get warm in the stockroom. The boys made a fire in the stove as soon as they came to work, and

380

they always put on a pot of coffee. Carrying a tin box holding dried Oregon pears, which she had bought from Foxy yesterday, she went down.

There was nobody in the stockroom except two clerks whose names she did not know, noisily knocking open some boxes of goods. The pot was steaming on the stove. When she had breakfasted on coffee and dried pears, Marny brought her sewing and took her place by the window, to be out of the way when Mr. Chase arrived. She laughed to herself as she thought how happy Mr. Chase would be when he found she was about to remove her naughty presence from his domain.

The door from the salesroom opened and Marny looked up to see Foxy. He ambled over to where she sat.

"Morning, Marny," he said.

She smiled a greeting. "'Good morning. How was the circus?"

"Circus?" echoed Foxy. "'Oh fair, pretty fair." He lingered beside her, an earnest expression on his long toothy face. "Say, Marny."

"Why yes, Foxy, what is it?"

Foxy stood first on one big foot and then on the other. "Marny, I've got something to tell you."

Marny sighed tolerantly. From the look of him, his news was bad news. She had observed that people who liked to bring news liked it even better when the news was distressing. She remembered Foxy's relish when he had told her about the death of Delbert, which had not distressed her in the least. "What is it, Foxy?" she asked.

"It's about your friend—our friend," said Foxy. "The fellow that works here. Loren Shields."

With a start, Marny put down her sewing "Yes, Foxy? What about Loren?"

Foxy spoke with gloomy importance. "He's not doing well."

"Why, Foxy!" she protested. "'Ralph Watson said he was doing fine."

"That's what they thought," said Foxy. He was sorry about Loren, but also he was enjoying his moment of eminence in being the first to tell her. "'But not any more," he went on. "Loren's in a bad way, Marny."

She wished she knew how much she could rely on his accuracy. Yesterday she had intended asking Dwight to walk up the hill with her so she could drop in to see Kendra and ask how Loren was. But they had stood so long on Kearny Street, talking about the Calico Palace, that before she knew it the dark was coming down and she had put off her visit.

"What do you mean by a 'bad way,' Foxy?" she asked. "Tell me."

Foxy told her. Early this morning, as they were about to get the day started, Ralph had come in to tell the boys he would not be at work today. He had to help Mrs. Shields.

Ralph said that about four o'clock this morning Loren had been wakened by a tearing pain in his side. Kendra, who slept on a cot at the foot of the bed, had rushed down to wake Ralph and send him for Dr. Rollins. She had been badly frightened, Ralph said. So had he been himself when he came back with the doctor and saw how Loren looked. Loren was haggard with the pain, and drops of cold sweat were running down his face. He was trying not to cry out but he could not help it. Ralph had gone to tell Mr. Chase, and Mr. and Mrs. Chase had come right over to see if they could give any help. Mr. Chase had not come to the store yet.

"Loren's in a bad way," Foxy said again.

At this moment Mr. Fenway came in, and seeing Marny he walked over to her.

"'An ugly business, this, about Loren," he said sadly.

Marny said it certainly was.

"Best man we ever had around here," said Mr. Fenway. "Honest and dependable and a lot of good common sense." For once, his sadness fitted the occasion. "Ugly business, this. Well, Foxy, I guess you and I had better get to work."

Now that he had succeeded in being the first to tell the news, Foxy was willing to resume his normal occupations. He followed Mr. Fenway. Marny sat with her sewing in her lap, thinking about Loren. And Kendra.

Loren must be very sick if Ralph would not leave him to come to work. Ralph was serious about his duties. He would not have stayed away for a trivial reason. And Mr. Chase was not here either. It sounded as if Loren's state was alarming.

That nail must have bitten deeper than they guessed. Maybe it was a dirty nail.

Was Loren sick enough to die?

Oh, of course not! He was a healthy young man, he would get well.

But suppose he did not get well?

382

Marny had never had any talent for believing what she knew wasn't so. She knew that if Loren should die, it would not be a tragedy for Kendra. Kendra had married him in a time of shock and fear and loneliness, when Loren's sturdy goodness had been a refuge. It was not an unhappy marriage. If they both lived to old age, Kendra would have had as happy a marriage as most people, maybe happier than most people. But while Loren was deeply in love with Kendra, Kendra was not deeply in love with Loren. She was fond of him. If Loren should die, she would miss him. That sturdy goodness of his was not something to be lightly lost. But she would get over it.

Marny took up her sewing again, to soothe her impatience by keeping her hands busy while she waited for Dwight. Shortly before noon he came in, hearty and happy, his cheeks bright red from the fog. Pulling off his gloves he grabbed her hands in his.

"Shall we go?" he asked her. "You'll be surprised to see how much they've done already this morning."

Marny said she would go with him as soon as she had wrapped up. But, she asked, would it be all right if they went to see Kendra first, so she could ask about Loren? She would stay only a few minutes, then they could go down to the plaza and take their time about watching the carpenters.

Of course, of course, said Dwight, anything she wanted. He was sorry about Loren. Dwight had heard of Loren's injury but not of this turn for the worse. He hoped they would find that Foxy's report had been exaggerated.

Marny and Dwight walked up the hill, Marny receiving her usual tribute of bows and greetings from the men she passed, Dwight haughtily seeing to it that none of them came too close. They went by the *Alta California* building, smoke-smudged but intact; and the library, where Pocket was probably on duty right now. A few steps farther, they came to the little white house where Kendra lived.

Looking up at the house, Marny stopped. She caught Dwight's wrist in a frightened grasp. The fog around her was cold, but here she felt as if she had stepped into an even colder shadow.

The house looked closed, dark, withdrawn. The front shades were down. It looked like a place of sorrow.

Marny thought of the house as it had been the last time she

383

had stood there. On the door the cluster of fir sprigs tied with red ribbon. More beribboned evergreens at every window. The glow of firelight and candles from within. She thought of their Christmas dinner, of Kendra at the piano, Hiram joyously singing—

"And God bless you and send you
A happy New Year."

Only a week ago. Suddenly, she did not want Dwight going in with her. She said,

"Dwight, the fewer people around a sick man, the less noise to disturb him. Can't you wait for me somewhere? You might drop into the library and look at the papers that came in by the steamer yesterday."

Dwight was in a mood to please her. Besides, he was not a close friend of Loren's. He had come here only because she wanted him to.

"Oh sure, sure," he answered. "I'd like a look at the papers. And I'll come back for you—how soon?"

"Half an hour?"

"All right." Dwight glanced at the men going up and down the street and casting wishful looks at Marny. "I'll stand here till you're safe indoors, then I'll walk down to the library."

"Thanks." Marny gave him a smile, went up the steps and knocked. She waited a moment, and knocked again. The voice of Mrs. Chase called from within.

"Who is it, please?"

"It's Marny, Mrs. Chase." She repeated, "Marny."

"Oh yes," said Mrs. Chase, and she opened the door. Tipping his hat, Dwight turned toward the library. "Come in," Mrs. Chase said to Marny. She added, "Kendra's in no state to see most people, but I think she'll want to see you."

Marny stepped inside and closed the door behind her. They stood together in the dim little hallway. Before them the stairs went up toward the landing and the room where Loren lay ill. The doors leading into the hall were closed, except the door to the parlor, and the only light in the hall was what little came in around the edges of the lowered shades at the parlor windows. But even in the dimness Marny could see that Mrs. Chase's kindly face was drawn with grief and pity. In a low voice Marny said,

"I came to ask about Loren, Mrs. Chase."

Mrs. Chase somberly shook her head. "The doctor's doing all he can," she replied. Her voice too was very low. "But it looks like that nail tore something inside of him. I don't know enough to say what it might be."

Marny did not know enough either. She said, "Then it's true, what I was told—Loren is very ill indeed?"

Mrs. Chase nodded. Her lips were pressed together like lips trying to hold back a sob. Marny was surprised at such deep emotion. She had known that Mr. and Mrs. Chase thought highly of Loren, but she had not known Mrs. Chase cared for him as much as this. She asked,

"And how is Kendra?"

"Brave," Mrs. Chase answered almost under her breath. "Brave. Braver than anybody I ever knew. But"—she made a quick gesture across her eyes—"it's too much for her, Marny, too much. She's already worn out. One thing on top of another."

Marny gave a start. "What do you mean by 'another,' Mrs. Chase? Is something else wrong, besides Loren?"

Mrs. Chase gave her a long look. Her chin quivered as as if she were trying to speak and could not. Again she nodded, dumbly.

Marny's hand closed on Mrs. Chase's plump elbow. "What *is* it, Mrs. Chase? Why do you look at me like that? Mrs. Chase, what has *happened*?"

Tremors of fright ran through her as she waited for an answer. Mrs. Chase wet her lips. Tears came into her eyes. At length she managed to speak.

"Marny I guess it's all right to tell you."

She caught Marny's hands and held them as she began to talk. Now that she was talking, the words poured out of her in a feverish torrent. She repeated.

"I guess it's all right to tell you. We didn't know. Nobody knew. We didn't know till we came here this morning. Kendra had told Ralph and Serena not to say anything to anybody. She was afraid somebody might tell Loren and she didn't want him to know. She didn't know then how sick he was, nobody knew, but he was sick and in pain and she said why trouble him and make it harder? She told Ralph not to talk about it at the store because those boys blab so, the word might get back to Loren. She wouldn't even tell my husband. He stopped in two or three times to speak to Loren, and Loren seemed like he was doing pretty well—weak, of course, but pretty well—but he didn't know and my husband didn't know. But today, of course, we know. My husband has gone on down to the store because there wasn't anything he could do here, but before he left he promised Kendra he wouldn't say a word to anybody there. But now you've come to see her, and she's so fond of you, she'd tell you if I didn't, she knows you wouldn't let it out to Loren—"

Marny was trembling with impatience. "Mrs. Chase, what are you *talking* about?" she pled. "Say it, won't you?"

"I've been trying to say it but it's so hard to say," murmured Mrs. Chase. Tears came into her eyes again. She blinked them back, and looked up. Speaking with an effort, she said, "Marny, it's the baby."

Marny's breath caught in her throat. She gasped, "The baby!"

"Sh! Don't say it out loud, Loren might hear. Though I don't think he can, they keep his door closed all the time—"

"For the love of God," Marny begged, "tell me! What about the baby?"

Mrs. Chase steadied herself. "He caught cold that night," she answered. "It didn't show up till after daylight, after they had brought Loren home. It seemed like just a little cold. But it got worse. Now he can't breathe right. He's burning up with fever. The doctor has tried and tried but he can't do anything."

"And Loren," Marny said in a half whisper, "doesn't even know the baby is sick?"

Mrs. Chase shook her head. "They had moved the crib downstairs, so Loren and the baby wouldn't disturb each other. When they found the baby had a cold, Kendra didn't tell Loren. She thought Junior would be all right in a day or two, and Loren was hurt already, so she said why worry him? When Loren asked how Junior was, Kendra said he was fine. Loren said he'd like to see him and Kendra said she couldn't bring him up to the bedroom. She said the weather was so cold and damp, the doctor had told her not to take the baby out of his warm crib and carry him up these drafty stairs. Loren said this was right, keep him warm. Every day after that the baby has been getting worse, and every day she's kept smiling and telling Loren he was fine. But he's not. I saw him this morning."

Mrs. Chase's voice broke. The tears crept down her rosy cheeks as she said,

"Marny, that baby is *sick*. And Kendra knows it. Only a month old, and they're so weak and helpless when they're that little. Marny—I don't know about Loren but I think the baby is going to die."

51

Trembling with shock and pity, Marny held to the balustrade of the staircase. She remembered Loren's joy when he came into the Calico Palace to tell her his son was born. She thought of her first visit to Kendra after that. And of Kendra saying, "I'm so happy about him! I didn't know, I never dreamed, how much a baby makes up for."

"Oh God help her!" Marny murmured. "Kendra's baby!"

Mrs. Chase nodded, drying her tears. "Now I'll tell Kendra you're here," she said.

"If Kendra doesn't feel able to see me," said Marny, "it's all right. Just give her my love."

"I think she'll want to see you. She's with the baby now. Wait here."

Mrs. Chase went down the hall, past the door of the parlor, into the dining room. Marny remembered how happy they had been as they sat around the table there. How different it was now! On the table the baby's necessities, beside it the crib, and in the crib the baby, gasping his little life away.

—If I could only *do* something, she thought. Anything, to help.

But she could think of nothing she could do. She had no idea of nursing. She had never rocked a cradle nor changed a diaper in her life.

Kendra came out of the dining room, closing the door silently behind her. Even in the half-light it was plain that she had grown thinner during the past week. Marny went to meet her, put her arms around Kendra's shoulders and kissed her. "You dear brave girl," she said softly.

Kendra moved a step backward. "I'm so glad you're here," she said in a voice like a tired little thread. "But—please don't give me any sympathy. I can't bear it."

Beckoning Marny to come with her she went into the parlor. Marny followed.

In the parlor the air was stale and cold. Though this room too was dim there was more light here than in the hall, and Marny could see that Kendra's face was white and rigid. Her child was dying and she was facing the fact of it.

Kendra caught Marny's hands in a hard, nervous grip. Marny thought—She's drawing on her strength like drawing money out of a bank. She won't realize how much she's taking out until it's all used up.

Marny asked, "Kendra, is there *anything* I can do to help you?"

To her surprise Kendra nodded. "Yes. Be my best friend."

"Yes, dear," Marny said earnestly. "I am your best friend. Tell me what you want of me."

"I think—I want—you to listen," said Kendra. Her grip on Marny's hands was so tight it was almost painful. Marny guessed that every muscle in her body was tense. Kendra went on. "Marny, I can't say this to anybody else. But I can say it to you because you know already."

Her eyes, darkly circled, looked into Marny's with a desperate plea for understanding. Marny waited.

"Marny," said Kendra, "you know—you haven't said it but you know—I've never given anything to Loren. He has given to me and given to me. All I've done is take what he gave. Now I'm giving him something. He loves that child so much."

She was speaking steadily, with a bleak and terrible courage.

"I don't think—the doctor doesn't think—Loren is going to get well. If we're wrong, if he does get well, then he'll have to know. But if he doesn't get well, then—I'll have spared him what I'm going through now. If these are the last days of his life, I can give him peace in these days. Will you help me?"

Marny drew a deep breath to ease the tightness in her own chest. "I'll do anything I can, Kendra. But what can I do?"

388

"You can stay here," said Kendra. "I don't mean *do* anything. Serena and Ralph and Mrs. Chase and the doctor, they're doing everything. But you—if you will—just be around." She loosened her grip on Marny's hands and made a gesture toward the sofa. "You can sit here. Keep out of the way. But just—be around. It will make it easier, knowing you're here. I don't know why, but it will. So just be around. Will you?"

"Yes, Kendra. I'll stay as long as you want me."

"Thank you. Thank you." Kendra looked about the room, as if only half seeing what was before her. "If there's any coffee on the stove I'll tell Serena to bring you some. Thank you."

She went out. Marny opened a window. A wind was rising, blowing the fog. The air came damply against her face.

The door opened and Serena stood on the threshold. She spoke abrutly. "There isn't any coffee made but Mrs. Shields told me to put on a pot for you." Usually so pleasant of manner, today she was blunt, almost harsh. "It will be ready soon," she said.

"Thank you, Serena," said Marny. "Mrs. Shields is a brave—"

"Please—I can't talk about it," said Serena. She went out as abruptly as she had come in. Marny remembered that Serena knew, better than she herself, better even than Mrs. Chase, what Kendra was enduring. Serena had watched death come to a baby of her own. As she saw Kendra now, she was almost living through it again. No wonder her manner was brusque. She was covering the memory of pain.

There was a knock at the front door. Marny gave a start. Of course—Dwight Carson, here to escort her down to the plaza. She had forgotten he existed.

She went to the door, but found Serena already opening it. Dwight was there, and with him were Hiram and Pocket. Hiram was explaining. After his midday lunch he had dropped into the library, and had been reading a New York newspaper when Dwight came in. Dwight had told them both about Loren's attack, and they wanted to ask how he was. Could they come in for a minute or two?

"Mr. Shields is not well at all," said Serena. "I don't think you'd better come in." She was speaking hesitantly, afraid she might say too much. Kendra had told her not to drop any hint about the baby, lest it get to Loren.

389

"I'll speak to the gentlemen, Serena," Marny offered. She smiled at Serena reassuringly, as if they shared a conspiracy. "We won't disturb Mr. Shields." She indicated the parlor. "Come in here, won't you?"

The three men went in with her. Marny told them about Loren's waking before daybreak with that dagger of pain stabbing his side. She said nothing about the baby, but she told them Kendra had asked her to stay here the rest of the day. "So, I won't be going down to look at the Calico Palace," she said to Dwight.

Dwight saw that she was distressed. He laid it to her concern about Loren, for she had made no secret of the fact that Loren was seriously stricken. He yielded at once, kind and sympathetic, so sympathetic that she liked him more than ever. He would go on with the work, he said. Everything would be done right. She could trust him. Looking straight at him, Marny said sincerely,

"I do trust you, Dwight. I'd like to go with you now, but as long as my dear friend needs me I must stay here. Thank you for understanding."

Dwight smiled at her. Marny wondered if Pocket and Hiram caught the message that passed between them.

Dwight went out. They heard the door close after him. Pocket asked for more details about Loren. And how was Kendra?

"And can't we *do* something?" Hiram demanded.

Hiram and Pocket were both well dressed in dark suits and white shirts, though as usual Pocket's suit was lumpy with his possessions and Hiram's thick tawny hair was tumbled about as if it had never felt a comb. Marny answered them carefully.

"Hiram, Pocket, Loren is very ill. It seems the nail tore some internal organ, and the nail may have been rusty. I'm afraid it was. I came here, like you, to ask if there was any help I could give. Kendra asked me to stay. But as for you two—I think you'd better go. Mr. Chase has gone back to his work because he knew he was of no use here. I believe you should do the same. I'll tell Kendra you came in and she'll be grateful. Now please, I think she would want you to go."

"Oh no I don't," said Kendra's voice from the doorway.

She stood there, her face like something cut out of a rock. Her hands were gripping each other, her fingers twisting

390

around and around. She spoke again in that tight breathless voice.

"Hiram, Pocket—Serena told me you were here." Her lips moved in a trembly little smile. "You don't know—what it means—having my best friends with me. Please don't go."

Pocket and Hiram spoke together, assuring her that they would stay as long as she wanted them. Kendra drew a quick hard breath.

"You don't know—Marny, tell them about—I can't—"

"About what?" exclaimed Hiram.

Kendra untangled her hands and made a gesture toward the room where the baby was. "About—Marny will tell you."

She left them. Their eyes full of anxious questioning, the two men turned to Marny. Marny was listening to Kendra's footsteps going up the stairs, toward the room where Loren lay suffering pain of the body but mercifully spared Kendra's pain of the heart.

Pocket came and sat on the sofa by her. Hiram sat on the floor in front of her, his big rough hands linked around his knees.

"What did she want you to tell us?" Hiram asked.

Marny told them. She did not include what Kendra had said to her about giving Loren something in return for all he had given her. She told them simply that the baby was believed to be dying, and Loren knew nothing about it. Kendra was telling him, over and over, that the baby was well.

Hiram and Pocket looked at each other. Hiram scrambled to his feet, as if movement was a vent for his feelings.

"But can't we *do* something?" he demanded of the air.

Marny shook her head. Pocket gently reminded him,

"Sometimes, Hiram, people can't do anything."

Hiram stood there with a look of hurt disbelief. He hardly knew how to accept a situation where his own rugged vitality was of no use.

"There must be something!" he insisted, almost angrily.

Pocket stood up and went to him and spoke firmly. "Hiram, there's nothing we can do. Except stay here. Kendra wants us to stay. Maybe, at that, we're doing something. So sit in this chair, and keep your voice down if you can."

Hiram took the chair. They all three sat silently, doing nothing.

Mrs. Chase came in, bringing a tray on which there were

391

cups and a pot of coffee. The men sprang up, so swiftly that Marny thought it looked less like good manners than eagerness to loosen their taut muscles. As she set the tray on the table Mrs. Chase said,

"It's good of you folks to be here."

"How is the baby?" asked Pocket.

"He's just—there," said Mrs. Chase. Across her plump friendly face went a twitch of pity as she added, "But he won't be there much longer."

"And Loren?" asked Hiram.

"Conscious. In his right mind. But—" Mrs. Chase swallowed hard and went on. "The doctor has looked at his wound again. I helped him take off the wrappings. Dreadful." A shudder ran through her. "Festered, and blue lines shooting out of it. Dr. Rollins is going to stay here tonight. He'll give Loren a dose to make him sleep. I've got to go now. Good of you to be here."

She went out. Marny poured the coffee. Fresh and hot, it made them all feel stronger.

They waited. The parlor was chilly and unwelcoming. They had raised the window shades, but the light that came in was filtered to a dull gray by the fog. Everything in the room looked vaguely out of order. Kendra had never been the sort of housekeeper who insists that every knickknack have its place and stay there, but her home had always been well cared for. Now the room had a look of being forgotten.

Marny set down her empty cup.

"And I thought I had something to cry about," she murmured, "when I lost the Calico Palace!"

"Kendra's not crying," said Hiram.

"She doesn't dare to," said Pocket. "Not yet. She'll cry later."

"If she can hold out," said Marny.

"She will," said Hiram.

"Will you men come back tomorrow?" asked Marny, "if she wants you?"

Speaking together, they said they certainly would. Pocket said the library could get along without him or close up, he didn't care which. Hiram said if his partner Eustis couldn't take care of the bank for a few days, they would go broke and he didn't give a damn.

Again they fell silent. From outside they could hear the clop of hoofs, shouts of drivers, voices of men hailing each other as they went up and down the plank sidewalk. The noises from the street seemed to make heavier the silence in the room.

Mrs. Chase came in, with Ralph and Serena. "Do you think," asked Mrs. Chase, "you could eat something with us? We've set bread and cold beef on the kitchen table, and I've made cocoa."

Hiram and Pocket said they had had lunch and were not hungry again. Marny had had nothing to eat since her breakfast of coffee and dried pears, but she too felt no appetite.

"It's hard to eat," said Serena.

"You'd better, honey," Ralph said to her anxiously. "People have to keep on eating. Can't live on coffee."

He was right, of course, thought Marny. But she herself, like Serena, felt no interest in bread and beef.

They heard footsteps in the hall. Dr. Rollins came in, good, jovial Dr. Rollins, who had done the best he could. His face had a beaten look, the look of the doctor who has tried to save promising and useful lives, and has failed.

He closed the door behind him. They had all turned to him, and they knew what he was going to say before he said it.

"It's over with the baby," he announced bluntly.

Marny caught her breath with a little wordless sound. Serena choked back a sob. Mrs. Chase put her handkerchief to her eyes. Pocket said,

"You did all you could, doctor. We know that."

"He sure did," said Ralph. "We saw it."

Hiram drew a deep breath. He looked around at them all. "Now who," he asked, "is going to tell Kendra?"

Nobody answered.

But they did not have to tell her. As if she too had heard the doctor's footsteps as he came out of the room where he had watched over her baby, Kendra came downstairs from Loren's room. She opened the door to the parlor and stood in the doorway and looked around at them. For a moment nobody had courage to speak. Then the doctor cleared his throat.

"Mrs. Shields—" he began.

"Yes," said Kendra. Again she looked from one of them to another. In that strange monotone she said, "I think—I

393

know what you're trying to say. My baby. This—is this the end?"

"Yes, Mrs. Shields," said Dr. Rollins.

Marny put an arm around her. Kendra moved out of her embrace. "Please," she said, "please, I want to be by myself for a few minutes."

"Of course, dear," said Marny.

For a moment Kendra did not move. They saw that her hands were holding each other in such a clench that the knuckles were white. "Wait here for me," she said. Significantly, she said it again. "Here. In this room. Will you?"

"Right here," said Hiram.

Kendra left them. They heard her going down the hall and opening the door to the room where her baby lay in the crib, under the sheet Dr. Rollins had drawn up to cover him. They heard her close the door.

They waited. Mrs. Chase was wiping her eyes.

"What a sorrow," Pocket said in a low voice.

"There's no sorrow like it in the world," said Serena. "Nobody can tell you what the sorrow is."

She turned toward Ralph and hid her face on his shoulder. He put his arm around her. They stood together, remembering.

Hiram stood looking down at his big strong hands, as if he felt guilty before the helplessness of them.

It seemed a long time that they waited. At last Kendra came back. She stood in the doorway, facing them, white and rigid and almost fiercely strong. "Marny," she said, "may I speak to you?"

Marny went to her. Kendra said to the others,

"Wait here for me."

She led Marny into the hall. They stood by the front door where Kendra and Hiram had hung the Christmas wreath. Kendra held Marny's hands. As before, her grip was so hard it hurt.

"Marny, be my friend."

"Yes, Kendra."

"There's something I've got to do," said Kendra. "I want you to come upstairs with me and when I've done it you can come down and tell the others."

"Yes, Kendra."

They went upstairs together, to the door of Loren's room. Loren lay on the bed, gaunt and glitter-eyed with fever.

Leaving Marny in the doorway Kendra went in and stood by the bed. "Loren," she said, "it's Marny. She wanted to come up for a minute."

Loren managed to turn his head a little, and give Marny a weak smile. She smiled at him, and saw him shake as a pain tore at his side. Kendra knelt by the bed, her back to the door. Marny could not see her face.

In a weak voice Loren asked, "How's Junior?"

Kendra spoke with a great effort, but clearly. "He's well, Loren."

Loren murmured, "Mighty—fine baby—don't you think—Marny?"

"A beautiful baby," said Marny. She thought her words sounded like the clinks of a chain. Her hands were clenched at her sides. But Loren was not strong enough to notice anything amiss. With a terrible effort Kendra said,

"The baby is well and Dr. Rollins wants him to stay well. He told me not to bring him up here yet. It's still—so drafty—on the stairs."

Loren said, "Right." In a mumble so low Marny could barely hear him, he added, "Keep him warm. Thanks for—coming up—Marny."

With her hand behind her Kendra made a gesture, waving Marny away. Marny said,

"I just wanted to speak to you for a minute, Loren. I'll go down now."

Loren murmured an almost inaudible goodby. Marny felt sure it was the last word she would ever hear him speak. She turned and left Kendra with him, kneeling by the bed.

Marny went down to the parlor. She shut the door and stood in front of it and told them what Kendra had done. They listened—Pocket and Hiram, Ralph and Serena, Mrs. Chase, kindly Dr. Rollins. Serena sobbed. Mrs. Chase cried silently. Hiram said, "God, what guts."

Marny said, "If one of you, even by accident says a word to let Loren know she was lying—I'll shoot the one that does it."

"You needn't," said Pocket. "I'll do the shooting."

Serena dried her eyes and steadied herself. "Would it help," she asked, "if I went up to her?"

Marny was not sure what to say, but Pocket spoke without hesitation.

"No, ma'am it would not. This is something she has to do alone. When she wants us, she knows where we are."

Again they waited. Practical as always, Mrs. Chase went into the kitchen and brought back the pot of cocoa she had made a while ago. She filled a cup and brought it to Marny.

"Drink this," she ordered. "It's nourishing." She filled another cup. "And Serena, you drink this. Don't tell me you don't want it. Somebody's got to have some common sense around here."

Marny and Serena both obeyed her.

A few minutes later Kendra came in. Like Marny, she stood in front of the closed door, but at first she did not say anything. Mrs. Chase brought her a cup of cocoa, but she seemed not to see it.

"Won't you try to drink this, dear?" asked Mrs. Chase.

As if not hearing her, Kendra said to them all, "Marny told you what I said to Loren?"

"Yes," said Pocket. "We understand and we think you did right."

"Thank you," said Kendra. "And thank you for being here."

She stood where she was, not noticing Mrs. Chase, still waiting beside her with the cup.

The room was full of a dreadful silence. Nobody could say anything. It seemed as if nobody moved at all.

Then suddenly, Kendra winced. As if not aware of what she was doing, she put her hands up to her breasts. On her forehead was a swift spasm of pain. Her breasts, healthily full of milk the baby would never need, had begun to hurt.

Serena spoke. "I know what to do, Mrs. Shields. Come with me."

"I'll help you," said Mrs. Chase. In her bustling fashion she put the untouched cup of cocoa on the table and hurried back to Kendra, glad to have something, anything, to do.

As she opened the door to the hall the doctor said heartily, "I'll be with you in a minute, ladies."

Kendra and Serena and Mrs. Chase went out. Ralph stood awkwardly where he was. Dr. Rollins spoke to Marny and Pocket and Hiram.

"You folks had better leave now, I expect. It's going to be dark before long and you haven't brought any lanterns. I'll give Mrs. Shields a dose to make her sleep. She's got to get some rest. She's going to have a hard time the next few days. Maybe it would do her good if you came back to-morrow. Yes, I think it would do her good.'

"Tell her," said Hiram, "we'll be back in the morning."

"I'll tell her," said the doctor. "And now, I'll go help her out with what's got to be done. You folks run along. There's nothing you can do."

"Here's your shawl, Marny," said Pocket.

They went out. They had never felt so helpless in their lives.

They came back the next day, and the next. On the second day, which was New Year's Eve, Mr. Chase and Mr. Fenway were there too. With them was the pastor of the Baptist Church, built last summer higher up the hill on Washington Street, and a man from the new Green Oak cemetery north of town. While Dr. Rollins sat with Loren, making sure he would not know what was going on, the pastor said a prayer over the baby's little body and gave Kendra such comfort as he could. Then the man from the cemetery took the body away.

Kendra endured it all somehow. When they praised her courage she said only, "This is something I've got to do." Mr. Chase and Mr. Fenway went back to the store. But Marny and Pocket and Hiram sat in the parlor for the rest of the day, knowing their presence was in some way a help, though they could not have told just how.

That night there was a howling torrent of rain. But the next morning, New Year's Day, there was a strong wind and the sky cleared. The streets, however, were streaks of black slush, and when Hiram and Pocket came by the store, shivering and mud-spattered, they told Marny she should not try to climb the hill.

While she waited for them Marny had been playing solitaire. She was alone in the stockroom, for the boys had demanded a holiday and the store was closed. Gathering up her cards, she spoke with resolution. Certainly she could climb the hill. As long as Kendra needed her she would be there.

She told them Norman had come in earlier, and if Norman could get through the streets so could she. Norman had been in a jubilant mood. The steamer *Oregon* had sailed for the Isthmus at eight o'clock this morning, carrying sixty-two thousand ounces of gold and two hundred and eighty passengers. The vessel was so crowded that the passengers had staked out sleeping room anywhere they could find it, including several spaces they had chalked on the dining table. This did not concern Norman. What did concern him and made his heart rejoice was that so many of these passengers had bought their tickets at high prices from his and Marny's collection.

"If they could get to the steamer, half of them in that storm last night," said Marny, "I can get to Kendra's house. Besides, boys, I've been looking out of the window. I've seen quite a few dandies, all dressed up, setting out to make New Year's calls. If they can get around, so can I."

They saw that she had her high mud-boots ready beside her. Hiram said,

"You'll ruin your dress."

Marny retorted, "It's Kendra's dress."

Hiram looked helplessly at Pocket.

"It's no use," Pocket said to him. "Come on, Marny."

They started out, stepping cautiously on the rickety sidewalks. In spite of her care, several times Marny did go knee-deep into the mud, and by the time they reached Kendra's house Hiram's prediction was fulfilled: her skirt was drabbled and spattered, and torn by the rough edges of the planks beyond much hope of repair. Mrs. Chase met them at the door.

She told them their vigil was ended. Loren had died shortly before dawn, while the storm was still raging.

"And Kendra?" they all three asked together.

Mrs. Chase said that for Kendra, Nature had mercifully reasserted itself. Kendra had been up all night. When Loren died, Mr. and Mrs. Chase had been at home asleep, but this morning as soon as the storm ceased Ralph had come to tell them. They had come here at once. Ralph and Mr. Chase had folded up the cot that had been placed for Kendra at the foot of Loren's bed, and had set it up again in the parlor. Here, Kendra had simply fallen upon it. In hardly more than a minute she was lost in sleep, the deep, almost statuelike sleep that follows utter exhaustion of body and spirit.

"And she did what she tried to do?" asked Marny. "Loren never knew about the baby?"

Mrs. Chase gave them a smile that was proud and tender. "He never knew."

"Thank God," Pocket said softly, and Hiram said, "Amen."

Marny had a sense of relief. She ought to feel sorrow, she was thinking, at the death of so fine a man as Loren, but just now she only felt glad that this much of Kendra's ordeal was over.

Mrs. Chase was telling them that Mr. Chase had gone to see the pastor, to make arrangements for the funeral. "When they decide on the time," she said to Pocket, "you can post a notice on the wall of the reading room in the library."

Pocket said he would.

"And tell Kendra," said Marny, "if there's anything she wants me to do she can send word by Ralph, and I'll do it."

Mrs. Chase nodded. "You're a real sweet girl, Marny," she acknowledged.

They went back down the hill. As they reached the plaza Marny spoke eagerly. "Boys, I know you have a lot to do, to make up for all this lost time. But would you walk a few steps on Kearney Street with me so I can see how we're getting on with the Calico Palace?"

They would and they did. The new Calico Palace was growing apace. The last time Marny had stood here looking at it had been Saturday morning; now it was Tuesday, and in those few days how much had been done! The carpenters were at work. New Year's Day might be a holiday, but these ambitious Chinese did not care. It was not their New Year, and Yankee customs were less important to them than Yankee wages.

Kearney Street was all agog with recovery. The El Dorado was going up, the foundation was laid for the new Parker House. Denison's Exchange was nearly done. Tarpaper and toothpicks it might be, but at this rate Mr. Denison would be back in business long before the contractor's allotted sixteen days.

Marny gave a joyful sigh. When the old Calico Palace had burnt up she had felt as if a part of herself had died. Now, watching the new Calico Palace going up, she felt as if a new part of herself was being born.

She caught sight of Dwight Carson striding toward them over the planks that the carpenters had laid in the mud. When he reached them they told him about Loren's death. Dwight was genuinely sorry. What a pity, he said. A man

399

of rare worth, with everything to live for. He would certainly attend the funeral.

"Mighty good of you fellows," he said to Pocket and Hiram, "to bring Marny here. I suppose she'll want to see everything, won't you, Marny? I'll show her around. You boys needn't wait. I know you've got your own business to attend to."

Hiram and Pocket took the hint and went on their way. Dwight put a hand on Marny's elbow.

"Be careful of the mud, Marny. I'll show you the safe places."

"Since the mud has already wrecked my dress," said Marny, "a little more damage won't matter. I want to see *everything*."

He showed her. His enthusiasm was like sun and warmth after the heartrending days just behind her. How *nice* he was, she thought; how—what the Mexicans called *simpatico*. There was no real translation for *simpatico*. It was just a word to describe a person you liked.

By the time he had shown her all the work done on the Calico Palace, his watch said it was past two o'clock and Dwight said he was famished. He told her Delmonico's, saved from the fire, was serving first-class meals again, and wouldn't she go there with him? Marny was hungry too, but she hesitated. A woman in a restaurant was such a novelty, would she be given enough peace and quiet to eat a meal? And even more important, her skirt was torn and wet and bedraggled with mud, and she wasn't fit to be seen.

Dwight serenely answered her objections. He would see to it that she had peace and quiet. As for her dress, she would be sitting at table, nobody would see the mud spatters on her skirt, and from the waist up she was as neat as she always was, and as pleasant to look at.

This was not quite true. Marny glanced down at her sleeve, where a splash of mud had struck when a cart jogged past her. But the fact was, every man in the restaurant would be muddy because today it was impossible not to be, and it had been a long time since she had had a good dinner. She consented, and they walked along Kearny Street to Delmonico's.

Her entrance did cause a stir, and the twenty or thirty men present gave her a noisy welcome, but Dwight sat beside her with an air of proud challenge, and not one of them gave

400

her so much as a nudge of the elbow. The stewards brought her the best meal she had had since Kendra's holiday feast. The roast beef was really good, and with it were some rare treats just off a schooner from Honolulu—yams and slices of pumpkin, and for dessert bananas, and coconuts brought to the table and cracked there, so diners could have the meat fresh from the shell.

Dwight walked with her to the store. By the time they got there neither of them had any doubt that Marny would soon be sharing the luxury of those two rooms at the Gresham Hotel.

She let herself into the stockroom with the key Mr. Fenway had given her, and Dwight went back to supervise the work on the Calico Palace. Locking the door behind her, Marny sat down on a box to take off her boots so she would not track mud across the floor. As she stood up she heard another door closing, and saw Mr. Chase come out of the room where the safes were.

"Getting some papers of Loren's," he said. "Wanted the address of his brother in the States. Somebody's got to write to the family."

Mr. Chase spoke gruffly. Loren had been his friend, and writing such a letter was a task he did not relish. Marny was surprised that he had troubled himself to tell her why he was here. He seldom spoke to her unless he had to.

To her further surprise, when Mr. Chase had locked the door to the safe-room he came directly toward her. Standing awkwardly before her, he cleared his thoat as if he wanted to say something and was not sure how to go about it. He caught sight of the boots and used these for an opening.

"Say, that's mighty tidy of you," he said, "taking off your boots just inside the door. The trouble Fenway and I have with most folks! Why, those boys would have the place knee-deep in mud if we didn't keep after them."

She smiled at him. "I don't like a muddy floor any more than you do, Mr. Chase. So I try not to bring the mud inside."

Mr. Chase cleared his throat again. "You've got your good qualities, Marny," he blurted, as if embarrassed to say so. "You've got your faults, I'll admit that, but you've got your good qualities too."

Marny was so startled she was almost stricken dumb. In his mind, she knew, there were two kinds of women, the chaste and the unchaste, and the unchaste were bad women and that was the end of it. She was a professional card player who made no secret of her love affairs, and for him to admit that she had good qualities—this was something the like of which she was sure he had never done before. She could only say,

"Why, thank you, Mr. Chase."

Standing there, stocky and shy, he reminded her of a little boy about to confess a fault. He said,

"My wife—she's been telling me—how you stood by Kendra in her trouble. Now that was kind of you."

—Good heavens, thought Marny, this is really costing him an effort.

It was such a concession on his part that she wished she could do something for him in return. As she thought of this she had an inspiration. She held out her hand.

"Mr. Chase, I haven't been able to give much help. But now—you and Mrs. Chase have done so much, maybe there is something I can do to help you. Would you like to give me the address of Loren's brother? I can write the letter to him, you know."

Mr. Chase caught his breath in a gasp of gratitude. Not only was this a hard letter to write, but writing letters of any sort was not one of his best accomplishments.

"Would you, Marny? You'll tell him all about the accident, and how much everybody admired Loren, and sort of ease the shock of it all?"

"I'll do my best, Mr. Chase."

With one hand Mr. Chase stroked his chin, with the other he gave her the papers. He spoke gravely.

"Marny, I just want to say this one thing. You've got your faults, but you've got a heart of gold."

He turned around and walked off, to the side door. As he opened it he said over his shoulder,

"Well, goodby, Marny, I'll see you later. And I say again, you've got a heart of gold."

He went out.

The corner where Marny stood was dim. She hoped Mr. Chase had not seen that her lips were trembling with mirth.

Didn't Mr. Chase know he was uttering the oldest of trite old sayings? The bad woman with a heart of gold—what sentimental goose had first said that? In Athens? Egypt? Somebody had probably said it in the shadow of the pyramids, long before Rahab had given shelter to the spies of Israel.

Didn't Mr. Chase know that? No, he didn't know it. With sincere and earnest surprise, he had told her she had a heart of gold.

After the tension of the past few days Marny needed release and here it was. As she heard Mr. Chase turn the key in the lock outside she burst out laughing, and she laughed till she hurt.

52

Kendra never had any clear recollection of the next few weeks. She knew she walked around, she washed and dressed and combed her hair and tried to eat the food they brought her. But she was hardly aware of what she was doing. She was hardly aware of anything but her own heartbreak.

She knew people were being good to her. Ralph and Serena were loyal. Her other friends came to see her as often as they could. This was not very often, for the winter went on with wind and rain and torrents of mud, and sometimes for days together the streets were really dangerous. Pocket dropped in more frequently than the rest of them, because he now lived in the building that housed the library and so had only a few steps to walk. He was gentle and kind, and brought her the newspapers, but Kendra could not bestir herself to read them.

Whenever the street was passable Marny walked up the hill with Dwight, and had him wait for her at the library while she visited Kendra. Marny said she had sent word of the deaths of Loren and the baby to Loren's brother, Clifford Shields, who lived in Boston. Now she offered to write to Eva. Kendra gave her the address at Hampton Roads, and was grateful. She could not have written the letter herself, not yet.

Serena told her one day that Ralph had said Marny was no

longer staying in Mr. Fenway's room over the store. She had moved into the Gresham Hotel with Mr. Dwight Carson. Serena spoke in a voice of regret. "Oh dear," she said, "really, I thought she was trying to lead a better life."

Kendra murmured, "Marny has been very kind to me, Serena."

This was all she said. She was not able to take much interest in what Marny did. Or anything else. As Marny had foreseen, she had drawn on her reserves until now she was as limp as an empty sack.

She was not even much interested when Marny told her the new Calico Palace had opened. She thought—Some day I suppose I'll go to look at it. But she was still too numb to think of it more than this.

She received about forty letters. At first she let them pile up on the parlor table, not even alert enough to break the seals. But at length Marny said to her, "Why don't you open them, Kendra? Isn't it some comfort to know all these people care enough to write to you?"

So Kendra opened the letters, and received a surprise that was almost a shock.

Nine or ten of them were the sort she had expected, from acquaintances who sent their sympathy. One of these came from Dwight Carson, one from Hiram's partner, Mr. Eustis. Another came from Reginald Norrington, the squatty little agent from whom Loren had rented the house. There was even an awkwardly scrawled note that said, "Dear madam, I feel so sorry for you. I still remember what a good dinner you fixed for us the day we got here. Yours with love, Rosabel."

But most of the letters were not messages of sympathy at all. They were proposals of marriage.

Among these were a few scribbles from clumsy louts like the fellow who had wanted to marry her after she parted with Ted. But the rest were written by men of obvious education, who formally and respectfully begged permission to call and repeat their offers in person.

Kendra had heard it said that with San Francisco's huge oversupply of men, no widow here was likely to stay a widow long. But she had not dreamed that men of culture and worldly wisdom would try to marry a woman they had never even spoken to. Certainly she had not thought any man at all would suggest a new marriage so soon after her husband's

404

death. Marny too was surprised. Not even Marny had known how many men in California were reduced to such desperation as this.

Kendra thought later that it was the fact of these absurd and somehow pathetic offers that had first roused her to reach beyond her own despair. As she read one after another, she exclaimed to herself—How *lonely* people are!

She was lonely too. She felt more alone than she had ever felt. —But at least, she thought as she read the letters, these men are trying to do something about it. And so can I.

Like them, at least she could try. She was not going to sit here forever, enclosed in a shell of pain. She was going to look out of the shell. She had to do it, and she had to do it herself because nobody could do it for her.

She began getting exercise again by wrapping up against the rain and walking on the porch. In the rare breaks of sunshine she went outside. The next time Marny came to see her Kendra said, "Tell me what's going on in town."

"Good!" said Marny. "You're waking up."

"Yes," said Kendra. "I'm waking up."

Marny looked her over. They sat in the parlor drinking hot tea while the kettle steamed on the fire and the mist blew past the windows. "You *are* waking up, Kendra," Marny said after a moment. "Your color is coming back. You were white as a candle. And your voice—it's different. It sounds more the way it used to."

Kendra spoke in some perplexity. "My voice? I didn't know it had ever changed."

"You didn't hear yourself, Kendra. That metallic monotone. But you're getting natural again, dear, and I'm glad. Now let's see, what's going on. There's plenty going on."

She talked first about her own main interest, the Calico Palace.

The Calico Palace had been the last of the gambling houses to re-open after the fire. It had been six weeks in the building, an extravagantly long time in San Francisco. But oh, so grand, said Marny. Four stories high, with the finest pictures and the fanciest bars in town. Not very stout or solid—what could you expect in six weeks? But the roof did not let in the rain, and this was luxury enough.

The other gamblers had rushed back into business. The contractor who had promised to finish Denison's Exchange in sixteen days had actually done so in eleven. The "building"

405

now had a loud new band, and a new game called rondo, something like billiards but different. The place even had a new name. The United States Exchange they called it now, a mighty high-sounding title for a place as shaky as a chicken-coop.

Marny said the new El Dorado also had been raised with chicken-coop speed. Not as large as before, though they would probably add to it later. They had simply thrown up some walls and nailed on a roof so they could get back into business. Rents were so outrageous that nobody wanted to waste much time on building. Get something up, anything, get inside it and make money, this was the idea.

But Marny said she and Norman had not wasted time. As soon as the Calico Palace was well under way, Norman had rented a table in the public gambling room of the Gresham House, where he dealt cards every evening. As for herself, Marny said she had taken a private gambling room—or rather, a space curtained off by cotton blankets—also in the Gresham Hotel. Here she had dealt for a select group of gentlemen who used to patronize her parlor, while one of the Blackbeards stood guard and kept out the rabble.

But now they were all back at the Calico Palace. And business was great.

Marny drew a deep warm breath like a contented cat. Kendra, remembering what Serena had told her, felt herself smiling a little. She asked,

"Marny, are you having an affair?"

"Why yes, dear. Do you mind?"

"I don't think it's any of my business," said Kendra.

"Thank you. It isn't, of course, but I like you for saying so. Look." Marny reached inside her dress and brought out a little bundle wrapped in a handkerchief. She held it out.

Kendra looked inside, and caught her breath. The handkerchief held a necklace made of a gold chain with a pendant of two pink pearls and a black one. "How beautiful!" Kendra gasped.

Marny smiled. "Pearls from that diving place in Mexico—La Paz," she said. "Chain of California gold. Dwight had it made for me. I wear it every evening."

"Good heavens, Marny! Isn't that an invitation to thievery?"

"Yes, but we have iron shutters, and I always put this in the safe when we lock up. Dwight wants me to wear it."

She took back the precious little package, hid it inside her dress again, and went on.

"Oh, Dwight's a fine fellow, Kendra. And the new Calico Palace—we're so proud of it!"

"So everybody's happy?"

With a bit of a shrug, Marny shook her head. "Not everybody. Rosabel is not speaking to Norman. They've had a tiff."

"About what?"

"Oh dear, I don't know. I suppose the same old story, she wants to get married and he doesn't. I hope they make it up. I don't care which way, but I don't want Rosabel going off to the El Dorado or the Verandah. She brings in a lot of trade." Marny glanced at the clock. "Time I was getting into my mud-boots. Dwight will be here any minute."

Kendra had an idea. "I'd like to see all those new buildings around the plaza. May I walk down the hill with you?"

"Of course!" Marny answered with enthusiasm. "It'll be fine for you to go out and look around. Dwight will see you home—I'll have to set up my card table. Get your boots."

Kendra stood up. "You're good, Marny," she said, "to help me get my mind off myself."

"*You're* good, my dear, to want to get your mind off yourself. Some people must love trouble, they cling to it so, but you don't. Put on a warm shawl, Kendra, the fog's heavy today."

Kendra was surprised at how much more alive she felt after she had seen the plaza. The fire was only two months past, but today a stranger could hardly have told that there had been a fire at all. Everything in the burnt area had been replaced by something creaky-new. True, most of these structures did fit Dwight's description, tarpaper and toothpicks. Many were not even buildings, but cloth houses of canvas tacked over wooden frames. Some were nothing but tents with floors. But all of them—stores, restaurants, saloons, lodging houses, gambling casinos, Blossom's flower garden and its rivals—all were alive with business.

The sidewalks were full of people. In the roads wagons rattled and drivers yelled, in the plaza auctioneers bellowed their wares. Kendra did not go inside the Calico Palace. But she saw it, tall and tempting, windows bright through the fog, the transparencies with their promised delights beckoning men from the street.

The plaza had come to life again, full of mud and rats and

vigor and gold, crude, bawdy, and splendid. Kendra felt braced by merely being in the midst of so much energy. She envied these folk of the plaza. They had no pretenses. They knew what they wanted and they meant to get it. She wished she could be as sure as they were.

But later, as she looked back, it seemed to Kendra that all this time she had known exactly what she wanted. —How strange it is, she thought, and yet how logical, that we get what we *really* want in this world. And oh, how we pay for it!

She had not wanted what Loren had given her. She had wanted the plaza and the Calico Palace.

So now, three months after the deaths of Loren and the baby, here she was. In the Calico Palace, in the racket of Kearny Street. And she had paid a dreadful price.

She tried not to inflict her pain on other people. They could not ease it. Nothing but time could help her, and even with the merciful blurring of time she knew her wound would never quite heal. Nobody could give her the promise Pocket had given her at Shiny Gulch, that after a while she would reach a point where she did not care. This was not that sort of wound. To the end of her life there would be moments when the scar would hurt. —If my son had lived he would be five years old now, ten years old, twenty. I wonder how he would look? What he would be doing?

This would never go away. This was the price she had paid to come down to the plaza.

Mr. and Mrs. Chase had offered her a home, but she had declined. She let them think this was because she was too proud to accept, and preferred to earn her own living; and while they did not approve of the Calico Palace they admired what they thought was her courage in accepting a harsh necessity. But this was not her real reason.

It was true that Loren had not left much money. He had spent all he earned to give her the safety and sheltering she had not wanted. It had not occurred to him that he ought to be provident. Young and vigorous, he had never had a serious illness in his life. He had earned a good income and he had had every prospect of increasing it. He had loved Kendra and his greatest pleasure had been to give her everything he thought she wanted. Loren had left no debts, but he had left little else.

Kendra found this out when a boy brought her a letter

408

from Reginald Norrington, telling her the rent was overdue. Mr. Norrington's letter was obsequious. He said he had not troubled her sooner because of his respect for her grief. But this was March, the third month since her husband's demise. ("Demise" was the word used by Mr. Norrington.) He said if he had owned the property himself he would not be addressing her now. But she must realize he was not free, he had a duty to his client, the owner of the house she lived in. And so on, and on.

He sounded *greasy*, Kendra thought. She did owe the rent and she was ashamed that she had let it slip her mind; a reminder two lines long would have been enough. The day she received the letter she walked down the hill with Ralph. First she went to the store. Mr. Chase opened Loren's safe and gave a start of dismay when he learned the smallness of its contents. He told her to go to the bank of Eustis and Boyd. Maybe Loren had kept his money there.

Loren had not. He had not kept his money at all. He had poured it out with loving extravagance on the expensive house and the fine furniture, the plank sidewalk, the summer's water wagon and the winter's loads of firewood, on the best food and clothes to be bought in town, on a salary to Ralph and Serena to give her protection and relieve her of work. There was not much left.

Mr. Chase at the store, Hiram at the bank, urged her to accept aid. Hiram offered her a loan for as long as she wanted it, at no interest. Kendra said no.

She did not add that today's discovery had given her a sense of release. The neat little white house had never seemed to her like anything but a cage. Now she was free of it. She thought of the cheese rolls and cupcakes she had made when the Calico Palace was a tent in the mud. She could do this again and this was what she wanted to do.

She sent Ralph to Mr. Norrington's office with rent to the end of the month and a note saying she could not afford to keep the house longer than this. When she told Ralph and Serena they said this was quite all right. Serena was expecting her long wanted baby, and wouldn't have time to keep on working for Kendra anyway. They would find another place to live.

The very next day, Kendra received a second letter from Mr. Norrington. This one was even longer than the first, and more larded with apologies. Mr. Norrington had reported

409

matters to the owner of the property. The owner had been indignant that Mr. Norrington had troubled her at all. He had said if she could not pay the rent, she was welcome to live in the house as long as she pleased, rent free. He would consider it an honor to be allowed to give a home to the gracious lady.

As she read this letter, Kendra wrinkled her nose and said "Phew," as if there were a bad smell in the room. A whole house to herself, in swarming San Francisco—the man might as well have offered her a lump of gold as big as a pumpkin. And she had learned enough to know that you were not likely to get anything free in this world. This proposal was not like those she had received just after Loren died. Those strangers were at least offering her marriage. This one was simply offering her a high price for her favors.

She thought of Marny, and Marny's nugget necklace, and Marny's chain with the pendant of two pink pearls and a black one. Marny had her affairs, and Kendra did not care. She really did not. Marny's affairs were her own business. But herself, no. Even if she had not wanted to go back to the Calico Palace she would not have wanted to stay here on these terms. Maybe she was not consistent, maybe she was foolish. But this was the way she was.

She sent Ralph down the hill with a note to Marny, asking, "Do you want me back?"

Ralph brought her a speedy answer. "Yes. Yes. Yes. Yes. Yes. Yes. Yes. Hurry up. Marny."

Kendra sent a cool note to Mr. Norrington, declining to accept the owner's bounty. She sent most of her furniture to Chase and Fenway's to be sold for whatever it would bring. In its place she bought an iron cot, six feet long and twenty-seven inches wide, and tin boxes to keep her soap and candles from the rats. But she kept her excellent kitchen equipment, and with this and her personal belongings she went to the Calico Palace.

Up on the top floor, the Blackbeards moved some cases of liquor out of a closet ten feet by six, and told her this would be her bedroom. They set up a kitchen behind Marny's parlor on the second floor, next to a storeroom piled with firewood. Marny and Norman welcomed her with delight. Besides the cakes and rolls to be sold to the customers, Kendra promised to cook dinner for them, and for Dwight Carson when he was around. Lulu and Lolo would prepare meals for the

Blackbeards in a kitchen of their own, downstairs on the first floor.

Dwight still retained his two rooms at the Gresham Hotel. But he spent much of his leisure at the Calico Palace, because Marny had to live here if she was to be at her table in all weathers. Every evening she wore the chain with the pendant of two pink pearls and a black one.

Kendra did not have the comfort of her days on Washington Street. But she had a sense of being free, of being herself. She remembered how frightened she had been when she had made her cakes before, the loneliness and terror that had pushed her into that mistaken marriage. She had learned a lot since those days. She did not know, any more than she had known then, what lay ahead of her, but she did know now that she could face it.

She continued to get letters proposing marriage. The writers told her how many town lots they owned, how much gold they had piled up. Several of them sent her gifts, to prove how well they could afford to keep her. Kendra tore up the letters and sent back the gifts. She was not interested in getting married. The house she had lived in was quickly and expensively rented to two families who divided it between them and were glad to have so much space. Kendra, living between her kitchen and her bedroom ten feet by six, did not envy them. She was content to be where she was.

She rarely went into Marny's parlor. But she was part of the Calico Palace and she liked it. She liked the merriment around her, and she liked being in the middle of what was going on. San Francisco now had three newspapers and Kendra read them, but often she had heard the news before she read it. She heard it behind the scenes, from the bartenders, the croupiers, the dealers, from Marny and Norman and Dwight.

There was plenty of news. Now in the spring of 1850 San Francisco looked like a big city and was acting like one. Fantastic, Kendra and Marny said to each other, that this surging metropolis was the same sleepy village they had left when they went up to Shiny Gulch only two years ago.

It was the same place, but how different! People were pouring in from every nook and cranny of the earth. River steamers ran on schedule to carry these people between San Francisco and the mining camps. Those who stayed in town had dumped so many hills into the bay that there was no longer any such thing as the moon-shaped cove Kendra had seen from the deck of the *Cynthia*. Vessels that had been drawn close to shore for business were now grotesquely surrounded by land, with landsmen's buildings beside them. Men newly arrived were startled when they heard that Montgomery Street had once lain along the edge of the sea.

But farther out, the clutter in the bay continued to spread. Most of the captains who brought their vessels through the Golden Gate still did not get them out.

While nobody knew how many people lived here, anybody could see that San Francisco had the ways of a big city. If you had letters to mail you no longer had to climb the Clay Street hill to the post office; you simply dropped your letters into corner mailboxes. If you wanted fresh milk you could buy it from a cart that made rounds every day. The markets offered you abundant fresh produce, brought down by the river boats. At the more elegant saloons the barmen gave you a free lunch with your drinks, and the saloon-keepers vied with each other in the dainties they spread. The town now had a real theater, where you could see performances every evening. Or if you had lustier tastes, you could go to the exhibit called Model Artists. Here you would see girls posed in "living pictures," one of which was advertised as "Eve in the Garden of Eden."

The stores had luxuries gathered from the whole world. If you were literary you could buy books in many languages; if you were musical you could have a piano or a violin or a flute, and take lessons from one of the French or German teachers whose cards appeared in the papers every day. If you had gold dust enough to pay for them you could wear clothes as excellent as any you could have worn in Paris or New York; you could buy watches and jewelry, fine wines and perfumes, and toilet soap brought around the Horn from France. The bath-houses did a flourishing business. A great proportion of San Francisco's people came from backgrounds where they had been used to regular washing, and they kept up the custom here, though they knew they could not long stay clean.

For though San Francisco was a big city it was not like any other big city on earth. In the daytime you saw (and smelled) the endless rats fighting over the endless garbage in the street; if you walked in the street at night you felt the rats scampering around your ankles. Sometimes you stepped on one in

412

the dark and heard him squeal. All the streets were dark; there were still no lights. If you were out after nightfall and had no lantern, you hired one of the boys called "street pilots." These boys waited around the doors of saloons and gambling houses, and for a fee they would light you home.

If you borrowed money you still paid interest of ten to fifteen per cent a month. In the papers, among the advertisements of champagne and gorgeous raiment you saw just as many offers of Colt revolvers, without which few men cared to go out of doors.

But a grand town it was, dirty and dangerous and exciting and gloriously rich. On the first of May the steamer *Panama* puffed out by the Golden Gate, bound for the Isthmus. She carried a hundred and fifty passengers and ninety-three thousand ounces of gold. Kendra and Marny stood at an upper window and watched her go. When she was out of sight they went downstairs, each to her own department in the Calico Palace.

Three days later the Calico Palace was gone. On the fourth of May, 1850, Kearny Street burst into flames again, and all the blustering glory around the plaza turned again into a pile of ashes.

53

This new fire was like the fire of Christmas Eve, but more destructive because this time there was vastly more to be destroyed. The firebells clanged over the plaza an hour before daybreak. Startled from sleep, Kendra saw the terrifying light as it flared beyond her window, and with a cry she sprang out of bed. Shaking with fright, she threw on the quilted Chinese satin robe Marny had given her, grabbed her shoes, and opened the door.

Before the safes she saw Marny and Norman and Rosabel, wearing whatever had been handiest to snatch up. Dwight, who had been spending the night with Marny, stood at her side, ready to rescue whatever he could carry. As Kendra came out of her room Marny was giving him a poke of coins. Dangling between her fingers was the chain with the pendant of three pearls. At the same moment Norman sprang to his feet and thrust a poke into Kendra's hand. "Wrap this in something," he said sharply, and to everybody in general he shouted, "Have you got your guns? Then get *out!*"

They got out. As Norman unlocked the front door, Dwight called to the three girls to come with him and take shelter in his rooms at the Gresham Hotel. Carrying their guns and gold, they fought their way past the roaring fury. The fragile buildings cracked and toppled. The Calico Palace, strongest building on the plaza, had no distinction tonight except that it made the loudest noise when it fell in.

Their clothes were scorched and their hair singed as the fiery flakes blew around them. With every step they quaked with fear lest the flames catch the hotel, but at least they were spared this. The fire-fighters, with axes and gunpowder, broke the fire before it went so far. When they reached his rooms, Dwight told the girls to lock themselves in and have their guns ready, while he went to help keep back the fire.

Dwight's two rooms were each eight by ten feet, spacious for San Francisco. One was a bedroom, the other was furnished with a couch, a bookcase, a chair, and a drawing table. Between the rooms Dwight had left a narrow hallway, which he used as a closet for his clothes and other possessions. They knew they were lucky to have such a haven. But they knew also how much they had lost. Rosabel crumpled up in a corner and cried helplessly. Marny let her own poke of gold fall on the floor, and stood looking down at it, despair on her soot-smudged face. Kendra went to her and put a hand on her shoulder. Marny turned with a bleak smile.

"Maybe I should have stayed home and married a college professor," she said. "Think of all the thrills I'd be having now, pouring tea for the faculty wives."

Kendra gave Marny's shoulder an understanding squeeze. No matter how much this new defeat hurt her, Marny would raise the Calico Palace again.

By eleven o'clock in the morning most of the fire had been put out, though from the windows they could see smoke clouds hovering over the ruins, and here and there little flames still fluttering in piles of red embers. About noon Dwight came in, bringing a lunch of cold greasy beef and cold greasy potatoes. With a sad grin he said he knew the stuff was not fit to eat, but it was all he could get, and he had brought some good wine to help. As the girls had had nothing to eat since yesterday, they washed down the food with wine and thanks while Dwight told them about the destruction.

The fire had devoured the richest blocks in town, from Dupont Street to Montgomery. All the gambling palaces around the plaza were gone. So were Blossom's flower garden and the most sumptuous of its rivals. And not only these, but banks and hotels and stores and warehouses, and merchandise worth millions of dollars. The fire had been halted before it reached Chase and Fenway's, but the *Alta California* building was gone and so was Hiram's bank. Pocket's library had barely escaped, with a side wall of the building badly scorched. There had been no tally yet, said Dwight, of the persons who had been killed or hurt in the fire.

When they had finished lunch, while Dwight and Marny talked about their own plans, Kendra went to a window. As she looked over the stretch of smoke and rubble she felt sick.

She felt sicker still when Marny told her more of the news Dwight had brought. He went out, and Rosabel, who had drunk rather more of the wine than was strictly necessary to wash down the beef, curled up on the couch and fell asleep. Marny and Kendra sat by the table and talked.

Yes, said Marny, this fire had been like the first fire, but worse. And there was another hideous difference.

The Christmas fire had been a tragic accident. But this fire of May was no accident at all. Somebody had started it on purpose. Some fellow who had been lucky at looting last time and wanted to do it again. Or maybe one who had not been lucky last time and thought he might do better if he gave himself a second chance.

There was no question about it. Walking around San Francisco right now was a man gloating over the horror he had caused.

"Or maybe two or three men," said Marny. "Buddies. One to look out, one to pile the tinder, one to strike the match—"

"Oh, stop!" cried Kendra. "I don't believe it."

She stood up. She was still wearing the Chinese robe of quilted satin, scorched and dirty now. Marny's robe of brown wool was equally scorched and dirty. Neither of them had anything else to wear. Clothes, though, were trivial. Kendra had lost little in this fire because she had little to lose. But

415

she thought of Marny's Calico Palace, of Hiram's bank, of all the other property turned to ashes, of death and torture in the flames. She thought of what that other fire had cost herself, and she thought of the people whose lives had been blasted last night as her own life had been blasted last winter.

Such anguish was bitter enough when you knew it was nobody's fault, when everybody around you wanted to help. But for any human being to be so empty of humanity as to cause this with deliberate hands—she wanted to cry out that such a thing could not happen.

She walked to the end of the room. Rosabel, sound asleep on the couch, drew a deep easy breath. Kendra walked back and stood in front of Marny.

"I don't believe it," she said again. "Marny, people *can't* be that wicked!"

"Oh yes they can," Marny snapped back. "It's been tried before. Didn't you know that?"

No, Kendra had not known it. Marny was surprised. The whole story had been published in the papers. But this had been shortly after the first fire, at a time when Kendra had been too numb to read a paper or to remember any news she might have heard. In a voice harsh with anger Marny told her what had taken place.

About four o'clock on a Januray morning the customhouse watchman, making his regular round, had caught sight of smoke coming through a window of an unfinished house near by. He had sounded an alarm, and men living in the neighborhood had rushed out to join him in putting out the fire.

It was plain to them all, said Marny, that the fire had been set. Scattered over the floor of the half-built house had been a lot of chips and shavings left by the carpenters when they quit work the day before. The arsonist had pushed these chips and shavings into a pile, under an opening made for a window but not yet glassed in. He had put a match to the pile and slunk off to wait.

But by good fortune a drizzle had begun. The drops blowing in through the window had not been enough to quench the fire, but the shavings were dampened so that they smoldered and smoked instead of burning, and the watchman saw the smoke in time to give the alarm. There had been no damage to speak of, only a plank or two scorched. But the fact was there. Some scoundrel had tried to repeat the Christmas holocaust.

The same thing, said Marny, had happened last night. This time the arsonist had chosen his location more carefully. He had set the fire in the "building" called the United States Exchange, the one that had been run up in eleven days so Mr. Denison could hurry back into business. After closing time, two faro dealers had heard a noise and smelled smoke. Investigating, they had found a pile of flammable stuff—including some rags soaked in oil—burning under an open window. They had shouted an alarm, but nobody could stop this fire. There was no drizzle last night. With its wafer-thin walls and its room dividers of cotton blankets, the place had burned like kindling. The buildings on either side, not much more sturdy than the Exchange itself, were sizzling within a minute or two after the men had given the first alarm.

Like Kendra, Marny stood up and went to the window and looked over the ruins.

"If I knew who did it," she said, "I'd like to kill him."

Kendra, sitting in the chair by Dwight's drawing table, shrugged wearily. "What good would that do?"

"At least he couldn't burn up the Calico Palace again."

"Somebody else could," said Kendra, with a cynicism she had never felt before. "If one man is so evil there can be more."

"Well, a good shooting would ease my temper," Marny retorted. "And right now that would be reason enough."

For the next few weeks they lived in the Gresham Hotel. Marny shared Dwight's room, while in the other room Rosabel slept on the couch and Kendra on a mattress bought from Chase and Fenway's and laid in the middle of the floor. They were not comfortable, but they were less uncomfortable than most people in town, and they were thankful.

Hiram and Pocket came up the day after the fire. Hiram consulted with Dwight about a new building for the bank, and both he and Pocket offered the girls their services.

Hiram, who had been living over the bank, was now sharing Pocket's quarters in the library. In spite of the loss of the bank building Hiram was cheerful. He said he and his partner Eustis had rescued the safes, with most of their coins and dust and valuable papers. Now all they needed was a shelter for their business. Maybe it was too much to ask that the shelter be fireproof.

"It's not too much to ask," said Dwight. His voice was

417

stern with resolution. "There *are* such things as fireproof buildings. I'm going to build them. But not," he added fiercely, "in eleven days."

Hiram grinned. He admired such forcefulness. "Nobody asked you to," he said.

Taking lists of what the girls needed, Hiram and Pocket went off to Chase and Fenway's. Before long they came back laden with packages. Later the same day Mr. Fenway called. He told Rosabel the store had just received three fine new pianos, and he would be happy to have her come in any time it suited her, to try them and choose one for the Calico Palace. Rosabel said she would love to try the pianos as soon as she had a dress to wear, and while she was sewing on the dress would Mr. Fenway *please* make sure the pianos were in tune. Mr. Fenway solemnly promised to do so.

Kendra asked him to take a note to Serena Watson, asking if Serena would do some dressmaking. The next morning Serena came in to say she would be glad to have the work. A little extra money was always handy. (Serena was joyfully pregnant, but she was too kind to say she did not have to spend her time making baby clothes because Kendra had given her the clothes her own baby had left when he died.)

Almost shyly, Dwight asked Kendra if she would prepare meals for the four of them. He said her cooking, which he had sampled at the Calico Palace, had spoilt him for the meals served in the restaurants. He would gladly pay her whatever she asked.

"Don't be silly," Kendra exclaimed. "Of course I'll cook if you'll set up a kitchen. As for pay—aren't you giving me a place to live?"

But Marny told her privately, "Please let him pay you a little dust, Kendra. He wouldn't feel right otherwise. Dwight's the proud sort. And right now he's ashamed of himself."

"Ashamed? What for?"

"For the way his buildings went down in the fire. He's going to put up some fireproof buildings if it kills him. When he gets them up he's likely to set the town on fire himself, just to prove they won't burn."

So Kendra accepted a salary of half an ounce a day, which was the usual pay for barmaids. Dwight wanted to give her more, because cooking required more skill than pouring drinks. But he was providing the food, and Kendra said that as he was giving her both board and lodging she would take

418

no more. Dwight laughed, and offered Rosabel a salary to be Kendra's assistant. Rosabel was no expert at cooking, but she said she would like to learn. They managed very well.

For their kitchen, behind the hotel Dwight set up an iron house twelve by sixteen feet. These iron houses were brought out from the States in pieces. The edges were grooved, so that the parts slid together easily, and two men could put up such a house in a day. There was an opening for a stovepipe and others for windows, and Dwight put in panes and shutters. Kendra found it an adequate kitchen, not attractive to rats.

Every morning, before the wind began to blow up the dust, Kendra and Rosabel went out with baskets on their arms and guns at their belts, to buy their dinner. Often they stopped at Chase and Fenway's. While Kendra shopped, Rosabel played one of the new pianos, to the enjoyment of both Mr. Fenway and herself.

Not long after the fire, Kendra received two letters by the steamer mail. One came from Eva at Hampton Roads, the other from Loren's brother Clifford Shields in Boston. Both were written in response to Marny's letters telling about the deaths of Loren and the baby, and both were written to offer Kendra a home.

Eva's letter was graceful and gentle. "I know you are suffering heartbreak, my dear girl. But you are young, and life is still open to you. If you can come to us, you will be welcome. Your friend Miss Randolph did not mention your financial situation, but if there is any problem here, Alex will gladly defray your expenses."

The letter from Clifford Shields had a tone of real affection. He said Loren had written him about his happy marriage, and he was grateful to Kendra for having made it so. "I shall always regard you as my sister," wrote Clifford. "If you can come to Boston, my wife and I will be happy to receive you."

As she read the letters, Kendra shook her head.

—Thank you, she thought, but no. I am not going to accept anybody's kindness. Here with Marny and the Calico Palace, I'm independent and I'm *wanted*.

She declined the offers as graciously as she could, and went on doing the work she liked to do.

Marny too was working. As they had done when the Calico Palace burned for the first time, she and Norman and the Blackbeards had rented space in the hotel for their

419

gambling tables. Norman had taken a bedroom in the hotel, and invited Rosabel to share it, but she thrust out her lip at him and refused. "You'll let me stay with you, won't you?" she asked Kendra. "I'm mad at Norman."

"Of course you can stay with me," Kendra answered. She said no more, but she thought—You poor silly girl, can't you get it out of your head that Norman is going to marry you? He's not going to.

In their free time Norman and Marny conferred with Bruno Gregg about pictures, and bought equipment for the new Calico Palace. Sometimes Kendra went to the auction rooms with them. She enjoyed seeing the mirrors and hangings and fine furniture, and hearing the spiels of the auctioneers, and listening to Blossom and Blossom's colleagues outbidding each other for trappings to embellish their parlor houses.

Dwight spent many hours on his plans for the new building. He moved his drawing table into his bedroom so he would not be disturbed by Kendra and Rosabel. Two small buildings, both banks, though in the heart of the fire, had withstood it.

"That proves," Dwight said vehemently to Marny, "buildings *can* be made fireproof."

Marny was taking a rest from the card table while Kendra and Rosabel prepared dinner. Dwight sat by the drawing table, Marny stood looking out of the window. In the sunset light she saw the burnt-over district. The new buildings were shooting up as fast as before, most of them no better than those that had gone down in the fire. And yet, as Kendra had said, some villain might start another fire; or, careless as men were with their cigars, anybody might start one. In a voice of exasperation Marny exclaimed, "Won't people in San Francisco ever learn?"

"I'm learning," Dwight said tersely.

He pushed his chair back and stood up. Marny knew what he was thinking. The two banks that had survived the fire had been small buildings of brick reinforced with iron. Many people were voicing doubts that a large building, with several floors and many rooms, could be made fireproof.

Dwight said, "Size doesn't mean anything."

"I'm not worried," Marny answered. "You're good at your work, Dwight. I'm not concerned about people who say you can't do it."

" 'You can't do it!' " he echoed. Restlessly he walked to the window and stood by her, looking out. " 'You can't do it!' " he repeated angrily. "Like my father back in New York."

"Oh dear," Marny exclaimed with wry humor. "Was that your trouble? You've never told me about your father."

"You've never asked me," said Dwight.

Marny spoke quietly. "Dwight, I don't ask my friends what they did before I met them. Most people like to talk about themselves. But some don't. So, I don't ask. But I do wonder."

"You don't say anything about wondering," he remarked smiling.

"No, but I wonder about the people who came out from the States before the gold rush. People like you. Those who came here after the gold news got around, they're simple to understand. But those of us who came before then—we all had our own reasons, and they're different reasons with each one of us. Why would Hiram Boyd ship as a sailor to come around the Horn? Why would you leave New York and go to live in Honolulu, out at the end of the world?" She laughed shortly. "You don't have to tell me, Dwight."

"I've just told you," he answered. "Family trouble."

Marny thought of her own family. "Did they nag you and boss you?"

"Not exactly," said Dwight. "But I was the black sheep. We were three brothers. I was the one who was never going to amount to anything. I wouldn't take good advice. My father had a store. A good one, started by his father. He wanted to open some branches. He wanted the three of us to join him. The others were enthusiastic. I wasn't. I wanted to be a builder and I wanted to take my own risks. They couldn't understand why I wanted to try anything so chancy when I could go into the good old family business and be safe."

"Some people like to gamble," said Marny. "Some don't."

He nodded. "And I guess they'll never get together. Anyway, I came out here to the Pacific so I could do what I wanted."

"And not have to listen to any more good advice," she added.

"Exactly," he said. He went on, "I didn't run away and hide. They know where I am. My father writes to me now and then, asking if I haven't had adventures enough and why don't I come back to civilization."

"Do you think you'll ever go back?" she asked.

"Oh, some day," said Dwight. "But not yet."

He turned from the window and looked at her with proud affection.

"First," he said, "I'm going to build a fireproof Calico Palace for you."

"For me," she said softly.

"Yes, Marny dear," he answered. He smiled confidently. "For you."

Marny smiled back at him. Dwight meant what he said. Or at least he thought he did. He thought he was going to build that Calico Palace for her. But she was not the reason. He was going to build it for his father.

—For his father, she thought, and his brothers. He'll not go back to them until he has a fireproof building like a scalp on his belt. Maybe several fireproof buildings. If he can do it in San Francisco he can do it in New York. He'll show them.

—And as soon as he has those scalps on his belt, he'll leave me just where I am, and go back to his father.

—Well, that's all right, she reflected. It's all right, so long as he doesn't know I know it. A man so often complains about a woman. She doesn't understand me. Let him say it. Never, never let him guess you understand him so well.

Dwight cleared the lot for the Calico Palace and laid a foundation of wrought stone from China. He promised Norman and the Blackbeards that they could open the public room as soon as he had finished the first story, and use the small rooms behind it as living quarters. When he had finished the second story Marny could join them and open her parlor.

With the Calico Palace under way, Dwight turned his attention to Hiram's bank. (The name of the bank was still Eustis and Boyd, but Mr. Eustis was a bashful man, excellent at the work he did at his desk in a corner, but so quiet that the customers seldom knew he was there. Hiram's big jovial presence so filled up the place that except on formal documents the treasure house on Montgomery Street had no other name than "Hiram's bank.")

Early in June the first floor of the Calico Palace was ready. Norman moved in, and opened the public room. Rosabel stayed with Kendra and helped her with the cooking.

"Do you like this work?" Kendra asked her. "I mean, do you like it as well as playing the piano?"

"I like playing the piano better than anything," said Rosabel. "But I like cooking too."

422

They were working in their iron kitchen. The fire gave them a welcome warmth, for outdoors the wind was whistling through clouds of chilly June fog. Kendra had put a pork roast into the oven and was now boiling onions, while Rosabel sat by the table peeling potatoes. After a short silence Rosabel said,

"Norman told Marny the Calico Palace was doing fine. Just that one room so far, but it's full all the time."

Kendra said she was glad of this. After another minute or two Rosabel added,

"Norman wants me to come back and play the piano in the public room."

"I'll miss you," said Kendra. "You're a lot of help."

"I hate the public room," said Rosabel. "Getting pinched by every Tom-Dick-and-Harry down from the mines. At least in Marny's parlor they have some manners. I'm not going."

"I don't blame you," Kendra said positively.

"Besides," said Rosabel, "I like learning how to cook. I sure do wish I could cook like you, Kendra."

Kendra stirred the onions. "You're learning. But it does take practice. I'm afraid you won't have much time for cooking when Marny opens her parlor."

Rosabel dropped the paring knife with a clatter. "I'm not going back to Marny's parlor," she announced.

Kendra went to the table. She put her hand on Rosabel's shoulder. "If you want to help me make cakes and rolls," she said, "I'll be glad to teach you."

"I don't want to go back to the Calico Palace at all!" exclaimed Rosabel. Curling an ankle around a leg of her chair, she looked up at Kendra, her eyes wide and dark and appealing under their black velvet eyebrows. "I'm tired of living like that!" she said. "Nothing to count on. Nothing to look forward to. Nobody giving a damn what becomes of me. I want to be married like other people."

Rosabel sounded suddenly so alone and helpless. Kendra felt a rush of sympathy. She stroked Rosabel's puckered forehead. "Rosabel," she said gently, "I'm going to speak the truth, even if it hurts you. You'd better give up hoping for Norman. I don't think he's ever going to marry you."

Rosabel's soft little mouth set in a new hard line. She spoke clearly. "I don't want to marry Norman," she said.

"Oh, I'm glad of that," Kendra answered with relief.

"There are so many others. A pretty girl like you, you'll have all the proposals you want."

"I don't want any more proposals," snapped Rosabel. Forgetting the unpeeled potatoes, she stood up.

"Then what do you want?" Kendra asked in astonishment.

"I want to marry Mr. Fenway," said Rosabel, and she put her head on Kendra's shoulder and began to cry softly.

54

Rosabel reached inside her dress and took out a letter.

"Ralph Watson brought this over today," she said, still with a little choke in her voice. "It's from Mr. Fenway. Read it."

The letter was addressed to Miss Rosabel Fitzgerald. Kendra wondered if this was her real name, and doubted it. Not at all sure what to expect, she began to read.

On expensive paper, the letter was written painstakingly, with many flourishes. It was evidently a letter composed in advance, altered, polished, made as fine as possible, and at last, copied with care.

San Francisco
June 12, 1850

Dear Miss Rosabel,

This epistle brings you a respectful offer of marriage. Though thronged by admirers more worthy than myself, you will, I beg, do me the honor of considering my proposal.

For some time it has been my pleasure to observe your beauty and talent, and the smiles that brighten the hearts of those around you. Many times you have made my spirit glad. When I was a child back in New Bedford, Massachusetts, my mother had a piano and she played it like you. She looked like you too, black curly hair and big dark eyes like yours, and she had your good cheer and sweet disposition. My father was a seagoing man and when he was away my mother would pass the time playing the piano by the hour and I used to sit and listen and the music made me happy. I thought nobody could play the piano like my mother until I heard you.

Miss Rosabel, I believe I can provide for you very comfortably. Chase and I are doing a good business in the mercantile line. Besides the store, I own four lots bringing in good rents. I also have a fair sum in cash, safely put away.

I take the privilege, Miss Rosabel, of laying my heart, hand, and fortune at your feet.

Yours with deep regard,

Silas Fenway.

Kendra looked up. Rosabel stood waiting, eyes wide, lips parted.

"Isn't it the most beautiful letter you even read?" Rosabel asked. She sounded awestruck.

Kendra felt a catch in her throat. "He means every word of it," she said. "Have you answered it yet?"

Rosabel shook her head. "I—I don't know if I can," she returned. "I mean, I'm scared to try. He sounds so educated. I'm not educated like that."

"Why don't you send him word to come and see you here?" asked Kendra. "Then you can tell him you accept his offer."

"Oh no!" Rosabel exclaimed. "He wrote to me. I ought to write back."

She spoke with conviction, but with dread of the task. Kendra thought she understood why Rosabel had shown her the letter.

"Do you want me to help you, Rosabel?" she asked.

Rosabel's reply had a touching eagerness. "Oh Kendra! Would you?"

"I'll be glad to. This evening after dinner, when Marny has gone down to her card table, we'll write the letter. Tomorrow when Dwight goes out you can ask him to take it to Mr. Fenway."

"Oh you *are* so good!" exclaimed Rosabel. "I wish I could make up a beautiful letter. But I can't, I know I can't."

"Nobody can do everything," Kendra reminded her. "I wish I could play the piano like you. All I can do is tinkle tunes. You have real talent."

"Silas told me the other day I had real talent," Rosabel answered happily.

That evening Kendra composed a reply to Mr. Fenway. It was more flowery than she herself would have liked, but Rosabel wanted some fancy words and Kendra put them in. Rosabel copied the letter in her slow awkward handwriting, and the next morning Dwight took it with him. They did not tell him what was in it. Dwight assumed that he was delivering an order for dress goods.

About two hours later Mr. Fenway called at the hotel. Kendra and Rosabel were in the kitchen preparing the midday lunch when they heard a knock on the iron door. Rosabel started, with a quick smile as if she had already guessed who the caller was, and Kendra went to open the door. There stood Mr. Fenway, more carefully dressed than she had ever seen him, with a black silk cravat tied under his Adam's apple, and a high beaver hat in his hand. He bowed low.

"Good morning, madam. I was told that this is where I could find Miss Rosabel."

Before Kendra could answer she heard Rosabel's voice behind her. "Here I am, Silas!"

A smile appeared on Mr. Fenway's long narrow face. He bowed to Rosabel, and stepping over the threshold he said to Kendra, "I suppose Miss Rosabel has told you, she has made me the happiest of men?"

"Yes," said Kendra, "and I'm happy for you both."

Mr. Fenway gravely thanked her. He said he had come to ask Miss Rosabel to go out with him. They had many agreeable matters to talk over. Rosabel breathlessly asked if Kendra would mind preparing lunch alone.

"Not at all," said Kendra. "Go with Mr. Fenway. May I tell Marny the good news?"

"Oh yes," Rosabel exclaimed, and hurried off to put on her bonnet and shawl.

Marny heard the news over a game of solitaire. Her mouth popped open in astonishment. "Angels and ministers of grace defend us," she murmured.

Kendra said thoughtfully, "She really wants to marry him, Marny."

Marny considered. She nodded slowly. "Yes, I can see that she would. She's tired of knocking about, and he's prosperous and can keep her well. But Mr. Fenway—why does *he* want to marry *her?*"

"He says she reminds him of his mother."

Slowly, Marny put down the cards she had been holding.

She gave Kendra a long green stare. Then, abruptly, she burst out laughing.

"Kendra," she said, "Kendra, this is the craziest gold rush I ever got mixed up in."

They did not see Rosabel until afternoon. When she did come in she was in a hurry. She wanted only to change into a better dress. She said Mr. Fenway was going to take her to dinner at Delmonico's. Then they would go to the Olympic Amphitheater on Kearny Street to see the Spanish Ballet and Opera Troupe.

Mr. Fenway called for her, and they set out for the restaurant and the Olympic Amphitheater. Kendra had gone to bed on her floor-mattress, and was nearly asleep when she heard the key in the lock. She raised herself on an elbow, and heard Mr. Fenway's voice outside as he told Rosabel good night. By the cloudy moonlight she saw Rosabel come in.

"How was the show?" Kendra asked.

"It was grand!" sighed Rosabel. "The most beautiful show I ever saw. And such lovely singing! Do you mind if I light the candle?"

"Go ahead," said Kendra, and Rosabel struck a match. By the light Kendra could see her face, full of joy.

"Oh, it was beautiful," Rosabel sighed again.

Rosabel was fortunate to have seen the show that night. At eight o'clock the next morning the firebells clanged over the town again. Before noon the Olympic Amphitheater, and with it ten squares of the city, were in ruins.

But this time Marny and Norman were among the lucky people. The fire began just south of the plaza. The wind, blowing from the northwest, swept the flames into the blocks still farther south and away from the plaza resorts. The unfinished Calico Palace was not touched. Nor was the Verandah, nor the El Dorado nor the Bella Union, nor Blossom's house of joy, nor Hiram's half-built bank nor Pocket's library. Also untouched were the furnishings Marny and Norman had bought for the upper floors of the Calico Palace. These had been stored in a warehouse well away from the damaged neighborhood.

Marny lost nothing. But for four hours, while Norman and Chad and the Blackbeards guarded the Calico Palace from the swarming looters, Marny stood within scorching distance of the flames. She watched, she twisted her hands till they hurt, she shook with terror lest the wind change. By the time

427

the fire-fighters had stopped the blaze, and the smoke clouds were drifting toward the sandhills south of town, Marny was weak with exhaustion.

Dwight was as frightened as she was. He had promised that Hiram's bank and the Calico Palace would be fireproof. But they could not be fireproof as long as they were still half done, the upper windows nothing but holes through which sparks could blow in to ignite the wooden floors inside. By the time they were walking together back to the hotel, Dwight confessed to Marny, "I feel like a man who has lived through an earthquake."

Leaving her at the hotel, Dwight set out to get his workmen back to work. Marny went into the kitchen, where Kendra had put on the coffee pot and was warming up yesterday's soup. Marny dropped into a chair by the table, and sat leaning her forehead on her hand.

"Give me a cup of coffee, will you?" she asked. "And add a drop of brandy. A big drop of brandy."

Kendra complied. "Don't you want something to eat, Marny?"

"Not yet." Marny reached for the cup. "First let me get my nerves untangled."

Kendra sat down across from Marny. She said nothing, waiting while Marny sipped the coffee laced with brandy. After several minutes Marny said, "I wonder how many more fires I can live through without going to pieces."

Kendra wondered too. "Was it an accident this time?" she asked. "Or arson again?"

"I don't know," said Marny. She added wearily, "What difference does it make?"

She pushed her empty cup across the table. "May I have another one like that?"

Kendra filled the cup again and added the brandy. Marny smiled and thanked her. As she raised the cup she gave a questioning look around. "Where's Rosabel?"

"Mr. Fenway came to get her as soon as the fire started," said Kendra. "She hasn't come back."

"Maybe I should be like Rosabel," said Marny. "Catch a rich husband and let him do the worrying." She pondered the idea, and shook her head. "No, I don't think so. I'm not the domestic type."

Kendra spoke thoughtfully. "Haven't you ever thought of getting married?"

428

"Oh yes, I suppose every girl thinks of it sometimes." Marny paused a moment, sipped coffee, and went on. "I'm not opposed to marriage. For other people, I mean. But I just don't think I was meant for it. I'm a gambler and a poplolly and I'm doing fine."

Never without a pack of cards, when her cup was empty Marny reached into the pocket of her skirt and took them out.

"I'll tell my fortune," she said, "and see if there are any more disasters in my future."

She began laying out the cards, while Kendra watched. Kendra had observed before now that when Marny played any kind of solitaire game she played it cleanly. Marny was honest with herself.

As she finished her layout Marny exclaimed jubilantly. "Look at the kings! And all those lovely diamonds clustered around the queen. Men, money, and no sign of danger. Now please, may I have a bowl of soup? Thank you for being so patient." She swept up the cards. "I'm doing fine," she said again.

She said it still again when Dwight came in. Dwight brought her a present, a pair of earrings made of California gold, each earring made like a yellow California poppy with a pearl like a drop of dew on one petal. These pearls were white, to complement the necklace with the pearls of pink and black. Marny wore the full set when she dealt cards that evening.

The June fire took place on a Friday. By Monday the blackened area was alive with carpenters. Norman came pleading to Dwight. He said the Fourth of July would mean big doings in the plaza. There would be guns and music and speeches, and a spectacular flag-raising on a flagpole a hundred and eleven feet tall, a gift to San Francisco from the people of Oregon. Also, some brave young men—Pocket and Hiram among them—had organized fire-fighting squads, with great rivalry about which company would have the brightest engines and the fastest horses and the most resplendent uniforms. These volunteer firemen planned to present themselves formally on the Fourth, with ceremonies in the plaza and a parade of engines through the streets.

Norman reminded Dwight that crowds of people would be out. They would throng the bars and gambling houses. Couldn't Dwight have the second floor of the Calico Palace finished in time for Marny to open her parlor on the Fourth of July?

Dwight's answer was stern.

"Make up your mind," he retorted. "If you want a shack that will turn to flinders next time some rattlehead starts playing with matches, I can give you all four stories in time for the Fourth. But if you want a building that will stay there, let me do it my way."

"When I think," groaned Norman, "of the rent we pay that blood-sucker Norrington, whether we're making a good income or no income at all—"

Dwight was not touched. And impatient though he was, Norman was wise enough to yield. He returned to the public room of the Calico Palace. Marny went on with her private card game at the Gresham Hotel. Kendra continued preparing meals. Between meals she went with Rosabel to help her choose furnishings for her home.

True to his ways, Mr. Fenway was making careful preparation for his marriage. After looking at many sites he had said that the best part of town for a home was the section called Happy Valley, in the southern part of town. Happy Valley was a family neighborhood, growing as more wives came from the States to join their husbands. Amid the turmoil of the gold rush these ladies had made an island of their own. In Happy Valley you heard no raucous music, no click of rondo balls, no midnight tipplers singing in the street. Here Mr. Fenway had bought a lot and set up a readymade white house. Still cautious, he said he would build a brick house later, when he and his bride had lived in this area long enough to be sure they wanted to make it their permanent place of abode.

Meanwhile he had told Rosabel to buy whatever furnishings she liked and have the bills sent to him. All this was so new to Rosabel that she could not help being timorous. She was glad of Kendra's advice.

Kendra wondered how Rosabel had lived before she met Norman; if she had known her parents, if she had ever had any sort of home. Rosabel never told her, and she never asked.

But whatever lay behind her, it was plain that Rosabel was happy in the prospect of what lay ahead. So was Mr. Fenway. Seeing them together, Kendra could not question his genuine fondness. No doubt Rosabel had told him much that she had not told anybody else. And no doubt Mr. Fenway knew what he wanted and was getting it and did not care what anybody might think.

The celebration of the Fourth of July began the evening of the third. The heroes of the fire brigades met for preparations. By the time they had polished the engines and groomed the horses and put on their gorgeous livery and visited a few bars, they were too skittish to wait for tomorrow. They swarmed into the plaza, shook the earth with guns and fire-crackers, and finally, in the middle of the night, they hitched up the fire horses, scrambled upon the shiny new engines, and gleefully paraded all over town.

Men at Marny's card table, provoked by the racket, loudly wondered if these eager lads would ever be of use. Marny shrugged tolerantly.

She was planning to take a holiday tomorrow. Rosabel and Mr. Fenway were going to spend the day watching the festivities, and Kendra had invited Pocket and Hiram to dinner. Marny intended to sleep until noon.

But at five o'clock on the morning of the Fourth, the fire-bells woke her up. Some wretch had piled a lot of dry planks in the yard behind a saloon on Clay Street, and had set them afire. The engines rushed out with a clatter worse than that of last night. In a short, a very short time, they were clattering back again. The firemen had proved their worth. The fire was out. No damage had been done. The celebration could proceed as planned.

Pocket and Hiram came to dinner that evening. Kendra served roast beef, Dwight poured red wine, and they all made merry. Dwight and Kendra and Marny praised the quick work of the fire companies, and Marny added that such quick work was remarkable in view of the fact that so many of the boys must have been suffering from bottle fatigue. But though she laughed as she spoke, her mind was not at rest.

The firemen were brave men and gallant. They had put out the fire. But the hoodlums were still here. Marny feared there would be a next time, and a next time. The firemen's efforts might not always be enough.

However, the present was so engrossing that she did not think long about the past or the future. While the second floor of the Calico Palace had not been ready for the holiday,

431

it was ready two weeks later. Marny opened her parlor, and Dwight went on with the upper floors.

Dwight was building well. The walls of the Calico Palace were of brick, three feet thick, reinforced with iron. At the windows and doors were double iron shutters, with a space of two feet between each pair. Across the second floor front, in tall gilt letters, were the words CALICO PALACE. Hiram looking up at the stern dark walls, said newcomers were going to think this was the Californians' quaint way of naming the town jail.

But before long, Dwight had added a balcony with a decorative wrought iron railing, from which Marny and Norman and their friends could view the spectacles in the plaza. Every evening the sunken windows were bright, and the transparencies on the street floor gave passersby a tempting foretaste of the merriment within. When they went inside they did not notice the iron shutters; these were folded back and hidden by red velvet curtains looped with cords of yellow silk. Between the windows they saw the paintings of beautiful women, and here and there a scene from the golden hills. The gambling rooms of the Calico Palace were the most luxurious in town.

By this time nearly all signs of the fires of May and June were gone. All over the hills, new buildings were popping up like dandelions in spring. To be sure, the local clergymen spoke regretfully of the fact that the finest of these were temples of sin. The plaza preacher had quite a lot to say about the matter. But as long as the citizens flocked in with pokes of gold, Marny and Norman were not distressed.

When Marny opened her parlor in the Calico Palace, she and Kendra both set up bedrooms in the space behind it. Rosabel, wanting to keep out of Norman's way, stayed where she was in the Gresham Hotel for the few weeks left before her wedding. The ceremony took place early in August, in the Congregational Church on Jackson Street.

There were now seven churches in San Francisco. Mr. Fenway had contributed without bias to the whole group. Not, he explained, that he exactly held with any of them, but they did keep a lot of people out of devilment. He chose the Congregational Church for his wedding because this had been the one he had attended with his mother when he was a boy in New Bedford.

They had the ceremony at eleven o'clock in the morning so

432

the guests could get to shelter before the wind began to raise the dust clouds. Hiram and Pocket, handsomely attired, escorted Kendra, in a gray dress and bonnet which they told her were most becoming. Norman was not present, but Marny attended with Dwight. Marny wore a plain straw bonnet and a plain dark blue dress with a modest V-shaped opening at the throat. She also wore the chain with the pendant of two pink pearls and a black one.

She wore the chain because Dwight wanted her to. When he had said so, Marny had demurred. "Dwight, really, nobody wears that sort of jewelry in the morning! And never to church!" But Dwight said, "What do you care? Wear it anyway." So Marny put it on, though she privately remarked to Kendra, "The French word 'esclavage' has two meanings. It's the word for a woman's collar of jewels, it also means 'bondage.' The French are so definite."

But she spoke with good humor. If Dwight wanted her to wear the necklace as a badge of possession, she was willing. It was a small price to pay for watching the Calico Palace rise, strong and proud, above the plaza.

Mr. Fenway was a leading citizen, and the church was well filled. Mr. and Mrs. Chase were there—dubious, but loyal. Ralph Watson attended, though Serena did not. Serena's pregnancy was changing her figure, and she was too modest to appear thus at a wedding. But she had sent Rosabel a note of good wishes. Serena was happy to see a girl like Rosabel being reformed.

Foxy was there with the other packing boys, all scrubbed and shaved and combed to a state of discomfort, and looking as if their hands and feet were twice as big as usual. Also present were the other employees of Chase and Fenway, and a number of business acquaintances.

Among these was Captain Pollock. Kendra was surprised as she approached the church to see him coming toward it from another direction. But Hiram told her Chase and Fenway were planning an addition to their store, and the bricks were to come from Pollock's brickyard. It was good business, as well as courtesy, for him to attend the wedding of his customer.

Pollock saw Kendra as they were about to enter the church, and with a bow he stepped aside to let her go in ahead of him. She smiled and thanked him, but he did not smile back. Behind her were Dwight and Marny. Always formallly correct, Pollock waited another moment for Marny to precede him. As she passed, he gave her a stony look. His gaze moved from her face to her pearls and back again as though to show his disapproval of such display. The *Cynthia* was a rotting derelict, and Pollock would never forgive.

The ceremony was short and simple. Mr. Fenway appeared in a black suit and a white silk cravat, and his face was respectfully solemn. Rosabel wore a quiet dark dress and bonnet she had chosen on Kendra's advice. She looked pretty, and quite at ease. After the wedding there was a small party at Delmonico's. Rosabel was serene, and Mr. Fenway was remarkably cheerful as he poured the champagne.

Afterward, Rosabel and Mr. Fenway took a carriage to their home in Happy Valley. Kendra felt sure she would never see either of them in the Calico Palace again.

55

As Marny had had to get up earlier than usual to attend the wedding, by midnight she was sleepy. So instead of dealing until the regular closing time of two o'clock, she gave her table to the dealer from Boston. The bettors protested. They warned that as she was not used to retiring so early she probably would not go to sleep anyway. Marny retorted, "Oh yes I will. I'll pour a drink to make sure."

She paused at the bar to choose a bottle, and with this and a glass in her hands she went toward the cubbyhole she was using as a bedroom while the upper floors were still unfinished. Seeing a light under the door of Kendra's room, she knocked and went in. Kendra sat on the edge of her cot, sewing on a button, as awkwardly as usual. "Come down with me," Marny invited, "and let's make sure the back door is locked."

Glad of an excuse to stop sewing, Kendra took up her candle. Together they went down the back stairs. The door at the foot of the stairs was safely locked and bolted, though the iron inner doors had not yet been drawn into place. The little area between the stairs and the door was almost quiet, for this was the hour when the musicians in the first-floor room went out for their supper. With a grateful sigh Marny sat down on the stairs and poured her drink.

"Join me?" she asked Kendra.

"No thanks, I'm all right."

"I'm all right too," said Marny, "but I do think it's delightful, what can be done with grapes and grain." She took a sip and smiled.

Some boxes of bar supplies, not yet opened, were stacked in a corner. Kendra set her candlestick on the pile and sat on the stair by Marny. For a minute or so Marny sipped in comfort. Kendra was about to make a remark about the wedding when she saw Marny give a start. "What is it?" Kendra asked.

"I heard something, Listen."

Kendra listened. She heard it too. A little whimper, and another little whimper. The sounds came from outside, just beyond the closed door. Marny asked,

"Now what do you suppose that is?"

They listened again. The wind had quieted and they had no difficulty hearing the little moaning sounds, faint and pitiful. "It's an animal, crying," said Kendra. "Let's look."

She went to the door, slipped back the bolt, and drew the door open a few inches. As she did so, a white streak went past her and vanished in the darkness behind the staircase. From the black hiding place the little sounds began again, like quavers of terror. As Kendra closed the door, Marny set her glass on the stair and stood up too. Taking the candle from the pile of boxes where Kendra had placed it, she followed the quavers, and moved the candle so she could see into the black space behind the stairs.

"Oh Kendra," she exclaimed, "it's a kitten. A tiny scared lost kitten."

They both looked into the dark corner. It seemed that the kitten, frightened by the noise and lights of the plaza, maybe kicked by some fellow staggering away from a bar, had fled here to the inside of the block, and trembling with fear, had huddled against the door. The door was set into the wall, and the dark angle gave at least a bit of shelter from the hostile world. As Kendra opened the door the kitten had sensed something unknown, no doubt an enemy, and had run again, this time inside, and had taken refuge in the

435

first dark corner it saw. Here it was now, shivering with fear and hunger and wretchedness.

They could hardly tell what the kitten looked like. All they could see was a whitish blob. But they could tell that the kitten was miserable and no doubt famished.

Neither Kendra nor Marny had ever felt any particular interest in cats. But neither of them could bear to let a helpless creature go hungry while they had food.

"Is there any milk left?" Marny asked.

Milk, bought daily from the milk cart, was one of the most expensive commodities in San Francisco, but Marny was moved with too much sympathy to care. Kendra went up to the pantry, where she had set the milk by a window to keep cool. Taking the cover off the jar, she poured milk into a pan and brought it down, and set it by the staircase.

"Now then," she said to the quivering little blob in the corner.

At first the kitten was too scared to move. But milk was food, and the kitten was shaking with hunger. Marny and Kendra stepped back and stood very still so as to give the poor little thing nothing more to be afraid of. After a few minutes the kitten could resist no longer. It began to move from its hiding place. Slowly, tremulously, it came to the pan of milk. It looked around for danger, but Marny and Kendra remained motionless, watching. The kitten put out its pink tongue and touched the surface of the milk. The milk disappeared.

When they talked about it later Marny and Kendra could only use the word *disappeared*. The whole panful of milk seemed to go almost at a gulp. This done, the kitten ran and hid again behind the stairs.

"We can't leave it here," said Kendra. "When the Blackbeards open the door in the morning, the kitten will run out and get killed. Let's take it upstairs."

"All right," said Marny. "I'll send one of the boys out to put some sand in a box."

She bent to pick up the kitten. This was not easy, for the kitten was still shaking with fear, but it had no place to flee to, and Marny finally managed to get it between her hands. As she did so she gave a little cry of pity.

"Oh Kendra, the poor little wretch! I never felt anything so thin. Like a bag of sticks."

Kendra felt a sweep of compassion. An egg, she thought,

436

would be ideal nourishment for their foundling, but eggs were even more costly than milk. More than once a dozen eggs for her baking had cost the Calico Palace half an ounce of gold. "Marny," she asked, "could we spare an egg? I'll pay for it."

Marny answered promptly, "The egg is on the house."

Beating the precious egg into another pan of precious milk, while Marny stood beside her holding the kitten and trying to soothe its tremors, Kendra realized all of a sudden that what had swept over her just now was not merely compassion. It was love. She had so yearned for something to love again. Now she had it. A baby kitten, alone and forsaken and in desperate need. The kitten needed her and she needed the kitten, and she was going to keep it.

The kitten was so frightened that they decided to give it—for the present at least—a room of its own. They unlocked a storeroom that had a window, and here they put a folded blanket and a sandbox and the pan of milk with the egg.

"There now," Marny said to the kitten, "you have all the comforts. Your own little bed, your own little privy, your own little bedtime snack. Now whatever did I do with my own little glass of grog?"

The kitten, lapping up the milk and egg, did not look around.

When they saw the kitten by daylight they were shocked at its pitiful ugliness. Its fur had fallen off in patches, so that it had a look of being moth-eaten. Scrawny from starvation, it did feel like a bag of sticks. In its short little life it must have known nothing but abuse, for it was so tremulous that for days Marny and Kendra could feel its fear of them, even when they approached with pans of food.

Norman was not enthusiastic. "If it was a good big ship's cat," he said, "and could be of some use at rat-catching—"

"I want this kitten," said Kendra, "and I'm going to keep it. If I can't keep it here, any restaurant in town will be glad to have my cakes."

The kitten stayed. And after a few weeks of food and kindness, Marny and Kendra discovered one day that their ugly little stray had turned into a beauty.

Instead of being like a bag of sticks, the kitten now seemed to have hardly any bones at all, so easily it folded up to fit any way they held it in their hands. Its fur was thick

437

and white, with black markings as if somebody had shaken a pen over it, scattering blots. Its eyes were green, not a pert clover-green like Marny's, but a pale delicate shade, the green of the first new leaves of spring. "The eyes of an aristocrat," said Marny. No longer frightened, the kitten played and scampered about. They could pick it up whenever they pleased, and the kitten purred, and liked to be fondled.

They wanted to give a name to their little friend. But here they were in a quandary. Names had gender and so had cats, but this cat was still so young that they did not know how to make sure of its sex.

Still, the problem was not too difficult. One of the frequent gamblers in Marny's parlor was a veterinarian named Dr. Wardlaw. The next time he came in Marny asked for his aid. Chuckling with amusement, Dr. Wardlaw followed her into the hall behind the parlor and she brought him the kitten. A minute or two later Marny reported to Kendra, who was taking a pan of raisin cookies out of the oven.

"Our cat," announced Marny, "is a girl."

Kendra looked up with interest. "How did he tell?"

"It's really quite simple," said Marny. "He showed me. You upend the cat and look for a certain little button. A girl cat has two buttons, a boy cat has only one."

Marny went back to her card table, but after closing time she came into Kendra's room to discuss the question of a name. As the room had space for only one chair, Kendra sat on the cot with the kitten in her lap. She stroked its satiny fur and marveled that this kitten should be the same trembling castaway who had come crying to the door.

"Let's give her a *real* name," said Kendra. "Not Tabby or Snowball or something ordinary like that."

"Oh yes," Marny agreed. "Not a name that could belong to just any cat. Something that fits *this* cat."

They began to consider names.

"Natalie," said Kendra. "Madeline. Lucinda. Winifred."

"Diana," said Marny. "Clarice. Nicolette."

She paused thoughtfully. Kendra went on.

"Henrietta. Gwendolen. Lysiane. Geraldine—"

Marny echoed, "Geraldine."

"Do you like Geraldine?" asked Kendra.

"Yes," said Marny, "it has the right ring. It reminds me of something." With a frown of concentration she repeated,

438

"Geraldine. Geraldine. It fits. Why does it fit? Geraldine?" A light broke over her face and she sat up straight. "Oh yes! I know! Remember that spooky poem by Coleridge? Geraldine the beautiful waif, coming mysteriously out of the dark? Remember?"

"No, I don't remember," Kendra said laughing, "if I ever heard it. You're the one who knows things like that. What happens in the poem?"

"Why, the lady Christabel opens the castle door at midnight to bring in fair Geraldine, and then Geraldine turns out to be a witch."

Cuddling the kitten in her lap, Kendra demanded, "Do you think this innocent ball of fluff looks like a witch?"

"Geraldine in the poem didn't look like a witch either," said Marny. "She was beautiful. Our kitten is beautiful. Our kitten did come mysteriously out of the dark, like Geraldine; she did plead that she was lost and helpless, like Geraldine; the time was midnight, you did open the door."

"What became of Geraldine in the poem?" asked Kendra.

"Nobody knows. He never finished it."

"And we don't know what's going to become of our kitten," said Kendra, "nor of ourselves either. Yes, I think that's the right name."

So they called the kitten Geraldine.

Marny, who had never had a pet before, became as fond of the kitten as Kendra was. "I'm beginning to understand the charm of animals," she said a day or two later, stroking Geraldine's head while Geraldine purred with pleasure. "They love you quite as much as most people do, and they don't talk so much."

Kendra smiled and agreed. But Norman said grumpily, "Cats don't love anybody but themselves. When a cat shows liking for you, you can be sure the cat wants something."

"Why yes," Marny answered. "Isn't it remarkable, how many human traits they have?"

But though she answered, she did not argue. She knew Norman was in a grouchy mood. He missed Rosabel. He missed her for two reasons: first, because she had been a good companion; and second, because her presence had attracted the sort of patrons that Norman called bons garçons, because they spent money easily. Norman had good musicians both in the public room on the street floor and in Marny's parlor upstairs, but they were all men. The bons garçons

439

kept asking him when he was going to bring in another girl to take Rosabel's place at the piano. But a girl who combined Rosabel's talent with her clever charm would have been hard to find anywhere, and with the general scarcity of women in San Francisco Norman's hopes of replacing Rosabel were dim. He knew it was his own fault that he had lost her, and this did not improve his temper.

Now and then he paid attention to a girl, taking her to dinner or to a show at the new theater called the Dramatic Museum. None of the girls really pleased him much, though he did enjoy the shows. The Dramatic Museum was on California Street just below Kearny. It was a well managed theater, offering a variety of entertainments, sometimes a serious play, more often an evening of song and dance and comedy. Marny liked to go there with Dwight, leaving her card table to the Harvard man. The players protested her absence, but she always returned to the card table after the show and stayed there till closing time. She told them they appreciated her more for having had to wait for her.

Norman could scoff all he pleased at Marny and Kendra's adoption of a stray cat. But Hiram and Pocket and Dwight, though they had no great love for cats, all admitted that they might have done the same thing themselves, being soft-hearted. Dwight said he would get his carpenters to build Geraldine a home. He asked what structural plan would please her best.

Marny and Kendra had observed that Geraldine liked to sleep in a box, preferably one turned on its side so she could look out. Dwight designed a hut shaped like an oversized loaf of bread. He put air-holes at the back, and in front a latticed door so if Geraldine had to be shut up she could still see what was going on. At the top he fixed a handle, so the girls could pick up the hut and carry it around. The hut was light in weight, but strong and well made, for Dwight respected his work, whatever it was. They folded a soft old shawl and put it in for a bed, and Geraldine now had a more comfortable dwelling place than most people in San Francisco.

When the hut was finished Hiram and Pocket came over to admire it, bringing Geraldine a gift of fresh fish. With the pleasure of an artist whose work is well esteemed, Dwight led them both into Marny's parlor and treated them to refreshments, Pocket to cheese rolls and coffee, Hiram to the best whiskey at the bar.

Unlike Norman, Dwight was in good humor these days. He had finished Hiram's bank, a building of two stories and an underground vault. The Calico Palace was rising steadily, and now Dwight added a balcony at the back, so Geraldine would have a place to play. Here he set up a wondrously contrived wooden framework, on which Geraldine could climb when she felt like taking exercise, and he surrounded the balcony with a flat-topped railing where she could sit and look down at the world.

Besides the Calico Palace, Dwight had begun two smaller buildings. Marny told Kendra all his work was going well. Another reason for his cheer was that the buildings were costing less than he had expected.

Marny told her why. Men of business in Honolulu and the Atlantic ports had heard of the fires in San Francisco, the frantic rebuilding, and the high prices. Eager to profit by the need, hundreds of dealers had sent out bricks and lumber. Now, said Marny, they had glutted the town. A shipment of bricks that would have cost Dwight fifty ounces of gold last year, he could now buy for ten. Sometimes even less. The sellers were not happy, but Dwight and his fellow builders were in a gladsome mood.

People were doing a lot of building. Among others, the men of the fire companies were setting up reservoirs at strategic points about town, one of them in the plaza. The filling of each one was an occasion for ceremonies. On a September evening, with pomp and fanfare and torchlights, the firemen pumped water into the plaza reservoir. Marny went out on the front balcony to look, but she did not stay there long. The ceremony, merry as it was with its bands and shouting, gave her shivers. Any reminder of the fire danger always did.

Marny was not a fainthearted person. But she was anxious because the danger was real. Eleven days after the plaza reservoir was filled, the firebells roused the town again.

It was four o'clock in the morning. When the bells woke them up, Marny rushed to the safe; Kendra grabbed Geraldine.

Geraldine now slept in her hut on the back balcony. Kendra latched the door of the hut, where Geraldine had begun to cry, half in fright and half in anger at being thus disturbed. Carrying the hut, Kendra found Marny and Norman and

441

the Blackbeards in conference before the largest of their safes. Through an open window she could smell smoke and hear the clatter of the engines.

The Blackbeards had just been looking out of this window. Right now Troy Blackbeard was telling them the fire was burning to the north, and might not reach the plaza at all. The best thing to do was get dressed and be ready to leave if they had to, but meanwhile to stay here on guard.

This made sense. When Marny and Kendra had put on their clothes and their guns they stood at an upper window, each of them holding a poke of coins. Kendra had set Geraldine's hut on a chair beside them. The fire was roaring eastward toward Montgomery Street.

Marny spoke little. With nervous fingers she twisted the drawstring of the leather bag in her hands. Kendra was doing the same thing. The coins in the poke did not belong to her. She did not own as much of anything as Marny. But like Marny, she had her life to lose and her sound body to be crippled if the fire should come this way. She had good reason to be afraid.

From somewhere behind her she heard Norman's voice, loud and angry. Lolo, afraid for little Zack, was sobbing with panic. Norman was shouting to her to keep calm. Kendra said to Marny,

"Why doesn't *he* keep calm?"

"He's in a bad humor all round," Marny answered promptly, as if glad to be reminded of something besides the fire. "He wouldn't own it for all the gold in California, but he still misses Rosabel."

At the mention of Rosabel, Kendra caught her breath. "Oh good heavens—I hope the fire won't go as far as Chase and Fenway's!"

"I hope," Marny said savagely, "whoever started it gets burnt up in it."

They never found out whether or not her wish came true. Later that day they learned that this fire had started in a combination flophouse and saloon on Jackson Street. Nobody knew if it had been set on purpose or if some fellow had gone to sleep with a lighted cigar in his hand. The fire engines had responded promptly to the alarm, but the flophouse was in an area of flimsy wooden shelters and by the time the engines got there the whole neighborhood was ablaze.

The firemen fought gallantly, and they did manage to hold

the flames within limits. The fire did not reach the Calico Palace nor the El Dorado nor the Verandah, nor the other buildings on Kearny Street facing the plaza. But it raced across another block and damaged the *Alta California* building; it wrecked the office of the *Alta*'s major rival, the *Pacific News;* it destroyed several fine stores and warehouses; and more important to Marny and Kendra, it destroyed the building that housed Pocket's library and his living quarters.

That afternoon Pocket came to the Calico Palace with Dwight. Pocket had gone to Dwight's office to discuss the rebuilding of the library. By three o'clock they were both hungry, but several restaurants had been lost in the fire and the rest were crowded, and Dwight had said maybe Kendra would have some leftovers on hand. They brought steaks to replace what they intended to eat, and a package of liver for Geraldine. While Kendra served them a meal of bread and cold beef, they told her and Marny more details of the fire.

Pocket was cheerful about his own loss. He said he and his assistants had managed to save the mail entrusted to them. Most of his cash and dust were on deposit at Hiram's bank, and were safe in the vault. The fire had gone as far as Montgomery Street, but though several other buildings on the block had been wrecked, Hiram's bank had withstood the flames. Chase and Fenway's, at the edge of the burnt area, had barely escaped.

The store had escaped because of the new wing Messrs. Chase and Fenway were planning to build. They had bought a lot next to the store, and by great good fortune this lot was between the store and the fire. Right now the lot was empty but for the bricks they had bought from Captain Pollock's brickyard. Sparks that had fallen there last night had fizzled out.

Pocket said he had gone by the store this morning and had spoken to both Mr. Chase and Mr. Fenway. None of the earlier fires had come so close to them, and Mr. Chase said the fright had aged him ten years. Mr. Fenway was complaining that he was worn out from lack of sleep. He was also complaining about the extra work he would have to do because of the extra trade. Folks would be crowding in all day long to replace the stuff they had lost in the fire. When he went home tonight, he said, he was going to take a bolt of cream-colored satin to make a new dress for Rosabel.

443

Poor girl, she had had a bad scare last night and needed a cheering up. Bad times, these.

Pocket finished his bread and beef, and went off to add to Mr. Fenway's labors by buying clothes to take the place of those he had lost in the fire. Marny walked downstairs with Dwight. Half an hour later she came back into the kitchen, where Kendra was delighting Geraldine with a pan of the liver brought by Dwight and Pocket. Marny sat down at the kitchen table, took out her ever present pack of cards, and began to shuffle.

"Life," she said to Kendra, "is like a card game. No matter how the game goes, every loss is somebody's gain."

Kendra offered Marny a cup of coffee. Marny, laying out her cards, shook her head. Bringing a cup for herself, Kendra came to the table. Marny was smiling at the cards.

"Go on," said Kendra.

"Dwight Carson," Marny said without looking up, "is today the happiest man in San Francisco."

Kendra smiled too. She thought she knew what Marny was about to say. Marny said it.

"He has proved himself. He *can* put up a building that won't burn. He has done it."

She looked up, holding the queen of diamonds in her hand.

"Dwight is no villain," she continued. "He wouldn't set a fire to prove his competence. But he can't help being gleeful now that fate has proved it for him. Pocket's library, which Dwight did not build, went down in the fire. Hiram's bank, which he did build, is still there."

She went on laying out the cards. Kendra hoped they would show a rosy future, because while she had no faith in fortune telling she knew Marny had.

Pocket and Dwight had told them about Hiram's bank. Carefully designed, carefully constructed of brick and stone and malleable iron, the bank had no trace of the fire except smudges on the outside. Dwight had reason to be proud.

It meant that she and Marny had been fortunate too. The nugget she had found at Shiny Gulch, and her small savings of gold dust, were secure in Hiram's vault. Also in the vault unharmed (though Marny had probably not called this to Dwight's attention) were the jeweled pin and nugget necklace Archwood had given her, and various other ornaments Dwight did not want her to wear these days.

444

Marny finished her layout and studied it.

"Of course," she said, almost as if appealing to the cards, "even when the Calico Palace is finished, we can't be *sure* it's fireproof. We can't know unless a fire hits Kearny Street."

—The last thing she needs right now, Kendra thought, is sympathy. But she does need to be encouraged. I can't tell her the Calico Palace is fireproof because maybe it's not. I can't tell her Dwight is going to stay with the Calico Palace until it has proved itself, because maybe he won't. But I do want to help her somehow.

"Marny," she said, "my grandmother used to have a cook who was happy and wise. I suppose she was happy *because* she was wise. When I would run in, all upset about something that might happen next week, she used to say to me, 'Little girl, the way to live is, *get ready* for the maybe. Then forget it.'"

Marny's face lit with a smile. "Get ready for the maybe," she repeated. "Then forget it. That makes sense." She looked down at the cards again. "I don't see any disasters here. And Dwight does build well."

"So he does," said Kendra. "Now if you want to stop worrying, get busy and do something useful."

"Such as what?"

"Take out Geraldine's sandbox," said Kendra, "and put in some fresh sand."

"All right. Where's the box?"

"On Geraldine's balcony."

Marny gathered up the cards, put the pack into her pocket, and stood up. "I'll get it."

A few minutes later she returned, carrying the box, now filled with clean sand.

"Where do I put this? On the balcony again?"

"That's right."

Marny looked down at the pan of sand she was holding, and looked up at Kendra. "In times gone by," she said reflectively, "I used to have my hopes and my ambitions. I used to think about the days to come, and I wondered what the future held for me." She gave a sigh. "I thought of so many possible destinies," she went on. "But never, in my wildest thoughts, never did I dream that I would wind up being chambermaid to a cat."

445

56

Marny tried to get ready for the maybe. Maybe there would be another fire on the plaza. But three floors of the Calico Palace were finished now, the top floor was progressing every day, and if ever a building looked safe and felt safe, this one did. Over and over she reminded herself of the advice from Kendra's grandmother's cook. "Get ready. Then forget it."

The second part of the advice was the hard part. How could she forget, when every week or two the bells resounded with another fire alarm?

In all these alarms, rarely was there any question of accident. A policeman or night watchman would be attracted by a glimmer in the dark. Going nearer, he would find rubbish piled against the wall of a building and set alight; or shavings heaped on a wharf, crackling merrily, and matchsticks lying about. Nearly all the fires were set in the blocks between the plaza and the waterfront, where loot would be richest. The volunteer firemen, prompt and profane, were keeping the fires under control. But every alarm reminded Marny that some day the firemen might not get there in time.

"I'm so damn mad," she said to Kendra, "that sometimes I feel like I've got a fire of my own, right inside my skull."

She was not the only citizen enraged. Every sort of crime was increasing. People and more people were crowding into San Francisco, some of them with no purpose but to help themselves to anything they could lay hands on. Every night men were knocked down and robbed in the unlighted streets. The papers did not even try to list all the murders. And what was worse, the authorities were not doing much to change things.

There were a thousand rumors about why this was true. At Marny's bar and Hiram's bank and Pocket's library, men talked of bribery and corruption. More and more, they were

446

saying it was time they took justice into their own hands. They all began, with pious monotony, "I don't believe in lynch law, but . . ."

The safest streets were those around the plaza, because of the lights that streamed from the pleasure resorts. The safest people were women, because their rarity hedged them with a kind of aura. Even on ill-lighted streets, a man with a woman at his side was not likely to be attacked.

"Everything here is upside down," said Marny. "The most orderly part of town is the region of gamblers and fancy ladies; and when a man has to pass a dark alley he hires a streetwalker to protect him. Was there *ever* such a place in the world before?"

Still, if there was much to remind her of the dangers, there was also much to turn Marny's thoughts to happier matters.

Gold was streaming down from the placers. Much of this gold went out by the steamers, but a great deal of it never got any farther than Kearny Street. Marny could not find the days too worrisome when she was getting richer all the time. And if she did feel quaky now and then, she could always divert her mind by stepping out on the balcony to see what was going on in the plaza.

Something was always going on in the plaza. People in San Francisco liked to celebrate. The anniversary of a battle, the birthday of a hero, a stirring piece of news—at any such event they rushed to the plaza with bands and cheering. The day a steamer brought word that California was now a state of the Union, they rang bells and tooted horns and had a parade, and fired so many guns that it sounded like a war.

Admission to the Union was important. They had felt like exiles, remote and unrecognized here in this far outpost of their country. Now they were part of their country. They resented anybody who did not realize how important this was. At Marny's bar an innocent newcomer remarked to Hiram that the new Union Hotel was as fine a hostelry as the finest in the States. At this, Hiram and three other men at the bar exclaimed together, "Sir, we are *in* the States!"

The stranger hastily said, "Yes, yes, of course, excuse me." Before long, new arrivals learned to say "back East" instead of "in the States." If they did not learn fast enough, affronted Californians taught them.

Dwight finished Pocket's new building. A handsome structure of brick and iron, it stood on the site of the old building, on Washington Street facing the plaza. The reading rooms were in front, and behind them were living quarters for Pocket and his partner, Mr. Gilmore. When asked, Pocket said business was going along nicely, thank you.

While Pocket was still content to live in a room behind his office, Hiram was not. Hiram had moved into the new Union Hotel. This hotel, the best in San Francisco, stood in the same block as the Calico Palace, next door to the Parker House.

In the Parker House itself the whole second floor had been rented by a theatrical producer from New York, who turned it into a theater called the Jenny Lind. He brought in first-class actors, and the plays were good. San Francisco play-goers were not easy to please. Too many of them had come here from the leading cities of the world, and they were used to good theater. They liked the Dramatic Museum well enough, but the Museum offered mostly farces, and song-and-dance acts. The Jenny Lind actors gave real plays, and they did it well.

Marny and Dwight went there often. Marny told Kendra that not only were the plays good but the manager was a smart fellow. He had done something new: he had given his theater two entrances. One of these led through the barroom; the other opened directly into the theater itself. For the first time in San Francisco, you could get into a place of public entertainment without passing a bar.

Marny herself did not object to passing a bar. However, the ladies of Happy Valley did object. More and more successful men were sending home for their wives. The presence of these ladies in a public place gave it an air of quality. And at the Jenny Lind Theater, not only could they avoid the bar, but they could see to it that their husbands did the same.

The new idea worked. Of the four hundred seats in the theater, seldom were more than twenty or thirty occupied by women, and not all these women were matrons proud of their virtue. But in the expensive boxes, almost any evening you could see leading men of San Francisco with their wives.

While they pretended to ignore women not as chaste as themselves, these ladies did send Marny glances bright with interest. They had heard of her—it was hardly possible to live in San Francisco and not hear about Marny of the Calico Palace—and her green eyes and flamelike hair made her easy to recognize. They whispered. Was it true that she came of a fine family back East? That her father had been a college professor? Or was it a banker? Marny was amused. She conducted herself with propriety that matched their own, and let them whisper all they pleased.

Hiram came to see Kendra and asked if she would go to the plays with him. They sat together in a private gambling room not in use at the time, and Hiram spoke to her candidly across the card table.

"I know the calendar of good form back East," he said. "A widow isn't supposed to be seen until she has been a widow at least a year. But this isn't back East. Anyway, I think you're too smart to want to bury yourself alive."

Kendra smiled back at him. "I think it's silly," she answered, "to say that a woman who has been bereaved should sit at home wrapped in her grief. It's like saying that when you've been ill it's bad manners to try to get well. I'd like to go with you, thanks."

He reached across the table and squeezed her hand. She noticed that Hiram's hand was not as rough as it had been when he was working a rocker at Shiny Gulch. But it was still a big confident hand, hard and strong. "I always knew you had good sense, Kendra," he said.

The next evening she went with Hiram to the play, wearing a flowered silk dress she had borrowed from Marny. As usual, the audience was mostly men, and she received a shower of admiring glances as she sat down. Kendra wondered which of these men had sent her letters proposing marriage. She still received these letters, and tore them up half read.

She enjoyed the play. After this she went often to the theater, either with Hiram or with Hiram and Pocket together. Sometimes, when she and Hiram went there without Pocket, they caught sight of him with a girl friend of his own. He escorted various girls, and always they were attractive girls.

"Pocket has better luck with women than any other man in town," Hiram said to her with a chuckle. "Even in San Francisco, where a girl can be a crosseyed hunchback and still have admirers, Pocket can take his choice of them all."

Glancing at Pocket's profile, Kendra was not surprised. He was a handsome man. And a likable man. She wondered if he often thought of that girl back in Kentucky. He had said he did not care about her any more. Kendra was sure he did not. But though a wound might heal, she reflected, it could still leave a scar that would never go away.

Another evening as she entered the theater she saw Mr. Fenway and Rosabel. They were occupying a box with Hiram's partner, the quiet little banker Mr. Eustis, and a lady Kendra did not recognize. Hiram told her the lady was Mrs. Eustis, who had recently arrived from back East to join her husband. Kendra gave an exclamation. "Oh! I'm glad."

"Glad of what?" Hiram asked with a spark of mischief.

"I'm glad she's in a box with Rosabel. You know as well as I do how some women are, about a girl like Rosabel."

Hiram was laughing. "My pretty blue-eyed friend," he said, "you're not *that* innocent. Rosabel is now a married woman, but that's not all. She's married to a leading citizen, and a rich one. All her sins are forgotten."

"I told you, I'm glad," Kendra repeated. "This is what she wanted and I'm glad she's getting it."

Just then Rosabel turned her head and saw them, and they exchanged smiles of greeting. Rosabel wore a dress of pink-flowered satin, and in her hair pink satin flowers held with a jeweled pin. Her black curls danced on her cheeks, and she looked pretty and pampered and content. Kendra noticed that Mr. Fenway, though he kept his solemn dignity, also looked content.

After the play they all had a chat. Mrs. Eustis proved to be a nice little woman, with a good deal to say about the dreadful hardships she had endured while crossing the Isthmus. Rosabel listened demurely, but Kendra saw her lips twitch. The route across the Isthmus was now guarded by the United States Army. Along the way were American lodging houses where travelers could sleep, if not in luxury, at least without fear of being murdered before morning. Rosabel could remember when things had been otherwise. But she kept quiet and let Mrs. Eustis prattle.

When Mr. and Mrs. Eustis had said good night, Rosabel spoke to Kendra.

"Come to see me," she invited. "My house is all furnished now and ready for company."

Kendra thanked her. She was wondering if Rosabel was also going to invite Marny to call. —If she doesn't, thought Kendra, I won't go.

But even as she thought this, Rosabel was saying, "Drag Marny away from her card table and bring her with you."

She glanced at Mr. Fenway. "You'll drive them, won't you, Silas?"

Mr. Fenway said he would be glad to. Let them agree upon an afternoon, and he would call for Marny and Kendra in his carriage and escort them to Happy Valley.

The time now was November, and the afternoon they chose for their call proved to be cold and cloudy, but the carriage was well cushioned and Mr. Fenway tucked a warm robe over their knees. In Happy Valley the houses had a look of cheerful neatness. There were fresh curtains at the windows, potted ferns on the porches, and even children playing games in the yards. Mr. Fenway and Rosabel still lived in the readymade house he had set up before their marriage, but he said he approved of the neighborhood and expected to start a brick house shortly.

They found Rosabel in a parlor lighted and warmed by a large wood fire, welcome in the gray chill of the day. Besides the furniture Kendra had helped her select, the parlor had cushions and footstools, a bookcase full of books, and a really splendid rosewood piano. Near the fire was a table on which stood a silver tea service. Rosabel poured tea and passed little sandwiches, with no more fluttering than might have been expected of any bride not yet quite used to receiving callers in her own home. It was a pleasant home, well kept, and Kendra said so. Mr. Fenway, sipping tea and nibbling an olive sandwich, solemnly quoted Scripture.

"As the Good Book tells us, madam," said Mr. Fenway, "'a prudent wife is from the Lord.'"

Kendra asked Rosabel about her housekeeping arrangements. Rosabel said she had the services of a married couple who lived in a cottage Mr. Fenway had built for them on a corner of this lot. The man cut wood and took care of the horses, while his wife did laundry and housework. This, said Rosabel, left her time for her music. She was taking lessons from a Frenchman who came in twice a week, and oh, she did enjoy it! She had played the piano since she was a little girl, but she had not realized till now how much there was that she did not know.

Mr. Fenway listened proudly.

They chatted about the new theater and the actors, about new fashions on display in the stores. Mr. Fenway said they must hear Rosabel play her new piano. Kendra observed that the French teacher was a good one. Rosabel had been taking lessons only three months, but already her playing showed marked improvement. Kendra told her so, and Rosabel smiled gratefully.

It was time to go. They thanked Rosabel for a pleasant afternoon, and Mr. Fenway drove them back to the Calico Palace. Not until after they got there and Kendra had gone to her own room, did she realize that Rosabel had not asked them a single question about the Calico Palace. When she saw Marny, Kendra asked if she thought Rosabel ever felt homesick for what she had left behind.

Marny's forehead puckered as she considered this. "I don't know," she answered after a moment. "I wonder too. But I'll tell you this, Kendra. If she asks us to tea again, I'm going to smile sweetly and decline."

"Oh Marny! Why?"

"I haven't been so bored since I left Philadelphia," said Marny. She gave a sigh. "Sorry. I guess I'm just not the domestic type."

A few days after this, Dwight proudly told them they would no longer be disturbed by the noise of saws and hammers. The Calico Palace was finished. Here it stood, four stories high, the finest building on the plaza. And fireproof, said Dwight. This he promised.

But though he assured them the building would not burn, he had not forgotten that there were many articles inside it that would—curtains, carpets, furniture. To be sure of an escape route if a dropped cigar set an indoor fire and smoke blocked the open stairwell, Dwight had built a narrow iron staircase at the back, leading from the fourth floor to an iron door at the bottom. The iron staircase was steep and narrow. "But it means," said Dwight, "you can get out, and come back safe and sound the next day."

"Dwight," Marny said seriously, "you're good. You think of everything."

Dwight answered with pride. "I do try to."

There were now seven buildings in San Francisco that had been built under Dwight's supervision. These were the Calico Palace, Hiram's bank, Pocket's library, and four other banks and office buildings. They all stood in the rich area near the waterfront. Not only did they have walls of brick and iron, but Dwight had added to each one a new feature to increase its chances of safety. Their roofs were flat, and on each roof

452

Dwight had put a tank. This meant that each owner could flood his roof with water a foot deep, and thus protect it from windblown sparks and cinders. Dwight looked over his work with the air of a general who had prepared his forces so well that now he was eager for battle.

Marny looked at the tank and up at the clouds. "Now if it will only rain!"

She got her wish. Within a week after Dwight had told her the tank was ready, the clouds broke with a howling storm. Dwight's carefully planned gutters led the rainwater into the tank. For ten days the rain fell, broken only by a few snatches of sunshine, while Norman gleefully rubbed his hands and Marny laughed with joy. By the time the weather cleared, the tank was full and Marny exclaimed, "We have water enough for a dozen fires!"

"No we haven't," Dwight answered. But he added with a confident smile, "We have enough."

As Marny said to Kendra later, they were ready for the maybe. And not only was the Calico Palace strong, it was also comfortable. The living quarters on the fourth floor were as luxurious as those of the Union Hotel. The rooms were large, well lighted, and well furnished. Even Geraldine had a little room of her own, where she would be warm and dry when the weather made her balcony unpleasant. Lulu and Lolo kept the fourth floor in order, helped by the wife of one of the bartenders.

"How gloriously different," Marny exclaimed, "from the way I had to live last year! Shivering in the drafts, throwing the sheets out of the window when I needed fresh ones, and rats eating the soap and candles. How everything changes!"

But though she said "everything," she did not mean everything. Some details of her life had not changed. She lived in luxury, but she still wore her gun all day and kept it beside her all night. San Francisco was as dangerous as it had ever been.

However, lawless though it was, the town was showing more of the ways of the towns on the Atlantic side. While women were still hugely outnumbered, by this time the group of wives from back East was large enough for them to introduce Eastern social customs. The same storm that had filled the roof-tank of the Calico Palace had also blown down the frame of the unfinished Presbyterian Church. The ladies from back East announced a bazaar to help raise money for

453

rebuilding. After spending several weeks stitching on elegant trifles, shortly before Christmas they held the bazaar in the elegant Union Hotel.

Hiram and Pocket and Dwight dutifully attended. Afterwards they came to the Calico Palace laden with fancy work. They sent one of the barboys to summon Marny and Kendra to a private card room, where they had spread their purchases on the table. "Take what you want," Hiram said, "and give Lulu and Lolo the rest. We have tatting and tidies and tea aprons, reticules and penwipers and lamp mats—"

"How do you know what these doodads are?" Dwight asked with wondering laughter.

"I'm a minister's son," Hiram reminded him. "I know all about church bazaars. Help yourselves, girls."

The girls took some hemstitched handkerchiefs, and Kendra chose also a pincushion and Marny a hair-band of pale green ribbon trimmed with silk flowers. The men told them about the fair.

"It was a great occasion," said Hiram. "All the beauty and fashion were there. Mr. and Mrs. Eustis, Mr. and Mrs. Chase, Mr. and Mrs. Fenway—"

"And Mr. Hiram Boyd," Pocket said, "spending his money and winning more clients for his bank."

"And floundering and falling over my big feet among those dainty little ribbon-draped booths," said Hiram. He stood up. "Now that I've done my social duty, I'm going to Marny's bar."

"And I'd better get back to my card table," said Marny. "After a church fair almost next door, I have a feeling that a lot of fellows will be heading this way, to loosen up and act natural."

She was right. The Calico Palace had a rush of late business. When she left her card table Marny was happy, but weary indeed. The next evening she said she was tired of cards and felt like going out. She and Dwight went to see the show at the Dramatic Museum.

The audience here was not as select as that at the Jenny Lind, nor as dignified. When Dwight and Marny entered their box, she received noisy greetings from several patrons of her card table, who had evidently paused at the bar on their way in. She smiled back at them and so did Dwight. Dwight was proud to be seen escorting Marny, and to know he was the only man in town who had the privilege of doing so.

454

Looking over the audience, Marny saw Captain Pollock, but he was not one of those who greeted her. He gave no sign of seeing her at all. For a moment Marny wondered if he still actively disliked her, but the show was beginning. She turned her attention to the stage.

First there was music by the orchestra. After this, the program said, there would be a one-act farce, and then an interlude of songs by Miss Hortensia Vale. Marny had never heard of Miss Hortensia Vale, but Dwight said he had. She was newly arrived from the East, and he had been told she sang well. The program said Hortensia would give them songs to her own guitar music, and more songs to a piano accompaniment by a gentleman from Peru.

The farce was well played and Marny liked it. When the curtains parted again she saw Hortensia Vale, sitting on a beribboned ladder under an arch abloom with paper flowers. At one side of the stage was the piano. Evidently Hortensia was going to sing first to the music of her own guitar, for she held the guitar on her knee. She was not a beautiful girl, but she was a pleasing one, with fluffy brown hair and a merry smile. Her dress displayed her figure more lavishly than would have been thought proper at the Jenny Lind, but it was a good figure and this audience approved and applauded. Hortensia kissed her hand to them, and with easy grace she began to play her guitar.

Though Marny had no ear for music she could sense that the audience was listening with pleasure. Hortensia began to sing, with a saucy mirth.

"It's hard to be a lady in a town like San Francisco,
    A girl just has to do the best she can—
You have to be so brisk, oh! You take an awful risk, oh!
    For everywhere you look you see a man."

Marny laughed, and listened with growing interest. For while she was no judge of Hortensia's voice she could certainly see that the girl had personality. Marny was wondering if Hortensia could play the piano. The song went on.

"Oh, men are very plenty here beside the Golden Gate—
    Enough to please the most exacting shopper,
And when every man you see wants to take you on his knee,
    It's really hard to keep on being proper."

455

Her hearers were liking her more and more. Marny decided that she would tell Norman to come here tomorrow and find out if Hortensia could play the piano as well as sing. With her twinkling stage presence, as a piano player she would be worth a lot of gold dust at the Calico Palace.

Hortensia sang.

"If I'm out some rainy evening when the rats run helter-
    skelter,
  And the streets are waterfally and cascady,
If some stranger from the placers wants to carry me to
    shelter,
  I don't think I'll even try to be a lady!"

To great applause, she slipped down from the ladder. Dwight spoke to Marny.

"She's good, isn't she?"

Marny nodded with enthusiasm, and turned her eyes back to the stage. Hortensia was still bowing her thanks, laughing and enjoying it all. They wanted more, and she was glad to give it to them. Dwight added,

"And not bad looking, either. We must come here again to hear—Ah, Marny!"

Before his words were out Marny herself had given a cry of dismay. The firebells were ringing.

The whole audience had started from their seats. All through the theater there were shouts of fright. Every man there feared the fire might be burning something that belonged to him. Or that looters, in the general alarm, were starting to work. They wanted to get out and see to their property. Where were the doors? Nobody seemed to remember. They were pushing, elbowing, everybody demanding that everybody else make room. In another second there might have been panic.

But there was not. Dropping her guitar, Hortensia had almost leaped to the piano. She began to play.

She was playing a march. She was pounding it out with all her strength, thump, thump, thump, and loud, loud, loud. It was so loud that they heard it above their own frightened voices. The Dramatic Museum was not a large theater, and Hortensia's thumps resounded like sounds of command.

Her hearers began to move in more regular fashion, following the rhythm without realizing that they were doing so.

Their exit was not orderly, but at least nobody was being knocked down and trampled upon.

In their box above the main floor Marny and Dwight saw it all with astonished admiration. Dwight's hand gripped Marny's elbow. He had turned toward the door that led out of the box, but had paused at the imperious sound of Hortensia's music. Now he spoke, in a voice of respect.

"I said she was good!"

"She's better than good," said Marny. "She can think."

Now Marny was certain. She wanted Hortensia to take Rosabel's place at the Calico Palace. If, she recalled with a start of terror, if the Calico Palace was still there tomorrow.

On herself and Dwight, as on the rest of them, Hortensia's playing had had just the effect Hortensia had wanted it to have. It had slowed them down for half a minute. Now Dwight was urging her out of the box and the exit beyond it. He was no longer interested in Hortensia. As the cold outside air struck their faces he was saying,

"Hurry, Marny! Yonder it is—see the smoke? Over toward the waterfront. Looks like Sacramento Street. I've got some buildings in that area—come on, Marny!"

He was almost making her run. She did not care. A weight had been lifted off her mind. The fire was not on the plaza. At the joy of this knowledge she was light-hearted enough to feel a twinge of amusement as she thought Dwight seemed less concerned about her safety, or even his own, than about the test now being given his buildings. As he rushed her on toward the fire she heard him exclaim,

"It's nowhere near the Calico Palace!"

Almost out of breath, Marny managed to ask, "Should we flood the roof just to be sure?"

"We don't need to. The wind's blowing the wrong way."

His voice had a sound of disappointment. Dwight had so much wanted to prove that the largest and most challenging of his buildings could withstand a fire. And now the wind was blowing the wrong way. Marny wanted to laugh, and at the same time she felt almost sorry for him.

57

To the joy of Marny and the secret disappointment of Dwight, the Calico Palace was not endangered that night. The firemen held the flames in two blocks near the waterfront.

But when the fire was out Dwight was a happy man. For though the burnt area was small, in that area were two buildings that had been put up under his own direction. These were still standing. On both sides of each one, other buildings had gone down. But not Dwight's. The outer walls had been blackened, and stained by the floods of water the firemen had pumped from the sea, but there had been no real harm. The fire had taken place on a Saturday night; on Monday morning both Dwight's buildings were open for business.

Several days after the fire one of the newspapers published an article about Dwight's buildings. The writer urged other builders to study Dwight's methods and profit by them. He praised the roof tanks, and even more he praised Dwight's refusal to hurry.

"Mr. Carson knows," said the writer, "that a house is not meant to spring up overnight like a toadstool. Too many men in San Francisco seem not to know it."

Dwight bought fifty copies of the paper. Half of these he sent to his father and brothers and friends in New York. The rest he kept to gloat over.

His office was besieged by men who wanted him to put up banks and stores and hotels. Dwight declined. He was at work on two buildings now, he said, buildings he had begun before the fire. He could not undertake anything more until these were finished. But Marny told Kendra she thought Dwight was refusing new contracts because he was planning to go back to New York.

"He hasn't said so," Marny added, "but he spreads out the paper and taps his finger on the column about him. He says, 'This will show them I can do it. I've done it.'"

They were in the kitchen drinking chocolate. Marny stroked Geraldine, who lay curled up in her lap. She went on.

"I think he's not content to have somebody tell them he can do it. He wants to go home and *do* it."

"I can't blame him," said Kendra.

"Neither can I," said Marny. "What's the fun of having scalps at your belt unless you can go back to the wigwam and show them?" She set her empty cup in the saucer. "Time I went down and took over from the Harvard man."

The Harvard man had a name, but in the Calico Palace few people ever used it. Marny now had three dealers who had come from the famous universities of New England. They all three were members of churchly families, and all three had been named for New England's most famous clergyman. With three men named respectively Jonathan Edwards Bradford, Jonathan Edwards Braxton, and Jonathan Edwards Brand, nobody could keep them straight. So in Marny's parlor the three dealers were called by the names of their universities, Harvard, Yale, and Brown.

Marny and her learned assistants were good friends. They had a great deal in common.

Marny went down to take over from the Harvard man. Left alone, Kendra wondered if Marny would be lonesome when Dwight left her. Probably she would miss him for a while, as she had missed Archwood, then she would take another swain, as she had taken Dwight. Marny seemed determined to stay on the surface of life. She was not going to let anything, and certainly not anybody, affect her deeply. She did not want any soul-shaking experience. So far she had managed very well.

As only two city blocks had been wrecked, this fire had been far less costly than the earlier ones. At Marny's bar men said the total loss had been only about a hundred thousand ounces. They said "only" with ironic laughter. Only a hundred thousand ounces. Elsewhere, people might call this a big fire. But not people in San Francisco.

They laughed, but their laughter was harsh. This fire had been set on purpose. The men who started it had chosen a store that stood next to a warehouse, both filled with fine goods. They had been on the spot, waiting for plunder. As soon as they saw their fire successfully burning they had crept from dark corners, ready to carry off all they could steal. Some of these vultures had been caught and their loot re-

459

covered. But the men at the bar knew there were more of them, gathered in the saloons and flophouses around Clark's Point, eager to try again.

Marny's patrons struck the bar with angry fists. Again and again she heard them voicing the old refrain. "Those firebugs have got to be stopped. I don't believe in lynching, but... ."

They talked loud and long, but they did not lynch anybody. The fire had hurt the fortunes of only a few men, and the talkers at the bar found that other people's troubles were not too hard to bear.

As soon as the first excitement of the fire had abated Marny told Norman about Hortensia. Norman was interested at once. He bought a ticket to the Dramatic Museum and came back all aglow.

"She'll bring in the bons garçons," he said.

The next day he sent Hortensia a letter. Marny helped him write it.

Kendra asked Marny what inducements he had offered. She had no doubt that the manager of the Dramatic Museum would do his best to keep Hortensia there. The ships were bringing more women than last year, but this still meant only five or six women to each hundred men; and half of these were dimwitted sluts from Sydney and the South American ports, brought in by procurers for the back-alley brothels. A girl like Hortensia, attractive and talented, was hard to find.

Marny said Norman had promised that whatever salary Hortensia was receiving now, he would increase it. And being a smart man, Norman knew there was another lure quite as tempting as higher pay. This was a snug private room to sleep in. Lodging houses were springing up, as the newspaper had said, as fast as toadstools. But not even these were enough to take care of the people who kept coming, across the Isthmus, over the prairies, around the Horn. By inquiring, Norman had found that Hortensia lived in one of these shaky "hotels." She had a room eight feet by ten, which she had to share with another actress. In the letter Marny had helped him write, Norman had promised Hortensia that her compensation at the Calico Palace would include a room of her own.

"He said modestly," Marny explained, "that he could give her 'a single room, quite comfortable.' You'll note he said a *single* room. He doesn't want her to bring a gentleman friend."

"Has she got a gentleman friend?" asked Kendra.

"I don't know," said Marny, "but he's taking no chances. I believe Norman has hopes."

One of the barboys delivered the letter to Hortensia. He brought back an answer, written in a firm hand with only two misspelled words. Hortensia said if Mr. Norman Lamont would call for her she would visit the Calico Palace and discuss his offer.

Norman called for her that same afternoon, and brought her to the Calico Palace. Before asking about the salary or her hours of work, Hortensia said she wanted to see the promised bedroom. With wonder in her eyes she noted the rainproof window sash, the sturdy walls, the absence of rats. She exclaimed, "Why Mr. Lamont, it's like New Yor—" and interrupted herself. "Has the door got a key? And a bolt?"

Norman reluctantly said yes.

They went into his office and conferred about terms. Afterward, Norman walked with Hortensia to the Dramatic Museum, in time for her to prepare for her evening show.

"What did she say?" Marny asked eagerly when he came back.

Norman gave an expressive Latin shrug. "She said she'd think it over and let me know. What she meant was, she would give the theater chap his chance to offer her more than I did."

For a week, Norman and the theater chap bargained for Hortensia. Hortensia stood aside. She gave her show every evening, and after the show she came into the office of the theater chap, bringing her workbasket. While the two men argued Hortensia sewed. She rarely said anything. She merely sat there, like a lady cat who lets two tomcats fight over her, serenely washing her face while she waits to bestow her favors on whichever tom will win the duel.

Only once did her cool reserve show a crack. This was the evening of another church fair, this one in the armory of the California Guard on Dupont Street.

The purpose of this fair was to raise money for the unsuccessful miners who were staggering off the river boats, starving and sick. Norman and the theater chap were talking business. In a corner of the office, calm as ever, Hortensia sat with her sewing. All of a sudden a flutist known as Buster came rushing in to tell them the news.

Buster said the fair had been proceeding in the most refined manner, when who should drop in to spend money

461

but the owner of the El Dorado and his girl friend, madame of one of the town's more elegant brothels. How the church ladies recognized the girl friend, nobody was able to state. But recognize her they did. The ladies closed their booths and told their husbands the fair was ended. The miners might be sick and starving, but this was not important compared to such an affront to themselves. They were not going to sell their fancywork in the presence of Any Such Woman.

At this point in Buster's story, from the corner of the room came a sputter of mirth. Her hand against the back of her chair, her face buried in the crook of her elbow, Hortensia was shaking with giggles.

The three men began to laugh with her. "What did the husbands do?" asked Norman. "Did they order her to leave?"

"They didn't *order* her to do anything," answered Buster. "I guess they were afraid the El Dorado man might start shooting. They just *talked* to him, man to man. They explained to him how it was. They told him, if he didn't take her out, they didn't know *what* the ladies might do."

"I don't know either," murmured Norman.

"So he took her away," said Buster. "When she was gone the ladies opened the booths again. I guess they are still selling fancywork."

"Somebody is going to sell me a drink," said Norman. "I'll treat all round. What'll you have, Hortensia?"

Business talk was over for the evening. However, it was resumed the next day. Two days later Hortensia agreed to come to the Calico Palace.

When Marny heard about the incident at the fair, she said to Norman, "Please find out for me,—was one of the ladies present named Mrs. Posey?"

Norman made inquiry and told Marny she was right. "How did you know?"

Marny patted the pocket where she carried her cards. "Maybe the cards told me," she answered.

Hortensia came to the Calico Palace in time to play the piano at Christmas. Later, when they knew her better, she told Marny and Kendra that she had made up her mind to accept Norman's offer as soon as she saw that cozy bedroom. But Norman did not know this and neither did the theater chap. She had been quite willing to keep them in suspense a few days while they pushed up the price.

Kendra was amused, Marny admiring. "Just what I would have done myself," said Marny. "I told you she had sense."

When Hortensia moved into the cozy bedroom she moved in alone. Hortensia had no gentleman friend. She told Marny and Kendra she had left New York because of trouble with a gentleman there. She had bought her own steamer ticket and had crossed the Isthmus with no escort. "The whole party stayed together," she said. "I didn't need a man then and I don't need one now."

In the parlor she laughed and flirted, but she guarded her bedroom key. However, Norman still had hopes.

"At least," Marny said thoughtfully to Kendra, "I've noticed that since she came to us, Norman's temper has improved."

Marny had warned Kendra that Christmas would be a big day, which meant—for the staff of the Calico Palace—an exhausting one. "Holidays are for fun," said Marny, "but they're hard on the people who sell the fun. You'd better do extra baking for a couple of days in advance, and you'll be baking from dawn to midnight Christmas Day." She gave Kendra's hand a sympathetic pat. "Sorry, dear, but that's the way it is."

Kendra was not sorry. Christmas was not going to be a happy anniversary for her. She was glad she would be too busy to brood over her heartbreak of a year ago.

On the evening of Christmas Day, Hiram wandered into the kitchen. "Mind if I stop for a few minutes?" he asked.

Kendra was mixing a fresh bowl of batter while a batch of her cupcakes baked in the oven. "Glad to have you," she said, with a gesture toward the stove. "I've made coffee for Marny when she comes in for a rest. Pour a cup for yourself."

Hiram did so. "Won't you have one?"

"Not yet," she returned, laughing a little as she stirred the batter. "Not until I get those cakes out of the oven and these in. Then I can sit down."

Hiram carefully placed his big self on a chair and sipped coffee. Lolo came in with empty trays and stayed to grease the pans for the cakes Kendra was mixing now. Hiram watched as they worked. "I'd offer to help," he said in a voice of apology, "but I don't know how."

"I don't need you," Kendra assured him. "You manage a bank, which I can't; I cook, which you can't."

Hiram good-naturedly agreed. In spite of the stout walls,

463

the racket from the first floor rose to meet the racket from Marny's parlor, where Hortensia was pounding the piano with all her might. Other sounds of mirth suggested gleeful parties in the private card rooms. Marny came in, mopping her brow with her handkerchief. She plopped herself into a chair and sighed gratefully as Hiram set a cup of coffee before her. They heard a burst of laughter from somewhere, and Hiram commented,

"Business sounds good."

"Business is stupendous," said Marny. "And tomorrow we'll do more business, selling fizz-powders at the bar." She sipped her coffee complacently. "I don't think the fizz-powders do any good, but the boys imagine they feel better if they take something. Especially something that tastes bad and costs money. So, I'm glad to oblige."

Kendra took the cakes out of the oven, put a plateful on the table, and arranged the rest on the trays Lolo had brought in. While Lolo carried the trays into the parlor Kendra put the fresh pans into the oven. Hiram brought her a cup of coffee and she sat down at the table. They all three began to munch hot cupcakes.

"Aren't these luscious?" Marny exclaimed.

Hiram said Kendra was the best cook in the world.

When Marny had gone back to her card game, Hiram told Kendra he had come here to bring her an invitation. Tomorrow, while tonight's merrymakers were taking fizz-powders, wouldn't she take dinner with him at the Union Hotel?

"I can't promise a meal as good as those you cook," said Hiram, "but it's the best restaurant in town, and it's not bad. We can have an early dinner and go to a show."

"I'd like that," said Kendra. She looked straight at him across their empty cups. "You're good to me, Hiram," she said sincerely.

"No I'm not," said Hiram. He spoke with decision. "I enjoy your company." He paused a moment and added gravely, "And I'm proud if I can help you do what you're already doing so well."

"Thank you," Kendra said in a low voice. She paused a moment, and then added, "I don't want to talk about last year—that's too hard—but you do help, Hiram."

"That's all I need to know," he returned. He pushed back his chair. "Thanks for the goodies. Now I'll run along."

He stood up, turned as if to leave, hesitated, and turned

464

back to face her, standing with his big hands holding the back of his chair.

"Kendra, I've been wanting to tell you something," he blurted, and stopped.

She said, "Yes, Hiram?"

"I've been putting it off," he said jerkily, "because—well, I didn't know how to say it. I still don't know how. I think a lot of you—I'm sure you know that—but just why I like you so much—it's hard to find words for it."

As she looked up at him Kendra's lips parted in astonishment. Not because Hiram had told her he liked her—as he had said, she knew this already—but for the first time since she had known him she saw Hiram actually looking bashful.

"But all the same," said Hiram, "I want to tell you."

He went on, looking more bashful as he proceeded.

"Kendra, you belong to a special group of people. Rare people." He shifted his feet. "I learned a lot," he said, "when I was on the *Cynthia*. There were some old sea-dogs aboard that ship. They had a term for the sort of man they respected most. They said, 'He can take the wind as God sends it.' That's the group I'm talking about. The rare people who can take the wind as God sends it. And you can take it."

Startled, she protested swiftly. "I'm not that good, Hiram! I do try, but—"

"—but you *can* take it!" he broke in, almost angrily. His hands were tight on the chair back. "You're one of them. It's like—well, like a club. The most exclusive club on earth. Nobody can get in who doesn't belong. And by damn, Kendra, you belong."

He stopped short. Kendra did not answer because she could not. Her throat had closed up. Hiram drew a long hard breath. After a moment he exclaimed,

"I know, Kendra. Other people—people like me—we can tell who belongs. Even though we don't."

Kendra had heard him with growing surprise. She had been fairly stunned into silence; then as he spoke his last line it was as if her amazement exploded into words. She cried out,

"But you do belong, Hiram!"

He shook his big untidy head. "No," he said. He spoke in a quiet voice, strange after the vehemence of what he had just been saying. "No," he repeated. He added with a rueful little smile, "I'm trying to get into the club. But I'm not in yet."

"What are you talking about?" she demanded. "Why not?"

Hiram shook his head again. He gave her another regretful smile. "If I had guts enough to tell you, Kendra," he said, "I'd belong."

Then he pushed, he almost threw, the chair against the table, and turned around.

"Good night," he said abruptly, and banged the door as he went out.

When Hiram called for her the next evening he said nothing more about the most exclusive club on earth. He was in good spirits, but he kept the conversation on everyday subjects.

Their dinner at the Union Hotel was excellent, and in the dining room Kendra saw some of the wealthiest men in town. She remembered how, on their way back from Shiny Gulch, Hiram had told her he intended to get rich. He was evidently doing so. Not many men, in San Francisco or anywhere else, could pay such prices as those of the Union Hotel.

After dinner they went to the play at the Jenny Lind. When it was over Hiram walked with her back to the Calico Palace, and she thanked him for a pleasant evening.

This was exactly what it had been. Pleasant, but not outstanding. Kendra had a vague feeling of disappointment.

In the days that followed, Hiram came into the Calico Palace as often as before. He bought drinks and played cards, and several times he and Kendra went again to dinner and a play. But he made no reference to what he had said to her Christmas evening. It was as if he wanted to forget he had said it. Kendra kept away from the subject, since it was plain that he wanted her to do so, but she did wish she could understand him.

They all had many other matters to talk about. The weather was proving amazingly agreeable. Everybody who had slogged through last year's mud had dreaded the return of the rainy season, but this winter they were having little rain and many days of sun. Pocket and Hiram both said their business was good. The Calico Palace was full every night. While Hortensia did not play the piano as well as Rosabel, she played quite well enough to please the bons garçons in the parlor. Every evening a group of listeners gathered around her, and to Marny's astonishment, Captain Pollock was often among them.

Heretofore, Captain Pollock had stayed away from the

Calico Palace. At least, he had not been into Marny's parlor, and if he had patronized the tables in the big public room downstairs, nobody had told her about it. When he came into the parlor now, he stayed away from her card table. He would spend a while at some other game, go to the bar for a drink, and glass in hand, join the men by the piano. Marny recalled that she had seen him in the audience the first time she had heard Hortensia play. As Pollock had no scruples about lady-chasing when he was in port, Marny wondered if he was one of those who hoped Hortensia would relax her present chaste behavior.

If so, he was having no more success than the rest of them. To Norman's dismay, and that of various others, Hortensia still locked her bedroom door.

Marny had no interest in what Captain Pollock did, but Norman was her friend. Sympathizing but stern, she advised him, "Let her alone."

Norman grunted.

"There are other girls in town," said Marny. She smiled. "Norman, if you're too precipitate—"

"Too what?"

"If you're in too much of a hurry," Marny amended herself, "you're likely to lose out altogether. But if you'll bide your time, I think you'll get what you want."

Norman perked up. "You do? Why?"

"She protests too much," said Marny. "Don't you remember, she told us she came here because she'd had trouble with a man and wanted to get away. She's still mad with men in general. That won't last. It never does. But while it lasts, you'd better go chase somebody else."

Though her advice was not what he wanted to hear, Norman knew it was wise. As Marny had observed before, Norman had scant ethics but a lot of plain sense. Hortensia was an asset to the Calico Palace. If she was not happy here she could leave tomorrow for any of a dozen other establishments. And as Marny had reminded him, there were other girls in town.

To the surprise of nobody—least of all Marny—not long after Christmas Dwight bought a ticket to New York. The buildings he had been working on at the time of the fire were neither large nor complex, and they were not hard to finish.

467

Dwight pushed them to completion, and early in February he took a steamer for the Isthmus.

As with Archwood, Marny cheerfully said goodby to Dwight and wished him well. "He's a fine fellow and I like him," she said to Kendra, "but I never did expect this to last forever. I've had plenty of practice in saying goodby."

Kendra wondered if Marny was never going to get tired of saying goodby. For all her mirth and merriment, Marny was essentially alone. Kendra herself had had plenty of practice in loneliness, and she did not like it.

But right now, if Marny continued to be alone it was because she wanted to. Hardly was Dwight's steamer across the horizon before she was beset by admirers. Some of them made their offers in person, others wrote letters. Some swore they would keep her in luxury undreamed of, others wanted to marry her. Marny said no to them all. She was gracious but firm. "I like men," she said to Kendra, "but sometimes I get tired of them."

The day after Dwight's steamer sailed Marny went to the vault of Hiram's bank and took out her nugget necklace.

"It's my favorite ornament," she explained.

She wore it that evening. Kendra guessed that she was wearing it not only because it was her favorite ornament, but because it was a badge of independence. Dwight had been a fine fellow but he had also been exceedingly possessive. Marny had not forgotten the day he had insisted that she wear his pearls to the wedding.

But she had genuinely liked Dwight. A few evenings later, drinking chocolate between shifts at her card table, she frankly told Kendra she missed him. Geraldine came purring around her ankles and Marny picked her up.

"I'm glad we have a kitten," said Marny, stroking Geraldine's fur. "She's a lot of company."

Kendra came to the table with a cup of her own. Marny went on,

"I love our kitten. Only she's hardly a kitten any more, she's growing. Have you noticed, Kendra? Pretty soon she'll be a cat."

Under Marny's affectionate stroking, Geraldine stretched and sighed with pleasure. Kendra exclaimed, almost with envy, "And she needs so little to make her happy!"

Marny smiled and nodded. "Plenty to eat, plenty of cuddling, a warm place to sleep—oh, it's so simple to be a cat!"

She added that it was time she took over her table from the Harvard man. She put Geraldine on the floor and drew the nugget necklace out of the pocket of her dress. Between shifts at the card table she liked to take off the necklace. The nuggets were heavy, and after an hour or so they grew wearisome on her neck. She fastened the catch and made sure her pretty little Colt was in place at her belt. Marny had never fired her gun in the parlor, though several times when some fellow became a nuisance she had whipped out the gun and held it on the offender until the guards could lead him outside. But she always wore it, and she frequently practiced using it. She made no secret of this; she wanted it known that she could take care of herself.

Watching her, impulsively Kendra exclaimed, "Marny, it's none of my business, but—don't you think you'll ever want anything that—well, that will *last?*"

"I don't know," answered Marny. "I don't even know if there is any such thing."

"I don't either," Kendra said frankly, "but I keep hoping there is."

She looked at Geraldine, curled up in a warm corner, blissfully content. "As you said, Marny—it's so simple to be a cat!"

Marny laughed in agreement, waved goodby, and went back to her parlor.

58

The very next day, Marny and Kendra learned that it was not so simple to be a cat.

Shortly before noon, when Kendra went to Geraldine's room with a pan of chopped meat, she found that their kitten had changed overnight. Usually Geraldine ran to meet her, eager to get her pan of food. But today Geraldine was not concerned about food. She was crying, dashing from wall to wall, rolling on the floor, and otherwise behaving in a most

469

alarming fashion. Frightened, Kendra shut Geraldine in the room and went to call Marny.

Wrapped in her woolen robe, her hair like a copper-red shawl on her shoulders, Marny was having coffee at the kitchen table. She listened sleepily, and sleepily began to laugh. As she did so, Kendra had a flash of enlightenment.

"Do you suppose," she exclaimed, "our kitten has turned into a cat?"

"It does seem so," said Marny. "I've never seen a cat in a mood for love, but I've been told this is the way they carry on. We'll ask the vet."

They sent one of the barboys to the office of Dr. Wardlaw. The doctor came in later that day, was led up to Geraldine's room, looked her over, and smiled wisely.

"You're right, girls," he said. "She's grown up."

He told them not to let her have kittens yet. Give her a bit more time. Marny and Kendra looked at each other, startled.

"Do we want her to have kittens?" Marny asked.

"I hadn't thought of it," said Kendra.

"You girls don't know much about cats, do you?" said Dr. Wardlaw.

"No," Marny owned modestly, "we don't."

"We'll think about the kittens," said Kendra.

"You'd better," said the doctor.

Over her squalls and protests, they locked up the room with Geraldine inside it.

For two more days and nights, Geraldine continued her shameless conduct. Lovesick tomcats gathered on the dump heap behind the Calico Palace. They tried to climb the brick walls. All night they yowled. To human ears their tones were dreadful noises, but Geraldine heard them as the sweetest of love songs.

It did not last long. On the third night Geraldine yawned and went to sleep. The next day she had forgotten all about the matter. From the innocent look of her nobody would have thought she could ever have behaved like such a hussy.

Her suitors went their way. The early California spring began. The hills turned green, and beds of wild flowers began to bloom on the slopes. As Valentine's Day came near, Kendra made heart-shaped cookies for sale, Marny hung pictures of cupids on her parlor walls, and Hortensia played romantic ballads on the piano. Hiram and Pocket sent Geraldine a feather cushion, and a white lace valentine with a tender sentiment signed Tom Katz.

But in San Francisco nobody lived long in peace. Besides the usual assaults and burglaries on dark streets, every few days they heard a new fire alarm; and not long after Valentine's Day there was a riot in the plaza.

The turmoil in the plaza was not a public execution but it was very nearly one. A storekeeper, alone in his store one evening, had been beaten up by two ruffians who left him unconscious on the floor and made off with his cash box. Now two men had been arrested and charged with the crime. The day they were brought in, several thousand citizens rushed to the plaza shouting that they wanted the prisoners hanged right here and right now.

The storekeeper had not died, and the assault was no worse than hundreds that had gone before it. But for some reason this one had tipped the scales of the people's endurance. They were in a mood to hang somebody. The pair now being charged looked like just the sort they wanted to hang.

The men in custody were useless fellows, not noted for habits of temperance or steady work. Still, there was no clear proof that they were the men who had attacked the storekeeper. But for two days the plaza seethed like a pot of boiling water.

While the tumult raged, the resorts around the plaza put on airs of desperate gaiety and went on with business. In the Calico Palace, Marny dealt cards and Norman moved about with gallantry and grace. Kendra baked cakes, Hortensia played the piano, the croupiers and bartenders stanchly stayed at their posts. The Blackbeards and their assistants managed to keep the peace indoors. But they all quaked lest the men yelling for law and order outside should lose their tempers and start behaving like the men who had roused their wrath. And in the midst of all the other commotion Geraldine had another attack of love trouble.

Marny and Kendra had decided that they wanted Geraldine to have a family. They had planned that when the time came they would put her into the little house Dwight had made, and carry her to Dr. Wardlaw's office. The doctor had promised that he would make her acquainted with a handsome tomcat worthy to be the father of her children.

But with those thousands of men storming outside, they could not follow their plan. All they could do now was shut the door of Geraldine's room and let her do some storming of her own.

In the plaza, citizens with cooler heads were begging for order. At last, about one o'clock on the second night of the uproar, the cooler heads prevailed. Tired and sleepy, the crowd began to disperse. A good many of the men came to the bars of the Calico Palace. Over their drinks they muttered that they were going home *this* time, but if the crimes did not lessen somebody was going to get hanged for sure.

Hiram came up to Marny's parlor to make certain she and Kendra were all right. Marny told him they had suffered nothing but loss of sleep, "and being scared half to death," she added, "but we're used to that." Hiram had time for only one drink at the bar before Norman tapped him on the shoulder and said, "Closing time."

Closing the Calico Palace tonight took longer than usual, but with their customary persistence the Blackbeards and the other guards managed to do it. They were expert at getting the building empty of everybody who did not belong here. They started on the top floor and worked down, and two watchmen stayed on guard until the gambling rooms opened in the morning, just in case the Blackbeards had missed a prowler. So far, they never had.

When the customers had gone, Marny went to the bar and poured a drink. She sipped it thankfully. Her head ached and so did her arms and legs and back, tense with long apprehension. She was glad to reflect that the men who had been making all that racket must be as weary as she was, so the plaza would be quiet tomorrow and she could catch up on her sleep. She poured another drink, lighted a candle, and with the glass in one hand and the candlestick in the other she went upstairs.

Kendra's door was closed and Marny heard no sound from beyond it. Probably Kendra was already asleep. Marny was crossing the landing to her own room when she saw Norman coming toward her. He too had a glass in his hand.

"Come and sit down a minute," he said, speaking in an undertone so as not to disturb the sleepers. "Something I want to tell you."

They sat down on the top step of the staircase and Marny placed the candlestick between them.

She smothered a yawn. "Make it brief," she pled.

Norman turned his glass between his hands. His face was grave, as if he was about to broach a matter of importance.

Norman had never tried to make love to Marny. She was too smart to attract his amorous thoughts. Norman's idea was that while a smart co-worker was a good thing, no man in his right mind would want a ladylove who could beat him at cards. But the fact that he and Marny had never been lovers and were never going to be, kept the way open for them to be friends. He talked to her with a candor he rarely showed anybody else.

After thinking how best to say it, Norman spoke.

"Marny, I've made a decision."

"Yes, Norman?"

"I've decided," said Norman, "to ask Hortensia to marry me."

Marny was taking a swallow from her glass. She choked on it, and coughed. "Norman," she exclaimed when she could speak, "how many drinks have you had?"

"This is my first this evening. No, I'm serious, Marny."

From Marny's throat came a small wordless sound of wonder. Norman had spurned many girls who would have been glad to marry him. Over and over he had told her he was never going to get married, couldn't see why any man would want to tie himself up like that. She could not help her astonishment. After a moment Norman continued,

"I wanted to tell you, so we could talk it over. Don't you think it's a good idea?"

Marny considered this. After a pause she said, "Norman, if you get married you'll have to do a lot of changing."

"I know," said Norman.

"What I mean is, don't be in a hurry. Think it over."

"I've thought it over," Norman answered firmly. "And I'll tell you something, Marny. It's time I did some changing. I know I don't look it but I'm past forty years old. I'm beginning to want things I used to not want. Like a permanent arrangement. A couple of kids. Things like that."

Norman sounded like a man who meant what he said. Marny sipped her drink and waited for him to go on.

He laughed a little. "And I'll tell you why I like Hortensia," he said. "She's no milksop. Remember how she made us raise her price? She's a *person*. Wouldn't get dull. She'd keep a man interested."

This time Marny answered, and her voice too was firm.

"Hortensia wouldn't put up with any running about, either," she reminded him. "Have you thought of that?"

"Of course I've thought of it!" he returned, almost indignantly. "Like I told you, I'm ready to settle down. Hortensia's a fine girl and I'll treat her right. I'll tell you something else, Marny, Hortensia's a *nice* girl. She may have done a bit of running about herself, but no more. She's kept her door locked ever since she's been here." He added proudly, "To everybody."

"Yes, I know," Marny said with a faint amusement. "You really have thought about this, haven't you?"

"Yes I have. I don't jump into important things without thinking. You ought to know that by now."

He was in earnest, but Marny could not help wondering how long this was going to last. However, she reflected as he talked on, Hortensia could take care of herself. She had left New York determined to come to California, but without money enough for the journey. She had told them how she had worked her way, going as far as she could pay for and then getting a theatrical engagement and earning money to take her farther, until at last in New Orleans she had earned enough to buy a ticket for the Isthmus route. If Hortensia married Norman she could cope with him. And Norman was, in many ways, a good catch. He had money and he was making more; and as he had said of Hortensia, he would never be dull.

He was demanding, "Don't you think it's a good idea?"

"I just wanted to make sure, Norman," she answered. "And yes, now that we've talked about it, I think it's a good idea." She drained her glass and stood up.

Norman stood up too. He was smiling all over his face. —Good heavens, thought Marny, he *looks* like a joyful bridegroom.

Norman picked up the candlestick and handed it to her. "You're a good girl, Marny," he said, and gave her cheek a pat.

They said good night and went to their own rooms. After the confusion of the past two days Marny was so tired that she went to sleep quickly, and stayed asleep until noon the next day. She woke feeling well. The sun was shining and the air had a zesty tingle. Marny washed her face, pinned back her hair, put on a robe and started downstairs for breakfast.

At the kitchen door she met Kendra. Marny started to say

474

"Good morning," but before she could speak she saw that Kendra's face was full of trouble. "What's wrong?" Marny exclaimed.

"It's Geraldine," said Kendra. She sounded almost breathless with concern. "Geraldine is gone, Marny. She ran away last night."

"Oh Kendra!" Marny gasped. "You mean she got out—into that mob in the plaza?"

Kendra nodded.

"And half of them toppling drunk," Marny said in a voice of dread.

Kendra nodded again. Their eyes met, and they did not need to tell each other what they were thinking. Those men shouting in the plaza could have killed Geraldine without even seeing her. It would have been easy for a little cat to be trampled in such a frantic mob. Even if she had not been hurt last night, there were all the dangers of today. She could be crushed by a wagon wheel, or her bones broken by the hoofs of a horse. They thought of Geraldine dying in agony, or lost in a cellar and starving.

Marny shivered. "When did you see her last, Kendra?"

"Late yesterday. Come in and I'll tell you about it."

They sat at the kitchen table and Kendra brought Marny a cup of coffee. She said she had gone to Geraldine's room shortly before dark with food and fresh water. Geraldine had made no secret of the fact that she wanted to run out and take a lover, but Kendra had left the pans and shut the door with Geraldine safely inside. Then, when she went to Geraldine's room this morning, the door was ajar and Geraldine had fled.

There was no way to be sure just when she had escaped or how. Everybody had been upset last night. In the confusion, someone could easily have opened the door to Geraldine's room by mistake, and left it unlatched. Kendra had asked the Blackbeards if they had seen Geraldine running around when they were closing up last night. They had said no.

Marny drank two cups of coffee, but when Kendra brought her a hot waffle she had a hard time making herself eat half of it. Kendra was not surprised; she had no appetite either. Marny dressed and went to her card table, glad she had to keep her mind on the cards and not think of Geraldine. She had never dreamed she could feel this way about a cat.

When the Harvard man came to relieve her at the cards,

Hortensia followed her to the door. "I'm so sorry about Geraldine!" Hortensia whispered.

—Hortensia is a nice girl, Marny thought as she went out of the parlor. I wonder if Norman has spoken to her yet. I don't know and I don't care. Oh Geraldine! I wonder if she's still alive. Please, God, if she has to get killed don't let it hurt her very much.

Day after day, they kept hoping they would find Geraldine somewhere in the building. If she had run downstairs while the place was full of men she might have been scared by so many strangers. Maybe she had hidden somewhere and now could not get out of her hiding place. Marny and Kendra looked and looked. They could not find her. At night they listened at the door by which Geraldine had first come in, hoping they would hear her calling from outside. Night after night they heard nothing but the wind, and sometimes a spatter of rain, and revelers singing their way home. Sadly, they came upstairs.

"We might as well give up," Marny said at last.

"We can always find another cat," said Kendra, "but—"

She paused and Marny finished the sentence. "—but it won't be the same cat. It won't be Geraldine."

They sat at the kitchen table, Marny drinking chocolate while she took a break from the cards. Geraldine had been gone ten days.

Kendra glanced at the clock. It was nearly midnight and she was tired. In the oven was her last batch of cakes for the day. When these were done she could go to bed. "Maybe," she said wearily, "we ought to forget about Geraldine."

"I wish I could!" Marny retorted. "Damn cats. I wish I'd never seen a cat. I'm never going to adopt another cat as long as I live. If anybody had told me—Kendra! What's the matter?"

Kendra had given a start. She was holding up a hand in warning. "Hush! I heard something."

Now Marny heard it too, from just beyond the kitchen door. The mew of a cat.

Marny set down her cup so abruptly that she spilt chocolate on the table. Kendra had sprung to her feet and flung open the door.

Into the kitchen walked Geraldine. She came in calmly, and with the utmost self-assurance looked up at them and

476

made the sound that they had learned meant in cat language, "I am hungry and you will please do something about it."

Kendra snatched her up and held her close. Marny glared at her.

"You miserable beast," said Marny, "I could gladly hang *you* in the plaza."

Geraldine replied that she was hungry and they would please do something about it.

Kendra was already doing something about it. Even as she spoke Marny had been holding out her hands. Now she cuddled Geraldine in her lap, murmuring endearments while Kendra took the food pan from the shelf where she had sadly placed it. She had no chopped meat ready, so as on the night of Geraldine's arrival she filled the pan with expensive milk and embellished the milk with an expensive egg.

Geraldine was thinner than she used to be and her fur was stained with mud, but she showed no sign of having been hurt. Like most cats she preferred meat to milk, but just now she was hungry enough to be glad of whatever was set before her. While she lapped her eggnog Marny and Kendra asked each other questions.

It was not hard to guess how Geraldine had come in. The big front door was always swinging as customers came and went, and cats had a way of slipping past people's legs. But where had she been all this time? How had she taken care of herself? Where had she slept? What had she eaten? And how, oh how, had she escaped the trampling mob, the wheels, the hoofs?

"We'll never know," said Kendra.

"I told you," said Marny, "Geraldine was a witch. Back in the Middle Ages some people used to say all cats were witches. Maybe they were right."

Having finished her eggnog, Geraldine chose a warm spot near the stove and began to wash herself. She had an air of velvety content.

"No more crying for love," Kendra said as they watched. "She's had it."

"Yes," said Marny, "she left her maiden bower and she's a maid no more. Kendra, our little friend has learned the ways of the world."

A few evenings later Dr. Wardlaw dropped into Marny's parlor and she consulted him about Geraldine. Dr. Wardlaw took Geraldine into his hands, smiled and nodded. Yes, they should turn the maiden bower into a nursery. Geraldine had run away in late February. The kittens would appear toward the end of April.

As she went back to her card table Marny felt a sense of responsibility. But as she shuffled the cards she also felt a glow of affection.

She still felt it as she came upstairs after closing time. How many kittens would there be? She did not know; she must ask Dr. Wardlaw. Would Geraldine's little house do for a lying-in chamber? She supposed so; she would ask him about this too.

As she neared the fourth floor landing she heard steps, as of someone pacing. Marny raised her candle and looked. The pacer was Norman. As he saw her he hurried to meet her.

Norman's face was drawn and almost pasty. He was handsomely dressed, but his hair was disordered, his collar awry.

"Marny!" he exclaimed, almost in a gasp. "I thought you'd never get here. Marny, tell me what's wrong!"

"What's wrong?" she echoed stupidly as she reached the top step.

Norman gripped her shoulder. "Marny, what's wrong with Hortensia?" He caught his breath. "Marny—she turned me down."

59

Marny had almost forgotten Norman's plan to propose marriage to Hortensia. Her distress at the loss of Geraldine and her joy at Geraldine's return had crowded Norman out of her thoughts. In the rare moments when she did recall what he had told her she had supposed that when he had anything more to say he would say it.

She remembered now that Hortensia had gone out this evening. All the employees of the Calico Palace had their days of leisure, and Hortensia had reminded Marny that today it was her turn. "Mr. Devore will play the piano," said Hortensia. "I'm going to a show." She had not said who was to be her escort and Marny had not thought to ask. The games at her table had been brisk all evening and she had not troubled her head about Hortensia again.

She had not even noticed Norman's absence. When he made his tours of the gambling rooms he was careful not to disturb the players, and Marny concentrated so closely on her cards that often she could not have said whether or not he had been into the parlor all evening.

Now it appeared that Norman and Hortensia had spent this evening together. He had asked her to marry him and she had said no. Norman was in a state of shock.

Again, as when he had told Marny of his decision, they sat down on the top step of the stairs. With stammering astonishment, Norman told her what had taken place.

He could barely believe it himself. Norman had carefully arranged his program. He had never before asked any woman to marry him, and having determined upon this momentous deed he had intended to make it an occasion worth remembering.

He had not been impatient. He had waited until there was a good comedy at the Jenny Lind. Norman did not like serious plays and neither did Hortensia; they both preferred to laugh. When he had asked Hortensia to go with him she had accepted gladly, saying she had a new dress and this was just the time to wear it.

Before the show they had taken dinner at the Union Hotel. With her pretty dress and vivacious manner Hortensia had drawn much attention from the men in the dining room, who had looked at her with admiration and at Norman with envy. Then Norman and Hortensia had gone on to the theater, where he had reserved two of the best seats in the house.

And Hortensia had enjoyed the play. He could tell. He was no innocent lamb about women. He knew when a woman was really having a good time and when she was merely trying to make him think she was. Afterward they came back to the Calico Palace. He conducted her into the largest and most sumptuously furnished of the private card rooms—he had left orders that it was to be kept for him this evening—and a bartender brought them the best champagne from the bar. Hortensia's mood had been as sparkly as the champagne, until he made his carefully planned and carefully worded proposal of marriage. Then she had gone cold. She had said no.

She had not been coquettish, not teasing like a girl who intends to say yes but wants to be begged. She had not even asked for time to think it over. She had said, simply and clearly, that she had not guessed this was what he had had in mind when he asked her to go out with him. Norman had escorted many girls to many shows. Hortensia had thought he wanted her company for one evening, not for the rest of his life. And now, would he please let her go to her own room?

And that, Norman told Marny, was all.

"What's the *matter* with her, Marny?" he pled.

Marny did not know what to answer, and Norman did not wait for an answer anyway.

"I didn't say a rude word to her, Marny!" he rushed on. "I was perfectly respectful every minute. I was going to *marry* her!"

Compared to the blow Norman had received tonight, Rosabel's desertion had been a trifle. He had been sorry to lose Rosabel, but the loss had done no great damage to his self-esteem. He had, in fact, turned down Rosabel by holding out against marriage.

But Hortensia! This he could not comprehend. Over and over he kept saying, "But I was going to *marry* her!"

Marny did feel sympathy for him, but she was also tempted to laugh. Norman had not once asked himself if Hortensia would want him; he had asked only if he wanted Hortensia. He had decided that he did. So he had offered the greatest concession of his life, and she had spurned it.

"What's wrong?" he demanded. "I'm not old or fat. And I've got money. I don't mean dust, I mean *money*."

Marny knew this was true. She knew the exact profits of the Calico Palace, and she knew Norman was canny about money. Hortensia had no income but her salary. From a financial standpoint Norman was a mighty desirable suitor.

—Of course, Marny thought as his words poured out, he *is* a good deal older than she is, even though he thinks he doesn't look it. And he hasn't exactly led an exemplary life. But neither, I suspect, has Hortensia. And they have been getting along well since she came here. She likes him. Still, there's a difference between liking a man and wanting to marry him.

"Norman," said Marny, "would you be willing to let me talk this over with Kendra?"

Norman was startled. It was bad enough to have Marny

know a woman could turn him down; it would be unbearable to have the news spread about.

"Kendra knows more about marriage than we do," Marny urged.

"What good could she do me?" he asked.

"Maybe she can find out why Hortensia said no. She can ask her what the trouble is. Yes, Norman," Marny exclaimed, "that's it. Let Kendra speak to Hortensia. Women talk more frankly to other women than they do to men."

Norman hesitated for a while longer, but his curiosity at last prevailed over his pride. "All right," he said. "You tell Kendra to find out what's the matter with Hortensia."

"I'll tell her. And now please, Norman, it's nearly morning."

When Marny went into the parlor the next afternoon Hortensia was already at the piano, playing tunes. Marny went to the card table and told the Harvard man to take a rest.

Later that day she told Kendra about Norman's plight. Kendra too was surprised at Norman's wish to get married. "But really, Marny," she said, "do you think it's any of our business?"

"No," said Marny, "but I'm sorry for him, Kendra! He's so upset he doesn't know east from west or up from down. Please help him out."

"What do you want me to do?"

"Stay in your room tomorrow," said Marny. "Read a new book. If you haven't got any new books Norman will get some for you. Don't do any cooking. We can manage without cakes in the parlor, and one of the boys will bring you dinner from the Union Hotel. Keep yourself available. I'll ask Hortensia to come in and talk to you."

The next day Kendra went to the kitchen only for breakfast, and left Lulu cleaning up while she came back to her own room. She took up one of the new novels Norman had provided, and was reading when she heard a knock. Laying her book aside she went to open the door, and met Hortensia.

"Marny said you wanted to see me," Hortensia said abruptly.

Hortensia was wearing one of the plain dresses she usually wore behind the scenes, to spare the fancier clothes she wore in the parlor. Her dress was neat and her hair was brushed, but her face had a stubborn look.

Kendra opened the door wide. "Won't you come in?"

Hortensia came in. She sat down on the edge of the bed. The bed had a counterpane of flowered chintz. Looking down at it, and following the design with her finger, Hortensia spoke shortly.

"Look here, Kendra. I think I know what you want to talk about. You can tell Norman he's treated me right and I like working here, but if he wants me to leave I'll start packing right now."

Kendra drew a chair neader the bed and sat down. "He hasn't insulted you, Hortensia," she said, as gently as she could. "He asked you to marry him."

"And I said no. What's wrong with that?"

"Nothing. Nobody is saying you ought to marry him, Hortensia. But you said no and you didn't give him any reason. He's really hurt. More hurt than you know."

"He'll get over it," said Hortensia. She looked up, and with a flash of wise humor she added, "Norman hasn't got the sort of heart that breaks easy."

This was so true that at first Kendra could not think of an answer. Hortensia looked down at her hands, folded now on her knee.

At length Kendra spoke again. "Hortensia, you just told me Norman had treated you right. So now, won't you treat him right? Won't you let him know why you turned him down?"

Hortensia still looked at her hands. She did not answer.

"You don't have to speak to him yourself," said Kendra. "I'll do it. Tell me something I can tell him. Just so he'll understand why it is you don't want to marry him."

For a while Hortensia still said nothing. Kendra waited. At last Hortensia blurted,

"I don't want to marry anybody. I've tried marriage and it's a rotten stinking mess. That's why I came to California. To get away from the man I married back in New York."

She had tried to be defiant, but on the last words her voice broke. She grabbed Kendra's pillow and buried her face, trying to smother her sobs.

Kendra sat on the bed and put an arm around Hortensia's trembling shoulders. When she could control her voice Hortensia looked up. "Lend me a handkerchief, will you? Thanks. I'm sorry, Kendra."

"Don't be sorry. We all cry sometimes. It's good for us."

Kendra waited, saying no more. Hortensia swabbed her eyes dry and looked up again.

"You're nice," said Hortensia.

After another pause, Kendra asked, "Do you want to tell me about it? You don't have to," she added quickly. "If you'd rather not, I'll never speak of it again."

Twisting the handkerchief, damp and bedraggled now, Hortensia murmured, "I guess it's all right to tell you. I didn't do anything disgraceful. I just fell in love with the wrong man."

She kicked at the leg of the bedside table.

"I was working in a theater. I was getting on fine. There were men around the stage door every night and sometimes I went out with one of them, but I didn't like living that way. I really didn't, Kendra. I wanted to settle down. My mother was a married woman, God rest her soul, and I wanted to be one too. And I wanted some babies. I like babies. So I got married. He played a violin in the orchestra and he was good-looking and I fell in love with him. I really fell in love. I thought he loved me back."

Her voice almost broke again, but she swallowed hard and managed to go on.

"We got along all right, fussed sometimes but I guess everybody does, and I was going to have a baby and I was real happy about it. And then one day I stumbled and took a bad fall and I had a miscarriage and I nearly bled to death and I was terribly sick. Of course it was expensive, doctors and all, and a lot of trouble, and one day he walked out and left me."

Kendra gave a start of horror. "You mean he left you *alone*?"

"Yes. Just like that. I guess I would have died except the orchestra leader came around to ask why my husband hadn't shown up for work, and he found me. I wasn't more than half conscious, could hardly talk. He hurried out and told the people at the theater and they came to help me. Theater people always help each other. They're good. The men took up a collection for me and the girls nursed me and after a while I got well."

"And that's why you came to California?"

"Wait a minute," said Hortensia. "I haven't finished. I got well, like I told you, and I went back to work. I even got a raise in salary. I'm good on a stage. Ask Marny. So then, would you believe it, that boiled cabbage of a man turned up again. He said I should forgive him, he really did love me after all. But I knew he had come back because I was making good money and he had a right to it because he was my husband."

Kendra thought of the heartless girl Pocket had loved. The iniquity of some people!

Hortensia went on. "And what could I do? There I was, stuck with that rat, and no way to get rid of him. Oh, I guess if you're rich enough and can get high-priced lawyers they can do something about it, but I couldn't. So I did what a lot of people are doing these days, I changed my name and set out for California."

"And you're still married to him, Hortensia?"

"I guess so," Hortensia said wearily. She gave a terse little laugh. "It's kind of a relief," she added, "to get this off my chest."

"Why haven't you talked about it before?" asked Kendra. "As you said yourself, you didn't do anything disgraceful."

"Well—I guess I didn't want any of you to know I was such a halfwit. I was ashamed of myself for marrying that rotten egg. And then—something else—" Hortensia hesitated.

"Yes?" Kendra prompted her, and added, "Don't tell me if you'd rather not."

"Oh, I guess I might as well tell you," said Hortensia. "I'm telling you everything else. One day just after I came to work at the Calico Palace, I was in Chase and Fenway's with Marny, and a lady came in pushing a baby carriage. She knew Marny, and Marny introduced us. Her name was Mrs. Watson, Serena Watson. She asked how you were, and told me she used to work for you. She had a baby boy, such a pretty baby."

Kendra felt a pain in her throat, a pain of regret for her own child and envy of Serena. She tried to swallow the pain as Hortensia went on.

"I admired the baby and let him put his hand around my finger the way babies do. But it made me feel sad because I thought if I'd had mine I could have been playing with my baby instead of hers. After a while she went on about her shopping, and then Marny told me not to talk to you about Mrs. Watson's baby. Marny said it would make you sad because you had had a baby that died. I could understand this, because I thought if it made me so sorrowful to lose one

484

that wasn't even born, it must be ever so much worse to have one and love it and then have it die. So I didn't say anything about mine—Oh Kendra, Marny was right! Your eyes are getting all teary. I'm so sorry! I shouldn't have said anything now. I'm really sorry, Kendra!"

Kendra had given Hortensia her own handkerchief. She went to the bureau and took a fresh one out of the drawer and dried her eyes.

"It's all right, Hortensia!" she said, making herself smile. "I'll be seeing other women with babies as long as I live and I'd better get used to it." She sat on the bed by Hortensia. "Well, now we know all about each other. It makes us friends."

Hortensia nodded. "You're nice, Kendra," she said again.

Kendra wanted to shed no more tears. She made haste to turn the conversation back to Hortensia's concerns.

"Now let me be sure of this, Hortensia. You're not free to marry."

"That's right."

"Very well. Will you let me tell Norman?"

"Well, yes, I suppose so. I'm ashamed of it all, as I said, but I don't want to hurt his feelings. He's never done anything to me. You tell him how it is."

Kendra said she would tell him how it was. However—though she did not say so—she doubted that this would make Norman give up his wooing. Norman was a man who went after what he wanted.

Kendra was right. When she told Norman that Hortensia had refused him because she was legally married, he exclaimed, "Is that all?" and burst out laughing.

His joy had two sources. First—and possibly the more important of the two—was relief that she had not found him displeasing. Now he could again look into the mirror without doubt of his charms for women. Second, as he told Kendra, there was no place on earth where it was so easy for a woman to get a divorce as in California. Here where women had such rare value, the judges dealt with them gallantly. The prevailing attitude was that if a man was lucky enough to have a wife, especially a pretty wife, it was his business to keep her happy. If he did not do so, he had better give her up to some man who would.

Hortensia had a worthless husband? Then, said Norman, shuffle him out of the deck.

He asked Kendra to say nothing to Hortensia except that she had told him about that first marriage. He said he would speak to a lawyer, then he would tell Hortensia about the divorce himself.

The next day Norman went to see Pocket and asked him to recommend a lawyer. In the library Pocket met most of the leading men of San Francisco, and Norman knew he was both perceptive and honest. Pocket suggested a certain Mr. Stone, who had an office on Montgomery Street. Norman walked down to Montgomery Street and called on him.

Mr. Stone's office was large for San Francisco, and furnished with quiet excellence. Mr. Stone himself was young, like most other men who had come to California, but he had a becoming gravity and an air of competence.

A shrewd observer of men, Norman approved of him at once. Facing Mr. Stone across the desk, Norman told Hortensia's story.

Mr. Stone listened closely, now and then giving a sober nod. He asked if the lady's husband was still in New York.

Norman said yes.

In that case, warned Mr. Stone, the divorce might be—ah —expensive.

Norman said he would pay whatever was necessary. "In coin," he added clearly.

The discreet Mr. Stone permitted himself to smile.

He said a letter must be sent to the husband at his last known address, saying the lady intended to divorce him and offering him a chance to reply. If the husband did not answer, or could not be found, the matter would proceed without him. But the effort must be made. Also, the lady must have testimony supporting what she said. She would need affidavits from her friends in New York, such as the orchestra leader who had found her deserted and half dead, and the actresses who had nursed her back to health.

As soon as the lady had signed formal charges, said Mr. Stone, he would write to his legal correspondents in New York. They would attend to these matters. He could not say how long this would take. Letters sent by way of the Isthmus now reached the Atlantic seaboard in six or eight weeks, but if Hortensia's friends had changed their addresses since she left, it might take some time to locate them. However, his associates would do their best.

Norman said he would bring the lady to Mr. Stone's office

tomorrow. He took out a purse and laid several gold coins on the desk. "Your retainer, sir," he said.

With affable dignity Mr. Stone accepted the coins.

Norman felt a sense of triumph as he left the office. It was all so simple.

When he reached the Calico Palace the parlor was full of men, and Hortensia was in her place at the piano. Norman was not a man to spoil his plans by being too hasty. Instead of interrupting her he waited until the next morning. Before the parlor was open to customers he asked Hortensia if she would let him say a few words to her in private. After some hesitation she said yes.

Norman led her into the empty parlor, where they could talk freely. Standing at the bar, he took a notebook and pencil out of his pocket and prepared to use the bar as a desk.

He told Hortensia about the leniency of the California courts toward women who wanted divorces. He told her about his visit to Mr. Stone. Now what, he asked, was the name of this fellow she had married?

Hortensia's mouth was set in the same stubborn line it had shown when she came to Kendra's room, but Norman did not notice this. Tersely she answered, "Rupert Williams."

"And your name? I mean before you were married."

Hortensia's expression did not change. In the same voice she replied, "Elsie Glutch. On the stage I was Laura Lester."

Norman asked several more questions, and wrote down Hortensia's replies. "All right," he said at length, closing the notebook. "We'll go to see that man Stone this afternoon. Never mind the piano. We'll give Stone all this information and he'll get your divorce. Then you and I can get married."

Hortensia said steadily, "I don't want to get married."

"What!" cried Norman. Now he was back where he had been before he learned about Hortensia's husband. The image in the mirror was crumpling again. "What's wrong, Hortensia?" he demanded. "You—you're not in love with somebody else, are you? Like that moony-eyed sea captain who's been hanging around you?"

"Certainly not," said Hortensia.

"Then what's wrong with me?" Norman pled in dismay. "I gave that lawyer a retainer in *coins*. Gold coins! And now you don't want the divorce!"

"Oh yes, I want the divorce," Hortensia said quickly. For

487

the first time today she was speaking with spirit. "I didn't know," she went on, "how much easier it was to get divorced in California than in New York. But since it is, I want to be rid of that polecat for good. I'll pay the lawyer as fast as I can earn the money. I don't want you to pay him because—" she repeated with emphasis "—because I don't want to get married."

Norman caught his breath "What have I done?" he begged. "Tell me why you don't like me!"

"You haven't done anything," she answered. Her voice had a quaver he had never heard there before. "I do like you." Hortensia pressed her wrist against her mouth, struggling for self-command. When she could speak she burst out, "Don't you understand, Norman? I don't want ever again to get into anything I can't get out of!"

A smile broke over Norman's frightened face. "But that's what I've been telling you, Hortensia! In California you *can* get out of it. You can get out of it any time you want to."

Hortensia gave a little gasp. Standing with an elbow on the bar, she stared at him. Norman hurried on.

"Hortensia, I swear to God I'll treat you right. But if I didn't do what you wanted, in California a judge would cut the marriage right in two and you could walk out. Not only walk out, you could take a poke of your husband's money with you."

Hortensia's eyes were wide with wonder. "Is that in the lawbooks?"

"I don't think they wrote it down exactly that way. But that's the way it's done in San Francisco."

"You mean really, Norman?" she asked with awe. "If I was married to you and didn't like it—no terrible reason but just didn't like it—I wouldn't have to put up with you?"

"If you didn't like me," Norman replied solemnly, "you wouldn't have to put up with me."

Norman had never been so humble in his life. Hortensia had won a victory and she had won it without even trying. If Marny had been there, Marny could have told her how great a victory it was.

60

Hortensia wanted to make up her own mind in her own way. She did not consult Mr. Stone nor did she ask advice of Pocket. She went to Hiram's bank, but she did not consult Hiram because he was Pocket's close friend and would be likely to favor the same lawyer. Instead, she went to the desk of the quiet little Mr. Eustis. She asked Mr. Eustis for the name of a lawyer who would give her counsel about a divorce.

Mr. Eustis did not approve of divorce. But neither did he approve of many other things that brought patrons to his bank. Two of his major depositors were Norman and Blossom, and he took care of their money while strictly objecting to the way they earned it. So though he opposed divorce, when Hortensia made her request Mr. Eustis considered it earnestly. He suggested a lawyer named Mr. Lang.

Hortensia made several visits to Mr. Lang. After each visit she came back to her piano, giving no reports. To Norman's eager queries she replied, "Don't hurry me up. I'll let you know."

Kendra was sympathetic. But Marny preferred the ways of Geraldine.

"When Geraldine is in love," said Marny, "she does as she pleases and asks advice of nobody. It's much simpler."

Geraldine, now getting big around the middle, purred and stretched. Geraldine was well content with the state of things.

Marny too was well content. With the Calico Palace flourishing, and herself working hard to keep it so, she had decided she deserved a little more luxury. Next to the bedroom was a smaller room that she had been using as a storeroom for glassware. But now that the stores of San Francisco were stocked as well as those in the East, she could buy anything she wanted at any time and had no need to keep so much on hand. She had cleared out the little storeroom and had engaged a carpenter to cut a door between this and her bedroom, so she would have two rooms for herself instead of one.

"We'll call it a boudoir," she said to Kendra. "You can use it too, as a refuge when you get mad. Do you know what the word 'boudoir' really means?"

"Of course not," Kendra answered laughing. "You know I'm not as intellectual as you are. What does it mean?"

"It means a pouting room," said Marny. "Everybody ought to have one. We all need a place where we can slam the door and shut ourselves up when we feel contrary. That is, a boudoir."

While Marny planned her boudoir, Norman fumed until Marny said he too needed a pouting room. At last, after leaving him in doubt for two weeks, Hortensia announced her decision.

She came into the kitchen late one afternoon while Hiram was having coffee with Marny and Kendra. With the calm good cheer of a person who has no misgivings, Hortensia told them she was going to marry Norman as soon as she had received her divorce.

They wished her happiness, and went with her into the parlor, to give Norman their congratulations. Norman was beaming, and regretting only that the divorce would take time because they had to wait for those affidavits from New York. He was a happy man, said Norman, but he would have been even happier if he and Hortensia could have been married tomorrow.

Kendra was glad the matter was settled, though she did not believe that even in San Francisco a woman could get a divorce merely by telling the judge she wanted one. When she and Hiram sat again at the kitchen table, she asked him if this was the case.

"Not quite," Hiram answered with some amusement. "I'm sure Hortensia's lawyer made that plain to her. But the laws *are* easier here than back East, and the courts are mighty partial toward women. I don't know a great deal about it, but I've no doubt Hortensia knows it all now."

"I'd like to see Hortensia happy," said Kendra. "I'm sorry she has to wait for those papers from New York." Adding, "I think my cookies are done," Kendra stood up and opened the oven door.

She arranged the cookies on a tray and took them to the parlor. When she came back Hiram spoke to her eagerly.

"I've had an idea," he said. "Maybe Hortensia won't have to wait for those papers."

"Why not?"

"I'm no lawyer," said Hiram, "but I should think one live witness would be worth a dozen affidavits. And maybe she can get a witness right here."

He explained. There were hundreds of New Yorkers in San Francisco, and more were constantly arriving. Old friends were always meeting each other unexpectedly in the street.

Kendra remembered Ted's meeting with Gene Spencer, and she was sure Hiram was remembering it too, but neither of them said so. Hiram went on,

"California is full of actors and musicians from New York. Isn't it possible, even likely, that among them is somebody who knows Hortensia? Who can come with her into court and give direct evidence of how her husband treated her?"

"It's certainly possible," Kendra agreed. "But how would you go about finding such a person?"

"Advertise," Hiram answered promptly. "If Hortensia has friends in California they haven't known she was here because she's using a new name. Norman can advertise for somebody who knows her by her real name, or the stage name she used in New York. It's worth trying."

"Yes it is," Kendra said with enthusiasm. "Hiram, it's so worth trying that I think you ought to tell Norman right now. He can go around to the newspapers tomorrow."

"Fine, I'll do that. I'll tell him to advertise in the Sacramento papers too. They have theaters there."

He went out, and came back to say he had left word at Marny's bar that when Mr. Lamont had leisure, Mr. Boyd had something of interest to say to him.

After a while one of the bartenders came to the kitchen with the message that Mr. Lamont was waiting for Mr. Boyd in one of the private rooms. Hiram went out. When he came back he was carrying one of the bar's biggest glasses, liberally supplied with a drink.

Kendra, who was putting in another pan of cookies, shut the oven door and came to meet him.

"Tell me about it. What did Norman say?"

Settling his big person into a chair, Hiram began to laugh. "Norman says it's a great idea. Doesn't know why he didn't think of it himself. Doesn't know what's wrong with those expensive lawyers, taking his money and poor dear Hortensia's

491

money and not having a simple idea like this. Kendra, he—"
Hiram's laughter began to choke him.

She had sat down across the table from him. "What's the
matter?" she asked in astonishment .

Wiping his eyes on the back of his hand, Hiram managed
to say, "Kendra, he—he offered me a tip."

She laughed too, but she knew Norman better than he
did. "Norman never in his life did anything he didn't expect
to be paid for," she said. "He doesn't understand that some
people will do a favor because they enjoy doing it."

"I suppose you're right," Hiram answered mirthfully. "He
was certainly startled when I declined the tip. I told him I'd
take a drink of whiskey on the house, but nothing more."
Hiram held up his glass. "And look at the size of the drink
he gave me."

"At least," said Kendra, "he feels better because he's given
you a little something in payment. And you deserve the drink.
You did solve his problem."

"I hope so." Hiram twirled the glass between his hands. He
looked at it, his face suddenly grave.

"That's why you're good as a banker," Kendra went on.
"You're good at solving problems."

"Yes," Hiram returned, without looking up. "Other people's." He gazed at the glass. Hiram was thinking, and he
was not thinking about Norman.

Kendra waited for him to go on, but he said no more.
Moodily, he sipped his drink. With an impulsive movement
she went around the table and stood by him. "Hiram," she
said, "if you have a problem of your own—can I help?
Would you like to tell me?"

Hiram gave a start. "Tell you?" He pushed back his chair
and stood up. "Never mind. Forget it."

"All right, I'll forget it," Kendra said quickly, though she
knew she would not. She changed the subject. "Stay and
have dinner with us. I'm going to serve ham, and sweet
potatoes fried in the ham drippings."

"No, thanks." He smiled down at her contritely. "Honestly,
Kendra, I'm sorry. I didn't mean to mention a problem. The
words sort of came out by themselves. I'm acting like a
schoolboy and I'm ashamed of myself. Now I'd better get
along."

He went out, banging the door behind him.

Kendra looked down at the glass on the table, still holding

half of Norman's generous drink. She wondered what was the matter with Hiram these days. Why was it?—she and Hiram had dined together, had gone to plays together, had sat here in the kitchen laughing and chatting, eating cakes and drinking coffee, and he had seemed quite at ease; but as soon as the slightest touch of intimacy slipped into their talk, that curious veil came down between them. Why was this? There was some reason why he hesitated, and drew back, with a shyness he showed nowhere else.

A light began to dawn in her thoughts. Was Hiram falling in love with her?

Maybe he was, and maybe he did not want to. If he did not want to, he had a reason. Else, why should he fear to tell her?

Kendra stood still, looking at the door Hiram had banged behind him.

—If he told me, she asked herself, would I take him?

—Yes, she answered herself, I would.

Her answer was clear. She had liked Hiram ever since the day they had had a moment's flirtation on the *Cynthia*. She had thought then that the big rusty-bearded sailor would be fun to know. At Shiny Gulch, when she had had romantic thoughts about nobody but Ted, Hiram *had* been fun to know. Later, when she had been forsaken and alone, Hiram had been her friend. Later still, when she had endured her stunning heartbreak after the Chirstmas fire, Hiram had stood by her with a steadfastness that she would remember as long as she lived.

But never had he spoken a loverlike word. Never had he talked to her in such confidence as Pocket had when he told her about the girl he had loved. Still, she felt closer to Hiram than to Pocket, or to anybody else she knew.

Would she like to go to bed with him?

She certainly would.

Kendra had not felt this way about any man since her heart got rid of Ted. And she had never felt about Ted as she was beginning to feel about Hiram. In those days she had been too young, too—how should she say it to herself?— too unripe. Today she was older, and wiser. She was ready to understand a man far more complex than Ted, ready as she could not have been when they all rode up to Shiny Gulch together.

She thought of Hiram—strong, but with a trembling spot

493

of self-doubt. Whatever it was he feared, she would do all she could to help him conquer it; or if he could not conquer it, to endure it. He would help her in the same way to bear her own shortcomings. Hiram had told her she had strength—guts, he called it. But she knew how often she had yearned to crumple up on a loving shoulder and shake with weakness. He could give her this. And he would. As was true of so many brusque and aggressive men, Hiram's character had a deep undercurrent of tenderness.

Yes, if he asked her to marry him she would do it.

He had not asked her. Maybe he never would. Maybe she was mistaken and he was not in love with her. But she did not think so.

She could, of course, go after him. Women did this often. She had done it once herself.

Kendra felt her face pucker. She walked across the room and stood before the mirror she had hung on the kitchen wall.

"No," she said to her reflection. "You've tried that. And remember what it brought you. Ted had a reason for keeping away from you but you wouldn't let him. Maybe Hiram has a reason too. Don't do it again. Don't be the same kind of fool twice. If you're going to make mistakes—and you are, everybody does—at least for heaven's sake make some new ones!"

With her fist she struck the back of a chair, so hard that the chair fell over and clattered on the floor. Kendra straightened it, and clenched her jaw as she set about slicing the sweet potatoes.

Norman promptly placed a notice in the San Francisco and Sacramento papers. Hiram helped him write it. The notice said:

"A certain person is interested in the welfare of an actress known on the New York stage as Laura Lester. Her real name is Elsie Glutch, later Mrs. Rupert Williams. If any reader of this newspaper is acquainted with this lady, he will find it worth while to answer."

(Norman meant what he said. If he could find an old friend of Hortensia's whose testimony would hasten her divorce, he was quite willing to pay for it.)

Again Norman wanted to give Hiram some sort of reward. Hiram, however, shook his head. He reminded Norman

494

that their advertisement might have no results. Nobody could find a witness unless the witness was there to be found. And as three weeks went by without bringing an answer, Norman's hopes began to droop and Hiram feared that he had not solved the problem after all.

Meanwhile, though he often dropped into the Calico Palace, Hiram said no more to Kendra about a problem. Kendra resolutely said nothing about it either. She was glad she had Geraldine and the unborn kittens to occupy her mind. Geraldine was giving her and Marny a lot to do.

Dr. Wardlaw had advised them not to let the kittens be born in Geraldine's room because of the balcony. He reminded them that a cat liked to carry her kittens around and hide them. If the balcony door should by chance be left ajar Geraldine would probably take the kittens out there. Newborn kittens could not see. They might easily squirm their way under the rail, and fall. No, they had better start their lives in a safer place.

Marny said the kittens could be born in the boudoir next to her bedroom. The boudoir was not yet furnished, and she and Kendra could fit it up as a lying-in chamber.

They had observed that in recent weeks Geraldine had preferred to sleep, and sit, above floor level. When they brought her little hut into the boudoir they set it on a table. They hired a carpenter to build a little staircase leading from the floor to the entrance of the hut, so Geraldine could carry her kittens up and down as she pleased. This done, they arranged baskets and boxes here and there about the room. Now Geraldine could inspect the premises and choose the place where she wanted her children to be born. Dr. Wardlaw told them she would almost certainly choose the hut, but a cat liked to make up her own mind. Later, when the kittens were born, she would have the baskets and boxes as hiding places.

Through the second half of April the weather was mild, with a rare lot of sunshine. They set another table by the window, and on it placed the feather cushion Hiram and Pocket had given Geraldine as a valentine present. During these last few days Geraldine spent most of her time here, basking in the sun.

On the twenty-fifth of April, Marny woke up shortly before noon. She said later that before she opened her eyes she had known what was happening on the other side of the boudoir door. Had she heard something in her sleep, or merely guessed it? She could not say. But when she went into the boudoir she was not surprised to find that Geraldine was no longer alone.

In the hut Geraldine lay on her side, purring a lullaby, and snuggled up close to her was a cluster of kittens, taking their first meal on earth. She regarded Marny with friendly eyes, for Geraldine knew Marny and trusted her, but Marny was careful not to touch the kittens yet. She knelt before the hut and counted. Geraldine had four kittens. Two were black and white like Geraldine herself; the other two were calico, black and white and gold.

—She must have had a golden boy for a lover, thought Marny. And they're going to be beautiful!

She hurried to comb her hair and put on a robe so she could go down to the kitchen and tell Kendra.

The kittens thrived and waxed fat. On the second day of May, when they were a week old, Marny caught sight of Dr. Wardlaw having a drink at the bar. As soon as the Harvard man came to relieve her at the card table she went to the bar and asked the doctor to come up and see the kittens.

A few minutes later she came into the kitchen, where Kendra was putting cheese rolls into the oven.

"Dr. Wardlaw says," announced Marny, "the calico cats are girls. All black-white-and-gold cats are girls. At least, he says he never saw one that wasn't. And the plain black-and-white pair are toms. And they are darlings and I love them every one."

"So do I," said Kendra. "Shall we call one of the toms Jupiter?"

"Yes, I like that. Every tomcat thinks he's king of the world, or ought to be. And let's call one of the girls Pandora, because cats are always poking into things that are none of their business."

After some further discussion they decided to name Jupiter's brother Emperor, and call him Empy. "And the other girl," said Kendra—"well, she's a calico cat and she was born in the Calico Palace. Let's name her Calico."

"Good," said Marny. "So there they are. Jupiter, Empy, Pandora, Calico." Accepting the cup of coffee Kendra was offering her, Marny continued, "Thanks, and now I have

496

some news. One of Norman's efforts has finally brought an answer."

"Oh, I'm so glad!" Kendra exclaimed. "When did he get it? Today?"

Marny nodded. She said that as she had been about to go into the parlor to deal her first game, Norman had stopped her at the door to show her a letter he had just received.

The letter had come from Sacramento. It was a genuine letter from a genuine friend of Hortensia's. The writer had signed himself Jefferson Quellen, and Hortensia had recognized the name at once. Jeff Quellen, she said, was a singer of comic songs, and he was married to a dancer named Daisy.

Jeff Quellen wrote that he and Daisy had reached San Francisco by an Isthmus steamer several months ago. They had stopped here only a few days, because they had answered an advertisement of a theatrical producer from Sacramento, and had been engaged. For some weeks they had appeared at the theater in Sacramento. Then in the spring when the mountain snows melted, the company had gone on a tour of mining towns. It was not until they came back to Sacramento, the day before this letter was written, that they had seen the notice in the Sacramento *Placer Times*.

Mr. Quellen said he and Daisy knew Laura Lester well, had been in the same show with her. She was a fine girl and he sure hoped she was not having any trouble. Not that he meant to blab, but she had had enough of same before she left New York.

The letter was not scholarly in phrasing nor the words perfectly spelled, but it was the letter Norman had been waiting for. He blissfully told Marny he would bring Mr. and Mrs. Quellen to town at once. And the next time Hiram Boyd came in, would she see to it that he got drinks on the house?

61

Marny went up to her bedroom to re-do her hair before going back to the cards. Leaving the rolls to bake, Kendra poured a cup of coffee for herself and sat down at the kitchen table to look at the *Alta*.

The *Alta* was as contradictory as San Francisco itself, a hodge-podge of the best and the worst, of proud achievement and brazen crime. She saw two paragraphs side by side. One of them boasted of the city's culture: the concerts and theaters, churches and book-stores, fine tailors and fashionable shops. The column next to it reported more brawls, more thefts, more men attacked in dark streets and murdered for their pocketbooks. She read that three steamers had left yesterday for the Isthmus, carrying passengers and a hundred and fifty thousand ounces of gold. But in a camp near Stockton the angry miners had set up an outdoor court of their own. In one day they had hanged five horse-thieves to a tree. Looking for more pleasant news, Kendra saw an advertisement for five hundred dozen silk-and-ivory fans.

Now what hopeful shipper back East, she wondered, had sent out five hundred dozen fans to be sold in San Francisco? There were not five hundred dozen women in town. Wouldn't they ever *learn?*

"Howdy!" said men's voices at the kitchen door.

Pocket and Hiram came in. They brought a gift of liver for Geraldine, and for herself and Marny oranges from Honolulu. Before she could speak her thanks Pocket was exclaiming, "Do I smell cheese rolls?" Pocket was exceedingly fond of cheese rolls.

She said he was right, but he would have to wait until the rolls were done.

"Then let's go out to the front balcony," said Pocket, "and get some air. It's a beautiful shiny day."

She consented, and called Lolo to watch the baking.

Pocket gave Lolo instructions that she was to come to the front balcony and tell him, the minute, the very minute, she took the cheese rolls to the parlor. Lolo promised. Kendra went out with Pocket and Hiram.

Dwight Carson had built this floor of the Calico Palace with a hall that led between Marny's parlor on one side and several private card rooms on the other. At the end of the hall was the door to the front balcony.

The hall was dim, and full of sounds from invisible sources—Hortensia's piano, the click of roulette balls, the clink of coins. They smelled cigar smoke and whiskey, and from behind the closed doors of the private rooms they heard voices. Most of the private rooms were occupied, though it was not yet evening. Business at the Calico Palace was good.

As they reached the balcony door they heard footsteps behind them, and looking around they saw Marny on her way back to the parlor to take over her table from the Harvard man. She came to join them instead.

"Darlings!" she exclaimed to Pocket and Hiram. "I'm so glad to see you. Oh yes, I can take a few minutes more."

Hiram opened the door to the balcony. As they went out he said "Damn!" With his big foot he angrily crushed a cigar stub, still glowing, that somebody had thrown away.

"Why can't they be careful?" he demanded.

Neither Hiram nor Pocket ever smoked, and Hiram at least had slight patience with people who did. Pocket, who had patience with nearly everybody, gave a soft answer to Hiram's wrath. "This building is supposed to be fireproof."

"Do they want to make us prove it?" Hiram retorted.

Pocket looked gravely across the plaza. The streets were resounding with the usual racket, and puffs of wind were raising the dust in whirligigs, but the day was, as he had said, shiny and beautiful. In front of them the sun was setting in a pile of ruddy clouds.

"If we have another fire—" Pocket began, and stopped.

As he did so Marny said dryly, "You needn't be so careful of my nerves. I've heard the rumors."

"What rumors?" asked Kendra.

At the same time Hiram was saying, "Bar talk." He looked across the plaza at the sunset.

Kendra asked again, "Bar talk about what?"

"Oh, some of the fellows," returned Marny, "are saying the Sydney ducks had such fun at the looting party in May of last year that they want to celebrate the anniversary. Which means, they're planning another fire so they can loot some more. Is that what you boys have heard?"

"Yes ma'am," answered Pocket, "I've heard it in the library. They tell me that's the talk in the saloons around Clark's Point."

Kendra felt a shiver. She thought back. Last year's greatest fire had taken place on the fourth of May. That was the fire that had driven herself and Marny and Rosabel to take shelter in Dwight Carson's rooms at the Gresham Hotel. Since then there had been more fires, but these had been small compared to the holocaust of May fourth.

That fire had been deliberately set. She remembered Marny's telling her about the faro dealers who had discovered the oil-soaked rags burning in the United States Exchange.

Now the year was moving close to another fourth of May. The people of San Francisco had rebuilt their city. They had made it larger, stronger, more splendid than it had been last year. Today the principal streets were lined with buildings of brick and granite. Looking at the lordly structures around the plaza, Kendra wondered—could any man want to turn these into rubble? To repeat last year's destruction, with its horrible accompaniment of heartbreak and agony and death? Could any man be so evil?

Yes, she knew now that some men *were* so evil. It had been done before. It could be done again.

Kendra thought of the five men hanged to a tree in the mining camp near Stockton. She knew this had happened in other mining camps as well. People had to protect themselves from theft and murder. Was this the only way they could do it?

She brought her mind back to the talk around her. Marny was telling the men about the letter Norman had received from Jeff Quellen. "So it seems, Hiram," said Marny, "your idea has worked. Hortensia can get her divorce right now. Yes, Lolo?" she asked, as the door opened again and Lolo came out on the balcony.

Lolo said she had come to tell Mr. Pocket that the cheese rolls, steaming hot, were now on sale in the parlor. And fresh coffee. Pocket said he would go in at once.

"I'll go in too," said Marny. "It's time I got back to work. Are you coming to the parlor, Hiram?"

"After a while."

"Good. Norman has left orders that your drinks are on the house."

She blew him a kiss as she and Pocket went in with Lolo. Hiram and Kendra were left alone on the balcony.

Hiram stood with both his big hands on the rail, as he and Kendra looked down at the plaza and the blustery streets around it. Wagons and carriages and horseback riders clattered through the dust. The sidewalks swarmed with men buying supplies for the summer ahead in the gold country. There were hundreds of men in sight. They had come from nearly every country on earth; their skins were white and black and yellow and brown; their languages made pandemonium in the air.

The city was growing and changing so fast that men who went away for only a few weeks were confused when they came back, and had to ask their way around. The streets were always full of people, and everybody seemed to be always in a hurry. It had become almost a proverb that in San Francisco even lazy people had to move quickly, because if they did not the rushing crowds would push them down and walk over them. As he watched and listened, Hiram drew a long proud breath.

"Say what you please," he murmured, almost as if talking to himself, "it's a magnificent town."

"Yes it is," said Kendra. "I like being part of it." She looked down at the surging vitality of the streets, and back at him. "Remember how it was when we left to ride up to Shiny Gulch?—these streets just tracks half grown over with weeds, and here and there a lone human being plodding along?"

Plodding—as she spoke the word, she thought what a strange word it was to use about San Francisco. Hiram was saying.

"Do I remember! And only three years ago. You know that, Kendra, but don't you still find it hard to believe?"

They talked about the transformation. That shantytown of nine hundred people, and now this brilliant city. Three years.

"You said it right," Kendra told Hiram. "I know it's true, but I find it hard to believe. San Francisco is so different now!"

There was a pause. Hiram had turned his eyes away from

501

the plaza and was looking down at her. Over his face came a slow, thoughtful smile. He said, "No more different than you are."

"Than I am?" she echoed. "Hiram, I know I've changed, but—" she made a gesture toward the town—"have I changed this much?"

"Yes," said Hiram.

"Tell me what you mean."

He considered, and spoke. "Three years ago, you were a mighty attractive girl. But you were—how shall I say it?— *unfinished*. You were like San Francisco, just the beginning of what you were going to become. I don't mean you're complete now. Any more than San Francisco is complete. But the difference between what you were then and what you are now, is the same sort of difference. You are both showing what you really are. And you're both more exciting than you used to be. Oh damn, now I'm getting sentimental. I'd better go to Marny's parlor and take one of those free drinks."

Down came the veil between them, again. Before he had finished his last sentence Hiram was holding the door open for her to go through ahead of him.

They both turned indoors.

In the hall the sounds of the plaza gave way to the clinks and clicks and music of indoors. From one of the private card rooms came a burst of laughter. Kendra heard the voices of two persons, male and female. She guessed that they were not playing cards.

The door to the next room stood open, and the room was empty. Hiram glanced in. "Whoever played here last," he remarked, "lost some cards."

Kendra saw several cards on the floor. "Marny has plenty of fresh packs," she answered.

She glanced at Hiram as she spoke. He was looking down at her. They had both paused by the door. For a moment they stood there, looking at each other. Then all of a sudden Hiram said, "You beautiful darling," and Kendra found herself in his arms.

They had a moment. But it was only a moment. There was a sound of footsteps. Somebody was approaching.

Kendra pushed herself out of his arms and slipped into the empty card room. The door swung behind her; she did not look to see if it had closed or not. She crossed the room

502

and stood by the window, aware of nothing but her new certainty.

—He does love me. And I love him. This is *it*. This is love. I never felt like this about any other man. It's different because I'm different. What Hiram said is true.

She heard the door bang. Of course, the door would bang. Hiram could not come into any room without banging the door. Pocket could, and usually did, move so quietly that you had to see him before you knew he was there. But not Hiram. He made noise like an army.

She turned from the window. Hiram stood by the closed door, facing her. He spoke.

"There now, I've done it. Now you know I'm in love with you. I've been in love with you since—I don't know since when."

Kendra remembered Loren. She exclaimed, "Don't tell me since we were on the *Cynthia!*"

"Of course not. You were a pretty girl then, no more. That's what I've just been telling you. And not since we rode up to Shiny Gulch, either. I don't know when it began. All I know is, I'm in love with you now. Am I a fool?"

"No!" she returned quickly. "You are not a fool. I love you too."

"Then—" he began, and stopped, tongue-tied with that same strange, baffling shyness. He stood, literally, with his back to the wall, and he looked as if he felt that way too.

They stood looking at each other across the card table. "Hiram," she pled, "*what* is it you've been trying to tell me?"

Hiram pulled out a chair and slumped into it. He crossed his arms on the table and dropped his head upon them. His thick rust-colored hair tumbled all about.

A hard silence lay in the room. Neither of them ever knew how long a silence it was. But at last, Hiram raised his head and looked at her. He spoke, almost timidly.

"Kendra—you said you loved me back."

She went around the table to him. Standing beside him, she put her hand on his shoulder. "Yes, Hiram, I do."

He looked up, into her eyes. "Does that mean—" he smiled, like a little boy "—for always? Marriage?"

"Yes," she said.

"You're sure?"

"I've never been so sure of anything in my life."

But he was still timid. "Even—even if I don't belong to the club?"

"What club, Hiram?"

"The one I told you about. The most exclusive club in the world. The people who can take the wind as God sends it. You belong. I don't."

Her hand tightened on his shoulder. "Hiram, Hiram my dear, *what* are you trying to say?"

"I suppose," he answered harshly, "I'm trying to say I'm the biggest coward this side of the Rocky Mountains."

She waited. This was a time for her to say nothing.

Again there was a silence, and again it seemed a long silence. Kendra stood with her hand on his shoulder, and he looked up at her, and she wondered what he had to tell her. He looked so strong, he had seemed so sure of himself, but now he was not. Now he was frightened of something, something that he knew and she did not. At last he said,

"Sit down over there. I've got to tell you. I'll tell you."

She obeyed him. She went around to the other side of the table and sat down. Looking straight at her over his crossed arms, Hiram asked,

"Kendra, what do you know about me?"

She thought before she answered. "I don't know much about what you left behind you," she said at length. "I mean, what you did before you shipped on the *Cynthia*. You said you were a minister's son and you grew up in New York State."

"That's not much, is it?" said Hiram. "Haven't you ever wished you knew more?"

She had, but she spoke of what she did know. "Hiram, it's been said a thousand times that all of us who came to California before the gold rush had some mighty good reason for leaving home. I don't know what yours was. But I do know this. You're the finest man I ever met. Whatever your reason was, I know it wasn't anything low or mean or dishonorable."

He was listening with eager intentness. Kendra smiled at him.

"I'm a lot wiser now, Hiram, than I was when I made a romantic hero out of Ted Parks. You're another sort of man. You're not a man who acts without thinking and then runs away. You're not a halfway person."

Almost breathlessly he said, "Thank you, Kendra. Thank you, my darling."

504

"Now," she asked, "whatever it is you've got to say, can't you say it?"

Hiram drew a deep breath. On the table before him his big hard hands doubled into fists. "Kendra," he blurted, "I don't know who I am."

Startled and perplexed, she did not answer at once. When she did answer, all she could say was, "What are you talking about?"

"Just that," he retorted. His voice was rough, almost angry. Now that he was saying it, his words poured out in a torrent. "I don't know who I am. I don't know what my name is, where I came from, what I inherited, what sort of children I'd give you. Don't you understand, for God's sake? I don't know who I am."

"No," she exclaimed, "I don't understand."

Hiram's chin dropped to his chest. He rested his forehead on one hand and the fingers pushed up through his shaggy hair. "All right," he said in a muffled voice. "I knew if I ever managed to tell you this I'd do it badly. I'll say it as plainly as I can."

She murmured, foolishly, "You said you were a minister's son—"

Hiram jerked up his head and interrupted her. "I'm nobody's son. They found me in a garbage can."

He drew another deep hard breath. Kendra waited. After a while he went on.

"The church stood under some trees, a little way back from the highway that led up from New York City. At intervals the women of the congregation used to come in and give the place a housecleaning. They would sweep and dust and polish and wash the windows, all that sort of thing. Afterward their husbands would join them and they would have supper in the social hall. The rubbish from the cleaning, and the leftover scraps of food, went into a garbage can that stood outside. The next morning the janitor would carry it to the town dump. Well, one morning after a cleaning party, on top of the trash in the garbage can the janitor found a newborn child."

Hiram stopped. While he talked he had not been looking at her. He had been looking down at his big strong hands. It was a way he had, looking at his hands when he was confronted with a situation before which his own strength was no good. It was as if he was reproaching his hands for being

505

useless. Now as he stopped talking he still did not raise his eyes.

Kendra kept quiet. She felt sure he had more to tell her and did not want to be interrupted till he was ready for an answer. She was right; after a moment or two he went on.

"That child was me. I was whimpering, so the janitor knew I was alive. If he had come by a little later I suppose I would have been dead. Poor fellow, he was shocked half out of his wits. He ran to the minister's home and gasped out news of what he had found. The minister and his wife—Mr. and Mrs. Boyd—came and saw me. They carried me home and took care of me."

Hiram gave his head a slow shake.

"They tried to find out who had put me there, but they couldn't. In a small town where everybody knew everybody else, nobody knew anything about this. I had been brought there from somewhere else. In the night somebody had passed along the highway, with a child nobody wanted. Whoever that somebody was, he caught sight of the garbage can beside the church. Of course the church would be empty that time of night. A good chance to throw away the child and go on without being seen."

Hiram stopped again, and drew another hard breath before he spoke again.

"The Boyds were kindly people. They kept me and gave me their name and let me grow up with their own children. I'm grateful for all they did for me. As long as I'm alive they won't want for anything."

There was another break. Hiram sat as if gathering strength to go on talking about the hurt that for so long had been festering within him.

"They were kind. But—children aren't kind. Children are hideously cruel. They don't know it. They don't know they're being cruel when they catch bugs and pull off the wings. I had been found in a garbage can. Everybody in town knew this. When I went to school the other boys taunted me with it. 'Hiram's a piece of trash! They found Hiram in a garbage can!' "

He smiled bitterly.

"Pretty soon, I learned. As I grew bigger, I grew bigger than most of them. I beat them up. That kept them quiet, but they never forgot it and neither did I. In little towns like that, nobody forgets anything. I made up my mind that when

I grew up I would go out to the end of the world where nobody knew I came out of a garbage can. I'm here. But that doesn't change the fact. I still don't know who I am. Behind me, there's still the garbage can."

At last he looked up at her. He gave her another of those hard, bitter smiles.

"Kendra, telling you this is about the hardest thing I've ever done. But now I've told it. Now you know. Do you still want me?"

Kendra gave him a smile in return. Unlike his, her smile was not bitter, but tender and gentle. She reached across the table and put her hands on his. She said softly,

"Hiram, is that all?"

"All?" He jerked his hands away and again he doubled them into fists. "All? Don't you understand? For all I know my mother may have been a streetwalker and my father a murderer. Maybe I was born of imbeciles or lunatics. I don't *know*. And you don't know either, Kendra."

"But I know *you!*" she retorted. "You're not an imbecile nor a lunatic nor a murderer—Hiram, does anybody ever really know all about the ancestors behind him?"

As she spoke, his eyes had widened. His lips had parted with astonishment that was almost unbelief. In a voice low and strange for him, he asked, "You'll risk it?"

"Yes, Hiram," she said quietly.

A smile broke over his face like a light. For a little time neither of them said anything else. They simply sat there and looked at each other across the card table, and were happy. Then Kendra asked,

"Hiram, why was it so hard for you to tell me this?"

Hiram reached out and took both her hands in his. It cost him an effort to answer. But he answered. He said,

"Because—I was afraid—when you found out—you would say no. I could stand anything but that. I couldn't stand being thrown away again. Or maybe I could—I mean, maybe I could stand being thrown away by somebody else. But not by you."

His hands tightened on hers.

"Now you know everything," he said, "and I'm glad you do. You know what a shivering coward I am and you love me anyway. Kendra, you genuinely don't think it's important?"

507

"No, Hiram," she returned steadily. "I think you've been making it a great deal more important than it is."

"You do? Why?"

"There are thousands of people," said Kendra, "who have adopted their children. Those children grow up safe and happy."

"But those children," he exclaimed, "were *wanted*."

Hiram pushed back his chair and stood up.

"Kendra," he went on, "maybe I've been making it important because all my life I've known nobody wanted me. My parents, whoever they were, certainly didn't want me or they wouldn't have thrown me away. My foster-parents didn't want me—why should they? They had their own children. I was an extra burden they carried from a sense of duty. They never said so, they were always kind. That's it. They were *kind*."

Hiram drew a short breath.

"You wouldn't understand that," he said slowly, as he stood looking down at her. "You had real parents. You were wanted, you were loved, you were somebody's child—"

At this Kendra stood up too, so abruptly that her chair fell over behind her. Hiram stared at her in amazement. She was staring at him too. For the first time she was realizing that Hiram did not know about her parents' elopement and her years of being put away in boarding schools because nobody wanted her. She had never told him about her lonely sense of being nobody's child.

She knew who her parents were; she had that much advantage over him. They had not thrown her into a garbage can. But her mother had grasped at the first chance she had to get rid of her, by handing her over to her grandmother and ignoring her as much as appearances would allow. Her grandmother had kept her out of the way as much as possible. If ever there was an unwanted child, it was herself.

Hiram did not know this. He did not know how much understanding she had to give him, any more than she had known how much he needed it. She used to think of Hiram as being utterly strong and confident. It was dawning upon her that nobody was utterly strong and confident. Everybody needed help from other people.

Hiram stood still, where he was, speechless. Her own silence and her own surprise had given him a shock. Kendra walked around the table and stood before him and held out

508

her hands. He took them in his and looked down at her with love and a wondering awe.

"You do want me then, Kendra?" he asked.

Kendra's throat had closed up. She could not answer. She nodded, dumbly, then all of a sudden she found that his arms were around her and she was crying, her head on his shoulder while his big hands soothed her as if she had been a child. After a little while she managed to look up, tears still on her cheeks.

"Hiram," she said chokily, "you need me, but no more than I need you. You and I—oh Hiram, I have so much to tell you!"

62

They had dinner at the Union Hotel, leaving the others to dine on whatever Lulu and Lolo saw fit to serve them. Before going out Hiram engaged this card room for the rest of the evening. When they came in they sat down to talk, and they talked for hours, and nothing they said seemed ordinary. Every line provoked laughter or tears, and sometimes both. Kendra had never laughed so much in one evening, nor cried so much either. But even the tears were delightful, for every time he saw her eyes grow misty Hiram kissed her and made her laugh again.

At last, when they heard Marny pass the door on her way to the kitchen for chocolate, they went to meet her, walking hand in hand like two children, and told her they were going to be married. Marny kissed them both and wished them all the joy in the world.

"Are you surprised?" asked Hiram.

Marny began to laugh. "Certainly not. Anybody could see you were in love with Kendra. But I thought you were never going to get around to saying so."

"I suppose," Hiram returned modestly, "I'm just a bashful swain."

She laughed again and gave him an affectionate pat on the cheek. "I've observed," she said, "that big tough men like you are often bashful when it comes to speaking tender lines. Don't apologize."

"I haven't," retorted Hiram, "and I won't."

When Marny came down the next morning Kendra told her letters had already come by messenger from both Pocket and Hiram. Pocket's letter said he rejoiced at the news. Hiram's letter said he would be over this evening to take her out to dinner again and then to a play, and would she please wear the blue silk dress with the flouncy sleeves because this was the one he liked best.

Marny smiled across her coffee cup. "He's really in love with you, Kendra. I wish you so much happiness—" she sobered, and reached to take Kendra's hand in hers. "And this time, dear, I think you're going to have it."

That evening Kendra put on the blue dress with the flouncy sleeves, and when Hiram came in he brought her a blue silk folding fan with ivory sticks. He also brought silk-and-ivory fans for Marny and Hortensia and Lulu and Lolo—all chosen, he said, from among the five hundred dozen that had been advertised in the *Alta*. The fans, of varied colors and designs, were beautiful, and the girls thanked him. Hiram and Kendra went off together.

Marny had an unexciting dinner of beef and potatoes, prepared by Lulu. After dinner she went up to her room for a breathing space before going back to work.

Marny's bedroom was well furnished, with soft deep rugs on the floor and a satin quilt on the bed, a long mirror, heavy curtains to keep her from being waked up by the morning light, and on the table a whale oil lamp with a shade of frosted glass. She lit the lamp and looked at herself in the mirror.

She was wearing a black satin dress with a flourish of white cobweb lawn across the bosom. Around her waist was a gun belt—black leather tonight, so as not to be too obvious against her black dress—with her little gun tucked into the holster. Her only ornaments were her nugget necklace and a pair of plain gold earrings. When she dealt cards she never wore rings or bracelets. Marny smiled at her reflection. She was a striking person, no doubt about it, with her trim figure, her flamboyant red hair and green eyes. After all this time in the mists of San Francisco she had no freckles left but a few golden dots that made a butterfly pattern, hardly more than a shadow, across her nose and cheeks. That trace of freckles seemed to be there to remind onlookers that while she was not really beautiful, she was uniquely herself.

She wanted to see how the kittens were. The big whale oil lamp was too heavy to be easily carried about, so lighting a smaller lamp she went into the boudoir. She set the lamp on the side table and bent to look into the hut.

The kittens were now eight days old, and how they had grown! They were still tiny, but so much bigger than they had been at first. No wonder, for they seemed to be always nursing. Luckily Geraldine was putting away prodigious quantities of food and could give them all the milk they wanted. Right now the kittens were curled up beside her, on a soft old blanket folded and tucked into the hut to make a bed. Geraldine was purring, happy as a cat could be.

Marny went back to the bedroom. The air was growing chilly, and the rippling curtains reminded her that while there was not much wind yet, it might get stronger as the night went on. She set down the lamp and went to close the windows.

The windows looked over the roofs that sloped downhill toward the bay. San Francisco still had no street lights, but here between the plaza and the waterfront the town was never quite dark, and as this was a Saturday night there were even more lights than usual. In the bay were five hundred vessels, most of them with lights of their own. Marny saw an Isthmus steamer, and other coastwise craft, and tall-masted seagoing vessels from many ports, and the busy little steamers that chugged between San Francisco and the placer country. Farther out she could see the lost ships, rotting and falling to pieces in the water.

She closed the windows and drew the curtains. Making sure the outer doors of bedroom and boudoir were locked, and the door between the rooms closed so the kittens would have to stay where they belonged, she started downstairs.

Around her she heard laughter, music, all the merry sounds of the plaza on a Saturday night. She went down to the first floor and cracked open the door behind the bar of the public room.

What a racket!—but the men seemed to be having fun. In this room they now had two female dealers, French girls who had come to California to seek their fortunes. Marny could see them, smoking little black cigars and bestowing seductive smiles upon the players.

The bar was doing a rush of business. On the platform at one end of the room the orchestra was playing. At the end of the bar near the orchestra four men were warbling the words that went with the tune. Along the bar other men clinked glasses and made comments of their own. In front of the bar a boozy patriot was prancing up and down, waving a flag and announcing that he was prepared to carve the gizzard out of the first fool duck of a foreigner who questioned the right of a trueborn American to do exactly as he pleased in his own country.

"Things going all right, Marny?" asked a voice at her side.

She turned to see Troy Blackbeard. "Yes, Troy, so far. Except, that fellow with the flag—don't you think we'd better get him out before he starts a war?"

Troy grinned. The Blackbeards liked Marny. Not only did she play fair and mind her own business, but she was one of the few people who went to the trouble of telling them apart and calling them by different names. After all, a man may like his twin but he also likes to be treated as a person in his own right instead of half a unit.

"We'll keep an eye on him," Troy promised.

"Good. I'll go on up to the parlor."

She went up to the parlor. As she crossed the room a score of men called greetings. Marny smiled at them and waved. She noticed that Pollock was here again tonight, as usual in the group around Hortensia. He was not one of those who greeted Marny as she passed.

Marny was not distressed. She told the Harvard man to go to dinner, and took his place at the card table.

She had an agreeable evening. Her table was crowded with as many players as she could take care of. Nobody made trouble. When she paused to stretch, she noted that play was brisk at all the tables, and while the bar was noisy the noise was good humored. The cards were kind to her, and she felt a glow of good luck.

At ten o'clock she left her game to the Harvard man and went out for a rest. In the kitchen a pot of chocolate was ready on the stove. Marny filled a cup and carried it upstairs to her own room.

She lit the whale oil lamp, took off the heavy nugget necklace and dropped it into the pocket of her skirt, took up

512

the cup and tasted the chocolate. Evidently Lulu or Lolo had made it tonight. Marny could always tell when Kendra had not made the chocolate. As she drank, she reflected that she was going to miss Kendra.

Certainly she did not begrudge Kendra her present happiness. Kendra had had more than her share of trouble and she had met it with courage. She deserved to be happy now.

—But I do wish, Marny thought as she set down her empty cup, that Lulu and Lolo could learn to cook like her.

She heard a little call from the boudoir. Geraldine had heard her come in, and had caught her scent under the door. In cat language, Geraldine was calling, "Come and pay some attention to me."

Marny lit the small lamp and carried it into the boudoir. Geraldine was standing by the door, but as Marny came in she sprang to the table top and rejoined her babies in the hut. Setting the lamp on the side table Marny bent to talk to them. The gun at her belt felt heavy. She should have taken it off, and given her waist a rest along with her neck.

No matter. The kittens were so adorable. Marny would never understand the way they liked to lie in a pile on top of each other. —You'd think, she reflected, that they would smother, or at least be mighty uncomfortable. But evidently not.

"You darlings," she said to them. "Jupiter and Empy and Pandora and Calico. I love you all."

As she stood up she was wondering—When Kendra leaves the Calico Palace, how shall we divide the kittens? I suppose we'll each take a boy and a girl. But which of us will get Geraldine? She's the one who came to the door at midnight. Oh well, we'll decide somehow.

Marny said good night to the kittens and started to leave them.

"Stop!" ordered a voice as she turned around.

In the doorway between the boudoir and the bedroom stood Captain Pollock. He held a gun in his hand, and the gun was pointed at herself.

Almost by instinct Marny's hand flashed to her belt. But at the same moment he barked,

"Stop!"

Marny stopped.

Pollock ordered, "Put your hands in front of you."

Without thought or reason, Marny obeyed.

513

"Don't move," said Pollock, "and don't scream."

Marny did not move or scream. For that moment she was benumbed. She felt nothing but stark, absolute terror.

They faced each other. Marny stood still, her elbows bent, her hands in front of her as though she were carrying an invisible tray. Pollock too stood motionless, his gun ready to fire.

Now that she had passed that first instant of shock, Marny's wits began to clear. She became aware of every detail, with such acuteness as she had seldom felt before. She saw the lamplight pouring through the doorway behind him, and the light from the smaller lamp on the table in front of him, making his features plain; she saw his neat chestnut hair and beard, the excellent quality of his clothes and his well-kept boots; and she saw his strong competent hand on the gun. The gun was a Colt Army Revolver. This was a favorite type of gun in San Francisco and Marny had seen it often. It weighed four pounds, it was a pistol of .44 caliber, and it could easily blow her—or anybody else—right out of the world.

She heard the sounds of the Calico Palace—music, voices, footsteps, opening and closing of doors, the muffled roar of the plaza and the streets beyond. The noise seemed loud, and it seemed to be all round her, like a wall enclosing the silence where she and Pollock stood.

She had thought she was well guarded. But Pollock was a clever man, and crafty. He was here on the fourth floor now. No doubt he had been here before, more than once. Leaving the parlor as if to go home, he must have found a way to elude the guards and slip up the stairs. Pollock had had a purpose in his mind and he had cleared the way.

And she had thought—they all had thought—he came to the Calico Palace because he liked Hortensia and her music! Of course, this was what he had meant them to think.

What did he want? Whatever it was, his plan had served him well. She was alone with him and he was holding the gun. He glared at her, full of hate, and she saw his eyes.

His eyes were open wide, so wide that she could see white above and below the blue irises. With rising terror Marny realized that Pollock did not look quite sane.

He began to talk.

"You are an evil woman." His voice was harsh with rage.

514

"Now you are going to pay for what you have taken from me."

Marny knew it was no use to answer. Pollock went on voicing his fury.

"You have taken everything good I ever had." He still spoke roughly, unevenly. "You have killed my ship. You have destroyed my prospects. Since you forced yourself upon the *Cynthia,* I have had nothing but misfortune."

"Do you think I can work—black magic?" she exclaimed.

He went on as if he had not heard her. Probably he had not.

"I tried to repair the blight you brought upon me," he said. "I went into business. Honorable business. Not like your career of wrecking men's lives. I dealt in brick and lumber. I wanted to help build this city—"

While he talked, her thoughts were taking shape. Pollock had made the same mistake as so many other men: he had chosen to deal in goods of which the supply had outrun the need. Since the Eastern shippers had overloaded the market, prices of brick and lumber were ruinously down.

Kendra had shown her that absurd item about the five hundred dozen fans. Pollock did not deal in fans. But like many other men lost in the swamp of unwanted merchandise, he was bankrupt or nearly so. And he was blaming her for this, as he had blamed her for the fate of the *Cynthia.*

With utter hatred, he was telling her so. His present trouble, like the other, was her fault. She had demonized his destiny. He believed every word he was saying.

Whatever he wanted of her, Pollock intended to get it or kill her. Maybe both.

At her side, below the level of her elbow, Marny heard little protesting sounds from the hut. Geraldine did not understand Pollock's words, but she had sensed that he was not a friend. Geraldine was saying to Marny, "I don't like this man. Make him go away."

Pollock heard Geraldine too. "What's that?" he snarled.

Marny said, "A cat." (—What stupid conversation, she thought, when he may shoot me dead any minute.)

"Cat" Pollock repeated. He spat out the word as if it were a dirty word. "Fit company for you. You look like a cat."

The sounds of hilarity rose from the floors below them. Marny was agonizingly conscious of the little weapon at her belt. If only she could put her hand on it! She could whip out the gun and fire it in a second. But oh, how to get that second?

If somebody would only come to the door! Hortensia, to say, "Kendra left us a plate of raisin tarts." Or Lolo: "Marny, Norman says what's keeping you so long?" Or Norman himself, to tell her he was taking coins out of a safe to replenish a table where the play was going against the house.

Coins. Gold. Of course, this was what Pollock wanted. If he told her to open the safes she would have to do so. This was what he was telling her now.

"You are going to pay me in gold," he thundered at her. "I shall walk away from this den of sin with what is rightly mine. It will be no more than what I should have had today if you had not destroyed my ship and my hopes. You she-devil!" he roared.

Such hatred was deadly. And Marny was realizing that if he killed her here he would have a good chance to get away. He could rob the safes and then shoot her, and run down the iron staircase at the back while the guards were rushing up the main stairs from the gambling rooms.

Or maybe he would not need to flee by the back stairs. He could crack her head with that gun as easily as he could shoot her with it. She would crumple up silently, and Pollock could walk down the main stairs and leave by the front door, his coat over his arm to hide the pokes of gold he was carrying.

Marny's heart was pounding and her skin felt clammy under her clothes. She did not know how much longer she could breathe without choking. In the hut Geraldine mewed angrily. Geraldine had plenty of breath.

Pollock was saying, "Do as I tell you." He turned his command into a question. "Will you do as I tell you?"

Stiff with fear, Marny gasped, "Yes."

(—If I am quite docile, she thought, maybe I can hold him until somebody comes up to this floor. Somebody will come up here for something, sometime—if only I can stay alive that long.)

Pollock was speaking again. "You will give me your gold. Gold nuggets, gold dust, gold coins. First I want your nugget necklace."

The nugget necklace was in the pocket of her skirt, where

she had dropped it when she came into the bedroom. But Pollock did not know this.

"I'm not wearing the necklace," said Marny.

"You are not wearing it *now*," he retorted with contempt. "But you were wearing it tonight while you dealt cards. You were wearing it when you opened your bedroom door. You took it off after you came in. Now," he commanded her with an evil smile, "you will tell me where it is."

Marny felt starved for air. She tried to draw a deeper breath, but she could not. If only she could think of some excuse to move her hands, she could reach her gun.

"All right, I'll give you the necklace," she said. "I'll get it."

"You will not!" Pollock snapped. "I will get it. And I will not move my eyes from you while I am getting it. Tell me where it is."

Again Marny tried to draw a deep breath. It was no use. She could not.

"Do you hear me?" Pollock demanded. *"I want that nugget necklace.* Tell me where it is."

In Marny's mind, from out of the depth of her breathless terror, rose an idea.

She wet her lips. "I hid the necklace when I took it off," she said. "When I take it off I always put it in a secret hiding place."

Pollock gave her a smile of triumph. The smile was like a cut across his face, showing his teeth. "Where is this hiding place?"

"It's in this room," said Marny.

His eyes did not shift and his gun did not waver. "Tell me where it is."

"It's a place where nobody would ever think of looking," said Marny. "My cat is in this little hut here by me, with her kittens. They are lying on a blanket. I hid the necklace under the blanket. If you will slip your hand under the blanket you can find the necklace and take it out."

Still watching her to make sure she did not move, Pollock took a step farther into the room. He took another step, and another. He reached the table on which stood the hut. He was very careful. Still looking at her, still holding the gun on her, he lowered himself on one knee to the level of the little doorway at the front of the hut. Marny followed him with her eyes.

Pollock held the gun in his right hand. Without looking

into the hut, with his left hand he felt along the front edge until he found the doorway. He felt the edge of the blanket on which lay the kittens and Geraldine. His face upturned toward Marny, he slipped his hand under the blanket.

With a cry of rage Geraldine leaped at him. She leaped right at his face. Her claws went into his cheeks. Pollock gave a gasp of shock, his head jerked, and by this time Marny had her gun in her hand. She fired.

63

The report of her gun was the most welcome sound Marny had ever heard. At almost the same instant she heard another and louder report, as Pollock's hand dropped to his side and his gun went off. Pollock stumbled to the floor. His bullet whacked the rug with a violence that nearly threw Marny down beside him.

She caught her balance against the wall, dizzy but not hurt. Her relief was so overwhelming that at first she did not notice anything around her. But as the spinning in her head began to lessen she saw that she had struck Pollock in his right leg, slightly below the knee. Blood was seeping from the wound and making a splotch on the rug, not far from the place where his bullet had torn a jagged hole in the rug and splintered the planks beneath. Pollock's face showed the marks of Geraldine's claws. Drops of blood were trickling across his cheeks.

As for Geraldine, she had gone down to the floor with him, and the shots had sent her ducking under the table. But hearing no more shots she had crept out again, and stood glaring at Pollock and growling awful threats of what she would do to him if he troubled her kittens any more. Though Pollock had been half stunned for a minute, now Marny saw that he was moving, pushing himself toward the spot where his gun had fallen.

The sight of him cleared the last confusion from her mind. Swooping like a bird of prey, she grabbed the gun before he

518

could do so. Pollock tried to stand up, but his injured leg doubled under him and he fell on the floor again. Marny heard him groan, less in pain than in rage because he could not reach her.

At the same time, she became aware of other sounds—banging doors, hurrying footsteps, cries and questions from a multitude of throats. Into the room burst Troy Blackbeard and Norman, demanding to know what the gunfire was about. From outside the room she heard Duke Blackbeard shouting to the gamblers who were suddenly crowding the halls, "Keep back! Stay where you are!"

Norman was staring down at the man on the floor. "My God, Marny!" he exclaimed, almost doubting what he saw. "Is that Captain Pollock? What's been going on here?"

Troy had put an arm around Marny's shoulders. "Did he hurt you, Marny?"

She shook her head. The Colt Army Revolver felt terribly heavy in her hand. She gave it to Troy, and leaned on him, glad of his support. Her other hand, still holding her own little gun, hung limply at her side. Troy took that gun too. She was glad he took it, for she felt hardly strong enough to hold anything. Now that her danger was past, it seemed to her that she had never been so tired in her life.

Norman went to the door and began to give orders.

"Tell them there's been a little trouble but everything's all right now. Burglar tried to get in and Marny fired. She got him, and we're about to throw him out. No, she's not hurt. Tell them to go on with the games. Everything's under control."

Except for her own tremulous nerves, Marny observed that everything really was under control. Pollock had managed to raise himself on an elbow, and was mumbling furiously, but with his leg wound he was helpless and no menace to anybody. Geraldine was on her way back to her maternal duties, climbing the little staircase that led to the table top where stood her hut. Geraldine too had observed that everything was under control. No doubt she attributed this to her own excellent management, and she was right.

Duke Blackbeard came to join Troy. Norman gave more instructions.

"Him," Norman said with contempt, indicating Pollock by a gesture as if such a villain did not deserve to be identified by a name, "we can't have him bleeding all over the place

519

like that. These rugs are expensive. Tie him up with a towel or something. That horse-doctor—Wardlaw—he's been playing roulette in the parlor. Tell Wardlaw to put on a bandage. And him," Norman continued, with another jerk of his thumb toward Pollock, "drag him out of here."

While Duke Blackbeard brought towels from Marny's washstand to stanch Pollock's bleeding until Dr. Wardlaw could attend to the wound, Troy continued to take care of Marny. With clumsy gentleness, while she leaned on him as though on a crutch, Troy led her into the bedroom. Norman followed them. Troy helped her sit down in an armchair, and spoke in a reassuring tone.

"We'll get that man outside, Marny. He's not much hurt. He won't die of it."

"Too bad," said Norman.

Marny did not ask herself whether she was glad or sorry she had not given Pollock a fatal wound. She was too shaky to care.

She must have looked as weak as she felt, for Troy was saying to Norman, "You'd better bring her some brandy."

Norman went out. Laying Pollock's gun and Marny's on the dressing table beside her, Troy returned to the other room. Through the open doorway Marny saw the two Blackbeards raise Pollock between them and drag him outside.

Norman came in with the brandy and poured a drink into Marny's toothbrush glass. As he brought it to her he caught sight of the army revolver on the dressing table. Norman picked it up.

"He came at you with *this*, Marny?"

She nodded.

Norman profanely voiced his wrath. "What did he want?"

"He wanted me to open the safes."

"Thieving bastard," said Norman. "What's the matter with him anyway? He's a leading citizen. At least he puts on airs like one. Well, it just goes to show, you never know who you can trust."

Norman sighed as he contemplated this evidence of human depravity. Marny reached for her own little gun and drew it nearer. She did not expect to need it any more tonight, but it was a six-shot revolver and still held five cartridges. She liked having it close by.

Lulu and Lolo and Hortensia came to ask if they could

do anything. Norman said no, and told them to go on as if nothing had happened. He himself stayed with Marny until Troy came back to report that all was well. Dr. Wardlaw had put a bandage on Pollock's wound. The Blackbeards had searched his pockets and confiscated all the keys they found there, to be sure of getting the one with which he had entered Marny's room. This done, they had put him into a wheelbarrow kept at the back of the building to carry off rubbish, and had trundled him to the hotel where he lived, nearby on Jackson Street. He was out of the Calico Palace and they had warned him that every soul who worked here would be given orders to shoot if he ever crossed the threshold again.

The gamblers were back at their games. Shooting sprees were too common in San Francisco to cause much concern except to the persons involved. Norman said, with wistful chivalry, "I don't suppose you feel like dealing any more tonight, Marny?"

"No," she answered, "I don't," and she ignored his disappointed face. "I'd like to see Kendra when she comes in," Marny added, "but in the meantime, please, I'd like to be by myself."

Norman yielded. He and Troy left her alone.

Marny changed her black satin dress and parlor shoes for a long loose robe and a pair of soft slippers. She took down her hair, and shook it around her shoulders. Pouring another drink of brandy into the toothbrush glass, she stretched out in the armchair, her feet resting on a hassock. Within reach on the dressing table lay her nugget necklace and her little gun, and in the table drawer was a pack of cards. When she had finished this drink, she reflected, she would take out the cards and ask them if she should still be afraid of Pollock or if in the future she could feel secure.

She was sipping the brandy when she heard a knock, and Kendra came in. Marny thought she had never seen Kendra looking so well. Kendra wore the blue silk dress and carried a dark wrap over her arm. The night airs had ruffled her hair into a pretty disorder. The dress matched the blue of her eyes, her cheeks were bright, her whole appearance was that of a woman aglow with joy. Such happiness shared itself. Leaning back in her chair and looking up at Kendra, Marny almost forgot her own ordeal.

"Where's Hiram?" Marny asked.

521

"Waiting. He didn't come with me because Norman told us you wanted to be alone. Do you want Hiram to come in? He'll understand if you say no."

"Of course I want him to come in," said Marny. "I was tired of so many people fluttering around, that's all. You and Hiram will be a comfort."

Kendra brought Hiram. As he reached Marny he gave her a big warm grin and took her hand in a big warm grasp. Hiram was festively dressed, in a black broadcloth suit and a ruffled white shirt and gloves of pearl gray kid, and he carried a high silk hat in his hand. "A fine man you've got, Kendra," Marny remarked.

"I like him," Kendra said happily.

"We like each other," said Hiram. "But right now," he went on, "we're concerned about you. Can we help?"

Marny glanced at Kendra. "I suppose they told you what happened?"

"Not all the details," said Kendra. "We didn't wait for those. But don't bother to tell us now. Don't try to do anything but get over the shock."

Marny gave her a grateful smile. "I do feel shivery," she confessed. "Am I still scared or is the wind rising?"

"You're still scared," said Hiram. "The wind is gentle tonight, what sailors call a lady's wind. Now if you'd like to go to sleep you can do it without worrying. I'll stand guard at the door, all night if you want me."

Marny drew the deep sort of breath she had not been able to draw while Pollock stood before her. "You're a dear man, Hiram, and I may want you to stay, but I'm not sleepy yet. It seems like hours since I left the parlor, but it really isn't late." She glanced at the clock, which showed the time to be not yet twelve. Marny rarely went to bed before three. She reached into the dressing table drawer and took out the pack of cards.

"I might have known it," said Hiram. He and Kendra both laughed understandingly.

Marny reached for his hand and stood up. "First I'd like to see how Geraldine is doing. Geraldine saved my life—I'll tell you about it later."

The three of them went into the boudoir. In the hut, Geraldine and family were snugly asleep.

Marny gave herself a long stretch. "I'm feeling better. Let's

522

go back to the bedroom and I'll lay out the cards and tell our—"

Her voice broke with a gasp. A shudder ran through her whole body.

"Oh God," she cried out, "Not tonight! I can't stand any more!"

They had all three recoiled at the same moment. As Marny gasped her terror Kendra had given a cry that was almost a scream, and Hiram had burst out in fury, "Those damned baboons! Again!"

The firebells were ringing.

At that instant, as Marny and Kendra and Hiram stood half paralyzed with shock, while the bells clanged over the plaza and other shouts of rage and horror broke out in the streets, they knew what was happening. The truth came to them as it came to the rest of San Francisco.

Those thieving murderers of Clark's Point were doing exactly what they had said they were going to do. They had planned it with taunting care. The clock showed the time to be nearly midnight. A few more ticks, and the date would be the fourth of May, anniversary of last year's great fire.

The hoodlums had talked about their purpose. With contemptuous laughter they had observed that the decent people simply could not believe them. But they had meant what they said. They wanted another spree of good looting and they were going to get it. They were burning up the town again.

All through that night one thought kept repeating itself in Marny's mind, over and over with compulsive sameness. —I've been through this before. Why must I go through it again, and again? I'm tired of it. I'm *tired*.

The thought kept coming back even when she was not thinking, even when all she felt was resentment at this horrendous monotony. She did resent it. She resented the lack of imagination among the hoodlums.

—They might at least do something different, she said to herself. Not the same thing all over again.

But it *was* the same thing all over again, only larger and more destructive than ever before. This fire, the fifth great fire she had seen in San Francisco, was the worst fire of them all.

The fire had been set in a paint store on Clay Street facing

523

the plaza. The store was owned by two men named Baker and Meserve. Because of the flammable nature of their stock, the partners had agreed that one of them would stay every evening after employees and customers had left, and go through the building to look for any lamp or candle that might have been forgotten. Tonight it had been the turn of Mr. Meserve. He had searched the store, made sure all was dark, locked the doors, and gone home.

Several hours later a man crossing the plaza happened to glance at a window in the upper story of the paint store. Through the windowpane he saw a little bright flicker. He shouted an alarm. The bells began to ring, the engines responded with their usual bang and clatter as the firemen raced them through the streets. They dashed to the plaza as fast as they could, but it was not fast enough. When the man in the plaza gave the alarm the flame was no bigger than a woman's handkerchief, but it grew and ripped through the building with appalling speed. Before the first engine reached the plaza the whole upper story of the paint store was crackling like a matchbox. In less than a minute the buildings on either side were burning too, and the fire was rushing down Clay Street toward Kearny Street and the Calico Palace.

For chance, or fate, or whatever you wanted to name it, had intervened. When the first alarm sounded, the breeze over the city was hardly more than a zephyr, blowing gently from the west. But as if the firebells had roused some sleeping god of the storms, almost at that same moment this "lady's wind," as Hiram had called it, turned into a gale.

The gale swept the fire eastward. It blew with such force that the firemen had barely begun to play their hose on the paint store when they saw flames tear into the sky from a restaurant on Kearny Street. Before they could move their engines they saw more flames rising from banks and business houses a block farther east on Montgomery. In a fearfully few minutes the richest quarter of the city was tottering and the wind was driving the fire on toward the waterfront and the shipping in the bay.

Marny and Hiram and Kendra had run along the hall from Marny's room to a front window overlooking the plaza. As they saw the fire leaping so close to them Kendra gave a start of horror and Hiram wheeled around toward her.

"Get out!" he shouted.

524

Kendra said breathlessly, "This building is supposed to be—"

"I don't care what it's supposed to be. Get out, I say!" Hiram grabbed her hands. He was about to draw her toward the stairs when he saw Marny running down the hall, not toward the stairs but back toward her bedroom. He ran after her, almost dragging Kendra with him, and caught the sleeve of Marny's robe. "Where the hell are you going?"

She answered with a force equal to his own. "I'm on my way to get a few things I need. And Kendra needs a few things too. If you want her to go into the street tonight without a gun you're a fool." Marny jerked at the sleeve he was holding. "Turn me loose."

Kendra spoke with emphasis. "Hiram, she's right."

From the floors below they heard men shouting, glasses breaking, chairs and tables falling over. The gamblers were scuffling as they tried to gather up their own or other men's wagers, banging doors as they ran out to save whatever they could. Hiram spoke to Marny, more calmly this time.

"Of course you're right, Marny. I always want to be in too much of a hurry. Get your gun."

They hurried back toward the bedrooms. Kendra ran into her room to get her own gun. It was the same revolver that Archwood had bought for her from a gambler, in the days when the Calico Palace had been a tent and she used to carry her cupcakes across the vacant lot on a tray. She had not worn the gun for so long that she fumbled and had to call Hiram to help her put it into the holster and buckle the belt.

As for Marny, the compulsive words had already begun to run through her head like a jingle. —I've been through this before. Why again, and again? And why does it happen again that I'm wearing a long clumsy robe to trail behind me and get in the way? I've been through every bit of this before. I'm tired of it.

She did not take time to get dressed, but she did pause to change her bedroom slippers for a pair of strong shoes. She had not forgotten her flight through the Christmas fire in those thin party slippers that broke to pieces in the mud.

Her thoughts were racing. The Calico Palace might or might not be fireproof. But no building was proof against looters unless it was guarded. Maybe Norman would want her to stay and stand by some door or window with her gun. If he wanted her here she was not going to run away. But if she did leave the building she was going to take Geraldine with her, and the kittens. Geraldine had saved her life and she was going to take care of Geraldine.

Already, at the first alarm, she had latched the door of Geraldine's hut to keep her and the kittens inside. Now she dipped a towel into the water pitcher, wrung it out, and draped it over the hut. This would protect the cats from flying sparks. She cut a slash in the towel, through which she could grasp the handle and carry the hut like a traveling bag. When Hiram and Kendra came back along the hall Marny met them at the door of her room, her gun in one hand and the other hand holding the hut, with Geraldine crying with fright and anger inside it. Marny said,

"She thinks there's entirely too much going on around here. I think so too."

As she spoke, Norman and the Blackbeards came hurrying up the stairs. At sight of Marny and Kendra, Norman paused and said to the Blackbeards,

"You go on up. I'll be there in a minute." He said to Marny, "We're on our way to open the roof tank."

"Oh please God," she murmured fervently, "let it work." Hiram added, "Amen," and Kendra whispered a hope of her own. As the Blackbeards went on toward the stairs that would take them to the roof, Marny spoke to Norman. "Is there any help I can give you here, Norman? If there is, I'll stay."

Norman gave her a shrewd, almost humorous look. "Marny, you're so wobbly tonight, as a guard you wouldn't be worth a fried egg."

Marny smiled. She liked his merciless candor.

"Come on!" Hiram exclaimed. He was waiting impatiently, his arm around Kendra. Marny could go or stay as she pleased, but he was in haste to get Kendra outside. Norman was saying to Marny,

"Take this with you." He held out a poke heavy with coins.

"I can't," said Marny. "My hands are full."

Norman glanced at the gun, which he approved of, then his gaze fell on the hut covered with the wet towel. His eyes bulged. "What's that?"

Marny said steadily, "The cats."

"Cats!" he exploded. "Leave those damn cats. Take this poke."

526

"I won't," said Marny.

"Dwight Carson guaranteed—"

"If the building is safe, the poke is safe. If the building burns, the coins will melt. But I'm looking after Geraldine."

"Come *on!*" shouted Hiram.

In a sputter of unholy words Norman told Marny her mind was failing and it would not distress him if she and the cats all got burned to a crisp. Leaving him to sputter, Marny went with Hiram and Kendra toward the staircase, but as she neared the top step she turned to call over her shoulder.

"Norman, Captain Pollock's revolver is on the table in my room. It might come in handy."

Without answering, Norman stalked off. Hiram held out his hand toward Geraldine's hut.

"Want me to carry that, Marny?"

"Thanks," she said briefly, and gave the hut to him. "It's an awkward load," she added. "We'll take turns carrying it."

"Now," said Hiram, "let's go."

They started down. On the lower flights, gamblers and their lady friends were hurrying toward the front door.

Gun in one hand and Geraldine's hut in the other, Hiram went ahead of Marny and Kendra to make sure the staircase was clear. They pressed close behind him. All around them they heard a medley of noises—creaks and crashes and screams of fear, the jangle of firebells and the rising roar of the flames. Then, from over their heads, they heard a clank of machinery and a rush of water.

Marny caught her breath. "Oh, thank God!" she cried.

She ran on down the stairs, panting, and at the same time almost laughing in her thankfulness. Norman had opened the roof tank. Stored in the tank, as Marny well knew, were eighty-two thousand gallons of water. Would it save the Calico Palace? This she did not know.

At the main exit one of the bartenders stood guard with the dealer from Harvard. Marny and Kendra and Hiram made their way outside, into the glare and smoke and turmoil of Kearny Street.

The blaze was so strong that they could see as clearly as by daylight. Hundreds, maybe thousands, of people were crowding the streets around the plaza. As usual, some of them were doing useful work, some were slipping off with whatever they had managed to steal, others were running around in hysterics, getting nowhere. (—I've seen it all before, thought Marny.)

The plaza itself was speedily filling up with a variety of things as men dragged their possessions out of buildings on fire or in danger of it, and piled them in the open square—bales and barrels and trunks, beds, tables, mirrors, paintings, safes, account books, anything they could grab and move. Through her own confusion Marny found herself wondering how anybody was going to find his own stuff tomorrow, even if the looters had not carried it off and hidden it somewhere else.

On the south side of the plaza, to their left, they heard a crash as the walls of the old City Hotel tumbled in. The other buildings on Clay Street were blazing wrecks. But to their right, they saw that the fire had not reached Washington Street. The firemen were sending streams of water from the plaza reservoir toward the *Alta* office and Pocket's library and Blossom's flower garden and the other buildings on that side. Hiram and Kendra and Marny pushed along Kearny Street toward Washington, bumping into people and being bumped, but somehow fighting their way.

The air was hot like a blast from a desert. Sparks and fragments of burning stuff were blowing wildly in the wind, but the El Dorado, at the corner of Washington and Kearny, had not caught fire. Neither had the Verandah, on the opposite corner. Roofs of both buildings were astir with men fighting to keep them safe. In Washington Street, all the way up the hill, other men were hitching mules to wagons and throwing in their valuables, yelling with rage when the fire engines got in their way. The wind turned their words into senseless tumult.

The wind was still blowing the fire eastward. Hiram and Kendra and Marny pushed their way into Washington Street and began to struggle up the hill, westward toward Dupont. The wind blew violently against them. Behind them the wind was sending the fire through the block on Montgomery Street where stood Hiram's bank.

They were not talking; their fight to get up the hill left them no strength for it. A man howling in panic rushed out of Blossom's house, gave a blank look at the glare, and then, as though out of his senses, he dashed down into the fire instead of way from it. At the same time they heard a fireman

528

exclaim, "Hiram! Thank God you're here to help us." He thrust a length of hose toward Hiram's hand.

Hiram stopped. Up to this minute his only thought had been to get Kendra to a place of refuge. But he too belonged to a fire company. If other men could ignore their own concerns in the common peril, so could he. He said, "Marny, take the cats."

As she grasped the carrying handle Hiram took the hose and went to work. Shouting to be heard above the uproar he ordered, "Go on up the hill! Don't stop for anything—keep going—go *into* the wind!"

Through the screams and crashes the girls said "Yes," but he probably did not hear. They fought their way upward. As they struggled along they caught sight of Pocket, busy with a hose. He saw them, and like Hiram he called, "Keep going, girls! Up the hill—into the wind!" They went on. The hut bumped against Marny's knee with every step she took. Panting, sweating, stumbling, she and Kendra pushed on up the hill.

The whole street was a jumble—people, mules, wagons, wheelbarrows. A few other women were climbing the hill, some of them carrying babies; and many men, bent nearly double under the loads they carried on their backs. Nobody seemed to notice other people except to shove them out of the way.

Around them roared the wind.

In San Francisco they were used to the wind, this exasperating wind that blew off men's hats and whirled women's skirts around their knees, raised the dust clouds and spattered sand against the windowpanes, and at night woke sleepers with its rattling of doors and shutters. They were used to the wind. Many of them even liked it, and laughed at the tricks it played.

But tonight the wind was not teasing them or playing tricks on them. The wind was ravaging their city like a maniac army. The wind had no mercy. Borne by the wind, the fire roared in triumph. Its thunder was so loud that it made all other sounds indistinct. The fire was louder than the shouts of the fireman and the hissing of the hose, louder than the crash of bricks and timber, louder than the screams of panic in the street. It even blurred the death shrieks of men and women who were caught in burning buildings and could not get out. Tomorrow, when the facts began to be told, people who had lived through the fire were going to hear about "fireproof" iron doors that had not been properly fitted. The doors had warped in the heat, so that they could not be opened, and the victims trapped behind them had been cooked as though in iron ovens.

Marny and Kendra slogged up Washington Street. Slowly, they made their way across Dupont, across Stockton, across Powell, up and up the hill. They were gasping, coughing, fighting the mob around them and fighting the wind. The wind met them fiercely. But they were thankful, for as long as it blew into their faces it was driving the fire away from them. Behind them they heard the fire and the hideous confusion of the other sounds under its roaring. They dared not stop and look back.

At last, when the street had faded to a weed-grown track, they came to the high ridge that overlooked the city. Gasping with weariness, they paused. Marny set Geraldine's hut on the ground, and she and Kendra sank, almost fell, among the weeds beside it. They half sat, half lay there, huddled together, panting.

Here on this bleak height the only signs of habitation were a few scattered shanties, creaking and groaning in the wind. Milling about among the shanties were other people who like themselves had fled the fire. Some sat on the ground, not speaking or moving, staring ahead of them with blank faces and glassy eyes as though made idiotic by shock. Some were running around in panic, sobbing and wailing in broken words. Men stood by their carts or piles of goods, guns in their hands, on the watch for looters, while the would-be looters hopefully prowled around.

Marny and Kendra were only half aware of the crowd around them. What they really saw, downhill in front of them, was San Francisco on fire. They saw it, and heard it, like the ruin of a nightmare city. This fire was so vast that, as they learned later, it lit the sky in Monterey, ninety miles down the coast. By that tremendous light they could see everything as clearly as though by the sun of noon.

For the first few minutes it all seemed a formless pandemonium of flame and smoke and crashing walls and the rolling thunder of the fire itself. Then gradually they began to see what the terrible light was showing them. They saw walls like shells around flames that burned inside and streamed out through the windows. They saw other walls crack like glass, and totter, and fall to pieces, breaking the bones of anyone who might be in the way. For long stretches on the streets everything had already been wrecked, and the streets now showed nothing but piles of fiery embers.

Marny sat with one arm across Geraldine's hut, protectively, the other arm around her knees. Shivering with dread, she watched the spreading horror. Dwight had promised her the Calico Palace would be fireproof. But could any structure on earth stand unscathed in the midst of such havoc as this?

She had thought she was too tired to move. But she had to see more than she was seeing now. She struggled to her feet and looked across the roofs that went like steps down the hill. She turned her head, her eyes searching. The roofs hid part of the plaza area, but she could see Kearny Street.

Kearny Street was blazing. But among the flames were some walls that had not fallen, and one of these was the front wall of the Calico Palace. How much was left behind that front wall Marny could not tell.

The walls of the El Dorado were still standing, and so were those of its rival the Verandah. For all she knew the insides of the buildings might be gutted; still, the solid look of the walls gave her hope. But the Parker House was a smoking wreck. Next door to the Parker House was the magnificent Union Hotel where Hiram lived, five stories high and long believed safe. As Marny looked, the front wall of the Union Hotel cracked slantwise from corner to corner. In another moment the wall crashed forward into the street, scattering thousands of red-hot bricks and sending up a sheet of flame that seemed almost to split the sky.

It occurred to Marny that now Hiram was in the same state as herself on the night of the Christmas fire: he had nothing to wear. The compulsive line began again. —I've been through it all before.

And the Calico Palace was only two doors away from the Union Hotel.

Marny dropped her head till her chin met her chest. "Please, God!" she whispered. "Don't make me go through that again!"

But after a moment or two she looked up; she could not help looking. The fire had ravaged everything on the Clay Street side of the plaza, but Marny gave a sigh of joy as she

531

saw that the firemen were still keeping it away from Washington Street. This meant that Pocket's library was still there, and the office of the *Alta California,* and Blossom's flower garden. Marny wondered how the plaza preacher was going to explain why the Lord had let the fire destroy so many places of respectable business while it spared the fanciest brothel in town. She saw men hurrying in and out of the *Alta* office, risking their lives to bring the facts of the fire so the paper could give a true account in the morning. —Brave men, she thought.

All through the burning district she could see a great many men, their movements clear in the great light. She saw men in frenzy tearing about like puppets pulled by crazy hands; and other men, brave men, fighting to save as much of the city as they could. They were holding hose that shot jets of water upon blazing walls; they were rescuing injured people who could not help themselves; in the streets ahead of the fire's progress they were sending off blasts of gunpowder, trying to make gaps too wide for the flames to cross. Those brave men were offering all they had. When the fire had burnt itself out some of them would no longer be alive.

As she thought of this, Marny thought of Hiram. She turned and looked at Kendra, curled up among the weeds. Kendra had put a hand over her eyes as though to shut out the view in front of her. Marny saw the fire reflected in the gleam of tears on her cheeks. Kendra too was thinking of Hiram.

Marny sat down on the grass and put her arm around Kendra's shoulders. She said nothing, but Kendra sensed her sympathy. After a moment, without looking up, Kendra spoke.

"Marny."

"Yes, dear," Marny answered gently.

"Marny," said Kendra, "if Hiram doesn't live through this, I don't want to live through it either."

—What can I say to her? wondered Marny. A nice hollow platitude like, 'Oh now, you mustn't feel that way'? If I said any such thing she'd slap me and she ought to.

Marny said, "Kendra dear, I can't answer."

"I don't want you to answer," said Kendra. "I just want to say it. I've lost everything else I ever had. I've tried to be brave. Marny, you know I've tried."

532

"You've not only tried, Kendra. You've been brave. The bravest person I ever knew."

"I'm not going to try any longer," said Kendra. "Marny, I can't take any more."

Marny raised her hand from Kendra's shoulder and stroked her hair. There was nothing for her to say. She let Kendra go on talking.

"I've just found him, Marny. And if I lose him now, I can't stand it." Kendra raised her head and looked down at the blazing city. "Marny, when we came in tonight from the theater, I've never been so happy. A whole new world was opening in front of me. And now that I've had a glimpse of it—" She shuddered. "Marny, maybe I'm a coward. But if I lose Hiram, I don't want to look for anything else. I'm not going to try any more."

There was a silence between them. On the other side of Marny, in the hut, Geraldine and the kittens had fallen asleep, worn out by too much excitement. Marny wished it were as easy as this for Kendra. But it was not. People were more complex than cats.

At length she spoke. "Kendra, I can't offer you any help. But I'm your friend and whatever happens I'll stand by you. That's all I can say."

"I know," answered Kendra. "Thank you for saying it. And thank you for listening to me."

Again they lapsed into silence. Around them were the voices of all those other people, below them the roar and tumult of the fire, and the city falling to pieces.

64

The fire burned on and on and on. It burned for hours. Neither Kendra nor Marny could have told how many hours. Their sense of time was as confused as everything else tonight.

They shivered in the screaming wind. In front of them, down the hill, the city was crashing. At every crash Kendra thought of death under the falling timbers. At every crash she sent up a prayer. —Oh God, not Hiram. Please God, not Hiram.

She remembered how willingly Hiram had stayed to fight the fire. He could not honorably have done otherwise. —But oh, she cried to herself, I wish he could have been a coward just this once!

Even as the thought came into her mind she knew she did not wish any such thing. Hiram was not a halfway person. She could not have loved him if he had been. She had had one experience with that sort of man. Kendra heard another crash and saw a million sparks shoot into the sky.

—Please God, not Hiram.

Hunched among the weeds at Kendra's side, Marny was nearly numb with weariness. As Norman had reminded her, that encounter with Pollock had tensed her nerves before the fire began. Now the reaction had set in, as Norman had known it would. She thought if she tried to stand up again she might fall down.

Through her weariness she began to notice that there was a light around her different from the glare of the fire. Daylight. —Good heavens, she thought, it's morning. Tomorrow morning. We've been here all night.

Looking over the bay, she could see the sun shimmering through the smoke clouds. She saw too that the blaze was no longer as fierce as it had been. Tongues of flame were still shooting up through the smoke, but the fire was burning itself out. Maybe, she thought despairingly, because there was not much left to burn.

Her arms and legs felt cramped. She stretched, and leaned over to look again into Geraldine's hut. Geraldine was still asleep, with the tiny kittens cuddled against her. Marny sat up again, laying her arm across the hut as before. She curled her fingers around the carrying handle. Happy little cats. They had no idea of what an evil world they lived in. Still holding the handle, she looked down again at the ruins, wondering how much longer it would take for the fire to finish its work.

All of a sudden, a hard rough hand covered hers and she felt rude fingers pushing her own fingers off the handle. Marny jerked herself around. A man with dirty clothes and a dirty stink was grabbing the hut, sure that any box so tenderly guarded must hold something worth money.

Marny forgot her fatigue. Before her mind had formed a

534

conscious thought she had leaped to her feet and at the same time whipped out her gun. Uttering a wordless sound of rage, she fired.

But though she had forgotten her fatigue, it was still there. Her hand was not steady. Her shot missed, and the bullet buried itself in the ground. She heard a cry of alarm from Kendra and exclamations from all around her, as with a mocking laugh the looter gripped the handle of the hut and started to run.

But he did not take a second step. Before Marny could fire again she heard another crack from another pistol. The looter fell sprawling. The hut dropped from his hand and turned over on its side.

Marny's knees were shaking. She felt Kendra's hand on her elbow, helping her to stand. Murmuring, "Thank you," Marny turned her head, and to her amazement she saw that Kendra's other hand held a gun.

Marny gasped. "You—? How did you do it?"

"I—I don't know," said Kendra. "It—just happened." She sounded as amazed as Marny herself, and looked down at the gun as if surprised to find it in her hand. She added, "You—you said I would need it tonight."

The man on the ground sat up, groaning in pain and anger. At the same moment another man's voice demanded, "What's going on here?"

By the new daylight they saw Pocket coming toward them. He held a murderous-looking gun of his own, and with an air of authority he was ordering other people out of his way. As he saw Marny and Kendra he stopped, and looked from them to the unsavory fellow on the ground, who now sat whining as he contemplated a wound in his right forearm.

"What was he up to?" Pocket demanded.

A man in the crowd pushed forward. "He tried to steal a box from these ladies."

"And got a bullet for his trouble," said Pocket. "Good work. If I'd seen him first I'd have shot him myself. I'm on patrol duty, looking out for looters." From one of his pockets he drew a big handkerchief and threw it to the whimpering man on the ground. "Wrap this around your arm and get going." To the others he said, "Well, I guess he won't steal with that hand for a while. Who shot him?"

"Kendra," said Marny.

"Kendra!" Pocket repeated. He spoke to her admiringly, a slow grin spreading across his face. "Smart girl. I tell you frankly, ma'am, I didn't know you could do it."

"Neither did I," said Kendra. "But I did it, and it made me feel better."

Again her voice had a note of surprise. She did feel better. She felt less helpless in the face of the holocaust.

"I'd like to sit down," said Marny, and without further ado she let herself crumple up among the weeds. A frowsy woman, apparently the looter's girl friend, had stumbled toward him. She was kneeling at his side, tying Pocket's handkerchief around his arm and wailing in alcoholic profanities. Holding his gun ready, Pocket made his way to the noisy pair. With his usual steady confidence he took a gun from the man's pocket and transferred it to his own. This done, he picked up the hut, where Geraldine was now storming angrily, and brought it back to Marny and Kendra.

"You heard me tell the folks I'm on patrol duty," said Pocket. "My job is to walk up and down Washington Street between here and Kearny, looking for looters. When you've rested a bit longer, you can walk down to the library with me. It's safe there now."

He told them—and a number of others who had gathered to listen—that the fire was, as Marny had noticed, burning itself out. The flames had crossed Washington Street below Kearny, but not above. This meant that the Washington Street side of the plaza was unhurt. But looters were creeping about, so he and several other men, the best shots in their fire company, had been detailed to patrol the street.

To Kendra's questions he replied that he had last seen Hiram about two hours ago. At that time Hiram had been fighting the fire, and though his clothes were scorched Hiram himself had not been injured. As for the Calico Palace, the walls were standing, but each fire company had its own district and Pocket had not been close enough to the Calico Palace to know if there was damage inside.

Marny told herself to be patient. As she looked up at him from where she sat on the ground, it occurred to her that she had never seen Pocket's pockets so un-stuffed. Some of them looked actually empty. The library kept earlier hours than the Calico Palace. Marny guessed that he had been in bed asleep when he heard the midnight alarm, and had sprung up and thrown on his clothes, and rushed out without pausing to gather his usual baggage.

Pocket was saying, "It's time you ladies had some peace and quiet."

He gave Marny a particular look of concern. Pocket had not heard about Marny's meeting with Captain Pollock, but his quick eyes and his warmth of heart had told him that she was close to the limit of what she could bear. He went on, "And it's time I got back on patrol. Kendra, will you carry the cats?"

Marny dragged herself up. Pocket resumed patrol, this time heading downhill, looking for troublemakers and now and then finding one and sternly sending him on his way. The girls walked behind him, down the weedy track to where it widened and met the plank sidewalk, and on toward the plaza. While this part of the street was not on fire, it was as chaotic as it had been when they climbed. Still, the walk was easier going down.

They came at last to the library. Here Pocket's partner, Mr. Gilmore, stood on guard with several of their clerks. Pocket told Mr. Gilmore that Marny and Kendra were to have his bedroom. They followed Pocket inside, through the reading rooms, to the back of the building where his bedroom was. When they tried to thank him Pocket said he had no time to listen. He hurried out to go back on duty.

Pocket did not live in such luxury as Hiram had enjoyed in the Union Hotel. The room was small and plainly furnished. The bed covers had been hastily thrown back, and over the chairs and washstand and chest of drawers were scattered the possessions that Pocket had not had time to put into his pockets. But to Marny and Kendra the untidy little room was a blessed haven. Marny dropped across the bed. Kendra set Geraldine's hut on the floor and stretched out by Marny.

They did not talk, but they were still too tense to sleep. The night behind them had been an ordeal, the day ahead was an agonizing uncertainty. —How is it with Hiram? How is it with the Calico Palace? How will it be with me, after this?

In the hut Geraldine cried bitterly. "I am bruised and hungry and miserable," she moaned in cat language. "Why do you treat me like this? Don't you love me any more?"

After a while they heard loud thumping footsteps, the bedroom door burst open, and a big voice exclaimed, "Hi, Pocket! Anybody home?"

They sat up, and Kendra sprang off the bed with a scream of delight.

"Hiram!"

He grabbed her in his arms. Together they demanded of each other, "Are you all right?"

They were both all right. Kendra's blue silk dress and theater cloak were torn and ruined; Hiram's fine broadcloth suit was in tatters, he had blisters on his hands and many bruises all over, but who cared? He had no important hurts and neither had she, and they were together again.

Across Kendra's shoulder Hiram asked, "And you, Marny?"

"How is the Calico Palace?" she returned breathlessly.

On Hiram's smudgy face she saw a big broad smile. "Marny, the Calico Palace is still there."

"Then I'm all right," said Marny.

Her voice cracked. She crumpled up on the bed and hid her face in Pocket's pillow and pushed her fingers up through her wind-blown hair and sobbed. The Calico Palace was still there.

Hiram waited until her sobs quieted. Then, sitting on the bed between her and Kendra, he told them more about the fire. He said Dwight Carson had built as well as he had promised he would. Not only was the Calico Palace intact, but so was Hiram's bank. On the block where the bank stood, every other building had gone down. But the bank, with its roof tank and its perfectly adjusted iron doors and shutters, had withstood the fire.

Chase and Fenway's store was a total loss and so was their warehouse. However, they were luckier than some men, for they both still had their dwellings. The fire had not reached the home of Mr. Chase on Washington Street, and it had not gone as far south as Happy Valley where lived Mr. Fenway and Rosabel. "And they have coins and gold dust," Hiram added proudly, "safe in our vault. So they can start rebuilding right away."

Marny dried her eyes on Pocket's pillowcase. "Hiram, is it safe for me to walk down to Kearny Street? I'd like to go to sleep in my own bed."

Kendra said she too would like to go back to the Calico Palace. Hiram considered. Kearny Street was piled with

538

smoking debris, and timbers were still falling. However, he had come here by walking diagonally across the plaza, scrambling among the barrels and boxes and other things piled there. They could do the same.

"If you can stand a lot of ugly sights," he warned them.

"We'll have to stand that sometime," said Marny. "Why not now?"

"All right," said Hiram. "I'll go with you."

"You're already worn out!" Kendra protested.

Hiram chuckled. Of course he was tired, he said. But he was also hungry. The Union Hotel was gone, and so were most of the other hotels and restaurants. Hiram was hoping, if he saw Marny and Kendra safely to the Calico Palace, Kendra would give him some breakfast.

While he was speaking Pocket came in. Kendra said she would give breakfast to them both, and they whistled joyfully. "Then Hiram and I will come back here," said Pocket, "and catch up on our sleep so we'll be ready for more guard duty tonight. I don't think there'll be much looting this morning. Nobody slept last night, and even the greediest thieves can't stay awake forever." He reached for Geraldine's hut. "Let's go."

Hiram stood up, but he paused, suddenly grave. "Wait a minute, Pocket. I've just remembered, there's something I want to tell Marny." He put his hand on her shoulder. "Marny, early this morning our squad found Captain Pollock. Dead."

She gave a start. "Oh Hiram! You mean burned up?"

"No. There wasn't a mark on him. He was in the street, near the hotel he lived in. Smothered by the smoke. He got out somehow, but he couldn't get away. With a wound in the leg below the knee, a man can't walk."

"Then I killed him, didn't I?" Marny said slowly. "Hiram, I didn't mean to kill him." She caught her voice. "Or—maybe I did. I don't know. It happened so fast, and I was so scared, I honestly don't know if I meant to kill him or not."

"What's this," exclaimed Pocket, "about somebody killing Captain Pollock?"

"You tell him, Marny," said Hiram.

Marny told him. "I don't know," she repeated at the end of her narrative, "whether or not I meant to kill him. But this makes me feel guilty, somehow."

Pocket had listened without comment, standing at the foot

539

of the bed. Now he smiled at her, and his smile was reassuring and serene.

"You didn't mean to kill him, Marny."

She asked eagerly, "How do you know?"

"If you shot him below the knee," Pocket said calmly, "you did some pretty accurate aiming. That's exactly the right place to hit a man when you have to protect yourself but you don't want to kill him. He falls down but he hasn't got a fatal wound. And you knew that, whether or not you had it in the top side of your mind just then. You aimed right and you didn't mean to kill him."

Marny gave a sigh of relief. Kendra squeezed her hand.

Hiram vigorously agreed with Pocket. "And you didn't kill him, Marny. It was the hoodlums who set this fire that killed him."

Pocket shook his head. He spoke with thoughtful slowness. "You know, Hiram, I think it's closer to the truth to say Pollock killed himself. If he hadn't tried to rob Marny he wouldn't have been hurt. And if he hadn't been hurt, he would have had a good chance to get away from the fire." Pocket smiled an odd little smile. "Evil people," he added, "have a way of killing themselves."

There was a pause. Pocket spoke to Marny again.

"And now that I think of it, Marny, Pollock might have been bankrupt yesterday but if he'd been an honest man he would have been rich today."

"What do you mean?" the other three exclaimed.

"He told Marny," Pocket answered with tranquil assurance, "he had a right to steal from her because he couldn't sell his bricks and lumber. Well, they were a drug on the market last night, but they sure aren't today. Three-quarters of San Francisco has been burned up and folks have got to rebuild. They'll be buying all the bricks and lumber they can get. Pollock's brickyard and lumber yard are down at the south end of town below Happy Valley. That area wasn't touched by the fire." Pocket picked up Geraldine's hut. "Well, folks, I'm famished. Let's go to the Calico Palace and get that breakfast."

Yesterday they could have walked from the library to the Calico Palace in about ten minutes. This morning they had to pick their way among the piles of rescued stuff in the

540

plaza, and the fallen bricks and timbers in Kearny Street, and they had to go around piles of rubble that only half covered the bodies beneath. They had to pause and listen to the frantic words of men who had lost everything they owned, and to other men who pled, "Have you seen So-and-So?—I can't find him—I'm afraid he—" and could not finish the sentence. Today the walk took a long time and it seemed longer.

They spoke little. They were too tired, and too sickened by the tragedies around them. But later that day Marny remembered Pocket's saying through his teeth, almost mumbling, more as if talking to himself than to her, "Human creatures did this. Did it on purpose."

"Some of those human creatures," Marny reminded him grimly, "got killed in it."

Pocket returned, "Not enough."

His voice was low but savage. Mild as his temper was, right now if Pocket had recognized one of the men who had set this fire, she did not doubt that Pocket would have shot him.

The Calico Palace was safe. The windowpanes were slivered; the brick walls were splotched with soot and water; at the street-floor windows Bruno Gregg's handsome transparencies had burned to shreds; the tall gilt letters that had spelled CALICO PALACE across the second-floor front had curled and cracked like autumn leaves; but the building itself stood firm amid the wreckage around it. Troy Blackbeard, on guard at the main door, told them Lulu and Lolo and Zack had gone to bed and to sleep. Norman and Hortensia sat on the staircase reviving their strength with bread and cheese and a bottle of wine. Norman said Hortensia had been great last night, just great. Didn't lose her head for a minute. Packed a bag for each of them so they would have clothes and coins if they had to run. "Now what," he demanded of Pocket, "are you doing with those damn cats?"

"Bringing them home," said Pocket.

Norman shrugged in wonder.

While Kendra was setting out a meal, Marny filled pans with food and water and carried them up to Geraldine's room, Pocket following her with the hut. Marny shuddered as she saw the bloodstain on the rug, and the damaged spot where Pollock's bullet had struck the floor when his gun went off. Only last night. So much had happened since then, it seemed long ago.

Pocket unlatched the door of the hut, and now they found they had a small tragedy of their own. One of the kittens was dead, the one they had named Empy.

"I suppose," Marny said sorrowfully, "Empy got hurt when that slug dropped the hut. Damn his thieving fingers. I wish Kendra had shot his hand off."

Pocket glanced at Geraldine, who was eating her breakfast with gusto. He said consolingly, "I don't think cats can count. If Geraldine had lost all her kittens she would miss them, but with three left I don't believe she will know the fourth is gone." He went to the door that led into the hall. "I'll dispose of this one."

"At least," Marny said, "I'm glad it's not the kitten we named Calico for the Calico Palace. That would have worried me. A bad sign for the future." She added abruptly, "All right, laugh at me if you want to. Kendra thinks I'm silly to be this way, but this is the way I am."

"I'm not laughing at you," Pocket answered with a touch of surprise. "I don't laugh at people. If they're different from me, maybe they're right."

She smiled at him. "You're a smart fellow, Pocket."

"Thank you ma'am," said Pocket. He opened the door. "I'll see you in the kitchen."

In the kitchen they gobbled a meal of cold leftovers (the idea of making a fire in the stove was too horrifying to be considered). The men went back to the library, while Marny and Kendra went to their own rooms and speedily fell asleep.

When Marny woke up that afternoon she felt surprisingly well. She got out of bed and stretched, put on her slippers, and went to the mirror.

"You *are* a mess," she said to her reflection. "Well, you've cleaned yourself up before and you can do it again. And this time you have something to wear."

She walked over to the window and looked down at what used to be the city, still smoking in the sunset. The sight was heartbreaking, blocks and blocks of rubble, and walls standing here and there like black tombstones.

The desolation was not complete. Not only was the Calico Palace standing, but so were the El Dorado and the Verandah. The north side of the plaza was not burned, and the fire had nowhere gone west of Dupont Street. And even in the blackest area Hiram's bank was not the only building that had shown itself to be fireproof. Marny could see several others, and there might be more beyond her range of vision. Already she could see men walking about, making notes, planning to start over. The sight of them was cheering. They had rebuilt before, they would do it again.

This was Sunday afternoon. Marny and Norman and their helpers spent Monday cleaning up. At three o'clock Tuesday afternoon the Calico Palace opened for business, and it stayed open until two o'clock the next morning. Through the whole eleven hours the bars and gambling rooms were thronged. Men's nerves were taut, their tempers on edge. It was some consolation to gather with other men and talk about their losses. There were more arguments than usual, and more men than usual who had to be carried out instead of walking. But as there were also more profits than usual, Marny and Norman bore the disorders without complaint.

In the days following the fire the *Alta* published long lists of buildings destroyed and names of persons who had lost their lives in the fire or died later of injuries. But the paper also had notes of cheer. Eustis and Boyd announced that all coins and gold dust deposited in their vault were safe and available on demand. Chase and Fenway inserted a card of thanks to the firemen who had made their way into the burning store and brought out a strongbox holding important papers. Mr. Reginald Norrington informed the public that he was now doing business in an office on Dupont Street, where he would receive the rents owed to his clients. If any firemen had given help to Mr. Norrington when his own office burned he did not say so, at least not in print. Words of thanks would have required extra lines and added to the price of his announcement.

But other men were not so thrifty. Day after day the *Alta* carried columns of notices thanking the firemen for their heroism. The paper also published a list of the buildings in the burnt area that survived the fire. There were not many. But the fire had proved that Dwight Carson had done what he had said he could do. There were seven buildings in San Francisco that had been put up under Dwight's direction. Six of the seven—all but Pocket's library—had stood in the district devastated by the fire. All six—the Calico Palace, Hiram's bank, and four others—were still standing. All were open for business.

And now Dwight was putting up buildings in New York. As Marny thought of this, she had an idea. She sent for Bruno Gregg and told him that when he had finished the new transparencies she would have another job for him.

65

On the second morning after the fire, Kendra told Marny she and Hiram were going to be married in nine days.

They had not planned to be married so soon. But that night of dread had shown them how little security they had. "We are not going to trust the future," Kendra said to Marny. "We are going to grab some happiness right now."

They rented a lot in Happy Valley, bought one of the readymade cottages from China, and hired Chinese carpenters to put the pieces together. They bought furniture—and Hiram bought clothes—from the auctioneers who spent their days shouting in the plaza. The furniture was tawdry and Hiram's new suits did not fit him very well, but these matters were not important. He and Kendra wanted to be married, and that was important.

Between the fire and the wedding Hiram stayed with Mr. and Mrs. Eustis. They invited him to have the ceremony in their home.

Marny smilingly declined Kendra's invitation to attend. "I know you and Hiram want me, darling," she said, "but I seriously doubt that Mrs. Eustis does. I'll come to see you in your own house after you've moved in."

Kendra had to yield.

Meanwhile, San Francisco lay in ruins but life went on. Pocket and Mr. Gilmore cleared out a storeroom and turned it into living quarters for their clerks. Norman put cots into several of the private card rooms, so the dealers and bartenders would have somewhere to sleep. They were not comfortable, but any roof was better than none.

Few citizens were comfortable, but many of them were devising ways to get rich among the ashes. Some men set up tents, where they rented sleeping space. Others contrived outdoor cookshops—stoves blackening the air with smoke, and beside each stove a trestle where the customers stood up to eat their meals. Three days after the fire a group of enterprising tradesmen opened a market on the Clay Street hill. While the cottage was being set up Kendra continued to prepare meals at the Calico Palace, and Hiram came in every day for lunch. She shopped at the market, escorted by one of the bartenders.

It was not easy to get to the market, or anywhere else. The citizens were trying to clean up, but streets in the burned area were still almost impassable. When she went out Kendra wore her high boots and gathered up her skirts with both hands, while the barman carried the market basket in one hand and kept the other on his gun. They walked over pots and pans and kettles, broken dishes and charred pieces of furniture, liquor bottles melted into shapeless chunks, piles of foodstuffs that had roasted in the blaze and now lay rotting underfoot. It was not a pleasant journey.

But the market speedily became a meeting place where people came to look for their friends or get news of them. Kendra met Ralph and Serena there one day, Serena carrying the market basket while Ralph carried the baby, for they could not push a baby carriage through the jumble in the street. They were both in cheerful humor. They lived on Powell Street, where the fire had not reached them. They told Kendra two clerks from Chase and Fenway's were using their parlor as a bedroom. Not convenient, but the poor fellows had nowhere else to stay and in times like these folks had to be neighborly.

The next morning Kendra met Rosabel at the market, accompanied by Mrs. Chase. Rosabel told Kendra she was going to have a baby and Mrs. Chase was helping her with everything and being a perfect dear. Of course they were both distressed about the loss of the store, she said. But they still had their homes, and their husbands would soon rebuild the store.

Kendra reported this to Marny when she came in. Marny, sitting at the table with a cup of chocolate before her and Bruno's sketches in her hand, listened with puzzled amusement.

"I'm glad Rosabel is happy," she said at length. "I was doubtful when she got married. Such a change. But maybe,"

545

Marny added, with surprise that she did not try to conceal, "maybe this is what she wanted all the time."

"It's what a lot of women want, Marny," Kendra reminded her. "Homes of their own, and children, and a peaceful life."

"I suppose so. At least, it's what a lot of them get."

Kendra did not remind Marny that this was what she wanted herself. There were some things Marny simply did not understand.

Hiram and Kendra were married in a ceremony brief and simple, as they both wanted. Mr. and Mrs. Chase were there, and Mr. Fenway and Rosabel; Pocket and Mr. Gilmore, several employees of the bank, and of course Mr. and Mrs. Eustis. Nobody else but the minister. Marny stayed away, and Kendra knew Mr. and Mrs. Eustis were relieved that she did. After the ceremony Hiram and Kendra went to the readymade cottage with its patchy walls and shaky furniture, and as she looked around it Kendra had never felt so completely at home in any other spot.

At the Calico Palace, Marny was busy with her own affairs. Besides her regular hours of work she was directing the replacement of Bruno's transparencies and the repairs that had to be made to other outside decorations. While this left her scant leisure, it was good to be rebuilding San Francisco.

But Marny knew, as the rest of the city knew, that not everybody wanted to rebuild. A few of the hoodlums had died in the fire, but more of them had not. The day after Hiram and Kendra were married some scoundrel tried to burn the Verandah.

Not long before daybreak, when the Verandah had been closed and locked for several hours, a watchman outside caught sight of a flame through the window of a storeroom behind the bar. He gave the alarm and the firemen promptly put out the fire. But they used a great deal of strong language when they saw how the villain had set it.

Marny heard the details from Pocket a few days later. Pocket had come into the parlor and bought a cup of coffee at the refreshment table. When Marny started out for coffee of her own, Pocket asked if he might follow her to the kitchen. "I want to tell you somehing," he said.

She was glad to see him. Pocket was a member of the company that had put out the fire, and he could give her more details about it than the papers had printed.

In the kitchen, she brought her own cup to the table.

"How are you these days?" Pocket asked as they sat down. She answered with a candid sigh. "Pocket, I'm scared."

"Because of that fire?"

"Yes. We think the Calico Palace is well guarded. But so is the Verandah. Tell me how it was done."

Pocket said the villain's technique had been simple. While the Verandah was open and full of customers, he had moved away from the other men drinking at the bar and had slipped into the storeroom. Here he had laid down a "slow match"— a long hempen string soaked in a solution of saltpeter and lime. He had lit one end of the string, put some oil-soaked rags at the other end, and slipped back to the bar before anybody missed him. Since fire crept along a slow match at the rate of about one foot an hour, a man could light such a string three or four feet long and leave the building well before the flame reached the rags and blazed up.

Marny shivered as she listened. While the fire of May fourth had shown that the Calico Palace itself was fireproof, the costly furnishings inside it were not, and neither were the people who lived there. Pocket was saying,

"I suppose this ruffian felt cheated because the Verandah had stood through the big fire and he missed some loot he expected. So he tried again."

"That's the spirit of San Francisco," Marny commented dryly. "Never give up."

Pocket laid his hand over hers. He looked straight into her eyes.

"Our side isn't giving up either," he said, slowly and gravely. "That's why I came here today, to tell you so. I knew you'd be worried." He repeated with resolution, "We are not giving up, Marny."

His manner had such significance that Marny was startled. "What do you mean by that?"

"I'm on my way to a meeting," Pocket returned. "Hiram will be there, and Mr. Chase and Mr. Fenway and Mr. Eustis, and a good many others. We're going to clean up San Francisco."

Marny answered with admiration. "Pocket, you really meant that, don't you?"

"We really mean it," said Pocket. He stood up. "Now it's time for me to go."

"All right, and thanks for coming in. You've cheered me up."

Pocket went to the door, waving goodby over his shoulder. He had an air of quiet confidence, like a man on his way to a task which he felt himself quite capable of performing. Pocket had a heart full of kindness, but as she saw him now Marny was reminded of what the poet Dryden had said long ago. "Beware the fury of a patient man."

In the days that followed, both Pocket and Hiram made frequent visits to the Calico Palace. Often Kendra came with them. On these occasions they brought steaks or chops, and Kendra cooked dinner for them all. Kendra was glowing with happiness. She and Hiram had chosen the site of their permanent home, and had engaged an architect to draw plans for the house they would live in. Meanwhile the readymade cottage, cramped and drafty though it was, gave them a joyous haven.

Hiram sometimes left Kendra with Marny while he went to the meetings, and Marny told her the news of the Calico Palace. Kendra was glad to hear that Hortensia's divorce was under way. Hortensia's friends Jeff and Daisy Quellen had come down from Sacramento, and were being lodged at Norman's expense in one of the rooming houses that had shot up since the fire. The Quellens were a witty and amusing pair and the four of them were having a good time together. Marny thought it likely that Hortensia was no longer locking her bedroom door, because Norman's temper was so much improved of late.

Pocket and Hiram rarely spoke of what went on at their meetings. If Hiram had told Kendra anything she did not say so, and Marny did not ask. It was enough to know these men were making ready to clean up San Francisco.

Marny knew, as well as they knew, how desperately San Francisco needed cleaning up. Except in the central district where businessmen hired their own guards and patrolled their own streets, the hoodlums had turned the town into a place of constant terror. Robberies, assaults, and even murders occurred nearly every day. Taxes were high, but policemen were meanly paid and often they quit because they were not paid at all. Few lawbreakers were arrested; still fewer were ever convicted; and the men who did go to jail had little trouble getting out.

With the horrors of the May fire, the decent citizens had reached the end of their endurance. They no longer doubted that the "government" was sharing the spoils of crime, and nothing would be done to stop the rampage unless they did it themselves. Five weeks after the fire, Marny and the rest of San Francisco learned what had been going on at the meetings.

A group of two hundred responsible men made the announcement. They asked that their names and their intentions be published in the papers. They said they had organized a Committee of Vigilance and they were going to make the town safe to live in.

Their program was definite. They had a written constitution, a meeting place, and a signal. One of their number was to be always on duty at a fire engine building on the plaza. The signal—two quick strokes on the firebell, repeated at one-minute intervals—would call them together at any time.

The hoodlums were warned. But they were not impressed. For so long they had been having their own way, carousing in crime while honest men worked, that few of them could believe the carnival was over. The first day after the Vigilantes were formally organized, the bell rang to tell them they were needed.

It was late in the afternoon. Hiram and Pocket and Kendra were all together in the kitchen of the Calico Palace. While they waited for Marny to take a break from her card table, Kendra was arranging steaks in a pan, Pocket was drinking coffee, while Hiram was holding a glass of whiskey and water and grumbling because there was no ice in it. For some months now the San Francisco bars had had ice, cut from the frozen mountain lakes and brought down on the river boats, but this week the boats were late. The bars had no ice and patrons of the bars were loudly complaining.

Marny came into the kitchen, and Hiram greeted her with a lift of his glass. "Join me in a warm drink?"

"No thanks. Your day's work is over, mine has just begun. I'll take coffee." She shook her head at him. "And if you don't like warm drinks don't buy them."

Hiram laughed as she spoke. "Yes, I'm a spoilt brat."

"So am I," said Marny. "I miss the ice as much as anybody." Pocket brought her a cup of coffee and she began to sip.

Kendra set the pan of steaks aside. "When do you want dinner?" she asked.

The men glanced questioningly at Marny. "At my next

break, if that's all right," she said. "Hiram will have time for another of our warm drinks."

"Fine," said Pocket, and Hiram added,

"Suits me. Maybe I'll have time for two of your—"

His words were interrupted by a sharp noise from outside—a double clang, and then a pause.

"What's that?" cried Kendra, and Marny gasped,

"If it's another fire—"

"Hush!" ordered Hiram. Both he and Pocket had sprung to their feet. Hiram took out his watch and held up a hand for silence. The double clang sounded again.

"It's not a fire," said Pocket.

His voice had an ominous note. He and Hiram looked at each other, stern-faced.

Hiram said, "It's our signal." He put away his watch and felt his holster as if to make sure his gun was there. He turned to Kendra. "My darling, I don't know what this means, but I've got to leave you."

She was trembling, but she made herself speak steadily. "I know you must, Hiram."

Hiram put his arm around her. Marny and Pocket stood silently while he said, "If I don't come back tonight, you'll understand it's because I can't." With regret as deep as Kendra's he spoke to Marny. "If I don't come back, she can stay here?"

"Of course."

The double clang sounded again. Hiram tightened his arm around Kendra and kissed her. "It's a war, Kendra," he reminded her. "If we don't win now, they will."

He and Pocket went to the door. On the threshold Pocket turned and waved goodby, and Hiram blew Kendra another kiss. Pocket closed the door, quietly, as he did everything.

Marny put a hand on Kendra's shoulder. "Hiram's right, dear," she said. "This is a war."

"I know," said Kendra.

"Go on and cry," said Marny.

Kendra answered with sudden force. "I don't feel like crying. I'm mad. I'm burning up inside. Those miserable wretches." She drew a deep determined breath to calm her nerves. With a glance at the steaks that now Hiram would not share, she asked, "Dinner at your next break, as you said?"

"Yes, please," said Marny. She made herself be casual. "Well, time I got back to work."

When she returned to the parlor most of the men she had left there were on their way out. One or two were leaving because they belonged to the Vigilance Committee, others because they wanted to see if the committee was serious in its intent, the rest for no reason except that the signal bell had promised some excitement and they wanted to be on hand.

But the men of the Vigilance Committee were not only serious, they were too serious to act in haste. They gathered at their temporary headquarters in a hotel just beyond the southern limit of the fire. Here they went into their meeting room and closed the doors.

The men who had rushed out of the Calico Palace began to drift back. They stood around, talked, went out again to ask for news, came in again to discuss what they had heard. Marny continued her game, pausing now and then to hear the talk. By bits and pieces she learned what was going on.

The men told her the Vigilance Committee had been summoned to sit in judgment on a well-known desperado, one of those who had been keeping the city in fear. He was a man named Jenkins, a big fellow of enormous strength. Jenkins was an Englishman who had been deported to one of the convict colonies of Australia. Hearing of the gold strike in California, Jenkins had taken ship from Sydney to San Francisco. There was no record of his having earned an honest dollar since he got here.

Late this afternoon Jenkins had crept into a shipping office on the waterfront, grabbed a safe heavy with money, and made off with it in a rowboat. Men at work on the wharf had seen him and shouted an alarm. In two or three minutes half a dozen other boats were chasing him.

He was strong, but he was outnumbered, and his pursuers managed to tie him up and take him to the fire station. The committee member on duty there gave the signal. When the committee had assembled at their meeting place, Jenkins' captors presented their case.

Here, they said, was a man whose latest crime had been seen by scores of witnesses, most of them present and ready to testify. Did the gentlemen mean what they said or didn't they?

They did.

Jenkins was put on trial. The trial lasted a long time, for there were many witnesses to be heard. They made their statements, while outside the building hundreds of persons, both men and women, gathered to wait for the verdict. There was no disorder among them. There was almost no sound. They spoke in hushed voiecs. They waited tensely. They waited through the long June twilight and they were still waiting by the light of the moon.

In Marny's parlor, men were restless, uneasy. They fidgeted about, now at the bar, then at a card table, then making bets at dice or roulette, then starting the round again. With her usual self-possession Hortensia played the piano, but tonight even her most devoted hearers did not sit and listen. They wanted to keep moving. The bartenders poured drinks, and said almost nothing except an occasional "Sorry" when a drinker lamented the lack of ice. At the bar, some men said Jenkins would never get out of this. Others said the hoodlums would surely put up a fight, and rescue him. Like the crowd waiting outdoors, they spoke in undertones. They walked softly. Marny had never known the room to be so quiet. This was a moment of crisis. War was declared and they were waiting for the first gun.

It seemed a long time, though the Harvard man came promptly at his regular hour to take her place so she could go to dinner. Marny finished her deal and spoke to him.

"Can I talk to you a minute, Harvard?"

Harvard went with her into the back hall. He had been out, and he was expecting her question.

"How is it going?" she asked.

"All quiet so far," he answered. "Now and then a man comes out on a balcony and urges everybody to be patient. He tells nothing. But rumors get around, you know."

"Rumors of what?" she asked in a low voice.

With a swift gesture, the Harvard man drew his hand across his neck.

Marny was not surprised, but she felt a chill.

"It had to come to this sometime," said the Harvard man.

"Yes," she answered, "it had to. All right, you can take over. We're having no trouble here."

Marny went to the kitchen. At another time the aroma of the steaks on the fire would have been tempting; tonight she only wished she did not have to eat. Kendra sat by the table, trying to read this morning's *Alta*. She stood up as Marny came in.

"I've made some soup to start," she said.

"Thanks," said Marny.

She took a chair. Kendra brought her a cup of soup. Marny's throat felt tight. She wondered if she could get the soup down. She knew she would feel better if she did, so she tasted it. The soup was a clear vegetable broth, brewed with Kendra's customary skill, and Marny tasted it again.

Kendra too had heard the rumor, brought by Lulu and Lolo, who had heard it from the Blackbeards. When she had poured a cup of soup for herself she sat down facing Marny at the table.

"Are they going to hang that man?" she asked abruptly.

"That's the talk," Marny told her.

For a few moments they were silent. Marny sipped the broth. Kendra asked, again abruptly, "Marny, if you were on that committee—would you vote for execution?"

Marny looked at her cup. She looked at the sugar bowl. She looked at a scrap of paper that had blown into a corner. She looked up at Kendra. She said, "Yes."

Kendra knitted her fingers on the table before her. "So would I," she said.

Marny continued. "It's terrible. But we've found out, there are some men so evil that nothing but terror will stop them."

"They're going to be stopped," said Kendra. She spoke almost fiercely. "Marny, Hiram and I have both been through a lot of storms. Now we want peace. We love each other. We want to have children and we want a home where they can be safe. We mean to have it."

"I think," Marny said firmly, "right now the Vigilantes are giving you a chance to have it."

She finished the soup. It did make her feel better, so that she ate the rest of her dinner with appetite. She went to her room to tidy up, and returned to the parlor.

In the parlor there were more men than before, and through the evening the number kept increasing. But there was still that strange lack of noise. Marny thought the very air felt tense with expectancy.

The time went on and on. Marny dealt cards, Hortensia played the piano, the barmen poured drinks. The roulette ball clicked on the wheel, the faro players sat in blank silence.

At last, the parlor door burst open and Troy Blackbeard almost threw himself into the room. Every soul there stopped and stared. Troy shouted,

"Trial's over. Jenkins is guilty. They're going to hang him in the plaza."

Before his words were finished, drinks were splashing, glasses breaking, chairs falling over as men sprang up and rushed to the door. Such was their haste that as the lucky gamblers swept up their winnings, if they dropped a coin or two on the carpet few of them paused to pick it up.

Marny gathered her cards and walked across the room to the bar. Only Wilfred the chief bartender was still there; his assistants had dashed out with the rest. "It looks like the end of my working day," Marny said with a sigh of relief. "I'll have a nip. A good one."

With an understanding smile Wilfred poured the drink. Still standing at the bar, Marny looked around. Beside the piano Hortensia and Norman were talking in low tones. Troy Blackbeard was coming toward the bar, and with him was the Harvard man. As they reached the bar Troy was saying, "No need for such a hurry. They're not going to hang him this minute."

"I wish they'd get it over with," Marny said fervently.

"They will, before long," said Troy. "But Mr. Brannan—he made the announcement about the verdict—he said they'd sent for a minister."

"Has Jenkins got any religion?" she asked.

"I don't know," said Troy. "At least they're giving him a chance."

Norman joined them at the bar. Watch in hand, he spoke to Troy. "It's nearly two o'clock. Let's get everybody out who doesn't belong here, and lock up."

"Right," said Troy.

"Find your brother," said Norman. Unlike Marny, he had never learned to tell the Blackbeards apart. "Tell him nobody gets in. Come on, Wilfred, and help us."

The men went out. Marny picked up her drink and went to a front window. Opening the curtains she looked down at the crowd gathering in the plaza. Hortensia came and stood by her. They watched, saying nothing, as people and more people came from all directions. Behind her Marny heard a door open, and turned to see Kendra entering the parlor. Kendra joined them at the window.

"Are you going to watch?" Kendra asked.

"I don't know," said Marny.

Hortensia spoke. "We're already watching, aren't we?"

"I don't want to see it," said Marny, "and yet I do want to. Times like this, I don't understand myself at all."

Hortensia glanced at the drink in Marny's hand. "That's a good idea," she said. She went to the bar and came back with a drink of her own.

The three of them stood there by the open window. They could not help looking. The plaza lay before them, and above was a brilliant full moon to show them all that went on.

They saw the Vigilantes approaching.

The men had marched from their headquarters to the corner of Clay and Montgomery streets, and then up Clay Street to the plaza. Heading the line was a group with Jenkins handcuffed in the midst of them, their guns ready in case his friends should attempt to set him free. Behind these guards the other Vigilantes marched two and two, their guns also ready for whatever might happen. From the window their faces were not distinct, but their attitude was plain. They were doing what they felt had to be done. These men had fought their way to California over the plains, across the Isthmus, around the Horn. Many of them, like Mr. Chase, were fathers of families; others, like Hiram, hoped to be. They had built their city and they did not intend to stand by and see it turned into a jungle.

Behind the marching Vigilantes surged the crowd that had been waiting so long outside their meeting room. Altogether, a thousand persons or more had gathered before the place of execution. But still, as had been true all through these grim hours, the people were almost weirdly quiet. Those who spoke, spoke in whispers. From the open window of the Calico Palace, with the throng so close beneath them, Marny and Kendra and Hortensia could hear almost nothing at all.

"Social note," said Marny. "As the papers so often observe, 'There were many well-dressed women present.'"

"I'm sort of surprised," said Hortensia, "to see so many women."

"We're present, aren't we?" Kendra said shortly.

"Yes, I'm present," said Marny, "and I still don't know what I'm doing here."

Neither did Kendra and Hortensia know what they were

doing here. But they all knew they could not have gone to their own rooms and shut themselves up while this was taking place. No use asking why. They could not.

The Vigilantes took Jenkins to the old adobe building in the plaza, the one that Morse and Vernon had pointed out to Kendra as the army barracks as they rode up the hill the day she reached San Francisco. Here they halted. In response to a gun at his ribs, Jenkins halted too. Still in the midst of that curious silence, the nine men elected to perform the execution approached him. They brought a rope with a noose at one end.

Up to now Jenkins had kept an attitude of sullen defiance, as if sure his friends would come to save him. But now suddenly he seemed to realize that while his fellow criminals were not afraid to set fires in empty rooms or knock down men walking alone in dark alleys, they were not going to risk their lives by facing men ready to fight back. As the noose came near he began to bellow like an animal. In spite of his handcuffs he struggled hard and horribly. But his captors, moving with steady resolution, put the noose over his head.

Standing at the window of the Calico Palace, Marny and Kendra and Hortensia shuddered and felt gooseflesh breaking out on their skin. Still they could not move nor look away. They could not.

In the plaza, the nine executioners went about their task. Once the noose was in place they threw the other end of the rope over a crossbeam at one side of the building. While Jenkins yelled and fought, the nine men grasped this end of the rope and drew up his great brutish body.

Indoors by the window, Marny and Kendra and Hortensia quivered as they watched. They knew Jenkin's howls were no more horrible than the shrieks of the victims roasted alive in the fires, nor his pains of death as painful as those others had been. But cold sweat trickled down their bodies and they trembled beyond control. Hortensia muttered thickly, "If only he didn't *kick* so!"

It did not last long. In a few seconds more the body hung motionless from the beam. Now that Jenkin's voice was stilled, in the plaza there was still no noise. Nothing but that strange chilling silence.

The body hung there for hours, guarded by relays of

Vigilantes. It was the quietest night the plaza had known in a long time.

Marny and Kendra and Hortensia did not stay to watch the guarding of the body. They shut the window and drew the curtains and wondered if they could sleep tonight and decided not to try, at least not for a while. Shaking all over, Kendra dropped into a chair by Marny's card table and hid her face in her hands. Hortensia went to the bar and poured another drink. Marny followed her. Kendra heard the clink of glass, and then felt a hand on her arm and heard Marny speak her name.

She raised her head. Marny stood beside her with a glass of brandy.

"Drink this," said Marny. "That's an order."

Kendra obeyed, and the brandy put warmth into her shuddering body. Marny brought a drink for herself from the bar, and with Hortensia she came back to the card table and sat down too.

For a minute or two they sat there without speaking. Then, as Marny sipped her drink, suddenly she began to laugh. It was a strange dark laughter, almost like sobs.

"For heaven's sake," Kendra demanded, "what's funny about it?"

"Nothing," Marny returned. "But I had a funny idea. Just think—a hundred years from now, people will be calling this the good old days."

66

When Marny came into her parlor the next afternoon the talk there was vehemently in favor of the hanging. A few men shook their heads, but only a few. Only a few, and most of these were men recently arrived, who had not lived through San Francisco's years of unpunished crime. The others not only approved, but added, "If it had been done this time last year we'd all be better off now. Oh damn it, Wilfred, you mean there's still no ice?"

Marny was tired today; they were all tired. None of them had had much sleep. When Marny and Kendra had finally decided to go to bed they had made up the bed in Kendra's old room and had told each other good night. Marny did not know if Kendra had slept well; she knew she herself had not. She fell asleep and woke up, and fell asleep again and woke up again, over and over. When she finally woke up for good, about noon, and went down to the kitchen for breakfast, Lolo told her Hiram had called for Kendra earlier and they had gone home together.

Marny drank three cups of coffee. She wondered if her head was clear enough to take her through the games, and consoled herself with the reminder that few if any of the players would feel any brighter than she did.

Shortly before dark, when she went to the kitchen for chocolate, she found Hiram and Pocket waiting for her there. They stood up as she entered, and Hiram said,

"We came to ask how you feel after last night."

Marny gave a sigh. "It was a night fraught with goings on, wasn't it?"

Pocket poured chocolate from the pot on the stove and brought it to her. He said, "Hiram asked how you felt."

They all sat down at the table. "Frankly," said Marny, "I feel pretty terrible. First time I ever saw a man hanged practically in my own front yard. Or anywhere else, for that matter. I'm still on edge."

"So are we all," Hiram confessed. "We're not used to this sort of thing either."

"At the same time," said Pocket, "I feel like a man who's had a load fall off his back. For so long, this has been about to happen. Now it's happening. At last we're doing something instead of saying something ought to be done."

"Do you think," she asked hopefully, "they've been scared into good behavior?"

"Oh no," Pocket and Hiram answered together. Hiram went on,

"We're on our way to another meeting now. Already talk is going around, about how the hoodlums are planning to get back at us. More burglaries. Another fire. A few more murders in the street. Nobody knows what they're going to try. But," he added with emphasis, "we're ready for them."

Marny spoke earnestly. "And you'll act again if you have to?"

558

"Yes," Hiram replied without hesitation. "We will. If they aren't convinced by one hanging, there'll be more."

"We mean that," Pocket said quietly.

Marny gave them a smile. "Bad men," she said, "so often make the mistake of thinking good men are softies. Those villains are going to be mighty shocked when they find you can be tougher than they are."

"Thanks," said Hiram. He stood up again. "Now it's time to go."

"We just wanted to see you," Pocket said politely.

They went out, and Marny realized that she felt stronger. She went up to her room and put on her nugget necklace and pinned a saucy black velvet bow in her hair. When the Blackbeards locked up for the night her table showed a cheering profit.

The next morning the *Alta* published an editorial approving the execution of Jenkins. The day after that, the paper published the constitution of the Vigilance Committee and the names of its members.

The Vigilantes went ahead, grimly and openly. Armed groups of men guarded the wharfs, boarding incoming vessels and seeing to it that no more convicted felons were allowed to land. Other groups visited known criminals and advised them to leave town. They spoke so forcefully that some rascals hastened to board the river boats, but to the dismay of those left behind, the returning steamers brought news that the men of the inland towns were forming Vigilance Committees of their own.

The elected officials were storming. They cried in rage that the work of the Vigilantes was illegal.

"Sure it's illegal," Hiram remarked on a visit to Marny. "So are murder and arson and burglary. They should have thought of that."

"Things are improving around here," said Marny. "You boys are making the town fit to live in and the ice boats are running again."

Hiram had come in to bring her a box of almond cookies Kendra had sent. They sat at the kitchen table, where Marny, in peignoir and bedroom slippers, was sipping her breakfast coffee.

"When you leave here, Hiram," she asked, "will you go back to the bank?"

"Why yes. Can I attend to something for you?"

"Would you take a few minutes extra," asked Marny, "and walk with me to the library? I want to speak to Pocket. It won't take me long to get dressed."

"It's still rough walking," he reminded her. "Wouldn't you rather I took Pocket a message, and saved you the trouble of getting there and back?"

Marny shook her head. "Thank you, but this is a sort of personal matter. I'd like to talk to him myself. In his office."

"All right," said Hiram. "In that case I'll be glad to go with you."

"Fine," said Marny. "One of the clerks can see me back."

She went out, leaving Hiram reading the *Alta* and munching an almond cooky. When she came back she was wearing a dark blue silk dress and a bonnet with a matching ribbon. She carried an artist's portfolio, the sort Bruno Gregg used for holding his sketches. If Hiram felt any curiosity he did not say so, and she was grateful to him for minding his own business.

They went into the street and began to make their way through the clutter. The fire was now six weeks past. While much of the rubble had been carted away, much of it had not, and the cleared spaces were choked with piles of brick and lumber brought in for rebuilding. The streets resounded with saws and hammers. On the Clay Street side of the plaza, workmen were breaking up the charred remains of the old City Hotel and piling the pieces into wagons.

They were sorry to see it go. San Francisco had few landmarks left from the time when this had been a scraggly little town out at the end of the world. Their memories of those days were gathering a sheen of romance. This was absurd and they knew it, but none the less it was true.

At the library, carpenters stood on ladders replacing a lintel scorched by flying sparks. Hiram led Marny to a side entrance and up a staircase to the door of Pocket's office. He knocked, and getting no answer he opened the door.

"Wait here," he said. "I'll find Pocket."

He clattered down the stairs. Holding the portfolio under her arm, Marny stepped over the threshold. As she looked around she felt a nip of surprise.

She did not know how she had thought Pocket's office would look, but she had not expected such an air of quiet competence. Without thinking much about it, she had allowed the chaos of Pocket's pockets to give her the impression that he was a bit of a scatterbrain. A dear fellow, of course, liked and trusted by everybody, but not a man with an organized mind. She told herself now that she should have known better. The library was not a flamboyant enterprise—compared to the Calico Palace it was a modest affair—but it was patronized by the most highly respected men in town and it undoubtedly made a profit. Locations facing the plaza were expensive. Marny well knew the rent she and Norman paid Mr. Norrington. No business managed by a scatterbrain could long stay here.

Pocket's office was a corner room lighted by three windows. The furniture was good. Marny saw a well-made desk, with a leather chair in front of it and a lamp on a stand at one side. Near the desk was a solid-looking table across which two armchairs faced each other. On the table lay some businesslike papers, and one chair was pushed back as if Pocket had been working on the papers when he was called elsewhere. Between the windows were bookcases, and on the wall hung a lithograph of the Golden Gate and a framed street map of San Francisco. While not severely neat, the room had a general look of being in order, the workroom of a man who had a clear head and knew what he was about.

Marny turned as she heard footsteps behind her.

Pocket came in, his hand out and his face bright with a smile of welcome. A good-looking man, Marny thought, with his firm jaw and regular features, and well dressed in a dark business suit and a crisp white shirt. "Glad to see you, ma'am," he was saying. He crossed to the table and drew out a chair. "Sit down."

Marny spoke frankly. "Pocket, if it's not convenient for you to talk to me now, say so. I can wait, or I can come back later."

"It's perfectly convenient right this minute," he assured her, standing with his hands on the chair back.

Marny made a gesture toward the table. Lying there was a large sheet of paper with some sort of diagram on it, several smaller sheets covered with figures, and a lot of pencils. "I did interrupt something," she demurred.

He shook his head. "Nothing but a chat with Mr. Fenway."

"Anything important?"

"Just passing the time of day, ma'am. Mr. Fenway came in to get a paper he asked me to keep for him after the fire.

561

I gave it to him, and we were gabbling a bit when Hiram came in to say you wanted me."

"All right," said Marny. She took the chair he was offering her. As she sat down Pocket gave her an endearing smile.

"Hiram told me this was a personal matter. Want me to shut the door?"

"Yes, you nice thoughtful man, I wish you would."

Pocket complied. He came back to the table and sat down across from her, pushing his own papers to one side. Marny laid the portfolio on the table. She took off her gloves and laid them beside it, and came directly to the purpose of her visit.

"Pocket, I want a favor. Will you write a letter for me?"

"Why yes ma'am," he answered amiably. "Glad to oblige."

"It's a letter I want written," said Marny, "but I don't want to write it myself. And it's not one that I'd want a lawyer or some other stranger to write for me. It's got to be a friend."

"I'm a friend," said Pocket.

"Yes you are," she returned with decision. "And what's more, you can keep your mouth shut." She smiled at him. "Promise?"

"Yes ma'am," said Pocket. He smiled back at her. In a businesslike voice he asked, "Now who's this letter going to?"

"Dwight Carson," she answered. "In New York."

If Pocket was surprised he did not show it. He simply said, "Dwight Carson, yes ma'am. What do you want me to tell him?"

"I want you to tell him about his buildings," said Marny. "Tell him all seven stood through the fire. Tell him six of them—all but this—stood while everything around them burned."

Pocket nodded. "I'll do that."

"When the *Alta* gets to New York," Marny continued, "he'll see his buildings in the list of those that survived. But I want him to have details, more than the paper has room to give. His work means a lot to him. I don't think he ever told anybody in San Francisco but me, how much it means." She opened the portfolio. "I've had Bruno make these sketches. Each picture shows one of Dwight's buildings the way it looks now, standing solid among the cinders around it."

She handed him the sketches. Pocket examined them with approval. "Mighty clear. Bruno does good work." Raising his eyes, Pocket added, "And Marny, this whole business—writing to Dwight Carson, and having these pictures made for him—this is a right friendly thing for you to do."

Marny smiled. "When you write to him, tell him how fast the Calico Palace got back into business, and Hiram's bank, and all the rest. Tell him everything you can think of that he might want to know."

"Everything," said Pocket.

"And please," Marny went on, "there's another bit of instruction I want to give you."

"Yes ma'am?"

Marny picked up a pencil and turned it between her fingers. "Pocket, when you write about the Calico Palace, don't mention me in particular. You can say, 'Norman and Marny and Hortensia are all back at work as usual'—that will let him know I didn't break my neck jumping out of a window, if he's still interested. But don't say anything to suggest that he and I ever knew each other personally."

"I understand," said Pocket.

Marny flashed him a look of esteem. "You know," she returned, "I believe you do understand. Not everybody would. You've got what the ladies in Philadelphia used to call 'delicacy of mind.'"

His lips twitched humorously. "I never heard that one before."

"Whether or not you ever heard of it," said Marny, "you've got it." She looked down at the pencil in her hand. "Pocket, when Dwight gets that letter, he'll want to show it around. If you say anything special about me, he might be embarrassed to show it around. That makes sense, doesn't it?"

"Yes, ma'am," Pocket said quietly, "it makes sense." He added, "And you know, Marny, I think you're right delicate-minded yourself."

Marny did not answer this. She said, "And you won't tell him I suggested this letter."

"No ma'am," said Pocket. "Now, how shall I go about that? Let me think."

He reflected. After a minute or so he said,

"I'll say I'm writing to thank him for taking a load off my mind. Since his other buildings stood up, there's no reason for me to worry about the library if those hoodlums should set another fire. Is that a good reason?"

"An excellent reason," said Marny, "because you'll be telling the truth. It *is* a load off your mind."

"You're mighty right it is," he agreed with emphasis. "Every time I look around and see those other six buildings still there, I'm reminded that if they are fireproof this one almost certainly is too. It's a cheering thought. I was plenty scared that night."

Marny drew a tremulous breath. "Pocket, when I think back on that night—when I remember those hours of looking down at the fire and wondering if the Calico Palace would stand through it—I can't tell you how scared I was."

"You don't need to tell me," he said with sympathy. "I know how tough it would have been for you to lose it."

Marny shivered at the thought. There was a pause. Pocket gave her a look of comradeship, real and warm. He went on,

"If you should lose a strongbox full of gold, gold worth as much as the Calico Palace, that would be hard. But not as hard as losing the Calico Palace."

There was another pause before Marny answered. When she did, her answer was another question. "Pocket, how did you know that?"

He considered a moment or two. "Well ma'am," he said, "when a person loses money, or a thing he's bought with money, if he still has his health he can generally get it again."

She listened, saying nothing. Pocket continued,

"But when a person loses something he's put thoughts into, something he's created, he's losing part of his own self. It's like a part of him dying."

Marny remembered how she had felt when she watched the old Calico Palace fall to pieces the night of the first fire. She had felt then as if a part of herself had died.

"And the Calico Palace," Pocket said, "is *you*. Every picture, every rug and table and pack of cards and every bottle at the bar, is part of you. Isn't that right?"

"Yes," Marny said candidly. "That's right. I love the Calico Palace. I love it more than anything else I've ever had. That's why I'm so grateful to Dwight for building it the way he did."

Pocket leaned back in his chair. He looked at her thoughtfully, his warm hazel eyes admiring the locks of red hair escaping under the brim of her bonnet, her well-fitted dark blue dress, her strong supple hands. Before his scrutiny Marny laughed a little.

"After all this time, don't you know how I look?"

"I like the way you look," said Pocket.

"Thank you. And now it's time I let you get back to work."

"Not yet." He tapped the papers on the table. "There's no hurry about this."

"Well, it's time I got to my cards."

He shook his head. "No it's not. If you started now you'd have about a twelve-hour day, and you don't love the Calico Palace that much. Not even if it *is* all you've got."

"Pocket! I didn't say that."

"Well, I'm saying it," replied Pocket. "That's why you were so terrified about losing it." He looked at her keenly as he asked, "Don't you ever want anything more than that, Marny?"

Marny stared at him across the table. Pocket had never spoken to her like this before. She exclaimed, "What are you talking about?"

"You," said Pocket.

"You're not being very polite."

"I'm not trying to be polite," he returned. "I can be polite without any trouble. But it's a lot of trouble to be honest, and I'm being honest now. You're a pretty fine person, Marny, and you deserve more than you've got."

Marny was hearing him with astonishment. "Such as what?"

Pocket looked straight at her. "Marny, it's not much to be in love with a pile of brick and iron. Don't you ever want something that can love you back?"

"Pocket," she said in a voice of wonder, "what are you trying to tell me?"

"Men are always falling in love with you," he said.

"In San Francisco," she replied tersely, "that doesn't mean a thing. I'm not the trustful sort."

"But you're the lovable sort," said Pocket. "You're mighty lovable."

"Oh, *damn!*" burst out Marny. She looked down. Her forehead on her hand, in a low voice she said, "Pocket, we've been such good friends. Don't go and spoil it now!"

"What am I spoiling?" he asked. He sounded genuinely surprised.

She answered without looking up. "Pocket, I've thought

often, one reason I like you and Hiram so much is you've both let me alone. You've treated me like a person, not just a female body."

She stopped abruptly. Pocket said nothing. He sat listening, waiting for her to go on. Still without looking up, Marny added,

"In this town every woman not absolutely repulsive gets chased until she's tired of it. We like to be noticed, we like to have men think we're attractive—but what we get here—it's a pestiferous nuisance."

"Now you listen to me," said Pocket. He spoke in the voice of a man who meant to be heard. "I've lived here as long as you have. Longer. I know what you're talking about. I don't wonder you get tired of it. But I'm talking about something else."

Her head still down on her hand, Marny said, "I wish you'd stop talking about it."

"I won't stop," Pocket said firmly, "and you're going to hear me. I've thought about you quite a lot in the past few weeks. And I've found out—I was really surprised to find it out, Marny, but I did—I've found out that I love you and I want to help you be happy. And I believe if we were married—"

Marny's head jerked up. "Married?" She gave a short little laugh. "Pocket, don't be a fool. Why on earth do you want to marry me?"

"Because I love you," said Pocket.

Marny's eyes met his across the table. "All right, you innocent country bumpkin, let's get this straight. I'm not the domestic type."

"No, and I'm not an innocent country bumpkin, either," said Pocket. He spoke with humorous derision. But more seriously, he added, "Marny I've thought about this long and hard. I do love you."

As she heard him, Marny was shaking her head in disbelief. "Pocket, how long have you been thinking about this? When did you make up your mind?"

"After the fire," said Pocket.

His words puzzled her. She had seen Pocket several times since the fire, and not once had he made an ardent gesture. "What did the fire have to do with it?" she asked.

"I'll tell you how it was," said Pocket. "You remember that morning, when we were all together and Hiram told you

Captain Pollock was dead, and then you told me how he had come at you with that big revolver?"

"Yes, I remember."

"That's when it started," said Pocket. "Not all of a sudden. Right then, when we were talking about Pollock, I thought what a rat he was and what a coward, and if he died in the fire it was no more than he deserved. I was pretty tired just then, not in shape to do any real thinking. But after I got organized, back in the routine of business, it kept coming back to me. I thought about it. I couldn't stop thinking about it. I got mad and every minute I thought about it I got more mad. That man wanting to kill you, and you with nobody to take your part but a cat."

Marny said nothing. She listened, her eyes intently on him.

He continued, "And all the time here was I, about as good a shot as you could find this side of the Rocky Mountains, and I wasn't anywhere near you. After a while it came to me, the reason I was so mad. I was mad at Pollock, of course, but mostly I was mad at myself. Mad at myself for letting you stay so long with nobody around who really cared what became of you, when all the time I could have been right there. I do care what becomes of you, Marny. I was so surprised it was almost a shock, when I found out how much I cared. But then I knew it was love."

67

Marny sat still, her fingers laced on the table before her. She looked down at her hands, those strong, talented hands, more skillful with cards than any other hands in San Francisco. At length, without raising her eyes, she spoke.

"Pocket, that's beautiful. I'm touched. I'm truly touched. But before I say any more, give me time to think."

She stood up and walked over to a window. Standing there, she looked at the pane without noticing what lay beyond it. Pocket stood up too. Pocket was never able to remain seated while a woman was standing, whatever her reason. After a while, without turning around, Marny said,

"Pocket, I know you like me. But I don't think you want to marry me."

"Oh yes I do," he assured her promptly.

"But why?"

He answered with artless candor. "Why Marny, because I love you."

"Oh Pocket," she exclaimed, "how do you know you love me?"

Pocket considered. After a moment he said, "Marny, on a clear night when you look up at the sky and it's full of stars, how do you know it's beautiful?"

She gave a soft little laugh. "You're too romantic to be real, Pocket, but you're a dear."

"But I mean it that way," he answered with boyish astonishment. He reflected for another moment, and added, "Maybe you're wondering why I took so long to find out that I loved you, when we've known each other so well. I'll tell you. Back in Kentucky, I had some trouble about a girl. I told Kendra—has she ever said anything about it to you?"

Marny shook her head. "If you told Kendra something in confidence, she wouldn't pass it on."

"It was a bad experience," said Pocket. "It hurt me deep down. I told Kendra I was over it. Well, I *was* over it. I mean, it didn't hurt any more. But I think the girl had left me—well, numb. Not hurting any more, but not feeling anything either. I've had plenty to do with women since then. I like women, but I didn't feel anything like love for any of them. I think my heart was sort of knocked unconscious and had to come back to life. And that took time."

Marny did not answer. She stood running a finger back and forth along the windowsill. Still standing by the table where she had left him, Pocket went on,

"But my heart isn't numb any more. I do love you, Marny."

There was another pause. Marny stood with her face turned away from him. She felt distraught. Pocket had said he loved her, and Pocket was one of the sincerest persons she had ever known. And while Norman could tell Hortensia about the ease with which California women could get rid of unwanted husbands, Marny knew this would not be true of herself. She had an independent spirit, but she did not have the sort of callousness it would take to throw away a man like Pocket as

568

she would have thrown away a broken chair. His words had shaken her deeply, and Marny objected to this reminder that she had any depths to be shaken.

At length she turned toward him, her back to the window.

"You haven't forgogtten," she said, "I've done a good deal of shopping around."

"I know," he replied serenely.

"And for more reasons than love."

"I understand."

"Do you?"

"All right, all right," said Pocket. "You've had affairs with half the population. So have I. The other half. And of course, you know we're both lying."

"Why do you say that?"

Pocket smiled, slowly and wisely. "Because, my dear girl, you're too fastidious. And as for me—I'm pretty good, Marny, and I'll brag as much as any other man, but I'm not *that* good."

Marny laughed as she heard him. "Pocket, I do like you," she said. But she sobered quickly. "Very well, let's leave it at that. I've had several lovers. Aren't you afraid I might want to change again?"

"You might," said Pocket. "But if you did you'd say so, and leave. You wouldn't cheat."

"How do you know I wouldn't?"

"Because I know you," said Pocket. "I've learned a lot since I let that other girl knock my heart numb. You're honest. You don't cheat yourself when you play solitaire. So you don't cheat the other players when you're gambling. A person who's honest with himself is honest with other people."

Marny thoughtfully pulled at a lock of red hair that had slipped down over her cheek. "Yes, I remember Shakespeare had something to say about that. You're right, if I were married I wouldn't do any dodging about. It's too much trouble."

"It's no trouble for some women," said Pocket, "but you like a simple uncluttered life. Now will you marry me?"

Marny looked at the windowpane, and back at him. "I can't cook," she said.

"Then," said Pocket, "we'd better plan to live in a hotel."

"Oh Pocket," she exclaimed, "let's stop this nonsense. We're not planning anything. We couldn't be married. We're too different. We don't like the same things."

"What would that matter, as long as we liked each other?"

Again, as when she sat by the table, Marny looked at her hands. She spread out her fingers, as if taking pride in how firm and competent they were. "It would matter!" she protested. "You don't drink, you don't gamble—" At those words she looked up, her green eyes bright with curiosity. "Pocket, why don't you?"

"Why don't I what?"

"Well, why don't you ever touch liquor?"

At her question, Pocket began to laugh. His laughter was almost a giggle, like that of a little boy caught in a bit of harmless mischief. "If I tell you, will you keep my secret?"

"Yes, of course, but why is it a secret?"

"Because," said Pocket, "it's kind of embarrassing. The fact is, Marny, I don't drink because I can't."

"Don't tell me you belong to the sort of people who take one little sample and then can't stop till they're dead drunk. I don't believe it."

"I've never been drunk in my life," said Pocket. "I can't get drunk. Liquor doesn't make me drunk, it puts me to sleep. One little sample and I start to yawn. Two little samples and I'm sound asleep with my head on the table. I can't help it. That's the way I am. I've watched men at bars, raising their glasses and having fun, and I wonder how they feel. I'd like to find out, but I can't stay awake long enough." His lips were quivering with amusement. "Now what else is it you wanted to know?"

Still standing by the window, Marny asked, "Why don't you gamble?"

"Same reason. It puts me to sleep."

She did not understand this, and he explained,

"I mean, it bores me. I can't get interested."

Reaching into the pocket of her skirt, Marny took out her ever-present pack of cards. "I like playing cards," she reminded him. "For you or anybody else, I don't mean to stop."

"I haven't asked you to stop."

Marny thought this over. When she spoke again she spoke seriously. "Pocket, I like you. I think I like you better than anybody else I know. But marriage—no. I'm not the marrying type."

"You're the type I want," he said with assurance.

"No," said Marny. She thought a moment, then went on.

570

"I have a lot of respect for you, Pocket, and I'm proud that you want me. But it wouldn't work." She came back to his table and picked up her gloves. "Now I'd better go. I'll get back to my business and you can get back to yours."

He shook his head, but she touched the papers lying on the table.

"You were at work this morning. Now go back to it."

"I'd rather talk to you," said Pocket.

He spoke with confident good humor, but Marny wanted to discuss this subject no more. To keep the talk away from herself she touched the big sheet with the diagram on it. "What's this? It looks like a street map."

"That's what it is," said Pocket. "A copy of that map on the wall."

Marny picked up the sheet. The map was clear and well detailed. With a glance at the sheets covered with figures she asked, "What are you doing? Or maybe you'd rather not tell me."

"Why no ma'am," said Pocket, "I don't mind telling you. I own some property around town. And most of the buildings," he added with a rueful smile, "were not put up by Dwight Carson. They went down in the fire, which means a big job of rebuilding. I've been figuring costs."

While he talked, Marny had been looking over the map. "These X-marks in boxes," she said inquiringly. "They aren't in the wall map. What do they mean?"

"They mark my lots," said Pocket.

"Oh, I see. Then you own—*Pocket!*"

"Yes ma'am?"

Marny lowered the map. Her green eyes were big with amazement. In a shocked voice she asked, "Pocket—do you own *all* these lots?"

"Yes ma'am," he answered simply.

Thunderstruck, Marny gasped, "Pocket—you must own half of Montgomery Street!"

"Oh no," he returned modestly. "Not that much."

Marny's eyes were searching the map. "And you own this lot we're standing on."

"Yes ma'am," said Pocket.

"And these lots on Kearny Street!" said Marny. "You own the ground under the Calico Palace—"

"Yes ma'am."

571

"—so you're the landlord who's been squeezing us for that outrageous rent, all this time—"

"Nobody would have let you have it for less," Pocket said without concern. "If you want a spot on the plaza you've got to pay for it."

"—and you're the bloodsucker who gets all those other rents from Norrington—"

"Not all," said Pocket. "Norrington collects rents for other owners besides me."

"—and you own the house Loren and Kendra lived in," Marny continued sharply, still studying the map. "You're that nameless cavalier who offered Kendra the house rent free after Loren died. Yes, she told me about that. Oh Pocket," Marny exclaimed with reproach, "you're a skirt-chaser but you're not a fool! Didn't you know Kendra wouldn't say yes to any such proposition?"

"Now this I won't take," Pocket interrupted her sternly. "I didn't have any such notion in the back of my mind. I didn't know Norrington had dunned her for the rent until he told me she couldn't pay. I knew what Kendra had been through. I was there, same as you were. I told Norrington never to dun another tenant of mine without getting my approval first, and told him to let Kendra have the house as long as she pleased. It didn't occur to me she'd read my offer the way she did. I just didn't think of it, that's all."

Marny regarded him with a faint smile, as if reproving a naughty boy. "You *are* pretty simple-minded sometimes," she remarked.

"I'm afraid so," he admitted meekly. "Anyway, that's how it was. But when I heard she was going back to the Calico Palace, I thought if I really wanted to do her a service I'd let her go. It was better for her to keep busy than to sit alone all day with nothing to do but brood about her sorrow. Don't you think so?"

"Yes, I think so. You're a nice fellow, Pocket. Even if you do have your witless moments." Marny had laid the map on the table again. Looking down at it, she stoked the design with her fingertips. "Pocket," she asked thoughtfully, "how long have you been buying town lots?"

"Ever since I've been in California," said Pocket. "When I got here nobody knew anything about gold, but with such a harbor and such fine ranch land around it, I could see that San Francisco was a settlement bound to grow. I bought

572

some lots in town while I was a clerk up at Sutter's Fort. That was four years ago, back in '47, before you got here."

"I'd love to know," said Marny, "what you paid for them in those days. Do you mind telling?"

"Why no ma'am. At an auction you could get a lot close to the water for fifty or a hundred dollars—"

"On Montgomery Street!"

"Yes ma'am. The town lots farther inland cost twelve dollars, and you paid three dollars and sixty-two cents more to register your title."

Marny thought of the fortune those lots would cost today. She gave a deep respectful sigh. "And you've been buying land ever since."

"Yes ma'am."

Marny looked down at the map. Pocket waited politely. She wondered if he had ever been noisy about anything, or impatient, or uncivil. Impulsively she looked up and spoke.

"Pocket, I asked you why you didn't drink or gamble, and you told me. Now tell me something else."

"Why of course," he answered. "Ask me anything."

He smiled at her, and his eyes met hers. They were standing on opposite sides of the table. What pleasant eyes he had, she thought, that hazelnut color of bright ruddy brown, with dark brows and lashes. She asked, "Pocket, why do you keep it a secret, how rich you are?"

"Why, it's not exactly a secret," he answered genially. "Hiram and Mr. Eustis know my holdings because I do business through their bank; and Norrington knows."

"But you don't live rich!" she exclaimed. "Why did you choose to live in that little room downstairs, when you might have had a suite in some comfortable place like the Union Hotel?"

"I'm right comfortable in my little room," said Pocket. "I don't have to go out in the wind and rain to get to my office, and anyway, I'm not a showy fellow."

"Oh for heaven's sake, Hiram wasn't being showy when he lived in the Union Hotel! Why shouldn't a man live well if he can afford it?"

"Hiram's a banker," said Pocket, as if this gave her a key to her question. "People expect a banker to be hard-hearted."

With a puzzled frown Marny asked, "What's that got to do with it?

"Quite a lot," said Pocket. He spoke with amusement. "Marny, rich men get *pestered* so. I'm not mean or stingy. I'm glad to help folks in trouble. But I won't be pestered by every whining lazybones in town."

Marny smiled in assent. "And you couldn't get a stony reputation if you tried."

"No, I couldn't," he answered with innocent regret. "You know, Marny, if a man has been raised to have manners, and if he has an easy voice and kindly ways, folks get the idea that he's not only soft-hearted, he's soft-headed. And if word goes out that he's rich too, then the leeches come swarming." Pocket gave a shrug and a sigh.

For a moment or two Marny said nothing. She looked at the map. Then, raising her head, in a wondering voice she asked, "Pocket—all this—why didn't you tell me?"

"Why should I?" he asked.

"You're a very rich man," said Marny.

"Well, yes, I suppose so."

"Don't 'suppose so.' Any man who has sense enough to acquire this much property in the right places has sense enough to know what it's worth. Now answer me this. When you asked me to marry you, why didn't you tell me how rich you were?"

"Why Marny," he said with surprise, "I didn't think of it. Why should I tell you?"

"Why shouldn't you?"

"Oh, it sounds—so mercenary. It sounds like I thought you were in love with money."

There was a moment of silence. Marny stood looking straight at him. She said clearly, "Pocket, when did I ever say a word, or do one single thing, to suggest to you that I was not in love with money?"

Pocket caught his breath. His eyes opened wider. "Why Marny!" he almost gasped. "If you had known I was rich— would you have said yes?"

She gave a short little laugh. "Now that it's too late, I might as well tell the truth. Of course I would."

"You would?" Pocket echoed.

Marny shrugged. "I would. But I didn't know you were a gold mine, so I didn't stake a claim."

Pocket gave the merriest chuckle she had heard from any man in a long time. He said, "All right, now you know. Will you marry me?"

68

Marny put her hand to her throat as if she felt herself choking. She stood staring at him. With an effort she found her voice. "May the Lord take care of you," she said slowly. "You don't know enough to take care of yourself."

"You haven't answered," said Pocket.

"I'm answering," she returned. "I'm saying I never met a man so stupid in my life."

"It's not stupid," said Pocket, "for a man to know what he wants."

"It's imbecilic," said Marny, "for a man to want a woman who'd be marrying him for his money."

Pocket gave his head an exasperated shake, like a teacher tired of trying to teach a pupil who did not want to learn. "Marny, I keep on telling you, I love you. And when I say that, I mean I want to give you what you want."

"Do you think I ought to want money so much?"

"How do I know what you 'ought' to want?" he exclaimed. "I don't know what I 'ought' to want myself. But I know what I do want, and I want you. Now will you say yes?"

"No!" said Marny. She shot the word at him like a bullet.

"But why not?" he demanded. This time his manner was forceful. "Tell me, Marny."

She did not answer.

Pocket repeated, "Tell me, Marny."

Marny took out the cards again. She looked down at them, fondling them, as she spoke. "It wouldn't be fair of me not to answer," she said slowly. "Pocket, you say you love me and I believe you. It would be easy for me to love you back. But marry you—no. Not you or anybody else."

More gently now, Pocket said, "Why not, Marny?"

Marny stroked the cards. "You think I would change when I got married. You think I'd be like Rosabel. A happy housewife. Pouring tea by the fire. Going to market to buy carrots

575

for dinner. Getting a thrill out of being approved of by Mrs. Eustis and Mrs. Chase—"

She stopped, because Pocket had burst out laughing and was holding a handkerchief over his lips to smother his mirth. When he could speak he said,

"Marny, I haven't got a fancy education like yours but I'm not half-witted." Crumpling the handkerchief, he pushed it back into his pocket. "I do not think," he said with emphasis, "that you would be in the least like Rosabel. I don't want you to be like Rosabel. If I love you the way you are why should I want you to be different?"

Marny's look was full of perplexity. "Then what do you want me to do?"

"I want you to marry me," said Pocket.

Marny shook her head. "You'd want me to give up the Calico Palace—"

"I would not," said Pocket. He stood with his hands thrust into the untidy pockets at either side of his coat. "Why do you keep imagining you can look into my mind and tell me what I want? I know what I want."

Marny looked down at her cards, as if drawing courage from her best friends. "Now that I'm telling you the truth, I'd better tell you all of it. Pocket, I don't want to get married because—because I'm scared."

This time Pocket was the one astonished. "Scared?" he repeated. "Of me?"

"Not of you," said Marny. "I'm scared of getting too close to anybody." She looked up, and almost fiercely she exclaimed, "I won't take any more well-meant meddling. I won't have any more attacks on—well, on *me*."

Her words snapped at him. She paused abruptly, as if startled and embarrassed by her own candor. Pocket realized that she had not finished all she had to tell him. He waited, and after a pause she went on.

"Maybe you don't understand that. But I've fought so long and hard for the freedom to be myself. Now I've got it, and that's my dearest treasure. I'll gamble with everything else, but not with that. For a minute there, I thought your bank account would be worth the risk. But as soon as you offered it to me, I knew it wasn't. Never again am I going to try to fit anybody's pattern but my own. All right, now you know."

Pocket did not reply at once. His look had changed. He was regarding her now with a new tenderness. Softly and lovingly, he said, "Marny, there's something about me you simply haven't got in your head yet. Put up those cards and let me explain."

Frankly baffled, Marny put away the cards. Pocket took her hands in both of his, and gently led her back to the chair. She yielded, though reluctantly, and sat down. Pocket went around to his side of the table and sat down too. He spoke to her earnestly.

"Marny, I've heard a lot of people talk about love. But they don't seem to mean what I mean. They say, "Because I love you, you must do what I want you to do.' That's not what I mean at all. What I mean is, because I love you, I want you to do what *you* want to do."

There was another pause. Marny cupped her chin in her hands and faced him. "I don't believe you," she said.

"Why not?" asked Pocket.

"Because," she returned, "there isn't anybody like that in the world."

"Yes there is," said Pocket. "There's me."

She shook her head.

"I'll say it again," said Pocket. "I want you to do what you want to do. I don't want to change one thing about you. I don't want you to be like me. I want you to be like *you*. There's a lot of difference."

Marny sat up straight. She struck the table a blow. "Oh, what a difference!"

She lifted her shoulders and dropped them as if trying to throw off a burden. When she spoke again she spoke slowly, again with a frankness she did not often show.

"Pocket, a lot of people have said they loved me. My family, my teachers, all those fine characters in Philadelphia. They said they loved me, then they tried to prove it by nearly driving me out of my mind. All they did, morning-noon-and-night, was try to make me different from the way I was. They could not understand that I wasn't like them and couldn't be like them. I couldn't change my nature any more than I could change the color of my eyes. I tried to please them."

Pocket was listening closely. He did not try to interrupt her. He realized that what she was saying had been piling up in her mind for a long time, and it was a relief for her to talk about it now.

"I tried to please them," Marny repeated, "and everything I did was wrong. Oh, I laugh about it now, but I laugh because I don't want anybody to know—I suppose I don't want to remember—that I had such a painful time growing up. No matter how hard I tried, I didn't fit. I was always out of place, I was always *wrong*. So at last I quit trying."

This time he asnwered her. "And none too soon," he said. His voice was low and full of compassion.

She smiled at him gratefully. Pocket said,

"But I've told you and told you, I don't want you to change. I'm in love with *you*. If you changed you'd be somebody else and I wouldn't be in love with that somebody else." He smiled at her, Pocket's sweet, engaging smile. "Now do you understand?"

Marny spoke with wonder. "And you don't want me to change in any way at all?"

"Not any way at all."

"You don't want me to leave the Calico Palace?"

"No," said Pocket.

"You wouldn't want me to live in some dim little cubbyhole, just to keep the leeches from pestering you?"

"Of course not. If I had an extravagant wife I could always say, 'She spends every cent as fast as it comes in, I can't give you anything.' "

Marny had not meant to laugh, but now she was laughing. She asked, "Where would we live?"

"One of my tenants," said Pocket, "is planning a hotel more sumptuous than the Union Hotel ever was. He could put in a suite for us. You'd plan the suite, and furnish it. I wouldn't know how. The fact is, Marny, I've never lived in real luxury. I'd like to try it." He began to laugh too. "You and I are a lot more alike than you realize. And as I mentioned before, I love you. It *would* work, Marny."

Marny looked down. She considered, long and thoughtfully. "I— wonder," she said slowly. "I wonder. Wait. Let me see."

She took out the cards.

Pocket pushed back his chair. He came around to her side of the table and stood looking down at the pack in her hand. "I see. You want to consult your friends."

Marny gave a start of defense. "Do you mind?" she flashed at him.

"Some day," Pocket answered patiently, "you're going to get it into that thick head of yours that I don't mind anything you do. I love you the way you are. Long before I asked you to marry me I knew you liked to ask the cards about your future. Why shouldn't you?"

Placated, Marny began to lay out the cards. Pocket stood by her and watched. All of a sudden Marny stopped, holding a card halfway between the pack and the table. "Pocket" she exclaimed.

"Yes ma'am?" said Pocket.

"I've just thought of something," said Marny, still holding the card in midair. "I don't need to ask the cards to foretell anything about this. I foretold it myself, a long time ago."

As she looked up from the layout to Pocket she saw a humorous quiver about his lips. "Yes," he said, "I remember."

"You do?"

Again Pocket pulled out a handkerchief—a different handkerchief this time, as he usually carried five or six—and again he was laughing.

"Why yes," he replied, "that day at Sutter's Fort when you found that Delbert had gone off with your dust."

With a teasing green twinkle, Marny nodded. Pocket went on,

"You said to me, 'Somewhere in the world there's some chump of a man who's going to pay me for this.'"

Marny was laughing too, her own soft silken laughter. "Yes, that's right. And I said, 'Trust me, Pocket. I'll find him.'" She reached up and used the card to stroke his cheek. "Pocket," she continued, and though she was laughing there was a note of astonishment in her voice, "Pocket, I do believe I've found that chump of a man."

Pocket too was still laughing. "It looks that way," he said.

But then Marny gave a start, and caught her breath. "Pocket—that's not exactly right. I didn't find you. You found me."

Tossing all the cards on the table, she stood up and grabbed his hands in hers and held them.

"Pocket, are those hoodlums going to set another fire?"

This time Pocket spoke gravely. "There's talk of it. I'm afraid they are."

Her grip on his hands tightened. "And that man—the tenant you were telling me about—he's still going to build that sumptuous hotel?"

"Why yes," Pocket answered smiling. Then he was grave again. "It's the same old war, Marny. The folks who want to build and the folks who want to destroy. I guess it'll be going on as long as the world lasts. Anyway, we know which side we're on."

Marny let go his hands. "We," she repeated. "*We*, Pocket!"

"Yes, dear," he said gently.

"Just think," she murmured, "I don't have to pretend any more that I like it when nobody cares what becomes of me."

Pocket put his arms around her and she dropped her head on his shoulder.

"You chump of a man," she whispered, "I'm so glad you found me."